THE LOHVIAN CYCLE II

The Dray Prescot Series

THE LOHVIAN CYCLE II

Kenneth Bulmer

writing as

Alan Burt Akers

Published by
Bladud Books

First published in 2012 by Bladud Books

Originally published separately in German by Heyne Verlag in 1992-3.

Scorpio Ablaze first published in English by Savanti Press in 1998, and republished using the original English manuscript by Mushroom eBooks in 2008.

Scorpio Drums and *Scorpio Triumph* first published in English by Mushroom eBooks from the original English manuscripts in 2008.

This omnibus paperback edition published in 2012 by Bladud Books, an imprint of Mushroom Publishing, Bath, BA1 4EB, United Kingdom

www.bladudbooks.com

ISBN 978-1-84319-896-3

Contents

SCORPIO ABLAZE

Dray Prescot

Dray Prescot tells us in muted tones of remembered horror of the time he spent as a slave of the Shanks and Katakis in the port town of Taranjin. Taranjin is the capital of Tarankar, a country on the west coast of South Loh. Here, Prescot has been sent by the Star Lords to drive the Shanks out. He has been forced to leave his new Companions from Loh—Mevancy nal Chardaz, a most spirited young lady, and Trylon Kuong, a young noble-man of honorable and romantic notions, and Llodi, a loyal fighting man and ex caravan guard. These folk are trying to follow Prescot, whom they know as Drajak the Sudden.

Prescot has had limited success in organizing the guerilla gangs in Tarankar, and his hopes are centered on a coalition of forces from allied Hamal, from his home, Vallia, and from Tsungfaril. Tsungfaril, a country across the desert to the east, has a new queen, Queen Kirsty with her con-sort Rodders. The Star Lords ordered Kirsty to be made queen of Tsungfaril. Now Prescot in Taranjin, employed to clean a Shank lord's armor aboard his flagship, is beginning to sense that he faces utter failure. He tries a last throw and places incendiary devices aboard Shank ships, and then is told to clean weapons—including a great Krozair longsword.

Prescot has been described as a man above middle height, with brown hair and level brown eyes, oddly brooding and dominating, with enor-mously broad shoulders and powerful physique. He has an unmistakable aura about him, a charisma known in Kregish as the yrium. He moves like a savage hunting animal, swift, quiet and lethal.

Under the twin sun, Antares, the planet Kregen is a world of wonder and terror, of beauty and horror. Now, in the streaming mingled lights of the Suns of Scorpio, Prescot takes up the Krozair brand. He hears a com-motion on the deck outside and sees Pazzian slaves about to be killed by the Shank lord using his trident.

He looks along the deck hearing the shrieks of pain and fear and sees the totally unexpected. He acts at once.

Alan Burt Akers

3

One

The Glitch Riders swept out of the dawn in a whirling welter of pounding hooves and spurting sand. Their furious onset billowing their desert robes laced with dust made them ghostly apparitions bursting from the half-light and shadows. Flashing blades swinging in lethal arcs and long slender lances stabbing mercilessly tumbled the sleepy caravan guards into instant ruin.

The first shrieks brought Mevancy to the flap of the tent in three lissom strides. She looked out with a caution ingrained in her. Directly before her a screaming guard running between the lines of tents threw up his arms and collapsed as the sharp narrow lance head pierced past his backbone.

The Glitch Rider reined up, withdrawing his lance, and his animal reared and his hooves pawed the dust-laden air. Mevancy saw that picture of primeval violence and mannish domination. The lance slanted down towards her, its head darkly stained. Under the brim of the turban-wrapped helmet and above the sand scarf, fierce dark eyes caught the radiance of the early suns and glittered upon her.

The Glitch Rider must have seen a defenseless woman's figure in the tent opening, a fine shapely woman clad in a single sheer yellow nightgown. He forced his animal's head around, hooves splaying sand, thrust the lance into its stirrup bucket and dismounted in a single smooth movement. A word into his mount's ear quieted the beast immediately. Beyond the opposite row of tents screams blistered into the dawn air. The Glitch Rider started for the tent in pleasurable anticipation. This was the kind of loot for which he and his companions attacked the desert caravans.

Mevancy nal Chardaz lifted her left arm and held it horizontally outstretched straight in front of her breast. Her arm pointed at the advancing warrior. Her clenched fist curled below the line of the horizontal. Blood suffused Mevancy's face. Her left fist twitched and there followed a glinting twinkle in the air. The Glitch Rider emitted just the one scream. His hands flew up to the red pudding that had been his face. The sand scarf flapped uselessly, shredded into pieces, blood stained. He doubled up, writhing, staggering, choking.

Mevancy went quickly back into the tent and snatched up her sword.

"What is it, Mevancy? What is that terrible noise?"

The girl in the other desert camp bed lifted her head and stared in understanding horror. The sounds were self-explanatory.

"Make yourself as small as possible, Bella. Make yourself look like a part of the tent. For an actress of your gifts..." and here Mevancy recognized her own cruelty. Still, she was feeling particularly aggravated and annoyed at the stupidity of the guards who had fallen down on their job, so she finished: "That should not be difficult."

Bella Chuan-Hsei gave a tiny shriek. Her hands pulled the sheet up tightly. Her arms were pink and smooth and firmly fleshed, glowing. Mevancy swung back to the tent opening. Her own forearms were granulated with a fine honeycomb of sunken points, the deadly bindles, some of which had destroyed the desert raider's face. What Mevancy did not say was that no Glitch Rider was going to enter this tent whilst she still swung a sword or could shoot off her bindles. She didn't say it because she felt that kind of fustian best left to Bella's orations upon the stage.

When she stepped out onto the sand the Glitch Rider was rolling about and greasy blood splattered between his fingers. She used her sword efficiently and gave him his quietus. She breathed deeply and almost steadily.

Noise racketed on in the camp and now the sliding screech of steel upon steel told that the caravan was coming awake and resisting the raiders. Because she had learned more of the tricks of the trade from Drajak the Sudden in their journeys, she caught the bridle of the Glitch Rider's mount and tied the reins to a tent peg. Booty, after all, was booty.

Around the corner of the next tent along a man ran swiftly into view. He cast a swift glance back. By the cut of his desert robes, the turban-wrapped helmet, the style of his sword, he could be nothing other than a Glitch Rider. Mevancy lifted her own blade.

He saw her and momentarily checked and then came on furiously.

She lifted her left arm before her, held straight with the fist tucked down. A shadow fleeted past the corner of the tent and there were Trylon Kuong and Llodi the Voice running swiftly after the raider.

The dust kicked into the air slicked on her tongue flatly, dry, and her nostrils stung. She faced the Glitcher, a slender handsome figure of defiance.

"Keep away, my lady!" yelled Llodi. His strangdja glittered as the twin suns pierced their mingled streaming light over the tops of the tents. Light began to illuminate the world.

"Not until I've bindled the shint!"

The Glitcher swung up his sword expecting to cut down this girl and get clear of his pursuers. For him, at least, the raid had gone wrong. He saw the tethered animal, a narrow-flanked, spiky-headed, six-legged wegener. He saw the sprawled body of his tribesman. Unhesitatingly he sprang for the wegener.

That sideways movement took him at an angle so that Mevancy's shot for his face splattered against the side of his helmet and shoulder. One or two of the little darts, her bindles, smacked into his cheek. He ignored the sudden and unexpected pain, reaching for the reins tied around the tent peg. Inflamed, Mevancy started for him, sword uplifted.

Kuong—young, limber, alive with a reckless passion in which honor and glory were all muddled up in his head—shouted in alarm.

"Mevancy!"

Llodi let rip a low growl of animal anger and fairly hurled himself on.

The glittering holly-leaf-shaped head of his strangdja, a killing instrument of cold steel, thrust forward as he charged. Llodi the Voice, a rough tough caravan guard who, had he been on watch, would never have been caught sleeping, put great store by his new friends, Trylon Kuong and the lady Mevancy—and, too, that hard and ferocious devil, Drajak the Sudden, who had so mysteriously disappeared. Oh, no, Llodi was not going to let anything nasty happen to the lady Mevancy.

The Glitcher reached the tethered wegener as Kuong leaped upon him and as Llodi thrust his strangdja forward past Kuong's hurtling body.

Sword and strangdja slashed and pierced the desert raider. He let rip a screech of agony, trying to swing about, trying to get his own sword into action, and Mevancy delivered a last cunning stroke that smashed him to his knees into the churned-up sand.

The three friends stood, together, over the body, and looked about for any more of these pestiferous Glitchers. They had no need to speak. They acted as a team.

A galloping wegener in his lolloping six-legged gait crashed past with his rider dangling from the saddle, his chest a mass of red under the crushed mail. Others appeared, running, and following them a vengeful mob of Kuong's personal guards mixed with caravan guards and mercenaries of other nobles and merchants traveling with the caravan.

"Bad cess to 'em," growled Llodi, grounding his strangdja. "What with murdering and thieving an' all."

"That's their way of life," observed Kuong. He glanced at Mevancy and the tiniest dent appeared in his forehead between his brows. "You are—well, Mevancy?"

"By Spurl!" She tossed back her dark hair, impatient with herself. "It was just that first sight of the Gahamond-forsaken bastard that startled me. He looked so—so—" She did not repeat the thought that had slammed through her brain at sight of the Glitcher—so mannish. Instead, she finished: "His damned evil eyes flashed like those of a risslaca."

"He was meat ripe for the chopping, my lady." Llodi sounded positive.

"Yes."

"Then," said Kuong briskly, in his best manner of young nobility, "it is time we had the first breakfast."

Not for the first time Mevancy saw with pleasure that briskness in Kuong, an attitude to life vastly different from the majority of his countrymen and women down here in Tsungfaril in Southern Loh. Of course, he was a Paol-ur-bliem, a man sentenced to the punishment of being reincarnated over and over again until he had purged himself of his own crime against the god Tsung-Tan seasons upon seasons ago.

Those who were not the Accursed, not paol-ur-bliem, lived only so that they might after death enter the paradise of Gilium. Their lackadaisical way of existing infuriated strangers who did not share their religious beliefs. Kuong had a goodly number of lifetimes to live before he could dream of entering Gilium and living in paradise for eternity.

Because Kuong was a trylon, the third highest rank of nobility, he could sit at the folding table with his friends and grandly eat the first breakfast whilst others cleaned up the camp. The Glitchers' bodies were stripped of everything useful and then taken out and dumped.

The caravan master, Nath the Horizons, a man whose face bore the creases of seeing vast distances across the desert, walked up to the table. He looked troubled. Gracefully, Kuong invited him to sit down and partake of the first breakfast.

"Thank you, lord. I bring grave news." He sat down but did not eat.

Levelly, Kuong said: "Tell me."

"Those shints. May Tsung-Tan in his infinite wisdom consign each one individually to the Death Jungles of Sichaz." The words were heavy, flat on the dusty air. "They slashed the water skins."

"Oh, no!" burst out Mevancy before she could stop herself.

"Aye, my lady. It is serious—"

"Water must be rationed at once." Kuong stood up. "We must gather up every last drop. We must know how much we have left."

Llodi stood up instantly and Nath the Horizons also rose, more slowly. He was an important man in the desert, and knew it; also he was not a lord.

"There may be just enough to see us all back to Makilorn. There is no question of going on our way farther west."

"Just so that we all arrive alive," breathed Kuong.

Mevancy threw him a quizzical glance. The young trylon, when he died, would be reincarnated into the chosen body of a newborn baby. It could well be thought he would welcome the chance of a genuine death so as to get his punishment over with as soon as possible. Yet Kuong did not, as far as Mevancy could see, appear to share that common ambition of all the Accursed, the paol-ur-bliem.

About to throw the dregs of her cup into the sand, an unthinking action, she hauled herself up. "Every last drop," she said.

"Aye."

"Reminds me of the time when old Perlandi got caught in that dratted sandstorm. We were short of water, then. But we survived."

"We will, my lady," said Llodi with gravity, "survive now."

She was about to agree in a rolling oath or two with Llodi when Nath the Horizons said in his heavy way: "If it is the will of Tsung-Tan, I shall accept that with joy, if he calls me up to Gilium at last."

Llodi and Mevancy exchanged impatient, annoyed glances. Still, neither wanted to question the fanatically held religious beliefs of these people.

Mevancy contented herself with: "Well, by Spurl, I have a great deal to do. I intend to return to Makilorn in one piece."

"And," said Kuong, looking into her flushed face, "so do I."

The caravan wrapped up and set off, heading east, and by agreement the second breakfast was omitted.

There was water, just, to get them through on savagely reduced rations.

When Mevancy suggested to Kuong, and he passed on the idea to Nath, that they should dump unnecessary impedimenta, thus lightening the load and increasing their speed, the reaction of most nobles was one of rejection.

"If we leave our tents and personal goods here in the desert," protested Laygon Fariang, a stout lord with a stutter, "they will be lost! The Glitchers may come back, there are bandits—oh, no, my slaves will carry their burdens."

"Quite right!" confirmed Stromni Yriang, purple-faced, jewel-bedecked.

"Well," temporized Kuong, "we will see."

In the event, when the caravan staggered with only half their animals left into the city of Makilorn, they left a trail of abandoned goods in their wake. No one sweated. Dust and sand caked them. They were a procession of ghosts stumbling to the banks of the River of Drifting Leaves.

Kuong's people had not suffered as badly as the slaves of the other nobles. By the same token, most of his possessions now lay dumped back in the wastes of sand. Going up to his villa, he said: "I'll send out for the gear. If it is still there."

"Which it won't be if those racketty Umblers stumble across it."

Even in their exhausted condition they had to smile at the thought of Umblers—erratic, incompetent diffs. Llodi finished: "They are a funny old lot, an' all, an' no mistake."

In Kuong's villa, Mevancy said decisively: "A bath. A long long soak."

Kuong's people bustled about. After bathing, a meal and then rest brought Mevancy, Llodi and Kuong back to normalcy. The experience had turned out not too badly in the end; it could easily have killed them all. They decided to walk across to the Mishuro villa early the next day to see Lunky and as Llodi said: "Find out if he's seen Drajak, an' all."

"Strange business," observed Kuong. "Oh, I know Drajak is a bit weird; but it's not like him to go off like that."

Mevancy opened her mouth, and closed it. She was a kregoinya as

Drajak was a kregoinye and they worked for the Everoinye. Drajak could have been snatched up by the Star Lords and sent somewhere else on Kregen. Mevancy knew all about that. That was how she and Drajak had met, in a burning building.

The guards stiffened up to attention as Kuong Vang Talin, the Trylon of Taranik, entered the Mishuro villa. Lunky greeted them with outstretched hands, puzzled at their return. When he'd heard the story he gave thanks to Tsung-Tan for their safe deliverance and then startled them.

"Drajak? Yes, he was here. But he's flown off again."

A light quick step brought their attention to a young man who bore a face remarkable for its clash of emotions. His forehead was broad and his features well formed with a rebellious set to his jaw. His red Lohvian hair was neatly trimmed. That young unlined face expressed baffled fury, scorn, self-pity and a growing rebellious determination.

Lunky introduced the young man as Rollo the Runner.

The moment the lahals were done with, Rollo burst out: "And damned ungrateful he is! By Chuzto! Just flew off and left me here to rot!"

"What is all this about flying?" demanded Kuong, not quite sure how to take this emphatic young man.

"Drajak had a boat that flew through the air," said Lunky.

"Yes!" Rollo waved his arms about. "He calls it a voller. Flew away and left me here." Only then was it borne in on Rollo just how his passionate words could be interpreted. Instantly he swung towards Lunky. "I beg your forgiveness, San Lunky. I did not mean—I am sure you realize—"

Not too long ago Lunky had been just such a young man; now with the death of his master he had become a most powerful Diviner. His face had filled out. He carried himself with poise and assurance. His marriage to Mistress Telsi would soon take place. And, since the discomfiture of the opposition party led by Shang-Li-Po, the party of which he and his friends formed the heart had come to power.

He said: "That is perfectly all right, Rollo. I do understand. I am doomed to lead an inactive life now. You may stride out to adventures—"

"Ha!" Rollo's fury burst out anew. "I may? When Drajak the Sudden sees fit, you mean. Where are the men he promised?"

"As to that, they will arrive in Tsung-Tan's good time."

"Did he," said Kuong, "explain where he'd been and why he didn't join us after we had—ah—rescued queen Leone?"

Mevancy remained silent. She could not be sure; but she felt fairly confident that the Everoinye had, indeed, taken Drajak up.

"No, trylon, not a word. But he had this wonderful flying boat." Talk of airboats aroused conflicting emotions in Loh. Lack of fliers was often given as one reason for the decline and collapse of the Empire of Loh. Conversation became general as Lunky led the party in for a splendid Kregan meal.

At one point, in answer to Rollo, Kuong said: "Our journey has merely been interrupted. We shall start west again with the first caravan."

"In that case, trylon," quoth Rollo the Runner, "I would ask leave to accompany you. I am doing no good here. Drajak has gone to Tarankar, so that is where I must go."

Looking at Rollo's determined young face, Mevancy saw clearly what an impression Drajak had made on this young man. Could other people see in her face the impression Drajak had made on her?

The episode with Leotes she had now firmly put away from her thoughts. He was paol-ur-bliem like Kuong. The new Repositers would be appointed by the college to collect every scrap of information about the lives of the Accursed in their care, thus ensuring continuity. Now, before Kuong could rush off again, he had to wait for his new Repositer. Lunky threw up his hands in regret, but, as he said: "This is your fate."

In the event Trylon Kuong received a small, sedate man with a nose more pointed than round, and a chin more round than pointed. He habitually put his hands into the opposite sleeves, and smiled. This was San Cheng.

Mevancy decided to reserve her opinion of him.

Some time elapsed in fresh preparations. Some of Kuong's gear was retrieved from the desert. A caravan formed and, at last, they could set off west for Taranik and Tarankar. The days in the desert passed as desert days do as the twin suns rose and set. The patient animals plodded on, and, eventually, via Orphasmot and the oases of Claransmot and Hanjhin, took the party to Taranik. Here, in this large and splendid oasis and its imposing lake, they were greeted by the Crebent left in charge by Kuong. T'sien-Fu was able to tell them that the flying boat had flown in and off and that Drajak the Sudden had asked after the very people with the trylon now.

"Well, at least we are following him," said Mevancy.

Whilst Kuong was in a hurry, it was needful for him to spend some time in his estates of Taranik. No further troubles had been experienced from the Glitch Riders, and the bandits were lying low. T'sien-Fu's mop of black hair quivered as he spoke to his lord. "But, lord, to go to Tarankar!"

Speaking with heavy gravity, Kuong said: "I have been ordered to go by the queen. Queen Kirsty is forming an army. It is necessary to find out all that we can."

"But, lord, the man Drajak in his flying boat has gone."

"It was our agreement to go together. Queyd-arn-tung!"*

With considerable reluctance, despite the urgency of their mission, the party left the peace and plenty of Kuong's estates of Taranik. The groves of trees, the cultivated fields, the herds of fine animals and the wonderful

---

* Queyd-arn-tung—No more need be said. A.B.A.

scent of Kregan flowers all called to the wanderer to pitch his tents and settle down here. The glitter of the twin suns off the lake was the last sight of water before She of the Sundering, the river marking the eastern boundary of Tarankar. Kuong took a last deep draught of the perfumed oasis air and then swung resolutely away into the desert.

The wasteland here was real desert, mile after mile of shifting sand. Known as the Glarkie Dunes, the barrier it formed was formidable.

Husbanding water and supplies, keeping steadily on, the party could only speculate what the future held for them.

At last came the day when Llodi, in the lead, hauled up and shaded his eyes, peering intently ahead. Kuong reined in beside him.

"Yes, Llodi. I think those are clouds."

"And mountains under 'em. That'll be the river, an' everything."

"I trust," said Mevancy, her sand scarf trailed across the lower half of her face, "I sincerely trust we may swim in the river."

"That is something to be discovered."

Although they did not urge their animals to a faster gait, the beasts soon snuffed water ahead and speeded up. San Cheng, his yellow robe flapping, held onto his saddle in a most awkward fashion. He carried a sword and Llodi, for one, promised himself not to stand too close to the Repositer if it came to a fight.

San Cheng had no need to give his history. He had been chosen early on showing signs of promise, had been trained up by the college, and would spend the rest of his life recording Kuong's doings and sayings. When this body inhabited by Kuong died the Diviners, now led by Lunky, would discover Kuong in the body of a new born baby. By that time it was highly probable that San Cheng's successor would be the trylon's Repositer.

Mevancy cried out and pointed.

"Look! That must be Drajak!"

Fleeting swiftly from the distant smudge of cloud and skimming over the desert towards them a dot rapidly grew in size and turned into a flying boat.

Mevancy started to wave and Rollo, after a single look, shouted: "No! No, my lady. We must hide!"

"Hide!" exclaimed Kuong. "Where, by Lohrhiang of the Springing Branch, can we hide in this hellish place?"

"What is it, Rollo?" Mevancy was appalled by Rollo's panic-stricken vehemence.

"Shanks!"

The flying vessel swooped down. Her brightly-painted squared-off upperworks glinted with gilding above the sleek black hull. Quite clearly her crew had seen the party below. Llodi clapped his heels in and started a blind rush off to the left, Rollo went galloping off to the right, San Cheng was carried off willy-nilly. Kuong cast a glance at Mevancy and ripped out his sword.

"From all I have heard about these Shanks," she said, speaking as evenly as she could, feeling her heart thudding, "we do not have much chance."

"Nevertheless—"

"Oh, yes, I agree. Your company has been pleasant, Kuong, and much appreciated." She drew her sword.

The Shanks flew with precision. Circling, they dropped nets, parties of fish-faced soldiers alighted. All Kuong's people were rounded up and of them all only two servants were killed. Everyone else was taken.

They resisted. They fought. Of course, they fought.

They were ruthlessly smashed down entangled in the nets, clubbed senseless.

Some awful time later, thrown down into a dark wooden-walled space deep within that black hull, they huddled together, nursing their cuts and bruises. The sight of these fishy people, these Shanks, affected Mevancy profoundly.

Used as any inhabitant of Kregen must be to the wonderful array of diffs, people who are not built as Homo sapiens sapiens is built, she still recoiled in revulsion. These Fish Faces repelled in a fashion at once nauseating, hideous and terrifying.

San Cheng simply sat with his hands thrust into the sleeves of his robe, head sunk on breast. Llodi was trying to prise a splinter of wood away from the wall. Some of Kuong's servants were crooning a slave dirge as old as slavery itself. Kuong said: "When we are taken out. There are no nets on us now."

Mevancy, on a breath, said: "Oh, yes!"

They all felt the bump shiver through the room and only then realized they had been flying through the air.

Rollo said: "You'll get used to it. Now, I do not stop fighting."

He, and the others, did not stop fighting as they were dragged out. Indifferently, the Shanks clubbed them down, hauling their kicking protesting bodies by ankles or wrists or hair. Mevancy had a chance to let fly with her bindles. Sensing this was the end, she did not husband her biological arsenal but let rip with both forearms.

Three Shanks screamed, dropping their weapons and clasping their ruined fishy faces. Others beat her to the deck and hauled on her hair, dragging her up to the top deck. Even then, in pain, half blind, she did not fail to note the callous treatment living Shanks afforded dead Fish Heads.

Repeatedly struck, dazed, Kuong and his party staggered from the flying ship, still attempting to struggle. Other ships lay on the landing field and the suns shone.

Now black-browed Katakis appeared to take over. These were slavers of Paz, man managers, utterly indifferent to other peoples' pains. They flashed their tails, to which were strapped six inches of daggered steel, and their whips rose and fell.

The slave coffle under the whips staggered on. Shouting and screaming, the line of slaves was hauled aboard another of the black hulled flying ships and thrust against the bulkhead. Mevancy lifted her head. On the deck a group of Shank officers glittered in scaled armor, glinting with gold, surrounding one who shone more magnificently than his aides. He, then, was the chief. He held a trident. Mevancy stiffened in fresh horror.

Perfectly clearly the whole situation was at once apparent. The Shanks had grown tired of the slaves' antics, annoyed and aggravated. The Shank lord would go along the line and thrust his trident deeply into each person's guts, twist and pull. That would be a dreadful object lesson to the rest.

Rollo surged forward and was beaten back by the smash of a trident butt.

The Fish Face lord thrust his trident into a Mionch who went down screaming to snap one of his long tusks against the deck.

The trident lifted. In the next heartbeat it would degut Mevancy.

A heavy throwing spear with red feathers flaunting where head joined shaft abruptly sprouted between the fish lord's shoulder blades. He went down at once. The other Shanks shrieked in uncomprehending rage, and ripped out their swords, lifted their tridents. They turned to stare down the deck.

Mevancy, sick with the horror and the stink of rotten fish, looked.

She did not really believe.

A voice of power and passion bellowed: "Hai Jikai! Hai Jikai, you murdering torturing kleeshes of Fish Faces! Hai Jikai!"

A bronzed and lithely muscular figure clad in a flaring scarlet breechclout leaped down the deck straight for the Shanks. A great two-handed longsword flamed under the Suns of Kregen.

"Hai Jikai!"

Two

Held in the cunning two-handed Krozair grip the glittering longsword slashed left and right. Two Shanks had no time to scream, collapsing in green gore. Most of the length of the Krozair brand still glittered in the lights of the twin suns.

As more of the surprised Fish Faces fell under the merciless blows, the glitter changed to an ominous green patina. It was absolutely vital to keep moving, to strike economically despite the red roaring passion of revengeful blood. The Katakis shouted confused orders and the Whiptail Chuktar tried to thrust with his bladed tail. The tail was severed by a slicing cut which went straight on to sunder his armor in a welter of blood.

"Come on! Come on! Grab weapons! Bratch!"

Llodi was the first to react. He snatched up a fallen trident and with a whooping shriek thrust a Shank clean through the guts.

Kuong and Mevancy retrieved swords and went to work.

Rollo got his fists around a trident and joined them.

The suddenness of it all, the shock, the abrupt death of the lord, tumbled the Fish Faces back in confusion. More died. The fight raged across the filthy deck.

Even then, we might not have done it—probably would not have done it—against this formidable opposition that swiftly threw more Shank soldiers into the fray. But acid was eating, eating at six membranes. The acid did not bite through evenly, so that the incendiary devices planted aboard six of the Shank flying ships ignited in sequence. With a great whoosh flames burst up from the ship next along the line. A bedlam of yells and shrieks broke from this vessel, the lord's flagship, as the incendiary device I'd planted in the magazine at last took fire.

Half a dozen Fish Faces leaped over the side. Others hesitated.

Striking with the Krozair brand I cleared a space.

"Rollo! I'll hold 'em. Get up to the controls!"

"But—Drajak—"

"Mevancy, go with Rollo! Come on. Runner, you know how to fly one of these contraptions! Move!"

Without another word Rollo started for the ladder to the next deck. The position of the controls was plain enough, in the armored box just for'ard of midships. Mevancy stuck a Kataki through and stepped on his tail as she ran with Rollo. She did not stop to cut his tail off. Normally one would cut off a Kataki's tail if the opportunity offered; but she'd stuck him good. She and Rollo vanished above.

Now other slaves were coming alive, were seeing salvation.

I knew none of the others, apart from my four friends. The killing frenzy that had given me impetus enough to break free from the slave mentality had to be channeled, organized, used. This fight was not over yet.

Flames roared over the after part of the flagship. Fire was sweeping through all six ships in which the fire eggs had been planted.

This ship, the lord's flagship, was a fine vessel. I had no compunction, in these latter days, in burning her. I just hoped we'd get her airborne before she was totally consumed.

Spouting flames, with Katakis and Shanks leaping over the side, the ship lurched. She lifted off and then fell back.

14

"Come on, Rollo, my lad. Come on!"

He took her up with a savage burst of power that threw many people to the deck. She nosed ahead and the flames streamed away aft. With Shanks and Katakis stumbling about, tripping over one another, falling to the deck, this was a splendid opportunity not to be wasted. There was not a shred of mercy in me as I raced on, striking with the green and red slimed longsword.

Mevancy's head appeared over the upper deck as I chopped a Fish Face and swung to degut a Whiptail.

"Cabbage! There's no one up here!"

She started to descend the ladder.

"Watch yourself, pigeon. There are a few of the shints down here."

Now the ship lifting up and moving forward faster and faster sent a tail of flame streaming back. The slaves—who were slaves no more—fought on. In a burning ship we leaped for the sky.

"Hunt 'em all down!" I bellowed. "Leave not one of the cramphs."

As you can see, I was in a right old paddy.

But, then, I'd been slave and had seen atrocities too dreadful to recount. My friends had been about to be murdered. And the scarlet breechclout and the Krozair brand had changed that, had altered fate.

With that swift onward rush of the flying ship through thin air the breeze swept in clean and sweet. The perennial stink of rotten fish diminished.

We went around the forward parts hunting slavers.

All the stern was now a single roaring mass of flames. When we were quite certain not a single Whiptail or Fish Face remained alive, we fell silent. Only the crackling roar of the flames and the windrush broke the silence.

Ripping a length of cloth from a Kataki face down in his own blood I cleaned the Krozair blade.

Mevancy's soft voice, full of questioning, said: "Cabbage?"

I tried to find a smile for her.

"Thank you, pigeon."

"What? You thank me? But—"

"I had failed here in Taranjin. All the land of Tarankar was lost, I thought. Then the Shanks and Katakis brought you and the others aboard."

Even as I spoke I recognized my own loquaciousness. All the same, by Krun, it had been a near run thing. I was recovering rapidly now.

She nodded. "Oh, yes, I see."

I think she did, at that.

Rollo walked up. He'd found a Lohvian longbow and was adjusting the quiver over his shoulder. He gave me a most peculiar look.

"I've read the stories, as I told you—Drajak."

"You looped the cords around the controls as I showed you?"

I sounded sharp.

"Of course." He sounded hurt. "I'm not that much of a fambly, am I?"

We were going along splendidly, burning and breaking up. How long the vessel would stay in one piece I couldn't say. Either that, and a sudden plunge to the earth, or we'd all crisp. Neither prospect pleased.

Kuong and Llodi were both looking queasy. That was not from the fight. That was because they were Lohvians and they had no experience here of flying ships. In an effort to reassure them, I said: "These flying contraptions are wonderful. We'll be all right." In the aftermath of a fight few people can react with complete normalcy. Our conversation was strained and unnatural. We'd get over that, too.

"I'm going below and aft. I want to see if we are being pursued."

Instantly, Mevancy snapped out: "You'll get singed."

His mind still on this marvelous experience of flying through thin air, Llodi said: "It's been a funny old day, what with this flying an' all."

That broke some dam of expression in us all. We all laughed.

Kuong said: "I'll come aft with you, Drajak."

So far, not one of them had commented on my appearance, except Rollo's oblique reference. He, alone of them all, knew my true identity. Yet the others had read the lurid tales of Dray Prescot, how he swung about the world of Kregen righting wrongs, rescuing damsels in distress, fighting oppression.

What you might call the trademarks of Dray Prescot were his scarlet breechcloth and the great Krozair longsword. Would they, I wondered futilely, then, would they connect up the clues? Could Rollo remain silent?

Well, that didn't matter much any more. I had the task, handed to me by the Star Lords, of clearing all the damned Shanks out of Tarankar and then of all Paz.

From the lower rear balcony, with the heat pulsing down over our heads, we could stare aft and see the armada of Shank flying ships in grim pursuit.

"How many?"

After a short space, Rollo said: "I make it twenty nine."

Wishing to be hard on the young hellion, I said: "Count again."

Whilst he did so I reflected that he'd overlooked one vessel flying immediately astern of another, and had counted the two as one.

Rollo grumped: "Oh, aye. Thirty."

"I suppose I needn't explain that the odd one out could be your death?"

"No, you needn't." He sounded most sharp.

"Let's get back on deck. It's unhealthily warm here."

Our streamer of smoke and flame trailing aft smudged across the sky. Truth to tell, there could be another thirty enemy hidden above that smoky tail, although I did not think so. We'd gained height in that first hectic escape and the Fish Faces were pressing on levelly and gaining height slowly so as not to fall back. From what now seemed only a few seasons ago when the Shanks had no vollers at all they had developed into competent aviators.

Back on deck Mevancy greeted me with: "You understand these flying boats. Surely you know a way to put out that fire?"

"Hell's Bells and Buckets of Blood, woman," I growled back at her. "I could spit on it, I suppose."

"Oh, you!"

Rollo, very brightly, said: "I'll check the controls."

I said: "I have an itch. Kuong—I fancy there is a Kataki or a Fish Face hiding still."

Instead of looking alarmed, Kuong brightened. "I agree with you, Drajak. I'll get some of these people organized. We'll smoke 'em out!"

"If we don't get smoked out first," sniffed Mevancy, very put out.

"Look, pigeon, in a wooden vessel like this all you can do is hope and pray. There isn't even the sea to bucket up. We can press the flames back by the speed we go. But, eventually, they will eat forward."

"Well, don't expect me to pull you out again."

Before I could stop myself, I'd rapped out: "No, thanks. I don't want another crack on the skull that paralyses me."

"What," she said in a voice of ice, "do you mean?"

Oh, well, Dray Prescot has a mouth large enough—at times—to accommodate a king size foot.

I said: "Nothing, pigeon. I'm going to the armory."

I didn't mean the armory but the lord's trophy room. If I didn't get there soon the place would burn.

As I stepped through the door past the bodies of the two Whiptails, I turned to call back to Mevancy, standing there with her hands on her hips, her head thrust forward and a most diabolical expression on her face.

"Get some people into chucking the bodies overside, will you?"

If I was in command then this vessel, burning or not, was going to be cleaned up as best we could.

The trophy room held a few objects I felt would be useful. The matched set of rapier and main gauche had come from Hamal and were ornately fancy.

We'd worked the etching trick on the Shank blades and although I'd seen none snap in the fight on the deck, I trusted the Fish Faces' weapons would break come the day. Just how long this fancy rapier set would last in a fight remained to be seen. A true Krozair brother or a Zeniccean Bladesman will allow only the most minimal of markings on his blade; the brudstern, a few secret marks and that is all. I don't trust fancy etched blades.

The lestenhide scabbard in the krosturr fashion could now be rehitched to its belt lockets. Now I needn't strut about with the brand naked in my fist. The coat of mesh mail was by a hand's-breadth too narrow for my shoulders, which was a pity. The legends may tell of Dray Prescot rushing about naked save for a scarlet breechclout, the truth is I like a spot of armor between my shoulder blades. The powerful Canopian crossbow would come in handy, though, by Vox.

As for the torn half of a flag from a Vallian Green Coat regiment of spearmen, well, now, that ought to be saved if possible. If we got out of this scrape whole I'd have immense pleasure in ceremoniously presenting the tresh to its owner regiment. By Vox, what a stroke that would be!

By the same token, then, I ought to take the lance pennon from Hyrklana. My lad Jaidur, Vax Neemusjid, was the King of Hyrklana. He'd like the lance pennon back for its parent regiment, too.

A shadow appeared at the door and in the same instant I was across the trophy room, the longsword out and snouting.

Mevancy said: "You are twitchy, cabbage."

I thrust the sword back into the scabbard.

"You'd better help yourself to what you want. This will all burn soon."

"Yes. Very well. Look, Drajak, we're both working for the Everoinye and you know I am in command. So just let me do the ordering about, right?"

There was absolutely nothing of sense I could say in reply.

Instead: "Decks all cleared?"

Her full and mobile mouth tightened. "There you go again. Just because you dress up like the Emperor of Vallia and have a large sword doesn't make you Dray Prescot, does it? I've read the books. I told you. Dray Prescot is far too much of a gentleman to act in the uncouth way you do. You can play act all you like, Drajak, you'll never be a Dray Prescot."

Well now!

"Sink me!" I burst out. "Whoever told you Dray Prescot was a gentleman was a double-dyed—"

"Now, now, cabbage! I know what I read. Now call some of the freed slaves for these weapons. They look useful."

"Very well. Oh—take this coat of mesh. It'll fit you. You'll find it useful." I held out the beautiful coat of links.

"Oh, you!" But she took it. Then she said: "Ask San Cheng to step in."

"San Cheng? Who's he?"

"Kuong's new Repositer. An odd little creature. Now, pigeon, move."

Feeling half satisfied and half dissatisfied with that minor confrontation with my lady spitfire I took myself off. San Cheng was pointed out to me and I told him to cut along to the Lady Mevancy in the trophy room.

He drew himself up, sharp nose and round chin high, hands in the sleeves of his robe. He said: "Whoever you are, you address me as san. Do I make myself clear?" He smiled. "I shall see the lady when I am ready."

This perked me up and a spot of deviltry entered my brain.

"You are not in Makilorn now. You are aboard a burning vessel under my command. You will obey the Lady Mevancy instantly, or I shall pick you up by the scruff of your grubby little neck and run you there. Dernun?"*

He flinched back. The old hateful Dray Prescot Devil Glare must have flashed across my face. He licked his lips. "Well, perhaps—"

"No perhaps about it, sunshine! Bratch!"†

Just then a shrieking started up and Kuong appeared along the deck with a crowd of the freed slaves. They were carrying something in a net.

They dumped their burden down, and it thrashed about with two arms and two legs and a daggered tail.

"You were right, Drajak! See!"

"I don't exactly smell 'em. But it's something like that."

The Kataki was hauled upright still enmeshed in the net. No bookmaker would take odds that this fellow hadn't used this very net to entrap and enslave ordinary decent people of Paz. And, now, the jibrfarils had sold their evil services to the Shanks. I stared upon this Whiptail with great disfavor. The fellow actually spoke and tried to bargain for his life.

"Look, doms—the Shanks made me do it—I'm a Pazzian like you—"

A shrieking chorus of hate burst from the slaves. I was pleased to note that Kuong had them under enough control that they hadn't torn the Whiptail limb from limb already. And, by my referring to them all collectively as slaves betrays something of what Kregen can do to a fellow's brains. Yes, some of these poor folk had been slaves before the Katakis took them up. Others had not. In my book they were all ex-slaves. But my book was not read down here in Tarankar. Some day, I trusted, it would.

Incidentally, I do not mean the books and plays and puppet shows regarding Dray Prescot of legend and song. Oh, no, I refer to the book with which we in Vallia were hoping to educate the rest of Paz.

Attracted by the commotion, Mevancy joined us. She carried the mesh coat over an arm, for the cunning of the armorers of the Dawn Lands with mesh iron has to be weighed to be believed. "Well, what's amiss now—ah!" She saw the Whiptail and instantly understood.

In an aside, I said: "This is where Caspar the Peaker could shine."

"Caspar? Oh, the Everoinye sent him off again."

"Busy fellow." Caspar was a kaogoinye, a licensed assassin for the Star Lords, and a remarkable artist into the bargain. "Where to?"

"He was warned and told me. Boromir of the Ashes."

"By the Black Chunkrah!" I didn't laugh aloud. But I felt the mirth. "That means either old Strom Irvil didn't make it, or that Caspar will have that charming numim aristo to contend with. I wish him luck of it, by Krun!"

---

* dernun? An imperative demand: 'Do you understand?' Not very polite. A.B.A.

† bratch! Move, jump, get on with it. Not as ferocious as the infamous grak! A.B.A.

19

Mevancy didn't know where away lay this Boromir of the Ashes.

The Kataki was trying to saw through the strands of the net with the dagger strapped to his tail. One of the ex-slaves, a hulking Brokelsh whose black body hair bristled vindictively, calmly leaned over and slashed the tail off.

"Now, now, Tuco!" exclaimed Kuong. "Plenty of time for that."

"Yes, lord. The shint deserves more than he'll get."

The Whiptail had the stump of his tail gripped in both hands and did not scream but stood staring in utter horror at the bloody end.

"Kill! Kill!" The people were becoming restless to the point where Kuong might not be able to hold them.

"The shint can tell us a few things if we ask him," suggested Mevancy.

"Such as?" I looked around. If something positive was not done at once then our authority was gone.

"Please!" the Kataki managed to gabble out. "Please. Spare me—"

This was a scene that I misliked intensely. There was, in reason, only one course of action left open to us. I said: "Whiptail. We shall show you the same mercy you showed Pazzian slaves."

He screamed.

"Over with him!" I bellowed. I used a powerful ordering tone, bullying these vengeful people into instant obedience. Yelling and laughing, screaming with delight, they lifted the Whiptail on a forest of upraised arms. He was run to the side, shrieking.

I didn't bother to step to the bulwarks to watch his long fall to the ground beneath.

Three

Cleaning up the world of Kregen by disposing of one Kataki was all very well. It did not solve any of our pressing problems.

Our pursuers neither gained on us nor fell back. As the Shanks habitually built their flying ships to a single pattern this was not surprising. There had been two or three different designs on view lately; but if they differed in speed as well as layout it was not apparent yet. In addition we were all feeling hungry and thirsty.

Provisions and water from the fore parts of the vessel were broken out. There seemed little reason at this time to impose severe rationing and the cooks appointed themselves and we all ate and drank reasonably well. When the twin suns set, which would be in short order, our pursuers could still follow us, a burning torch scorching the sky.

The fire crept forward only slowly for we were making a good clip and the breeze blew back splendidly.

Thus our progress south was measured by our pursuers and by the fire.

Here in Loh the Suns of Scorpio are called Luz and Walig. They duly set in bands of crimson and viridian across the western sky and only a single lesser moon of Kregen hurtled low across the heavens. Tuco, who had been volunteered by Kuong to stand lookout, came forward in haste.

"They've put lights in them flying things—and they're going away!"

Kuong, Mevancy and I went carefully down and aft to check and it was true. The Shanks had given up the chase. Clearly, they believed we would burn.

Back on deck I felt I had to be as tactful as possible in dealing with the susceptibilities of Mevancy, as well as Kuong. I said: "There is a plan—"

Mevancy snorted. "We all know about your plans, cabbage!"

"All the same, I think it will work. If you give it a try."

"Speak on, Drajak," said Kuong in his best trylonish manner.

"First of all, you'll have to understand a little of how the flying ships work. Rollo will have to play a major part. And we will all have to act very smartly, very smartly indeed, by Chozputz!"

When I outlined the plan there were some long faces, some grim faces, and one or two blank faces.

"I'm for giving it a try," quoth Rollo, stoutly.

"Very well. The fire will burn through before the night is out. So we must begin at once."

Selecting personnel to perform the various tasks demanded by my so-wonderful plan was not too difficult. One absolutely vital factor was to determine the exact wind direction. If we fouled up on that we'd crisp.

Taking Rollo, Kuong, Llodi, Mevancy and Tuco below to where in a Pazzian craft the silver boxes of lift and motion would be located, we found no silver boxes. Instead, in the small armored space reposed bronze boxes. They were mounted in brass and balass orbits in a fashion almost identical to the mountings with which I was familiar. I explained succinctly.

"When the boxes move closer we rise. When they are pulled apart we go down. When they revolve in their orbits we go forward or turn to the side. Here are the control wires leading down from the levers in the conning tower."

They digested this.

"Each one of you will be assigned a single task. You will have enough of the ex-slaves to help in carrying. The vital need is utmost speed. But that does not mean you drop a single item!"

"We'll run, what with the fire at our heels, an' all," commented Llodi.

"The whole operation will be carried out in strict sequence so that nobody gets in anybody else's way."

Tuco in his uncouth Brokelsh manner said: "I'll go last."

"I appreciate your offer, Tuco." Kuong was very much the grand noble. "But, as everyone realizes, that is a task devolving on me."

Talk about noblesse oblige! Mind you, from Kuong's point of view, if he did get himself killed he'd be born again in a new baby body.

That might be all right for him and his weird beliefs; if he dropped a vital element he'd shaft the rest of us. Shaft us rotten.

We sorted out the duties. Everyone was told twice what to do.

Then I had them recite what they had to do back to me.

Rollo was taking the control levers. He commented casually that he was becoming addicted to flying through thin air.

Each of the principals selected their assistants.

I said to Kuong: "Oh, trylon. Would you mind telling that Cheng fellow to get some people to carry out all the weapons they can?"

"Assuredly, Drajak. Still, he's not altogether a lost cause."

"I am heartened to hear it. Now. A few last words."

They heard me out in a waiting silence. We were risking much; no one had a better suggestion. At last we were ready. Everyone went to their posts and I went up with Rollo to the conning tower.

Just as we reached the armored box the aft fighting tower, eaten away by flames, fell by the board with an almighty crash and spewing fountains of sparks. A tall Gon girl, her long silver hair wrapped about her bare waist, looked in one of the slits of the tower to say: "Master. The sparks all blew that way." She pointed a few points off to larboard.

"Your name?"

"Glima, an' it please you, master."

"Thank you, Glima. That was smart work. I congratulate you."

Her drawn face broke into a smile that I couldn't see without a pang.

A glance through a top scuttle at the stars—those splendid stars of Kregen—located the wind direction for me. Now we had to find the right spot.

"Head her into the breeze, Rollo, my lad. I'll go for'ard and see what I can find. Glima, you will relay messages to Master Rollo."

"Yes, master."

Glima and I went forward into the eyes of the ship. In less than half a bur the Maiden with the Many Smiles would be up and by her fuzzy pinkish moonlight I ought to be able to scan the land. When that radiance broke across the land I saw we were flying over scrubland similar to much to the south. By heading those few points to larboard we were trending south eastward, which was not the direction in which I wished eventually to go.

Carefully studying the ground as it fleeted past, for we could not slow down, I waited as patiently as I could until a small river hove into view bordered by trees. Beyond it the ground looked flat. To try to touch down in the water would be of little use; the fire would rage contemptuous of the stream's waters to extinguish it. And we'd have to wade or swim ashore.

A few last meticulous observations ahead to check that there were no obstructions, then: "Run, Glima. Tell Rollo. Now!"

She was gone on bare flashing legs.

More quickly than I'd expected the flier's speed slackened and she nosed down with that reckless impetuosity I was coming to recognize as Rollo's special way of expressing his addiction to flying through thin air.

Still, he did it cleverly. When we hit we were barely moving forward. Now, below, my friends and their assistants should be hard at work. I rushed off to make sure no one got in anyone else's way. I gave a stentorian bellow as I hit the forward deck on my way to the conning tower.

"Cheng! Get your people moving! Bratch!"

The Repositer was standing staring at the roaring mass of flames engulfing the whole of the after part of the vessel. He jumped at my bellow. He had a sack of weapons slung over his shoulders and the people with other sacks were pushing past. He flung me a look compounded of hatred and fear and hurried to the side. He flung the sack over before following himself, which annoyed me. You don't treat weapons as thoughtlessly as that, not on Kregen.

The ex-slaves tended to jostle as they rushed for safety. You could hardly blame them for that, for now the heat was appreciable. The breeze was not all that strong, and whilst the flames were being blown aft, tongues and evil creeping streamers were eating their way forward.

Here came Kuong and the others, all carrying their appointed pieces. Rollo scrambled down from the conning tower with the control levers. The wires were dragged out and Llodi hauled them along with a will. Mevancy and Tuco were carrying the bronze boxes. All in all, as we scuttled like rats from the burning vessel, we must have presented a macabre sight.

Flames crackled and hissed. Smoke blackened the stars. The Maiden with the Many Smiles shone down refulgently, and fuzzy pink moonlight washed over men and women, over the doomed vessel. We ran and panted away until the heat was such that we could haul up and catch our breaths and watch the end.

Those people ordered to hack away as much as was practical of the forward parts of the flier had the heaviest burdens. One strapping Khibil was hauling a whole huge baulk of timber. I marked him.

I shouted: "Well done, all. It's no good gawping at the fire. Cooks! Get our own fires going and cook!"

This was a calculated risk; but a necessary one. My thoughts were that the Fish Faces might send a patrol out in the morning in curiosity to find out what had become of us. By that time, we'd be gone.

In the event we all ate and drank and then taking up our burdens trudged back to the stream where we could conceal ourselves among the trees.

Now even on Kregen, which is a truly remarkable world, everybody is not superhuman. Men and women react in unpredictable ways under unusual circumstances. So, all right. We had with us folk who were used to being slaves and their reactions to combat were thus modified. We had with us warriors, and their reactions to being made slave were unprintable. I decided we all needed a rest. The suggestion being made to Kuong and Mevancy resulted in immediate agreement. Some people had been injured by the Katakis as to need careful nursing. With our slender resources, this we provided.

Two days, I felt, would be sufficient for all but the worst cases. We had to bury one poor devil of a Fristle who'd been badly beaten. We carried out the necessary rites with due solemnity, commending him to his god, Tsung-Tan, and trusting he went up there in glory to Gilium rather than wandering hopelessly through the Death Jungles of Sichaz.

As the people rested and ate through the next two days I went along between the trees marking those I wanted. We were extremely cautious with fires, using them only for cooking. On the afternoon of the second day the lookouts raised the alarm and we all held still and silent as the Shank flying patrol passed overhead.

On the morning of the third day, as Luz and Walig rose into a marvelous Kregan dawn, Kuong and Mevancy, needing little prompting, set the folk to work.

In the fetching and carrying of tree trunks the big Khibil proved a most satisfactory substitute for a beast of burden. I didn't think of him in exactly that light, until the fact was pointed out, somewhat stuffily, by Kuong's Repositer. The Khibil's name was Quando the Iarvin.

I admit it. I stand guilty and condemned. I laughed.

Well, and why not, after all? My good companion and fellow kregoinye, Pompino the Iarvin, had once had a pretty little run in with a thief wearing the cognomen of Iarvin. A smart fellow, a lad who knows what's what, that's what Iarvin more or less means. Like all Khibils, this Quando knew his own worth and was well aware in his supercilious way he was a cut above the rest.

At least, he was a godsend when it came to lifting the trunks into place. Nothing fancy. That had to be my watchword. We built a raft-like platform and, perforce, had to plait ropes to tie the lot together. The bronze boxes were positioned and the control wires had to be drastically reduced in length as the levers were situated so close to them. Rollo took a deal of interest in all the technical aspects. I fancied he'd be turning into a second Oby, who'd started out desperate to be a kaidur in the Arena, and had wound up as an expert voller pilot and captain.

The body of the raft-like structure took shape. Rails were added and a light structure for shelter along the centre line. The controls were placed in front. I'd had experience building small personal vollers in Sumbakir in Hamal and that knowledge came in useful now.

When all was done I decreed another single day's holiday. Hunters had brought in game, we had the stream for water, and supplies of garsun flour were holding up. Palines, of course, grew freely along the stream.

On the day which Kuong and Mevancy had, between themselves, decided we should leave, the trylon said: "Do you have any special direction, Drajak?"

"Yes, Kuong. I'd like to go to the area just north of Clovang. I left some friends there I'd like to see are all right."

"That is away from the capital, Taranjin."

"Aye."

Mevancy said crisply: "We should be trying to link up with Queen Kirsty's army."

"If it's even formed yet, let alone started."

"Well, cabbage—"

"Also," I said, "we have some poor folk with us who ought to be dropped off in as safe a place as we can. There is fighting ahead."

"That is true, by Spurl!" flashed Mevancy.

"We will," said Kuong, "pick up Drajak's friends, drop off those who we feel are not capable. Then we can see how Queen Kirsty is doing."

Rollo insisted on handling the controls. With everyone packed aboard we soared away and up into the streaming mingled radiance of the Suns of Scorpio.

Four

Fan-Si couldn't stop laughing. She'd started the moment after she and the rest had crawled out of cover and she'd taken in me and the disreputable craft in which we flew.

"A witch did it," she declared, in between whooping in breaths to laugh some more. "Your wonderful voller was changed by a witch into this heap!"

"It certainly is—crude," observed Moglin. He stared at Fan-Si. "If you don't control yourself not only will you do yourself an injury, the prince may well decide to do it for himself. Fan-Si!"

I could see the Fristle fifi's reaction was only triggered by her amusement at the change from the smart voller in which she'd served as my Ship

Hikdar, or first lieutenant, to this lashed up heap. The continuance of her excited reaction, expressed as uncontrollable laughter, had other causes. These, I surmised, had to do with her feelings that she'd never expected to see me alive again.

Her man, Moglin the Flatch, an experienced Fristle Bowman of Loh, put his arm about Fan-Si's delectable waist, whereat she tried to flick him with her tail. He tugged her and, with a glance more than a trifle uneasy at me, kissed her. This stopped her laughing. When they broke away she was sobbing.

Larghos the Throstle shook his head. "Moggers always did have a way with women."

Around us stretched a respectable woodland, threaded by watercourses, with clearings in which flowers grew and struggled between themselves for the mastery of the suns lights. The air scented with Kregan sweetness. The little army I'd managed to scrape together out of various gangs remained still in being. They were upwards of eight hundred souls now, and they continued to carry out the tasks I had set them. They had suffered casualties.

These three were my Jiktars, my commanders of regiments, Moglin the Flatch, Larghos the Throstle, and Fan-Si, who loved to ride through the air aboard the voller. Well, where that was now only the Star Lords knew, for they had hoicked me up out of her and dumped me down in Taranjin— after an argument.

Mevancy, crisply, through thinned lips, said: "These are your friends."

With due respect for protocol, I made the pappattu. When the introductions were over, and Kuong had been particularly gracious, Mevancy rounded on me. Her always highly-colored face positively glowed.

"Well, now, cabbage. And what is all this prince nonsense?"

As they say in Clishdrin, sow the wind and reap the whirlwind. I'd been going around Kregen sowing many different names, and now here was my comeuppance. These three new comrades and the little army we ran knew me as Prince Chaadur na Dorfu, the Striker, Kurinfaril, their chief. Also, they knew this was not my real name. This had been done in my expectations of gaining a significant victory over the Shanks and the Schtarkins and chucking them out of Tarankar. As my plans had gone awry I was now stuck with two different names to be accounted for.

Kuong and Rollo were listening with great interest.

"Come on, cabbage. Prince?"

"The thing is," I began, most shiftily, and, what was worse, hearing that shiftiness in my voice. I sounded positively guilty as charged.

Kuong said: "You have always struck me as a man of great position, Drajak. One can tell these things. I, for one, would readily accept your assurances that you were a prince."

Now I know Kuong was a young noble, full of noble ideas. But, give it to him—you couldn't say fairer than he had, by Vox!

I said: "One of my names is Drajak. It is more than a simple use name. I chose to use my name of Prince Chaadur here to replace the leaders lost by these people when the Shanks overcame them. I do assure you, strange though it seems, I am a prince."

That was the truth, of course.

Mevancy shook her head. Not a beautiful woman, our Mevancy, but strong featured, well-built, radiant when animated, her beauty came all from deep inside her, an essential part of her spirit. "I—I always thought—suspected—there was something odd and special about you, cabbage—"

"Oh, aye, Most odd. Now can we get on? We have a lot to do."

Llodi stepped forward. His face looked troubled.

"What do I call you now, Drajak, what with you being a prince an' everything?"

"You call me Drajak as you have always done. It does not always suit me to be known as a prince."

"Oh, I see that an' all."

Rollo suddenly sneezed, largely and loudly. I ignored him. I knew damn well what he was about, the scamp.

He must be having a good laugh at these antics of names, knowing as he did that I was Dray Prescot. He was enjoying me wriggling on the hook of my own duplicity, laughing so hard inside he had to sneeze, by Krun!

During this fascinating period of name calling Fan-Si had recovered.

She approached me with her tail decorously looped at her rear. She was not wearing armor, against my express command, and I'd have a word with Moglin about that.

"Prince," she started, and rubbed her nose. "Prince—my girls—"

There were ten of them now, ten Fristle fifis, armed and armored—well, some of them—standing in an expectant line. These were the Jikai Vuvushis of our little army who had flown with me and hurled fire pots down on Shank flying ships.

I turned to Kuong. "Kuong—they have proved useful and brave and are grand fighting Jikai Vuvushis. I'd very much like to take them." I added, more grimly, for this revealed a darker side of the affair: "Also, I would not relish leaving them here."

At once he said: "The decision must now be yours, prince." He used that word prince unaffectedly. He was nowhere near as surprised or discomfited as I'd anticipated at my sudden elevation, and in that, as I saw later, I did him a grave injustice. A fine lad, Trylon Kuong of Taranik.

Not wanting to get into a maudlin or sentimental argument over rankings, I nodded. "Thank you. Very well, Fan-Si, get your girls aboard."

As was to be expected, the rest of the army being left behind started up their caterwauling. I raised my arms and they quietened down. There were not the whole eight hundred here, of course; there were enough to listen and repeat the message. That message was the same old fustian, elaborated on by a brief account of what had occurred in the capital city, Taranjin. I finished by assuring them that the Day would Dawn when the Freedom Armies would burst into the city to join the risen slaves, and the Armadas from Hamal and Vallia would arrive.

"In that great Day, all the Fish Faces will be driven out of Tarankar, and men and women can go back to living decent lives once again!"

They cheered; but the applause sounded thin.

We shouted the remberees and our crazily strung-together craft lifted off. She'd been given the name Deliverance. The name fitted, for she had saved us. Those of the freed slaves who wished to remain with the Freedom Army did so. Now Deliverance carried fighting men and women.

The interesting development of our relationships I noticed now was interesting, all right. By Makki Grodno's disgusting diseased nose and infected inner ear! It was fascinating, intriguing—and positively eerie.

No one—not Mevancy, not Kuong, not anybody—asked me what our plans were or what we were going to do. They didn't even ask where we were heading.

My initial intentions were to make the rounds of the scattered groups of Freedom Fighters. They had to be ready. Now that the Opaz-forsaken Shanks had brought in hired Katakis to take effective control of the slaves the anticipated slave revolt had become enormously more difficult. There were those who said, openly, that a slave uprising was now impossible.

The next thing was to make contact with the armadas flying here. Their arrival was problematical at the moment. Many mischances had contrived to hold them up. Rollo the Runner had been charged by me to stay in Makilorn to make contact and liaise with my Guard Corps. I couldn't really find it in my heart to blame him for joining Kuong and Mevancy and following me. All the same, at the moment I had no idea how the armadas were progressing.

Our shambling tree trunk raft of a flying boat sailed on serenely enough. The Shanks had copied the Hamalese way of organizing the power boxes in their orbits. I wondered just what was in those two bronze boxes. I'd had a few fraught excitements trying to find out what mix of minerals was placed in the Hamalese silver boxes. Without the correct mix you'd come up with a silver box that would lift a ship and grip her onto the ethereal-magnetic lines but would not give her any forward motion. We'd used those sub-silver boxes in Vallia because we'd had to. We'd built what we called vorlcas, box-like constructions that passed as ships. One bonus derived from the ships not having to sail the sea was that we did not need compass timber. We built the vorlcas with straight lines and slab sides, deck on deck. Because Vallian galleons were the best sailing ships of the outer oceans—apart from the Shanks' remarkable ocean going vessels—we could rig our sailing ships of the air with centuries old skills.

The armada from Vallia had consisted of vorlcas. They had been blown off course, involved in a fight, and were now down somewhere repairing. Where the armada from Hamal had got to I didn't know. They had sailing ships of the air, also, and these they called famblehoys.

I'd relieved Rollo at the controls and was standing up forward contemplating the multitude of problems confronting me. In order to save Paz an inordinate amount of back-breaking work had to be put in. I don't believe in feeling sorry for myself; but if ever I had, then I ought to have been feeling sorry for myself then, by Krun!

Mevancy came up and stood at my side, looking ahead, saying nothing.

There was no gainsaying she was a funny girl. She was not beautiful, as I have said; but she radiated an inner strength and beauty I found admirable. She had heard me speak of my lady—and I meant Delia—and had sniffed and been sarcastic. Mevancy had tacitly agreed a compact with Leotes before he'd given his life for her. Although, mind you, he was still alive in the body of a newborn baby. If you believed that. Now Mevancy had received the distinct, direct and definite answer from me that she was not and never could be my lady. Was Kuong next in line?

Presently, to break the silence that had become oppressive, I said:

"Mevancy. You'll have to learn piloting, like Rollo. Would you care to start now?"

She didn't turn to face me.

"In some things, I suppose, as you are a prince, you will give the orders. And I suppose flying this contraption would come under that." Now she turned to face me. Her splendid eyes fixed me with a direct and challenging gaze. "But in matters for the Everoinye, cabbage, remember. I am still in charge."

"Of course, pigeon."

"What did you mean, you know, about hitting your head when I was dragging you out of the burning building?"

"Do you remember how you got where you were after you'd collapsed trying to pull poor old Rafael out? I mean, got to the outside?"

"Rafael," she said, and looked down at her boots. Presently, she said: "Well—vaguely, not really—it was all so confused and hot—"

"Oh, aye. It was hot. Worse than back aboard the Shanks' flier."

She cocked an eye at me. "So?"

"So you don't remember. Well, it's not worth remembering."

"Now look here, Drajak, or prince, or whatever your name is. You set about those Katakis and Fish Heads smartly enough. I know you're no

Dray Prescot; but I will admit you put up a very good imitation. So you were supposed to be a weakling—"

I shouldn't have said it. But: "So I was after I hit my head."

Her lips clamped into a demanding line. "There you go again. It's—"

"Look, Mevancy. That's all over with now. I don't forget how you came back for me in the desert and the way you dealt with the vulture and the bandits. Now I suggest you allow me to teach you how to fly."

Her spirit was bold enough to rise to that challenge. She saw that she'd get no more out of me. By Krun! The poor girl had been dragged out of the burning building by me at the commands of the Star Lords. At the last minute I'd been temporarily knocked down by a falling beam and Mevancy had awoken and dragged me the last few yards. In that dragging she'd contrived to hit my head hard enough to paralyze me. Now she had to learn to fly.

Rollo the Runner walked up. He stood looking as Mevancy got the hang of keeping the airboat on a steady and level course. He didn't exactly smile condescendingly. I still had to fathom out his relationship with Kuong and Mevancy.

So, being a devious devil at heart, I said: "Rollo. Why don't you help Mevancy?"

I walked off down the treetrunk deck. Let 'em sort that one out!

Whatever agreement they reached the next couple of days as we reached the group led by Kov Nath the Ron and his kovneva, Layla, they did not come to blows nor did I see any argument. They were both forthright people, and one comment brought forth another. They'd gone through adventures together and that often, not always, tends to bind folk one to another.

Kuong had expressed his desire to learn to fly and I'd asked Rollo if he would oblige. He could scarcely refuse.

Needing to take myself off to think, I was about to leave the camp where the cooking fires had already been doused. I got past the last fire and Rollo cut across my path. He seemed to me to be walking in a jerky fashion and I frowned. I'd never seen him drunk. If anybody in my circle became drunk he had one more chance. The second drunken episode resulted in ejection. Drunks are not funny. Oh, sure, you laugh at their antics when cleverly reproduced on stage; real drunkenness is disgusting.

He said: "Lahal, Dray."

I stopped and remained silent, staring at him in the Moons' glow.

"There is not much time. Can you fly right away?"

"Of course, Deb-Lu. Where and what has happened?"

Rollo's voice changed from his own to the friendly wheezy tones of Deb-Lu-Quienyin. Deb-Lu was dwaburs away in Vallia, using his kharrna to project not his image but his vision and voice. As a most potent Wizard of Loh, Deb-Lu was a valued comrade. He spoke succinctly.

"An airboat is down north of you, outskirts of Chem. Most unhealthy. When you near the exact spot I'll guide you in."

"Right. A northerly course it is. Who's aboard?"

"Better ask me who isn't aboard."

My heart both sank and rose. By Zair! It would be like them all, like her, like—

Rollo said: "Deb-Lu has gone."

"Break camp. All aboard. We're flying north!"

Five

From Tarankar the west coast of Loh bulged out to the west in a great arc of coastline until, just south of the equator, it curved in again and then was drawn in a subtle sweep up to the northern point of the continent, the land of mountains and valleys, called Erthyrdrin, from whence hailed Seg. Chem sprawled all across the equator. There was no dividend for us in flying due north. We had no wish to tangle with the Fish Faces and their flying ships again. We could take the westerly route over the sea or the easterly over the desert. In deciding to go via the eastern route I was guided by a strong desire not to fall into the water if the bronze boxes failed. We took many pots of water, just in case we came down in the desert. Then we flew.

Pouring on the power, ferociously impatient, I took the controls and willed the little tree trunk craft onward.

People took one look at me and then kept out of my way.

Of them all it was Fan-Si who came forward, diffidently, tail flicking over one shoulder and then the other, to request that I allow someone else to pilot and took my rest.

That made sense, of course. The trouble is, when Delia is in danger, sense and I part company. I looked at the little Fristle fifi in a fashion that did not make her flinch back. Rather, I think she saw the dazed expression on my face and understood I was in the grip of a powerful emotion.

"Rest?" I said, stupidly.

"You'll fall down, else—prince."

Mevancy hove up then, tight-lipped. She gave me a look.

"Very well." They were right, of course. I'd be of no use if we arrived in the middle of trouble and I kept falling asleep. "We will fly through the night. Rollo will have to take the controls then."

Now, mark this. We were supposed to be engaged in freeing Tarankar from the Schtarkins. We were to have flown to arrange the Day of Uprising, to contact Queen Kirsty's army, to synchronize all the elements that should fuse to chuck the Fish Faces out. Yet no one questioned why we thus flew so madly north, away from Tarankar.

Interestingly enough, and I didn't believe it, with my brain whirling with fear and concern for Delia and the others, I slept. I closed my eyes and Mevancy was shaking my shoulder and saying: "It's morning, cabbage."

I sat up, blinking.

The truth of the matter was I'd been pushing myself too hard lately—although that is normal for me on Kregen, by Vox! Nature had done what she could to patch me up. I felt refreshed.

Mevancy's eyes were red.

"Did you sleep, pigeon?"

"A little. Over there—" and she pointed to the west "—is Sinnalix."

The early morning suns filled the sky with apple green and peach pink. The air breezed past like the bubbles in sparkling fresh spring water. This was a day to be up and doing, to be about great affairs on Kregen.

"Sinnalix," I said, deliberately repeating the name of her home country. "You are a kregoinya. I suppose the Everoinye wouldn't mind if you made a trip home. When we're done here."

"Oh, I'm not homesick, fambly!"

"It's no business of mine, then. Now, pigeon, breakfast!"

As we roared on over the rolling grasslands below, the desert far astern, the jungles ahead, we ate the first breakfast. Toilet facilities were arranged behind a canvas screen, and I allowed only wetted cloths—there was no pouring of pots of water over anybody. Llodi, who had found himself a strangdja, kept guard on the water supply. Any sensible person looking at the strangdja and seeing that wicked steel holly-leaf-shaped head would decide not to attempt to steal more than their fair share of water.

Something was bothering Mevancy.

An unnatural calm had fallen on me. We were going as fast as we could. We would reach the downed voller when we did. Only then would I know the true gravity of the situation, for Deb-Lu, probably quite rightly, had not put in another appearance.

Munching the last of my handful of palines and relishing the yellow berries as every single person of Kregen relishes them, I came across Mevancy sitting on the edge of the raft flier, her legs dangling overside. She was looking out to the west.

I said: "If you fall off, cabbage, I shall not stop to pick you up."

"She means so much to you, then?"

I was startled.

Mevancy went on in a low voice: "The lady of whom you have spoken."

"Yes."

Mevancy lifted up her shoulders and let them slump. She had one arm wrapped around a rail support. If she let go and tried to do anything foolish I would stop and catch her first.

The enormity of that thought suddenly made me feel insignificant. She'd thought she'd been in love with Leotes, and now she knew she had not been. I had the funny old thought that she and Kuong might make a go of it. Mevancy, although she had forearms covered with bindles with which she could destroy a man's face, was a different form of apim. She was a sport, a mutation, peculiar to her country. Kuong was apim. The match would be a good one.

Still, that was a subject I could not mention to her.

When Deb-Lu showed up to guide us in he did so in a lupal projection. You could not see through his body. There was no blue nimbus about his figure or halo about his head. He stood on the tree trunks smiling at me in his old familiar way—and his damned turban toppled almost over one ear until he shoved it straight.

"Jak! You have made good time."

He often called me Jak in remembrance of past and fraught times of mutual adventure. Also he knew my fad for aliases. Rollo came up and was most polite. A number of Kuong's people tended to congregate as far away from the sorcerer as they could get. There was no undue muttering. The existence of mages is a mere matter of fact upon Kregen.

Mevancy and Kuong stood silently at the side as I said: "Deb-Lu, perhaps you would be good enough to instruct Rollo in our course."

Rollo gave me a leery look. "You will allow me to fly?"

"Carry on."

Giving them no more time to talk I went as far forward as I could and stretched out on a projecting trunk. I clung on as a monkey clings to his mother as they swing through the trees. I looked down.

The trees were down there, all right. They were not brellam trees. The smells of the jungle wafting upwards in the hot air brought a spicy tickle to my nostrils. There was a sense of the whole body being bathed in exotic perfumes. The trees grew in great folds and swathes of ground, following the contours, and yet they did not form an unbroken canopy. Narrow watercourses threaded in what appeared haphazard directions and here the trees left the sky open. The ground was extremely stony, the streams being littered with boulders, and I guessed the topsoil lay only thinly over the rocks. The trees were not the incredibly tall giants of many of Kregen's jungles; they might be shorter of stature, they formed a massive living organism in which animal life flourished.

There was no need for that dramatic—and, if the truth be told, ostentatious—gesture on my part of going right forward so that I should be the first to spot the downed voller. We fleeted in over the treetops as Rollo held her in sure control and there was a wide-spaced clearing ahead, ringed by trees, shooting into view as we cleared the last branches.

The situation was at once plain and at once horrible.

The voller was of a type I did not recognize. She was barely visible for the multitude of ropelike lines stretching from the encircling trees across her decks and upperworks. These web-like structures were white and sticky and as I stared down more lashed out from the tree tops to fasten about the vessel. They were trying to pull her up so the cruel spined flowers about the trunks could devour their prey. The voller lurched up and to the accompaniment of a gust of foul-stinking air and a belching sucking sound, sagged back to her former position. The grass all about the clearing was of a bright brilliant green.

That ominous bright green lapped up all along the hull of the voller, like a thousand mouths trying to suck her down.

Rollo called down: "I do not need to tell you what that is!"

He'd saved us from one of these deadly shuckerchuns on our way south.

I pulled myself back from that ungainly perch and stood up. I was not feeling happy. I was feeling rather as though I'd like to poke out the eyes of whatever devils had a hand in this infernal affair.

"The shuckerchun is trying to pull the voller down. The trees are trying to pull her up. What are the damned things?"

"They're a kind of syatra," responded Rollo at once. "Some change in their environment changed them, too. They're called flitchlaks. They can whip a sticky tendril about you and whip you up to their flower in no time at all. Unholy things."

"The ground sucks down and the trees pull up," said Kuong with a voice heavy with concern. "They are in balance."

"If we cut the lines," observed Mevancy. "The voller will be sucked down."

Rollo swung our little craft in a circle about the clearing. Everybody looked down. Not a single sign of movement was visible on that tendril-infested vessel below.

I said: "Deb-Lu—can you let them know—?"

He nodded so that his turban almost tumbled off onto the floor of his chamber back home in Vallia. "Khe-Hi is already there, Jak. Just to hearten them, you understand."

As I turned back from the Wizard of Loh to stare sickly down at that frightful scene below, I caught a glimpse of Fan-Si creeping up to join the party in the bows. I heard her say in her sibilant Fristle whisper:

"But what can we do?"

The voller was held in suspension between the sucking shuckerchun and the lifting flitchlaks. The shuckerchun had evidently worked its way along under the ground. It moved slowly and the process would have taken a deal of time so that the trees had grown up again after their ancestors had been pulled under. My guess was that the shuckerchun was looking for a richer ground than that afforded by the thin topsoil and stony land here.

As for the flitchlaks, perhaps they welcomed a clearing there, even a clearing which vied with them for food. I could imagine the race between the two to snare game wandering into the lethal clearing.

But, as Fan-Si had said, what could we do?

The first and obvious solution I had immediately discarded. The danger to the people aboard the flying raft was unacceptable. But as I struggled and twisted my brains for a better solution I kept coming back to the obvious. I always enjoy an elegant solution to a problem. If the people kept steady aboard the raft, their peril could be controlled to a level that was acceptable. The elegance came in using the lethality of the problem for its own solution.

If I landed them somewhere nearby they might well be in as much peril, from flitchlaks, syatras, hungry reptiles or any of a hundred jungle dangers, as risking it with me aboard the flying raft. Anyway, I was in no mood to shilly-shally. I wanted this thing done, and done quickly.

So, seeing nothing else for it, I made up my mind.

"Llodi, Moggers, Larghos, Tuco—help me rip up these end timbers. Don't cut the lines, we'll need them to tie the trunks again."

With that I was off to the stern of the raft where I started in ripping up the end trunks. They stared at me somewhat blankly—only for a moment, though, by Krun! Only for a moment.

"Get stuck into it, you lollygagging bunch of hulus! Bratch!"

They jumped.

Following my impatient lead they carried the released timbers to the bows where they were placed from the front rail slanting down to the deck. Other shorter timber was placed across the front, and enough of a gap was left for me to see through. In short order we'd built a sloping triangular shelter over the controls.

"Now wrap those lines around. Tie 'em fast! That's the style."

Rollo said: "I can fit in there nicely enough. But to what purpose?"

I said: "You don't fit. I do."

"But—"

"You help to get everyone in the deck shelter and don't let 'em out."

"I see!" He snapped it out at me. "It's a crazy scheme! The flitchlaks will rip that flimsy shelter to pieces and snatch you out for lunch!"

I wasn't prepared to argue. I could have said the tendrils would not find it easy to get at me. If they did I happened to have a sword. All the same, elegant though my solution to the problem was, it remained a crazy scheme.

Inevitably, as I knew and accepted with a resignation I tried not to make too hasty, I had trouble with Trylon Kuong.

In his open, free way, he said: "I do not quite see what you seek to accomplish here. All the same, I shall stand with you."

Here was where the tomfoolery of being a prince paid off.

I said: "Your offer is befitting your courage, trylon. However, I'm the prince here, and I'm the one to do the job."

His face showed genuine disappointment. "Of course, prince."

We were pulling the last lines tight around the lash-up of logs. Just what these damned flitchlaks could do or not I just didn't know. Ominously enough, Rollo, who did know, kept up a gloomy, hurt silence. Mevancy looked nervous. "We can only take a few people at a time, cabbage. And while we're waiting the tendrils will grab us."

"I want the tendrils to grab us. As many as possible."

"What?"

"You keep your head inside the deck shelter. If a flitchlak's tendril grabs your head it won't remain between your shoulders."

"And, cabbage, what about yours?"

There was nothing to say to that. Just before I squeezed into the tiny triangular space abaft the controls I wondered if I ought to have found a spot to dump these people down. I was running them into hideous danger. My mind was decided in a most unpleasant—not to say frightening—way by the movements of the voller down there in the clearing.

The flitchlaks were bending over and all the time they had been bending further and further. They continued to shoot out fresh lines. The earlier ones were breaking under the strain. Whilst this scared me, it also heartened me, reinforcing the correctness of my decision. The balance we had at first discerned between sucking and pulling was now becoming an imbalance. Time had suddenly become vital.

Speed, of course, had always been essential.

If the confounded tendrils or tentacles or lianas fastened about the little flying raft before I'd conned her where I wanted her to be then the whole scheme would be in ruins. Into the bargain, we'd all be trapped.

A single yell back: "Everybody inside?" and Kuong's answering shout: "All in!" and I set myself. The controls felt slick and warm under my fingers. The air held a close mugginess in that confined space. There was one chance and one chance only. A single mistake and it'd be the Ice Floes of Sicce for us all, or, down here in Loh, the Death Jungles of Sichaz. I shoved the controls over to full speed and swung the little craft in a swinging sweep into the clearing.

Instantly the snaking white lines hissed past. They crisscrossed in a dazzling pattern. I swung and swerved about, feeling the momentary checks on speed as a line whipped across and held for an instant. Then the raft would lurch and the tendril snap and curl away and on we'd hurtle.

Straight down for the stranded voller I plunged. The white mass of tendrils festooning decks and superstructure looked as though a giant chef had gone mad with an icing bag and piped in maniac abandon. A clotted solid mass of the things clothed the ship. I aimed for my target and jinked and sideslipped and so in a wind-rushing storm slapped down hard.

The moment I touched the voller and sank some way into the clustered white tendrils line after line hissed past, wrapping the raft in a sticky cocoon.

Almost at once all vision ahead was lost. Only a faint gray light seeped past the flitchlaks' tentacles across the forward observation slit.

There was no need to see. I could feel it all. The lash and thump across my fragile shelter, the way the raft jumped. I waited.

I waited.

By the stinking putrescent nostrils and dangling eyeballs of Makki Grodno! I waited.

Apart from the thud of lines slamming across the logs I could feel the steady and deadly sinking beneath my feet. There was no doubt about it. The shuckerchun was winning the contest. Before long the voller would be sucked down, all the lines broken, and nothing would remain on the surface of Kregen of all my friends here.

This was it. I could wait no longer. I was gambling, yes; but I was not gambling entirely blind. If the shuckerchun sucked the voller down far enough, dragged her deeply enough below the surface, my fine gamble might not pay off. Now was the time!

Gently—oh, so gently!—I eased the control lever over.

If I had miscalculated...

At first, nothing happened. We did not rise. I moved the lever a fraction more. The raft lurched. I could feel the heavier touch to her, the sense of weight. Another fraction. We lifted. I could still see nothing ahead. A vast tearing ripping sound was followed at once by a slobbering sucking noise. A filthy stench gusted up.

I felt the elation.

We were lifting! We were rising! The sucking sound and the stench confirmed the feel of the controls. The handling told me we were rising up with the voller stuck to us by the flitchlaks' own tendrils.

Slowly we rose and then with a monstrous gush of effluvium we shot up into the air.

I took the combined crafts up and up and then thrust the levers over to take us away from that cursed clearing.

The first person to break out of the deck shelter and, sword in hand, slash away the white tendrils from my triangular haven was Kuong. With him were Mevancy and Llodi, and the others crowded up after. Suns shine broke across my face. I looked out at my new friends.

Then I simply ran for the raft's side and dropped over onto the confused mass of white tendrils, sword in fist.

Six

"Well, my grizzly graint. You do look a sight!"

So powerful were my emotions that after I'd hacked and hewed a way through the clinging sticky lines I'd simply burst into the control top and clasped her in my arms. I could feel her heart beating against mine. We trembled together, heart to heart, and nothing else mattered in all of Earth or Kregen.

Her face—radiant, radiant!—upturned to mine, that delicious half-smile, so mocking, so tender, so gut-rending, telling me that here she was, in my arms, all meant so much, so much—I managed to steady myself and become half aware of my surroundings.

"By Zair! All this sticky mess—and now it's all over you!"

She laughed, that laugh that sends razor blades up and down my spine, that makes my knees like bananas. Her brown hair with those outrageous chestnut tints, her eyes—her eyes!—her mouth of so soft and rich a red, smiling at me—by Vox, but what it is to be loved!

"We know about that sticky mess, dear heart, never worry."

She wore her russets, trim and compact about that superb figure. Rapier and main gauche swung from her belts, and her long Vallian dagger nestled in its own sheath. Her sandals were very plain and practical. A little jewelry, a little perfume, oh, no, she has no need to gild the lily.

There were other people in the control top. The armored box, round and warlike, housed the control levers. She gently disengaged herself, and said: "We tried to cut the lines and poor Nol the Arm was snatched up."

"Nol the Arm—a good lad, a Deldar in 1ESW—what a tragedy."

"Too right, my old dom," said a strong familiar wonderful voice. "We had to haul Inch in, for he was flailing away with his axe like a—"

I swung about, blindly, choked with emotion.

"Seg! Inch!"

"Oh, aye, my old dom. We're here."

"As Ngrangi is my witness!"

I stared at them, my splendid blade comrades. Seg, with his fey ways, his wild black hair and blue eyes, the finest bowman in two worlds, and Inch of Ng'groga, thin as a lath, seven feet tall, absolutely lethal with his two-handed Saxon pattern axe. They knew me. We'd had wild adventures in the old days—and more to come, by Krun!—and without the need for words we knew we'd all die for the others. And here came Korero the Shield, four-armed and tail-handed, magnificent and golden, a Kildoi of remarkable powers who carried two shields at my back in battle. And Balass the Hawk, his superb black face shining with joy, the best sword and shield man in the business. And—would you believe—young Oby who was not so young these days, a lad who'd been a mischievous sprite desperate to enter the Arena, and now a voller pilot and captain of this vessel. And the others, many of whom you have met in my narrative—the lads of First Emperor's Sword Watch, who are a mighty independent set of rascals, who arrange their own hierarchy, day by day, so that all are, in my eyes, chiefs.

Seg said: "Turko was coming but at the last minute he couldn't make it. There were a lot of other folk pixilated they didn't come."

"They've missed this little lot," said Inch. "My taboos—"

That broke the artificial situation. We all laughed. Dear old Inch and his taboos! He'd be standing on his head, or banging his head against a wall, to expiate his crime in breaking whatever taboo it was this time.

Seg said: "Milsi's below—"

"And so is Sasha," added Inch.

These two comrades had sent their ladies below to a greater safety than here. I looked at Delia.

"Well!" she flashed.

Seg said: "Milsi and Sasha agreed to do what was sensible and as their husbands asked them. But who can tell the empress?"

"Seg, dear. I'm not the empress any more. Your daughter Silda is the Empress of Vallia now."

Seg made such a comical face that we all laughed again. Yes, all right. This laughter was reaction, a fearful danger was past and now we had to recover. All the same, it was hard to remember that we were not the Emperor and Empress of Vallia. But Seg's next remark showed a deeper understanding. "I mean, Delia dear, that you are the Empress of Empresses, the Empress of Paz. And I was thinking how all mighty puffed up we are with titles these days, when only a short time ago we didn't have a copper ob between us and were often chained up as slaves—"

"I don't forget those days," said Inch, and his voice was, on a sudden, remarkably grim. "Now, if you will excuse me, I will be off to see about my taboos."

Now it is perfectly clear that all the people aboard were not in the control top. My memory may be perfect through the influence of the Savanti; all the same, in that moment emotion tended to make me jumble up the order of events. Most of the 1ESW lads and the other bright sparks who'd managed to wangle passage aboard were below. A head looked in the open door and a cutting voice said: "Cabbage! Rollo would rather like to know the course to steer. If you're not too busy, of course."

Everybody turned to look at the newcomer in the doorway.

The next instant and before anyone could say anything, a tall figure appeared alongside Mevancy and—somehow—Mevancy was no longer in the doorway. Another figure appeared and both rushed at me. I was engulfed by two beautiful women, both of whom totally ignored the sticky gunk smeared over me. Now Sasha is nearly as tall as Inch, and although slender is not as thin as a lath. And Milsi is warm and wonderful and every inch a queen. I kissed them both and then said: "I am glad my comrades have sensible wives. Unlike some people—"

Now Delia might have interrupted in some wise as: "If you think, Dray Prescot, I'm going to skulk below then you've another think coming." She did not. She was sensitive enough to the feelings of Milsi and Sasha, good comrades all. And that shows how stupid I can be—sensitive to feelings! My Delia, my Delia of Delphond, my Delia of the Blue Mountains, has so much of pure humanity I give thanks every day that she just is.

Well, we sorted ourselves out.

Making the pappattu took time. As you will easily comprehend, introducing so many people did take time; and I enjoyed it all. I had most certainly changed from the grizzly old graint of the Dray Prescot who had landed on Kregen all those seasons ago.

Eventually, I managed to say to Mevancy: "Pigeon—Rollo. Ask him to find a nice clearing by a stream. We all need to clean up."

Mevancy gave Delia a long long look. I think she realized now just what I had been trying to tell her. She maintained a nice cheery spirit and was pleasant all round. I found a great affection for her in those moments when she saw reality.

What she was really thinking and feeling I dreaded to know.

Rollo took us down into a clearing where the grass was not a bright and lethal green. We all went out to inspect the voller and the raft.

The tendrils had done their job. My elegant solution had worked. The flitchlaks had secured us to the flier safely. The lifting power in the Shank's bronze boxes had been more than ample to tear us free of the shuckerchun. Looking at some of the white tendrils, though, I saw how close a thing it had been. Many had broken and the rest were badly strained and ready to part.

Seg put his lips together, and puffed, and then he tut-tutted. He nodded to the serpentine weavings binding raft to voller. "That was a long chance, my old dom."

"A chance. Not too long. I'd already seen a voller haul herself out of a shuckerchun, a smallish ten-placer, and the Shank's bronze boxes are more powerful than that—more powerful than I'd thought."

Inch, over on my other side, was facing away and as Seg and I walked on in our tour of inspection, Inch walked backwards with us.

Now he said, lightly: "And we all know the story of that smallish ten place airboat! Your Guard Corps people are abrupt, to say the least."

Seg cut in: "They're a good-hearted bunch if you don't rub 'em up the wrong way. But, look at the keel, here. I don't like that."

No more did I. Between sinuous tree-tendrils and greedy ground a chunk of the hull by the keel had been torn away. We could look up into the interior of the vessel when she flew. It was an important enough point for us to go back aboard and down the ladders to the orlop. Here the extent of the damage was plain. One of the four massive baulks on which the armored box containing the silver boxes was located had been strained and splintered. The miracle was the timber hadn't fallen out through the hole in the bottom. The armored box had been built up out of iron plates riveted together. Two of these plates had popped their rivets when the whole box had twisted. I looked inside.

Dim though it was, I could see the silver boxes were still silver. They had not gone black. I pulled my head out and said: "Anyway, what in a Herrelldrin Hell were you doing down there? You had no power."

Inch said in his sad-funny way: "The silver boxes let us down, like they used to do, and no one knew why." His voice took on a defiant almost comic-bluster tone as he said: "Anyway, that clearing looked nice."

Seg said: "I thought you were expiating a taboo bust by walking backwards—"

"So?"

"So how did you get down the ladders?"

I knew what Seg meant. You can descend a ladder frontways or backwards; but if you have to walk backwards, what is the opposite of that in the ladder sense? Trust Seg and Inch to get themselves into a ludicrously trifling philosophical debate!

Inch looked shifty. "I cheated. That taboo bust will cost me a whole dish of palines at dinner."

"Oh, no!" I said. "Is there a crime bad enough to warrant the denial of palines after dinner?"

Inch said: "You come from Taboo Ng'groga and you'd better believe it."

The most wonderful voice in two worlds spoke from the hole in the hull: "Just how did you cheat, Inch, dear?"

"I slid down the ladders."

Seg roared his mirth and then broke out: "Frontwards or backwards?" whereat Inch made a cutting remark anent axes and bows, and they were off again, joyously slanging each other and teasingly refusing to be serious as is our custom in good times and bad. I turned to the rent in the hull.

"Where'd you get this voller? I've not seen her like before."

She pointed up. "Since neither you nor I can wriggle through the part of the hole visible, I will meet you on the deck. The cleaning goes on."

One does not need a second hint when Delia of Delphond hints. I grabbed a stick and pitched in with the rest in scraping and cleaning and getting the white sticky tendrils off. A deal of water and scrubbing would have to go on. Holystoning, well, that was a task of my boyhood and one I had myself ordered as the first luff of a ship of the line. I've remarked about cleanliness of decks apropos of the Fish Faces' filthy habits. I am well aware I'm prejudiced in this matter; but early training sears the brain.

An interesting glimpse was afforded me of Llodi and Tuco working alongside a couple of my lads of 1ESW with Moglin and Larghos on the other and I had the sudden and enlightening conviction that all those rascals would get on one with another in friendly fashion. If they didn't then I'd have to knock a few heads together.

By the time the voller was cleaned up I was able to gain an appreciation of her lines and build. She was a surprise, all right.

"We had a visit from the ambassador of Tomecdrin in Balintol." Delia brought out a dish of palines and we all dug in—all save poor Inch. She went on: "They'd heard we were over the Times of Troubles and wished to set up trading links. I must say, Drak and Silda received them in fine style."

"It was a good little shindig," observed Seg.

"You didn't—" I said. "You didn't... No. Of course not. Farris would have negotiated the purchase for the Air Service. No. Silly of me to imagine you needed to—"

"Farris is getting very old these days." Delia spoke gravely.

"He refuses the solution," said Inch. "In a funny way I can understand that. I don't blame him."

"But," I persisted. "You didn't actually—"

"Not," said Seg, "actually."

"A kind of loan before purchase," said Delia.

They all smiled sweetly upon me.

I started to groan in despair of my comrades and the problems I'd have with the ambassador from Tomecdrin. Then, in a blaze of glory, I realized. "By the Black Chunkrah! It's not up to me! It's all Drak and Silda's!" I beamed upon them. "A loan before purchase!"

"And the dratted thing broke down," said Delia, cuttingly.

"We will fix the Shanks' bronze boxes in the orbits in place of the Tomecdrin silver boxes. The bronze ones are very efficient."

"Pity we can't open 'em and find out how they differ."

"We'll do that, Seg, when we get home," said Delia.

"The damned Shanks," said Inch, with feeling. "Their ocean-going ships are superior to ours. Have the rotten Leem-Lovers better fliers, too?"

I gave him a quick glance. One did not hear that old expression 'Leem-Lovers' for the Shanks very much these days. It was still used. But in our circle Leem-Lover now really meant a degraded follower of the evil cult of Lem the Silver Leem—which remained still to be defeated.

"By the Veiled Froyvil! Even if they have, we'll still lick 'em!"

Seg was not boasting; he was stating a fact in which he believed.

"Oh, aye, by Ngrozyan the Axe!" said Inch. "That's true. All the same, it's a pity we can't build ships and fliers as good." As he spoke he made a dismissive gesture with his right hand, a movement at once violent and contemptuous. In the next instant his mass of long yellow hair tumbled free from its restraints and fell flowing about his shoulders. He gave an instinctive and rapid glance upwards. He needn't have bothered: the Maiden with the Many Smiles was not in the sky. Dear old Inch had not broken another of his unaccountable and inscrutable taboos.

After we'd done our bit in the cleaning exercise we'd gone down to the stream to wash. A kind of small pool had formed here above a raggedy tumble of boulders. The water looked most inviting. Across on the opposite bank the trees clustered, on this side we could see a tangle of fallen logs and the looseness of the stony soil. I heard a cheery call and Milsi and Sasha came walking down to us. As they passed some of my fellows of 1ESW the lads straightened up to attention. That was as much a tough old swod's tribute to beauty as to mere rank.

Milsi said: "And I suppose a swim is quite out of the question?"

There did not seem to be any danger in the water. None of us was deceived. Milsi was queen of lands along the River of Bloody Jaws. She understood only too well the terrors lurking beneath the placid surface.

"It's not worth the risk," said Seg, giving Milsi a light kiss on the cheek. "But if you wish, why, then I'll—"

"You, you great oaf, will not!" said Milsi instantly. I hid my smile. Milsi had picked up our harum-scarum ways in fine style.

"Yes, dear," said rough tough he-man Seg Segutorio.

There was a prodigious quantity of news to be learned. I gave them a quick run-down on my activities since, as Delia said in her sweetest and most cutting way: "Since you went out to fly a kite with Inky."

Now we blade comrades had been re-united and we'd talked and laughed and jabbed fun at one another, and every now and then others of our circle would join us—Balass the Hawk, Oby, Korero, any of the Chuktars of the regiment. The twin Suns of Scorpio passed across the heavens, and still we talked and laughed. We made, as I can attest, a brilliant company. I own it; I had become completely selfish. That I had every excuse does not really excuse me. I make no excuses for anything I may do that furthers the well-being of Delia, that goes without question. All the same, slowly—too slowly, really—I began to feel that little itch of unease.

Looking back from the stream to the voller showed me a casual grouping of my lads from the regiment. They did not form what you could call a line. Yet they were there, and they were a barrier.

To understand the mentality of my rascals of the First Emperor's Sword Watch you have to realize how they created themselves in the Times of Troubles specifically to protect the person of their emperor. They'd come from an amazing variety of sources. They had fought in many battles. Now they lived for their regiment, for their emperor, for themselves and for their honor. They had no private home lives—or very very few, a mere handful, who had acquired wives and children. They called their emperor their Kendur. No one outside the Guard Corps was—by their decree, not mine—allowed to call me that.

Given these facts, then, my constant absences from the lads of the Guard Corps was a source of intense frustration to them. They had dedicated their lives to my service, and I kept on slipping away from them. They understood some of the reasons why—after all, they could read the lurid accounts of Dray Prescot leaping around Kregen—and had fashioned a toleration to make their days worthwhile and livable. But, now, you couldn't blame them for assiduously carrying out their duties as they saw them.

Casually, I said: "I'm going to have a look at the voller. What d'you call her?"

Seg said: "She had some folderol name or other. Delia—"

"Shankjid," said Delia, firmly.

"H'm," I said, walking on slowly. "A mighty boastful name, that; but one I rather care for." Jid means bane. The name had to be true.

Directly before me stood two Fristle swods. A swod is the soldier in the ranks, the fellow on whose shoulders everything else rests. In the Guard regiments, although a guard is a juruk and therefore the lads could call themselves jurukkers, and often did, mostly they called themselves swods.

The two Fristles had magnificent cat-men's whiskers. They wore the red of the regiment, and armor, with weaponry girded about them. They held halberds horizontally. Standing against this barrier, Moglin the Flatch stared at the Fristles balefully. His bow slanted over his shoulder. Fan-Si stood as it were to his rear and side, and his arm was about her.

Moglin was saying: "...anybody at all messes with Fan-Si gets a shaft through the guts. Quick, by the barbed shafts of the True Trog Himself!"

Flarvil the Nose, the left hand Fristle, said: "You're fretting over nothing. The girl is safer here than anywhere else on Kregen."

"That's right," amplified Ortyghan the Dagger. "The Kendur don't allow anything like that." Then he said in a most indignant tone: "You are forgetting you're dealing with One ESW."

Then, because they were 1ESW and were romantic Fristles, despite being ferocious swods, Flarvil added, slyly: "Unless, in course, that sweet little Fan-Si prefers a fine upstanding guardsman."

Fan-Si did not exactly giggle; but her tail switched about delightfully.

Ortyghan the Dagger was given that cognomen because he often strapped a dagger to his tail. Fristles were taking up the habit. If the Opaz-forsaken Katakis could blade daggered steel, so could Fristles!

Seg and Delia walked alongside me, with Inch and Milsi and Sasha.

"By Odifor!" quoth Ortyghan, and his daggered tail flashed up over his shoulder. "Any fine girl with any sense would prefer a gallant fellow out of the Kendur's One ESW!" His laugh and that of Flarvil perfectly expressed their playfulness; I could see they teased poor Moglin.

Fan-Si saw that, too. She tugged Moglin. "Come on, Moggers. If they won't let us past to see the prince, then they won't."

"They call Prince Chaadur, Drajak the Sudden, an emperor." Moglin sounded disbelieving, uneasy. Fan-Si kept silent and pulled him away.

Three figures cut off the Fristles from my sight and three of the highest chiefs of 1ESW walked up to me, smiling yet grave. Dorgo the Clis, Naghan ti Lodkwara and Targon the Tapster, good comrades all, wanted to know if we were camping here for the night.

"I hadn't thought," I said, dragging my mind back to this minor decision and away from the dreadful mess I'd made with my new friends.

"Why not?" demanded Delia. "There is water, and the clearing is safe."

"We could all do with some sweet ibroi and the ship with some pungent ibroi," said Milsi, mentioning cleaning materials.

"That's true, by the Veiled Froyvil."

"So we will camp," I said.

"Quidang, jis," said Targon. "We're well equipped."

They'd see to that, all right. Kampeons all, old campaigners, able to look after themselves in the Furnace Fires of Inshurfraz. They'd set up watches and organize everything down to the last detail.

I looked about the clearing. People were already busy setting up the firepits and bringing food out of the voller. There'd be a right old shebang tonight. Over in a little group by themselves I spotted Kuong, Mevancy and Rollo. With a measure of guilt, I supposed they'd tried to walk over to see me, and the lads had politely stopped them, and turned them back. Llodi and Tuco, with Larghos, were joined by Moglin and Fan-Si.

Truly, I'd been remiss!

I said to Delia: "I've made rather a leem's nest of them."

She understood at once. "Well, no harm done if we smooth all now."

When Delia decides to be charming I seriously believe she could make a savage and malignant leem lap milk from her fingers.

Kuong was immediately overwhelmed. Rollo left off being supercilious. And Mevancy—ah, Mevancy! She flowered as Delia in the most natural way admitted her to a personal friendship. There was nothing supercilious about Delia, no hidden mockery. She understood with an intuition that never fails to astound me. Well, as I never tire of saying, there is no single lady of Earth or of Kregen to equal my Delia, my Delia of Delphond, my Delia of the Blue Mountain's.

After a bit, I said: "Before we start the party I must get the bronze boxes fitted into their orbits."

Milsi, half-pouting, said: "Must you, Dray, right away?"

Mevancy gave an enormous start. I suppose she'd understood from the moment we'd all met up. I suppose, understanding, she had not accepted that belief into her conscious mind. Now she had to face it.

Oddly enough, it was Llodi who said: "I was just getting used to calling you Prince Chaadur, Drajak. And now you're Dray Prescot an' all. Fair muddles a fellow up, it does, an' everything."

"Call me what you feel comfortable with," I said. "What you like." Then, very quickly, I added: "Only, not Kendur. The lads have a lien on that."

Mevancy's face was the color of the setting Zim. Slowly, she said: "I said you were never as good as the real Dray Prescot." For a dreadful moment I thought she was going to cry. Her voice was choked. "It's a funny old world, isn't it, cab— I mean, majister."

Sternly, I said: "If you do not call me cabbage, pigeon, I shall be most hurt."

"But—"

Delia took her arm in the most friendly fashion. "I have some nice clothes in a cedar trunk with crushed flowers. You must choose what you like. There are far too many for me."

In something of a daze, Mevancy went off with the divine Delia.

Well, we had the most enormous party that night, singing and dancing by the lights of the Moons. It was a high old time. There was ample to eat and enough to drink and no one was boorish enough to get drunk.

The night passed and although I could have wished that the Suns of Scorpio would wait before they rose into the dawn sky, rise they did and it was another day. Delia said: "Out, Emperor of Emperors," and one dainty foot delightfully joined to a rounded rosy limb gave me a right old thump and out I went, tumbling onto the cabin deck.

I sat up and a great smashing knocking on the cabin door was followed at once by Seg's bellow.

"Hai! Up and out! There's a confounded Shank airboat just flying over us!"

Seven

Oby's dreams of becoming a famous voller kampeon had become true. He was, as I could testify, if not the very best then one of the very best of pilots of Vallia. He held honorary rank of Chuktar in the Vallian Air Service; but he was employed as the emperor's personal pilot—that is, my personal pilot. Now he had no need to be told what to do.

He took Shankjid up with that smooth easy ascending curve that is the mark of the superb pilot. There was nothing left of the rapid jerky reckless-ness with which, say, Rollo, took up a flier. Rollo was a green novice beside Oby, yet Oby, once, had been just such a tearaway.

Clinging onto the companionway rail I managed to prevent myself from being hurled bodily back to the deck. Delia, on the step above me, swung back like a graceful willow leaning under the wind. With a smooth move-ment she regained her balance and was up the companionway ahead of me.

We burst out on deck to find a scene of busy and orderly uproar.

My lads of 1ESW are variously cavalry, infantry of any sort, artillery-men and engineers. They can turn their hand to any of the dark arts of war. Now they were preparing the varters along the bulwarks. Others were ascending to the fighting tops, while others laid out sand and water buck-ets. Contingents of bowmen were distributing themselves in coigns of vantage about the ship. In short, Shankjid was Clearing for Action.

Lifting up swiftly into the fresh morning air, I caught the last whiff of fragrance from the flowers and shrubs below. Now all the aromas about me were of battle and of a ship preparing for action.

Still, and despite all the years between, in these moments I missed the sights and sounds and scents of a ship of the line—the matches in their tubs, the rumble of guns on the hollow decks, the quick patter of the pow-der monkeys, and, above all, the move and tang of the sea.

Drums thundered through the ship and everyone fell silent.

Everyone nearby was looking at me.

I drew a breath and then pointed at the Shank vessel which was curving away and still above us.

"There is your enemy!" I shouted it out, big and bluff and strong. "Let us go and blatter the rast!"

"Hai!" they screeched in a savage chorus.

The Hai Jikais would come after we'd nobbled this cramph.

Oby's flying skill continued to prevent the Shank from doing as he wished and flying directly over us. When the firepots rained down our fire parties would spring into action. These aerial sailors would hurl firepots from their catapults; but they were very very careful over the procedure, and not too happy about it. Petard hoisting—what Kregans call snizzing—is catastrophic aboard a wooden vessel up in thin air.

Well, we survivors of the Shank lord's flagship knew that, by Vox!

Seg, clad in war harness and girded with swords, carried his great Loh-vian longbow in his bronzed fist. He cocked his handsome head up.

"He's a good flier up there; but I think Oby's got him by the short and curlies."

I looked at my blade comrade and, deliberately, I drew my eyebrows down. "You look out for yourself today, Seg. No stupid heroics."

My eyebrow antics, I could clearly see, made Seg want to burst out into delighted laughter. Still, he understood my feelings, for he growled: "I'd say the same to you, my old dom, if it would do any good." He gave me his funny quizzical look. "But it'd make no difference."

"You forget, I have Korero to shield me."

"Yes, and I have Tim Timutorio."

I gave Seg a sideways glance, taking my gaze from the Shank ship. Tim Timutorio, a Bowman of Loh from Seg's country of Erthyrdrin, had lost the use of three of the fingers of his right hand. How that bestiality had occurred no one had asked. Now he lifted a shield at Seg's back in battle.

"I am diffident in this—I wish you could get a Kildoi."

"Oh, old Tim will do. Perhaps Korero might know of a friend."

At that moment Inch rolled up. He had a bright red scarf wrapped tightly around his hair and his helmet perched somewhat. He carried a bow.

Seg said: "You don't actually hit anybody with that, Inch. You have to pull it back and let the stick thing in the middle fly off and hit your enemy. I thought you might care to know."

"I thank you most sincerely for your information, Seg. Why, I was wondering what had happened to the head off this haft—which is a skinny and puny little thing, to be sure."

"You wait 'til you try to pull it."

The bow happened to be strung, so we were spared the pantomime these two would have gone through over that. Inch was a good shot, anyway. He just preferred to charge and get stuck in with his axe.

I thought I'd give good old Seg a jolt.

The enemy ship had given up trying to fly over us and was now clawing for height. Height, in one sense, corresponded to the weather gauge in sailing ships of the sea. Oby was going up, too, and beginning to crowd the Shank. Now it is a fact that until great guns and steel ships were used on Earth's oceans, few ships were sunk by gunfire. Flame and explosion destroyed ships. Gunfire dismasted them, knocked out guns and killed crew, all in preparation for the final act—boarding. So the far less powerful ballistae and catapults could not even do the damage guns could do. A thirty-two pound roundshot driven by gunpowder, smashing into solid oak would make a hell of a mess; a chunk of rock from a catapult hitting the same solid oak would dong a nasty dint, the damage would be far less. So it was that everyone aboard knew we'd shoot it out, and try to extinguish any fires that were started, and perhaps set a few blazes going aboard the Fish Head, but that in the end it would have to be a boarding action that would settle the issue.

So, as I said, just to tickle old Seg up, I said: "I found a capital crossbow in the trophy room. I'll give it a shot."

Seg gave me a withering look, whereat I smiled.

Delia joined us carrying a splendid longbow. Well, she can shoot it out with the best. I heard a scuffle at my back and half turned as a hoarse voice said: "That Larghos is all puffed up on account of being a Bowman of Loh, an' all, Drajak. C'n I span that crossbow for you, Drajak?"

I held the weapon out. "Certainly."

He hitched his strangdja over his shoulder and grasped the crossbow. He looked pleased. I said: "You'll need your strangdja when we board, so don't get yourself killed before then."

"That's all right," he said in a cheerful way. "I'll be standing at your back, an' all, won't I?"

Seg and Inch both burst into delighted guffaws. Delia favored me with a look that said, quite clearly: "And you'd better not get yourself killed, either, Dray Prescot!"

The day's radiance shone down in mingled tints of jade and ruby. The air tasted like wine. The two ships circled, gaining height, acting like two contestants in the ring, seeking openings and weakness in the other. With a quick in-turn the Fish Face tried to cross our bows. The maneuver was carried out smartly. Even if the ensuing rake would not have the smashing impact of a gunfire rake, it would still be unhealthy. Oby was having none of that. Deftly he swung Shankjid in a tighter turn than the Shank's and the two vessels raced along parallel. Here was where the shooting would search out marksmanship and courage. Arrows rose from the Shank and shafts sped from us in reply. A massive chunk of rock went hurtling and skipping across the deck, carrying away two crewmen in a red splodge. As always, I felt the anger and the despair. Good folk being cruelly cut down by those damned reiving Shanks!

Our dustrectium smashed into the Fish Face.

We could see chunks of his bulwarks splintering and collapsing under the impact of our flung stones. Mind you, our bulwarks began to take on a chewed look. Korero hovered close. No arrow would pierce Delia whilst Korero stood watch and ward, for he knew my standing instruction in situations like this. He might be my shield bearer; his orders were to protect Delia. Powerful though Korero the Kildoi was, even he wouldn't be able to stop a flying granite boulder on his shields.

Seg said: "She's not like any Shank I've seen before."

I said: "They're building different patterns these days. She has a fighting top, when their first ships only had lower galleries."

Seg grunted. "Well, we have two fighting tops." He shot in his bow and reached for another arrow. "See that fellow bending to the varter on their quarterdeck? He has a damned red scarf—"

"I see him. What, a gold talen?"

"Done."

I knew I'd lose the wager. Seg seldom misses. Still, if we couldn't have a friendly shooting wager or two, just like the old days, what was Kregen coming to?

He said: "That's one gold you owe me. What about that monstrous mechanical object you laughingly refer to as a bow?"

Llodi stretched out and slapped the crossbow into my hands.

"All right. You're on. And you can choose."

"The next fellow on the same varter. He's already done too much damage as it is."

When I had duly reduced the crew of the ballista by one more, Seg sniffed and made no comment. Even he recognized that a crossbow was of more use in certain special circumstances. Llodi busily wound up his windlass. I stared about. The decks were beginning to take on that look of a shambles. There was no doubt that the Fish Face was pressing in. Clearly, he was getting the worst of this long range duel and wanted to come to close quarters, to board and so come to hand strokes.

Now whilst that was comforting in one way, it left a dilemma to the commander of Shankjid. The voller, a product of Tomecdrin in Balintol, was strange to me. She was a bit of a fantastical craft, with fighting tops rather like tiered wedding cakes, all angles and spikes and balconies. She was some thirty-five feet in breadth and about three times that in length, with two decks pierced for varters, twenty a side in two tiers. Now these were ordinary or common varters, not the superior gros-varters of Vallia. This was where the comforting bit came in, for we were out-shooting the Fish Head with our normal weapons.

The dilemma was whether to go on pounding the Schtarkin or to close and board. In other circumstances boarding was the final and decisive act. This was turning into a classical single ship encounter. Both vessels were of two decks, so they did not really fall into the category of frigates; but in everything else this was like one of the great frigate engagements of Earth.

The odd thing was, as the ships circled and swung about and ran parallel for a space, and as we shot and loosed, I was under the strongest illusion that as a passenger I was not in command. Oby was the captain. If Seg or Inch had exercised strategic or planning control, that was proper.

So the dilemma was not mine. I rather fancied I'd shoot the cramph up a little more before boarding. If you have an edge, use it.

Certainly, our shafts were taking a heavy toll of the Fish Faces.

Larghos the Throstle, who usually employed a strangdja, was a Bowman of Loh. He and Moglin the Flatch were shooting well and fluently. I caught a glimpse of Fan-Si lifting her bow.

I shouted, viciously: "Fan-Si! C'mere! Bratch!"

She walked up, swinging her tail, well-knowing what I wanted.

"I shall not be patient with you for very long! Go below and do not come back on deck without your armor! Dernun!"

She started to give me a saucy look, saw I was not joking, and scuttled off, her tail very much down.

Seg said: "They don't learn."

"No, because they're dead."

"Quite."

"Have a look at young Rollo. He wants to go off adventuring as a Bowman of Loh. I would value your opinion."

There was every indication that Rollo was in an inflated frame of mind. So far I hadn't told Seg that Rollo was in reality an apprentice Wizard of Loh. I'd told Delia last night and she'd laughed and whistled and said: "Dear Deb-Lu has a handful, there."

Now Rollo the Runner, as he called himself, shot with a neat delicacy that brought a grunt of approval from Seg. "Perhaps a little more extension," he said, his head a little on one side, studying technique. "He can be made into a fine bowman—if he'll listen, of course."

I said: "As to that, Seg, I'd rather he trains up to be what he is, a Wizard of Loh. Oh, and keep that close."

Inch said: "Can't he chuck a spell across there?"

"He's a novice. You'll have to wait until Deb-Lu is through with him."

A damned great chunk of stone blistered into the bulwark before our little group and as the splinters flew Korero and Tim slapped their shields across. The stone rebounded and fell away below. The Shank was hitting us well enough, and every now and then we could feel and hear a particularly shrewd knock echo and tremble through the vessel.

As often happened in single ship actions, there was going to be little left of either ship at the end.

We continued to shoot well. Fan-Si crept back on deck wearing armor. I ignored her. Milsi and Sasha, as befitted them, were shooting when the ranges came down. Everyone at the varters labored to shoot as rapidly as possible. And still Oby kept up his intricate maneuvers to baffle the Fish Face. By now, I began to think, we ought to be considering closing and boarding.

Kuong's Repositer, San Cheng, stuck closely by the trylon. He was doing his own particular duty in recording everything Kuong did. Later, this would be placed into the records so that Kuong, when he came back to Kregen as a newborn baby after his death, would know what he had done in this battle.

I said to Seg: "About time Oby closed, d'you think?"

"The notion had flitted through my skull. It's up to you."

"Do what?"

Inch said: "Get on with it, Dray. My shooting arm is tiring before I've swung my axe."

"But—Oby is the captain!"

At that moment, the coincidence perfectly explainable by the necessity of the next few moments, Glima turned up with a message from Oby.

"Majister—Captain Master Oby would like to know—"

"Thank you, Glima. Ask him to take her in, will you?"

"Quidang!" She was off, bare legs flashing, her long silver hair a shining girdle about her bare waist.

Llodi handed me the freshly-spanned crossbow.

The thought occurred to me that if I could be so sharp with Fan-Si, a fighting Jikai Vuvushi, over the wearing of armor, then surely Glima in her humbler yet essential role as messenger ought to merit the same consideration? Fan-Si detested armor because it restricted her, and in that I agreed yet felt the advantages in most circumstances outweighed the disadvantages. As a messenger, Glima would want to run as fast as she could. This, as they say in Clishdrin, would have to be taken under advisement.

With the crossbow in my hands I lined up against the most convenient target aboard the Fish Face. "This'll be the penultimate shot, Llodi. After that, we must clamber aboard somehow."

I loosed and handed the crossbow to Llodi.

Shankjid swerved sweetly in mid air. Oby had her in perfect control. We could see the bright colored upperworks of the Fish Head as his black hull slimed away out of sight below. Oby had him. We were ready to smash into him and our boarders go leaping across in a red roaring tide of destruction. Oh, yes, with a good ship under him there was no holding Oby. He had brought us into the perfect position to strike.

Inch said: "Time I went for'ard. Good hunting!" He vanished down the companionway heading for the forward fighting galleries.

Seg said: "I'll tell you somebody who'll say a few choice words when he hears what he's missed."

"Yeh," I said.

"Too right. Old Hack 'n' Slay will be livid."

Nath Javed, old Hack 'n' Slay, was away as a Chuktar in command of the 43rd Mixed Infantry Brigade. This consisted of a regiment of archers, one of churgurs and one of spearmen. This kind of formation had been found useful to bolster a sag in the line or to add impetus to a thrust. Well, he couldn't be an army commander and at the same time go adventuring with Seg and me. And, truth to tell, I somewhat missed him then.

"I'd better get down and for'ard myself."

"I'll shoot out a few more of 'em first."

"Can you keep the girls—?"

"I'll try."

There was little hope of stopping Delia from joining the boarding party. I'd mention it to her, in a forlorn hope she'd listen.

Seg lifted his bow and I started off and a distinct and sharp check jolted through the ship. Seg missed his shot. I caught the rail. Other folk had been staggered. The idea that we'd hit the Shank ship lasted only a moment; the check was not of that order of violence.

"What in a Herrelldrin Hell happened?" Seg was furious.

Ahead where only a moment ago the bright upperworks of the Shank had been slipping away so that our boarders lining the lower galleries could leap aboard, now they were rising up into view. Either we were going down or the Fish Head was climbing above us. Seg had his balance and calmly loosed into a pack of Fish Faces clustered on their sloping deck.

Glima ran up, and there was a trace of blood mingled with that silver hair at her waist. She panted.

"Captain Master Oby mentioned the glass eye and brass sword of Beng Thrax. Also he said by Kaidun. There is something wrong with the bronze boxes."

The Shank vessel was lifting, was turning. In only moments the Schtarkins would come raving down among us on our decks instead of us going roaring down on theirs. Again the voller jerked under my feet and her speed fell off. There was no other course for me, now.

"Hold 'em!" I yelled to the people on the deck. "I'll see what's the matter with these Opaz-confounded bronze boxes!"

I leaped for the companionway.

Eight

The cause of the trouble was instantly obvious.

What was to be done to rectify the problem was not as readily obvious.

Where that confounded shuckerchun had sucked off some of the strakes, the hole had been roughly patched with timber. The new wood was much lighter than the original scantlings. By the immutable laws of fate, the vaol-paol, two strikes had been scored in almost the same area.

I thought of that Shank varter crew Seg and I had reduced. Maybe their ballista had been the very one, keeping its aim true, to send two chunks of rock into this very spot. The patchings lay in splinters. The baulk of timber supporting the armored power box had been knocked all skew-whiff. The two iron plates with popped rivets had fallen off. So that the second strike had come whistling in and fair smashed into the bronze boxes.

No doubt that had been one of the gut hits I'd felt in the ship.

The bronze and balass orbits looked to be functioning reasonably well. The trouble was trickling from a corner of a bronze box. Tiny granules were trickling away from a crumpled corner. Now the exact mixture of minerals and other substances in the box was a most profound secret. Even though I'd been instrumental in seating Nedfar as Emperor of Hamal, I still didn't know the full composition of the silver boxes. A group variously known as the Faceless Nine kept that secret, and death was the reward for failed attempts to penetrate the mystery. That secret cabal had other names. Yet the damned Shanks had found ways to duplicate the powers of the silver boxes in their bronze boxes.

Well, it was no use crying over that now. Something had to be done, and done instanter.

As I watched, the orbits revolved as Oby tried to get Shankjid to rise and fly forward. I felt the ship lift a trifle; there was no detectable forward movement.

As is my custom I do not wear folderols and flying tassels and scarves and bullion and gold lace, particularly when going into battle. Any swod of mine is trim for action. So the only spare piece of cloth I had that I could get to quickly was—the brave old scarlet breechclout.

That came off as quick as thought and I wrapped it about the leaking bronze box.

The incongruousness of the action and the look of the thing was perfectly apparent to me—and perfectly unimportant.

Glima leaned down from the ladder and shouted: "The Fish Faces are aboard!"

So it was a case of us trying to resist them as they leaped on us, rather than us ravening down on them.

"Mind you keep out of the way, Glima! Or take armor from a dead Fish Face. D'you hear, girl?"

"I hear master. You have no breechclout—master."

"No. And I'll have yours if you don't get yourself to safety!"

At this she did give a giggle, which heartened me immensely.

The grimness of the situation was thrust viciously upon me in the next instant as a body came tumbling head over heels down the ladder. Glima gave a squeal and jumped out of the way. The dead swod—and I didn't know his name!—was young, heartbreakingly young. He still clutched the trident through his throat. I said: "To Opaz, my lad," and ripped his red breechclout off and wrapped it about my own nakedness. Then I went up on deck.

That classical single ship action had turned nasty.

The Shank flying ship hovered just off our bows and was pouring in shot after shot deep into Shankjid's hull. Our deck was covered by a sprawling mass of struggling fighters. The Shanks were aboard with a vengeance.

Balass the Hawk, shield high, sword low, was cutting a swathe through shrieking Fish Faces. Inch had reappeared on the upper deck and no one lived within the sweep of his axe. With all the superb skill of the master Bowman he truly is, Seg was shooting at selected targets. Very sensibly he had taken himself up to a vantage point and as I looked he shafted a Shank in the act of stabbing a trident into Chandarlie the Montro's back. Others of our company suddenly found their opponent reeling back with a long red-fletched arrow clear through them.

Kuong was fighting with that dedicated young man's application that worried me for his safety. Llodi's strangdja ran green. Tuco, also, was using a strangdja and laying about him. Larghos the Throstle and Moglin the Flatch, likewise, were employing strangdjas to deadly effect. There was no sign of Fan-Si, Mevancy, Milsi or Sasha. I looked for Delia and could not see her. The girls were Up To Something. I could smell it.

So I unlimbered the great Krozair longsword and rumbled down into the fight.

Shouts lifted, screeching. The Shanks were shrieking: "Ishti! Ishti!" Some of our folk felt inclined to waste breath in shouting back: "Vallia! Valka!" Most saved their efforts for fighting Shanks.

If what Rollo had said was true about his meeting with my lads of the Guard Corps, that they were thirsting for a good fight, then their wishes had been vouchsafed them. Now with every reason the fighting prowess of the various races of Shanks was greatly feared. Everyone knew the Fish Faces were violent and lethal in battle. Still, and if there is a twisted pride in this then for that I beg forgiveness, some folk of Paz are just as violently lethal—if not more so. Among that select company must be placed my Djangs of Djanduin, the Clansmen of Segesthes and the lads of the various regiments of my Guard Corps. The Bladesmen and rufflers of Ruathytu's Sacred Quarter, the Bladesmen—called Bravo Fighters—of Zenicce, do not have quite that same wild and untamed savageness. The Iron Legions of Hamal are drilled soldiers through and through, like the Canops. There is a world of difference between a soldier and a warrior. The wonder of it is, the jurukkers of my Guard Corps are warriors and soldiers.

Many of their names you know, far more you do not, for to weigh everyone's worth is impossible in so small a compass, and chance dictates who gets a mention and who does not. Also, there were quite a few newer men I did not know, for the Chiefs kept the regiments well filled up.

Seg saw me and left off that smooth flowing shooting rhythm to point off to starboard. Over there a gang of Fish Faces were trying to overwhelm a varter crew who resisted not only with sword and spear, but with spike and windlass handle. Soundlessly I rushed across the small space of open deck and the longsword twitched left and slashed right and two Fish Heads were no longer in possession of those fishy heads. I dragged in a breath. I had to control that mad passion to slay all these bastards who so mercilessly oppressed the ordinary people of Paz.

The next three Shanks went down smartly enough and the varter crew disposed of the remainder of that bunch. The raw stink of spilled green blood smoked into the air. There was no time to waste; more Fish Faces raced towards us, brandishing their tridents. If they thought to strike fear into the hearts of their enemies by this ferocious appearance, then in the normal course of normal battles for them they'd think correctly. Unfortunately for this particular Shank flying ship's crew, they were up against fellows who didn't go in for showiness and boasting and weapons brandishing. The proper place for weapons in the fists of my lads of the Guard Corps was not brandishing about in thin air but stuck into the guts of damned Opaz-forsaken Shanks.

Korero appeared beside me, two enormous shields upraised, a sword in his tail hand. He glowed golden in the light.

"You fambly!" he yelled at me. He was in a right old paddy. "I've been looking for you—"

I yelled back, at once alarmed, apprehensive—no, speak the truth—I was scared clean through. "Delia?"

The onrushing Shanks were almost upon us.

"She went with the rest of the ladies and that mad bunch of Fristle Jikai Vuvushis—"

Then we were at handstrokes. Korero, with four arm hands and a tail hand, could protect my back, protect his side, and attack on the other side. He was most comforting to have at my back, yet I wanted him with Delia, protecting her. We slashed that bunch of Fish Heads away and glared about for more.

"Well, Korero?"

"All the women went below."

They most definitely were Up To Something. I'd find out about it in due time—if they lived.

Some of the Schtarkins were trying to form a slender line along the deck. They could see the cumbering corpses of their own people, and, thank Zair, precious few of ours. They were forming up for a proper disciplined charge. They came on when they were ready, menacing, shrilling: "Ishti! Ishti!" Their scales coruscated in the morning light, their weapons glittered.

The leader fell down. The Fish Face next to him also fell down. Both had long red-fletched arrows through their eyeballs.

Now I know Seg has experimented with loosing two shafts from a bow at the same time. I doubted he'd be doing that right now. I took a heartbeat to glance away from the advancing Shanks. Seg was there, already bending a new shaft. In an adjoining coign of advantage stood Rollo in the act of drawing an arrow from his quiver. My lips thinned. If Rollo thought he could stand and shoot shot for shot with Seg Segutorio, then he was sadly mistaken. All the same, the lad was doing well, and I hoped he would survive this fight.

I wasn't prepared to hang about waiting for damned Shanks to charge me. I gave the briefest of forward jerks with my sword, snapped out, "Charge!" and went crashing off down the deck smack into the Fish Faces.

The lads were up with me, and a solid wall we smashed into the solid wall of Shanks. We hacked and thrust and parried and ducked and overthrew that neat Schtarkin line. We cut them down in their own blood.

When that little dust-up was over we'd cleared the after portion of the decks. We held our own voller from the stern forward to the front fighting top. Arrows were spouting down from there like bees buzzing from a hive. Forward of that the control top was isolated and the fighting was taking place in an attempt to push on forward up the deck. For the moment, Oby was up there in the control top separated from us.

Seg and Rollo jumped down from their positions halfway up the after fighting top and joined me. I was looking forward.

"There has to be a better way," I said, fretfully.

Rollo panted out: "Can't we go down a deck and run along and then jump up behind 'em?"

Korero said: "They're fighting down there just as we are up here."

I had to push my desperate fears for Delia out of my head. That I could not merely meant I had to live with my terrors for her and try to carry on, get this thing over with, so that she might be safe.

"We'd better go up there and get stuck in, give Inch and Balass a hand. And look out for young Kuong. He's all go."

"From what you say he believes in, my old dom, he don't care if he does get the chop."

"True."

"By the Veiled Froyvil! You can really find some weird ones in Loh!"

"Oh, aye," I said. "Particularly from the northernmost tip."

We were advancing on the enemy as we spoke, and we had a few more of our little personal licks in before we would come to handstrokes.

Rollo was looking from Seg to me and back, and shaking his head. He must have thought we were a right couple of nutters.

In a wild melee of clashing steel and the screech and slide of steel against iron we pressed forward. Men screamed and died. Others screamed and dragged themselves out of the thick of the conflict, nursing hideous wounds. Blood fouled the decks and ran greasily across the planking. This madness proves that human beings are all mad, for surely only mad people would countenance such insane behavior? True. But, as you know to your cost, there are times when madness is the only answer.

Seg fought with silent and applied magnificence. He shared my views. We barged our way through the press and soon saw Inch, as it were, enclosed in a ring of Schturgin dead.

The enemy flying ship hovered just above our bows. Dark and agile figures were clambering up the ropes and nets from our deck to hers.

For a single and stupid instant I imagined those frantic figures to be our lads boarding the Shank.

Seg rapped out: "The cramphs are pulling back."

"Aye."

The Fish Faces were leaving the fight and climbing back to their own vessel.

This was not the final victory. Some single ship actions have seen ship's companies boarding, being driven off, been boarded, thrusting the enemy back, and boarding again. A real ding-dong knock-out fight can last.

I said: "Now it's our turn to board."

"Indu," said Seg with great gravity, "bitably."

"Yes," I said. "Old Hack 'n' Slay'll be livid he missed this little lot. And I'll tell you another—"

"Nath na Kochwold. Surely."

As Kapt of the Phalanx Corps, Nath na Kochwold had to make the decision to relinquish his beloved brumbytes, the pikemen in the files, if he wished to become the governor of a province. What he really wanted to do was come adventuring with us, and no one in Vallia would take bets on what his final decision would be.

As I stared up at the Shank I fancied she was drifting down our starboard side. That movement was not ours; I didn't think Oby would get us to move again until we had repaired the leaking bronze box. Seg, looking up, said: "What now?"

"We can't reach her from the deck, that is certain. We might get aboard from our forward fighting top—"

"Whoever's up there has been shooting well."

Inch, wiping the blade of his axe, came up just then. He said: "The girls are up there. Didn't you know?"

Korero burst out: "So that was it!"

Well, I'd known the girls had been brewing something. They'd slipped below and then crept out and up to the top to have a fine view of the proceedings. They'd done good work, too.

The Shank was now drifting perilously close. If he could get only a little nearer he'd be chucking firepots down on us.

Fretfully, I said: "Can't Oby get us to lift, for the sweet sake of Opaz?"

Rollo snapped out: "I'll go and see." He was off like a hare.

Inch said: "I haven't got that one fathomed out yet."

Seg said: "He hasn't got himself fathomed out, either."

I said: "He's been learning a few things today."

Shankjid hung motionlessly. The Shank was turning and moving towards our starboard bow. Already the Chiefs of 1ESW were harrying out their fire fighting parties. Some of them had tried to follow up the retreating Shanks, hanging to the nets; but shouted orders caused them to drop back onto our deck before they dropped off into space.

Inexorably the Shank flying ship swerved in towards us.

So far neither combatant had thrown fire pots.

Seg turned that fey blue gaze of his on me. "They want to take us!" He jabbed his bow upwards. "That's why they haven't chucked any firepots."

"I agree." Inch was still finickily cleaning his axe. "They haven't seen a voller like this before. So they want to capture us."

There were good men dead scattered across the decks. The stink of blood smoked into the air. The suns shone. I felt the futility.

Balass said: "We gave them a bloody nose. They're coming back." His shield described a circle in the air. "Will they try again, or will they try to burn us?"

"Board or burn," said Korero. "We'll stuff their fishy faces where—"

"Korero!"

This was most unlike our reticent Kildoi, whose personal life remained a mystery to his comrades.

The Schtarkin swung on through the air above us. I felt at least three separate and distinct lurchings of Shankjid, a sluggish rise followed by an abrupt fall back to the original position. Oby was trying. No doubt Rollo was attempting to give advice.

Our fire parties stood by. We were as ready as we could be to resist whatever the Fish Face up there sprang on us.

Closer and closer he came. Seg grunted and leaned into his bow. There were Fish Heads lining the ship's lower fighting gallery, and that kind of target could not be resisted by Seg Segutorio.

Other archers took up the challenge, and return shots spat onto our decks. Up there the Shank's keel slid in over our deck perhaps two or three man heights above the fighting top. We all looked up.

There was no deadly flicker of flame I could see, linstocks held in fishy fists to light the pots. No flaming bundles of death tumbled down on us from above.

A Shank with an arrow through him did fall down onto our deck. He was speedily disposed of overside as Hikdar Larghos the Trevoilyan spoke and Deldar Nath the Veins said: "You heard the officer," and Swods Mangarl the Sofirst and Oglin Vandar jumped to scoop up wrists and ankles and with a swing fling the offal over the side. I didn't smile. But I thought of these lads of mine of the Guard Corps. Then I returned my attention to the enemy vessel.

I saw it all, saw it all in a heartbeat, and my own heart seemed to jump into my throat.

With an abrupt and vicious swoop the Shank dropped down. The Fish Face pilot didn't judge it perfectly. The keel crashed into our forward fighting top. Struts splintered and snapped. The Shank lifted for another try. Our forward fighting top leaned over, straining against the remaining struts. As I looked another strut parted. The top was now almost on its side, visibly moving further and further over and out to hang over the ship's gunwale.

A narrow door flapped open in the side of the top, the side that was now becoming the floor. A bundle flailing arms and legs tumbled out, screaming, to spin over and over and fall and fall down and down past the ship, down out of our sight into the ground below.

An arm reached out and after a struggle pulled the door closed.

The Shank ship was dropping down again for another attack.

In that top balanced on breaking struts over nothingness was all that mattered to me on Earth or Kregen.

On a sudden all I could see was redness. Half blind I raced for the ladder leading up to the toppling wreckage.

Nine

As I clambered up I could hear a savage snarling, growling noise, unutterably menacing, enough to send a shiver down your spine. Only after another three or four upward lunges was it borne in on me that the dreadful sound was coming from me. Instantly, I forced my mouth shut. Because Delia was in peril I had reverted to bestial primeval savagery. And I knew why. Had the danger come from some ferocious wild animal, or cruel barbarian, I'd have sailed in and chopped them indifferently, knowing they but obeyed their instincts. But this was different. The hand of blind fate threatened Delia and I felt helpless to influence with my sword the course of events.

The voller lurched and the toppling fighting top twisted and sank lower. I half-turned and screamed back.

"Tell Oby to keep her steady!"

"Get on, get on!" came a voice from just beneath me.

A single fleeting glance down showed me Seg and Inch clawing up the ladder. Inch's phenomenally long arms and legs swirled him up like a spider.

I'd served aboard sailing ships where you laid out along the yard arm in gales to turn your hair white. In no time at all Seg, Inch and I clung onto the broken top of the ladder, surrounded by a mess of splintered struts and snapped supports.

Below us the spiked and balconied tower now looked like a wedding cake that has been half consumed by ravenous wedding guests. I'd no memory of clawing up the ladder past the galleries. Men crowded them, ready to repel the imminent boarding.

The Shank hesitated—Opaz alone knew why—and swung up and around. Rocks and arrows spat from his lower fighting gallery.

"We're just targets, perched up here," observed Inch.

The round top trembled as another strut buckled. Had the Tomecdrin voller builders gone in for tripods or pole masts the whole lot might well have snapped clean off by now. The multi-strutted construction gave us a slender chance.

I started to crawl along the tangled raffle out towards the top.

Seg grasped my shoulder.

"That's no good! Get a rope over to them!"

I had to think, I had to get rid of this red roaring madness in my old vosk skull, I had to calm down. With a tremendous effort, I said: "Quidang, Seg! We can rip a line free from this raffle."

The bottom of the pillbox shaped top faced towards us, with the broken-off end of the ladder leading to the trapdoor. As we pulled a line free a face appeared at the trapdoor opening. She must have been standing on something to reach the trap—even on the shoulders of her comrades.

"Hurry up and throw," she said in a clear controlled voice.

There was no din of gunfire to drown out shouted words. I heard her perfectly clearly. I saw her only through a red haze.

I gathered up the line into a coil. This was down to me.

An arrow spat against the wood at my side.

The coil of rope swung backwards and forwards. I'd throw this underhand, unlike my days out West when I'd used a lariat. Seg moved at my back. Inch said: "You got the cramph."

Where my crossbow was I hadn't the faintest idea. Probably Llodi had stowed it somewhere safe before surging into combat. But Seg still had his bow. Trust Seg Segutorio not to abandon that! Now he was shooting back at Fish Faces loosing at us.

The rope felt hard and hairy yet greasy in my fingers. I swung with a last vicious jerk and hurled.

The line snapped across, uncoiling, sinuous as a serpent.

The end flicked across the opening and an arm grabbed—and missed.

Keeping my breathing as steady as I could, a great ragged gasping for air, I hauled the line in. "No good," I said. I saw the jagged end of a timber and I reached out and snapped that wood off as though it was a stick of sugar candy from a banje shop. With sure practiced speed the chunk of wood was lashed to the end of the line. I coiled again, swung again, and loosed again.

The wood went slap bang into the hole and Delia just had time to duck her head out of the way.

They hauled in and I waited feverishly, knowing they were tying the line around one of the ladies trapped in there. A Fristle climbed through the trap door and then another. They were trying to cross two at a time.

Inch grunted. "I've got the end lashed tight, Dray. If they fall we can pull them in."

"Aye. But this is going to take time, time!"

The Fristles began to crawl along the swaying perilous raffle of splintered struts. I hauled in pacing them. I watched, hardly able to breathe. Perhaps it might be better to tie off the line inside the top and have the girls grip onto it as they struggled across the gap. But, then, if they fell, they'd fall all the way down to the ground beneath or the hard deck of Shankjid. Time—it would take time and the damned Shank was up there, circling and preparing to come in again—and I knew with anger just who would be the last to cross. Anger, yes—and pride.

Also Milsi as a queen would claim priority over Sasha, a kovneva, and come across as the penultimate survivor. As I waited the thought crossed my mind that a kingdom ought to be found for Inch and Sasha. Something had to occupy my frenzied brain. The uselessness I felt then is a dark and horrible period I do not wish to dwell upon. The Fristle fifis reached safety and were assisted down by Moglin and Llodi who had climbed after us. The line was coiled and hurled back. Two more girls crossed.

Delia and Milsi could cross together. That would reduce the time. Sasha and Mevancy would then be the penultimate pair. I felt something wet drop onto my wrists, extended before me on the line. It was sweat from my forehead and face.

Oh, no, I do not wish to remember that black hell through which I passed as the girls crawled across the swaying mess of wreckage.

Twin shadows fell across us and I looked up to see the Shank dropping down. He'd evidently decided that he couldn't get his lower gallery close enough to our decks if he came down on top of the crushed tower and so was trying to land further aft. A single fleeting glance showed me men gathering to repel boarders.

The shadows passed away aft and I looked back as two more Fristle fifis clambered across the gap. When the wood-weighted rope flew back and the next two girls appeared I saw I had miscalculated. There was an horrendous clamor of mad thoughts clawing at me. The top had contained an odd number of women. Fan-Si and Mevancy started to cross.

When they were safe it was the turn of Sasha and Milsi.

I half turned.

"You'd better get them all down safely. And pitch in to help the lads." The senseless din of combat burst up from the after deck of the voller where Fish Face and jurukker clashed and smote and died.

Seg said: "I'll hang on—"

"Get Milsi down. Inch, get Sasha safe."

The others had already climbed down the rickety structure.

Mevancy had given me such a look as she passed. I do not know what she thought of the look on my face; but she went down without a word.

Seg and Inch and their ladies tried to argue. I shook my head and persuaded them to descend. Perched up here we remained mere targets.

Delia appeared at the trap door opening. She must have arranged a way to reach that from the side of the top that was not its floor. She gave me a cheeky wave and then laid into the line. All the time the top had been making doleful screeching noises as wood pressed against wood and splintered and parted. It sank lower, turning inwards now so that Delia had to climb upwards at an angle. I could see her movements, controlled as ever, as she climbed with neat and economical precision. Carefully, I kept enough slack on the line so as not to hinder her movements, and yet ready instantly to haul in if she fell.

She did not fall.

The whole damned top fell off.

The hollow round structure hit the bulwarks with a rending gonging sound. I set my teeth. That gong note was not a Passing Bell—never! The whole lot vanished over the side and Delia clinging like a monkey to the line swung pendulum fashion. She was not wearing one of the flying safety belts. Delia swirled in towards the tower.

I remember more falling than clambering down the ladder among the wreckage. I do recall my fists pained. I did not notice that at the time.

With a heartbeat to spare I reached the tangle directly opposite Delia's swinging form. Everything hazed about me into a ghastly blur. Now I have mentioned before, mention now, and will undoubtedly continue to mention, Delia of Delphond is no simpering weak shemale, no screaming blonde of fiction. Delia is resolute, quick, sharp-witted—apart from being the most beautiful woman in two worlds, of course—and now she saw what was going to happen. Everything took place in mere fragments of time. She would cannon into me with rib-crunching force and we'd both be hurled spinning sideways, seriously injured. So Delia in the tiny moment of time left to her worked her gorgeous body around in a sinuous series of swings so that she would pass just clear. With calm, precise and elegant movements she used herself as the bob of a pendulum and so swung past.

On her return swing I gathered her up in my arms and held her to my breast, close, close!

She said: "The Shanks are inconvenient, my love. They keep shooting at us."

Even as she spoke an arrow sprouted from the shattered wood beside us.

I had no need to ask fatuously: "Are you all right?" Anyway, there was no time for that. Headlong we tumbled down the ladder to the deck. The world of the voller, of noise of shouting and screaming, of the raw stink of blood, of violent action, smashed back into my consciousness.

"Oby's lost control—except for lift—"

"Can nothing be done about the bronze boxes?"

"I wrapped my breechclout around the break. It'll stop the damage getting worse—but that's all."

"Then we must take the Shank!"

Amid all the noise and confusion of battle she made that simple declaration without bombast or boasting but as a simple comment on our sole course of action remaining.

The enemy flier had managed to position himself so that his lower gallery overhung our stern. Screeching their hideous war cries the Shanks leaped aboard.

"Ishti! Ishti!" In a howling frenzied mob the Fish Faces charged.

We met them with a wall of steel and smashed them back with a charge more wild and savage than theirs. Inch swathed them away. Seg shot them to pieces. Balass surged forward as though through a corridor of toppling scaly forms. Korero remained with Delia, for she would not be denied. Everyone did his or her part, everyone fought as best they could.

We were all uplifted on the rush of blood in the head, nerved past the ordinary, driven to do extraordinary deeds. The Schtarkins either ran back to their ship or were cut down where they stood.

Our fellows started to clamber aboard her lower gallery, battling all the way. I had my fists around a black wooden stanchion and was about to haul myself aboard, the Krozair brand dangling by the sword knot, and a dagger between my teeth just in case of necessity.

A shrill voice lanced through the hubbub.

"Get off the Shank! Get off the Shank! He's afire!"

That was Rollo's voice, shrieking a desperate warning.

At the word so dreaded by sailors of wooden ships there was an immediate evacuation of the Schtarkin's lower gallery. We jumped back to our own deck where Seg was still methodically picking off Fish Heads.

A flicker of flame wavered like a flower in the breeze high on the enemy flier's poop. At first the gossamer strands were lost in the radiance of the suns. Swiftly the flames thickened into a crackling blaze and the black smoke blew down over us.

Oby's reaction came immediately the last of our people dropped back to the deck. That happened to be Sandar Na-Ku, a Pachak with a touch more of the calculated berserker in him to cause him to fight to the last. The moment Sandar hit the deck Oby dropped Shankjid and the voller plummeted.

Everyone lifted up on their toes, so swift was the descent.

Seg held onto his arrow and then let the string slowly forward. "We're drifting with the wind, my old dom. If that rast up there falls straight down he ought to miss us."

"But he's not falling," observed Inch, already thoughtfully wiping his axe. These two knew how to control the after passions of the madness of combat. This was not callousness on our part, just an acceptance of one unpalatable face of life in a turbulent age. Truth to tell, we had been fighting Shanks, and so the reactions were all of a different kind from those we experienced after fighting with warriors of Paz.

"He's burning, though," observed Sasha with great satisfaction.

Oby held us low above the ground. We were drifting aimlessly, pushed by the breeze. Up there the Shank began to move. He turned into the breeze and increased speed, clearly trying to keep the fire blazing away aft in a fiery streamer. Well, we knew all about that.

He stayed in sight for some time, a blazing meteor high against the sky slowly sinking to the horizon and finally disappearing beyond a cloud bank.

Often enough in my life on Kregen I've felt like saying, as you know: "Well, now what?" I said it to myself, then, aboard a crippled voller drifting over the forgotten jungles of Chem.

My comrades were acting in the ways I expected of them, thankful we were still alive after the fight, speaking mostly in low tones, sometimes breaking into a boisterous—and not altogether incongruous—laugh. Rollo stepped down the deck to us, looking a trifle wild. His shout about the fire had saved some of our fellows, no doubt of that. Mevancy appeared, looking flushed, her color high. People began to drift over so that soon most of them were looking down from various vantage points. I felt a most peculiar sense of Theatre in the air. Most odd.

What the hell was I going to do now, what say to them? What did they expect of their famous and puissant Dray Prescot now?

Mevancy said in a clear voice: "Well, cabbage. What happens now?"

"That's simple," I said, making it brisk, making it brusque. "Now we can get on with doing the job we're all down here for."

Ten

In pursuance of that policy—to use an amusingly pompous phrase beloved of the verbose governments of two worlds—we needed an army, a navy and an air force. We had one crippled flying ship.

"Once Deb-Lu or Khe-Hi regain contact," said Seg in his big confident way, "we'll soon have it all settled."

A few of us were gathered in the aft cabin of Shankjid. This was not a Council of War, for, as you know, I have little faith in them. This was a meeting where we might take a breath and plan. As always, the final decisions would have to be taken by me. Had I ever, I remember thinking as

65

we sat around talking and drinking there in the paneled after cabin of this strange voller, had I ever really got used to making Emperor's decisions? Oh, I made them smartly enough, as this narrative will testify. All the same, running a King's Ship is one thing, running an empire is quite another—or, is it? Do not the same imperatives apply? I half-turned to Seg and said: "You're right. And we badly need to know where the armada from Vallia has gone."

Delia said: "They are subject to the wind, just as we are now."

Inch nodded quickly. "True; but the lads are busy at work on the sails and spars. If Dray has anything to do with it, we'll be sailing soon."

"Thank Opaz for small mercies," I said. "The split in the bronze box—"

"But it didn't, you old worrier, so think forward!" Delia sounded quite sharp, by Krun!

Milsi, quite calmly, said: "I've always maintained that one day some use would be found for Dray Prescot's scarlet breechclout."

"That does seem a more suitable function for it," added Sasha with immense dignity.

We mere mortal men did not have the courage to exchange glances but stared busily at the ceiling or the floor. Eventually, Delia said: "If the prevailing wind has taken the Vallian fleet away then we can follow."

A trifle uneasily, I said: "With Khe-Hi's help, that is so. But I rather feel we ought to think about Queen Kirsty and her army, and about the rebellion in Tarankar, and about—"

"What, my old dom, do you think one sailing flying ship will avail against the Shank fleets?" Then, very very quickly, Seg added: "Of course, if we decide to go down there, I'll—"

"Quite," I said.

"Well?" demanded Delia.

"Precious little—except—"

"Except what?" demanded Inch. He had to sit a trifle crouched, for spacious as the cabin was, the overhead was too low for Inch and Sasha.

"Oh," I said, making an irritable gesture with my fingers. "We could go around the different gangs, help 'em, train 'em, give 'em heart."

"No." Delia shook that delightful head so the chestnut tints in her gorgeous hair caught the light and put a golden bronze halo about her. "Oh, no. Utter waste. When the time is ripe the gangs can close in on Taranjin. They will no doubt do their best; they may turn out to be most useful although I have my doubts on that score." Her voice hardened. "The Fish Faces have to be put down by armies and fleets trained to a better standard than theirs." Then with a tiny sigh, a puff of sound almost inaudible, so typical of her, she said: "I do wish Deb-Lu was here!"

I knew—and the knowledge was at once uplifting and shaming—that Delia wished the powerful Wizard of Loh here so that he could protect me.

Deb-Lu protected us all at a distance; Delia's concern for me was matched only by my concern for her. And, yet! And, yet I allowed her to go off on hair-brained adventures for the Sisters of the Rose and I knew she risked her life over and over again. What a fool I was! Yet because I loved her I could not stop her doing what she wished. Deb-Lu's distant protection was far more vital over Delia than anyone else. I agreed with Delia; I wished Deb-Lu-Quienyin, toppling turban and all, was here with us.

Following Delia's earlier remark, Inch said: "The Hamalese at least are well trained."

"And where in a Herrelldrin Hell have they gone to?" demanded Seg.

Milsi said: "Better to find them first. Then the vollers can tow the sailing fliers."

That was sensible. From my personal point of view, no matter how well-trained the Hamalese might be, their ships did not have the ferocious lads of my Guard Corps aboard.

"Where the blazes is Deb-Lu!" I stood up restlessly. "Sink me!" I burst out. "I won't be put down by a pack of Fish Faces!"

Delia looked at me with that special crinkle along her eyebrows, so I sat down and kept silent.

Each of us, in our way, knew what the other was thinking.

Balass the Hawk put his head in at the door, his powerful black face just sheened with sweat—it took a great deal to make Balass sweat. He said: "By the brass sword and glass eye of Beng Thrax! I might have known it. Here I am hauling ropes and lifting spars, and you lot are lolling about drinking parclear." He licked his lips. "By Kaidun! I'm parched!"

Sasha said: "Here, Balass, a fine sazz." She held up the goblet.

After Balass had drunk, he said: "Almost done. Want you to have a look at it, Dray. Oby isn't too sure of the exact pitch of the yards."

I smiled. "Young Oby feels degraded not having a voller's power under his feet. Handling a sailer will be good for him."

"He's come a long way," said Balass, "since the Jikhorkdun."

"Aye," I said. I didn't like the note of heaviness in my voice.

We all went out onto the deck into an immense bustle as the lads erected the masts we'd cut from tree trunks and crossed the yards. Oby was standing with his hands on his hips, his head thrown back, yelling at the hands tailing onto the braces as the yard swayed up. The fellows on the halyards eased the yard up carefully. They'd done this kind of work before, of course, as so often in the past the Emperor's Guard Corps had been forced to fly in sailing flying ships. Mistakes might be made; they'd get it right in the end.

Oby caught sight of me out of the corner of his eye, and in between shouts, called across: "Say when, Dray!"

I nodded. At the moment I considered appropriate, I yelled and the yard was snugged down. With only two masts and main course and fore course, the vessel would be a pig to steer. It was necessary, therefore, to rig fore sails and a funny little mizzen to carry a spanker.

Whilst all this was going on I went down to see if the emergency repairs done to the bronze box were holding. The minerals spilled had been carefully swept up and put in an empty jewel box for safety. My red breechclout had gone for laundry and the split had been thoroughly bound up with canvas and lashings. I shook my head. One day I'd figure out what all the minerals' sources were. What we had now in this vessel was the ability to lift up in the air. We had no forward power. Because the boxes gave us the ability to reach down into the aetheric-magnetic lines of force about the planet we could, as it were, extend a keel and so use that as the very necessary resistance to enable us to make boards and tack against the breeze. The skills of the sailor were required now.

All the deck activity cheered me up. Something I understood was happening, and we were creating a living ship out of a crippled hulk.

My new friends from Tsungfaril and Tarankar had been assigned quarters and they tended to keep to themselves, no doubt feeling somewhat out of it in the general bustle. Only Rollo—who was, of course, from Whonban and a Wizard of Walfarg—joined in. He was clearly intent on striking up a friendship with Oby in connection with vollers. And he dearly would love to strike up a friendship with Seg Segutorio in connection with Bowmen of Loh.

Everyone in two worlds has ambitions and motives, drives and needs. Maybe many folk don't even know what it is they want. When hope seems senseless in view of the current conditions, ambitions may shrivel; deep down in every person the needs crave on.

In the aftermath of that traumatic fight with the Shank voller we needed time to recuperate, to bring ourselves back to being ourselves. Rigging Shankjid as a sailing flying ship gave us something to do whilst we resumed normalcy. Or—as normal as anyone can be on that dreadful yet wonderful world of Kregen.

Yet that remark, too, is untrue. As you know, there are many many simple ordinary folk living on Kregen and leading ordinary simple lives. Not everyone is a rollicking adventuring hero swinging a sword. Sometimes, when I looked at Delia and saw her afresh and drank in her beauty and aliveness and sheer wonderful gloriousness, I could wish that I, too, was not who and what I was. But those dreams were foolish. The Star Lords would see to that. And, too, as you will readily perceive, these remarks indicate perfectly clearly that no matter who or what I or Delia might be, we would continue to love each other natheless.

Because Shankjid was—or had been—a voller flying under her own power she did not carry a vast quantity of spare rope so that my people had cut vines and lianas from the forest to twine and plait into substitute ropes and cables. I went off towards the stream to find a suitable source of lianas to make up for the spanker rigging.

Stepping away from the clearing it seemed to me that the forest closed in with uncanny rapidity. Our noise and activity had probably driven almost all the animal life away; anything not frightened off would prove unhealthy but would succumb to the varters. Moglin the Flatch with Larghos the Throstle walked towards me carrying a raffle of loose vines and Fan-Si trailed along lifting dangling ends. They passed me with a few short words, as one would hail good morning to an acquaintance across the street, and trudged on. I half turned, starting to sigh, and then I swung back as a voice at my shoulder said: "Drajak—Mevancy—she's not herself at all, what with what's been going on an' everything."

I was aware of two reactions. One, pleasure that Llodi had accepted the situation and continued to treat me as a friend, and second, a twinge of alarm over Mevancy. Unpredictable as she was, she could do just about anything as the situation that Llodi had accepted worked on her unstable emotions. There was concern in Llodi's voice as he said:

"She's down by the stream an' all, and she's not cutting vines."

"I'll see."

Llodi moved on with his bundle of lianas and a long trailing vine slithered after him through the clutter of the forest floor, hissing.

When I reached Mevancy sitting slumped under a tree by the bank, I did, indeed, see. She sat in that withdrawn almost fetal position that denotes intense misery. At my approach she started up in terror, as though I were a jungle monster after her blood.

Not quite sure of the best tack to take I opened my mouth and she said: "What a mess I'm in!"

I sat down beside her, comfortably stretching out my legs. Somewhere a little upstream and masked by low bushes someone was cutting vines. Other voices could be heard echoing. It would rain the tropical rain shortly, in the eternal recycling of rain forest water.

For a space of time neither of us spoke. Then she leaned sideways and put her head on my shoulder. She was not crying. In a voice like a child's lisp, she said: "If only I wasn't a Sinnalix!"

"Then you wouldn't have your bindles—"

"My bindles!" The venom with which she spat this out startled me.

"Your nasty little darts have proved more than useful in the past—"

"Oh, aye, cabbage, aye! And what they will cost me—"

"Cost you?"

"Yes, yes!" She was no longer speaking as a child but as a mature woman filled with spite and venom and frustration. "Don't you know?"

"Rumors—"

"Well, they're not rumors. I want to have children like any normal woman and if I have a girl I want her to have bindles to protect herself. But if I marry—Kuong, say—my daughters will be born as apims, without bindles studding their arms."

"I see—"

"No you don't, cabbage! If I want a daughter with bindles, as I do, of course, I must mate with a man of Sinnalix."

"I see the problem if it is Kuong now—"

"What do you mean, now?"

"Ah—well—"

She gave me a look and then in a gush of words blurted out: "The males of Sinnalix are brutish, misshapen and ugly. They are hideous in the sight of any woman. Their touch disgusts. Yet I must mate with one of them—"

I felt for her, of course. That prospect would chill the heart of the bravest girl, particularly as Mevancy went on to explain further that the Sinnalix males were vicious of temperament and delighted in dominating their beautiful women. The men were cruel to their wives.

"And if we shoot them with a burst of bindles, our punishment is—"

Well, it was highly unpleasant, not fatal, and prolonged.

I said: "And I suppose it is the same with the sons?"

"Yes. A Sinnalix male will produce a monstrosity like himself."

"But, pigeon, you told me your father was a good man who tried to enlighten the barbarism darkening Sinnalix—"

"Yes. I always think of him as my father, but, of course, he was my step-father. My real father, so mother told me, was a typical Sinnalix male. He was killed in a raid and my father married my mother, who was wealthy." Her voice carried no animation as she spoke of her childhood. She spoke in a dull, hopeless way. "If I'd married Vad Leotes, or if I wed Kuong, we will produce beautiful boys and lovely girls—without bindles."

She did have a problem. Perhaps just talking about it helped to calm her down. She explained more details, although given the situation was self-evident, they were hardly necessary.

There was a chance here to clear up the further situation of Mevancy and Kuong. I fancied she was in the after-the-storm mood to confide her secret thoughts and desires. Delia—and I felt sorry for Mevancy—had come as a shattering shock to the girl from Sinnalix. About to widen the conversation so as to ask if she wanted Kuong and would marry him, my first words were interrupted by a shriek from upstream. Instantly, Mevancy and I sprang up.

A splashing and bubbling located the source of the scream. A mass of silver hair swirled in the current.

"Glima!" I shouted. "She's fallen in the water!"

Flinging myself flat on the bank I reached out desperately. Into my fists I gathered a bunching double handful of Glima's silver hair. I felt myself roughly jerked forward and my chest went into the water, my arms out-stretched before me and my head up. "Mevancy!"

At once I felt her grip my ankles as I was dragged further forward. She held me. I started to swing Glima in to the bank and her head broke the surface. Her face turned to me, terrified, eyes closed, wet as a seal. I hauled in as gently as I could and called reassuringly to her.

"Glima. Open your eyes. Grab the root."

Just below me a tree root protruded from the soil of the bank. Glima, splashing and gasping, managed to grip the root. Mevancy started to pull me in. Glima's mouth contorted as she tried to breathe and scream at the same time. I let go of her hair with my left hand and took her right arm and pulled her in. Then I shouted: "Pigeon! Hold on!" and hauled Glima up.

Between me, Glima and the root, we hauled her out. Mevancy held onto me, Glima clung to her root until the last second, and I twisted and pulled.

Gasping water, Glima fell forward on the bank beside me.

Head down and held by Mevancy, I couldn't see Glima on the bank, and I was in no position to wriggle myself back up. I put my hand on the root to get a purchase. At that moment, Mevancy, concerned for Glima and thinking her rescued and me about to haul myself out, let go of my ankles.

There was no longer any danger. All I had to do was push myself up with my hands on the root. No problem.

The root snapped.

Headfirst I toppled into the stream. Instantly the current swept me away. White water spumed each side and shining black boulders shot past. The force of the current held me locked as though in a vice. A thumping great smash on the back of my head half dazed me. It began to rain in a solid downpour. A chip in a millrace, I was swept helplessly downstream.

Eleven

Smashed and pummeled by the water, bashed by black boulders, charged by drifting logs and lashed by overhanging branches—yes, I can say that unknown river in darkest Chem gave me one of the roughest rides of my career, a career, as you who have listened to my narrative can testify, not without its full freight of rough rides.

Away I went, hurly-burly, scattering foam as I tried, damn feebly, too, to claw a way to the bank and out of this maelstrom.

Rolling over and over like one of those confounded logs that kept battering at me, I saw streaming black and white water and then a whisk of a green-leaved bank and then the black branch-laced sky. The current possessed the power of a thousand leems. The boulders were positioned with the cunning animosity of Mak Grancesi the Malignant himself. I could feel the bruises starting up already. If I didn't hoick myself up out of this tout de suite I'd run my head full tilt into a rock, and as what there might be of brains oozed into the water, that would be the end of Dray Prescot.

One of those Opaz-forsaken branches that kept on whipping me as I thundered past proved the saving of my carcass. The thing took a vicious swipe at my head as I was rolling, all splashing and flailing arms and legs, and turning face uppermost. I reached up with arms and fists seeking life.

The grip I took was the grip of death. I felt the shock of the sudden check in my helter-skelter progress. I hung on, panting, and after a bit, gritting my teeth, started to haul myself up. By the time I'd got my legs up out of the clutching jaws of the stream and gripping the branch, I felt as though I'd been beaten with laths. When I got my breath back I swung leg over leg and fist over fist to the bank.

I wasn't fool enough to imagine my troubles were over. No, by Vox!

Here I was, dumped into a hostile jungle, pelted by rain so that visibility was practically nil, isolated, with only my wits and weapons to save me from becoming some predator's lunch. Well, as you know, this is no novel situation for Dray Prescot even if each situation is different one from the other. Previous experiences would be invaluable; the unexpected will always turn up and must therefore be expected.

Because this was Kregen, where you take your weapons for even the shortest trip, I was not unarmed. There were spare strings for the Lohvian longbow in the waterproof pouch on my belt. I had the Krozair longsword and the rapier and main gauche. My old sailor knife snugged over my right hip. And, inevitably and correctly, I wore the brave old scarlet breechclout.

Well, now...

As abruptly as it had begun, the rain stopped and the incessant hissing drumming was replaced by the steady drip drip drip as the leaves shed the surplus water. Everything began to steam like the hot rooms of the Baths of the Nine.

One fact was absolutely certain in this infuriating situation.

I must stay by the stream. Already it was beginning to broaden out into what might be called a river and although it still spumed and roared, and unpleasant rocks spouted white water along its course, the top cover concealed only the stretches close to the banks. There was no doubt whatsoever in my mind that Delia and my comrades would fly Shankjid down the river in search of me.

"A fire!" I exclaimed aloud. "By the disgusting diseased left kidney and the blighted liver of Makki Grodno! A fire!" And, for good measure, I added: "A goodly waft of smoke, by the black armpit hairs and leering squint of the Divine Lady of Belschutz! A fire and billow on billow of smoke!"

The river took a bend in its course a couple of hundred paces ahead and widened further. A jumble of boulders across the width formed a dam of sorts and the water smashed and spumed high sending rainbow colors glinting. The noise of the rapids beat steadily between the trees. In this section of the rain forest there would be no easy traveling by boat or canoe along the rivers. Among the pleasant scents wafting in the air one or two atrocious stinks told of vegetable life attracting animal life of a different order. I prowled along warily.

Sure enough, at the bend there was quite an expanse of blue sky above. Luz and Walig, the twin suns, sent opaline beams to cheer me up with the reflection that the whole wide world of Kregen was not one confounded jungle.

Among the dripping branches finding dry wood was a mere matter of stripping off the wet bark and digging out the soft and dry inside. If my flint and steel refused to work it would be the work of moments to fashion a fire-maker's bow and then of skillfully twirling until the tump caught. The tinder caught on the third strike and I blew gently.

A flicker of gossamer flame danced into life.

Well, I'd had just about enough of fires lately. Building the fire into a blaze had to be done carefully; but it was not long before I could pile on dampish wood and start the smoke roiling upwards.

As I straightened up ready to bring across a fresh branch, I saw a man standing among the trees about twenty paces off. He stood absolutely motionless, staring at me.

I stopped my movement. I stared back. The noises of the jungle screeched and howled about us.

There was something deuced odd about this fellow.

He was six or seven inches taller than I am and although his face in the shadows of the leaves looked shiny and plump there was a gauntness about his frame. He wore only a loincloth of a drab beige color and appeared to have no weapons. That, by Vox, in a hostile jungle of Kregen, was distinctly odd!

He moved forward and a shaft of mingled light fell across his face. The plumpness was emphasized by the shine; his face looked as shiny as the shell of a crab. I couldn't make out with any distinctness the morphology of his body. He had two legs all right; but of arms I could see none. Across his chest were crisscrossed shadows.

I called out: "Llahal, dom!"

I made no move to draw a weapon.

He moved further forward, leaving the shadows, stepping into the full rays of the suns. What were those crisscrossing ridges on his torso? He had two eyes, two ears, a nose and a mouth, and no sign of body hair. He advanced silently three or four more paces.

The situation grew odder by the minute. Now, I did not want to take my eyes off his, yet it was imperative that I looked carefully all around to see if he had any comrades ready to jump on my back.

I threw the branch onto the fire and in a continuation of the same movement looked left, right and rearwards. In that flashing surveillance I saw only jungle, river and sky.

He took advantage of the interruption to move swiftly forward so that when I looked at him again he was no more than five paces off. If he essayed a rush from there I could unlimber a weapon before he reached me. The jumble of shadows across his torso looked like a bundle of sticks. His head was fuller than I'd at first thought. I had not seen him blink once.

Again, I called: "Llahal, dom!" This time my voice was sharper and harder, demanding an answer—always assuming, of course, that he could speak.

He did speak. He made a gargling, hissing noise that closely resembled: "Schahal, schdom."

I opened my mouth to attempt a conversation. You must always be alert on Kregen if you wish to survive. I saw the bundle of sticks across his chest stir. They were not a bundle of sticks. They were his arms. From the shoulder they were jointed like a folding rule so that he had three elbows to each arm. Instead of hands he had serrated claws like those of a lobster or crab and I did not need to be told they were razor sharp. The arms straightened and slashed like flails. The fellow had a reach of five paces easily. He'd have had me if I hadn't given a convulsive leap backwards.

"Schnarra! Schnarra!" he screeched and rushed, those enormously long arms swinging and slashing before him. I dodged away. You know my views on wanton killing and its abhorrence. You also know my views on people who try to kill me. In this situation I judged the longsword to be the correct weapon in preference to the rapier.

The Krozair brand hissed free of the scabbard. The blade glittered once as it cut. A claw and the first elbow span away trailing blood. The thing screeched and the other arm flailed scythingly towards my head. The sword switched up and the second claw and forearm dropped.

Holding the stained blade up, I stood my ground, waiting to see what he would do, not wanting this grotesque encounter to continue.

He was hissing and shrilling, keening higher than the roar of the rapids. For a moment he swung his shortened arms before him and then, recognizing the futility of any further attacks, folded them up across his chest. He turned about and ran off into the jungle.

I felt, I admit, by the sweet name of Opaz, only regret for him. He had sought this encounter and initiated violence. Because of that he suffered. I walked a little way after him. There was no sign of him so I went back to the fire shaking my head at man's folly.

The severed limbs looked only pathetic. When I tested the claws they were, indeed, razor sharp. The forearm and claw would make a capital weapon. The creature reminded me of a Praying Mantis. The marvels and mysteries of Kregen under the Suns of Scorpio! I would have to ask Rollo or Mevancy for information on this fellow. If he lived with his kind in the jungle I just hoped he was a solitary.

You may well imagine I kept a sharp lookout after that, by Krun!

One or two animals blundered up from the trees but the fire discomfited them. I was not troubled by animal life and I kept well away from those vegetable predators I recognized—and well away from anything not like a simple ordinary forest tree.

Dark smoke wafted into the bright air.

A pang from my inward parts reminded me that I could do with a solid Kregen meal. If I was not found in the very near future I'd have to go hunting for my lunch.

As you may well imagine, just feeding a fire and trying to make white and black smoke waft high into the air took little intellectual capacity. I was left to ponder on all the multifarious problems facing me.

"By the Blade of Kurin!" I said to myself as I cleaned and polished up the Krozair brand. "I thought it was a truly smart move to get out from under the job of being Emperor of Vallia. And now everyone wants me to be the Emperor of Paz."

The divine Delia was being supportive and understanding but I felt it to be absolutely imperative that I knew without any misunderstanding her true feelings on this awkward matter. What the Star Lords wanted must also be taken into consideration. They considered I had the yrium, that blessed and cursed charisma, to organize all the lands of Paz against the Shanks. And there were others... Truly it was all a moil!

Of one thing I was passionately certain. I must do nothing to cause the Everoinye to hurl me contemptuously back to Earth.

Worrying over what might happen in the future can be highly unhealthy if your current actions cannot influence the course of events. Forward planning to meet contingencies, though, is highly rewarding. What ought to happen in the future seemed planned out well enough. What might happen, of course, was a zorca of a different horn. It was no good fretting. I stoked up the fire so that the suns paled and then hauled out the Krozair longsword.

Any fighting man must keep in trim. A spot of practice every day is required. So, there in that lost jungle clearing by the rapids in the bend of the river, I went through the Krozair manual of arms. Naturally, there was time only for the basic techniques but I chose to go through the routine from the Fifth Circle of the Artifices of the Sword. San Zefan, Krzy, had written down his Artifices some two and a half thousand seasons ago on the Island of Zy in the Eye of the World. Later artists of the sword had amplified and improved the basic work. Some had merely decorated it, so that these practitioners gave a showy performance. Only by continual practice and hard work does a swordsman stay alive—on Kregen.

Towards the end of the session I felt much calmer.

A voice much distorted and muffled said: "Do you thus fight phantoms, Dray?"

I swung about. Half visible in the sunlight on the bank of the river the figure of Deb-Lu-Quienyin wavered. His turban appeared to topple off his head and then in the heat distortions flow back again.

"Deb-Lu! Lahal and Lahal!"

As I spoke the ghostly figure shimmered, thickened and darkened. I thought the Wizard of Loh was putting more of his kharrna into his lupal projection. Then I saw this was not so. The face of Khe-Hi-Bjanching appeared in place of Deb-Lu's wise old visage, and then disappeared as Deb-Lu once more showed. They were both projecting into the same space.

"Khe-Hi! What is going on?"

"We face tremendous interference. I am in Whonban and Deb-Lu is in Vallia. The planes distort—" The fluttering voice keened into incoherence. A most unpleasant feeling of unease possessed me.

They both spoke together in a weird double-echo.

"We are maintaining our Observations. But the load is crippling. When we know more we will—" With a guttural gargling as of water running down a plughole the voices tailed off. The lupal projection flickered and died. I was alone.

These two comrades were powerful Wizards of Loh, well-versed in their arcane arts. Their thaumaturgy protected my comrades and myself. Yet here they were being baulked of a simple lupal communication by what must be an enormous and hostile force.

A snickering wheezing laugh sounded from the trees and I swung about, the sword snouting. Then I knew who that hostile force was.

Twelve

This time the bastard was surrounded by a bevy of half-naked girls. They were Bowmaids of Loh. They had sweet round faces and soft pouting lips and were sharp as barracudas and tough as old boots. There were eight of them, four each side of his damned throne chair. Their great Lohvian long-bows were half drawn in that practiced archer's grip. They could lift, draw, let fly, in the flicker of an eyelid.

He sat in that chair leaning slightly forward, bearded chin cupped in his left hand, looking broodingly at me. He wore robes of a smoky sullen red sweeping away from artificially widened shoulders over a scale shirt. He was studded with golden adornments. His right hand, bone white like the left, rested lightly on the haft of a double-headed axe between his booted feet. All this was as I had seen him before. He wore his helmet. To look at him you couldn't rightly say if he was a man wearing a fish-face helmet, or a fish-face with a man's face as neck adornment.

Scraped chalk white, that face out of nightmare. Paper-thin skin stretched over and revealed his facial bone structure. The open lipless mouth showed a double row of jagged fang-like teeth pressing outwards from wide jaws. His thin nostril slits pulsed. I looked at his eyes. The eyes of a devil, I'd said, blue-black yet filled with the mad red glow of rhodopsin, eerie, repellent, dominating.

The little scaled creature with the silver collar still crouched against his right leg. Now he had two naked girls, one with flowing yellow hair, one with short dark hair, twined against his booted left leg.

The snickering wheezing laugh sounded again.

Among the dark greens and rusty blacks of skin and scale drapings and the redness of his robes, a patch of white glimmered. Low down at the left side of the throne, a patch of dirty white, like a fish's belly, moved forward, and a red-black gash opened across it. From that slit the mocking laugh wheezed again. This was the face of an obscenity, neither apim nor true fish, a miscegenation that had been procreated with the worst of both sides. I stared, feeling slightly sick. But then, of course, the wonderful wise men and savants of Kregen, those scientists of the ancient times, who had wrought so playfully with the flora and fauna of Kregen, might also have created this corpse white, leech-like, horror.

The throne chair hung suspended three feet in the air. The Bowmaids of Loh stood on the same level.

From the slant of the twin shadows from the girls and the throne you could tell they were not here in this jungle clearing.

I breathed in hard, and breathed out, and said nothing and waited for what he might have to say. I kept a sharp lookout for his pet Arzuriel. I'd already disposed of Arzuriel once; but I'd learned he was a multi-dimensional creature and so could be expected to turn up again.

He saw me looking.

"Do not concern yourself, Dray Prescot. Arzuriel will come when I call."

I took another hard look at him, his throne, his clothes, his companions. They made a tableau of evil. You could feel the gust of depravity reeking from them. Opaz alone knew how many more of them there were in whatever foul den they hailed from. One thing was certain sure about that place—it stank.

Was it because I hadn't bothered to answer him that made him mad? The deep red of the rhodopsin in his eyes glared to match the sullen smoky red of his robes. He lifted his head. His left hand jutted forward, forefinger pointed directly at me. His nails were long and curved and sharp, like claws.

"You think you are so important, puny little apim! I tell you, you are less than nothing in my scheme of things."

The last time he'd appeared to me like this he'd been instrumental in stopping me from getting to where I ought to have been in time. What was he stopping me from doing this time?

As far as I could see, I was waiting for my friends to pick me up in Shankjid. The thought did occur to me that perhaps they wouldn't be able to see this tableau. I just stood there, poised, alert, the Krozair sword in my fists, ready.

"Fear has this effect, very often," he went on, lowering his pointing finger. "Like the risslaca and the woflo. I had heard you were a false jikai, Prescot, and found it hard to believe. Perhaps it is true?"

I looked at the Bowmaids. They were a toothsome bunch. All they wore in the way of uniform was a scale triangle in front and a few wisps of feathers here and there. The heftiest of them had three red feathers in a headband. She said something in a voice like a spoon hitting a glass. Two girls each side lowered and eased off their bows.

He saw me looking at the beauty parade and when I turned back I thought there was a dull flush of red along his cheekbones.

"We could have worked in concert, you and I, Dray Prescot. My plans call for a strong man to rule in Loh. I thought I had such a man; but he decided his own powers gave him strength to do as he wished." His voice took on something of the keening whine he'd used when he first spoke to me. He clearly felt deeply on this point. "My plans have not gone as I would have wished." Now the bright malice showed in that monstrous face. "But all that interference is ended."

He paused there. If he was puzzled I hadn't spoken he covered that well. All the time he sat in his chair and jabbered, he was destroying the picture of horror he presented. Familiarity might not, in this instance, breed contempt. He was an apparition, using his kharrna to project his image in lupu to this spot. And he brought his retinue along into the bargain. He had power all right. Enough power, as I surmised, to choke off the combined powers of Deb-Lu and Khe-Hi.

The little corpse-white thing half hidden in the shadows wriggled up. The massive head and crown inclined as the thing whispered into an ear. He straightened up. Those fearsome eyes, all blue-black and red, fixed me.

"N'gil suggests your fear is feigned."

I said nothing.

"N'gil wants to know if, even at this late hour, you would join us."

In a short time my friends should be along. The black and gray smoke from my fire was dying. But it ought to be enough. I wanted to get rid of this unnatural sorcerer and his gang before Shankjid arrived.

All the time he talked and I didn't I was watching the edge of the forest in case Arzuriel showed up. With his four tentacles, each with a head with jaws at its tip, he'd make a likely candidate for the monster gallery in the jungle. There was no sign of him.

"Well, Dray Prescot?"

"No thanks, Carazaar. Your kind of existence is too unhealthy for me."

N'gil drew in a hissing breath.

"I have told you you are a prince of fools, Dray Prescot, an onker of onkers, a get onker—"

I interrupted.

"I've been told that—many times—by people who could slow fry you in your own sorcery."

His ghastly face twisted. "I do not believe you."

"That's your privilege, Carazaar. Just don't say I didn't warn you."

Stretching to the rear and slightly to the sides of the throne the air was hazy, vague with half-seen moving shapes. No doubt that was some kind of reflection through the planes of Carazaar's hang out. From just above the throne a gasp sounded, clear and sharp, between my remark and Carazaar's immediate snarling retort.

I guessed that to be the woman with the plump white arms who carried Carazaar's fish-faced crown about for him. Would she like him?

Now from my previous experience I knew that a sword slash would go clean through this apparition. Of them all, so far, only Arzuriel had been solid, and he'd drifted through a brick wall to get at me. Could I rely, then, on the Bowmaids' shafts not going solidly through me?

Using the Krozair Disciplines I could knock the arrows out of the air. But, suppose they contained thaumaturgy of a superior order? Then the sword would go through the shaft without deflecting it, and the charmed arrow could penetrate me and stick me clear through. That was not a happy thought, no, by the Crooked Shaft of Hork the Squint!

Perhaps he saw the intention on my face, black thoughts giving me that old Dray Prescot Devil Look. I own I scowled.

His right fist gripped the double-headed axe. He lifted it high and shook it. It was pure Theatre.

"There is yet time, Dray Prescot, for you to change your mind."

The chair, the Bowmaids, the naked girls, the chained things, N'gil and Carazaar himself began to fade. I spoke up.

"Remberee, Carazaar. Don't call us, we'll call you."

The apparition blinked and was gone.

Thirteen

For too long a moment I just stood there. The vision of that reekingly evil character persisted. Two shadows, one red, the other green, drifted across the clearing before me, each suffused by a wash of color from the other sun. The Suns were sinking now and the rays slanted into the forest. I looked up.

Instantly I was running like a maniac—running into the nearest of the trees.

I'd expected to see Shankjid up there, sailing to my rescue.

The hull of the flier up there was midnight black.

So that's why that bastard Carazaar held me still!

If I could make the treeline I stood a chance of shaking off pursuit. Any fancy notion of standing stock still so I wouldn't be noticed was like hoping a hunk of red meat wouldn't be noticed by a hungry leem. Any idea of slipping over the bank and hiding in the river was just as foolish. Even if the Shanks up there didn't have Katakis with them, they wouldn't miss a trick like that.

If the Fish Faces did have Katakis with them, and the Whiptails had a pack of werstings, then I was in deep deep trouble.

Those black and white striped hunting dogs can run down a scent like a toddler can scent a banje shop two streets off.

The Fish Heads up there were on the ball. A rock flew past my head, gouged a chunk of dirt, rebounded on to slam into a trunk with force enough to spray chips of bark. I put my head down and ran. If they shot arrows off after me they missed. Probably their short bows weren't up to the job. By the time they got their varter reloaded I dived in between the trees. This time the rock mangled the head of a bush just out from the shadows.

Back in the clearing the flier had touched down. Shanks were jumping out, screeching their warcries, brandishing tridents. They glittered, sharp and cruel, in the declining suns light.

They started off towards me.

Now wandering about at night in a jungle is not a particularly healthy pastime, and not something I would recommend for light entertainment. Mind you, I've done it. Seg and I have had our share of nighttime jungles.

Here, though, there would be dangers of a different kind from those of the forests of South Pandahem. The vegetable carnivores would be just as lethal as the animal—more so, given certain circumstances.

With the utmost caution afforded by the need to travel fast, I headed deeper between the trees.

The obvious plan occurred to me. If I circled around I could hope to shake off the Fish Faces and then, when they gave up the chase and took off, I could sneak back into the clearing.

There'd been no sign of Katakis or werstings. As far as we knew, the Shanks did not have a tame form of bloodhound. The shadows dropped, deep black-green and a red as sullen as the red of Carazaar's robes.

I started to circle to my left.

Again, if what we believed of the Shanks was true, they disliked much foot activity far from the sea. There was the river. If I could cross that in some way—say by jumping along the boulders, or swinging on a liana—they might not believe I'd do that. They'd search out the section where I'd vanished into the trees as best they could, and then they'd give up. It wasn't much of a plan; it was the best I had.

There was no chance I'd venture deeper into the forest.

Now it was dark under the branches. Mist coiled promisingly. I slowed down to a quick walk, still searching every step, and listened out.

The sounds of men crashing along floated in the still, misty air. They appeared to be going straight on along the direction I'd first taken. Slowing right down, I continued to listen and scan all about. The odd thing was that I could still see remarkably well in a situation I knew must be murky. The mist cut off vision far more than the darkness.

And another thing—the stillness of the air. That was not nice at all. That meant my friends couldn't sail Shankjid. She was stuck wherever she'd reached when the breeze died.

With an abrupt crescendo of sound, a shrill screaming broke out off to my right and rear. I didn't exactly smile; but I felt a grim and ugly amusement. The Shanks had run into a denizen of the nighted jungle.

The uproar swelled and then died and went away. Presently the sounds drifted in again. The Fish Faces were on their way back to their ship.

I reached the river. Already a few stars glittered, high and remote from man's foolishness.

The smells of the jungle changed with the fall of night. Exotic blooms opened to drink of moons light sifting down between the branches, and other exotic blooms closed their petals to wait for the rise of the Suns. Something exceedingly nasty coughed way off to the right.

A few steps along the bank showed me a way to cross.

The outcrop of rock here, which caused the river to bend in its course and opened out the clearing, had tumbled boulders haphazardly. I jumped nimbly across as though playing hopscotch. I became no wetter than I already was.

Night sounds of the forest screeched and grunted and laughed all about. I went along the bank a little way looking towards the Shank ship. My fire had gone out but in the open there was enough light to pick out details. Some of the Fish Faces congregated about the voller and there was a quantity of arm waving and trident brandishing. The noise they made surged in hisses and splashes like a racing tide.

Settling down in the concealment of a rock I waited and watched. By this time I was ravenously hungry. The moment the Schtarkins took off I'd have to go hunting.

A number of unpleasant thoughts rose to collide in my old vosk skull of a head. Had Carazaar held me here after summoning the Shank voller? Or was she simply flying nearby and thus convenient for the task? Also, how did Carazaar know exactly where to find me? There was a most disturbing answer to that important question.

He had interfered with the lupal projections of Khe-Hi and Deb-Lu. As they worked their way through the planes so as to talk to me down here in Chem, could Carazaar track them? Had my two comrade Wizards of Loh actually brought Carazaar here?

Just who or what Carazaar was no one seemed to know. I say 'seemed' because our Wizards of Loh had not yet reported their investigations. Could it be that in investigating Carazaar they had summoned up greater powers? Powers able to do what Carazaar had done, and able for the future to harm us all most profoundly?

Of one thing I remained tenaciously sure. The cauls of protection afforded me and my family and friends remained operative. They must be. Otherwise, Carazaar would have dealt with us long ago.

A group of Shanks approached from the far side of the ship, making a deal of noise. I guessed they were reporting in their failure to find me. Did they know who they were hunting? I'd no way of telling. Maybe it was pure chance they'd drifted down and spotted me. Maybe they had nothing whatsoever to do with Carazaar. I could only make a guess, a judgment based on a cynical disbelief in too many coincidences, either happy or unfortunate. Carazaar's connection with the Shanks appeared to me to be indisputable. All those fishy symbols, for instance. This was a sad reflection. Here was another ally, along with the damned Katakis, taking sides with the Shanks against the folk of Paz.

The ensuing and obvious thought did occur to me. This clever sorcerer Carazaar, and his minions Arzuriel and N'gil—and how many other monstrous associates he had—might not hail from Paz at all. They might, as did the Shanks, come from over the curve of the world.

The nighttime insects were up and flying and attempting to bite and sting and suck. The crushed herb juice we smeared on ourselves to keep the insects off was wearing too thin after my immersion in the river so I spent a bur or two collecting the correct leaves and rubbing the juice over my body. I'd always felt that the scent gave a human some kind of camouflage in the forest against predators hunting primarily by smell. I'd no idea if I was right.

What were my people in Shankjid doing now? Probably going mad with frustration that the breeze had died. Still, the rising of the Suns should whistle up a wind, and if it wasn't too foul, they'd be here. If the Shank voller had not departed by then—I refused to contemplate what might happen then. I'd put money on my lads, though, by Krun!

I caught and skinned my supper, and going into the verge of the forest found a boulder to act as shield and so was able to build a tiny fire which kebabed the meat reasonably enough with a root or two. This was not a sumptuous Kregan meal and to follow there was only water from the stream. But I found some tropical palines and so assuaged the demands of the inner man.

The Shanks had not lit any fires so they were continuing to cook their fishy meals aboard their vessel. The ship hulked there in the clearing, bulky and dark and a damned nuisance. I collected up a number of sticks about a palm or so long and started to whittle them into points at both ends. The tree I selected stood just within the rim of the jungle yet not so far in as to be over-near another. It had a decent trunk with a crotch about twenty feet up. There was no difficulty climbing to the branch junction. With my old sailor knife I made holes in the trunk beneath me, circumferentially, so to speak, and stuck the sharp spikes in slanting down. If anything tried to get at me up the trunk he'd make enough noise negotiating the spikes to rouse me. I repeated the exercise on the two upper branches, this time with the points sticking upwards. Then I composed myself in the crotch and went to sleep.

Rather to my surprise I woke up with the dawn.

As a habitually light sleeper—well, as you know, drunken sleep on Kregen is often never awoken from—I'd expected some nocturnal incident. I awoke fresh and clear-eyed, and taking in deep draughts of that superb early morning air of Kregen, even in a rain forest, I looked about.

The Shanks were still there but from the activity going on looked as though they were about to depart. The naughty notion of sending a shaft after them, to help them on their way, did cross my mind, to be immediately rejected. I'd had enough trouble getting rid of 'em, I most certainly didn't want the cramphs chasing me again, no, by Vox!

Before the twin Suns of Scorpio had risen above the tree tops the voller lifted off. Her brightly painted upperworks foreshortened as she rose and that evil black hull turned with supple ease. She cleared off to the south west, going fast.

I let out a breath, said a few inhospitable words re all the different brands of Fish Faces, and climbed down from my night's lodging.

Fourteen

After a vigorous wash in the stream I enjoyed a breakfast that was a simple repetition of last night's supper. The dilemma in which I found myself was obvious.

Whilst it was needful to light a smoking fire to let my friends know where I was, the smoke might well bring the same Shank or another on patrol.

Also, and this dismayed me more than the smoke problem, the breeze that got up shifted around to the north. The brilliance of the suns and the freshness of the air suddenly seemed more chill. The sounds of the forest echoed with a greater menace. Even the scents soured.

There was one bright spot. Carazaar did not put in another appearance. Maybe his kharrna was limited, so that he used great chunks of it to accomplish his deeds, and was then incapable of action for some time. Maybe.

All the time I kept up a lookout for anything flying over, and for my Praying Mantis friend of the previous day.

After a bur or so of this futile shilly-shallying I saw there was nothing else for it. Shankjid could make her way north by a long and tedious succession of boards, tacking against that diabolical north wind. My lads ought to be able to deal with a single Shank voller, although from our recent experiences I harbored dark and shadowed doubts I would not share with a single soul. If they could not then we'd all be stuck down here in the jungles of Chem.

The fire lighting business had been underway for only a few moments before I stopped striking the flint and steel. Yesterday I'd decided that I had to be out in the open for my friends in Shankjid to spot me. That had been the reason I hadn't immediately made my way back upstream along the bank. They'd never see me under the tree cover.

But—Shankjid had not put in an appearance. This confounded foul breeze meant they could be anywhere trying to tack up north. I remained totally undecided on my best course of action.

The good night's sleep had freshened me up physically. It had done nothing to sharpen up the brain cells.

Reluctantly I came to the unpalatable conclusion that I had no other option. I had to light my fire and waft the smoke and trust in Opaz and hope that Five-handed Eos-Bakchi would smile on my endeavors.

With some frustrated savagery I struck flint and steel and the tump caught first time and a trifle of careful blowing brought a blaze. Soon smoke drifted into the air, blown southwards.

With some forethought I'd sited the fire near the northern edge of the clearing. If Carazaar put in an appearance, or some damned Shank voller, I could fade into the trees pronto.

The suns crept across the sky. I began to feel peckish.

This time I spotted the flier early. He sailed in from the south going steadily on a dead level course. One look—"By Makki Grodno's false wig and clotted nose! A stinking Fish Face!"

Instantly I dived into the shelter of the forest.

The voller was the same one. He'd come sniffing back, and no doubt this time meant to finish the job. I scowled.

Did the Schtarkins up there realize they were hunting a man who meant them mischief? They were keeping me from getting on with the task of slinging them out of Tarankar and out of Loh and eventually of all Paz. Even one day could be vital. I fumed—quite futilely.

The ship settled in the clearing. Fish Faces alighted. They fanned out and a mean looking bunch came over to inspect the fire.

Now if that miserable hunk of evil called Carazaar put in an appearance now...

Confident they hadn't seen me I hung around on the skirts of the forest, moving slowly and cautiously so as to keep the parties that ventured in some distance off. They were hunting methodically; but they still refused to go very far in among the trees. That was, of course, most sensible of them. Presently the voller lifted gently and slid into a narrow slot among the foliage on the southern edge of the clearing. She halted and lowered to the ground. Shanks started to cut branches, selecting those with plenty of leaves, and began to cover the voller. Pretty soon the vessel was camouflaged so as not to be visible from the air.

This was distinctly not good.

Whether or not they knew who I was, they were well aware the smoke was intended to attract my friends. They were waiting quietly in ambush.

The heat grew and the humidity closed clammily all about.

I made a brief lunch of suitable roots, not wishing to chance a fire. At its precise time the rain cannon-balled down, slashing into the leaves, bouncing in solid sheets in the clearing, drumming heavily, splashing into the river. When it ceased and everything steamed I looked with a deal of apprehension to the southward, hoping not to see Shankjid under a press of canvas sailing grandly into view.

The clearing sky revealed only clouds moving away.

The suns burned off the moisture. I gave Zim and Genodras ample time to dry things off. I collected a big leaf full of dry twigs. I set off around the clearing and I know my face bore a look of the utmost malevolence.

Perhaps Five-handed Eos-Bakchi, the Vallian spirit of fortune and good luck, did smile benignly upon me.

Crouched in the twinned shadows of a bush less than ten paces from the camouflaged vessel I looked across the clearing to its northern edge and saw movement there among the trees. The Shanks reacted instantly.

As they tumbled down from the voller and raced across the clearing half a dozen gangling figures broke cover from the north and then halted, staring at the Fish Faces. There were six of the weird Praying Mantis creatures.

They appeared to have no fear of the Shanks. Probably they had never seen a Fish Face before. One of them was minus two forearms. So he'd gone for help.

Moving forward silently I found a fleeting moment of pity for the strange jungle creatures. I hoped they'd have the sense to run off—but not before they'd served their purpose. I lost sight of them as the lower gallery of the voller cut them off. Now they would have to take their chances. Once they were in among the trees they'd be safe.

The familiar fishy reek stung my nostrils as I swung up into the gallery. The long narrow expanse was deserted. Working now with precision and speed I built a little pile of dry twigs, got the flint and steel going, puffed the fire alight. Underneath the voller the lower fighting gallery had been protected from the rain. Like any painted wooden ship of the air, she was dry—tinder dry. Swiftly the fire took hold.

I believe an unpleasant smile disfigured my mouth.

Eos-Bakchi smiled again. In a rope bower all neatly racked stood a line of fire pots. These were intended to be dropped upon the Shanks' victims from above. My good humor increased. A little snicking sound attracted my attention. A door was just sliding open at the end of the gallery.

I did not want the fire discovered just yet. With almost the speed of Seg Segutorio the Lohvian longbow was off my shoulder, an arrow was nocked and the stave lifted and bent. I believe it unnecessary to remark that during the rain the bow had been unstrung and restrung afterwards with a dry string. A Shank in a scale shirt walked through the open door and then looked stupidly at the rose-fletched shaft protruding from his chest. The pile had gone clean through the scale and through him.

He fell down with an odd wheezing sigh.

Waiting for a handful of heartbeats I saw no more. Probably he'd been off trying to get into the party chasing across the clearing after the strangers and had thus neglected his sentry duty here. Letting him lie I fired up the flame pots and hurled them with great satisfaction in a slew along the gallery. Everything began to burn. Time to go.

A wall of flame and smoke cut me off from the sliding door and the sprawled Fish Head. The stink of marine life mounted nauseatingly as fishy oils began to bubble. Lowering myself off the gallery back into the jungle at least brought the familiar raw, menacing, throat-choking stink of the rain forest to clear my nostrils of fish.

Shrill yells bounced about the clearing. The Praying Mantis people had gone and I could only hope they'd run off and not been shafted. The Shanks were running back towards their burning vessel like crazy men. I faded into the skirts of the trees and circled around. The spit and crackle of flames and the crashing of burned-through beams sounded as pleasant music in my ears. They couldn't have spotted me for no one chased after me.

The smoke blew at an angle across the clearing. I took notice. The wind had shifted, was now from the east. That should make life easier for Oby tacking Shankjid up northerly.

From the cover of leaves I peered out at the blazing vessel.

This summary justice was no more than they deserved. Oh, yes, they were consummate seamen, and were now proving themselves to be fine airmen. Perhaps there were overriding reasons why they had to come ravening around the curve of the world to raid our lands. But because they did, our imperative was to stop them. Burning ships is no business I take joy in, as you know. If it has to be done, do it with some dignity. I could take little delight in the sorry business, and certainly could not gloat over the destruction of any ship. Except, perhaps, well there have been occasions in my turbulent career when I tended to send up a little cheer when a ship burned. Once, I recall, they threw me overside with my pants alight... Still, she'd burned, she'd burned.

There was no way the Fish Faces were going to extinguish that fire. It had taken hold now, and spat and spluttered and had begun shooting out fat sparks all around like fireworks of Earth. The Shanks were now marooned here in the jungles of lost Chem. Could I feel sorry for them? Well, yes. In a remote way that detached me from petty animosity and allowed me to view the situation from the point of view of a man vis-à-vis another man, I could feel for them. But—one must harden the heart, summon up the blood, make strong the sinews when adversaries insist on knocking you over the head and stealing your land and property. Oh, yes, I could feel sorry for 'em; but they'd got what they deserved.

When a fresh shadow drifted across the clearing and the Shanks looked up as I did to see a voller flying over, I realized instantly that we were in a nip and tuck situation. The voller was from Hamal. She was of a small medium size, double decked with fighting galleries and two fighting tops. She looked hard and professional. I remembered Mathdi. She circled as her complement studied the situation below them.

If her captain had any sense, seeing the burning Shank ship and the castaway Fish Faces, he'd up sticks and sail off. The jungle would take care of Schtarkins who hated to venture far from the sea.

The Hamalese flier circled again.

If I was going to get myself rescued from this jungle then it behooved me to clip stirrup and slap leather as they say in Segesthes.

The trouble was, as soon as I made myself known the Shanks would take a most unhealthy interest in my welfare.

No use shilly-shallying about, no use hesitating. Saddle up!

I sprinted out into the clearing and started waving my arms like sema-phores.

Up there they could see I was apim and not a Fish Head. The voller remained in her circling pattern. I waved crazily and looked over towards the fire. Shanks were screeching and starting to run across towards me.

"Get down here!" I bellowed up. "Drop a ladder, or by Hanitcha the Har-rower, I'll never see the Sacred Quarter of Ruathytu again!"

That galvanized them into activity. The voller swooped down and a rope ladder unrolled and swung like a trapeze artist's nightmare.

There would be the one chance to grab that. Arrows began to fly from the voller and a few of the leading Shanks went down. So vengeful and lusting after my hide, so great was their fury for revenge, they didn't shoot at all but simply rushed in a shrieking mob.

The ladder swirled towards me, twisting. And it was just above the full stretch of my upflung arms. I braced myself, got set and felt all the glory of Kregen surging about me and infusing my veins with a beat of passionate blood. I wasn't going to be beaten by a pack of measly Fish Heads, no, nor by a giddily swinging rope ladder, no by Vox!

At the precise instant I judged correct, I felt a sharp nick along my upper left arm. As I put everything into a wild leap upwards I said to myself: "So the bastards have thought to shoot at me at last!"

The penultimate rung slapped hard into my fists, stingingly.

I was whipped away like a slinger's bullet.

I held on as a monkey holds on to his mother. I didn't intend to be cast off like that slinger's bullet.

A couple of tridents flashed past my twisting body. I hauled up. Climb-ing undulating rope ladders is a difficult art which had been mastered very quickly after I'd joined the Royal Navy. I went hand over hand like a mon-key and I didn't bother to use my feet.

When I stuck my head over the rail a whole line of heads along the bul-warks regarded me as though I was a devil springing up through a stage trapdoor.

"Lahal!" I called. "Permission to come aboard?" Before anyone on deck had time to reply I took a look down. The Fish Faces were hopping up and down like jumping beans. Tridents flashed in the light of the suns. Oh, yes, by Krun! They were good and mad! We swept away from them over the treetops and the last I saw of that ship's crew was their vessel still merrily burning and sending up coils of smoke.

A metallic voice above me said: "Lahal, majister. You are most welcome aboard." I didn't need to see the speaker to know he didn't mean what he'd just said. Twisting my head back up I sized up this fellow. He was a Khibil and his foxy face fairly bristled with arrogant whiskers. Supercilious, Khi-bils, and condescending with it. As far as they are concerned, every other race of diffs on Kregen is of far less consequence. He looked to be a smart spry specimen of his race, brisk and competent. But he didn't like me, and he had difficulty concealing that animosity.

With a last heave at the ladder and a lithe vault I was over the bulwark and braced on the deck. This Khibil was Hamalese. Hamal and Vallia had been mortal blood enemies for a long long time. Only recently had Emperor Nedfar and I patched up the differences and declared alliance. Old wounds smarted still. Old enmities had not been eradicated by the stroke of a pen or a handclasp. It was going to be back-watching time now.

"Lahal, majister," he said again. He was being punctilious. "Allow me to present myself. I am Jiktar Taranto ham Armit, Rango of Firthlad." He gestured gracefully to the woman who walked quietly to stand at his side. Her features glowed with Khibil health, foxy and shrewd, animate with self assurance. "My sister, the Rangicha Taranta."

"Majister," she said in a full voice. "Lahal." She might have been speaking over her shoulder to a casual acquaintance in the street.

"Lahal, Rangicha."

Her eyebrows came together. I was being polite, true. But she'd have much preferred me to have addressed her as my lady Taranta. Of such petty nuances in etiquette are sore subjects made.

To ease that subtle tension I looked about and then, unable to resist riling him some more, told the Ranga: "You run a tidy ship."

"Thank you, majister. I have been detailed to take you to Fleet Admiral Harulf ham Hilzim."

"Detailed?"

"Yes. I came looking for you. There was sorcery in it."

"Ah. I see." And I did. Deb-Lu had contacted his opposite number in Hamal who'd contacted the Hamalese fleet. The admiral had ordered this uppity Khibil to nip across and pick me up. I said: "Is a battle imminent?"

"Yes, majister. The Schturgins are in great force."

If that was the reason for his dislike then I could feel relief. We'd be back with the fleet in time for the fight, I did not doubt. What I did doubt, though, was that explanation for his malice. He'd probably fought hard for mad Empress Thyllis and resisted everyone until the end of the campaign. Then, with any other option far less attractive, he'd come over and joined Nedfar. And he still hated Vallians.

The thought did occur to wonder why old Harulf ham Hilzim had picked this Khibil Taranto ham Armit. I'd had little contact with Hilzim during my times in Ruathytu; but I knew him by sight.

As far as I could tell he was loyal to Nedfar. But, it could well be, he was not. There might be plots afoot to oust Nedfar and put in some puppet of a group of diehard Hamalese nationalists. That would put Nedfar's son Tyfar at risk, and with him my daughter Lela. This contemptuous Khibil Taranto would merit watching.

I didn't forget how damned fast and high he'd swung the rope ladder.

So, you see, even in the midst of all the problems confronting me down here in Loh, problems enough to last a sage man for a long time, fresh problems stemming from old troubles were rearing monstrously ugly heads of doubt and suspicion. All would have to be dealt with in the fullness of time.

As the voller fled across the dwaburs—her name was Dovad Daisy—Rango Taranto forced himself to the amenities.

No doubt he wouldn't quickly forget the time in Hamal when apim and diff forgot their old friendships, when diffs were regarded askance and excluded from positions of power. My blade comrade Rees had suffered from that disgusting chauvinism. The situation had been saved through the sheer necessity for Hamal to use all her resources in the war. Tolerance of diffs of whatever race and from whatever race seems to me a mark of the culture and civilization of any peoples. And, of course, the very word tolerance in itself expresses those things that are hurtful.

Well, they made me reasonably comfortable, showing me to a small cabin where I could wash and where some welcome food was provided. A hulking great fellow came in, knocking the door all sideways with his bulk, his huge face awash with whiskers. His eyes were all but invisible among the creases and the hair. His mouth was very red-lipped.

"Lahal, majister!" he roared out in a voice like a hailing trumpet.

I gave him a narrow stare, munching my palines.

"Lahal, Hikdar."

His face grew even more suffused. His hair fairly bristled.

"I am Ship Hikdar Sternum Hamparz, majister!"

I shook my head. "Sternum Hamparz is a slender young fellow without a beard with whom I had the honor to share bread at breakfast—oh—many many seasons ago in Ruathytu. I'll give you that Sternum served in the Hamalian Air Service; but he had not yet reached the dizzy heights of a Deldar, let alone a Hikdar, and a Ship Hikdar at that."

"Yes, majister. It was many many seasons ago. And you spilled the slursh over the fristle fifi serving us—"

"By Krun! It is you! Lahal and Lahal, Sternum!"

I jumped up and took his hand. He'd always been a rough and tumble fellow, even back then, and now look at him! And, too, this explained somewhat why Hilzim had sent the uppity Khibil. His First Lieutenant, Sternum Hamparz, would keep an eye on him.

We cracked a bur or two on news, and I was pleased to know Sternum had supported Nedfar from the first, although not meeting up with me in those campaigns. He told me that the fleet now were seeking the Shanks in high confidence. There were upwards of fifty vollers, and the Hamalese had even condescended to bring along some of the unpowered fliers they called famblehoys, towed by powered vollers. "Oh, yes, majister. We'll whack 'em. By Kuerden the Merciless! We'll give 'em a bloody nose!"

"They are—uh—competent opponents. Tough."

"Surely. But, by Krun, we have the beating of them!"

There was no sign of a crack in Sternum's confidence. After a time I was able to quiz him on the Khibil Taranto.

"Shrewd and deep, shrewd and deep. Managed to keep his head after the battle when he offered up his sword. He pretends to serve the emperor loyally. His thoughts stray in other directions, by Krun!"

I nodded. "As I suspected. And you—?"

"The emperor asked me—personally, mind, personally!—to sail with the Rango. I was called back to Ruathytu specially for this task. I was sorry to leave Prince Tyfar... Majister?"

He'd seen my face and he stopped speaking abruptly.

I said: "Sternum. You saw Prince Tyfar? And the Princess Lela?"

He licked those red lips buried among the hair. "Why, yes, majister. She and the prince were fighting the wild men over the mountains." I felt my heart go flip-flop. What it is to worry and fret over a loved one when they are far away and doing God knows what and running all manner of risks. Sometimes they get in touch, and they are so casual it stings. They say they visit crocodile farms. They say they canoe up a river filled with Head Hunters. They say they dive for pearls on coral reefs. And all the time you yourself sit at home and sweat blood.

All Sternum could confirm was that Lela and Tyfar were still alive when he'd reluctantly left them. The problems of the production of the minerals and powders for the silver boxes remained unsolved.

It would be trite to comment that this news once more reinforced the global extent of our commitments, that every action everywhere tied up with every action everywhere else—so to speak.

Sternum added that he had changed and grown up and went on to say that all those seasons ago when he had no idea I was Dray Prescot, arch enemy of Hamal, he still saw greatness in me. I stopped him then, knowing he referred to this damned yrium with which I am cursed—or blessed—and well understanding his initial confusion when my identity became known. This bluff red-faced fighting man was the perfect exemplar why Hamal and Vallia ought to remain firm friends against the outer foes. There were plenty of warriors just like him in Vallia.

A Fristle wearing a leather helmet with a green feather put his head in the door. "Hik! Fleet's in sight."

"Very good," said Hikdar Sternum Hamparz. He turned to me. "Shall we go on deck, majister?"

91

Fifteen

Despite everything else my first and overriding thought when we signaled the fleet was to ask information of my friends in Shankjid.

The flags fluttered to yards slung out from the fighting tops. The yeoman wrote on his slate and the young cadet brought the slate to Sternum.

He cocked a bushy eyebrow at me.

"No news, majister."

I kept my face stony.

"Thank you, Sternum. And you can knock off the majister bit. Just use jis. Like we do in Vallia."

"Quidang, jis!"

Written perfectly plainly on that hairy red visage and in his words and bearing was the message that he bore no animosity in my thus flaunting Vallia before him. Rather, he felt elation and pride that he was permitted to call an emperor jis. I didn't sigh. But I admit I felt a cheap kind of cheat. Then I chucked that stupid idea out of my old vosk skull of a head. To run an empire you need to be an emperor. The kind of emperor that is Dray Prescot I hope you have some inkling of by now.

Sternum pointed. "There's Skull Charger, nearest. Just past her is Havil Resplendent. Then—" he screwed up the hair about his eyes. "Yes, that's Hirrume Warrior and as usual with her Pride of Hanitcha." He made a small gesture. "Newish ships, both."

Well, that figured. I'd had a passing acquaintance with both those ship names before. Quite possibly there had been two other ships built between these two over there and those I'd destroyed. As far as I knew, King Doghamrei, who'd owned the old Hirrume Warrior, had disappeared.

The streaming mingled lights of the Suns of Scorpio threw long beams athwart the lines of ships. The vessels rode the level air. Line after line of them, proud, glittering, tall of castle and fighting top, crested with a host of fluttering flags. Yes, they made a splendid sight.

All were of Hamal.

They radiated confidence. You could feel the sheer zest for the coming battle as an aura about them. As for Dovad Daisy whose deck I trod, the crew were already back in various low dives in the lowest portions of Ruathytu spending their prize money.

Jiktar Taranto walked up with a swagger. He gave me a perfunctory salute.

"It is going to be a day, majister."

"Aye."

To Sternum, curtly: "See about finding our position in the line."

"Quidang, Jiktar," said Sternum. I did not miss the fact that he had not shortened Jiktar to the familiar Jik.

The old-fashioned courtesies in naval observances and orders to which I had been accustomed in the Royal Navy were paralleled to a considerable degree in the navy of Vallia. One could quite see why. Vallia had possessed a great sea going navy and custom and tradition would follow the ways of the sea. Hamal had no great sea-going navy. Her power flew. Even so, I didn't like Taranto's manner with his Ship Hikdar.

To ease whatever tension there might be, I walked to the rail, and leaned comfortably, and studied the armada spread between land and clouds.

Well, yes, they were an impressive lot. There were fifty-three of them. Many were skyships like Hirrume Warrior and Pride of Hanitcha, vast vessels of many decks and fighting tops and galleries. They were tiered fortresses of the sky. They carried batteries of varters and catapults. They carried regiments of marines. They were colossal machines of destruction floating through thin air.

Among the shoals of large ships flashed the smaller pinnaces, long boats, tiny two-place fliers, carrying messages, performing the multifarious tasks needful in any fleet.

The flagship, Pride of Ruathytu, was a veritable monster.

She was not towing a famblehoy and it was noticeable that that demeaning duty had been allocated to the smaller vessels.

Well, I supposed it made sense.

Flags broke from her yard arm. The yeoman screwed his telescope into his eye and the lad wrote on the slate as the yeoman called. The signal informed Jiktar Rango Taranto na Firthlad of his position, tucked in at the tail of the Sixteenth Wing at the rear of the larboard column.

Since the days of the great conflicts, now thankfully past, finding crewmen for fliers was easy enough, for the huge fleets of yesterday were no more. Likewise, the Hamalese Wing now consisted of nine vollers instead of twelve. The grand skyships, of course, tended to act in small squadrons or individually. Dovad Daisy turned in mid-air and sailed carefully below the fleet until she reached her place when her helmsman lifted and turned her into her slot. We rode at the very end of the fleet.

The Ship Deldar (sometimes written ship-Deldar) went forward supervising a painting party. His position equates with that of boatswain on Earth. He was short, rotund, built of muscle, hight Hondar the Frogan. The hands with their paint pots were going to smarten up the eyes in the bows of the vessel. It was vital that in the coming battle Dovad Daisy could see where she was going.

Whilst all this activity went on—and still no sign of the Shanks—I fretted over Shankjid. No, that is a lie. Delia was aboard that ship. I sweated blood.

A brightly painted pinnace darted down the column and swerved up to Dovad Daisy's quarterdeck rail. A most natty young Hikdar stepped aboard. He was smothered in gold lace, feathers festooned his hat, his face was a pink chinless round. He spoke up in a kind of chirrup.

"Hikdar Nath ham Homath. Lahal."

The ham Homaths were a family well known in Hamal, of power, wealth and influence. Even if the old vad had sided so heavily with Thyllis.

This young whippersnapper went chirruping on. "The c-in-c, Fleet Admiral, Harulf ham Hilzim, Vad of Quinvarn, requests the pleasure of the company of Dray Prescot—" here the youngster floundered, and, I thought, with design to embarrass. Then he chirruped on. "Dray Prescot, emperor, aboard the flagship, Pride of Ruathytu."

By this time they all knew damn well I'd abdicated the throne of Vallia. Yet the idea that I was supposed to be an Emperor of Paz over them all would be a hard nut to swallow. Still, I was a kind of emperor still.

"I shall be delighted," I said, curtly.

Sternum looked disappointed. Taranto didn't look as pleased as I would expect him to look.

No, I said to myself. No, by Vox! That devious one has designs on my person.

Much as I might have joyed in staying aboard his ship and playing him as one plays a giant fish on the end of a line knowing he is your supper and you'll starve if he gets away, I needed to be at the center. The flagship was obviously the place to be. I looked at Sternum and winked. He contorted all his features so that it appeared all the whiskers disappeared into some other dimension centered on his nose. Then he managed to splutter out: "We are all mightily sorry to see you go, jis! By Krun, yes!"

Taranto snapped out: "Majister."

Hikdar ham Homath was half bending and indicating with an elegant arm that I should step aboard his pinnace.

I said: "Thank you, all aboard Dovad Daisy. I shall not forget." Then I crossed to the rail and stepped aboard the admiral's pinnace.

As we whirled away with the breeze rushing past I saw Sternum at the rail, gazing after me, his whiskers fairly blowing everywhere.

The flagship, Pride of Ruathytu, was the largest skyship I'd seen up to that time. She was just simply immense. You could get lost aboard and not find your way back to your quarters in a sennight.

Homath knew his way to officers' country in the center castles.

The fore castles were given over to the marine officers. The ship bustled with activity. I surmised that the control tower would be a veritable fortress, sheathed in thick iron and protected by grilles it would take heat cutters to break through. As we went towards the admiral's quarters, the smells of tar and resin faded to be replaced by lavender water. This, I confess, made me grin a wicked grin. A whiff of boiling cabbage broke through the lavender scent, and Homath put a lace kerchief to his nose. I didn't blame him. Only idiots boil cabbages limp.

After various doors and sentries, we eventually arrived at the admiral's quarters and the admiral himself. Like anyone on Kregen who does not change much once they reach maturity until a few years before their death at two hundred or so, he looked just the same. He greeted me kindly and waved me to a chair and sent for wine. His face was burnt brown by suns and wind, his hair was Hamalese dark and his jaws were like those of a shark.

After some pleasantries, he said: "I, for one, will support your candidacy. I have the utmost regard for Nedfar. I know what you did for him. I am your man. The quicker we can unite all of Paz the better. There is no better man for the job than Dray Prescot." Before I could make any sensible reply, he added: "And I thank Havil the Green that I have not been picked for the job. No, by Kaerlan the Merciful!"

He wore a plain blue shirt and gray trousers. His belt was hard worn leather and the lockets of his thraxter were solid steel. He was, I sensed at once, a man after my own heart. I stood up and extended my hand.

"Welcome aboard, Harulf."

He smiled and we shook hands after the Hamalese fashion.

When we had reseated ourselves and he had poured more wine, he said: "All the same, majister, the task is daunting."

"Aye. Call me jis. Aye, the task is daunting. Still we have advantages the Shanks do not. They are dwaburs from home. We are down here in Loh, true; it is not too difficult to find our way home to Hamal."

"They are consummate sailors."

"That is indisputable. We just have to be better."

"The confidence of the fleet is high. I have pumped that up. But, privately, I have doubts."

"All I can say is I am impressed by your fleet, Harulf. I cannot say I have seen a better."

He glowed at that, briefly, and then said: "Aye, aye, jis. I've done what I can. But—and to be brutally frank—after we Hamalese fought one another, and the rifts remain, there are elements in the fleet of which I remain dubious. I am disquieted. There is a growing adherence to a creed of which I know nothing but am investigating."

I came alert at this. I stared at Harulf. I could feel heat on my temples. I said: "Tell me, Harulf, you do not mean Lem the Silver Leem?"

It seemed to me to be a whole parcel of lifetimes before he slowly nodded. His face was grim. "Aye, jis. That is their name."

I braced up. "Very good! Root and branch, Harulf, tear them up and burn their temples. Lem the Silver Leem is an evil creed."

"That I had gathered. My own pantryman's daughter went missing. By a pure fluke some ceremony or other was stumbled upon in the skyship Havil Resurgent. The little girl was—" He stopped then.

Very quickly, I said: "You need not amplify. I know. I have seen what they do to little girls. Lem must be put down. They will have it no other way."

"Put down and obliterated, by Krun!"

"Aye. Now—I am not sure if this evil cult of Lem the Silver Leem is in any way connected to the Shanks."

He looked at me, stricken. "You mean—jis—you mean, there are those of Paz who would ally with the Schtarkins?"

In a voice like shifting gravel I said: "Down in Tarankar the Katakis work for the Shanks."

"Katakis." He dismissed them. "Scum."

"Agreed, Harulf, agreed. But they are of Paz and they ought to work with us and not against us."

"If we can contrive that, jis, we will do so. If not, then..."

The edge of the sword is supposed to settle so many arguments!

The day was now waning and Harulf had duties to perform. He was clearly a man I could do business with. That he supported me as Emperor of Paz came as a surprise and a pleasure. We went up to the central top and the view of the armada spread about us was a breathtaking sight.

This central top was well armored; just below and for'ard the control top was the heavily armored box I'd anticipated.

You could certainly have put at least a half dozen, if not more, Shankjid's aboard this flying mammoth.

Harulf was proud of his fleet. He had every right to be. When the hails came in: "Sail ho!" and we all looked, there was only tense and brilliant anticipation of action and a great victory.

Out there, black against the glows of the twin suns, the Shanks hovered, waiting.

They looked like flecks of darkness hurled against the sky glow. I started to count. The shifting and treacherous light made accuracy difficult and I made a total of sixty. I felt that was probably an undercount.

"Fifty-eight," said Hikdar Nath ham Homath and he snapped his telescope shut with a grandiloquent air of finality.

Others in the fighting top voiced their opinions.

"Fifty-five or sixty-five," said Harulf, silencing the babble. "We will smash them. We have to."

The two fleets surged together.

There is no pleasure in recounting disaster.

The Hamalese fought. They fought like maddened leems. They fought like wounded graints. They fought like chavonths or strigicaws, cunning and lethal. The Hamalese fought. And the Shanks fought harder.

Ships burned. In the failing light, ships roared with flame, strewing the evening sky with lurid streamers of death. Ships fell. Men fell. Red roaring madness scorched across deck after deck.

Pride of Ruathytu burned.

The wonderful skyship, queen of the air, burned.

All about Shank vollers were swooping and darting and Hamalese vollers were dying.

Nath ham Homath, white to the lips, chattered away to himself in the fighting top as flames licked up from the deck. Harulf had gone for'ard some time ago to sort out a problem. A Shank veered away from us as our flames belched up.

I grabbed Nath ham Homath and hauled him up.

"Come on, sunshine. Time to leave."

"Fire," he babbled. "All on fire."

"Let's find that pinnace of yours."

"Shouldn't play with flint and steel—"

"Come on!" I took him by the arm and fairly hurled him down the ladder.

We didn't find his pinnace. We did come across a group of crazed men trying to launch a small flier and fighting over her possession. Homath appeared to regain a semblance of sanity and wanted to take the flier from the men by right of rank. I hauled him on. He'd have wound up with a slit throat, for sure. Now all the gigantic vessel above us burned. We crawled out onto the lower fighting gallery. Men were toppling off into the shadowed void beneath. The shrieks were pitiful in their intense abandonment to fate and destruction. A dark shadow drifted in below us.

I shook Homath.

"That's a voller down there. We must jump."

He looked down, and drew back, shuddering. "I can't!"

The voller below us looked familiar. She eased up, closer, and I was sure. Dovad Daisy. Now there was a turn up for the book.

Nearer and nearer the voller rose towards us. Bits and pieces of Pride of Ruathytu were falling all about, spitting flame.

At last I judged the flier could close no nearer. I took hold of Homath's fancy collar and dragged him over the edge of the fighting gallery. Judging the moment, I shoved him and myself, let go my hold, and we fell through thin air.

Sixteen

Other men were toppling from the fighting gallery.

Nath ham Homath broke a wrist and two ribs when he hit the deck. He'd not made any attempt to break his fall. With my habitual agility I managed to land catlike and escape serious injury, although I did feel as though some giant had trodden on me with seven league boots.

For that reason I was out of action in the subsequent moments. I was aware that the voller was swinging and moving. The burning bulk of Pride of Ruathytu above drifted away, sparking flame and burning debris.

By the time I'd got my breath back and my wits about me we were pulling away from the debacle.

I clambered up. The lights of the Suns struck slantingly in across the deck. I turned and looked back. The sky burned.

Ships were blazing like torches. Ships were falling wrapped in shrouds of fire. And through that whole incredible panorama the dark febrile shapes of the Shanks darted like piranha stripping the Hamalese to the bone.

A voice said: "I thank you, Taranto. I owe you my life."

The voice was mellifluous, full bodied, assured. I took a look. The speaker was burned about his clothes, which had been fancy like those of Nath ham Homath's. His rank was that of Jiktar and I judged him to be a nobleman. Taranto's twin sister, Taranta, was there, fussing.

"Oh, Naghan, you did frighten me so! I thought you would never jump!"

"It was a confounded long way! By Flem, Taranta, I thought the voller would rise closer!"

"We rose as high as we could, Naghan." Taranto spoke icily.

"I'm sure, I'm sure, my dear Taranto. Just that the void looked remarkably unhealthy, by Krun, remarkably unhealthy!"

A hand reached under my armpit as I listened to this interesting conversation and I was hoisted to my feet. Sternum's hoarse voice said in my ear: "Any busted bones, jis?"

"Nary a one, thank you, Sternum. Who is this Naghan fellow then?"

"Him? Why, he's Naghan ham Newsat, Strom of Livhavil. He's just gone through the bokkertu to marry the lady Taranta. She carried on something dreadful. Made her brother fly to the flagship to get Naghan off."

I glanced about. The suns were just about gone. Whether by chance or good airmanship Dovad Daisy escaped any further Shank attentions. She bore on through the air, heading north. North did not suit me. There was work to be done down south. There was Shankjid to find.

After a disaster of this magnitude, the people involved would be in shock. You couldn't expect the Hamalese, for all their reputed toughness, to carry on regardless. The survivors would need time to recuperate. I wasn't about to give them that time. There just wasn't time for that kind of time wasting.

I said to Sternum: "We must head south. There are things I must do down there. Important things for Paz."

"The Jiktar Rango Taranto is heading home for Hamal, jis."

"Yeh, I guessed that was where he was headed."

"The lads are a bit shaken—by Krun! I'm shaken!"

"Your fleet's been beaten. So you've been whacked. So all right. You come out fighting and smash up the Shanks next time. It's no use scuttling back to Hamal—"

"But we don't have a fleet any more, jis!"

"There are other fleets around here to take over."

"We-ell—"

"This is a set-back, Sternum. That's obvious. But that's all it is. It isn't the end. Now go round and have a word with your lads. Make them see we have to carry on down south." I gave him an eyeball to eyeball look. "I'll compromise if I have to. Just get the lads to take me down south to link up with my friends, and then you can scuttle off to Hamal like a whipped rark."

"What about the Jiktar Taranto?"

"I'll deal with him. If you and your lads agree to take Dovad Daisy down south, then down south we'll go. Dernun?"

"Quidang!"

Then he added. "And we won't scuttle off like a whipped rark, jis! No, by Havil the Green! We'll see what we'll do."

"What we can do for Paz."

"Aye, jis."

About this time I began to feel that I needed to catch up on all the sleep I'd been missing. You can drive the body so far—and if you've been educated in the navy of Nelson's day, then you can drive yourself well past any sane limits—but in the end nature catches up. The confrontation with Taranto and this Naghan and Taranta must come right away or be left until morning. I said: "How long will it take you to sound out the hands?"

"Two burs, three at the most."

"Then I'll come with you. Otherwise we'll all be asleep."

We made the rounds. I repeated the words I'd used on Sternum, pointing out our duty to Paz, that everything was not lost, and in the end coming down to the simple task of taking me to find my friends. You may well believe I promised rewards. I'd have given the kingdom to find Delia. I promised enough gold to keep them happy, and the odd thing was, because of the reputation I'd acquired through the lurid books and plays about Dray Prescot, they believed absolutely in my word.

When all was ready we went up to the quarterdeck.

Taranto and Taranta were astounded to see me.

Nath ham Homath had been carted off unconscious to have his ribs and wrist attended to. I'd been completely missed in the shadows, with Sternum to assist me.

This Naghan ham Newsat, Strom of Livhavil, said in his assured tones:

"Who is this fellow, then? Who gave him leave to come onto the quarter-deck?" And, to me: "Clear off, yetch, before I call the marines!"

I stepped forward from Sternum. The quarterdeck was well-lighted by the Maiden with the Many Smiles and the bunch of nobles stood erect like cut flowers in a vase. Naghan drew his sword.

I said: "You can put your sword away, strom." I turned to Taranto. "We are sailing south, Jiktar. Will you give the order, or shall I?"

He gobbled at that. "But we have been defeated! The Shanks!"

He would have gone on; but I silenced him.

"We have had a setback. Nothing more. Hurry up, Jiktar. Every moment you delay carries us further away from Tarankar."

"Tarankar!" shouted Strom Naghan. "Ho, guards! Clear this fellow away! Clap him in irons!"

There was no sign of guards or of irons.

Taranto, nervous now, spluttered out: "But, majister! Tarankar—that is a death trap now."

Strom Naghan caught that majister. He fixed me with a jowly look.

"Majister? Majister? You are Dray Prescot?" The sword in his hand trembled. It switched down into line. "I ought to chop you here and now, by Clem, here and now!"

The Krozair brand whipped free, it described a graceful evolution and Strom Naghan's thraxter flew up into the air, buried its point in the deck ten paces off and quivered like a tuning fork.

I put the point of the longsword against the fancy gold lacework collar. I said: "Jiktar Taranto. Give the order to turn this vessel to the south. This strom has no authority here."

Taranta let out a distressed little squeak and I suppose I felt a twinge of pity for her at seeing her affianced with a brutal longsword digging into his throat. Strom Naghan, for his part, had sense enough not to move a muscle. Taranto spluttered some more, then in his metallic voice snapped out: "Very well, majister. By Flem, it suits me ill, though." He turned to see Sternum close by. "Steer southerly, curse you!" he snarled out. Not, I considered, a seemly way to address your First Lieutenant.

The helmsman turned Dovad Daisy under the stars. Those constellations which had grown familiar to me since I'd first arrived in Loh revolved and we were heading south.

The longsword revolved itself and snicked back into the scabbard.

Strom Naghan let out a breath. Then he said: "We should have destroyed you when we had the chance. When you were dragged at the tail of a calsany through Ruathytu."

"You were there too, were you, strom."

"Aye! By Flem, I was there, and I joyed in every heartbeat of it!"

"That is all over now, strom. Now we fight Shanks."

"I fight Schtarkins well enough. But you have flipped my sword away. I cannot fight without a sword."

"Take your thraxter, strom, and fight Shanks. For if you cross me again you will fight nobody thereafter."

So, on that idiotic boast, the affair was concluded.

This had been one of the quickest and most peaceful mutinies I'd ever been involved in, by Vox. We fled southwards under the stars of Kregen. Delia! She was all that really mattered now.

Seventeen

Was this somewhat pathetic little mutiny one of the earliest examples of the power of an Emperor of Paz? I surmised that perhaps the idea of Paz could be projected to receptive minds. It had been in the past in a vague fashion. As the word spread, more and more like-minded people would take up the cause. If they didn't, they'd be doomed. The Shanks would see to that.

In this fabulous world of Kregen very often what the heart desires is achieved, and very often not, and it is what is done with the achievement that counts and the reaction to disappointment that matters.

We saw no signs of any other ships, either friendly or hostile, as we sped south. Sternum set watches; they saw nothing of Shank or survivor. There were good chances that some of the Hamalese had escaped as had Dovad Daisy. To destroy an entire fleet remains a difficult task and one very seldom ever accomplished, even in the greatest of sea victories.

I managed to catch a few winks of sleep, enough to keep me going, and stoked up the inner man. Along towards dawn Sternum, who, although not appearing to do so, must have had some sleep, came up looking grim. His jaw was set just so. He spread hairy hands in a gesture of utter disgust.

"Hai, Sternum, have you lost a zorca and found a calsany?"

"That Rangicha." He breathed in and out a few times, blowing his whiskers. "I've never understood why some folk of good breeding act like they do when they needn't. Young cadet Nalgre ti Mornlad told me. A smart lad. Going to be admiral of the fleet one day, if he survives."

"Sternum," I said, and he stopped speaking. "Told you what?"

"Oh—uh—yes, jis. This noble lady is trying to buy someone of the crew, anyone, to assassinate you."

"I suppose her fancy man Strom Naghan doesn't fancy his chances."

Sternum laughed. We were up in the bows, waiting for the dawn, and I still had a handful of palines to munch.

"All the same, jis, by Krun, it is a serious matter."

"I suppose so. I'll have a word with her."

Then Sternum surprised me again. He shifted his bulk about, for he had grown enormously from the stripling I'd known back in Ruathytu. He more blurted out than spoke coherently. "Jis. I have read the stories and seen the plays now they are freely available in Hamal after the censorship. What I would most like—"

I held up a hand. "If you have read, then you know the difficulty of taking very many folk on adventures."

"Oh, yes, jis, that I understand. No. What I would most like to do is join your Guard Corps. As a Hamalese, would that be possible for me?" His face screwed up into a hairy whirlpool.

As I say, he surprised me.

I thought for a moment. Then I said: "I don't see why not. Mind you, Sternum, I don't run the Guard. They're a damned independent lot and make up their own rules and regulations—"

"Which you have to ratify!"

"Sometimes I stop 'em doing something, that is true. Not often."

"Well—?"

"I'll have a word with one or two of my lads at the first opportunity."

"Thank you, jis, may Havil the Green smile on you."

"Um," I said.

After Sternum had taken himself off, mightily pleased, I decided on a course of action which did not please me but which I fancied might do the business quickly and cleanly. One of the crew approached by the Rangicha, a varterist hight Hoban the Brows, was sent to me by Sternum.

He stood uneasily as the Suns of Scorpio came up and flooded the world with their mingled streaming lights. His eyebrows were, indeed, of a profusion. "Hoban," I said, speaking easily. "Do you believe in Paz?"

He didn't rattle back a quick reply. He shifted on his bare feet again, looking at the deck between his toes. "Well, majister—"

"It is a simple question. It does not have a simple answer. I know you want to go home to Hamal. We all want to go home, by Krun! But we can't really run off home and leave the Shanks to smash everything up here, now can we?"

"I suppose not."

"You suppose correctly. Fighting against the Shanks and for all of Paz— including Hamal—means you believe in Paz."

"Yes, majister."

"Even if you're fighting for some folk who are not Hamalese."

"Yes, majister."

"Because we are all of Paz."

"Yes—"

"So when do you think you will assassinate me, Hoban?"

He shook all over. He couldn't lift his head to look me in the eye. A dribble of spittle trickled down his slanted chin.

"All right, Hoban. I am going to assume you never intended to assassinate me at the pleasure of Rangicha Taranta."

"No, no, majister!" He was spluttering and blubbering. "No, for I told the lady I would not! I said ask someone else!"

"Come with me." I started off down the deck.

Sternum was waiting with a small party, all heavily armed. With myself at their head and Hoban the Brows in the centre, we marched to the after-castle where Jiktar Rango Taranto had quartered his sister. I knocked on the door and then, without waiting for a reply, pushed it open and barged into the cabin.

She was half-dressed and at once she snatched up a robe and held it to herself. Her Khibil face flooded painfully with blood. A man's voice from further back behind the bed curtains said: "What is it, by Glem?"

"Leave my cabin at once!" she said. Her chin lifted. She pointed and then grabbed for the slipping robe. "How dare you! My brother—"

"You are being placed under arrest for plotting to murder the Emperor of Paz. Can you say anything in your defense?"

"Arrest? Murder? What nonsense!" But her breathing gusted unsteadily, and she put out a hand to steady herself, ignoring the robe.

"You will be placed in the cells until a court is assembled."

"You cannot! I am a Rangicha—my brother is the Rango!"

"There are many more important nobles than you or your brother where you are going. A court can be formed." I spoke briskly. "Of course, I can always pass judgment on you myself. That is something that emperors can do. I shall find you guilty of attempting to murder the emperor." I lifted my hand. "As for your punishment, I suppose the easiest way will be to throw you overboard. Good riddance to bad rubbish."

She was panting now, half-crouched, her face and hair wild.

Strom Naghan appeared from beyond the bed curtain. He'd used the time to dress himself, more or less, and now he stalked forward ready to add all his habitual authority. I stopped him dead in his tracks.

"Hand over your sword, strom. You are an accomplice in this and equally guilty with the lady. You will suffer the same fate. I did warn you."

His dark foxy face clouded into a thunderhead. Some Khibils have this dark hair; some, like my kregoinye comrade Pompino, tend to the auburn, red or ginger. He looked now as savage as a wild animal about to spring. His fist gripped his sword hilt.

I held out my hand. "Well, strom? Or do you wish to die here and now?"

What effort it cost him to unbuckle the sword belt and hurl it down on deck between us I couldn't know. It must have hurt.

"Also," I said, going on remorselessly with the business, for I wanted to end it as quickly as possible. "It is quite clear that Rango Taranto was in league with the would-be murderers. He must be taken up at once." I half turned. "Jiktar Sternum Hamparz! You are now in command. Take up the treacherous Rango and clap the three conspirators in irons. Dernun?"

After a single gulp, he was himself. He roared it out, joyfully.

"Quidang, Majister!"

The sorry affair was thus far concluded. Three highly indignant and upset nobles—not to say frightened nobles—were clapped in irons. A smooth-faced, light-haired lad dressed as a cadet stood nervously by the door as I went out. I gave him a look.

"Cadet Nalgre ti Mornlad?"

"Yes, majister—I mean, aye aye, majister."

"You did well, cadet. I shall not forget."

He flushed up at this. "Thank you, majister." Then, unable to hold back, he burst out: "Will you really throw them overboard?"

"Of course not! What an idea! No, no, Nalgre, they have to learn their lesson. We are about the business of fighting Shanks, and we need every-one we can."

"So you'll let them off, majister?"

"I certainly do not intend to have them executed. No, they'll be a little frightened, learn their lesson, and then they'll have to behave."

He looked up at me, clear-eyed. "They have not treated me well, they have abused me. But it is not for that I speak."

"Speak what?"

His smooth young face expressed perfect innocence. He said: "They say that with age comes wisdom. If it were me, I know they will continue to try to harm me. They will continue to hate you, majister, and try to kill you. I'd execute the three of them."

I stared at him, at that frail young face, and marveled. Of course, he spoke the way of wisdom common to kings and emperors. Of course. Once a man or woman has betrayed you, you can never trust them again. To be on the safe side, it is better to put them out of the way permanently. Maybe, after all, I was no good as an emperor.

Cadet Nalgre ti Mornlad's fresh young face abruptly went as blank as that of a codfish. His forehead glistened and his eyes dulled and then, shockingly, opened to their full width and glared upon me.

"Jak!" he said in a febrile voice. "It is Highly Difficult. There is Not Much Time Left."

"Go on, Deb Lu."

"This great devil Carazaar has the planes sealed. Difficult. Delia has gone to Taran—" The voice faltered and Nalgre swayed as though about to fall. I grasped his arm and stared into his eyes. His lips moved sluggishly. "The fleet—"

Nalgre moved in my grip and said: "Majister?"

"It is all right, Nalgre."

"But—"

"Quite. I thank you for your advice. Now go about your duties."

"Quidang, majister!"

He went off, somewhat puzzled, I fear, at the sudden lapse in his memory and concentration. He promised well, as Sternum had prophesied.

'Taran', Deb-Lu-Quienyin had said. That had to mean Tarankar. It was not likely to be Taranik. I frowned. It might be Taranjin, and in that case it meant Delia and my friends were running their heads into the leem's jaws.

It was easy enough to guess that Deb-Lu had managed to get the news of my rescue through to Delia. Now she was pushing ahead with the plan, confident I'd soon join her.

Deb-Lu had also said 'the fleet.' As far as I could see, he could only mean the fleet from Vallia if he spoke of our forces. If he spoke of the enemy—well, they probably must have more than one fleet operating over Loh.

A twinned shadow fleeted across the deck and I looked up, squinting against the blaze of the Suns.

I expected to see the shape of the raptor from the Star Lords, the Gdoinye, circling up there ready to hurl down mockery and contempt upon my head, calling me a get onker, chastising me in the name of the Everoinye. It was not so.

Up there, planing in gentle circles, sailed the white dove of the Savanti.

I felt surprise rush all through me.

Why should those mortal but superhuman folk of Aphrasöe the Swinging City send their dove to spy on me? They might be taking a fresh hand in the game. I gravely doubted that they were. But if they were, by the disgusting diseased liver and lights of Makki Grodno, what were they up to now?

Eighteen

"Despite all the difficulties, Deb-Lu is managing to maintain communications. We are in contact, even if tenuously."

"Highly tenuously, my old dom."

"But still in contact," said Delia, firmly, in her no-nonsense voice.

"We're all here," observed Inch.

"All!" I said, grumpily. "All!"

Well, I was being unfair. As we sat in the cabin of Shankjid deciding what to do next—although we all knew that well enough—about us rested the vorlcas of my Guard Corps. The lads, at least, were all here.

Maintaining her previous thought, Milsi said: "I do wish we had the fliers with us." She drew in a breath. "Those poor people of Hamal—"

"We may not have heard the last of them." Seg spoke with an abrupt shake of his shoulders, as though shaking off rain. We all looked sharply at him. In his native hills and valleys of Erthyrdrin they breed fey folk, folk with the Eye. Nobody spoke for a moment or two.

Then Sasha said: "Inch, dear. Surely we can get some warriors from Ng'groga to help?"

"Since I left home I have very little influence in Ng'groga, if any at all. It's the same with Seg. We're Vallians now."

"Aye, by the Veiled Froyvil. Vallians and Pazzians."

"Or Pazish," I said in a neutral voice.

"Or," said Delia in her cutting voice, "Pazese."

"Oh. Quite."

"And," she went on briskly. "I just hope Deb-Lu tells that son of ours to unglue his wings."

"I'm sure Drak will do all he can." Milsi spoke with tact and affection. "He knows his own mind."

I stood up. "We're doing no good going over and over the problems. I made a mess last time with these new friends of Loh. I don't want to make it worse. They all have their points."

"Some more than others." Seg spoke on a breath. "I wouldn't like Mevancy's bindles in my face, no by Vox!"

"That young Rollo," said Inch, shaking his bent head. "Deb-Lu is going to have a handful there, by Ngrangi."

"He seems very nice," said Milsi, somewhat primly.

We all laughed.

When we went out on deck the day was bright and breezy with layered clouds scudding overhead. Around us the fleet rested in a wide valley among hills. We'd met up, thankfully enough, about a hundred miles or so from the capital of Tarankar, Taranjin. That city was our objective.

How to take it, with the forces at our disposal, was the problem.

Whenever a fleet makes port of call, or in the case of a flying fleet, touches down, there are always multifarious tasks to perform. Patching, mending, carpentering, painting, there is no end to maintenance. The scene on that bright and breezy morning sparkled with activity.

As you may well imagine, there were a thousand and one calls on my time. Useless to list them all. Just take it from me, if there had been another couple of dozen burs in the Kregan day there still wouldn't have been time to see all those who wanted to see me or deal with all the questions hurled at my dizzied head. In the end, of course, as happened routinely when I was away, delegates dealt with the vast majority of importuning folk, those with grievances, those with ambitions, those with plans. We had, I may mention, no thomplods with us. We'd used those impressive animals with six legs each side and looking like haystacks in a so-called battle-winning plan. Their smell so offended most other saddle animals that they'd run off. It would have worked, too, had not the Shanks adopted the disgusting idea of smearing vosks with tar and setting them alight to charge madly at our thomplods and rout them first. They might employ that obnoxious trick again when we went up against them.

Mileon Ristemer, whose thomplod plan it was, remained with us today still with his regiment.

Delia had been delighted to see Nath Karidge again, the Beau Sabreur, the commander of her first personal regiment, EDLG, the Empress' Devoted Life Guard.

As for me, I'd spent a delirious time with my swods, my old sweats, my Guard—each one of them dear to me, each one of them a match for Vikatu the Dodger, the Old Sweat, the old hare, the archetypal old soldier of Vallia and of Paz on Kregen, paragon of military virtues and vices, a legendary figure of myth and romance. Oh, yes, we'd ripped up the night all the way to dawn.

Naghan ti Lodkwara, one of the chiefs of 1ESW, confided a clever plan to me during that time of carousing. "Kendur! We fly over them and land and blatter them into the sea!"

"A sound plan, Naghan."

Targon the Tapster, a chief of 1ESW, leaned towards us, and not slopping a drop from his winecup. "Sounder still, jis, if 1ESW land and line the waterfront. We'll catch 'em between two walls, then."

Solemnly, I nodded. No good pooh-poohing these notions. My lads believed they could carry out stratagems such as this, and they'd all get themselves killed trying.

Turning the conversation was not too difficult. All I had to do was say: "That reminds me of how the Phalanx stood at Kochwold—?" and they were off, refighting and reliving old battles.

I had not risen too early on the following day.

This enforced waiting grated on the nerves and frayed tempers short. All the same, stubborn as a graint as I am, I would not move until I considered we were ready.

Do not take the wrong idea from this report of the plans of my chiefs of 1ESW. That little fragment of conversation more aptly belonged to my Djangs. The initial members of the Emperor's Sword Watch had formed the unit themselves. That had been their own idea to protect me. They had learned their craft in the field. They were not novices. It was just that, like Nath na Kochwold and his Phalanx, they believed themselves invincible.

Just before an intriguing incident occurred in the air I took thought regarding Jiktar Sternum Hamparz and his request. There was no use dreaming that he'd get into 1ESW. The Emperor's Yellow Jackets, the second corps in seniority in the Guard, would take him. Probably they'd start him off in 4EYJ, possibly 3EYJ, and then see how he did. 2EYJ had retained its training function as a fighting unit, and I fancied Sternum had learned his battlecraft. Although there was no doubt that anyone at all could learn from my Guard Corps.

When the agreement came through that he could join 4EYJ, Sternum's hairy face positively sprouted with pleasure and pride. He started to thank me: "By Krun, jis—well, I don't know—by Havil the Green—"

I stopped him in his tracks.

"Krun is accepted because I use it. Havil the Green may well not be. No man in Vallia is forced to follow any religious creed he does not wish to follow and no man or woman is persecuted for their religion. All the same, a trifle of tact would be sensible."

"Quidang, jis!"

"If you must apostrophize some supernatural deity try Chusto, or Chozputz. I have found them most comforting."

"I have never heard of them—"

"No. I made them up. They have proved most useful."

His barely visible eye among the hair closed in a massive conspiratorial wink. "I fly your course, jis!"

He shifted his kit out of Dovad Daisy. Unsure what to do with her and her confounded hoity-toity Khibil lords and ladies, I felt it best to send her back. She'd be a liability in any fight and—she was Hamalese and not Vallian. It was a hard decision; but, I thought, the right one.

Delia and my friends said nothing about that; I had some gyp from some of the others about losing a ship we needed.

Mevancy, of course, was cutting.

"I am concerned over the reactions of the Everoinye, cabbage. By Spurl! If they start thinking we are not doing all we can against—"

"I know it seems to me the Star Lords may be superhuman and possess all these wonderful powers, it also seems to me they are idiots from time to time. I just hope they're not cretinous enough now to imagine what you suggest."

She drew in a breath and her flushed face paled a trifle. "Oh, you! If they take exception to your words—"

"By Vox! They have done and no doubt will again, pigeon."

Then Kuong and Rollo joined us as we talked in the shade of a fine broad-leaved tree at the edge of the landing area where the fleet was moored. We'd resumed a little of our old intimacy; there was still some way to go yet before we were back to the old friendships.

Just across the way in the blaze of the suns, Splendor of Opaz was exercising her flutduin squadrons. The magnificent birds soared aloft from their perching poles jutting from the sides of the ship. They were flown by Valkans and they were superb. Down here in flierless Loh the sight of these gorgeous birds spreading wide wings and carrying people through thin air smacked of miracles akin to those of their own Wizards of Loh.

Mevancy heaved up a sigh.

"I'd love to do that—but—"

"If you fasten up the straps of your clerketer, you're safe enough."

"And they fight up there?"

Now it was my turn to heave up a sigh; I did not. If you have to fight then you have to fight with all you've got.

"Yes."

Rollo in his enthusiastic way said: "I'm confident I could still hit the mark from the back of one of those birds."

Kuong's brown fist gripped the hilt of his lynxter. "A sword will be of little use up there, Drajak."

"True. You need a lance, a toonon, perhaps a lengthened strangdja."

Just then a flutduin swooped down over our heads and volplaned neatly up to avoid the tree. A bulky man waved down.

A voice bellowed through the windrush: "Hai! Groundlings! It's wonderful up here an' all! You can see for dwaburs and dwaburs an' everything!"

We all gaped up.

Then Rollo, in a determined voice snapped out: "That settles it!" He started off with a purposeful stride towards Splendor of Opaz.

Kuong hurried to march at his side and after a momentary hesitation, Mevancy ran to catch up. They shouted back over their shoulders: "Just watch us!"

So, then, I did heave up that sigh. Scatterbrained, the lot of 'em, by Krun!

In addition, this little incident indicated to me that perhaps they were really over the shock of discovering their new friend Drajak was an emperor—well, an emperor of sorts—and were feeling their way back to our old comradeship. There was some way to go yet, though.

You will understand that I cannot at this moment mention all the old comrades and friends who had flown in with the fleet and were now my companions in the adventures ahead. You do not live a life on Kregen and travel widely without making a vast number of acquaintances as well as friends. And, of course, enemies also. Take it from me, the days were filled from suns-up to suns-down with activity.

News of Queen Kirsty's impending arrival reached us. She'd driven her forces across the desert and into Tarankar. She'd avoided aerial observation. This, I confess, had been the one great stumbling block to our plan. Now that Kirsty was actually in the country and approaching, we could form our final plans for the onslaught.

Our ships and people were spread out and camouflaged. A few times we saw Schtarkins flying over patrolling. Stopping the lads taking off in our lone voller and tackling them proved a task too, by Vox!

As the Fish Faces had been lavish of late with their distribution of fire pots, I had a large number made up and stowed carefully. Misuse of fire pots is a hazardous and lethal business.

Now—for Queen Kirsty.

I'd given orders for her army to be quartered some way off from the Guard Corps' fleet. This seemed a merely sensible precaution.

Determined to put as brave a face as possible on it, I went over to see her and Rodders. I'd put on a simple white tunic for the occasion—well, I must admit, the tunic had a fancy gold-stitched hem—and wore my usual arsenal of weapons. To Delia, I'd said—not at all sure—"It's probably best if I see them by myself to start off with—yes?" To which the divine Delia had replied, with a typical little tilt to her delicious chin: "Yes. If the woman is as cutting as you say she is." Delia laughed. "That will spare me the enjoyment of watching you squirm." To which I had replied: "If I know Kirsty, squirm is the word, my heart."

And Delia said, very sharply: "Take care, my heart. You will take a squadron of 1ESW."

"I'd thought to—"

"Good!"

So, there I was, being ushered into Queen Kirsty's tent which was of a size and luxuriously furnished. Rodders sat at her side. She looked not quite just the same. There was even more maturity in the set of her jaw. There was, I remember, a strong scent of jasmine on the air within the colored tent.

"Drajak," she said in her sharp way, yet I felt she was being as gracious as she could. "We missed you. Where have you been?"

And Rodders, big and vigorous and a fighting man after my own heart, chimed in: "Lahal and welcome, Drajak. We have need of men like you for the battles ahead."

So—they didn't know. No one had told them.

Carefully, I said: "I came here to scout the Shanks. Kuong is here, too. We face a formidable task."

Rodders in his professional paktun way started to make an observation. Kirsty held up her hand and Rodders stopped speaking. She said: "I understand this Dray Prescot will bring powerful forces to assist us. He comes from Vallia. Also, I think Hamal will help."

Gravely, I told them about the Hamalese debacle.

Rodders looked angry. I thought I detected the merest whiff of a white tinge along Kirsty's stubborn jaw.

"I had heard tales of these Hamalese," Queen Kirsty spoke with some acerbity, "which I could not fully credit. Now I can understand their veracity. They appear less than dogs."

"Our army—" began Rodders.

All the intensity in Kirsty's face concentrated and came together. Her high square shoulders lifted. "Our army will fight!"

Rodders put a hand through that brilliant red Lohvian hair of his. His eyes met mine in a swift fleeting glance, a man to man look of understanding. Oh, yes, with Rodders to command, Queen Kirsty's army would fight.

The trouble was, I was convinced that Kirsty had no idea of the magnitude of the problem, and I doubted if Rodders was fully aware.

I went on to explain that the gangs who were hiding out in the countryside around Taranjin were divided. They were continually hunted from the air by Shank patrols. They could handle that as we did and as I'd trained up the combined bands of the Kov and Kovneva of Borrakesh. The political divisions were a more serious threat to our success. Just who, the question was asked, just who would form the government of Tarankar after the Shanks had been expelled? The old usurpers, the Riffims, who had taken control of Tarankar and subjugated the native inhabitants, were now all gone, destroyed by the Fish Faces. Who would rule Tarankar?

I'd made a vow that, by Vox, Krun and Djan, it wasn't going to be me!

For reasons of state it might prove necessary that I, in an official capacity, should take part in any negotiations to appoint any new ruler or rulers of Tarankar. The thought may have occurred to Kuong Vang Talin, the Trylon of Taranik, that he might well become chief of the government here. I couldn't say if it had. It may have done and it might not have done. If the squabbling guerilla gangs were left to their own devices, the country would never settle down and the Shanks would find easy pickings when they returned.

Kirsty was never slow on the uptake.

"So they squabble amongst themselves." She put that determined jaw into her fist, leaning forward, her intense gaze bent on me as though I were a specimen in a jar. "Good! Divided they will never be able to oppose—" She stopped herself speaking with a clearly visible effort. She would not deign to disclose, let alone discuss, her plans with the lower orders.

I said: "Divided they pose little threat to the Fish Faces." I gave her a mean look. "If you wish to place the crown of Tarankar upon your head alongside that of Tsungfaril, you will meet opposition."

She drew in a sharp little breath just short of a gasp.

"You presume on our graciousness, Drajak!"

Rodders shifted in his seat, and his great Lohvian longbow, perched against the arm, slipped forward. He retrieved with instinctive reflex, smooth and easy, like any master Bowman of Loh.

"You would find," I went on with heavy emphasis, "the problems of ruling these two countries well nigh insuperable—"

"Drajak!" she flamed out. "Hold your tongue lest—lest—"

"Kirsty," breathed Rodders in her ear.

Her breast rose and fell within the silken sheath. She put a hand to her throat. Then: "You had best leave us for now, Drajak, for we are not unmindful of your services. We do not wish you to incur our displeasure." She made a graceful gesture, recovering her composure. "Rodders will find a place for you in my army."

I gave them both a brief nod apiece and took myself off. What a hoity-toity madam! The Star Lords had insisted that she be made queen of Tsungfaril. You could quite see some of their reasons, by Krun!

That they didn't yet know the fellow they knew as Drajak was really Dray Prescot, potential Emperor of Paz, meant only that they'd find out in due time when the gods smiled. They did so by chance, as Delia delighted in telling me. "Kuong made his courtesy call, and—"

"Of course. Well, I'm glad I wasn't there to witness it."

"A very prickly lady, your friend Kirsty. Queen of Tsungfaril and wants to be Queen of Tarankar."

"Yes. I think she has little hope."

"Yet, according to you, your precious Everoinye picked her to be queen and there was a great deal of trouble making her so."

"Trouble and a half!" We were walking out in the rays of the suns with some lads of 1EYJ pacing us. The ships lay all about hidden under trees and camouflage netting. The flutduins were exercising, flying in swooping circles, letting their wings taste the air. I felt some concern that they might be spotted by a Shank aerial patrol; but flutduins need to spread their wings. A handful of beautiful and tough girls followed us along, clad in russet leathers and armed with whip, claw and rapier. They were Sisters of the Rose, and they were Jikai Vuvushis, Battle Maidens. Delia had taken them onto her staff and was considering forming a full sized regiment, bearing in mind the squeamishness I still had not thrown off after all these seasons on Kregen. Walking and chatting with them were a brilliant group of cavaliers from 1EDLG. They'd vote the Jikai Vuvushis in, as Lasal the Vakka was their witness! The air rang with the sounds of carpenters and smiths and riggers working in the ships. The fragrant scent of tar smoked up, for although these ships might never ride the waves, tar is a beneficial substance aboard ship. A zorca troop cantered past, weapons gleaming, followed by a nikvove troop. All in all, the whole scene was one of activity and brightness and life.

Soon, horribly soon, these people must be flung headlong into a battle they had slim chances of winning.

If they were not, then quite apart from the further spread of the Fish Faces, the Star Lords would summon me for judgment—and punishment.

When at last Kirsty and Rodders paid their courtesy call on me, I deliberately pitched the whole thing into a low key. I was just as simply dressed. I waited for them at the gangplank of Shankjid and I welcomed them aboard in a natural way—at least, I hoped it was natural—giving them the Lahal and watching as they observed the fantamyrrh.

During the brief conversation over miscils and palines and sazz, Kirsty did say in her sharp way: "You deceived me, majister. Did you consider the embarrassment I would suffer when I found out your trick?"

"There is no need for that."

I didn't add that by acting correctly at the time any backward look could not make her feel embarrassed.

Rodders said: "Now I wonder about that wager, majister. From all I read of Dray Prescot and his friend Seg Segutorio, they are bowmen to test the best in Erthyrdrin."

"Seg don't test 'em," I said, dryly. "He beats 'em."

The reception finished on a more friendly note as Delia set to work in her subtle, devious and downright cunning way to make Kirsty regain some composure. I suppose she'd gone back over her memories, searching for some horrible faux pas she'd made, and hoping desperately not to find a single one. We sent them off more cheerful than when they'd arrived.

Delia said in a voice like the cat that has supped the cream: "They accepted tacitly, without question, the fact that you are emperor."

"Oh, aye, my heart. I'm some kind of emperor. As, indeed, you are more than some kind of empress. But of what? I cannot believe that anyone of Paz is going to swallow that without—"

"Hush! Tsleetha-tsleethi. Softly-softly. We've made a start."

In these later passages I realize I must sound puffed with self-importance, bloated with self-esteem, stupid with self-glory and power.

This is not so. It has been said that respect equals power. Sometimes I caught a little dent between Delia's eyebrows when Mevancy called me cabbage, say, or Llodi addressed me as Drajak. Yet she knew the reasons for these ways of going on. If I was going wrong in my handling of the emperor's slot, Delia would put me right. If the people didn't want me to be their leader, then, by Djan-kadjiryon, I'd be only too happy to leave!

Delia walked with her graceful litheness to stand at the opening of the tent, holding to a rope. I caught my breath. Blood-thumping and heart-stopping is Delia, empress of majesty. Khe-Hi-Bjanching walked into the tent past Delia, turning to smile at her and nod respectfully. He wore a simple saffron robe with a silver hem and a flat hat of some obscure provenance, girdled with little golden hearts.

"Delia!" he said. "Dray! Good news!"

He wasn't actually there in the tent with us. As far as we knew he was still in Whonban to the north. His unlined face and lively expression summed up a fellow whose much-loved wife had recently had twins.

Delia turned back and crossed to me as I moved towards her. We touched hands as the Wizard of Loh went on.

"Fleet Admiral Harulf ham Hilzim has gathered some survivors of that dreadful battle. He's on his way. Better to wait for him—"

The figure of Khe-Hi wavered. His saffron robe suffused with a bloody red. His voice trailed off. Just before he disappeared the last we heard was: "The interference—Deb-Lu will—Remberee!"

"Remberee, Khe-Hi," said Delia, gravely, speaking to the air.

This item of news livened us up. With a handful of vollers we could materially improve the chances of the unpowered vorlcas. Kirsty's army moved out, traveling by night, hiding by day. They were well-provisioned. When they were set, the Vallian fleet would fly. The gangs would close in, no doubt still wrangling about the power sharing to come after the victory.

On the morning of the day specified for the fleet to move, I stepped outside the tent and scanned the early sky. A few clouds, the brilliance of the suns, a scattering of birds.

Delia said: "Where in a Herrelldrin Hell are they?"

Seg ambled over from his tent, screwing his face up to the sky.

"Well, my old dom, we didn't expect 'em, so we'll do without 'em."

"I suppose we'll have to," I grumped.

Although Inch is a head taller than us it gave him no advantage in seeing now. He stuck his head out of his own tent and looked up. "What are you moaning about?" he demanded. A hand thrust through the opening and a rigid finger pointed up. "Look!"

We swung about. Drifting low above the trees a voller flew into sight, and another, and then more.

Yells broke from the camps. "The Hamalese! By Vox, the Hamalese!"

To say this reminded me of our gallant Prussian allies after Ligny arriving at Waterloo is probably unnecessary. But the thought was there.

The vollers looked knocked about. They flew their flags bravely. They swung in good formation to make touch downs in open areas. Just how it happened was never ascertained, even at the Court of Inquiry. Two fliers touched. They collided with considerable force and in the contrary and frighteningly vicious way of these things, they both burst into flames.

Smoking and spewing flames they fell to the ground.

A shocked silence constrained everyone. Not for some time did normalcy return to the camp as we set about the breakfasts and then the final preparations for departure. I gave Hilzim a great welcome; but I saw the shadows in his face. The accident had shaken us all. As we flew off for the grand attack on Taranjin, was this a portent for the future?

Nineteen

The maps of Taranjin were pored over again and again until we knew every back street and alley. Like many cities of Kregen at this time, Taranjin was a higgledy-piggledy mess. Well, when a cornered rat fights he or she likes to have a tortuous corkscrewy maze of alleys in which to surprise the adversary.

Our advance was materially assisted in that the Shank aerial fleet had gone north to deal with the Hamalese. They flew patrols; they could be avoided. There were only a couple of quick flare-ups and in both the Fish Face went down, burning. Below us spread the outskirts of the city and the tiny dots of the gangs of Freedom Fighters closing in.

I spoke to Balass the Hawk as he stood at the rail, impassive in armor, shield resting on the deck, his black face intent on the scene below. "That Fan-Si, Balass."

"Oh, aye. A pretty enough little Fristle fifi. Wild, though."

"Too wild at times. By Kaidun! She willfully won't wear her armor, even when the consequences are spelled out to her."

Balass cocked an eye at me. "It gets in the way at times."

Even for folk who spend a very great deal of time in armor, still, it can get in the way at times. I sighed. "See if you can make sure she wears her armor, Balass. All her friends are with us here."

"I can but tell her. If she takes it off I can't buckle it on."

Then Targon the Tapster came up with a query and Balass and I left the topic of willful little Fristle fifis.

Balass would take command of a group of folk who were associated with us in a loose kind of way—auxiliaries, almost. I'd told Llodi that I didn't want him in that group, and detailed Korero the Shield to take Llodi under his wing as a supernumerary to help out in that department.

Delia said: "And I'll look out for Mevancy."

"She's good; she's not a Jikai Vuvushi—"

"I've told her to reserve her bindles for emergencies. She'll do all right, and my girls will chip in."

Seg laughed. "I'm saddled with that young rip Rollo."

"He did well when we saw that Shank off—"

"Oh, aye. By the Veiled Froyvil! We've all got to do well now!"

Well, that was true enough—hurtfully true.

Seg favored me with one of his sideways looks that always seem to sum me up complete. "You using that unmentionable again?"

"Llodi is with Korero; but he'll span for me."

"Um."

"I'll keep my own longbow, though. Don't fret."

"I trust Erthanfydd the Meticulous has cast his intolerant eye—?"

"Of a surety."

"Remember," said Seg, and he half lifted a fist, "remember the Battle of Jholaix?"

"Aye."

"I was working it out. This coming fight may seem the same, apart from the town element. But it's different."

I knew exactly what he meant. At Jholaix our vorlcas had acted like a fleet, a single organism under sail. Anyway, we'd been fighting against the Hamalese, then. Jholaix had been fought before the creation of the Vallian Phalanx Force, before Delia and I were empress and emperor. Looking back, did it seem to me the days were freer then, more sunny, more open and careless? Maybe. Ahead and below the sea sparkled and the city of Taranjin lay spread before us. The time for action had arrived, the time for dreaming had passed.

One last single pang hit me then. Jholaix had been fought whilst we were waiting for Velia, who was now dead, to be born.

"Sail ho!"

The shout scythed through the air, shrill and excited.

We all looked up.

At first sight it appeared the sky was filled with ships.

We saw the banners. Those treshes flew back bravely as this fleet circled us. Red and yellow. A yellow saltire and cross on a scarlet field—the Union Flag of Vallia!

I cocked an eye up at my own flag, Old Superb, flying above, the yellow cross on the scarlet field. There were many other treshes, flags of the provinces of Vallia, flags of nobles, a brilliant field of color over the fleet.

Seg said: "I make it fifty, and Drak isn't with 'em."

Delia said, on a breath: "He'll be far too busy running Vallia."

"Look there," I said, sharply, pointing. "Hyrklana. And if I'm not mistaken that's Jaidur's flag."

"Yes," said his mother at my side. "Oh, yes!"

A couple of two-place fliers span up and headed towards us.

The Admiral of the Vallian Fleet, Vangar ti Valkanium, stepped aboard with a quick salute and then he stepped smartly aside as a brisk bustling figure jumped down, shouting.

"Dray! I am here!" Then: "Delia! My most humble respects!"

"Good grief!" I said. "What's got into you?" For this was Nath na Kochwold, the stern disciplinarian, the Kapt of the Phalanx Force.

"Out into the field at last, out adventuring, that's what!"

Vangar ti Valkanium was just as upright and scrubbed and filled with the same integrity as when I'd first met him, all those seasons ago in The Rose of Valka by the Great Northern Cut of Vondium. "Nath has been like a child on his birthday all the trip, Dray. He won't sit still."

"Well, there's work for him." I looked meaningfully at Vangar. "How is the Lord Farris?"

Vangar scowled. "He is not well, and he won't stop working." Vangar's scowl deepened. "He knows I don't want his damned job until—well, until there is nothing else. If only he'd rest!"

"He scraped up this force for us down here? What of the emperor?"

Vangar nodded. "Farris has found these ships from somewhere—well, I know how he did it, of course. The emperor concurred, although he is in dire need of ships himself."

Delia said, sharply: "Tell me, Vangar!"

"Those idiots of the Bloody Menahem."

At that moment the second flier touched down and Jaidur leaped out. He looked fit, bronzed, active; but there was an odd look to him I didn't like. That almost sullen and resigned look only partially lifted as he greeted his mother. Over his shoulder she looked at me, our gazes locked. We both understood there was trouble at home in Hyrklana.

Seg said: "Welcome all. The Shank fleet must have been following you—"

"For," chimed in Inch, "there they are!"

Up over the horizon rim floated the Shank fleet, dark against the suns' glitter.

Nath na Kochwold burst out: "Put me and the lads down, and you can have your aerial battle, Vangar. Keep 'em off our necks."

I said to Nath: "Which Phalanx?" for I knew Drak would be able to spare only one.

"Fifth."

"Ah," I said. "Ninth and Tenth Kerchuris. I have fond memories of the Tenth. Very prickly."

We had been going through a profound alteration of the Phalanx organization before I'd been wrenched away from Valka by the Star Lords. Drak had given that task to me as something to do, and Nath and I had worked hard on tables and command charts to rig the Phalanx Force for its role in the new reduced army needed after the Times of Troubles.

Nath was looking at me expectantly. So was Vangar. So was Oby. So, by Zair, were a lot of folk! The usual dilemma confronted me.

I could not be in two places at once—not unless the Everoinye willed it, as they had done on a number of notable occasions. Where I chose to fight would have considerable weight in the battle.

The Shank fleet fleeting on so swiftly towards us presented now a much less formidable menace. This newly arrived Vallia fleet might consist of ancient vollers, patched fliers, a rabble of the air; they were true vollers, with their own power. My place was with the lads of my Guard Corps.

The moment I told them my decision, Vangar rapped out: "As I guessed. I'll be off back to my flagship. Opaz fly with you—"

"And with you, Vangar."

Jaidur barely looked at us as he kissed Delia and then flew off to his Hyrklanian flagship. He must have traveled hard and fast to get here and join in. Delia looked at me. But we said nothing for now.

We knew the coming battle was going to be a messy fight. All the disparate elements would combine in an untidy way. To try to bring some kind of order—very difficult beforehand and practically impossible once contact was joined—I'd organized some of the flutduin troops into a messenger service. Normally one used fluttcleppers or volcleppers for merkers; our messengers would use the superb flutduins.

One such messenger group had been placed at Kuong's disposal. I told him he would be our liaison with Queen Kirsty and her army. When they burst in with the Freedom Fighters, the slaves must rise. The Vallians would be landing inside the city by then. Vangar, we all trusted, would hold off the Shanks' aerial attack.

I said to Nath na Kochwold: "I trust you have other troops besides the Fifth Phalanx?"

"Oh, yes," he said, not quite off-handedly, but almost. He prized the pike-wielding brumbytes of his Phalanx above rubies, did Nath! "Churgurs, kreutzin, archers, spearmen, artillery, cavalry—although not much of that, by Vox! A brigade of totrixmen, lance and bow, and a brigade of swarths."

"Zorcas? Nikvoves?"

He shook his head so the bright red feathers in his pikeman's helmet fluttered. "No. I had Drig's own trouble finding zorcas for my commanders—and myself. Some regimental infantry Jiktars are riding the poor man's zorca and old Jik Ortyg nov Thandin is riding a preysany."

"A preysany! A Vallian regimental commander riding an animal only a whisker removed from a calsany! We must be scraping the barrel!" Delia pulled her rapier around in an irritable gesture. She and I, we both knew the intolerable costs of blasphemous wars.

Nath agreed and then, with a smile that was almost a leer, said: "You might be interested to know I have the Forty Third Mixed Infantry Brigade with me." He saw the way Seg and I brightened up. "Yes, I thought so! Well, by Vox, I'm out having some fun this time!"

He added that to balance the brigade a regiment of kreutzin had been detailed to cover the heavy infantry, spearmen and archers.

Whilst all these very necessary preliminaries had been taking place Kirsty had moved her army up into the open and together with the gangs of Freedom Fighters was advancing at a smart trot.

Overhead the aerial fights began as the Shanks tried to break through Vangar and disrupt the ground attack. Hilzim's Hamalese vollers played a full part, and already ships were burning.

Nath cocked an eye at me.

His voller-towed vorlcas were dropping down into the city. If the slaves rose at sight of these fighting men chasing Fish Faces we ought to have Taranjin sewed up. My Guard Corps might not even be engaged—a development that would please me and displease the lads.

Everything was going swimmingly. The air battle was swinging in our favor. The ground battle had already seen Kirsty's army breaking through and the streets awash with Shank blood as Vallians cut swathes through their fishy ranks. And, uncommitted, we retained a powerful reserve.

"I must join—" began Nath.

"Of course. Opaz be with you."

He was off at once, streaking down to his beloved Phalanx. Not, I fancied, that they'd do much more than hold the wider streets and avenues this day, and let the other fighting men clear the alleys.

Our Flutduin squadrons worried the Fish Faces. The superb birds cavorted above the Shank vollers, swirling and tormenting, and their riders—young men and women of Valka—flung firepots with savage abandon. Many a fine Shank flier burned at the hands of the flutduin squadrons. And there were more than one or two of those brave youngsters brought down with a shaft skewering through them, or their flyer badly wounded.

But the day was going well.

We'd held the vorlcas of the Guard Corps to windward of the city so as to be able to sail down to any spot we selected. I was beginning to consider actually landing to hold our position instead of continually tacking back and forth, which can be a wearying exercise.

A merker flew up from the city where already smoke was fanning out in palls and concealing much of what went forward down there. It seemed to me that the battling fleets were nearer than they had been. I pointed this out to Seg and Inch.

"You're right, my old dom."

"Our fleet is being pushed back! By Ngrangi—we're losing!"

A boil of figures spewed from the city, animated manikins running and falling—and the ferocious forms of Fish Faces following with deadly tridents stabbing, stabbing...

"What, in the name of the Heavenly Twins, is going on?" demanded Delia.

I kept silent. Milsi said: "It's going wrong."

"It certainly is not going well," spat Sasha.

Targon, Lodkwara, the other chiefs, crowded in silently. They were all staring at me with hungry eyes. There was no doubt now.

I opened my mouth to give the orders that would send my lads of my Guard Corps down to blood and death, when Deb-Lu-Quienyin walked across from the companionway. He was not smiling. He pushed his turban straight with an irritable gesture. He looked firm and solid.

"Delia! Jak! Lahal all. The interference has ceased. Khe-Hi is off to perform our very necessary functions. But I Fear Mischief Here."

I said: "We were winning. Now we are losing."

The hush about the deck allowed the awful noises of the battle to racket in nauseatingly. Deb-Lu spread his fingers. "I see. Then he has placed all his kharrna into this single effort."

"Which," growled out Seg, "looks like succeeding unless we nip him in the bud damn quick."

What the ordinary crewman, the ordinary swod, thought of sorcerers suddenly appearing might remain conjectural; I knew that if our mages failed us now, the arch demon Carazaar would triumph.

Clearly, now, without a single doubt, he worked with or for the Shanks. Maybe, even, he controlled the Fish Faces.

The merker from Kuong confirmed that Kirsty's forces were being thrust back. Everywhere, on the ground, in the air, we were being beaten.

"What can be done, Deb-Lu?"

"Khe-Hi and I have formed a plan which—" He looked uneasy. "It is not certain. There is great danger." He wouldn't look at me, so I guessed that whatever he and Khe-Hi had hatched up demanded my presence. "The planes," he went on. "They cannot be controlled by any single person."

"Something must be done," rapped out Delia. "And done right now!"

A shout ripped through the air from a lookout. What he screamed was incoherent. Everybody felt the force of terror in that wild shriek and we all looked up into the brightness of the sky.

He sailed up there, the arch demon, sitting in his throne and peering down at us mortals below. The throne was as I had last seen it with its chained naked girls and savage beasts, with the glitter of gems and gold. A cloud suffused with yellow light swam beneath the throne and shards and sparks of fire, blue, green, yellow, spat like lightnings all about. The picture he presented was one of terror and of glory, of power and of punishment. A light shone from that awesome apparition and spread to encompass the city and the battling armies. Sparks spat from the chair in bolts of living flame. Everywhere the forces of the Shanks pressed on victoriously.

Calmly, firm among all the terror, Seg lifted his bow.

"Useless, Seg," said Deb-Lu. "There is only one way." He swung about and now he looked at me, long and low beneath his eyebrows.

Delia abruptly clutched my arm and I felt her tremble against me. "Dray—are you prepared for the gamble?"

"If it's the only way," I said, "then let's do it!"

Twenty

"Right," said Seg. "Let us do it!"

"Aye," said Inch, very sharply.

"Aye!" roared out from the lads gathered about.

Deb-Lu shook his head and his turban fell off and rolled—and instantly vanished. Deb-Lu's right side was illuminated by a samphron oil lamp. We were bathed in the rays of Luz and Walig.

"No, no. Khe-Hi and I—One Only. We can manage only one."

"Me! Let me! No, me!" The cacophony burst up as everyone yelled their demands to be allowed to go to almost certain death.

I didn't want to go to death, certain, almost certain or otherwise. I glanced swiftly at Delia. She stood straight and lissom, holding herself erect, a faint flush along her cheekbones. She stared back at me, solemnly, her lustrous brown eyes full on me, weighing me, weighing the idiot who is Dray Prescot, knowing already, as I knew, the only outcome of this situation.

I held up my hand.

Instantly, stillness and quietness fell over the babble.

"I am ready, san."

Deb-Lu glanced back, tilting his turbanless head so the red Lohvian hair gleamed in the samphron oil lamp's beam. He said something we could not hear to someone further back in his room. When he turned back I sensed a freshness in him, a lightening to his spirit.

"Jak! Khe-Hi has hit upon a Capital Scheme. Ling-Li also... It Will Work, I am Assured of it... Capital—"

Still speaking, the phantom image of Deb-Lu-Quienyin vanished.

I waited. We all waited, hushed, expectant. We stood motionlessly, held by the thrall of our beliefs.

Nothing happened.

Nothing happened, that is, on the decks of Shankjid. But a very great deal was happening down there in and around Taranjin.

Kirsty's forces were now just about on the verge of breaking and that would be followed by a full scale rout. Masses of black smoke swept across the city obscuring buildings and streets. The noise spurted up as though a cavern of maniacal giants forged weapons for the gods. Whatever the Vallian forces were doing, they were certainly not putting pressure on the Shanks driving forward against Kirsty. In the air Shank vollers span and twisted and Hamalese and Vallian vollers fought back stubbornly. For a moment—a moment only and not a heartbeat longer—I fancied our aerial fleet would hold the Schtarkins. They still had not yet fathomed a way of countering the flutduins who tormented them so, even with the thaumaturgical assistance of Carazaar.

121

And that arch demon?

His cloud-supported throne hung above the town. Sparks and bolts of light flamed from it. Scintillant dots of fire broke away like molten gold, dripping and dropping in curtains of flame.

Whatever he was up to, he was swinging the battle in favor of the Fish Faces. Unless our Wizards of Loh could counter Carazaar's thaumaturgy very quickly, the battle was lost.

The stink and taste of the conflict gagged in my throat. The flat raw stench of burning clogged nostrils and coated tongues. And my Guard Corps stood there, and now they were shifting from foot to foot impatiently, and the coughing to attract attention broke like waves upon a rocky shore.

They would not be held much longer.

Yet if I gave the word and sent them joyously down into the battle, the slaughter and the carnage, how could they triumph against sorcery of so potent a power as that against which we now strove?

Where in a Herrelldrin Hell were Deb-Lu and Khe-Hi?

Delia still held my arm, and I felt her firm grip as a solid comfort. Seg breathed evenly and lightly and Inch was running his fingers up and down the haft of his great Saxon pattern axe. Just to the rear of Delia stood some of her Jikai Vuvushis, and these Battle Maidens, as she had told me, were not all from the Sisters of the Rose. As I turned my head to look back to follow Carazaar's hectic career across the heavens, his cloud-supported, flame-encrusted throne swooped down and out of sight below. My gaze, following him, was arrested by the group of women.

Clad in fighting gear, lissom and strong, firm of feature, they presented a picture that could only be described as noble. About to turn back I halted as one Jikai Vuvushi spoke to her companion. She was a Hikdar, and although I was a mere man, I knew she was a member of the Sisters of Voxyra. Her face was very pale under the tan and two globules of sweat trickled down her temples from under her helmet. She leaned closer to the Hikdar at her side, and although she intended a whisper, I did not doubt, her words reached me clearly.

"I knew ill would come of it, Scanda, when the prayer-idol of Our Lady Zunida the Laudable was stolen—"

"Hush, Merle," whispered back Hikdar Scanda. "Our Lady will still protect us."

"Oh, yes. But I still wish I knew who had stolen her prayer-idol."

This tiny fragment of conversation, caught and held like a stray fish in a net, lasted only for a heartbeat or so, and then I was back with the pressing disasters of the moment. There was time for me to wonder who would wish to steal a prayer-idol of a minor and semi-secret religious sect of whom I had heard no ill word.

Seg growled out: "We'll have to go down, my old dom."

"Aye," said Inch, meaningfully.

The chiefs of my Guard Corps, assembled on the deck of Shankjid, clearly shared that pragmatic view.

Stonily, I spoke in a loud voice so that all might hear. "Give San Quienyin and San Bjanching a little more time."

A little sigh like a summer breeze across a cornfield rippled across the crowded deck. The barrage of coughing lessened. I said, speaking curtly: "Go see where that devil in his flying throne has got to."

I was surprised to see Cadet Nalgre ti Mornlad come racing back with the information. He must have smuggled himself aboard from Dovad Daisy, probably with Sternum's help. He yelped: "He's going up again!"

With that the coruscating throne skittered into view on the other beam and swung in a wide arc over us. Carazaar was watching us, ready to counter any move we might make.

"By Ngrozyan the Axe!" snarled Inch. "I'd like to—"

"Quite, dear," said Sasha, staring venomously at the glittering glory of evil flying high over us.

"Is there nothing we can do?" demanded Milsi, furiously.

Seg lifted and lowered that famous Lohvian longbow. "It's wizard's work now, my heart."

"And have they migrated to Cottmer's Caverns?" Delia fairly ripped it out. "By Vox! We must do something!"

Yet we all knew there was nothing sensible we could do until our comrade Wizards of Loh had completed their thaumaturgy.

Nalgre the Erkensator walked across with a pewter tray loaded with goblets of sazz. Delia snapped out: "See that everyone has a drink, Nalgre, please. It's going to be thirsty work soon."

"Quidang, jes."

The sazz was flavored with blackcurrant and tickled my throat going down. Carazaar carried out another circle, flaming like a comet across the heavens. The lads shifted from foot to foot, and managed to remain steady. What was going on aboard the other ships of the fleet I hated to imagine. They were all flying flags that implored action.

Without any rush of displaced air—for he was not really there at all— Deb-Lu appeared once more on the deck before me.

His wise old face looked haggard. "It Is Accomplished, Jak." He swallowed. "Khe-Hi calls down the blessings and the protection of the Seven Arcades upon your head. Go with Opaz."

I was standing on a yellow soft surface that undulated like a cranky boat in a seaway. Tall twisting smoke pillars rose ahead and the sky was a mere yellow shell of fire. A breeze blew into my face bringing the stinks of the charnel house, yet the wind did not disturb my hair or bend the rising columns of smoke. All about me hung a yellow luminosity.

Out from the opening between the smoke columns waddled a creature of nightmare. Two scaled and stunted legs supported a torso and a flat squamous head, its eyes filled with malice below naked bone ridges. Four tentacular arms weaved patterns in the air before the thing, and each arm bore a round head with twin eyes alongside a wide and fang-filled mouth. I'd had a mouthful of arm scrunched off by one of those heads, and I'd lopped the four of them, and thrust my sword into the thing's guts. But it had not been killed. Oh, no. For this was Arzuriel, Carazaar's pet horror.

Arzuriel waddled directly towards me and I leaped forward.

Before, he and his master had delayed me long enough to prevent me saving the life of San Tuong Mishuro. Now they were trying to delay me so that the Fish Faces could complete their victory over us.

The Krozair brand switched up and sideways and down and across four times. Four round furiously snapping heads rolled upon the yellow cloud.

Hurdling the collapsing body I recognized well enough that this was not the end of Arzuriel, for he was a multi-dimensional creature.

The ground swayed and I judged it to be a cloud, the same damned cloud Carazaar and his confounded throne chair were riding upon!

Through the pillars of smoke I leaped and heat smote me. Just ahead a wall of smoke and flame broke up, blindingly, streaking all my vision with black tears. I didn't think. I just put my head down and went blindly hurtling on. I crashed through the wall of fire. Scorching heat stung my body. I felt the breath burning my lungs. Then I was through and there he was, there he was, the arch devil himself!

Instantly a long Lohvian black-fletched arrow spat viciously past my left ear.

The keening hissing voice said: "Stand, Dray Prescot. Stand still!"

That was N'gil, the little leech-like miscegenation of fish and some other unholy offspring. The red gash of his mouth opened across the corpse-gray of his face. "Your forces suffer destruction!"

Now was this little unhealthy lot still an apparition? I did not think so. I realized then as I plunged on just what Deb-Lu and Khe-Hi had accomplished.

Another arrow zinged in and this time it was aimed to strike. Remembering my previous doleful thoughts concerning these Bowmaids of Loh's possible ability to shoot magical shafts that I could not deflect, I dodged aside and ran on. Another arrow flew.

This time I had to knock it aside with the longsword. The feel and sound as the brand struck the shaft aside came most sweetly to me.

"Stop, Dray Prescot!" The wheezing voice of Carazaar came like a freezing breath from the Ice Floes of Sicce. "You do ill here!"

The footing across the yellow cloud might be treacherous. I'd learned to hold a balance running out along the yardarm on a dirty night. I fairly flew along, and now I was knocking shafts out of the air with contemptuous ease. I was wrought up. I admit that. This stinking devil in his throne stood for all the things I and my friends were combating in Paz on Kregen. He would drag us all down and see us all slain or enslaved just so his friends the Shanks could ride triumphant over us. Well, I'd have him! Oh, yes, I admit it, I admit it, I, Dray Prescot, went plunging headlong on, in as furious a frame of mind as I'd ever been in.

That demonic frame of mind would easily encompass the destruction of the Bowmaids of Loh. They worked for this devil; ergo, they must be obliterated with him, along with his pets.

He was no apparition. My Krozair brand would slice through his body and bring the blood spurting out. The sharp point would burst his heart. The keen edge would slit his throat. I knew if I once hit him I would not stop until he was ripped and torn into tiny pieces.

Carazaar's devilish face, scraped white, pinched, reflected a sudden, new and shocking concept. His eyes of that elusive blue-black hue with the mad glare of rhodopsin, smoky red, glared hotly upon me. Over the yellow cloud I raced on. I was nearer now, nearer than he could ever have expected. A hissing snarl of warning spat from N'gil.

I quite expected Carazaar to lift the double-handed axe, double-bitted, and step down from his throne to challenge me.

Some hope!

He cursed at the Bowmaids, and their leader answered tartly. I braced myself. His sorcery was very great. It is a nonsense to imagine a simple fighting man with his sword can take on and successfully defeat a wizard in full possession of his magical skills. All this now was taking place only because sorcery was acting against sorcery.

From the figure of Carazaar in the throne a figure of Carazaar picked up the axe and stepped down onto the yellow cloud. Carazaar sat in his throne surrounded by his pets, his chail sheom, his creatures, and Carazaar strutted before me, axe cocked over his shoulder, smoldering eyes boring into mine, ready to fight!

Had, I wondered, Deb-Lu and Khe-Hi foreseen this?

Which of these two devils was real, which was the apparition?

With a snarl as vicious as his own I hurtled on. There was only one way to find out now!

Abruptly, shockingly, just before I reached him—there were two Carazaars before me, and the third laughing in the throne!

A two-handed axe against a two-handed sword.

It all depends on skill.

Perhaps this bastard for all his cleverness and sorcery was not aware of what a Krozair longsword was capable of. He pressed on—both of him pressed on—confidently. I used a neat and subtle twin-attack devised by

Pur Zanath na Zenrik three hundred seasons ago. The Krozair brand sliced left and spilled one set of guts through the scale mail, then, without halting, checked the sweep of the second axe and so drove the point into the second set of guts.

I stepped back.

The two bodies vanished before they hit the yellow cloud.

There was no sign of the Bowmaids.

N'gil was shrieking unintelligibly.

The little scaled creature by his right boot jumped up and down in a frenzy against his chains.

The two naked girls, one with streaming yellow hair, the other with short dark hair, stirred, and turned, and looked at me. I saw the entreaty in their eyes. I leaned forward with a snarl.

The Krozair blade, darkly stained, lifted. It slashed down.

That superb sword sliced empty air.

Carazaar and his minions were gone. The smoke wafted away. The yellow cloud thinned and dissipated. I was falling.

Clutching with the grip of death onto the hilt of my sword I fell. Down and down I plummeted and all about me the bright air rang and resounded with the awful din of battle.

That hell-spawned hell-hound of evil had escaped!

I turned over slowly in the air and saw below me the city spread out and the smoke and flame, the battling hordes caught in the frenzy of combat. The ships carrying my Guard Corps were landing, row after row. A change had overtaken the fight. No longer were Kirsty's people running. No longer were the forces of Paz reeling back. Now they were advancing, pressing on, grimly determined to clinch the victory.

Carazaar's baleful influence had been banished.

That was most satisfactory. As for me—well, I was like to hit the ground so hard I'd drill a personal hole right down to Cottmer's Caverns.

A feather-light touch held me. I was still descending. But now I was going down slowly, gently, and when I hit the ground I'd feel no more than if I'd jumped off the back of a zorca.

"Good old Deb-Lu and Khe-Hi!" I said aloud.

They had successfully placed me on the same plane as that occupied by Carazaar. Rightly, they had foreseen dangers. As I saw it, Carazaar's nerve had failed. There was no doubt at all in my mind that he could have summoned up demons, monsters of unspeakable horror. He had chosen to test me himself—even if he'd cheated and used two facsimiles. The very swiftness of my Krozair attack and the sudden double destruction in the midst of his own self-assurance had undone him. And bad cess to him!

Also, there was absolutely no doubt in my mind that we hadn't seen the last of Carazaar.

126

As I drifted feather-light into the conflict, the strongest conviction was borne in on me that Carazaar had too much invested in all that had gone before, all his schemes, all his dreams of impossible dominion, to fade from the scene now.

Oh, no, that rast would be back.

Then all that dire speculation was washed away in the sight of what was going on in one of the town's squares. A mass of struggling Fish Faces and Katakis surged like stampeding cattle. Many ran and fell to be trampled by their fellows. Many threw away their weapons. A few, a very few, trapped at the tail of the rout, attempted to strike back at what pursued them. At what pursued them! What a sight they made, the brumbytes of the Fifth Phalanx, helmets low, shields high, pikes all in line and thrusting remorselessly on! Nothing could stand in the way of that headlong charge. Over the din of battle rang the chanted paeans of the brumbytes, fierce, devoted pikemen, grim in their dedication to their corps, to their leader and to Vallia.

Slanting in my fall, I saw I would pass over that square and touch down in a cross street a few blocks further on.

Here I landed with a spring in my legs, instantly ready for action. A group of Schtarkins rushed crazily down the street pursued by a bunch of my lads from 3EYJ. There was no mistaking their yellow jackets and the ferocity of their onslaught. All over the city brilliant little cameos like this were being enacted as our forces mopped up the enemy.

They hullabalooed on and vanished past the corner. Directly across the side street the swift stumbling forms of Katakis burst into view. The whiptails were now clearly ruing their alliance with the Shanks. The magnificently uniformed troopers of Karidge's EDLG galloped after them and great was the execution thereof. Then I looked again, and blinked and smiled. Amidst all the clamor of battle there was no mistaking the stentorian bellow of the massive figure astride a zorca urging on a running group of swordsmen. Nath Javed, Old Hack 'n' Slay, was in there with the best, hurling his brigade on to the utter destruction of the foe.

In the momentum of the pursuit he did not spot me in the shadows of the buildings. I did not call out. He had his duty to perform and he would carry out that duty whilst breath persisted in his body.

Now there was no doubt we had the upper hand in Taranjin. The baleful influence of Carazaar had been removed. If the Shanks did not take to their ships and escape then none would survive.

I cut through an alley and came out unexpectedly onto a scene I had no wish to see. Four Katakis surrounded the lissom form of a girl. She fought them magnificently with rapier and Claw, striking and dancing as though limned in light. I recognized Deldar Paline Asatha and in the instant I dashed forward a cruel trident thrust past her defense and stabbed her in the body. She did not fall and her Claw sliced the face from the whiptail. But she had been sorely hurt. She stumbled. Then I took the head off the nearest Kataki in a spouting welter of blood. The other two span about and the Krozair brand lunged between corselet rim and helmet of the first, withdrew and twitched across to slice the right arm from the other. He screamed incredulously and Paline put her rapier neatly into his eye.

The Jikai Vuvushi looked at me with wide, drugged eyes.

I caught her in the crook of my left arm. "It is all right, Paline. You've done for them."

"Majister!" Blood welled up between her lips. Gently I placed her on the ground and stripped clothes from the Katakis to cover her, keep her warm. "The Puncture Ladies will be here directly."

"Majister." She reached up a blood-dabbled hand, trying to form words. "The Empress! The Katakis—"

I felt all my blood rush to my head so that I thought my skull would explode.

Then I felt deathly cold.

"Paline! Where—?"

She pointed across the street into the continuation of the alley.

I remember the coldness of the alley and the stroke of the Suns across my head as I burst into the avenue beyond. They must have recognized the worth of their prisoner, and slavers to their cores determined to gain some merchandise from this debacle. They were just mounting up. Their zorcas looked a mettlesome bunch, and there were more zorcas than Katakis after the battle. They saw me. Delia was lying unconscious across a zorca and the Kataki's snaggle-fanged mouth split into a derisive and hating grin. He gave his animal a thwack and he bounded off. There were six others and they galloped off after their leader.

The zorca didn't particularly want me to mount up. He tried to curvet away, and I had absolutely no remorse as, zorca-man though I am, I gave him a belt to make him behave. He quietened and I flung myself on his back. The whiptails carrying Delia off were now spurring down the street. I could see no one else in view. I gave the zorca the flat of my blade and he started and neighed and then went hell for leather after the others.

I'd catch them. I'd catch all seven of them and I'd slay all seven of them. No one was going to take my Delia from me, my Delia of Delphond, my Delia of the Blue Mountains.

The zorca ran because he understood a demon sat on his back and would unhesitatingly lash him without mercy. I hit him again. We were catching the Katakis. One looked back and yelled.

The stench of battle, the noise, the sights, all flowed away into a hollow silence between my ears. I could see only Delia and the Katakis. A blue mist hovered before my eyes. I felt cold.

At first I didn't understand, so wrapped up in agony and fury and determination. Then I did understand.

I did not want to believe.

"No!" I screamed it up as I'd never shrieked at the Star Lords before. "No! Give me time, give me time!"

The blue mist thickened. I lost sight of the whiptails and Delia. All around me the blueness grew. The shape of the phantom Scorpion hovered above, gigantic, absolute, not to be ignored.

Up I went. Up and up, drawn into the blueness of the Scorpion of the Everoinye. There was no arbitration. The Star Lords wanted me.

Screaming incoherently, I felt myself flung into the gulfs of nothingness, bathed in cold, destroyed to my heart, whilst my Delia was hurried off into a captivity I could not contemplate in reason.

Delia! Delia! Delia! Ahead of me lay only a black nothingness.

SCORPIO DRUMS

Dray Prescot

Of himself, Dray Prescot presents an enigmatic and compelling figure. He is dynamic, dominating, demanding, yet we sense in him a vulnerability completely at odds with his given character within his narrative. He has been described as a man above middle height with brown hair and level brown eyes, with enormously broad shoulders and powerful physique. There is about him an abrasive honesty and indomitable courage. He moves like a savage hunting cat, quiet and lethal. Reared in the cruelly harsh conditions of Nelson's navy, he has been transported to the savage and exotic world of Kregen, four hundred light years from Earth, under the double star Antares, the twin Suns of Scorpio.

There he has made a new life for himself. He has gained fame and fortune, has been blessed with good comrades and a family, and, most of all, by Delia of Delphond, Delia of the Blue Mountains. He has recently given up the job of being Emperor of Vallia, only to be pitchforked into the task of uniting all the varied continents and islands of Paz, one half of Kregen, to resist the reiving onslaughts of the Shanks from Schan, the other half of Kregen. People are beginning to call him the Emperor of Emperors, the Emperor of Paz.

Down in the southern continent of Loh he has met new friends in the task of throwing the Shanks out of Tarankar, a country on the west coast. The capital city of Taranjin, under attack by Prescot's forces, was on the point of being taken when Carazaar, a superhuman being apparently working with the Shanks, sorcerously interfered. Prescot's comrade Wizards of Loh were able to place him on Carazaar's plane where in a ferociously brief fight Carazaar decamped in confusion, leaving the forces of Paz to sweep on to victory. Prescot enters the city to assist in the rout of the Shanks and their slaving allies, the whiptailed Katakis. To his horror he sees Delia being carried off by a group of the slavers, galloping off astride zorcas. Frenziedly he charges after them...

Alan Burt Akers

One

The whiptails carrying Delia off were now spurring down the street, I could see no one else in view. I gave the zorca the flat of my blade and he started and neighed and then went hell for leather after the others.

I'd catch them. I'd catch all seven of them and I'd slay all seven of them. No one was going to take my Delia from me, my Delia of Delphond, my Delia of the Blue Mountains.

The zorca ran because he understood a demon sat on his back and would unhesitatingly lash him without mercy. I hit him again. We were catching the Katakis. One looked back and yelled.

The stench of battle, the noise, the sights, all flowed away into a hollow silence between my ears. I could see only Delia and the Katakis. A blue mist hovered before my eyes. I felt cold.

I did not want to believe.

"No!" I screamed it up as I'd never shrieked at the Star Lords before. "No! Give me time, give me time!"

The blue mist thickened. I lost sight of the whiptails and Delia. All around me the blueness grew. The shape of the phantom Scorpion hovered above, gigantic, absolute, not to be ignored.

Up I went. Up and up, drawn into the blueness of the Scorpion of the Everoinye. There was no arbitration. The Star Lords wanted me.

Screaming incoherently, I felt myself flung into the gulfs of nothingness, bathed in cold, destroyed to my heart, whilst my Delia was hurried off into a captivity I could not contemplate in reason.

Delia! Delia! Delia! Ahead of me lay only a black nothingness.

The feel of the zorca between my knees remained one sensation among the many battering at my consciousness. Blueness twined about me. The Star Lords through their blue phantom Scorpion had hauled up the animal in addition and as I felt as though I was strapped to a giant Catherine Wheel that tiny touch remained a reminder of common flesh and blood.

Delia was being carried of into an all too easily imagined horror. If I went mad I could be of no further use to her. The vital necessity of keeping fast hold of all my faculties must be my sole aim now. I had to deal with the Star Lords and get back to Taranjin as fast as possible, otherwise—I must not, must not, think of the otherwise.

I, Dray Prescot, Pur Dray, Krozair of Zy and Lord of Strombor, after the first decision to retain my sanity, must think solely of handling the Everoinye and of returning from whence I had been brought.

Of course, there was a horrific chance that the fumble-fingered Scorpion might drop me as he had once before.

The blueness, a continuing symptom of my travels with the Star Lords, lasted for a very short time and then I felt myself lifted from the back of the zorca. I went tumbling headlong across a wooden deck. So I knew where I was.

I sat up. Yes. I was sitting on the deck of the narrow double-ended craft and all around stretched glittering blue sea.

Standing up I scanned the horizons. Nothing betwixt sea and the shining remote silver sky met my gaze.

The scents of seaweed and ozone and tar meant nothing to me.

"All right, Star Lords!" I bellowed up, head flung back. I was about to go on with something like: "What in a Herrelldrin Hell do you want this time, you bunch of nurdling great onkers?' when I clamped my lips shut.

Recently I'd wondered on and off that if I'd treated the Star Lords with some of the awed respect other kregoinye treated them they might have treated me better. I seriously doubted that. All the same, it might be a clever scheme to eat humble pie, as they say in Clishdrin, and bow and scrape, kowtow to them, not arouse the anger which could fling me back four hundred light years to the planet of my birth.

So, all right, then! By the pustular eyeballs and disgusting nostrils of Makki Grodno! I'd fool the Everoinye, fool 'em rotten.

The clanging voice rang across the boat.

"Dray Prescot!"

I took a look around the boat as she bobbed in the sea; but of course there was no one aboard but me.

Speaking carefully, as it were thinking of every word before uttering it, I said: "It is imperative that I return at once. It is vitally important. The Empress Delia—"

They interrupted then, as I said that name and felt the scoring whiplashes burning across my mind, and struggled to hold my sanity. "We are aware of that situation. There is time."

"Time!" The sensation of heat suffused my body. The Star Lords could tamper with the time flow and had flung me about within the Time Stream. Hope burst up in me. I shouted up: "Put me back when—"

"It is not for you to tell us what or what not to do."

"Of course not," I said at once.

A pause followed that. These were superbeings, old beyond computation, entities who had once been as human as I. Could they truly still remember and understand humanity? I had doubted that in the past and had come to believe I'd been mistaken.

So, now, would they be deceived by my unnatural acquiescence to their wishes?

What I took to be a different voice said: "You have obeyed our orders, Dray Prescot. We knew you possessed the yrium and you have proved that you can use your gift of superior charisma wisely—sometimes. Taranjin has been cleared of the invaders from Schan."

Instead of bellowing up that I knew that, by Krun, and what need was there for them to repeat old news? I said: "What is to be done next?"

Unmistakably, a tone of gloom tinged the next words.

"There will be more invaders."

In my wrought up frame of mind I struggled to think what I could say to that. Previously I'd have burst out with intemperate words, a tirade of vituperation against Shanks and Star Lords. I had to think. I said: "And you will place me down to fight them?"

They didn't even bother to reply to so crass a remark.

I began to wonder if they could see right through me, for in our last meeting I'd argued and convinced them against their original wishes. I'd altered a decision of the Everoinye. Now I was acting the Yes-man with such humility I guessed they must suspect me.

So I summoned up a tiny scrap of courage and with a whisper of belligerence, said: "What about my voller? You took my airboat away. It's about time you gave her back."

"In due time."

"And I didn't meet a feller called Wulk—"

"He is away on another case."

Oh, yes, that was the word they used, in its Kregish as well as Terrestrial meaning. On a case. Well, now.

"There are other pressing matters to be dealt with. We will return you to an appropriate moment—"

"I have your word?"

That was, of course, an utterly fatuous question. Of what use had these superbeings for words, and honor, and promises? They stood aloof. They played with the destinies of peoples and nations. Of what significance the life of a solitary individual?

I said: "Star Lords, do you play a game with whoever rules in Schan?"

The silence remained unbroken for a long time. I refused to break it. Sweating with desperate impatience though I was, I'd play these Everoinye at their own game. My question was deadly serious. If idle minds had the ability, might not they play games, side against side, and use us poor mortals as pawns?

The boat barely moved in the sea. The silver sky shone lustrously above and the sea sparkled a brilliant blue, shot with silken streaks. Wherever we were, we were highly unlikely to be on Kregen with its two suns and seven moons. No birds sailed through that limpid light. Occasionally a huge and beautiful fish would leap in a graceful arc and plunge back into the water.

The Star Lords were going to return me to an appropriate moment. That meant they'd plunk me down back on Kregen in the burning city of Taranjin in time to save my Delia. I had to believe for the sanity of my mind and soul.

Delia, her Kataki captors, the whole turmoil of the battle, were all frozen away there, waiting on the Star Lords whim for my return.

That, I must believe.

Towards one end of the boat rose a small deckhouse. I walked along the planking, feeling warmth on my toes, and tried the door. It was locked.

What, I wondered, lay below deck?

Two steering oars were swung up into their beckets at this end of the craft, and true to dwaprijjer fashion a second pair were lashed at the other. Either end could be bow or stern. The pirates infesting the Ivilian Keys used them with great élan, and they were known in other parts of Kregen. At the moment this particular craft had neither oars nor mast. I fancied she had a fair turn of speed. Something wet dropped onto my chest, and I realized the sweat was running down my face and dripping off my chin. Madness hovered close, close, then.

The Everoinye could manipulate time; but I was convinced their command was chancy, for they had made mistakes in the past. My ploy in asking if all the fraught happenings that shook Kregen were merely a game, and we were all merely pieces upon a giant Jikaida board, was delaying my return back through time.

Mind you, the question was not a true ploy, for I wanted to know the answer. I wanted to know for the dignity of my fellow sufferers.

At length they deigned to reply.

At their first words I felt anger and resentment, for it was clear they were as usual fobbing me off.

"It is not for you to question us on matters you cannot understand, Dray Prescot. The answer is not simple. No, we do not regard the threat from the Shanks as a game. But there are, as there must be, game elements in the handling of the situation."

This was something. "Men and women get killed at this game."

I must have spoken in a return of truculence, for the answer lashed out: "We acknowledge your usefulness to us in the past, Dray Prescot. The future need not follow that pattern."

I breathed in and I breathed out.

Tsleetha-tsleethi, softly-softly! "You have, then, many kregoinye to call on? There are many men and women on Kregen serving you?"

"Few people are fitted to serve. That does not concern you."

"I understand." I swallowed down. "Will you return me now—please?"

"You will be returned to the appropriate place and time. There are many tasks set to your hand. But, first—"

The boat soared aloft, up and up into that distant silver sky. I held on, the breath short in my throat. Mist enveloped the boat and tendrils of clammy vapor clung about me. I knew what was going to happen next, and was ready for it. When the boat abruptly plunged down and down, shrieking through thin air, I realized I was only half prepared. My ears banged and I gulped down and hung on and waited.

We roared on down, and below a wide and open land opened up, green fields and wending rivers and scattered white-walled towns. If we tried to land on dry land we'd splinter into shivers. A tiny lake, like a little eye peering myopically upwards, flashed blue in the radiance of the twin Suns of Scorpio.

The dwaprijjer hit the water in a long splashing slide that started at one bank and brought the sharp curved end to a rocking halt in the reeds of the other. The feel of good Kregen air and the streaming mingled magnificence of Zim and Genodras all about drove me forward.

Over the sharp prow I leaped and hurled myself into the reeds. Muddy water splashed up my thighs. A few floundering steps saw me to firmer ground where I halted to take stock of my surroundings.

I was, of course, completely naked. That was the usual way when the Everoinye hurled me down somewhere to sort out their dirty work for them. I refused to allow dismay or desperation to enter my mind. I had a job to do as a kregoinye. When that was done the Star Lords would send me back to see about those slaving Katakis.

At one time I'd fumed at what I'd considered the incompetence of the Star Lords in thus flinging me down naked and weaponless. There was one very good reason for that practice. They expected resourcefulness from their agents. Clothes and weapons must be obtained in the field. If I'd landed dressed in the costume of one part of Kregen in an entirely differently-dressed region, I'd be spotted instantly as a foreigner. Perhaps the Star Lords were not as stupid as I'd bad-mouthed them. In all the dazzlingly varied cultures of Kregen a naked man, sharp and determined, might fare better than one marked down as a stranger.

When I had been dropped down in armor and wearing swords, usually, the reasons had been good ones.

There was a counter argument, exemplified by the time I'd been sent to Vienna. All the same, naked and weaponless, I started up the slope away from the lake.

The land hereabouts looked a trifle wild and untended, not a wilderness but rather a sorry land left uncultivated for too long. Rank grasses grew in swathes of green, and the heads of wild flowers, red, blue, violet, peeped above. There was a line of a track where the ground had been trodden by occasional usage. Along this track came a group of arguing and gesticulating people. Back a few ulms lay the red-tiled roofs and white walls of a small town, a fantastic spire flashing gold in the suns light.

I dropped into the concealment of a clump of grass.

The dress of this mob indicated their status and origins.

They wore plain workaday clothes of tunics and loincloths fashioned not from silks but from cottons, and a few wore woolen garments manufactured in the Walfonian style of Walfarg. All the women wore face veils of thick material, dark and concealing, quite different from the filmy sherissas worn on holiday or days of feasting. Many of them brandished meat cleavers, and rolling pins, with a pitchfork or two. They were your common or garden mob, bolstered by mob fever and capable of committing deeds they afterwards wouldn't understand how on Kregen they could do such horrible things. I had no whiff of grapeshot to disperse them. When I saw the girl being dragged along in their centre the whiff of grapeshot couldn't have been used anyway.

The argument, clearly, was what they were going to do to the girl. With the lake at my back, I had an idea of which argument would win.

So—here was the task set to my hands by the Star Lords. This was quite like old times!

When I saw the captive girl more clearly, and recognized her, I understood a little more. The first and last time I'd seen her she'd been haranguing a mob. The damned fool Scorpion had dropped me, fumble-fingered me down into a right old peccadillo. Now I saw he'd been on the way to the girl so that I could drag her away from the mob anger. She'd got away all right, how I didn't know, and I'd then followed my own destiny for a space. Now, here she was again, up to her ears in trouble.

The track ended at the lakeside about fifty paces away. By the time the mob reached the water they'd decided exactly what to do.

Moving with care I edged along towards them.

They were tying ropes to the girl's wrists and a weighted sack to the ropes. They screamed abuse all the time, and the women in particular jumped up and down in frenzied hatred. You could see their point of view and I admit at the very first I'd been surprised the Star Lords wanted this girl preserved for posterity. I edged closer.

In all the hullabaloo the girl was hoisted up and swung backwards and forwards. "Ob! Dwa! So!" the mob chanted to the swing. On 'So!' she flew up sideways. She didn't spin as she turned over and splashed into the water. I hadn't heard her scream once, although in the noise and shrieks of rage she might have been screaming as loudly as anyone else. Bubbles rose and broke. Ripples moved away in neat interlocked concentric rings.

The noise of the mob abruptly ceased. They clustered among the reeds and stared out across the lake. There was fascination in their faces, awe at what they had done. Only later would remorse set in—if it ever would.

The water closed around me, warm and caressing. A fat fish flicked near-transparent fins and lazed away. I finned towards the blue-tinged shape of the girl and the sack as they drifted to the bottom.

She had her mouth shut and was flailing away with her legs. Her hair twisted like a candle flame. She was hardly conscious of my presence.

There was little time. She would not have long to live without breathing. I had no knife so I took the sacking material in both hands, gripping, and used my muscles. A resistance—I felt my muscles jump and bulge—the sack ripped open and a tumbled mass of pebbles spewed out.

Instantly I grasped the girl about the waist and dragged her down. Down. Savagely I thrust against the water, forcing myself along away from the bank, the girl clamped to my side.

She could not last much longer.

The dwaprijjer of the Star Lords would have flown back to wherever they garaged their conveyances. This bank of the lake was occupied by a hostile rabble, armed with cleavers and pitchforks. There was only one sensible alternative.

When I judged we'd gone far enough I rose to the surface.

She let out a huge gasp as her head broke free and whooped an enormous lungful of air. Still holding her I trod water and turned to look back. A great wet floppy stinging mass went squashily smack around my face and for a moment I could see nothing save a few thin streaks of light. Tangled strands choked my mouth. I felt choked.

The damned girl had shaken her head as one does and her hair had slapped smack about my eyes and mouth, near blinding and choking me.

I dragged the dripping hair free and snarled: "Can you swim, girl?"

It did not matter if she could not, for I'd swim with her; that was the most polite thing I felt I could say at the time.

The ropes around her wrists came off quickly enough. As I had let her go she sank down and then rose again.

The moment her head broke water she glared at me. "Yes."

"Then swim to the other side before they run around."

"They will not do that."

She spoke with arrogant confidence. All the same, she turned and started a careful breaststroke, moving along in a series of sedate frog undulations. The people had seen us. They were jumping up and down and shrieking imprecations. Some started to run around the lake. Most of them stayed where they'd thrown the girl in. Very soon those who'd started to circumnavigate the water stopped, and then trailed back. She'd been right.

She had no need of my assistance as we crossed the lake. I did stay in the rear just in case, although from the little I knew of her from what I'd heard, I judged she was a capable woman.

She clambered out, all glistening and firmly brown, for she was as naked as I was. I was not prepared to let her know I knew who she was, for my own very obvious if devious reasons.

Just upslope from the bank blew a stand of trees and the land beyond was hidden by this slight eminence. She stretched her arms up, her body taut and firm, and swung them around a few times. She must have thought she was dead. Then she'd been saved. Tough though she must be, she'd need a little time and meditation to get over that experience.

"I thank you, walfger. I am beholden to you."

The quaintness of her expression could not conceal her sincerity. I nodded. There was, it seemed to me, nothing appropriate to say.

"I am Mul-lu-Manting. Lahal. You are?"

"Drajak, known as the Sudden. Lahal."

The last—and first—time I'd seen her haranguing the mob in the central kyro of Changwutung she'd worn fancy silken robes and curved leather armor across breast and hips, with swords and a Lohvian longbow. She had the red hair of your true Lohvian. My informants had told me a deal about her, and I had surmised more. I was not sure if she was a fully-trained Jikai Vuvushi, a Battle Maiden. She did not wear the veil which lent credence to the idea she was a Fighting Lady; she could just as easily be a Witch of Loh. Rather, had been, for she ranted against the Witches and Wizards of Walfarg, blaming them and the kings on the throne for the collapse and loss of the old Empire of Walfarg, the Empire of Loh. Her ambition, which she preached with fanatical fervor, was to recreate the old Empire of Loh, ruled as before by Queens of Pain.

She was studying me frankly. Her face, that hard strong face, womanly handsome, would not be called pretty. Like Mevancy, she drew her beauty from inner truths and strengths. To an addle-pated fellow she might be nothing; to a man with eyes to see she would hold undeniable attractions.

After a moment, I said: "Why didn't they chase us here?"

She made a brief gesture towards the tree-lined crest.

"Beyond there lies the enclosure of Scharn, an ibdrin. I knew you were a stranger when you asked me to swim to this side."

"Ibdrins do not worry me, Mul-lu-Manting."

"Nor me. Now I need something to eat, something to drink, and something to wear—in that order."

I didn't smile; but I appreciated her priorities.

We walked up the slope together. She went with a loping stride, very free and lissom, and I knew I would need to discover more of her history. After all, the Everoinye had singled her out for salvation. Over the rise the land spread away in a sweep of moorland. The tall and lightning-shattered trunk of a single tree projected sternly a hundred paces ahead. This was the locus of the spirit land. Folk hereabouts believed that the souls or spirits of murdered or violently-killed people clustered here waiting for vengeance. You might never have murdered anyone in your life: you weren't fool enough to chance going near an ibdrin where a spirit might mistake you for the killer. Oh, no! By Lhun, no!

At the top she stopped stock-still, legs apart, fists jammed on hips, jaw outthrust, brow drawn down. She stared broodingly at the miserable landscape.

Half to herself, she said: "And that is Walfarg. Desolate, dun and dreary. Gone to seed. Producing no good." She moved and a hard toe kicked the rank grass stems. "Give me the strength to go on!"

I kept quieter than a church mouse.

Her face beneath that flaring red Lohvian hair expressed bitterness, sorrow, anger. There was no scrap of resignation I could see. She became aware of my scrutiny and like a person suddenly awoken from a deep dream-filled sleep, she started. Brusquely, she said: "I am for Shamfrin, a city where I have friends."

"As you said, Mul-lu-Manting, I am a stranger in these parts."

"You may, if you wish, Drajak the Sudden, accompany me."

Deliberately, I did not reply at once. Truth to tell, now I had rescued her, saved her for the purposes of the Star Lords, my interest in her was over. She was still in the throes of coming to terms with the dreadful experience through which she had just suffered. She might need a friendly shoulder on which to lean and cry. She was tough, yes; she was still a human being. And, at the same time, I did feel a personal responsibility for her. That was one of the odd, and if I acknowledged it, infuriating things about my working for the Star Lords. I tended to feel partial towards those I rescued.

The other grand discovery here was obvious. I would have said, previously, that Mul-lu-Manting had been saved for the inscrutable purposes of the Star Lords. Well, by Vox! This time was different. They'd saved her because she wanted and preached a new Empire of Loh. The word inscrutable no longer applied. Then, because I am Dray Prescot with sometimes a mind like a flea on a griddle, devious to the point of re-entry, I considered the opposite. The Everoinye had saved her because her message about a new Empire of Loh was counter-productive. People gave her a bad time when she preached a new crusade, and in their apathy her attempts merely strengthened their hostility to her and her ideas.

As for myself, there was no immediate decision. I could see advantages and disadvantages to the rebirth of the Empire of Loh. The advantages would come in our fight against the Opaz-forsaken Shanks. The disadvantages were all too familiar, by Krun!

She pointed to a small black and white speck on the western horizon.

"There is Shamfrin. Those oafs caught me as I passed through their disgusting little village." She cocked an eye up at me. "You do not ask why they tried to kill me, and would have, but for—"

"Their reasons and your business are not mine."

"Oh!"

"Do not misunderstand me. I have problems of my own."

Then—then, dear Zair, then! I realized. I felt myself shaking all over. I know I must have lost color, for Mul-lu-Manting gave me a most peculiar stare, and started back. I realized! The Star Lords had promised. I'd done their job for them, completed the task, saved this Mul-lu-Manting. And here I was, still, down here, here in the same spot. I gazed around in a dazed and stupefied way. The Everoinye had promised! They'd said they would return me in good time, back to burning Taranjin, back to save my Delia from those devils of Katakis.

And I was still here. I gazed about, like a lunatic. Delia! Why would not the Star Lords return me? Why?

Two

Madness hovered close. The Star Lords had promised! Why didn't they send down their phantom blue Scorpion as they had done so many times and snatch me up, to return me to Taranjin so that I might take all I loved in two worlds from those devilish slaving Katakis? Why?

"What is the matter with you, man?"

"What?"

"I said, what is the matter with you, man. You look awful."

The scene around me swam back into focus. No longer were my eyes filled with the excruciating vision of Delia being carried off by Whiptails. Mul-lu-Manting was giving me that same peculiar stare, at once a look of questioning, of arrogant demands that I did not go sick on her, and of a smidgen—I believe—of genuine concern.

"It's all right."

"Well, by Lhun, buck your ideas up. We have a way to march yet."

There was only one explanation. There was more work here at hand. When I'd done what the Star Lords wanted with this demanding madam, then and only then would they return me to Taranjin and all that mattered in two worlds.

If that was the way of it, well, by the Black Chunkrah! I'd do it, do it damned sharpish, and then dare the Everoinye to welsh on the deal.

"Your feet are all right, walfgera?"*

"I'll reach the city."

If she was not really tough then she both acted and talked so. She quite clearly wished to be tough and appear hard and strong. I didn't know if she was. This little trip to the city on the horizon was scarcely likely to test her, although tender feet treading bare over prickly ground are devastatingly quickly rendered painful past walking.

So we set off. There was an element of the strange to me here; I'd been in similar situations before and not been truly comfortable. Oh, no. This

---

* walfgera: feminine form of walfger. *A.B.A.*

had nothing to do with striding out without clothes with a naked woman matching me stride for stride. Nothing particularly odd about that, at least on Kregen. But, on Kregen, the true and uncomfortable oddness lay in thus marching on without a weapon, without a sword or bow, without a spear, without even a knife. That, on that marvelous yet horrific world four hundred light years from Earth, is likely to get you killed by someone who does have a sword or spear.

Then again, that is true only of certain locations. You can find some spots of Kregen where you may walk freely and safely without a sword baldricked over your shoulder. Some spots. A few.

The moorland type ground offered precious little in the way of a stick to be used as a shillelagh or blatterer. Just for the feel of it I picked up the thickest stalk I could find and swished it about as we walked. I did not cut off the heads of the few flowers we passed. That cretinous behavior belongs to the stupid and unpleasant variety of so-called human. The same sort of sub-species who probably delights in pulling wings off flies. You meet 'em, you meet 'em.

Thinking of my lack of a weapon, to be fair, there are societies of Kregen who live in contempt of pointed and edged weapons. These are what on Earth are termed Martial Arts exponents. Of them all, I suppose to be honest and without boasting, the Krozairs of the Eye of the World stand in the forefront; but they do not despise weapons. For that, you must go to the people of my comrade Turko's home, the Khamorros. Many and many a poor wight has sought to stick a sword through the guts of a high kham and found his sword a hundred paces away and he himself tied in a knot with his hands and feet all mixed up. Then, too, the Martial Monks of Djanduin know more than somewhat of the arcana of facing edged and pointed weapons with only your own naked body to serve as your weapon.

We had marched some way in silence. Now Mul-lu-Manting half-turned her head as we went along and said: "You are not of Walfarg. Nor, I judge, are you of Loh."

"That is true."

"Well?" The single word held all of expectant arrogance.

"You have heard of Segesthes?"

"Of course. The easternmost continental mass of Paz."

"Do you know aught of Segesthes?"

"Balintol is a mysterious place. There are many wonderful cities and strange races there."

"The cities mostly fringe the southern coasts. To the north, inland, there are almost limitless expanses, the Great Plains."

"Ah!" she said. "That makes sense. You are a Clansman."

"Aye."

I did feel a trifle of amusement. The Clansmen of Segesthes hold themselves aloof among the plains, yet their ferocious reputation had spread as far west and south as this.

She digested this information in silence for a handful of paces, then snapped out: "So, here in Loh, you are a paktun. You know why I have no clothes, for those shints of villagers stole them. But you?"

"I have been a mercenary in my time, yes."

"A zhanpaktun, I do not doubt, a hyr paktun. And someone snatched your golden pakzhan from its chains around your neck, and stole your clothes into the bargain. Ha! By Lhun, that must have been a sight!"

"It wasn't quite like that—" I started to say when a flicker of movement from stunted bushes off to the left caught my attention. I stopped walking, and took the woman's arm into my grip, halting her.

"What—?"

"Keep still."

"By Hlo-Hli, you onker! What d'you mean—" She was struggling to free her arm.

Curtly, I snapped out: "Look over there, and shut up."

She looked. Whether or not she would have obeyed that more than churlish command I couldn't say; she stopped wriggling when she saw the fellow who came strutting over towards us. She gasped.

"A Kanzai Warrior Brother!"

"Precisely. And he's bad news."

"But they don't—what's he doing—we must run! Hlo-Hli Herself have mercy on me! Run, you onker, run!"

"He will throw a Star of Death. You cannot outrun that."

She was panting now, her breast going up and down like a gig in a seaway. Her red hair draggled forward, still wet despite the rays of Luz and Walig. She tried to twist her arm free of my grip.

"Stand still, Manting! We will just talk quietly to him."

She moaned. "I know what is said of them..."

"Your virtue is safe, if that worries you. They are Warrior Brothers, Adepts, devoted to their Disciplines. Each has a mission. Generally, they try to rid the world of Kregen of vermin."

"And he will consider me as vermin?"

"Unlikely."

There are many weird and wonderful creeds and Disciplines on the equally weird and wonderful world of Kregen. Of the Kanzai Brotherhood I knew little. Their training is harsh. They are usually chosen from the more militant races. Their concept of honor may, to the ideas of an ordinary fellow like myself, seem a trifle warped. All the same, I'd dealt with them before and, Opaz willing, would do so again.

He strode on boldly, his laminated armor a mass of glinting points of light from rivet and studding. The wide brim of his helmet swept back over his shoulders, and the front was crowned with a skull. Dulled metal and polished leather clothed him. He wore swords, and he could produce an amazing variety of specialist weapons from the pouches strapped to his harness.

Holding myself as relaxed as I was able, I re-dedicated myself to the Disciplines of the Krozairs of Zy, and awaited his arrival.

He halted in a little willy-willy of dust. I could smell the oils of leather and of metal wafting from him. Added to that he exuded a strong rank odor of body sweat. His face glared at me, rather like the blunt end of a tent peg. His eyes, narrow and bright, dark with secret knowledge, sized up the girl and me.

"Lahal, dom," I said, before he opened his rat-trap of a mouth.

"It is Llahal, dom." He spoke harshly, rattlingly, as I expected.

He was, of course, perfectly correct. That guttural double-L makes of the Lahal with which you greet a friend the Llahal, the general greeting for a stranger.

I nodded. "As you wish, dom."

"You have seen a shint of a Rapa with blue feathers and a double-handed axe?" It was more of a demand than a question.

Half-turning to Manting, I said so the Kanzai could hear: "Have you seen such a fellow?"

"No." She was still shaking.

"No more have I."

He eyed us with those bright dark eyes. In a twinkling he could snatch up a Star of Death and hurl it with unerring accuracy.

"His name is Ralafon the Kaktu."

"I regret I can not be of assistance to you."

He stood absolutely still, braced on those strapped legs.

Then, I suppose because although humanity had been trained out of him after a lifetime of bloodshed, simple human curiosity remained, he said: "Your clothes?"

Manting opened her mouth and I said, sharply: "Damned villagers."

"A village? Good. Perhaps that Shuvu-forsaken Rapa has sought shelter there. They would not take his clothes from him."

"Not until he was dead," I said, equably.

He ducked his head in a quick, instinctive gesture.

"Yes. He is of the Tolkvar Sect."

Who the hell the Tolkvar Sect was I didn't know.

Every day, they say, on Kregen, you may learn a new name. And, as I have said, it behooves you to remember names if you do not want your throat cut. I did not take my gaze from him, waiting.

Now, let me make this clear. I had absolutely no wish to fight him. I just wanted to get this task for the Everoinye over and get back to Taranjin and

Delia. If he started something I could have no mercy, not with the burdens on my shoulders.

"We are going to Shamfrin. We would like to arrive before the suns go down." I spoke carefully.

"She of the Blushes will be up soon enough."

With seven moons in the sky any Kregan can tell the time and prognosticate when a certain moon is due. So why had the Kanzai said so obvious a thing unless he had an ulterior motive?

"We must get on, then." I spoke with a tinge more hardness.

Now, as I have said, I swear I did not want to fight this fellow. He was looking at us, sharp and bright, and I knew, I just knew, that what he intended to propose would not fit in with my own plans. I suppose some imp of deviltry, I plead in extenuation, tempted me. Perhaps Hoko the Amusingly Malicious leered enticingly at me, or Khokkak the Meddler suggested mischief, both spirits of deviltry in the pantheons of Kregen. At any rate, I spoke up, and I still insist I did not want a fight.

"Kanzai," I said, crisply. I pointed to the fancy gold-edged blue scarf slung around his neck in a most dashing way. "The lady is bereft of clothes. I would consider it a favor if you clothed her nakedness."

He just didn't believe this. He opened his mouth, and closed it, and half ducked his head in that flaring-brimmed helmet.

"Cramph," he got out, at last, chewing the word like a cheekful of cham, making the insult stick. "Cramph. You are fortunate. I do not dispose of you instantly because I have a task—"

Well, by Krun, I'd guessed that! And there was no time left to lollygag about. I'd just have to take him, armor and swords and all. I leaped.

He was taken completely by surprise. My fingers were gripping his throat, high above the laminated neck ring, thumbs thrusting his Adam's Apple deeply back against his spine, before he had time to gasp.

He was choking away and his eyes stuck out like gob-stoppers; but he was a Kanzai Brother, an Adept. He struggled and fought back.

His knee smashed past my side, my movement instinctive the moment I sensed his. His arms raked up and his hands clamped about my wrists. I could still think clearly for I had not slipped into that fighting mesmerism that makes every move part of a natural rhythm. My opinion of Kanzai techniques went down, if this was an example. He'd reacted to my attack in a defensive response and gone for my wrists. A Krozair Brother would have gone instantly onto the offensive, probably a gauntlet in the face. I kept my head tucked down in anticipation.

We glared eyeball to eyeball, our noses almost touching, the helmet a frame for this struggling, wriggling, constricting contest.

He kept on dragging at my wrists and trying to knee me. He was getting nowhere with those tactics. If the minor devils had lured me into this, perhaps they had one more stab at me, this time to my discomfiture. Being Dray Prescot, I am the antithesis of the boaster; equally, I detest silly show-iness, Vulgar Ostentation. I have no excuse for what happened next.

I shifted grips, leaving my left hand at his throat whilst my right dropped to the hilt of one of his swords.

The silver-wire wrapped hilt was in my grasp. I gave his throat an extra dig and, suddenly, he was toppling away from me, falling over in a flail of arms and legs, and I went on over him, my left hand ripped away from his throat and my right slipping helplessly from the sword.

I rolled over three times and jumped up like a flea. The moment my feet hit the dusty ground I leaped sideways and the Kanzai's flung Star of Death hissed past my ear, a little whirring horror of silvery steel. He'd have another of these Shuriken-like killers in his fingers in the next second. I hurled myself forward—and then saw I'd never reach him before he threw.

The whole world of Kregen fined down to that single silver streak flash-ing towards my eyes.

Three

I did not think. There was no time to think. Only afterwards could words be found to express what occurred. Everything was instinct, an instinct trained and honed by the Disciplines of the Krozairs of Zy.

Mul-lu-Manting, afterwards, was of little help. She could only say of what happened, whispering: "It was all a flurry. Arms and legs and blood and dust. I did not really look."

As for myself, I remember spurts and flashes of scarlet and yellow strik-ing across my eyes, and the evil silver glint of the Star of Death flashing towards my face, and of the grunt the Kanzai made.

To recollect violence in after days is not pleasant, either.

What happened, I think, was this.

There were two options open to me as the Shuriken swooped at me. The Kregans make their Stars of Death asymmetrical, so that their flight is not in a ballistic line. The little whirring death dealers swoop cunningly, curv-ing into face-destroying contact. So a deflection would be tricky. It could be, had been done. To obstruct the naked human arm in way of a descend-ing blow is always painful. The Star of Death might well spin at the last fraction of a second and so stick me. The other option was to duck out of the way fast enough. The Star of Death was traveling rapidly and my move-ment might not carry my head clear in time.

These apparently nice calculations, of course, just did not exist in the heartbeat between throwing and reaction. This explanation may appear to lack the melodramatic blood and guts demanded by sensation-seekers. It would seem to them cold and lifeless, not blood-stirring. To the true aficionado of Martial Arts quite the reverse is true. To such a one, the super-quick and instinctive response has to be trained and disciplined into the correct reaction. Instinct tends always to try to save our necks, and sometimes that—as this Kanzai Adept had shown—is not always the most efficient way of doing what is required. This time, the saving of my neck was done as prescribed by Mother Nature.

I ducked.

The Star of Death flashed past, hissing, and I was lunging forward.

He got his sword out before I hit him. Well, he would, being who he was.

Inside the first slash I bundled headlong. Body contact shocked all through me as my naked flesh smashed into his armor.

That was the first time he grunted.

My try for his throat was blocked by a savage sideways jerk. His sword arm was in my left fist. Correction, his elbow was in my left fist. I gripped, twisted, yanked, wrenched. So much for my left flank. My right flank had to be protected from the dagger in his left hand and the first slanting upward movement of my arm forced the blow away to the side. Missing his throat, I stuck my fingers for his eyes.

He tore himself backwards, still struggling furiously to free his sword arm. Only my middle finger connected, a ramrod of bone.

I felt the jolt of contact as I caught him on the bridge of his nose, which was squat and spatulate. That didn't bother him; to some folk of Kregen it would have brought water to their eyes.

The next moment I had to deal with that pesky dagger again.

A change of tactics was called for. With his sword out of action the dagger became the focal point of the combat. I did not make an attempt to deflect or block the next blow. I twisted a trifle and took his fist into my grip. He wore the large, ornate and truth-to-tell clumsy gauntlets of his calling, and I just crushed down hard. I did not break any bones, but his hand slowly opened. I say slowly. In comparison with the rest of it, his fist opened like a flower, gently.

Once more trying to be clever I made a grab for the dagger but it fell away to the dust.

He essayed another bold move and shoved himself forward bodily like a rugby scrum forward. I went staggering back and almost lost his right elbow. To let him know he had better desist, and desist quickly, that elbow was given a right rollicking wrenching about. That was when he grunted for the second time.

Bracing myself, I halted his drive, and shoved him back.

His left hand must have been smarting; but he doubled it up into a fist inside the gauntlet and hammered a blow at my ribs. That I could parry, and curl my arm inside his, and so grip and twine and pull. Evidently, he was not aware of that particular technique for he allowed it as a novice on the mat would do. A simple pull, and a reversal, a foot tucked behind his, a roll and a lunge and he went over slantingly backwards and sideways. As he went I released his sword arm. As he sprawled I was able to jump on him.

After that, as they say in Clishdrin, it was all over bar the shouting.

I had his own sword point poised above his throat, and then I dug the steel in a little, just a little, so as not to draw blood.

That was when he grunted for the third time.

There was blood on me and it was my own damn blood.

In the ferocity of the combat I couldn't exactly say when I'd caught the little scratch; but, as Mul-lu-Manting said, there was blood.

If I make this contest sound easy—it was not. There was no primitiveness of a foot behind a foot and a push to unbalance him. Oh no, by Zair! That technique was harshly taught and painfully learned and was delicate as to balance and timing and not for novices. He lay on his back glaring up at me past the blade of his sword.

I said, and I own that although I was not panting, I took a breath before I spoke. "Do you bare the throat?"

This ritual request from Jikaida seemed appropriate.

He couldn't nod his head, not with the brand's point indenting the skin. He growled out in a surly fashion. "And if I do not?"

When I answered I must have displayed that demoniac face folk call the Dray Prescot Devil Look. He licked his lips, which were dust caked inside the helmet, and said, very quickly: "Aye, dom, aye. I bare the throat."

"Unbuckle your harness."

Flat on the ground he could still do that. When I let him up his two swords and the empty scabbards and his pouches remained there. I motioned with the lynxter I carried and he stepped away from his armaments.

I touched the harness with my foot. "This is an interesting sword, dom."

He was rubbing his throat and glaring. Some saliva ran down his chin. "It is a drexer from Vallia."

"Oh. The thraxter is from Havilfar, that I know. Where did you come across this drexer?"

If he thought my interest in a sword after such a fight was odd, he gave no indication. "It was given to me by a comrade."

"His name?" That snapped out more sharply than I intended.

"Larghos Vom ti Ferlinsmot."

I hadn't seen Larghos for many a season and I doubted if that crusty old kampeon had become a Kanzai Brother. If he'd given a drexer, which is a superior sword of Vallia, to this fellow, then I knew I'd done right in refraining from slaying him. I said: "Then I must ask you for the loan of the blade. You have other swords."

He didn't answer, still chafing his neck. Now and then he let a little grunt past his thin lips.

"That pretty blue scarf with the golden edges. I must now ask you to let the lady have it to clothe herself."

He fairly tore it off and hurled it at Manting. It fell to the dust in a crumple.

I said: "Not the action of a true walfger, although the Kanzais may have other ways of treating ladies." I put a snap into my words. "Pick it up and hand it across properly."

Now was his chance to grab the girl and use her as a hostage. He didn't try. By this time I believe he had the message that he wouldn't win with that gambit. He picked up the scarf and before he passed it over he actually dusted it off. I quite liked that.

"Now that scrap of red at your waist, under the armor. That will be a nice red sash, I believe. I'll have that, too, if you don't mind."

He had to strip off some of his armor to get the sash out. It was not a brilliant scarlet, being more of a bright crimson; it would serve me well enough. When I pulled it around myself and tucked the ends in, I own I felt a new man. Of such petty symbols is morale built!

His three swords were each swung from their lockets on separate belts, so I could strap the drexer's belt around me and haul tight.

He moistened his lips again. "Your name, dom?"

"Drajak the Sudden. And you?"

"Noring the Ovoinach. Yes, you are sudden."

"You are for the village and this Rapa, we are for Shamfrin. I would we could part in peace."

At that time I knew little of the Kanzai Brotherhood. I had been told their humanity had been trained out of them. They went about the world on missions in pursuance of their own ends. Yet the very fact they called themselves a Brotherhood indicated feelings, one for the others. They were not, I judged, evil in the mundane meaning of the word.

He shifted a foot in the dust.

"I surprise myself," he said in that harsh, uncompromising voice. His face had regained some of the color it had lost during and after the fight. The rank smell of sweat hung on the still air. "I would not willingly go up against you in fair combat. Peace from a Kanzai Brother is possible only to a dead adversary—or to one who does not threaten us."

"Well, by Chusto!" I burst out. "Sink me! I don't threaten you!"

"If that is the truth in your heart."

"It damn well is, and it is not for you to harangue, Kanzai."

He nodded, a quick yet formal bow. "Very well. Let us part in peace."

I didn't offer to shake hands. I moved off a little way as he retrieved his harness and sheathed the lynxter and dagger. If he threw another Star of Death I had the sword to deflect it.

He straightened up and started to march off with a swing. After half a dozen paces he stopped and turned about.

"Remberee, Drajak the Sudden."

"Remberee," I called back. "Remberee, Noring the Ovoinach."

Four

To the majority of people of Paz, the Clansmen of Segesthes appear as archetypal savage barbarians. My Clansmen, I hasten to add, I hope needlessly, are not barbarians. Some of the clans farther off are a trifle hairy, I suppose. But if you wish to describe someone as savage and destructive and barbaric, you can call him or her a Clansman.

The clans of the Great Plains are nomads, of course. Nomads, in their eternal marches across the grazing lands, do not in general assist the onward march of progress and civilization. Nomads are essentially living a static way of life. And, too, something of that harsh living is caught in the very word Clansman. A girl or a woman of the clanners will call herself a Clansman unselfconsciously, for she is of the clans.

All this in explanation of Mul-lu-Manting. She had heard of the clanners and she had seen what she had seen, and she could still look me straight in the eye, her shakes forgotten. As we trudged on towards Shamfrin she resumed her normal attitude. That meant she began to try to convert me to the creed of the New Empire of Loh.

Even in the most populated nations of Kregen the land area is so extensive that vast tracts remain comparatively uninhabited. Stretches like that over which Mul-lu-Manting and I now walked existed between cities. Well aware of the sudden and ferocious habits of Nature upon Kregen I walked with a light step and a wary glance. Leem, themselves, the archetype of feral destruction, might be sniffing on our scent. At the least I expected savage hunting beasts like chavonths or strigicaws, mortils or prychans. The white walls of Shamfrin approached as the Suns of Scorpio declined and we walked only the last ulm by the light of She of the Veils.

Other cities and towns I had visited in Walfarg had given me the strong impression of weirdness. They were different from other cities in unexpected ways and therefore were strange beyond the normal strangeness of foreignness. The white walls and red roofs might well appear to be familiar; their architecture caught the eye at odd angles, leaning, overtoppling, pile on pile piled on arcades of gloom in the depths.

The light of the moon guided us the last distance through cultivated fields where the fuzzy pink and golden light caught the sleeping heads of the crops, shadowing and highlighting stalk and leaf and ear. That light was sufficient for the guards to see clearly and they had not yet closed the gates as we approached. A few stragglers moved along with us, and a Quoffa hauling an immense cart piled with nameless objects; a string of pack calsanys, and a lone rider astride a lictrix passed under the gatehouse with us.

We were not challenged.

"They are confident, then," commented Manting.

The guards were Bowmen of Loh, so they had some right to be confident.

I said, only half to myself: "Mul-lu, you may call me an onker if you wish."

"Oh?"

"I should have taken a little gold from our Kanzai brother. Where are we to stay tonight?"

"I have friends in Shamfrin—onker."

I did not smile; but I own I felt relief. Being stranded in an unknown and probably hostile town without cash is an unpleasant bore I've experienced before this, as you know; but I'd cope with it somehow. With a woman tagging along the problem is more acute. If this Manting ranter had pals here, well, they might be fanatical Empire of Loh advocates. I might be in for an evening of ear bashing.

In that streaming moonlight we walked quietly along and, I can tell you, I walked lightly and with the drexer loose in the scabbard.

Manting knew her way all right and we passed massive buildings with walls peppered with lights and with many people coming and going, and carriages twinkling along and the smell of evening on the warm air. A long prospect of arcades was broken by a square, and this kyro had been set out with many small canopied stalls. Here vendors were shouting their wares in strident voices. The variety was amazing, from shoes and shirts to cooking pots and cucumbers, and idols of Vutch-Ikar with pot bellies and staring eyes. Mul-lu-Manting glanced sideways at the mass of idols' heads.

"Vutch-Ikar." She sniffed with vast contempt. "A male god and a false god. Yet he is not a false god because he is male."

I moved sideways sharply to avoid a calsany loaded with sacks whose driver simply let the animal blunder on, well knowing people would jump out of the way. The sense of moonlight streaming down overhead and the scatter of stars, was entirely lost. Now I felt enclosed and shut in by walls of vendors' booths, by shouting people, by dust and the smells of commerce.

Lanterns and torches flared in my face as Manting went on: "When the empire was lost, Vutch-Ikar was the fashionable god. People took the true Hlo-Hli too much for granted."

I felt compelled to say: "What about Raffi of the Lightning and Thunder?" I nodded to a stall loaded with idols of the god. "She was always a goddess of the pantheon, before and after the fall. And, anyway," I added, "those statues are rather pretty. She looks quite nice."

She sniffed again. I hoped I was not consciously teasing her. "You pretend to know a vast deal of Lohvian history, remarkable for a barbarian clanner, Drajak!"

"Oh, we barbarians have our hidden sides too, you know."

We pushed through the rest of the jangled confusion of the market into the balance of the arcades where quite soon Manting led off along a side street. The houses here were smaller and then we had reached the door she sought and she knocked. She rapped two, one, three. At this secret knock the door disclosed a small square aperture barred with black iron beyond which a moustached face glowered out, two gimlet eyes boring into Manting.

What she said I didn't hear; but the door opened and we went in.

A form swathed in voluminous robes like a bundle of laundry was topped by a round doughy face. The gimlet eyes sized me up. The damp mouth beneath that moustache opened and she said: "A man."

"Yes, Nola, a man. He has been useful."

This moustached lady, Nola, sniffed. I began to suspect this contemptuous sniffing was the trademark of these folk. She stepped aside and Manting led on along the dimly lit corridor to what was clearly a general living room at the end. Here a broad scrubbed wooden table at the centre was surrounded by bentwood chairs. The walls were covered by shelves and cupboards. A stove stood along one wall and washing facilities opposite. The smells were what one would expect—stale food, disinfectant, sweat—but mingled with them the unmistakable scents of expensive perfumes.

There were four women sitting at the table preparing a meal and a fifth pottering at the stove. They were not all alike, and they were not all the same as Manting; they were, all five of them, near enough to fool one on a dark night. I guessed this was the coven headquarters acting as the powerhouse for ideas and energy for the new Empire of Loh.

Introductions were made and I sat quietly and got on with a hunk of bread until the meal was ready, and I said very little, only politely answering questions with the most convenient lies that came into my mind and listening to what was said.

The women and Manting had news to impart and gossip to exchange. The bread had gone down nicely, thank you, and intending to display no interest in what was being said, I glanced at a couple of books on the table. One made me think back to Sosie na Arkasson, for it was The Quest of Kyr Nath. The other book made my lip twist down wryly. The first words of the first chapter were: "A foot scraped in the shadows." Oh, yes. The tall stories of the adventures of Dray Prescot had reached here, in uncaring Loh. And, of course, thinking back to the Black Feathers of the Great Chyyan made me sweat with terror afresh for new perils endangering Delia. What in a Herrelldrin Hell were the Star Lords doing keeping me hanging about here when I should be back there in burning Taranjin and seeing off those damned Katakis and taking Delia into my arms where she belonged?

Foolish to imagine the Everoinye heard and answered my passionate internal demand. Yet one of the women, Lola the Assandra, was saying: "Yes, Mul-lu, I'm afraid we do stand in some peril since you left."

"Tell me."

"Ferlie was pelted with filth when she tried to speak, and she was followed back. They know where we live."

Nola sniffed. "Let 'em come. I have my rolling pin." The moustache looked fierce above the damp mouth, the gimlet eyes mean.

Mul-lu-Manting looked more annoyed than apprehensive. "I had the word of the Kovneva Shernly, her personal word, that we would not be molested."

"The kovneva shares our views." Lola cut slices of vegetable with precise tiny cuts. "The kov does not."

"Yes," put in Ferlie, whose pronounced perfume was now explained. "And I'm sure he encourages the common folk against us. Because—"

"Because he is frightened of his wife!" snapped Manting.

The explanation for this state of affairs was simple enough. During the time of the Empire of Loh, the nobility, like this Kov of Shamfrin, were very much under the thumb of the Queens of Pain. A kov, which is more or less like the terrestrial duke, is the highest rank of nobility—apart from a hyr kov or arch kov—and nowadays in the relaxed atmosphere after the fall of the empire, the nobility exercised much greater authority. His wife, this Kovneva Shernly na Shamfrin, might quite like to see a return of the empire and the Queens of Pain, the kov her husband most certainly did not.

The mineral oil lamp on the table cast shadows across Manting's face, as suddenly, out of the blue, she burst out: "When they tied that sack of stones to me, and I felt the water all about me, I—" She shivered, and put her palms flat against her face. Lola the Assandra stood up at once,

155

dropping her knife, and went around the table. She held Manting's head against her bosom, stroking her hair, soothing her.

A slightly-built, dark curly-haired girl with bright eyes, said: "If the barbarian had not been there, Mul-lu—"

"Hush, Tilly." But Lola spoke gently.

By the time we'd washed and sat down to the meal, Manting had recovered her composure. Her cheeks were flushed. She spoke up sharply enough and between herself and Lola dominated the conversation. I felt a sneaking admiration for her. She had been through a devilishly unpleasant ordeal.

The youngster, Tilly, seemed a bright spark. She gave me a slanting look from her dark eyes, and said: "For a barbarian he has nice table manners. Don't you think, Mul-lu?"

Mul-lu-Manting did not look up from her plate. "Manners do not make the man in Loh, Tilly."

"Maybe," said Tilly, pertly. "But they often make a woman!"

"Tilly!" snapped out Lola, and Tilly looked quickly down at her plate. She was quite unrepentant, that was obvious.

As is my wont in these circumstances I offered to do the washing up, and was accepted for the job. In addition I was sent out with two buckets for water from the well at the cross roads at the end of the street, and then sent back for two more. After that they gave me a whole silver piece and I lugged back two bundles of firewood. I felt I'd earned my supper.

Lola held out her hand. "Where is the change, Drajak?"

In handing her the copper coins from the wood vendor I felt we'd come to an unspoken agreement. They'd trusted me with silver. I'd done what they asked, and had not run off. Had I done so, I wondered, what female trickery had they up their sleeves to thwart that dastardly male plan?

After that, amid much clanking and clanging, they brought out weapons, spread them upon cloths laid across the table, brought out oil and rags, and went to work. There were harnesses of armor, curved to fit girls, and helmets of the Lohvian quoinrin pattern. The skulls were drawn and beaten with neckflaps and nasals, and although not a devotee of the quoinrin helmet, I'd used them in my time and found them serviceable.

"Come on, Drajak, bratch!" snapped Lola, and I set to.

"Brick dust and spit," I said. "That's what I'm more accustomed to."

Tilly laughed at this. So we sat, talking desultorily, cleaning.

Then Manting said: "I did not think Clansmen, being nomads, knew anything of bricks for building."

To stir her up a trifle, I said: "Only when we knock 'em down."

"Oh!" said one of the women, startled.

"Barbarians!" sniffed Lola the Assandra.

So, as you can see, we were getting along like a house on fire, as they say in Clishdrin.

When I felt it appropriate, I took up the drexer from the Kanzai and gave that a good clean and polish.

Despite my good intentions, and the very real necessity of not doing so, I found myself more and more fretting in the direst terror for Delia.

Like a ripsaw through knotty pine, Manting's words jolted me.

"What's the matter with you, Drajak? Has the meal upset you?"

"No, no," I managed to say. The meal had been soup with ingredients of unknown provenance. "Very nice." Then, speaking honestly as I had with Mevancy, I said: "I was thinking of a lady."

"I see." Manting's nose pinched in and her mouth clamped shut.

"A barbarianess!" said Tilly, with a little laugh.

This was no good. I had to concentrate on what was happening now. So, back to myself, I heard the sounds first.

I stood up.

Lola tilted her head.

Mul-lu-Manting said: "They know where we live, now, you said, Ferlie. Well, they have come for us."

Outside the house the sounds of trampling feet, the chink of weapons, drifted into the quiet room. Most ominous of all the half-bestial sounds of voices raised in chanting chorus, menacing, infinitely threatening, swelled closer and closer in a dire litany of vengeful destruction.

Hastily, the women began to strap on their armor. I took up the drexer. This was going to be a nasty little fracas. If I got myself killed in the doing of the Star Lords' wishes, and my Delia was not saved, then I'd never forgive the Everoinye, no, never!

The women all looked determined. They handled their weapons in such wise that showed they knew how to use them, even if they might not be highly skilled. Overblown sentiments like dire litanies and vengeful destructions however melodramatically infantile were absolutely spot on here. Those crowds outside were out for blood.

Mul-lu-Manting started to speak and I cut her off sharply.

"Is there a back way out of here?"

"Do what?"

"You heard."

She was clearly taken aback. A stone rattled against the door at the end of the corridor. "You mean you'd run away, Drajak?"

"Too right! By Lhun, woman! They'll rip us to shreds!"

She swished her sword about. She only had two more strapped about her waist, so she was not heavily over-armed by Kregan standards. "Almost, Drajak the Sudden, almost, I gave you the jikai—"

"Well," I fairly snarled back, "don't bother. I'll shove some furniture against the front door. You lead off out the back."

"You are not in command here, man," Lola told me, curtly.

"Well, whoever is better unglue her wings—that is, had better put her slippery shoes on—before it's too late."

Whilst we thus stood jabbering, more stones rattled against the door and a resounding and meaty thud announced the onslaught of a battering ram.

"That's it!" I fairly snatched up the table and hurled myself along the passage. The table, jammed against the door, wouldn't hold the mob for long. It might just give us time to nip over the wall at the back. If there was any damned back exit from this benighted place.

When I returned to the living room the women were standing, rather like statues, glaring at me. Tilly giggled in nervous reaction to her own fear. "It takes four of us to lift that table."

"Where's the back way?" I shouted. I was growing warm.

Mul-lu-Manting jumped at my tone. "Just the same," she said, and her voice hardened. "Just as it was when we lost the empire. The women fought and the men ran away. Jikarna, the lot of you."*

The noise outside resembled a circus of beasts just before feeding time. Now I was well aware I wouldn't run off and leave these stubborn women—and not just because the Star Lords wanted me to protect Manting, either—but they didn't know that. I started for the rear door of the living room. I exaggerated my stride to indicate I meant what I was doing.

Tilly broke the impasse. She ran after me, dropped her sword, bent to snatch it up with a beautiful flowing movement, and squeaked out: "Wait for me, Drajak! I'll show you the way!"

I looked back. Nola was running her plump hand up and down a spear shaft; but—and this is true—she did have a rolling pin thrust into her belt. Lola the Assandra was turning her head to look down the corridor and then back at me. As for Mul-lu-Manting, that fiery woman was about to march down the corridor, sword up, ready to chop the whole damned mob of 'em out there.

"Tilly! Lead on. You others, follow and make it sharp. And watch for any of the crowd out at the back." With that I rushed across the room and dived down the passage.

The table was jumping at each blow like a poor ill-used animal under the lash. I scooped Manting up with my left arm around her waist, feeling the lack of armor there, span about, and started back with her carted along like a roll of carpet, head first, feet last.

She started in yelling at me, and hit me—fortunately she did not strike me with her sword. I just tightened my grip on that waist of hers and hurried along. No one was left in the living room so I went through the far opening and back-heeled it shut after us. A lantern glowed ahead, and moved up and down. Someone had waited for me, then. I took a mental wager, and when I saw Tilly by the back door holding the light I won my bet.

---

* jikarna: coward. A.B.A.

"Mul-lu!" exclaimed Tilly, and I realized she was not horrified but amused at her companion's position. I wasn't going to put Manting down yet, no, by Krun!

"Get on, Tilly. And thank you for waiting."

Mul-lu was raving on about a Walfargian's honor—I took no notice. If there did happen to be a crowd waiting at the back then she'd have plenty of opportunity to see how well her ideas of honor served her in a dirty street knock-down, drag-out fight.

She of the Veils and Tilly's lantern revealed a shadowed courtyard. The so-called back door of these living quarters led onto a common yard along with other back doors in the block. Moonlight splashed down over the dilapidated arch over the gateway on our left side. Tilly led us quickly over the cobbles. I strained to listen and could pick up no sounds of a waiting mob.

The wooden gate, somewhat worn away at the edges, stood half-open. In the street outside the women grouped in a huddle. They reminded me rather of a forlorn group of birds huddling on a fence in the rain. Events had overtaken them. They weren't out of the wood yet.

"Right, Lola. Which way now?"

"It is for Mul-lu to say. She is our leader."

Mul-lu let out a squeak and a volley of oaths the burden of which was that I'd better put her down right this minute, or—

"Or what, Mul-lu? I warn you, if you try to fight this mob single-handed again I shall stop you again."

I slapped her down on the soles of her feet—hard.

Her red Lohvian hair, dark under the moonlight, flopped about her eyes. She brushed it away savagely, as though knocking me down.

"Who appointed you my keeper, Drajak the Sudden?"

The irony of that gave my lips a twitch.

I said: "Lead on to somewhere safe, Mul-lu. Then we can discuss the mysteries of your future and fate."

"You're a damned impertinent man!"

"For the sweet sake of Hlo-Hli Herself! Lead on, woman!"

"He's right, Mul-lu," chattered Tilly.

Even Nola, holding her spear like a soup ladle, nodded agreement.

Well, eventually we all trailed off along the street. We kept up a sharp lookout. The bestial mob sounds gradually faded.

"They'll break in and wreck our house," said Lola. She spoke with a deal of annoyance and regret.

A woman of somewhat vulpine looks and wearing a heavily chased breastplate, Nan-ni-Oboling, spat out: "We couldn't have gone back there again, anyway. It is our possessions I'm furious about."

"As we were prevented from fighting for them we shall have to find more." Manting shot the remark directly at me. I did not reply.

"We'd better go to my brothers," said Lola. She spoke as though going to her brothers was like going to the dentist without acupuncture.

"No good." Manting said. "He's known to them."

Lindy-ma-Sendiyin said: "Well, where to then?" She had a florid face under the helmet brim and sounded petulant. She'd been the first to follow Tilly at the beginning of our escape.

Now Tilly perked up. "Let's go to my sisters."

"You said she was never fond of us." Manting gave Tilly a look.

"She thought you were silly to try to bring back the past, and she didn't like the way I liked you."

"Jealousy." Mul-lu-Manting sniffed.

"We'd been close, very close. You can—"

"Oh, yes. Well, then. Wenda!"*

So our forlorn little band traipsed along the moon-shadowed streets, past dark arcades reeking with menace under that towering architecture, until we reached a block not much different from that we'd just left.

Here, Tilly's sister, Milly, a few seasons older, let us in. From the very first it was apparent that she was more than not fond of the followers of the New Empire of Loh. Still, she brought cakes and fruits and her husband Lanlo the Plump poured wine. The general tenor of the conversation, although formal, reassured me. These two, Milly and Lanlo, were not about to betray us.

There was no striking family resemblance between Milly and Tilly. The older sister struck me as a person who thought far more about things than the younger. Lanlo was plump, true; he held within himself a strength that had to come from a source of power. I noticed among the cheap decorations of the walls, the flower paintings, the images and the draped shawls, a small oval picture. All it contained was a blue equilateral triangle outlined in yellow, point down. I'd seen that symbol before.

Lanlo saw me looking at the blue triangle.

Speaking very quietly, I said: "I see you are a Pilgrim."

His miniscule start of surprise was well-controlled. He might be plump; his face was hard enough and his eyes shrewd. "You are a Wayfarer, Drajak?"

I shook my head. "Unfortunately, no. I have met only two Pathfinders, good people both. And I say unfortunately for I have a very great interest in finding my way through the paths to the truths that will unlock the power of miracles and magic."

He smiled. "You say 'will' unlock. You do, then, believe?"

"Yes."

"Yet you say you are not—?"

"Time, Lanlo, time. It seems I'm always in the middle of something going on, in the thick of things. Like tonight."

---

* wenda!: let's go! A.B.A.

"Yes. But you must also, then, believe in the New Empire of Loh?"

This put me in a trifle of a quandary. To cover my hesitation I took another cup of wine from Milly with a thank you. She said: "They will never succeed in bringing back the old Queens of Pain to Loh."

Taking a breath I explained my meeting with Mul-lu-Manting and the subsequent events in such a way they seemed natural—and these happenings are not at all unusual on Kregen. "No, I am not committed to a return of the empire. I've not really contemplated that. I am interested in Alternative Magic and what powers for good will come of success."

If the Star Lords, in having me protecting Mul-lu-Manting, were indicating they wanted the Empire of Loh to return, then I'd have to go along with that. Arguing with the Everoinye had cost me dear in the past. My most recent conversation with them gave a pointer to future conduct—perhaps.

"Alternative Magic." Lanlo spoke the words almost with reverence. "This is what we strive for, so that from a man or woman's own head will stream the power to move mountains."

"One day," I said. I spoke quite sincerely.

"Oh, yes." Milly spoke decisively. "Most certainly, one day."

Then the others drifted over across the room and we began to sort out sleeping arrangements. We'd had a long day.

Five

Bright and early the next morning Milly said she had to go out for the shopping. She selected her veil with care. I knew there existed a complex system of color, design and embroidery styles marking off one Lohvian woman's veil from another's. That was one subject of research I had not pursued. These blank-walled courtyard houses were clearly the urban development of the famous walled gardens of Loh. Once I'd imagined that veils and walled gardens, mysterious though they might be, were all there were to the great continent of Loh. That opinion was in process of revision.

I told Lanlo in a quiet moment whilst the women were all chattering away in the kitchen that the two Pilgrims I'd known were San Ornol Wanlicheng and his disciple—if that was the right word—Xinthe.

"I do not have the pleasure of their acquaintance, Drajak. We are a thin community spread widely. And new members, although sought, are difficult to find and even more difficult to keep."

"So there's no central organization?"

"Not really. We are able to send messages to those we know through a loose network. And Lisa the Forthright acts as our—mentor, guru, leader? —she is a truly remarkable woman."

"Well, San Ornol and Xinthe live in Changwutung. I'm sure they'll be glad to hear from you. Mention me. I think they'd like that."

"It will be a pleasure, Drajak."

Here, then, were two more people, Lanlo the Plump and Milly, who besides being Pilgrims in search of Alternative Magic, were two more of those pleasant nice folk of Kregen.

As though to confirm that, Lanlo heaved up a sigh. "We do not hold with this New Empire of Loh, yet we cannot turn them out into the street. The damage has been done. Some way will have to be found for them to escape Shamfrin."

These were my sentiments. Thinking that, the thought I'd toyed with recurred. The Star Lords had once been human like me. Suppose they had reached their awesome powers through the study of the Paths, through Alternative Magic? Then suppose some of the Pilgrims succeeded, and others followed the corners through the Paths. Even if the powers they gained were only a fraction of those of the Everoinye, what would be the Star Lords' reaction? Would jealousy drive them to denying the new Star Lords? Would they destroy them? Or would they welcome them, as new companions in their aeons old designs? I just didn't know, and was most reluctant to guess, by Vox, yes!

"You look troubled, Drajak. I think it is not as bad as you imagine. We can puzzle a way for these women to leave safely."

"The sooner the better."

"Assuredly."

Without undue emphasis yet not casually, I asked him if he'd heard of an evil wizard called Carazaar. I termed him evil because I'd been told he was evil and he'd certainly done some dastardly things to me.

"No, Drajak, never."

I mentioned the Wizard of Walfarg, Na-Si-Fantong. He laughed. "Oh, yes. Everyone has heard how he was kicked out of Kothmir. Tried to steal a valuable necklace."

"And he's not been heard of since."

"Not to my knowledge. I'll ask Milly when she gets back from the shopping."

The shopping duly deposited in the kitchen, where the women of the brave New Empire of Loh began to prepare the second breakfast, Milly, too, laughed as her husband had.

"Well, you hear such things in the markets. Quaenci—you know, Lanlo, her husband has the gregarian stall—well, she did tell me there was a rumor this great wizard of Walfarg had gone from Kothmir to Murn-Chem. That is a mortal long way south past the jungles."

"Highly unpleasant," confirmed Lanlo with a shiver.

I thanked Milly and she went on to tell us that she had contracted with Lop-eared Nath to take us out tonight in his Quoffa cart. "No one will suspect a thing. All he wants is gold."

"Um," I said, and I own I spoke glumly.

To my surprise the women had gold and silver secreted about their persons. Manting and I, of course, were penniless.

"We have enough," declared Milly when the coins were laid on her scrubbed table. "As soon as the suns are gone, we move."

So that was that.

Kregans, like Terrans, treasure favorite stories. Many plotlines run along familiar grooves. In this situation where we were trying to leave a city inconspicuously in a lumbering country cart, we were not running from the lord's brutal guards. Oh, no. This was different. The women of the New Empire of Loh were running from the people.

So that made me more than ever uneasy.

Milly went on speaking. "And, Lanlo, I saw Naghan the Boorish and told him—"

"Milly! Milly! How many more times must I ask you—?"

"Oh, you're too soft! I call that man Naghan boorish because he is boorish! I wish you could work somewhere else. He said he was most annoyed you did not go in to work today. And he was boorish when he told me, may Hlo-Hli Herself afflict him with boils."

"Milly!"

I felt amused by this, and sobered, too, at the reflection of what these peoples' lives were like in the normal way. Lanlo worked as a cashier in a bakery and he'd taken the day off to assist us.

The day wore on and somehow we did not all go stark staring raving out of frustration and boredom and waiting fever. Milly had more errands to run in the afternoon. When she returned she confirmed that Lop-eared Nath had his cart ready. Then, turning to me, she added: "You were asking about that fatuous Wizard of Walfarg, Na-Si-Fantong. Well, I made some enquiries." She looked pleased with herself.

"Thank you, Milly." I spoke gravely.

Whilst I wouldn't actually swear she preened herself as she told me her news, she was in her simple way genuinely delighted she could be so useful to a stranger, even if he was a friend of her empty-headed sister.

"He did go off to Murn-Chem according to one story. But I also heard that he had one of those flying things that so hurt the old empire. He was supposed to have gone to Notesov. Well, the funny thing is, Nanli the egg-woman and Lorca—you know, Lanlo, him with the huge wart by his nose, has a fish-stall—well, both of them heard from their children only this sennight and what do you think?"

"I, my dear," said Lanlo, "cannot imagine."

"Well, of course you can't! It's so funny. Well, Nanli's son—you remember, little Tonli, always had big ears—he's gone for a paktun and he was in Notesov and the wizard's not been seen there and they heard he'd gone to Murn-Chem." She took a breath. "Fancy that! Now, what do you think—?"

Just about then I think we all got it. Still, Lanlo spoke in his quiet way to his wife, saying: "I've no idea."

She was consumed with pleasure at the way she'd told her news. "Well, listen to this! Lorca's son is in Murn-Chem and he'd heard Na-Si-Fantong was in Notesov! There! What d'you think of that?"

"Remarkable, my dear, quite remarkable."

"Stupid wizards," ground out Mul-lu-Manting. "Don't believe a thing you hear about them."

The women of the New Empire of Loh were contemptuous of Wizards of Loh—a frightening concept to the rest of Paz—because they were held partly accountable for the fall of the old empire.

Tilly spoke up in her bright way. "That means the wizard covered his tracks. He could be anywhere." She cocked that saucy eye at me. "Anyway, Drajak, what's so special about him?"

"Well, he's a Wizard of Walfarg for a start—"

"Fumbling fools!" commented Manting with some bitterness. Anyone would think from her vehemence that the old empire had crumbled away only this minute before her very eyes.

All this passed the time to nightfall. We ate well and drank moderately. Lanlo insisted I take the loan of a short cape in a fetching shade of violet to cover me up. Truth to tell, the weather was warm enough and I am well used to wandering about wearing only the brave old scarlet breechclout. This fancy cape would serve to make me blend in more with other men wearing short capes. Mul-lu-Manting had taken the opportunity of clothing herself in a swathing robe back at the house before the attack. Her armor, like that of the other women, would mark them out. The women insisted on wearing their armor and swathing themselves in ordinary robes from Milly's wardrobe. Her sister's visit was costing her and her husband dear.

Tilly's question about the specialness of Fantong had been avoided in Manting's outburst. I did not intend to tell these women that Fantong was seeking to collect nine ruby-like gems. The whole thing was called the Skantiklar. He'd stolen the necklace in Kothmir and everyone laughed at the way he'd been kicked out and chortled over his discomfiture, for the necklace had been recovered. The trouble was, Fantong had removed the one gem he required from the necklace. I knew he had this gem. How many more did he have, and how many more were there to find? There was one in Makilorn he'd failed to get. What did he want the nine ruby-like gems for? Power, I supposed.

Mind you, then I was interested in Na-Si-Fantong only from an idle curiosity. For one thing, I didn't like his middle name. My own comrade Wizard of Loh, Deb-Lu-Quienyin, a staunch friend through thick and thin, had observed that this Fantong fellow would bear watching. We both could only speculate on the reasons for Fantong's pursuit of the Skantiklar.

With the decline of the Suns of Scorpio, Zim and Genodras, which here in Loh are called Luz and Walig, we could venture out. She of the Veils, often called down here She of the Blushes, would light our evening way; but until the Twins rose to circle each other endlessly as they circled Kregen, the fuzzy golden-rose light would not unduly discommode us. Lop-eared Nath had his cart ready.

I thanked Milly and Lanlo the Plump. There was no need to put warmth into my voice; I felt respect and affection for them, representing as they did one of the more admirable aspects of Kregen.

Then I said: "One last favor. Veils. The women will be seen as War Women without."

Milly opened her mouth and Mul-lu-Manting cut in sharply.

"Had we wished to wear veils we could have walked out as ordinary silly women without trouble."

Lola shook her head. "No. We do not wear veils."

All the women—including Milly—burned spots of rising annoyance on their cheeks. They were clearly quite capable of sparking off a continuation of an old argument.

Nola patted her stomach where the rolling pin nestled under her folds of cloth. "We are not Warrior Women in the common parlance. We do not claim to be Jikai Vuvushis. But my rolling pin will deal with a man quicker than a Bowmaid of Loh can shaft him. Ha!"

Tilly sniffed. "I would have gone for a Bowmaid but Milly—"

"I was quite right, too! Still, perhaps if I'd let you, you wouldn't have taken up with this lot."

Mul-lu-Manting opened her mouth, quite clearly to make some remark that would fuel the row, and it was my turn to cut in sharply.

"If you women stand here arguing all night we'll never get you away. Now, come on!"

They all turned their heads to stare at me. So I must have rapped that out a trifle brusquely.

"Men!" said Nola of the Rolling Pin. And she sniffed.

We said the remberees and the women made small respectful gestures to the idol of Hlo-Hli in her niche with two dips burning.

She of the Veils shone down refulgently, and Nath of the Quoffa cart did, indeed, possess lop-ears.

"Hurry up and get in," he said in a surly tone.

"I," I said, in what I trusted was not a lofty tone, "will walk at the side."

"As you wish, dom."

The women climbed in the back and heaping straw was piled over them. I made sure good handfuls concealed all the protuberances. The Quoffa with his huge patient face, rather like a perambulating hearthrug, heaved at the shafts and off we went.

We were not, I had to remind myself, escaping from the local bigwig, whether king or kov. In some of the more insalubrious places of Kregen punishments are handed out that make a rational mind cringe. For allowing prisoners to escape, for instance, a common penalty is for the offender to be castrated and to have his right eye, hand and foot removed. Life after that, to say the least, by Krun, is not to be lightly contemplated.

As we passed along the street by the light of the moon I had to contemplate the serious possibility that this Lop-eared Nath would betray us. He could sell us down the river for a handful of silver. Consequently, as usual, I marched warily and the drexer could be up and snouting forward into an opponent's guts in less than a heartbeat.

These confounded cantankerous women! Why, by the Furnace Fires of Inshurfraz, couldn't they wear veils like sensible females here? Then all this nonsense of skulking off hidden in a Quoffa cart wouldn't have been necessary. I tell you, I stalked along in a most foul humor.

Anyway, was this sniffing madam, Mul-lu-Manting, worth all the bother? The Star Lords quite evidently thought so. They either wanted the Empire of Loh re-created or they wanted it to remain defunct. To the Bat Caves of Gratz with the lot of 'em! Why couldn't they tell me which way they wanted the monkey to jump?

Lop-eared Nath hawked up, and spat, and said in a dripping tone of voice: "Nice little lot of shemale flesh there, dom."

I said: "I shall not hit you now. If you repeat your filthy remarks you will be thrashed senseless. Dernun!"*

He blurted out: "By Hornli! You're damned sharp! I only—"

"I know what you only, Lop-eared Nath. Shut the black-fanged winespout. And, again, Dernun?"

He hawked up and spat again. He was only half-looking at me, eyes downcast. Then, reluctantly, he growled out: "Quidang!"

"Dondo!"† I walked on and I made sure I walked a little astern of this flea-bitten Lop-eared Nath.

Thinking in these unpleasant ways of the Black Spider Caves of Gratz, and allied unpleasantnesses, like Kov Koronin's Dungeons of Dolor and the Stromicha Senteva's Crushing Bed, I tried to cheer myself up with the reflection that, by Vox, we weren't there!

Mind you, on Kregen which, as I may have mentioned, is a world of

---

* dernun: 'do you understand?' Not very polite. *A.B.A.*

† dondo!: good! *A.B.A.*

marvel as well as horror, we could well be in far worse case at any moment. So, looking everywhere, I walked on alongside the straw-covered cart where the girls in their armor—and without veils!—huddled.

Whether or not my unpleasant spat at Lop-eared Nath made him repent of any ideas of treachery or not I couldn't say. I can say we went on without undue haste and without any hindrance through the moonlight until we reached the gates just as they were about to be closed. There was a quantity of amused jibing at Lop-eared Nath and his Quoffa cart—and then we were through under the gateway and trudging along the dusty ribbon of road. Mul-lu-Manting pushed her head out through the straw and said: "It seems we are safe now, Drajak. You have my thanks. Now we are for Chanshong, a nicer place than Shamfrin, where we have friends."

I felt disinclined to leave the women now. My job would be done when the Everoinye said it was done—not a mur before.

There was no need for me to worry my head on that score.

There was no time for a single remberee.

Up I went, clothed in blueness, the lambency of the phantom blue Scorpion of the Star Lords blazing in my eyes. The coldness touched me and then passed by. I felt something hard smash against my thighs and instinctively, as a rider, I gripped on. I was sitting in the saddle of a zorca.

So I knew.

I heaved up a huge prayer of relief, trying to see through the haze of slowly-dissipating blueness.

My clothes and armor were with me, and quite involuntarily, without even a pause, I gripped the great Krozair longsword in my fist. The noise, the smells, the sensations of a burning city burst in on me. Smoke roiled across the street, as the blueness at last vanished. Smoke lay like a blanket over the city, a blanket splattered with blood.

Up that street I had urged my steed on, chasing after the seven Katakis who were abducting Delia. I recognized the street. I peered ahead as the smoke writhed in heat-driven coils. The Star Lords had kept their promise. They had returned me to Taranjin at the precise moment I had been taken away. I felt sensations of all manner of varieties overpowering me—I wanted to hurl mocking thanks at the Star Lords, to screech defiance, to curse the Opaz-forsaken Katakis and their slaving ways, to encourage the zorca between my knees to greater efforts, to call on Vox and Krun and Djan—oh, yes, I rode on amid a welter of powerful emotions.

Smoke wafted across my face, stinging my eyes, clogging my mouth.

The smoke cleared. I stared eagerly down the street as my zorca galloped swiftly on. I wanted to see Delia again, and the doomed Katakis abducting her.

I stared down the street.

The street was empty.

Six

The street was empty.

"No!" The cry of agony broke from me with lung-bursting horror. "No! Star Lords—No!"

Ahead of me as my fleet zorca galloped on, the street lay deserted. The smoke choked down, heat smote from burning walls, the whole terrible panorama of man's stupid inhumanity extended as though in condemnation all about. I felt numbed. I felt as though liquid fire surged through my veins. My whole body burned. Delia! Where was Delia now?

My head throbbed. I could feel my heart thundering away. Pressure swelled my wrists. Delia! Delia!

The Everoinye had betrayed me.

Well, their power over me might be real and awesome, never again would I do a single thing for them—never, ever. I could not think coherently. I know I must have been completely mad for those moments. Nothing on Kregen or Earth mattered now. The whole lot could be taken over by the Shanks. See if I'd care. Oh, no, as the zorca raced on along the burning street and my eyes stung and pained and my throat choked with a lump of agony, oh no—life was dead for me.

A shout reached me, a harsh, demanding, ordering kind of Kataki shout.

"Out of the way, cramph!"

As the finish of my life had sunk in and madness overtaken me I'd eased up in the saddle and the zorca, grateful for the rest, had slowed down. Now I was in someone's way.

I looked back over my shoulder.

Perhaps only Opaz alone knows my feelings then.

I have—metaphorically—climbed back out of the grave. I have served my time in the Black Marble Quarries of Zenicce. I have slaved in the Heavenly Mines of Hamal. I have believed my Delia dead before now, and rejoiced when she was found alive. But this time, this time a wholly new sensation afflicted me—a sensation I cannot wholly describe. To be dead and then to be alive. Yes. To lose and then to win. Yes. But more—oh, yes, much more!

She rode her zorca surrounded by the seven Katakis, and they spurred on in their vile way, ready to cut me down if I did not get out of their way.

She looked—as always—gorgeous. The spots of color on her cheeks blazed her contemptuous anger for these Whiptails.

I held the Krozair brand. What had happened was now quite clear. The Star Lords' command of the Time Flow was chancy at best. They'd dumped me down in front of the Katakis instead of chasing them. To be honest—I fancied as I turned to look back that a fellow astride a zorca was actually chasing after the Whiptails. If I had seen him, almost an apparition, then that fellow would have been me.

The zorca span about and raised his head where the long straight spiral horn cut a shaft of ivory whiteness against the dark smoke.

"You are a dead man, shint!" The foremost Kataki swung his lynxter about his head in a gesture intended to intimidate.

When the Star Lords had tweaked me up to go off to rescue Mul-lu-Manting, I'd seen Delia unconscious across the saddle of a Kataki's animal. In the time stream muddle, time itself must have folded, so that Delia had regained consciousness and could stare with such defiant disdain upon the Jibrfarils.

In not at all the same way as the brawl with the Kanzai, this confrontation proceeded along its way with suppleness and speed. The first Kataki fell off his zorca with his head hanging by a few shreds of skin. Six. The next tried to spear me and he fell off his zorca with his guts hanging out. Five. The next swung a cunning and powerful axe-blow at my head and he fell off his zorca without a right arm. Four. His comrade thrust the wicked holly-leaf-shaped head of a strangdja, and he chose to be clever and aim at my own mount. He miscalculated and so he fell off his zorca with the back of his skull thrusting past his nose. Three. The next two were also clever and tried to work as a pair. One slashed with his lynxter as the other thrust with his spear. Both of them fell off their zorcas, separated from different portions of their anatomy and their inward parts disgorging themselves onto the dust of the street. One.

This was the fellow who held onto Delia's zorca and no doubt the same one who had ridden with her unconscious body draped over his saddle.

He said in that harsh guttural of your dyed-in-the-wool Whiptail: "Dom—you may take the girl—" His tail with its six inches of bladed steel waved over his head. "She is of value—dom."

Whilst it was comforting to know a damned slaving Kataki was feeling terror in his guts, peril for Delia remained. If this damned fellow caught on to the fact that Delia was important to me, he could hold her as a hostage and try to bargain.

I said: "Just let go of her bridle—dom. You may ride off."

Delia, of course, being Delia, had immediately sized up the situation. She sat and she sat silently.

The Kataki let go the bridle. He eyed me warily. Unpleasant folk, Katakis. Slavers, slavemasters and traders, they are called Jibrfarils with reason, for that more or less means lovers of pain giving. This representative of an obnoxious race of diffs sidled his zorca away, and then slapped in those cruel and unnecessary spurs. He galloped off.

Delia said: "Lahal, husband." This, above all else, revealed her emotions.

I wanted to burst out with a whole barrage of romantic declarations, of undying love, of passion, of desperate fears for her safety—all the turgid stuff of Kregan dramatic romances. Delia felt all that, and knew the right time and place.

I was facing her and she was looking at me—and past me.

"Dray, my dear, move quickly aside."

I simply did as she ordered. The Kataki's arrow from his short bow spat down onto the cobbles.

"Well, now," said my Delia. "How ungrateful can you get?"

I unlimbered the Lohvian longbow. "You can get dead."

My first shaft, as Seg Segutorio would have approved—nay, insisted—hit the mark and the Kataki threw up his arms and he fell off his zorca with the red-fletched Valkan arrow through him.

"I had noted there were seven of 'em and seven of 'em I'd marked."

"I do believe you marked them."

"I must tell you where I've been—all crazy stuff about Loh."

Her face tightened. "The Everoinye?"

"Yes."

"Will it ever end?"

"Impossible to say. I've a theory when we've finally persuaded the Shanks not to come raiding us over the curve of the world—"

"Then it will end?"

"I very much doubt it, my heart."

Then I pushed all this nonsense of the destinies of empires away. I dismounted and held my hand for Delia's foot—is there a foot of so dainty a fashion in two worlds? A foot that has marched all the livelong way through the Hostile Territories? She alighted and turned to look at me from the corners of her eyes. I felt—well, I am Dray Prescot, etc., etc.—I felt my ears go red. I started to say something—I've no idea what—and she put a pink finger to my lips.

So I put my arms about her and after a time we strolled across the Kataki-littered street to a house that had not burned properly and found a heap of straw. Later, I mentioned the straw, and laughed, and we wondered how Mul-lu-Manting and her straw covered Quoffa cart were getting along.

"And you really did suspect that Lop-eared Nath of something?"

"Assuredly. He was cut out for the part of a villain."

"Well, we have had our share of villains, my love."

"Oh, aye," I said, comfortably, stretching back on the straw so I could admire the way Delia sat up talking. "And we'll meet a whole regiment of 'em in the future. That's certain."

"Yes. This Carazaar—"

"I've been told he's evil and I tend to believe it."

170

"I was not at all sure—Deb-Lu said he was confident—but when you went off up to Carazaar's plane—well—"

I'd described my very very swift fight with the simulacra of Carazaar and she had shivered and hugged me and then laughed to reassure me. Now her true worries were being revealed.

Eventually—much later—we thought we'd better be making a move. After a great battle there are always many things to be done.

"If I know Nath na Kochwold he'll have teams of fire fighters out. We ought to save what we can of Taranjin."

In the succeeding days we saved Taranjin and saw to all the multifarious problems besetting people after war. The Shanks had gone. My friends and comrades were relieved and pleased to see me safely back on this mortal plane, and it was easy to guess many had given me up for lost. As Seg said: "Well, my old dom, they say leems have more than one life."

His wife the queen said serenely: "Only cunning old leems."

"That, Milsi," observed Inch with some acerbity, "is quite right."

I knew what they were getting at, well enough. I growled out: "What happened to the damned Fish Faces?"

Sasha, almost as tall as Inch, said: "They flew off in the ships they had left. Their sailing ships were long gone."

Delia glanced at me, and I nodded and said: "Sounds as though they'd sent their sailers back to Schan to pick up reinforcements—more vollers, more settlers. I don't like the sound of that."

"Not one little bit," said Delia.

During this period immediately following the Battle of Taranjin, religious ceremonies were held to mark the occasion. More than one noumjiksirn had to take place. A noumjiksirn is the Kregen form of a wake, a serious yet carousing way of remembering fallen comrades. And, believe me, there were names in the casualty lists I hated to see there.

Nath Javed, old Hack 'n' Slay, came to pay his respects, and stayed for a night of revelry with my lads of the Guard Corps. He did not ask to join any of the guard regiments. I did not ask him why, for I had the idea he felt if he was a freer agent he could come adventuring with us again. He praised up his Mixed Infantry Brigade and took shameless advantage of his friendship with the Emperor of Emperors to wheedle extra medals and rewards for his men. I felt any man under old Hack 'n' Slay's command would fight well and deserved his bob.

So, of course, there were endless parades in which the bobs were handed out, proudly worn, and whilst the flags waved and the bands played, shown to the recipients' family and friends.

A fine healthy spot had been chosen for the erection of the rows of hospital tents. The needlemen and puncture ladies kept at work for long hours and with their techniques could alleviate pain. They could not always save a wounded person; at least he or she died painlessly. Among the wounded were a score or so of Katakis.

I issued absolutely no instructions concerning these Whiptails, rather like Pontius Pilate, and yet was gratified to find, as I had suspected, that the doctors treated the damned slavers as just more patients. When they were fit their fate would have to be determined by the courts.

In the normal way of things I would have begun to chafe at this kind of life. Surely, what we were doing was valuable and needed to be done. All the same, usually I'd be itchy to get off back home. On this occasion I fancied I was stringing fate along and hoping to be able to settle up some more scores for the Everoinye.

At least, that was how I phrased it myself, all jumbled up in my old vosk skull of a head.

Delia spotted all that without any trouble. Well, being Delia, she would, wouldn't she? She said:

"Now, you grizzly old graint, you want another chance to have a go at this Carazaar. Come on, now, admit it!"

"Don't have to, to you. Of course, I suppose that is why we're hanging about down here in Loh instead of going where we belong, back to Esser Rarioch and Valkanium and—"

"Naturally."

"So," I said, only now realizing the enormity of what I'd been doing, my unconscious selfishness, my unthinking brutality, "we will leave for home first thing in the morning. My Val! What a selfish brute I am! Exposing you to potential danger when Esser Rarioch—it makes me shudder. Well, my heart, my eyes are open and—"

"Fambly," she said, and she stopped any further words with her lips. Now kissing Delia is an occupation fraught with peril for me—for I can go on kissing her and forget all about anything else. After some time we eventually disentangled ourselves and she said, very prim and proper with her hair in charming disarray: "So we shall just await what happens. And the nearer we are to the action the less distance we'll have to fly to reach it. Dernun, husband?"

I pulled her towards me again and before the world vanished once more I whispered: "I think we'd better ask Deb-Lu down here."

"A splendid notion—"

Towards suns set of that day we were contracted to go to dinner with Queen Kirsty and Rodders. Kuong and Mevancy would be there. Some of the guard commanders had been invited. The do would be formal. "I suppose," I said, trying to fix the high and ornate collar around the back of my neck, "we do have to wear these mazillas?"

"Oh, Dray, dear, do shut up!"

"I know, I know. This'll be Kirsty trying to show everyone how important she is. She's already starting her campaign to become Queen of Tarankar as well as Tsungfaril."

"So that's why we have to dress formally, like Vallians."

"I told Mul-lu-Manting I was a Clansman. With this blasted collar up at the back of my head it would have been profitable if I'd stayed a barbarian."

"Dray, dear, do stop whingeing."

"It's all right for you. You look marvelous! As for me, I look a right pop-injay rigged out like this."

"Nonsense. You look extraordinarily handsome and commanding. Any-one can see why you've been chosen to be the Emperor of Paz."

"No one asked me, though, did they?"

"Because you can't refuse. There is no one better fitted."

"Well, at least, you're the Empress of Empresses, the Empress of Paz."

"And no one asked me, did they?"

I said: "If you really do not want to go on with this empress and emperor nonsense, I shall pack it in." I looked at her and all I could see in all the wide world of Kregen was her face, isolated as it were from every other mundane object, serene and lovely and well—entirely useless to attempt to carry on that line of thought rationally. I finished: "I can refuse the job. A single word from you and I will refuse."

"And the Everoinye?"

The anger welled up inside me and had to be quashed, forced back and away. Yes. The Star Lords would see to it.

"I could try."

"The last time you defied them to the end you were banned to your funny little world with only one silver moon and only one yellow sun and no diffs at all, only apims."

"Twenty one Earthly years. A period I hate to recall. If only there were a way to take you with me—"

"To a miserable little world like that!"

"Oh, no. Earth is a most wonderful world."

"Well, yes," she conceded. "You have told me wonderful stories of the marvels of Earth. All the same, to leave Esser Rarioch, to abandon the Blue Mountains, never to see Delphond again!"

"Not to be contemplated."

"There's nothing else for it."

"Um," I said, a remark I considered at the time to be remarkably acute and to the point at issue. "Um."

"So you see," said the divine Delia, Delia of the Blue Mountains, Delia of Delphond, "we are doomed to our fate."

"The Empress and Emperor of Empresses and Emperors." I rolled the empty words around my mouth like bile. "Empress and Emperor of Paz. Ha! Let's hope you get some pretty frocks out of it!"

Seven

Many airboats and flying sailing ships were employed in the constant carriage of food and equipment in and wounded and people on leave out. The land of Tarankar had been sore wounded in the recent wars and would need time for Mother Nature to repair the damage. In the interim, those countries of Paz that banded together to fight the Shanks, provided each according to the country's means.

A couple of days after Kirsty and Rodder's dinner—which had passed off very well—Seg and I were inspecting a regiment of archers due to fly off on leave.

Seg's tall handsome figure moved slowly down the lines. His black hair and fey blue eyes of Erthyrdrin marked him as a Bowman of Erthyrdrin, the best of all the Bowmen of Loh. The archers stiffened under his intolerant gaze. I say intolerant because that Seg surely was when it came to matters concerning toxophily; otherwise he was often too tolerant. That had lost him a kovnate in the past. Turko, who had taken over, had sorted things out with true rigor and justice. Now Seg reached the end of the ranks, turned to me, and with that mischievous glint in his blue eyes remarked, in a voice loud enough to be heard twenty archers off: "Reasonable, I suppose, for a rabble. Leave? They're due for leave? Well now..."

You could see the lads in the ranks rolling their eyes at this and wanting to squirm and being unable for they were standing to attention.

"Who did you say was in command, majister?"

Seg took delight in thus giving me pompous titles when on parade.

The Jiktar in command had, of course, marched two paces to Seg's rear during the inspection, as was proper. When I mention customs similar to those on Earth many of them had been introduced by me. So, of course, Hyr Kov Seg Segutorio knew very well who commanded.

"Jiktar Ortyg Vondal ti Dernsmot commands here."

"And the brigade chuktar, majister?"

"Chuktar Nath Javed."

"H'm," quoth Seg, and looked down his nose, and, with the eye away from the regiment, winked at me. This was not truly pantomime. If you took it as being funny, as indeed you very well might, you could be accused of tormenting the lads. The practical approach of Seg's was always to keep the swods in the ranks on their toes.

I said: "Kov. There are three other regiments I must inspect. One of churgurs, one of spearmen and one of kreutzin." Now churgurs are your heavily armored sword and shield men and kreutzin are your unarmored or lightly armored light infantry, your voltigeurs. Seg might inspect them with me if he cared to; his overriding concern was with bowmen.

"Quidang, majister! The regiment will pass muster."

I nodded to Jiktar Ortyg Vondal. "Well done, Jik. Get the lads off on leave as soon as possible. Carry on."

"Quidang, majister." Then he turned and raised his helmet with the brave feathers flying. "Hai for the emperor! Hai!"

The regiment responded with great vigor, roaring it out, their leave passes safe. I lifted a hand in salute, touched my zorca, and with Seg at my side rode off to the rest of the brigade.

"Well, my old dom, old Hack 'n' Slay really has brought them to a fine pitch. I am impressed."

"They did well in the fight."

"Aye."

The remaining three regiments of the 43rd Mixed Infantry Brigade stood rank on rank, immaculate, drilled, and the bobs shone upon their armor. Their chuktar nudged his zorca out to meet us, saluted gravely. His bulky figure in a kax of simple iron, unadorned, his helmet with only the regulation feathers of his rank, the rest of his war harness plain and practical, spoke eloquently of the professional fighting man, a warrior to his fingertips.

He carried the usual arsenal of weapons favored by warriors of Kregen.

"Majister!" he bellowed. "The Forty Third await the honor of your inspection."

I knew why he'd waited like this; he wanted to let Seg get on with the archers first. Now he'd ride along with us and his eye would be just as intolerant as Seg's had been.

"Chuktar!" I rapped it out, military, sharp, demanding.

So we inspected old Hack 'n' Slay's brigade and, indeed, they were a formation of which to be proud. When the inspection was over, Nath Javed reined in. His face, usually the color of the setting sun Zim, flushed up even more as I congratulated him. "My thanks, majister, on behalf of my men." He did look pleased. Whilst Seg and I took delight in play-acting at titles and ranks, we knew they carried much weight. Nath Javed, known as Nath the Impenitent, had always avowed he detested nobles and emperors. Then he'd gone adventuring with Seg and me and had changed his mind with regard to some at least of the nobility. He knew our views and shared them. But like the good commander he was he was jealous of the name of his units.

"So they're all off on leave, then, Nath."

"Aye, majister. The whole brigade."

"And you?"

Seg laughed. "Need you ask?"

Nath the Impenitent licked his lips. He glanced at Seg. "Well, now, Horkandur. You read my mind." He called us Seg the Horkandur and Jak the Bogandur when formality was past.

"We missed you on our last outing."

"I bemoaned my fate, I can tell you, by Vox!"

I said: "If anything turns up, Nath, you're in."

"My thanks, Bogandur."

"Now—who's for a wet?"

We raced the zorcas off the parade ground to a refreshment area set up where the officers of the brigade could wash away the dust. For a goodly time we talked and then the ships arrived, floating down like thistledown, and it was time for the brigade to ship out home. Amid the yells of 'Remberee!' the 43rd took off.

Delia, Milsi and Sasha cantered over. All three looked stunning.

"Inch?" Seg said.

Sasha made a face, Milsi laughed, and Delia said: "We left him standing on his head trying to drink a cup of water. I do not know which one of his taboos he broke this time."

"It was not squish pie." Sasha had her own taboos and she'd often be found doing the most extraordinary contortions in expiation.

A voice called: "Lahal all."

We swung about to see a fellow with a kind happy face, cheerfully lined, walking towards us. He wore a plain robe and an enormous turban that looked on the point of toppling off. He carried a plain varnished wooden staff.

"Deb-Lu!" we all said.

This puissant Wizard of Loh was our comrade who lived with us in Vallia or Valka and who could go into lupu and transmit his image like this to talk to us and advise us. He held out his hand to me as though offering a Vallian handshake. His apparition looked quite real. Jokingly, I held out my own hand to grasp the illusion and—lo!—my fingers met firm flesh.

"Deb-Lu!" I exclaimed. "You're real!"

"By the Seven Arcades, Jak! I hope I am—the journey took longer than I expected and we have only just touched down, as you saw, and I am famished and my throat is afire."

"How wonderful!" Delia welcomed Deb-Lu-Quienyin and the others joined in as we escorted the Wizard of Loh to the refreshments.

The moment Deb-Lu had repaired the ravages of the flight, he spoke to us using Capital Letters. "A Matter we considered Light is now Highly Significant." Whenever he spoke in those clearly audible Capital Letters we knew things were afoot. "The Skantiklar."

"Oho!" I said. "So you've been finding things out."

"Not Enough, Not Enough. I know How, most of Where, but the Why remains Obscure."

"The Who," said Delia, "being Na-Si-Fantong." She shook her head, the suns' light catching those outrageous chestnut tints in her hair and making of her curls a halo. "I don't like that Si in his name."

"Brings a sour taint," said Seg. His folk of Erthyrdrin, as we all did well

176

to remember, possessed the Eye. Now Seg's fey blue eyes betrayed concern for the future, a concern I imagined must be linked to the past.

"Seg." Milsi touched his arm. "You—?"

"I expect I'm just being foolish, being an onker."

"No, Seg." Deb-Lu sounded grave. "We must all take great care in our dealings with this Fantong. He Is Trouble."

I, for one, and I know Delia for another, felt a chill of unease.

"Khe-Hi and Ling-Li now have more time to spend away from the nursery." Deb-Lu chuckled a typical old sorcerer's chuckle. "They are working and between us we'll make it all come out right. Dray! You do not need to be so despondent!"

"Trouble," I said. "Trouble follows me about like—like—"

"Like something to keep you out of mischief," said Delia briskly.

"Now, then." Deb-Lu rubbed his hands together. "Where's this young feller, Ra-Lu-Quonling, then? Wheel him out."

Seg had already sent for Rollo the Runner. Only a small and select group knew that Rollo should really be a Wizard of Walfarg but had been expelled for missing lessons, dreaming after a girl who'd let him down. What he really wanted to do was to go for a Bowman of Loh. Seg had measured him and pronounced him first class material; I was going to insist that Rollo go along the path ordained by his birthright. Deb-Lu would sort him out.

I said: "Deb-Lu, Ra-Lu-Quonling is known as Rollo the Runner and few are aware of the truth. I think it best—"

"Of course, Dray, no problem. I'll just go along and start as I mean to go on. I won't shake him up too much."

We all smiled. Rollo was in for a bit of stick from the word go. After that, as we all knew, Rollo would find himself in the hands of a kindly master of whom advantage would be taken all too frequently.

Just after that a shout attracted our attention. The shout expressed shocked incredulity. We all looked to see old Hack 'n' Slay pointing out to sea, his other hand resting on the shoulder of the sentry who'd shouted.

Just sailing into sight around the curve of the headland and taking the normal approach to the wharves of Taranjin, a convoy of ships ploughed steadily on. Those ships all had tall thin sails over their lean black hulls. Their upperworks were squared off, brutal, in stark contrast to the sleek streamlined hulls of Paz. Exclamations running the gamut of emotions broke from everyone. The majority expressed indignation, surprised contempt that after they'd been so soundly thrashed the damned reiving Shanks had the temerity to return.

"Well, now." Seg looked pleased.

I wasn't so sure. Delia gave me a quick glance and then looked away.

"What's the excitement? What have I been missing—by Ngrangi and the Mystic Axe without Taboos! I don't believe it!"

"They're real enough," grunted Nath Javed. "And my brigade not here!"

Needless to say that the chiefs of my Guard Corps were on hand. Less than one percent of the Guard had taken leave. Their lives were wrapped up with their Corps and with their emperor, their Kendur. Volodu the Lungs lifted his massive battered trumpet and looked at me. Each dent in that trumpet represented a foeman dealt with. I nodded and Volodu blew Assembly. Some of the Fifth Phalanx had gone on leave; enough remained for a sizeable force to form up. Nath na Kochwold, as ever blazing with energy, left the refreshment area at a dead run to join his brumbytes.

I turned to Vangar ti Valkanium. "Still, Vangar, despite the land forces, it's all down to you."

Vangar's scrubbed face showed dedication to duty imposed by unshakeable beliefs—beliefs in Vallia and Valka, in Opaz. "We'll be aloft in no time. I'm an Airman, Dray; it will not please me to burn ships."

"Not Shank ships?"

"To capture them would be more useful."

Seg said: "I like the idea. But the execution?"

Inch said: "Execution is the correct word for Shanks."

"It is clear," I pointed out, "that the Shanks are unaware they've lost Taranjin. These are reinforcements. No ship must be allowed to land her troops."

"So where did the beaten Shank aerial fleets go?"

Everybody looked at Delia as she spoke, and no one could give an answer to what was a mighty ponderable question.

Vangar snapped up a smart salute and within an incredibly short time his vollers and flying sailers rose from their berths. What the consternation aboard the Schtarkin ships must be like we could only surmise. When the Fish Faces began to burn and the sky filled with greasy smoke I own I, for one, felt regret at splendid ships burning. Even damned Shank ships.

Eight

Amidst all these tangled threads of peoples' lives where Fate had thrown me, what gave me great pleasure was the way Deb-Lu-Quienyin and Ra-Lu-Quonling, known as Rollo the Runner, got along. Rollo might be rebellious and headstrong; he had a head on his shoulders and was quickly aware of the essential quality of Deb-Lu. Rollo said to me: "Y'know, Drajak, you made me go back to learning to be a Wizard of Walfarg. Seg told me—I wormed it out of him—that I was good enough to be a first class Bowman of Loh. Still, I'm not sorry, now, that I'm to be a sorcerer."

"And mind you respect and take care of Deb-Lu if that should ever be necessary."

Rollo looked at me down his nose, all the old arrogance blazing forth. "D'you think I don't know that?"

"I think you do."

He nodded, and, head high, stalked off.

After the abortive attempt by the Fish Heads to land more troops our general feelings were that we could hope to see a reduction in raiding activity. Delia's question troubled us all. Where had the flying Shanks gone?

Deb-Lu set the task for Rollo, as training.

"Wherever the devils have gone," growled Inch, leaning on his axe, "some poor folk are suffering."

When I had the chance of a private word with Deb-Lu I spoke with great care. Nobody employed Wizards of Loh. They accepted you as a client—or not, if they didn't care for you. I said: "I am glad young Rollo is buckling down to the work you set for him. Please forgive me if I wonder if the task of searching for the Shanks is of importance enough—that is, Rollo always said he was not very good at going into lupu, and—"

"Jak, Jak! Finding the Shanks is enormously important, of course. And Rollo has got to sharpen up his techniques. You really are asking me why I do not try. The answer is the Skantiklar obsesses me. There lies our true danger for the future."

"But—"

"We will find the Shanks, never fear, and send a fleet." He pushed his turban straight and scratched his nose. "No. By Hlo-Hli, it's this Na-Si-Fantong. We have been busy discovering the locations of the nine rubies. Not that they are ordinary rubies, of course."

"Of course."

He perked up at my tone. "You need not feel bitter about this, Jak. The Fish Faces are, as far as we know, the greatest menace facing Paz."

"Absolutely. As far as we know?"

"Aye, Dray. There is a mystery about this Fantong and the Skantiklar that I feel—and at the moment I've no proof—I sense strongly is of the utmost importance. If Paz is undermined, who will halt the Shanks?"

"Well, Deb-Lu, I just hope that young rip Rollo unglues his wings. We need to stop the damned Shanks wherever they are."

The next few days passed uneventfully—or as uneventfully as you can ever expect on Kregen. Our lad Jaidur had flown off back to his Kingdom of Hyrklana. Delia and I had talked about his moodiness and the problems he faced at home and could see no sensible solutions.

The Hamalian fleet had also flown home; but their Fleet Admiral, Vad Harulf ham Hilzim, who was a loyal friend in Paz, had sworn he would be right back at the first news of fresh troubles.

Queen Kirsty and her consort, Rodders, remained with their mercenary army. Kirsty intended to be able to parade a show of strength when it came to choosing the next queen of Tarankar. I'd told her the job of running two countries separated by inhospitable desert would be difficult; she'd simply shrugged and said: "The whole of Loh—and beyond the seas—was ruled by the old Queens of Pain. I don't see why I cannot."

If she thought she was going to get herself the job of being the next Queen of Pain—to be Empress of Loh—she had another think coming, by Krun! Whilst Mul-lu-Manting might fancy being Empress of Loh, I had by this time come to a certain decision on that score. Well, all right, then. Contrary to my usual custom I will let you into the secret—well, not so much a secret as a desired secret course of action. If the Star Lords wanted a New Empire of Loh—or even a New Empire of Walfarg—to form, then form it would. I doubted if it would be allowed to extend overseas. With the whole of Loh to be ruled by a single person, that person would have to be very good indeed. I was not convinced it would be a good idea, either. Anyway, should it all come to pass, the person I wanted to run Loh was Mevancy. So that was the great secret. And, naturally, Mevancy didn't know.

Because Delia is Delia, Mevancy could act quite naturally in the presence of the empress. They were well on the way to becoming genuine friends. I'd told Delia of this little plan and she'd laughed and hugged me and said: "Well, you grizzly old graint, so there are a few brains in that vosk skull you call a head."

Then, on a day with dark clouds scudding over the sea, Rollo reported he'd located the Fish Faces.

The continent of Havilfar hooked a trifle west and south of Loh, the Tamish Channel, Djanduin—all memories, memories! Off the extreme south west coast of Loh lay the forbidden Island of Tambu. Beyond that, of course, were Bet-Aqsa and Ba-Domek. On the latter island was situated Aphrasöe, the Swinging City, whose Savanti had first brought me to Kregen.

Should the Shanks be foolish enough to try to land on Ba-Domek—well, perhaps they had at one time or another and what had happened to them had kept them quiet, for a long time. Rollo said they'd gone to Tambu, had picked up reinforcements sent out after those we had destroyed, and were setting up a powerful base.

Our reactions were predictable. We sent scouting forces who reported the truth of Rollo's discoveries. We called on the countries of Paz loyal to the scheme of Pazzian resistance to the Fish Heads for their contributions, in men—and women—in ships and weapons, food and gold. This would all take time.

"Now," said Deb-Lu, scratching his nose. "Now we have what we are doing with the Fish Faces sorted out, we can get on with the Skantiklar."

That there could be anything more important than the Shanks came to me with a profound shock. Carazaar, Deb-Lu believed, was quiescent after his late defeat.

"I'll tell you something that ought to amuse you, Dray."

"Yes?"

"There are nine gems. We know Fantong has the one he stole in Kothmir. There is one in Makilorn, among Kirsty's jewels. And there is one in the ceremonial regalia of Vallia. What d'you think of that?"

"By Vox! How charming."

"And so we must have worn it, many times, all unknowingly." Delia tinkled a laugh. "How quaint."

"So that leaves six," said Deb-Lu.

"Well, the rumors were that Fantong was going to Murn-Chem or Notesov. Damned jungles."

"Yes, Dray—" and Delia fixed me with a gimlet eye "—and if you think you are running off again on your own—think again, sunshine."

"You will recall, will you not, that I fell in the water?"

"Oh, you'll find any excuse!" And we both burst out laughing.

"All the same," put in Seg. "The gems in Makilorn and Vallia are vulnerable to a clever thief with some magic."

"I have placed a caul of protection about the jewel in Vallia." Deb-Lu did not sound testy so much as impatient. "Makilorn is being attended to by Khe-Hi." He made a quick gesture. "It may be I shall have to go across there myself. Inconvenient."

"What of the other six?" said Inch.

"Once I fix a lead on Fantong he should lead us to the gems."

"He is a very clever and slippery customer, Deb-Lu." I frowned. "You caught a glimpse of him on some steps I remember."

"Oh, yes. As I said then, a Capital Adversary."

What I expected happened with expected rapidity. Nath Javed, old Hack 'n' Slay, face a brilliant scarlet, said: "The expedition against the Fish Heads in Tambu is being formed. My brigade, the Forty Third, will be coming back off leave and joining in. Now, Bogandur, what of—?"

"The decision must be yours, Nath."

"You would release me from command of the brigade if I so chose?"

"I would."

"Then I will delay my decision until you are ready to set off. In the meantime I will make sure that Jiktar Volans is an even better brigade commander than I am."

"I wouldn't tell him too much, Nath. We might not go."

He gave me that big bold confident look. "Don't you worry about that, Jak. We're going. I can smell it!"

I tended to think he was right.

Another Nath—Nath na Kochwold—was an altogether more difficult headache. He was the Kapt of the whole of Vallia's Phalanx Force and was down here in Loh with the Fifth to—as he put it—go off on a spot of adventuring. Now the Tambu affair had come up, could he bear to leave his beloved Phalanx, the brumbytes all aligned in their files driving on with pikes leveled, could he bring himself to abandon them?

When Deb-Lu, on a morning of bright suns shine and a brisk little breeze, came in to tell me he had located Fantong, only then was I brought up face to face with the problem confronting me.

With the Fish Faces busily establishing a powerful base on an island of Paz, how could I possibly contemplate any other course of action save taking the expedition over there and sorting out the Shanks?

This was the personal problem I'd overlooked. Now it rose up and gave me an almighty thwacking. "Deb-Lu! I can't go off chasing after mysterious red gems, and mysterious sorcerers! I've got the Shanks to fight!"

"Your forces will fight well enough without you. You are not indispensable—"

"I never claimed to be—"

"But you are in other circumstances. You have to go yourself."

"Now look here, Deb-Lu! Is this damned Skantiklar really all this important? I mean—"

"By the Seven Arcades, Dray! You know the power that he will gain when he can unite all nine gems. You know what his middle name is. Doesn't that give you a clue to what he's up to?"

I sagged back. "Oh, no. No, no, he couldn't do that."

"But he could."

"You say you've located him?"

"Yes."

"I'll gather the lads, the ones we need. We'll start off before the hour of mid. There is no time to lose."

Nine

Of course, it was not as simple as that.

I should have known. I, Dray Prescot, Lord of Strombor and Krozair of Zy, had had experience before of organizing expeditions.

Everyone wanted to go along and let someone else go and bash the Shanks. The time we'd had this trouble when I'd needed to go down to Hyrklana to see about Naghan the Gnat, and Tilly, and Oby, the solution had been taken out of my hands. This time, too, was different because I shamelessly worked on the lads' loyalty. "Paz!" I declaimed. "There lies our duty. Where I must go is sorcerer's work—all for the good of Paz—and your duty is to go and blatter Fish Faces."

"But—Kendur!"

In the end we agreed that I ought to accept the First Emperor's Sword Watch, the First Emperor's Yellow Jackets, and—because Delia was going along—the Empress's Devoted Life Guard. Nath Karidge, the Beau Sabreur who commanded EDLG, commented acidly that it was about time he got to join in with an adventure. In addition, small parties of the other regiments, selected by lot, were to accompany us. I heard of enormous sums being promised to buy a lucky person's place in the expedition. There were few takers.

All the same, we were venturing up into Chem, among those blasted jungles again, and a useful fighting force might well be vital. We had no idea of what we would be facing.

Rollo told me: "Drajak! If I am not allowed to go with San Quienyin then I shall cast a most awful hex upon you."

I said: "It lies with Deb-Lu whether or not you go."

"I'll fix it with the san," he said, and if he'd had a beard he'd have been muttering in it.

San Deb-Lu-Quienyin's heart was too soft to deny his apprentice.

Mevancy came to see me, very flushed of face, not beautiful to outward seeming, all her fire and spirit from within. "Cabbage! You will take us, will you not? Kuong and Llodi? They sent me to speak for them as you are so aloof in these days."

"By the diseased liver and lights of Makki Grodno! I know I'm damned well aloof—it's all the damned work I have to do. Of course you can come along, pigeon, and my warmest welcome to Kuong and Llodi. By Chusto, pigeon, are we or are we not comrades?"

"Aye, cabbage. And you and I are kregoinye for the Everoinye."

"Well, I've just done a job for them up in Walfarg, as you know." I'd told her all about it as a fellow kregoinye. "If they want us again, we'll soon know."

"The situation remains as is, then. You are the emperor; but I am the senior kregoinye and I run our affairs for the Star Lords."

"You run the ship, pigeon."

What the hell—I wasn't going to disabuse her of her notions.

In the end we got everything sorted out, and, by Krun, it wasn't finished by the hour of mid. Oh, no, by the time all the argy-bargying had been completed and the dust had settled down, we were well into the hour of mid on the following day. Nath na Kochwold, faced with going adventuring with us or going into a battle against the Fish Faces with his Phalanx, just dithered.

When, sweating, annoyed with himself, almost shamefaced, he came in and said: "Well, Dray, I've made up my mind. I cannot abandon my Phalanx," I felt relief. He would be a splendid companion on an adventure; he would be far more valuable running the battles ahead. I held out my hand.

"We've been through a lot together, Nath. You will turf those Fish Heads out of Tambu neck and crop."

"Aye. We have and I will!"

One last soul came to see me with reference to going on the adventure—Ian Vandrop, his goatee neatly trimmed, his spare, athletic figure dressed now in the yellow of EYJ, still with the pakzhan at his throat.

"Since my regiment was disbanded after the Time of Troubles, jis, I've been seconded here and there and have accomplished nothing of consequence."

"Your value is undisputed. You are now an ord-Jiktar—"

"Without a proper command. You told me my grandfather was once kind to you, and you have been kind to me. Jis, I ask you, may I go on this expedition with you?"

Well, how in a Herrelldrin Hell could I refuse?

Jiktar Ian Vandrop departed, beaming.

The handsome black face and powerful figure of Balass the Hawk showed up as Vandrop departed. He was doing some arithmetic on his fingers.

"Now look here, Dray! That gaggle of—of—well, that bunch you foisted off on me. They're all assuming they're coming along."

"They're all right, Balass—"

"Of course they're all right. Am I to remain their nursemaid?"

"You're so damned good at it."

"Very well, then. And if I catch that Fan-Si without her armor again, I'll—well, I'll do something, by Kaidun!"

So the party for the expedition formed.

When the little squadron took off and sailed up into the streaming mingled radiance of the Suns of Scorpio I still couldn't believe what I was doing. Was I really flying off on some hare-brained scheme to snatch a gem before some damned sorcerer could get his grubby little paws on it, instead of leading a powerful force to smash the Opaz-forsaken Shanks into oblivion? What in a Herrelldrin Hell did I think I was up to?

So then, of course, Delia walked up with her superb swing and said: "Now, then, Dray. Brassud! Pay attention to what Deb-Lu tells us."

"It's all so—so—"

"Yes. And will be more so if you don't perk your ideas up."

"Deb-Lu did say how important all this is—so, obviously, it is."

"As dear old Hack 'n' Slay would say: 'Indisputably.'"

"Indisputably."

184

So, as I often remark, my Delia can see through me as easily as glass.

Na-Si-Fantong's whereabouts, he had no doubt considered, had been cunningly camouflaged by misdirecting rumors. Murn-Chem and Notesov lay far enough apart, by Krun. A line drawn between the two, originating at the centers of the two respective countries offered a beginning. Deb-Lu narrowed down the area and with Khe-Hi and Ling-Li assisting, at last defined the location. All the maps showed was jungle. Damned jungle!

"It'll be hot work," observed Inch. "Also, by Ngrangi, there will be far too many opportunities for me to break a taboo or three."

"By the Veiled Froyvil, you broomstick—I believe you enjoy busting a taboo for the sake of standing on your head or whatever—"

"Seg!" exclaimed Milsi, trying to stop from laughing.

Sasha inclined her head. "He may be my husband, and I may have my own taboos—Inch is Inch and maybe Seg has the right of it."

"There you go!" said Seg, cheerfully, as though he'd just won a thousand talens.

All this time the squadron sailed on through the limpid air. Trust my blade comrades not to take a little trip like this too seriously. When we got down to handstrokes they'd operate with swift and lethal efficiency; until then, why, dom, the world is wide, the suns are shining and the breeze is sweet on your face.

Now, if Seg was the Inspector General of Archers, then Balass was the Inspector General of churgurs, the heavily-armored sword and shield men. Both had a tremendous regard for the swods in the ranks, the ordinary soldier on whose shoulders the whole military edifice rested. This by way of explanation for what happened to the scouts. All the kreutzin volunteered, as was to be expected, and a party of a dozen selected, led by Hikdar Ronal the Waspish, went off to check under the trees.

They did not return.

"Deb-Lu?"

He pulled his ear where his turban had slipped. "Very strange. I can—ah—detect nothing apart from residual magic. Odd."

Jiktar Thana ti Vincentsmot spoke up. "Another party will have to go down and find out. I shall lead it personally."

Again, how strange this was. In the old days there'd have been no nonsense of sending in scouts first. I'd have been first, as always.

The second party did not return.

"This is becoming unpleasant." Seg sounded grim.

"Aye," I said. "We'll have to take a look."

Deb-Lu shoved his turban straight. His plain varnished wooden staff glistened in the light of the suns. "Take Rollo with you."

Rollo pushed forward in the group on the deck. "You don't have to tell me. I'm volunteering."

At that the usual uproar of voices of folk all desperately anxious to venture down to what could easily be a nasty death caused a babble of volunteering. In the end we had it sorted out. I said: "Deb-Lu, give us two burs after we dip under the trees. Then you must do what you think best."

In efficiently run navies captains and admirals do not go running off in landing parties every time they make landfall on an unknown coast. If they did so, promotion would be swift for those left alive. But, here you see my cunning. I was not the captain, Oby was the skipper. I refused to allow the girls to go with us.

"If you think, Dray Prescot, I'm letting you go gallivanting off—"

"We're only going to look under the trees."

"Then there's nothing stopping me going along."

"Or me," said Sasha and Milsi together.

Seg said: "It's no good, my old dom. You can't win this one."

"They'll only get into some other mischief if they stay," said Inch.

Short of not going myself, I was stuck. We climbed into a small voller, observing the fantamyrrh, and Delia took the controls. Down we swooped, leaving the squadron hovering in the bright air, down and through a tiny gap between the treetops.

I expected the heat and gloom of other rain forests. We looked down and below us a great city spread out in granite walls and towers and battlements. Trees grew everywhere, spaced out, soaring up to spread their branches to form the canopy above. The effect was at once eerie and superb.

No one said anything for a space as Delia swung the voller in circles. I sniffed. There was very little scent on the humid air and that was odd. Then Seg said: "They can't like suns light."

"They're all probably anemic." Inch did not look up from staring over the side. "Look! There are people."

Following his pointing finger I made out a shadowed avenue with a considerable crowd of people. Just what they were doing I couldn't guess. They did not move and were extremely quiet. No one looked up at us. At the end of the avenue a platz opened up and this was crowded with people. Everybody was quite obviously standing still and listening to what the nobs on the platform had to say. This was a grand occasion of some sort.

The quietness over everything remained impressive.

I'd never experienced crowds who could stand so still and quietly before. Other avenues opened from the central kyro and these held a few people. The folk here were dotted along the avenue and you'd swear they were hurrying along to the square. So why didn't they get along? Why did they halt half way? Their clothes were bright enough, swathing robes for some, breechclouts and bare chests for others.

Delia said, very sharply: "The vollers!"

Sure enough, the two vollers which had taken down the scouting parties were landed on the flat roof of a sizeable building. From there they could lift off easily. They appeared undamaged. And—the crews were still aboard, peering over the sides, just as we were.

"The first one landed," said Seg. "And the second landed to see what happened to the first," went on Inch. And Delia finished: "So we land to make number three."

Rollo said: "It is clear, now. Some kind of enchantment has been cast upon this city. Everyone is in a state of paralysis. Animation is suspended. If we go lower we will be caught—"

Before he could finish a bolt of fire lanced up from a tower below. The blazing mass missed the voller by a whisker. The noise and the heat as it flashed past stunned us.

"Up, Delia, up!"

Another lance of fire, spitting and hissing—the voller started to rise—a third and the airboat rocked like a cockleshell in a gale—we were whirling over and over and the whole world filled with fire. We began to fall.

Ten

We were falling straight down, tumbling out of the air. Below us lay some damned magic which would entrap us and paralyze us. The airboat lurched as another fireball hissed past in a confusion of fire and spitting sparks.

At the controls Delia remained firmly in command. She is a brilliant pilot and she used her skill to right the voller and bring her up in a long soaring slant that was not a direct line. Only four more bolts of fire were let off, and then the shooter must have given up, recognizing that the pilot was better than he was.

Up and up we lifted. The humid air tasted sweet then, by Krun!

Up between the leaves Delia took us and then—out in the radiance of the Suns we soared with the breeze in our faces.

Milsi said: "Oh, Delia—!"

Sasha started to say: "Flying skill—" and didn't finish.

Inch said: "That rast down there couldn't hit Delia; but he needs us to go down and sort him out."

Seg just leaned forward and gave Delia a little kiss on the cheek.

My Val! What it is to know my Delia!

Rollo said: "Deb-Lu will sort this out." Then, probably because he was the youngest and brashest aboard, he said what really had been eloquently said already. "You fly a mean voller, majestrix."

Delia, without the slightest sign of a smile touching her lips, said: "Why, thank you, Rollo."

He didn't get it. We others did, though, knowing Delia was sending young Rollo up in the nicest possible way. Every now and then his habitual arrogance would break out. Anyway, he fancied himself as a voller pilot.

Back aboard, plans were made to deal with this unforeseen situation.

"Everyone is absolutely motionless, like statues," said Rollo.

"Yes, yes." Deb-Lu nodded. "There are many ways to achieve that."

"And the fireballs—"

"Nasty, brutish, ignorant—yet unfortunately effective."

I'd seen Deb-Lu and Khe-Hi hurling fireballs against a certain sorcerer and his accomplice to form that awe-inspiring if horrific Quern of Gramarye between them. Oh, yes, I didn't want anything to do with bolts of fire chucked at my head.

Delia, crisply, said: "If everyone down there is turned to stone, who is hurling firebolts?"

Rollo coughed, and said: "They only started when we began to lift up. The other two vollers went on down and weren't shot at. Could the firebolts be shot off without a living person to trigger them?"

"That would present little problem," commented Deb-Lu.

"Or," I said, "that could be Fantong down there already and he's got some protection against the freezing spell."

"Quite possible."

"Let's go down there heavy-handed and blatter him." That was Inch.

"You can cancel the spell?" Seg turned to the Wizard of Loh.

"I shall need to know what kind it is first. I said I was aware only of residual magic below the trees. Whoever placed this glamour must have been careless. It will be most interesting to find out."

"The power it must have taken," said Rollo. "Surely that must show up?"

"And for how long it's been going on for."

"Let us," I said, "get on with it."

Something of the old intemperate Dray Prescot must have echoed in my words. At any rate, the plans were immediately finalized and the whole squadron dropped carefully down between the leaves.

The scene looked exactly as it had before. How long, I wondered, had this city been doomed to motionless timelessness?

The ships spread out. A firebolt lashed up when it was clear the ships were not intending to drop lower. Each pilot had been given the most explicit instructions. They were to keep on moving and weaving and on no account were they to allow their ships to be hit.

Deb-Lu-Quienyin, as always in these situations, lost all his friendly comicalness. He became remote, awe-inspiring, a sorcerer practicing his arcane arts. He held up his hands, an extravagant gesture for him. He looked with a long down-drawn stare upon the tower from which the fire-bolts spat. I knew what we were in for.

The moment Deb-Lu drew upon his kharrna and instigated his protection the spinning succession of firebolts spat up at us. All the other ships would be safe now. Now, we alone could be fried and crisped like best vosk rashers.

Halfway between the tower and our ship a dish of light grew. It spun in a multitude of colors, spitting sparks. And it grew. This was the Quern of Gramarye. Deb-Lu and the mage below were putting forth their powers. At first the spinning light moved towards us. Deb-Lu exerted more power, his face calm, composed, without a trickle of sweat. The Quern of Gramarye moved back through the air, approached the tower.

As the plasma of thaumaturgy overflowed so it shot off sparks and flames and heat from the disc of light. Nearer and nearer the tower it crept. With the remorseless logic of his profession, Deb-Lu knew what must be done.

Coruscating with light, shooting off great discharges of molten matter, spinning like a crazy Catherine Wheel, the Quern of Gramarye smashed back. The tower was engulfed in flame. Chunks of masonry broke off and flew through the air like crumbs from a snapped bread roll. Destruction shattered the top of the tower. Stone slagged and dripped like treacle.

No more bolts of fire lanced from that tower.

We were all impressed. Of us all, I suppose Rollo understood most. He said, in a low voice: "There is much to learn."

"Aye, my boy," Deb-Lu-Quienyin told him, perfectly composed after his demonstration of sorcerous power. "There always is."

"Now," said Delia. "We can deal with the rest of it."

"Ask Oby to bring the ship directly over that crowd of people on the platform in the central kyro." Deb-Lu was brisk. "And make sure we don't drop down."

We all trooped off to the lower galleries as Oby brought the voller in over the platz. A ceremony was being performed down there—rather, a ceremony had been in process of being performed when everyone became frozen. Customs vary wildly all over Kregen, of course. But it took little nous to see this was a wedding. The man in splendid robes, the woman in even more sumptuous robes, her face veiled, stood side by side, holding hands. The priest marrying them looked a wily old devil, lined with seasons of power. Either side of the pair stood their relations and all were dressed up with gold and jewels, in swathing robes of fine silks. Represented there were money, power and prestige.

Deb-Lu said: "There. That's the culprit."

Among all that glittering show the fellow standing on the next lower platform looked out of place. Where everyone wore grand robes for this important wedding, his clothes were a simple blue and silver breechclout and a light short cape of pale blue. He wore no weapons where the others, men and women both, were festooned with armaments in the Kregan way.

Open across his palms lay a book. He was in the act of reading from its pages. The book—it was obviously a hyr lif—was bound in skin of a pale sallow yellow, banded with gold bars and chained to his waist belt by a golden chain. Downturned, his face was difficult to see.

"Another of those idiots of Almuensis," observed Rollo.

"Not altogether idiots, they do have real powers." Deb-Lu's voice carried a mild note of reproval.

"They must do." Delia spoke decisively. "If that's the fellow who's done all this."

"A Sorcerer of the Cult of Almuensis. Yes. But Rollo is right in one thing." Deb-Lu's wheezy voice brightened at the joke. "He, I expect, had been bribed to stop the wedding by someone who wanted to marry one or other of the parties involved. So he cast something like "To hold and detain," or perhaps "To render immoveable." He worked it all right. The only trouble was—patently obvious, by Hlo-Hli!"

Well, yes, we could all see that.

"I doubt if he's the fellow who set up the fireballs, then," I said. "At the moment the fireballs remain a mystery. Once we can remove this enchantment from the city we might take a look at the remains of the tower."

"That leaves us little option." Deb-Lu sounded quite pleased. He always welcomed a challenge in the ethereal planes of higher thaumaturgy. "I shall try the most simple and obvious way first." He started in giving orders and the crew sprang to do his bidding. When a Wizard of Loh asks you to do something, you bratch, you jump very quickly!

Deb-Lu's simple idea saw Oby coaxing the ship gently forward, guided by Rollo at the beginning of a chain of crewmen all passing along directions. Inch held the rope, having bagged the job before anyone else. The rest of us looked on and offered comments. Rollo, perched right forward, called out "left a bit" and "right a bit" until he had us lined up. Inch dangled the rope with its knotted-on wicker basket, trying to keep it steady.

Keeping the unease I felt out of my voice, I said: "If we bring the book aboard, won't that—?"

"No danger of that." Deb-Lu squinted his eyes down past Inch. The wicker basket was irritatingly spinning. Inch tried to steady it. "The effect has occurred. The Almuensis Culter made a mistake, that's all." Deb-Lu sounded much more cheerful. "A not uncommon happening."

"Got it!" called Inch. His lanky form bent and then straightened. The book lay snugged in the basket. Inch hauled in with a will.

Nobody offered to rush forward and lift up the book when Inch swung the basket over the rail onto the deck.

Down below us the city continued to show no life or movement.

"Most Interesting," observed our own Wizard of Loh. "A few jolly evenings of reading ahead. Excellent!"

Rollo came charging along the narrow gallery from the bows and scooped the book up. He did not close it but left it open at the page and handed it across to Deb-Lu. We all saw the sudden graciousness with which he passed the book over. Both sorcerers, the experienced mage and the apprentice, recognized the power in those pages. I looked at the paper; it was a high quality vellum, and not paper from Aphrasöe.

There was a good chance the binding was made from a virgin's skin.

I said: "How did you break the chain?"

The golden end dangled and looked half-melted.

Rollo looked across swiftly, and his teeth flashed.

Deb-Lu's wheezy voice was as modest as ever. "Not too difficult. The chain held no extra applied kharrna."

The more you witnessed what Wizards of Loh could do without mumbo-jumbo, the more they impressed you.

"I'll just give a little study..." Deb-Lu's voice trailed off. He began to read.

Quietly, Rollo said: "There are two sorts of kharrna—at least, two to my current knowledge. There may be more, and study will reveal them when the san considers I am ready. One is passive, the other active. Passive kharrna exists in all the objects of nature. Active kharrna is that within and controlled by a wizard. This comes only from study." He took a meaningful breath. "Hard study, by Hlo-Hli!"

I smiled inwardly at this. Deb-Lu really was taming this tearaway to good use.

Seg said: "I'm for a wet. Anybody?"

This was a highly sensible suggestion.

Emder and Tim Timutorio brought up the sazz and parclear. As we all wet our throstles Deb-Lu looked up. He nodded in satisfaction and Rollo, who was watching carefully, caught the toppling turban.

"Kharrna." Deb-Lu's eyebrows drew down. "There is a division of active kharrna, applied kharrna, as you very well know, Rollo. Also you are aware that it is not customary for an adept to discuss his art outside."

Rollo did not look so much put down or disciplined as uncomfortable.

"Now," said Deb-Lu briskly. "When you wish to undo something it is always useful to know how it was done. The mistake was not easy to make; this fellow down there made it. I can redo and then undo."

"Hold on a moment, Deb-Lu." I rubbed my chin. "Now this fellow froze himself along with the rest of the city. We are hoping Fantong will lead us where we want to go. Wouldn't it be useful if we could walk about down there and everyone else remained frozen?"

"Now I know exactly how it was done I can reverse the—well, never mind that." Deb-Lu pondered, the book open on the table before him. Rollo stood to one side, looking at the book. Presently, Deb-Lu lifted his head. "All right. By a combination I can do that."

"Excellent!"

Rollo said: "But there will be an area around—"

"Oh, quite," confirmed Deb-Lu. "If you approach near a frozen person the applied kharrna you're carrying will interact and wake them up."

"We'll just have to steer clear of any ugly customers, then."

Delia, who has a sharp eye when it comes to matters of cleanliness and always keeps our residences spotless said: "There's no dust down there. If they've been like that for some time you'd expect dust everywhere."

"And the rain," pointed out Milsi, whose realm lay along the forested River of Bloody Jaws.

"The answer is," said Rollo, "that the aura prevents rain and dust falling." He threw a quick glance at his master to see if Deb-Lu wished to amplify, and then went on: "The air is inanimate down there."

"Then how do we breathe?" demanded Seg.

"By the same means you will wake up a frozen person. You will also reanimate the air about you as you go."

"Nice to be a bit lofty, then," observed Inch.

"Except," said Sasha, giving her husband a look, "when you get your ears frostbitten."

This old chestnut produced the expected smiles. Mind you, I am making all this sound as though we did not have a care in the world. The truth, obviously, was that we were embroiled with magic of a very high order.

Every step could lead to disaster. There were grim days ahead.

"How long, san, d'you think these folk have been like it?" Hack 'n' Slay looked meanly over the side. He and Seg and I had gone up against magic before, and we didn't relish all the memories.

"A good few seasons, I'd judge. But I can't tell exactly."

"We'd best get on with it," I said, rousing myself. "Let's go and get our scouts and their vollers back."

This was accomplished. The scouts were uninjured, for the airboats had made gentle landings, and the kreutzin were astounded at the rapidity with which we'd joined them. They gaped when they were told.

After that we landed in a deserted avenue well away from the main platz. Exploration parties were detailed off with instructions not to go near enough to any living souls to awaken them. From our experiences with our scouts we were a trifle perturbed to discover that the distance varied and did not seem predictable. Deb-Lu commented that it was probably down to the person's own possession of kharrna. It appeared that everyone had one form of kharrna, at least. I got the impression, a fleeting one only, that

Deb-Lu's slight hesitation as he spoke might indicate that there were other forms of thaumaturgical energy besides kharrna.

As they say—so rightly—in Clishdrin, "Anything can happen on Kregen and it probably will."

An imposing domed building looked promising. I found myself walking up a sloping ramp with my comrades towards half-open bronze doors. Whether or not magic was abroad on the air, that air still carried the scents of the rain forest, and I guessed we brought them with us. Weird, the sorcerer's game, and not to be trifled with, by Krun!

We went in cautiously. There were no lights or windows and the interior looked gloomy and not at all inviting.

"By the Veiled Froyvil, this is a miserable dump!"

"Light up the torches," commanded Delia.

The lights showed us a considerable area and that consisted of curved walls of dull stone and ranked statues of all manner of diffs in armor.

"A mausoleum?" Milsi sounded doubtful.

"They build them like this over in Chem of the Cataracts." Sasha spoke with authority. "They burn the corpses, though."

"Yeh," added Inch. "Frightened their ibs will come out at night and chase 'em."

This domed building didn't appear to hold much promise to me. I swung about and headed off for the door and the suns shine. A shout reached me as I stepped outside.

"Drajak! Here—this looks interesting."

Rollo was beckoning from a doorway farther along. I sauntered across. Other parties were foraging about in and out of doorways. For our explorations we were fortunate that almost all the citizens were congregated in the main kyro. I stepped in after Rollo, blinking. "Well?"

This was a side entrance and a few windows admitted ruby and jade streamers of light. Tall double-doors of ivory, studded in gold, stood imposingly to one side, away from the mausoleum. Above the centre of the architrave a shining golden statue glowered down on us. Its long sinuous neck thrust forward, the small head darting, as it were, at us, the jaws stuffed with needle teeth. The scaled body and tail and clawed legs were sculpted in perfect detail, and the strongly curved wings were outspread as though the xichun was about to leap into the air and descend to devour us.

"Xichun!" said Rollo, in a savage voice. "Well, we've had our fill of them, may Jallalak the Merciless be contumed!"

"He don't look a pretty sight, not with them teeth an' all," said a voice at my back.

Mevancy's voice said: "We'd better go in and take a look, anyway, cabbage."

"I suppose so, pigeon."

I pushed against one leaf and Rollo the other. The four of us stepped through into a bright blaze of light.

"Go carefully!" I snapped out very sharply.

Foolish fatuous words!

The soft sibilant hissing at our backs made us all swing about. A stone slab descended with a swift remorseless rush beyond the opened door. The two doors closed inwards, shutting with a thud followed by an ominous click.

"Caught!" I exclaimed in blazing wrath. "Trapped like a fly in a flick-flick plant!"

The floor tilted. We staggered and then slid in a tumbled heap down and down the long slope into a light of intolerable brilliance.

Eleven

My eyes were clamped shut against that brightness yet the light struck through, black spots danced among a deep and menacing redness before me. We hit bottom in a wild tangle, with Mevancy's hair in my mouth and my leg fiercely gripped by a pair of powerful fists. We rolled over and over on straw that stank like a cess pit, and eventually cracked into a stone wall.

"By Spurl!" choked out Mevancy. "What happened?"

The fists gripping my legs went away. "Jangflor alone knows, and he ain't telling, not with us down here an' all."

I spat and got rid of pleasantly scented hair and sat up. I kept my eyes shut; but I knew Rollo and Mevancy and Llodi with his enormous purple flower of a nose would be sorting themselves out. If we couldn't see where we were, how in a Herrelldrin Hell were we to see where we were going?

Rollo said: "Hold on a moment. I'll try—"

The rest of us had the sense to remain still and silent. After a short time Rollo let rip a snort and said: "All hold on, form a chain, and I hope, by Chusto, I'm going in the right direction."

I got my arm about Mevancy's waist and Llodi gripped onto me. With Rollo in the lead, we staggered up and started blindly off.

I felt the coolness drop over me and the malefic red light faded before my eyes. Gingerly, I opened one eyelid.

The light beat down with a soft pulse of ivory and pearl, very soothing after the searing blast scorching our eyes. Facing me, a wall of veined marble stretched to a low ceiling. In my ears the splashing thunder of water echoed off the walls. The air smelled musky, of the earth, and cool and refreshing after the heat of the jungles of Chem outside.

"That's better!" Rollo's voice carried satisfaction as well as relief. Whatever he'd done he'd pulled us through the inferno.

"With a trapped slope like that an' everything," observed Llodi, "you'd expect spikes at the bottom. Not straw."

"We are expected," said Mevancy in a choked voice.

I swung about.

The wall at my side, built of the same veined marble, contained three doors, all closed. Over them an inscription had been picked out in gold.

The four of us, we all stood up and looked at that invitation. Beautiful calligraphy in the flowing Kregan script, it caught our absorbed attention.

ADVENTURERS! WELCOME TO THE REALM OF THE DRUMS!
MAY YOUR WAY LIE STRAIGHT AND YOUR END IN FIRE!

Rollo said in a shocked voice, an exclamation jerked from him: "By the Seven Arcades! May Hlo-Hli smile on us now!"

Mevancy said: "You know what this means?"

"It is a legend, a myth from the old days—"

"The old days of the Empire of Loh?"

"Yes."

"Well, as we're down here an' all, you'd better tell us."

Rollo sat down, plump, onto the floor.

We all waited until he'd gathered himself together. He wet his lips. He held both hands together, fingers entwined—and I judged that was to stop his hands from shaking.

"The city," he said, at last, "the city above us. That is the City of Eternal Twilight."

"Well," observed Mevancy in a level voice. "That seems a sensible name. They live under the trees." She was, I saw with pleasure, determined to keep on a level keel in these eerie surroundings.

"The city was built over a vast underground complex, caverns and caves and chambers and corridors. Rumors passed surreptitiously and some were written down in secret documents. A treasure beyond imagination is buried here. That knowledge was passed down from Queen to Queen, from wizard to wizard. Expeditions went forth to bring back the treasure—"

"In course," said Llodi, "none of 'em came back."

"Right." Rollo stood up. He took a breath. "The whole place is protected. It was said the people of the Realm of the Drums were not of the same stock as those of the City of Eternal Twilight. There are—"

"There will be," I said, trying to be casual and yet positive at the same time. "Monsters and Magic."

195

"Monsters and Magic."

"Well, by Spurl!" growled out Mevancy. "Let us try to find a way back and tell the others."

We all looked back at the opening where that intolerable light blazed down.

"The ramp will be unclimbable." Rollo rolled his shoulders. "And I cannot guarantee to pass that awful light."

"Then we must find another way out," snapped Mevancy.

Now in all this, you will understand, one thought dominated my mind. I had no fears for Delia when she was with Seg and Inch and our comrades. We had a little army and a squadron of vollers up there. They might explore into the corridor with the tall double doors and the statue of the golden xichun and they'd never find the way in past the slab of stone that would look exactly like the rest of the corridor wall.

I mentioned that to the others, and went on: "We're on our own down here unless—Rollo, can you contact Deb-Lu?"

He shook his head. He looked not so much sullen as frustrated. "No, Drajak, no. Deb-Lu said there was only residual magic and he was right—for the city. Here there is magic of an order surpassing anything I can achieve. It is all about us."

"And presumably concealed from above."

"Yes."

"Well, there's only one thing for it. Mevancy is right. We've got to find our way out."

"Yeh," said Llodi. "I just wish I had my strangdja."

That must have been jerked out of his hand as we fell, for his had been the two fists wrapped about my legs. Otherwise, we had all our weapons. The noise of the water battered into this small room. I looked at the three closed doors. They were all painted black and looked the same.

"So that's the way of it," I said in an extremely ugly voice.

"The inscription suggests our way should lie straight." Mevancy's hands rubbed together briskly. "And our end a fiery one. Well, we don't take the middle door!"

"Right or left?"

"The noise of the water appears to be coming from the left," said Rollo.

"Let's have a look." I marched across to the left hand black door.

Now when you go adventuring into places other folk of a mean character have made as unpleasant as they can, there are certain ways of going about simple things like opening doors. I once knew a fellow who carried a large oil can with him and whenever he came to a door that opened towards him he carefully oiled the hinges. That way he could open the door silently. He was caught and devoured by some monster crab beetle going into a room whose door opened away from him.

Even at this very first door I felt back on familiar, if ugly, territory. The standard procedure was to listen and smell and be quiet and judge the opportune moment. Just how our fortunes would fare depended as much on circumstances as the way we bent those circumstances to our advantage. The black door opened silently and the pervasive pearly light showed a narrow flight of stone steps. The steps led up.

"That's a relief!" said Mevancy.

Llodi said: "I'll go first."

I said: "You'll do no such thing. Use your bowstave to prod the steps."

He no doubt thought me a trifle touchy, still he unlimbered his bow and prodded away at the steps. Even then I couldn't be sure if that pressure would simulate the weight of a foot. I needn't have bothered.

The third step up released a shower of darts that whistled high over our heads from slots. Mevancy said: "Oh!" Llodi sucked in his cheeks. Rollo mumbled something to himself.

The door at the top was shut and locked and there was no way we could open it.

"Solid marble by the look of it," said Rollo, savagely.

So we trooped down and went along to the right hand door.

This opened onto a stairway leading down to a door at its foot.

"Let us at least have a look at the middle door," Mevancy said.

Here we found the source of the noise of rushing water. The corridor led straight ahead and a spring welled up just inside the door and the water channeled along parallel to the corridor. All that appeared to be perfectly satisfactory. The oddness lay in the walls. They were formed of packed earth, well soaked by water. Long thin white lines snaked in and out of the earth. My fist gripped onto my sword hilt in instinctive reaction. The wriggling lines in the earth remained still.

"Of course," said Mevancy. "With all the granite in the city the trees must have somewhere to stretch their roots."

"The stasis spell freezing the people keeps rain off," pointed out Rollo. "The trees will gain some moisture from rain on their leaves; but this underground water must exist all over the city."

A nasty thought occurred to me then that I felt prudent not to communicate to my companions.

"Do we or do we not go straight ahead?" Mevancy wanted to know.

"If we go down an' all we'll be deeper and it'll be harder to get back up."

"The question is," said Rollo with a zephyr of his old arrogance, "do we or do we not obey the instructions in the inscription?"

"Hardly instructions, Rollo. You're suggesting the words are a challenge?" I said.

"Implicitly, yes. 'May your way lie straight.' What does that mean? Are they wishing us well, or—"

197

"They?" snapped Mevancy.

"Whoever built this damned place. Long dead now, I don't doubt, although with Wizards of Walfarg you never can tell. They had treasures to guard and they knew greedy people would try to steal the treasures. So they protected them as best they could. Dead or alive, Rollo is right, we are responding to a challenge."

"Yeh, and I don't fancy going down, not with whatever horrors an' all you've promised us down there an' everything."

"But, Llodi," said Mevancy with a hint of exasperation, "if we don't go down we'll be doing what the inscription wants."

This situation was pressing in on my comrades and for all their good humor and courage they were, like me, ordinary human beings. Nerves were being frayed. How long would it be before words grew harder and hard words changed into blows? That I had to prevent, somehow.

"Let's take a look along the corridor of the roots," I said. "If it's no good we can always come back and nip down the stairs."

Mevancy's sniff was not of the same order as the sniff of Mul-lu-Manting. "Very well, cabbage. You and Llodi go and see, then, we'll—"

"No, pigeon." I spoke gently. "We all stick together."

"That, I think," Rollo spoke judiciously, "would be wise."

So off we trooped along between the roots which grew everywhere. The water was perfectly sweet and clean and safe to drink. At the far end a door admitted us to another corridor of exactly the same character. I squinted along the wall, and then turned and squinted back the way we'd come.

"Clever. The corridor is not quite straight with the last. It goes off a fraction, but that's—"

"That's enough to confuse you altogether later on!" burst out Rollo.

"Let's go along to the next corridor—"

"All right, Llodi. But that's all."

This time the corridor ended in an intersection of six branches. The stream of water divided into five and sparkled on. Little brick-built bridges crossed the streams. I stopped.

Mevancy said it for us all. "A maze!"

"All right, by Jangflor! You win. Let's go down the steps."

Had we, I wondered, done the right thing? Perhaps the designers of these underground ways had calculated that we would not go straight on just because of their inscription. Then I ceased to fret over that one. No matter which way we went, we were heading into trouble.

The pearly light continued to pervade the air. The walls were well-constructed of cut stone. There was, down here, some dust about, but in general the passageways were as clean as though recently swept. We saw no one. That passage opened into a wide, rough-hewn cavern. A large number of small dark objects lay on the stone floor.

"Keep away from 'em," said Rollo. "If we wake them up they'll be fluttering about our ears and biting our faces."

We edged around the wall of the cavern and left the bats sleeping.

"I wonder."

"What do you wonder, Mevancy?"

"Why, the bats have to eat. They fly out over the countryside at night, in this case the rain forest. They have to have ways in and out."

"Probably small holes high in the roof." Rollo made it gentle.

I was harsh. "They find their food down here."

"Well, cabbage, it was just a thought!"

"D'you want to wake the bats up and find out an' everything?"

"I think not." Rollo was already walking on. "They'd flap about our ears and try to bite us to death."

We marched on in silence after that along a short passageway that connected into the next chamber.

Two steps from the entrance we all halted sharply; very sharply, by Krun! Standing snarling at us with whiskers bristling and black gums pulled back from yellow teeth, a vorlind looked about to spring. This particular vorlind was a big fellow, with a spotted hide of orange and black, a tail that now stood straight out like a poker, and pads and claws that could remove your head as neatly as a headsman's axe.

We whispered in that cathedral like place as though the vorlind could overhear us. "How much kharrna does he have, Rollo?"

"It is impossible to say accurately. Another two steps and—"

"Get around the spotty-lind," said Llodi in his hoarse voice, using one of the slang names for vorlinds. I wish I had my strangdja!"

Edging past the vorlind so as not to awaken him was easy enough. The danger might well come from the walls. I never do like leaning against walls in these kinds of situation. I mentioned this to the others, and we kept as much room as possible between the rock and our shoulders.

Nothing else of interest met our gazes in that cavern so we pressed on to the next. Rollo said he was trying to keep a map in his head. Llodi said he'd have a go, too—an' everything.

This cavern stretched away and the pearly light being much reduced here meant we could not see the far end. Those shadows up there looked damned ominous. Cautiously moving forward we followed the center line. The fellow up ahead must have been doing that, just as we were. Little good it had done him. He lay in the path with his head crushed in.

"By Hlo-Hli, we won't wake him up!"

"Thassa spotty-lind done that."

"Aye."

"But," pointed out Mevancy, "the vorlind isn't frozen here. So—"

"Just where the shadows cluster thickly, I think," I said.

We advanced with great care to see the tableau revealed through the gloom as we drew closer. A man very much like the poor fellow back in the path was marching on. Like his fellow he wore only a breechclout of a mustardy color. He carried a wicker basket on each end of a yoke over his shoulders. Just in front of him marched a guard, a Rapa whose feathers thrust stiffly and whose vulturine beak curved cruelly. He was armored in banded iron and carried swords and a whip. His kind I had met very very early in my acquaintance with the peoples of Kregen. Another slave marched on ahead of the Rapa and other figures were dimly discernable further on.

To one side and only just visible in the shadows crouched the motionless form of a vorlind, tail outthrust, red eyes glaring upon the men.

"What a picture!" Mevancy was saying. "Fascinating!" Rollo sucked in his cheeks. Llodi didn't say a word, nor did I. We both heard the coughing snarl from the shadows beside us.

We swiveled about.

From the gloom the ferocious form all teeth and claws leaped full on us.

Twelve

Llodi dived one way clutching Rollo and I dived the other clutching Mevancy. Both of us clambered to our feet. The vorlind was standing with his massive head swinging left and right. His muscles must have betrayed him after the stasis and his leap failed. His red eyes glared on me and then on Llodi and then his head swung back to me.

"By Spurl!" spat out Mevancy, sitting up. She held out her arm.

"No, pigeon," I said, quickly, jerkily, watching the vorlind and Mevancy from the corner of my eye. "Save 'em. Later."

Llodi was preparing to rush in with me, catch the beast from two sides. I supposed that was what we'd have to do. I hate this kind of thing, where a noble beast is only acting to his nature. Mind you, if his nature is to take my head off, then noble or not, he has to be stopped.

"Stop, Llodi! I'll shaft the poor thing."

My sword snicked back into the scabbard and the Lohvian longbow came off my shoulder. All this took very little time. Had that spotty-lind not suddenly been woken up from stasis he'd have been chomping by now. I fitted nock to string, drew and loosed and the arrow went splunk! into the vorlind just abaft his neck. The vorlind, unlike the leem, has only one heart. He only has six legs, unlike the leem. This fellow just keeled over.

Rollo lowered his bow where he stood alongside Llodi. "No need for me, then."

The lad had been quick, then, recovering and getting his bow ready. As Seg would have done, I took out my knife and retrieved my shaft.

"The problem is," Rollo was saying. "Who and what are they?"

"Friendly or hostile," amplified Mevancy.

"If we wake 'em up we'll have more people to help an' all."

"A shrewd point, Llodi."

I said: "We'll have to nobble that vorlind first."

There was a certain sharp brittleness in our conversation. We'd just been through an experience that would affect us. Right now we had to come to terms with our emotions. Mind you, Llodi, a tough bird if ever there was one, whose profession was as a caravan guard, had seen worse sights than a poor dead hunting cat. Mevancy had been through the mill. She was employed by the Star Lords and they do not use weaklings. As for Rollo, young as he was he had seen certain sights in my company already. No, all in all, I felt that our group would retain cohesion and reason.

Regarding the vorlind, Llodi grunted: "Shaft the beast."

"A regrettable necessity," remarked Rollo, who had quickly picked up my scruples and foibles.

"Only if we wake 'em up."

"As to that, pigeon, could we walk off and leave that tableau? It's weird enough as it is. But when they unfreeze another poor damned slave is going to have his head taken off."

Llodi lifted his bow and let fly. He might be employed as a strangdjim, he remained a Bowman of Loh. I judged the beast would not wake up.

"Before we unfreeze 'em," I said, "let us scout along their line and see what manner of folk they are. We'll have to watch out for—"

"Everything, cabbage!" cut in Mevancy.

"Too right, pigeon. I was, though, talking of vorlinds."

"Them and the rest of the nasties an' everything."

What I refrained from telling my companions was that although the evil institution was accepted as an everyday part of normal life down here in Loh, slavery was abhorrent to me. I'd been slave enough times, and had been mercilessly whipped by just such dominating Rapa guards. Oh, yes, by Zair! And slavery had been taboo to me whilst still on Earth.

So whoever was leading this frozen party had better measure up!

When we reached the head of the column, of course and as you would expect—how to judge the quality of a man from outward seeming? Much is revealed, of course. More is hidden. This fellow wore a black jutting beard, his face was brown and seamed, he wore expensive and fancy clothes and was girded with swords. His costume had once been white with much gold; now it was grimed and torn. Just abaft him stood a massive Brokelsh, all bristling body hair and pugnacity, carrying armor. To his side another Brokelsh carried the lord's other weapons. The lord himself carried a bow. The lead group were followed by half a dozen guards of various races, then a string of slaves carrying bundles and wicker baskets, more guards, more slaves, until the end was reached where we'd first encountered them. I fancied the slave at the tail end had a bad leg and was hobbling to keep up. In all there were some twenty guards and fifty slaves. I could not see a single female in the party.

"No spotty-linds within range, Drajak."

"Right. Now, are we all agreed to wake 'em up?"

Mevancy, being a woman and therefore a trifle of a schemer in these affairs, said: "I'd like to scout ahead for a way. If there are more vorlinds up there, we could warn these people." She arched her eyebrows at us. "They ought to be grateful, by Spurl, then, surely!"

"Capital!" exclaimed Rollo. "I'll go."

"We'll all go," I said in what I realized was a menacing voice.

We found six more up the pathway and dispatched them all. We had been talking a whole lot lately. All four of us had waxed positively loquacious. This had to be caused by our uncanny surroundings.

"All set? Right. Let's walk in."

Seeing that column of men come to life was amazing enough. They walked on in the first instance as though nothing had happened. Their knees moved up and down and their legs swung forward. But something had happened. Muscles had grown stiff, even though the spell mitigated the full effects. Some stumbled, some fell, all cried out in terror and despair.

Those cries told me something of their recent history.

The two Brokelsh dropped their burdens and sprang—clumsily—to the assistance of their lord. "Lynxor!" The Lohvian word for lord rang in the cavern and I tried to detect meaning. Did they really care for their master? They looked as though they meant business, for they caught him before he fell and supported him. I suppose they were fussing over him. This cheered me up in one direction and made me doubt in another. Obviously.

We four stepped forward and we all had a shaft nocked and the string half drawn.

"Llahal, doms!" I shouted in a firm, demanding voice. "Llahal!"

The reactions should not have astonished us. But they did.

A shrieking wail screeched up from the slaves, they dropped their bundles and baskets and ran madly back along the path. The guards milled about trying to form a line to front us. Bows lifted.

"We are not demons!" I bellowed. "We are travelers like yourselves!"

It was touch and go.

The lord straightened up. He held a lynxter, the sword pointed at us and did not tremble.

"Stand!" he said in a clear, crisp voice.

He'd dropped his bow and drawn his sword sharpish enough, by Krun!

"Llahal, lynxor." I made the greeting even more demanding than before. I looked hard at him, at his pale cheeks, his dark eyes, that stiff small black beard. I lowered the bow. "We seek the way out of this maze." I gestured with the bow. "There are beasts we shafted up there."

"Beasts? Vorlinds, yes, we have been pestered by them." He wasn't sure yet, not quite sure of us. He turned abruptly to the guards. "Fetch the poor people back before they run into more mischief."

"Quidang!" rapped the lead Rapa who wore more feathers than the others among his own. He was the cadade, the captain of the guard. He belted out quick orders and some of the guard went running off after the witless slaves. I felt I could take an easier breath.

"Your name?" He sheathed his sword.

I made the pappattu, introducing us, and he announced himself as Chan Holomin, Strom of Wioldrin. Strom being roughly equivalent to a terrestrial count made him a member of the higher nobility. Where Wioldrin was I didn't know; I fancied he hailed from Walfarg.

Further to smooth over this meeting, I said: "We felt a tremor, and weakness took us. Then we saw you in like case."

The guards were returning with the runaways and the hullabaloo quietened down. He pulled at that stiff beard. "I felt most peculiar, by Wurzam! We have traveled a long way and have not previously been troubled by sorcerers." He gave us a sharp glance.

Before he could frame in words what he was thinking I cut in: "We suspected sorcery, too. I suppose there must be a great deal of it down here."

He asked about our travels and we assured him there was no way out that way and in the end we agreed to cut off to the side of the cavern, wary of savage cats, and seek a fresh opening. Mevancy set herself to learn all she could. Chan admitted he was out for adventure and could not resist the challenge from the moment he first heard of the Realm of the Drums. By clever, seemingly innocuous questions, Mevancy drew forth the startling information that Chan and his party had ventured in here some five hundred seasons ago. All that time they'd stood there, clear of dust and decay, waiting all unknowingly to be released from the stasis spell.

Just how many others were there down here, all frozen?

He said he'd ventured in from an opening in the walls, sneaking in from the forest under cover of night, not wishing to let his presence be known to the inhabitants of the City of Eternal Twilight. He had a map of the way to get here; once inside he was as lost as us. Then he said: "It is told that the great and puissant Queen Satra ventured here. As everyone knows, she mysteriously vanished a few seasons ago. I am beginning to believe the rumors are correct. You could wander about down here for a lifetime."

One minor mystery was cleared up as Chan talked on. It was clear to us he was glad of the company. He'd started with over two hundred people, so he was considerably reduced. The mystery was this—the inscription we had come across indicated adventurers were expected. The folk of the City of Twilight knew about the labyrinth under their feet and never ventured down. They usually admitted anyone foolish enough to try to descend. Queen Satra, omnipotent, had accepted the challenge and taken a huge retinue down with her. That, at least, was the rumor which Chan now believed true.

"So you sneaked in after her, on the quiet?"

He started to bristle up at the crudity of my remark; then he smiled a trifle ruefully. "You are blunt, Drajak the Sudden. Yes."

His reaction heartened me. If he turned out to be your usual unpleasant example of so-called nobility we'd take our chances on our own. If he proved to be a reasonable traveling companion then we would, as I phrased it to myself, allow him to accompany us.

There was, indeed, a fresh opening in the side of the cave. I had a quick quiet word with Rollo. "Your map?"

"Still holding it in my head. I'd welcome pens and paper, though."

"We'll try this Chan fellow, later on."

"Seems a reasonable sort, I suppose."

"Mevancy is prepared to trust him."

"I bet friend Llodi isn't, by Hlo-Hli!"

The opening led into a rough-hewn passageway which wound round and about so that I felt sorry for poor Rollo trying to keep a track of it all in his head. I said to Chan: "Did you make a map as you went along?"

He gave an odd sideways look. He hesitated, and then said: "We began in that fashion. But Orgli, my stylor, was eaten by a syatra. After that every way we went led nowhere. I think, Drajak the Sudden, we are all resigned to our fate."

"Nonsense!" I exclaimed, probably with more force than I intended.

Again Chan favored me with that leery look. Llodi, marching along on my heels, said in an unnaturally loud voice: "I agree with you, Prince Drajak!" He went on: "Why, the king your father would never surrender!"

Chan jumped. So that was it! Good old Llodi! He'd spotted the way this strom didn't relish the familiarity with which I spoke to him.

I said with some acerbity: "Now, Llodi, you know I am incognito."

At once Mevancy jumped in. "Please forgive him, majister."

Rollo joined in. "Please, majister. One has to become accustomed to calling Prince Drajak simply Drajak the Sudden."

My comrades meant well, of course. But was I always to be encompassed around with stupid titles? Still, they'd passed the issue off and the deception might help us. Then I smiled inwardly. It was no deception!

"You are forgiven," I said with my most imperial manner.

"Majister," Chan started up. "Had I known, I would—"

"Now, Strom Chan. Just call me Drajak. And what is that shadow ahead, just past that buttress?"

We all stopped abruptly. Up there the pearly light dimmed. If every time we came across perils the light faded, the prospects loomed even more unpleasantly. I could see pretty clearly, though, and made out a humped shape with prongs upon its back. As we stared, four red eyes opened. Four red eyes regarded us balefully and a gusting stench wafted upon us.

"A stinkback!" Chan held out his hand. "Axe!"

One of his Brokelsh slapped the haft of the axe into his fist.

"Bowmen!" ordered Chan in a firm voice. Then, to us, he said: "They are the very devil. Armored. You have to chop through them."

Rapas stepped up smartly enough and let fly. Some of their arrows chinkled off the scaled hide, others lodged, and one red eye vanished. At once a crescendo of screeching bellowed up, the stench increased, and the stinkback charged.

I stepped in front of Mevancy, the Krozair longsword snouting. "Get out of the way, pigeon!"

"I'll—" she began.

I glimpsed Rollo hauling her back and Llodi stepping up with his sword at the ready. He said, through his teeth: "I wish I had me good old strangdja now, what with them scales an' all."

The next few moments were a pandemonium of thrashing claws and smiting steel, of a Rapa staggering back without his beak, of Chan leaping with me and of us smiting together. Llodi went in low, thrusting.

He bounced back.

Blow after blow rained down. Chan staggered as a claw ripped at him. I managed to get another eye and then I smashed the Krozair brand down onto the junction of forelimb and shoulder. The leg was not severed; it dangled. Llodi was up and at my side, panting, slashing his sword down. Chan got back into the fight and a couple of Rapas edged in from the side and used their strangdjas. Huge, slashing blows hacked the stinkback to pieces.

When it was all over the place stank disgustingly.

"Move out!" yelled Chan. Then he glanced quickly at me, and I said: "Carry on, Chan."

We hurried past the poor dead beast.

Up ahead the floor began to curve to the right and descend.

"By the nit-infested and tangled curls of the Divine Lady of Belschutz!" I said to myself. "Down!" Then I pondered as we walked on and down into the pearly radiance. We might very well have to go down again, and deeper and deeper, before we could find a way up and out. That was the nasty habit of these labyrinth builders, by Krun!

That is, if there was a way out.

As though reading my thoughts, Rollo said: "If Strom Chan came in through an opening in the walls, then surely we must be able to find that way out? Or another opening?"

"We'll find a way out." I spoke bluffly, putting confidence into my voice. "And we'll take some treasure with us, for good measure."

"By Wurzam! I'm with you, Drajak!" exclaimed Chan.

I gave him a twitch of my top lip to show I appreciated that.

Then he said: "I had wondered about that sword you carry. It appeared hopelessly unbalanced. Yet it did as much damage as a strangdja."

"It is a competent weapon." I wasn't going to be drawn on the terrible destructive abilities of a true Krozair longsword, nor its origins.

The passage continued down and the walls began to smooth out, still with the mark of cold chisels upon them. Mevancy contrived to walk alongside.

"Cabbage—you pushed me out of the way."

"Aye."

"I intend to stand and—"

"I know you do, pigeon."

"Well, then?"

"Well, then, remember the Star Lords would be most displeased with me if I let you get killed. And I shudder to think what the Empress Delia would say to anybody who returned and I did not."

Now, of course, that was a cruel and heartless thing to say to her.

Her face, always flushed by reason of her need for a high blood pressure to shoot her bindles, reddened even more. She blinked rapidly. For a dreadful moment I thought she would burst into tears—I swear I thought I saw a sparkle on her eyelids. Then she stuck a shoulder in the air and stalked off to walk with Rollo.

By the Black Chunkrah! The last thing I wanted was to become even more involved in Mevancy's emotional problems. She had enough worries over selecting a proper father for any daughters she might have so that they would be born with bindles on their forearms. She stalked on ahead with Rollo.

"You have to admire her, though, Drajak, what with her being a girl an' everything."

"Oh, I do, Llodi, I do."

Now, why in a Herrelldrin Hell did that come out as though I were mocking the poor girl? I had a tremendous admiration and affection for Mevancy. She contrived an inner beauty that shone out to captivate mere men.

Llodi grunted and said: "I missed me strangdja, back there."

Now what I said next must be heard in context. I said: "There will be plenty of fights to come. There'll be spare weapons aplenty."

"I s'pose so, what with these monsters an' all."

Llodi would find his strangdja, of that I had no doubt. We were in for a stormy passage before we won free of this labyrinth. Now, if you view looting a corpse with abhorrence, you are absolutely right in general. In particular, sometimes, it is necessary or customary. As a paktun, an acknowledged mercenary of standing, would automatically take the pakai, the string of trophy rings, from a vanquished rival, so he would expect his own pakai to be taken from him. He was entitled to his trophies of victory. In the same way any mercenary, any soldier, will take what he needs from the dead. And any mercenary, certainly, and many a soldier, when dead and looking down from whatever heaven he inhabits, will nod when a living mortal in need rifles through the possessions on his dead body, and say: "Thy need is greater than mine."

There's little use for swords and armor buried with dead warriors. Modern archaeologists welcome the fact. No respectful warrior would ransack the tomb of another—unless pressing considerations swept aside the morality of it. So if any of you following my narrative imagine I have ever advocated stealing from dead bodies here on Earth, you are sadly mistaken. That, of course, refers to civilian life. There is a strong and vibrant civilian life on Kregen, as I have said; but Kregen is Kregen, and Kregen is not Earth, by Zair!

All this by way of explanation of the dart that streaked from the hidden wall slit.

The smells were left to the rear and we debouched into a chamber that was no longer a cavern, for the walls were masonry, and many areas were covered with tapestries. The pearly light suffused the whole large area with that soft and lambent glow so soothing to the eyes. Tables and chairs stood about, and chests banded in black iron were piled against one wall.

"Ha!" exclaimed Chan, and strode forward eagerly.

Most of the chests were rotted and the black iron rusting. Chan stopped. He tugged his beard. "Worthless—or camouflage?"

"Or, lord," said Dravka, the Brokelsh who carried his armor. "Trapped?"

The other Brokelsh, Braga, turned and beckoned curtly. The Rapa cadade was quite clearly used to this. A couple of his guards ran a slave up to the Brokelsh. The slave, a shaven-haired Gon, just stood there with eyes half-closed, mouth slack and drooling a little. The finest of trembles vibrated his limbs. He looked like a limp propped-up sack.

Two Rapa guards slapped their strangdjas into their outside hands and grasped the Gon with their inside fists and ran him forward. They intended to catapult him towards the chests and retire. It did not quite work out like that.

They thrust the Gon on so that he staggered, tangle-footed. He crashed down and his shaven skull cracked against a chest. Everybody knew something terrible would follow. One of the Rapas put a surprised hand to his throat above the corselet rim. The streaking flash of metal from the wall slit had existed for a heartbeat. The sliver of the dart stood in his throat. He looked dazed. Then he fell with a crash.

"Hlo-Hli have mercy!" exclaimed Chan.

The Gon lay there with a thin trickle of dark blood trailing across that shaven skull where already the white spikes of hair were growing through.

The Rapa guard on the floor jerked out in convulsions. He choked. Black liquid welled from his beak. Chan looked down and his face betrayed exhaustion and tension and fear. He said: "We have seen this before. Poor Rogrifor will take a long time to die—in agony. In mercy, Rhagran," he said to the Rapa captain of the guard. "Despatch him."

"May Rhapaporgolam the Reiver of Souls take him!" and the sword sliced delicately across the man's throat.

Llodi started to say something and I stopped him. "I will speak to Chan in the matter of the strangdja."

The dead guard's weapon lay on the floor. I said to Chan: "You will do me a favor, Strom Chan, if you allow my comrade Llodi to take the strangdja."

"Of course, of course." He was tugging his beard and staring down on the dead Rapa.

So, in this wise, Llodi gained possession of a strangdja, that feared weapon of Chem with its holly-leaf shaped head of metal spikes and edges that can take off a head with the easiest of ease.

Thirteen

The chests proved worthless.

The Gon, scared past caring, slowly recovered. We had lost the life of a man for nothing. Except—one of the guards, a Brukaj very heavily built, picked up a small diamond ring. His stubborn bulldog face looked sullen as the Rapa cadade made him hand the ring over.

"This is for the lord, Benormy, make no mistake!"

"Yes, Jik."

Chan took the ring into his fingers and turned it about.

"Magic," he pronounced. "At least, we have salvaged something from this shambles."

Rollo and I exchanged glances. Chan was no Wizard of Walfarg. Rollo said, quietly: "In Walfarg at the time Chan was alive—I mean, well, you know what I mean—the land was soaked in sorcery. Some artifact can be given applied kharrna and function for a time."

"I've never put much store by magic rings."

"Nor I. Far too chancy. Nowadays, when we wizards are hanging on by our fingernails in Whonban, Loh in general shares these doubts."

A memory of Marta Renberg ghosted in, and I wished Korero with his shields could march at my back.

Listening, Mevancy said: "You know, by Spurl—it's going to come as a tremendous shock to Chan when he finds out the date."

"To go down here when the Empire of Loh is the most puissant force in this part of Paz, and to come out when it is a dusty memory. Quite!"

"If he gets out." Llodi was polishing up his new acquisition.

"Don't you start, Llodi!"

There being nothing of further interest in that cavern, we all trailed off through the far opening. The pearly light persisted.

"We must guide ourselves to a plan." I sounded testy.

"It is not easy when the passageways turn and curve." Chan's face held much of that depressed look of defeat. "We can only go on in the best way we can."

This particular passageway held straight for a good long run. Some way along we passed the skeleton of a Khibil. Nothing else save the yellowed bones on the floor indicated his companions had gathered up what there was and marched on. We gave floor, walls and ceiling a thorough examination before we pressed on. Nothing startling occurred; but the tension of expected disaster crackled in the still air.

We reached an intersection where two doors in the opposite walls indicated decisions of direction were required. Chan said: "I am weary, hungry and thirsty. We have found fresh provisions down here, so I would like to rest, and my guards and people."

Mevancy said at once: "A capital notion, strom."

So I realized, and I suppose Rollo and Llodi likewise, that I was famished and dry. A wet was strictly in order here and now.

Chan turned to his cadade and nodded to the left hand door, which had a flaked blue paint over gray. Rhagran pointed at the door and said: "Benormy and Domesti! Check that room out."

The Brukaj and an Och started forward. They moved readily enough, yet they weren't happy about the assignment. Well, by Vox, who would be?

They opened the door carefully and went cautiously in whilst a pair of Rapa bowmen positioned themselves ready to shoot in support. After a short interval, the Och came to the door and said: "All clear, lord."

Chan nodded. "Dondo! Let us go in and rest."

The room, walled in stone, looked bare and inhospitable.

I said: "I'll check the other room. It might be more inviting."

"Yeh," said Llodi. "Inviting to what?"

"You could be right, still—"

Mevancy stared at me, flushed. "Oh, you!" she said.

That cheered me up. The door of peeling varnished wood opened smoothly. I looked in and felt surprise. At my side Rollo sucked in his breath. Llodi said: "That's more like it, what with them couches an' all."

The place was sumptuously furnished with couches and chairs and tables, with tapestries on the walls. As usual, we brought the scents with us. Half a dozen tripods held amphorae. Llodi licked his lips.

"Well, now," I said, not going in. "This could be illusion. This could be trapped to the eyeballs. Rollo?"

"No illusion. As for traps, we must test."

Intrigued by our reactions, Chan came over. He turned to speak—over his shoulder. "Rhagran!"

This time the cadade chose a pair of strapping Hytaks. Their hard faces under the helmet brims showed no expression. Their armor and weapons, as always with Hytaks, were in impeccable condition. Not apim, Homo sapiens sapiens like me, the Hytak is a diff with only two arms and two legs. He does have a sinuous tail to which he often straps an edged blade. The backbone of many armies and many mercenary bands, hytakim are valued as fighting men and women. These two were twins. In they marched and poked and prodded, with exquisite care. Nothing happened. At length, the room was pronounced safe.

The amphorae contained a nice light yellow and I felt the smoothness as it went down. "By Mother Zinzu the Blessed!" I said, and I deliberately wiped my hand over my mouth. "I needed that!" Just how you'd judge the age of the vintage I didn't care to contemplate. As to its provenance, it could have been shipped in from almost anywhere during the time when Loh had trading links extending over most of this part of Paz.

We ate and drank, the cadade set watches, and we settled down to some much needed rest. This City of Eternal Twilight was just one of the famous Lost Cities of Chem. If they were all like this, then—!

Chan and that damned silly magic ring bothered me. I had no truck with foolishness of that kind. Yet, here I was supposedly chasing after magic rubies. Na-Si-Fantong believed in the power of the Skantiklar, and so did Deb-Lu. So how could I, a mere mortal, disbelieve?

Thinking of the powers of thaumaturgy, I wondered how Deb-Lu had got on in his investigation of the tower—or what was left of it—from which we had been shot at by fireballs. If that was Na-Si-Fantong's handiwork then that meant he had left some device or another assistant sorcerer up there. He could be down here now, and, as I surmised, he would also have negated the sleep spell. Did I want to run into him? That would bring this affair to a head; it might not be to my advantage, by Krun!

Chan would not hear of my standing a watch.

Later I said to Rollo and Llodi: "See? That's what you get for saying I'm a prince. I don't stand a watch. Ha!"

Eventually I went off to sleep with my perennial last thought. By Zair! She had to be safe with all that chivalry about her, and Deb-Lu!

In the all-pervasive light where no such thing as night existed, we reckoned that morning dawned when we were all rested sufficiently to continue.

Chan stretched. "By Wurzam! Had my mother and father treated me differently I might not have caught this disease of adventuring. When I think of my estates in Wioldrin, the plans I had for the conservatory and the rose arbors, I wonder. And there is Susy-Lee-Sarin. Ah! Hlo-Hli Herself must aid me to return, for Susy and I are to be wed." He tugged his beard. "When I return I do not think I shall go adventuring again. Susy will rule me with a very different rod."

"You'll return to your Susy, strom," I said, making it positive.

He did not employ a slave overseer. Very often hired guards when in charge of slaves are heedlessly cruel. These Rapas carried whips. I had noticed that Chan appeared concerned over the well-being of his slaves, whom he called his people. That, of course, could be because they were carrying the treasures found along the way. At any rate, so far I had not seen a whip used.

Around the corner of the room where we had rested, further doors, carefully opened, revealed more rooms. This appeared to be a complex of guard rooms. Apart from the room where we had rested, all appeared uninhabited. I had to remind myself that this underground labyrinth was in use, was peopled by the folk of the Realm of the Drums. The stasis spell had caught them as well as the people of the City of Eternal Twilight. Things down here existed as they had done for at least five hundred seasons. And they were as fresh as they had ever been.

We went on. I said to Rollo: "What chance is there of you being aware of the nearness of Na-Si-Fantong?"

"In all this kharrna down here, not much."

"Well, if we run into him—"

Rollo said with great loftiness: "We will do what we can."

He walked on ahead, for we were at the tail of the procession. The rock walls here were rough-cut once more. A slave had cut his foot, a young quanim, with pointed ears and long chin. He carried a bundle wrapped in sacking and he dropped back. A Rapa guard stalked past. I turned to look back.

Among the slaves there were Fristles, although none served in Chan's guard. The cat-folk and the bird-folk more often than not did not get along together. There were no Pachaks, Khibils or Chuliks, either, in the guard.

The Rapa guard swiveled his head to look towards the head of the column. He had dark feathers, and looked the typical vulturine Rapa I had first encountered upon Kregen. The column turned a corner up ahead. The Rapa unlimbered his whip. He hit the young quanim.

"Up, shint! Move, or I'll stripe you! Grak!"

That disgusting word grak is a word calculated to cow, to make a slave run until he falls dead. It is a word and an idea I detest.

The quanim shoved up with his bundle. Blood dribbled from his foot. The Rapa hit him again, quite needlessly. The youngster yelled.

I went back towards them. Oh, yes, I know. This is something that Dray Prescot cannot keep his big nose out of. It was quite clear that Strom Chan looked after his slaves, his people. This Rapa would never dare act like this in the presence of his lord.

I caught hold of the Rapa's shoulder, swung him about, and hit him on his big curved beak. He was so surprised he staggered back, dropping his whip. His dark feathers bristled. "Get up ahead, beakim. Bratch!"

He stared at me for a moment, his eyes mean. Then he picked up his whip and slouched off.

The quanim looked terrified. I said: "It's all right. Your lord does not allow whipping. Now cut along ahead."

"Thank you, master." He hobbled off.

I took a breath. Thank Opaz! I had been fully prepared for a most ugly scene, and it had passed off this easily.

I started off. The quanim ahead disappeared around the corner with his bundle. For just those few moments I was alone in the corridor.

Reaching the corner I swung around it—and stopped dead.

I gaped.

The corridor was empty. No one. Not a single solitary living soul marched along ahead. The rocky passage stretched to another corner about a hundred paces off. There was no sound. The expedition had vanished.

Fourteen

This was uncanny. I walked on, testing every step carefully, until I reached the next corner. The corridor here went on a long way in that pearly light. There was no sign of anyone. I went back to the first corner and searched around, looking for anything that might explain this mystery.

I yelled, after a bit, exasperated. "Mevancy! Llodi! Rollo!"

Not a dicky bird. Where in a Herrelldrin Hell had they gone?

I couldn't find any signs of cracks to indicate secret doors. I banged on the walls and floor. The rock rang back mockingly.

By Makki-Grodno's leprous left earlobe and putrescent right eyeball! Where the blue blazes had they gone?

I searched around quite uselessly for some time. After that I felt my best course would be to go on. We had to meet up again, surely?

Going on alone for me is both a pleasure and a source of concern. Any adventure can be heightened by the presence of good comrades. Adventuring alone is rewarding in quite different ways. I may say I kept an excruciatingly sharp lookout, testing any and everything that did not look right.

Corridor followed corridor. There were many doors now, lining the walls. I looked in a few to find nothing. After a time I kept on and ignored the rooms, reasoning that if my comrades were in any of them I'd hear. Coming out into a larger hall in the smooth light I saw a man lying on the floor. His booted feet were entangled in a rug. I stopped.

Not being sure just how close I had to be to wake him, I waited. He did not stir. I looked closer. Then I let out a breath.

Looking all about, I walked over to the corpse. He'd had his armor caved in by a blow I judged to have been of enormous force. His body had not rotted away, so he'd been killed just before the stasis spell came into effect. Logically, then, he'd be one of Queen Satra's party.

His helmet, dislodged, revealed his shaven skull with his pigtail, dyed red and yellow, twisted at the back. One of his tusks rising at the corners of his mouth had broken off at the gold band. In death he had lost some of his color; but his skin still showed that oily yellow sheen. Although I'd evidence to suggest that Chuliks were not entirely devoid of humanity, as is often said of them, their harsh military training from birth creates a race of diffs notably lacking in humanity. In service all over Paz they are among the most highly paid mercenaries.

His usual arsenal of weaponry was missing. His comrades had helped themselves in the paktun way. A broken stux lay near his fist. The throwing spear had snapped just below the cross quillons. These were very small, almost mere ornaments, at the base of the foot-long head. Developed to be hurled in hunting for vosks, large blundering stupid—if succulent—animals, the stux might have to be used to stop a maddened creature's charge. So that is why the check pieces were fixed, to stop the vosk clawing his way up the shaft to stick his tusks into you.

I said: "Mikshu the Treacherous—or whoever—smile on you, Chulik."

Passing on, I reflected that I'd not studied Chulik history or religion as much as I had other diffs'. Likshu or Mikshu—well, yes, there must be a difference. In the same way I knew a fair amount of Walfargian history; but detail was hazy. I walked on into another chamber. All these areas were natural caverns, I felt, and the rumble and roar of water now became constant. Another body lay to one side, a Fristle, and this catman had likewise been stripped of weapons. His armor, also, was gone.

A long thin sliver had been passed through his body from below to top. He'd been skewered from a round hole in the floor. I studied this with attention. How—he'd been marching along and triggered the trap and up popped his death. So he was probably in the vanguard. This meant that because of the stasis, no one who lived here had come along to reset the trap. Wherever traps had been let off, they were now harmless. That made me guess that Chan's party since meeting us had been lucky or we'd been traipsing along after another party.

In this chamber a few chests had been tumbled to one side, smashed open, flung down. The thought occurred to me that these caches of chests in these particular rough caverns were not window dressing, were not necessarily traps, were not even required; but they might be genuine.

The searchers had not been altogether thorough and a kick revealed an unopened lid. I kicked it open. Inside a mass of jewels flamed and sparkled like a furnace fire. Splendid gems! I looked at them, and laughed, and walked on. I did not want to be slowed down by junk.

I say I looked at them. Oh, yes, by Krun, I looked! There was not a single red jewel among them.

Further on I crossed a cavern in which a chasm emitted clouds of steam. The far opening admitted me to a corridor more gloomy than usual and with wisps of steam being sucked along with me. It grew hotter.

Somehow or other I found I could see quite well in the gloom. I stopped. I saw a marvel. A plant grew from the roof, a corpse-white plant growing from a thick stem. Venus flytrap growths surrounded that trunk, and fleshy tentacles extended out to catch its prey. The spine-barbed leaves glistened slickly. The marvel was this, the syatra grew upside down. Its roots were firmly embedded in the earth above the roof and its tentacles sought food in the passage below.

It had found some sustenance. A portion of a naked girl could be glimpsed between the spines of one of the growths.

If I approached the syatra it would unfreeze. There was just room to squeeze past against the far wall of the corridor. Clearly, this poor girl had been careless or unlucky and had been seized up. Then—and I have seen sights in my time on Kregen, I felt it, then—another portion of the girl showed between the spines of another of the growths.

Remember, I told myself, remember the frog and the scorpion. A syatra will live, therefore it will do what it has to do. What, I couldn't help wondering, did the inhabitants of the Realm of the Drums make of it?

Shoving up against the wall I began to edge past, my Krozair brand naked in my fist. If the syatra struck he'd lose a tentacle or three...

The plant awoke, the portions of the naked girl vanished as the spined lids clacked shut. Steam coiled up as the tentacles began to lash about trying to seize me up, and stuff me down in a trap adjoining the bits of the girl. I had only to lop one fleshy tentacle that groped too close. It fell to writhe on the ground. Then I had edged past and was clear.

There were three more syatras before the tunnel opened into a cavern. The air hung close and humid. Vapors rose from cracks in the floor where a rich yellow grass grew luxuriantly. Just in front of me a small hairless animal, very much like a piglet, cropped the grass motionlessly. Ahead and as far into the cavern as I could see, covering the ceiling, the corpse white syatras grew. Fleshy tentacles hung down, spined traps gaped open. More than one syatra had a piglet-beast in tentacle or trap.

The nearest syatra contained another girl in its tentacle. A second tentacle had pulled. Each sinuous length was about to deposit its bit of the girl in its trap. There was no way through there, so I would have to retrace my steps through the cavern of the chasm and take another fork. The way I had chosen had looked the best and most open way.

Until, that was, I'd run across the syatras.

So, I retreated in face of a superior force and found my way back across the steaming cavern of the chasm until I could turn off and continue ahead along a different track.

Once again the walls became squared off and tool marks showed. The light improved. Whilst I had no real idea of the design of this place I had the notion that the rougher portions existed on the perimeter. That would make sense, anyway, up to a point. The way continued on and I did not relax my caution. A glitter of gold drew my gaze. As I walked on I passed a handful of gold pieces, then a few more, then a pile, then a stream of gold. Further progress brought me to a box, splintered at the corner, with gems spilling out. Again, there were no rubies. Going on carefully, I found a sack of gems, which I checked, and a slew of precious objects—cups, trays, bracelets, necklaces—all heavily jeweled.

At a corner a woman lay sprawled in the way. The curved fangs of a lavonth had ripped out her throat. The lavonth, about the size of a greyhound, with his zig-zag of tawny and umbre, had found the woman on the ground, I felt sure. Her feet were bruised and bloody. She must have taken her boots off at a halt—foolishly—and been unable to pull them on again. She wore a deeply double-curved kax, its iron polished to a mirror brightness that had not dulled in all these hundreds of seasons. She had two swords and a longbow and quiver. Her colors were red and yellow. These were not the scarlet and yellow of Vallia but the madder and gold of Walfarg. The blood dribbling from her throat showed starkly against her flesh.

All this evidence was easy enough to read, so there was no help for it but that I must shaft the lavonth. This I did and then went on with a word to Hlo-Hli Herself to care for the woman's ib.

The next two corpses were much like the last, strong-featured women with heavily-double-curved armor. These two had died with swords in their fists, facing something that had done for them. There was not dust enough to reveal any clawprints. Again commending these Jikai Vuvushis to Hlo-Hli, I pressed on.

The next parcel of evidence appeared confusing at first; but a few moments of study soon deciphered the clues. Against the wall lay the body of a man, stripped of armor and weapons. Just beyond him lay a woman whose body had been chewed by whatever killed her. She was fully armed and armored.

All the Jikai Vuvushis so far had been apims. The man, as it happened, was a Brukaj; I did not think that had anything to do with the picture that was unfolding as I marched on.

In a cavern lay many corpses jumbled together. Again, the evidence looked contradictory. Some of the corpses had decayed into skeletons, others were in the same state as when the owner of the flesh and blood had died. Still, once more the clues were not too difficult to understand.

That particular cavern ended at the head of a flight of steps that, whilst they were broad enough, went on down a damn long way into shadows. The air of menace that breathed up the stairs hung like a palpable mist. There was nothing else for it. I started on down, testing everything.

Of course, there were corpses strewing the stairs like a dreadful flung-handful of rags. They had all been stripped of weapons and armor, men and women alike. I kept a lookout for anyone still with weapons and found none.

The first one I found with weapons lay at the first corner of the first tunnel after the foot of the stairs. I could imagine the terror that must have overcome them. Even when I went into a large chamber where food jars and baskets lay overturned and in the wildest confusion, I could still imagine them shivering with fear. There was good food in there, and wine, and I stoked the inner man. I was not tired; but I rested a whick and then pushed on refreshed.

Now I do not wish to give the impression that the passageways and caverns were choked with corpses; of course they were not. There were enough, though, to indicate the horrors through which these parties were going. For some way I walked on without seeing any corpses or skeletons and I began to wonder if I'd taken the wrong fork at intersections. I was going straight ahead, as the inscription had advised, confident that the parties ahead had done the same.

By this time I was getting the feel of this Realm of the Drums. People still lived here—of course, all those hundreds of seasons ago—but there were less of them. A lot less, I judged from what I'd seen of the abandoned caverns. Somewhere far below must be the currently inhabited portions. Had any expeditions ventured that far down? How was Na-Si-Fantong's expedition coming along? And—the question I had to look at squarely—had Delia and my comrades found a way to start down here?

At the entrance to a room lay the half-naked body of a young girl. She was a Sybli; gentle, innocent, extremely beautiful girls are Syblians. The real name for these diffs is Ennschafften, and they are naive and simple folk.

She wore only a yellowish breechclout. The edges had been embroidered with a plain stitch in a lighter yellow. Around her neck hung a black bead necklace. Syblis are employed as house servants or slaves, usually, for the men are very strong and perform arduous tasks admirably. This poor girl had been a slave. I could envisage with even greater clarity the mental turmoil up ahead, the state of the party.

Proof of that came very shortly when a box, flung down all those seasons ago, revealed expensive feminine toilet articles, brushes, combs, mirrors, pots of unguents. Here lay a girl's secret beauty.

This fresh evidence relieved my mind of the concern that I'd taken a different path. If there was chivalry in this, a small jikai, I was not going to belabor that in my own mind. No, by Zair!

As is any wise old delver's custom, one keeps a wary eye upon the ceiling. In a plain corridor a dark splodge on the ceiling abruptly came to life as I passed under. A quick leap—a damned quick leap, by Vox!—carried me clear. I whirled to face, sword snouting. The thing had missed and now hung on a thread anchored in a crack in the ceiling. It was a wide flat creature, like a cartwheel of tentacles and stingers and unpleasantnesses. If that lot fell on your head you'd snuff it, as sure as Zim and Genodras rise.

Giving the thing a good look, I went on, leaving it slowly reeling itself in back up to the ceiling.

There were more of these pesky nuisances. If you were quick you could dodge. They did add a new zest to proceedings. I confess I continued to feel the eerie business of waking people and things up as you approached most uncanny. It sent a shiver up my spine. What lay around the next corner, frozen in sorcerous sleep, ready to wake up as I neared and jump on me? Yet that danger was quite different from the expected dangers in delving.

Lots of the little piglet-like creatures scuttled to life as I passed. They were usually a bright orange in color, although some were dark brown or fawn and a few were bright pink. All were hairless, with little round ears, and snouts, and curly tails. You could imagine one as a pet.

One of them had been caught by a cartwheel of tentacles dropping from the roof and was already half-digested. The scene in the centre of the corridor ahead would come to life if I passed. Yet the piglet was dead and the round tentacular monster had to eat. I would not slay that one. I passed by and the piglet was duly consumed.

I sniffed. Yes, there was no doubt of it. An expensive perfume wafted on the air. Yet we brought our own scents in with us—the answer, of course, was that in activating the air we activated particularly strong smells. The scene at the mouth of the cavern before me explained the perfume.

I stopped stock-still and studied the layout. The weirdness was that these people, this drama, was unfolding with breakneck speed to death, yet I could stand and study it with detachment. Odd, by Djan, deuced odd!

From the roof a tentacled cartwheel was dropping towards the head of a girl. She was clad in half-armor of ornate and expensive style, with much goldwork. Her helmet had fallen off. Her swords were sheathed. Her face expressed the most awful fear, a terror frozen there for hundreds of seasons. Her hair was the red of Loh with a darker infusion that brought the widow's peak down over the centre of her forehead as a challenging statement of identity. Her face was pallid to chalkiness. Her eyes were large and kohled and brilliant—brilliant with terror. Her figure in the armor was of a pleasing shape. All in all, she was a most proper Jikai Vuvushi.

Crouching with her back to this girl, another girl held a slender dagger. She was a Sybli, twin to the first I had seen. Her back was to me; I could imagine the expression on that simple pretty face.

Advancing on her stalked the crocodilian shape of a Magor. His scales reflected the pearly light. His jaws were agape and the teeth, ragged and uneven, looked capable of cutting the Sybli girl in half. His eyes glared with rhodopsin, red and mad with blood lust. Feral and lethal, Magors, in their natural swampy habitat. Down here they must be consumed by hatred. Semi-intelligent, Magors? Or brainless beasts only? No one was prepared to give an authoritative answer to that—not yet. His claws reached out.

So, this was the problem.

The moment I advanced the tableau would come to life.

The tentacled cartwheel would drop on one girl and the Magor would charge and destroy the other.

I, Dray Prescot, just stood there. I'd walked into a real juicy one this time, by Zim-Zair!

Fifteen

I'd shaft the damned Magor. One arrow wouldn't stop his mad onslaught. He'd need a quiver full to stop him, and even then he might not stop until he'd wrapped those ugly jaws around the girl's body.

As for the tentacled cartwheel, I could shaft him but he'd still drop on the girl's head and shoulders and his acid secretions would begin to work.

I unlimbered the Lohvian longbow and selected a shaft fletched with rose red feathers from Valka. I took up an easy stance and shot in my bow. A score of shafts slugged into the Magor. His opened jaws bristled with shafts. His eyes were gone and I'd managed to put four good shots into the high muscles of his forelegs.

I put the longbow down. I did off all my harness of war until I stood forth clad only in the brave old scarlet breechclout.

Flexing my muscles I eyed the task. Quick. By Djan Kadjiryon! I'd have to be damned quick. There'd be no second chance. In, do it, out. Still that uncanny feeling persisted that I could thus stand and size up the situation, contemplate action, when in reality those two girls were within heartbeats of mutilation and death. Weird, by Vox!

A few deep breaths, a quick consignment of my carcass to Opaz, and I sprang forward.

The tentacled cartwheel dropped on his thread. The Magor had been snarling his ferocious intent and now those sounds changed. His onward rush continued. Blood spurted from his mouth and eyes.

In a windmill of motion I moved forward in a straight line at right angles to the Magor's charge. The Jikai Vuvushi went up under one arm and the Sybli up under the other. Their legs flew up into the air. On, on! With a ferocious spurt of energy I surged out from under the thrashing mass of tentacles. They hit the ground with a squashing thud. I felt the Magor stumble past as we leaped out of his way. I didn't look back. Head-long the three of us tumbled up the passage and then I tripped and down we all came in a bundle of naked arms and legs and whirling hair.

"Thank Opaz and all the Names!" I said to myself.

The little Sybli had passed out from terror. The armored woman was yelling blue bloody murder. Both reactions were perfectly normal.

Disentangling myself from the women was startlingly more difficult than expected. The Sybli's arms flopped over my face as I tried to shift her head with its crop of dark hair—shades of Mevancy! The Jikai Vuvushi staggered up, reeling, staring about. She saw me, I think, in a daze of terror. She kicked me.

Her sandals were hard. At her second kick I took her foot into my palm and stopped her from kicking me. I glared up into her pallid face.

"You are safe now, woman."

"You—Let me go! I shall—guards, guards!"

I said: "Sit down and compose yourself. You have no guards left."

I tugged gently and she fell down. I pushed her back against the wall—I judged that any traps had already been triggered—and said: "Just take a few deep breaths. You have been through a terrible experience but you are safe now."

"You are a dead man."

Now I've heard that said before, and in exactly those same tones. So I had no need for the picture to be drawn out for me. In view of that, and because I value my hide, I decided I had to cover my tracks and organize a logical defense that would hold water. Quite obviously this little madam was an important personage. She could be a princess or something like that. Whatever she might be, she was probably in that class whose person is sacred. Any common person who touched her would be put to death in the appropriate fashion. She crouched back against the wall. Her pale face tilted up to me, her dark eyes wide, that widow's peak of hair forming a wedge of menace over her forehead. Her lips were red, glistening, pouting half open. Her teeth were very small and white.

Her fist clenched over the armor at her breast. She panted.

I started to say: "If you were to be saved—"

She interrupted without even listening to me. "I do not know you. I do not know everyone in the expedition. But," she was looking at me as someone might look at a strange creature brought up from the depths of the sea. "But I think, had I seen you, I would not have forgotten."

This was time for a little push of pike. I said: "You would have died if that thing had dropped on you."

She shuddered. "The stangsi! Disgusting!" She put her left hand against the ground and pushed herself up. She staggered forward a step and recovered. She whipped out her sword. "Loathsome! Forfeit to the White Hot Pincers of Vorwal the Relentless!"

The tentacled cartwheel, the stangsi, fluttered about on the floor, no doubt recovering himself after his missed strike. Just how he was feeling I didn't know. The Sybli had fainted. This domineering girl in armor no doubt associated her feelings of release from the stasis as a part of all the unpleasantness surrounding this experience.

She stepped forward and lifted the sword. The stangsi was completely defenseless.

"Is that necessary?" I spoke in a hard, gravel-shifting voice, and she jumped. To the side the Magor lay speckled with my shafts. "The thing can't harm you now."

In a hating voice, she said: "I'll make sure of that." She cut down and lifted the sword and slashed again. She cut the thing to pieces.

"So you have recovered," I said. "Now we can make the pappattu."

She held the sword, smeared with a greasy substance, away from her. Her eyebrows lifted. "Are you a fool besides a dead man?"

I was about to make some flippant reply, when she held out the sword, and went on: "Here, clean this. And grak!"

Now I am perfectly prepared to clean the sword of a young lady. This is all a part of the mixed up chivalry in my old vosk skull of a head. Still, there are ways and ways of making the request. I did not reply. I went over to the Magor and whipped out my old sailor knife and began to retrieve my shafts. As I did this I was not fool enough not to keep an eye on her.

She started to work herself up into a temper. Again, this was all a natural reaction. I went on working quietly. She burst out: "Shint! I told you! Clean my sword!"

One of the arrows had gone in deeply and I was having to cut as deeply to ease it out. One had broken on a scale, and this annoyed me. I said: "You can see it is necessary to retrieve these arrows. There may be more Magors."

"I shall not tell you again! You defile my person, now you defy me." She was waving the smeared sword about wildly. "What kind of man are you?"

A soft little voice whispered up from the side. "Majestrix. He is a jikai—a great jikai."

We both turned to see the little Sybli girl just sitting up. She was pretty, no doubt of it, as Syblians are. The yellow stitching on her loincloth and the black beads indicated a superior slave status.

"Oh, Folly, so you've decided to help your mistress, have you, instead of sleeping. Well, clean this sword, or you'll be striped."

"Yes, mistress."

At least, that disposed of the confrontation over cleaning the sword.

Now this Sybli slave, whose name was Folly, had been gripping a dagger, a long slender dagger, and facing the Magor. There was no sign of the dagger now. She was trusted to clean weapons, or, was she? I watched as Folly used her own loincloth to clean the muck off the blade. She seemed to handle the weapon without cutting herself.

Majestrix, Folly had called the girl in armor. Majestrix is given only to the royal females. So, unless she was a queen or an empress, this hoity-toity little madam was a princess. Another damned princess!

My logical defense in the handling of her sacred person appeared to be working, judging by the recent conversation. The cleaning of the sword had been unfortunate; but that appeared resolved. I fancied I'd better make sure.

I said: "I regret that I do not have the honor of your acquaintance. I am Drajak, known as Drajak the Sudden. Lahal."

She stared at me, not as though I was bereft of my senses, but as though I was a buffoon play-acting or drunk.

"What d'you mean, you don't know me?"

"Precisely that."

"You call me majestrix and bow and scrape, or—"

"Listen, woman! Haven't you realized yet that I'm not with your expedition! I don't know who you are, except a bad tempered little girl."

She gasped and Folly squeaked: "Oh!"

The pretty face of the Sybli turned to me like a flower turning to the sun.

She continued to lift her loincloth and clean the sword all the time she spoke. "Jikai, you are in the presence of Princess Licria—"

"Princess Licria, Princess Majestrix of Walfarg!" rapped out this princess, rattling it off with pride and relish.

I said: "Did you come down here with Queen Satra?"

Her nose pinched in. Her jaw thrust forward. "Will you or will you not address me properly?"

That quite clearly meant she had accepted the situation.

"I shall treat you with the respect you deserve. I do not bow and scrape. I judge you to be a brave girl in a situation of horror. Let us go forward together as allies."

"Horror, yes, horror." In her little paddy over titles and bowing and scraping she'd pushed aside her situation. Now it rushed back on her with stunning force. She stared about and I saw the way those red lips trembled and I was able to move smoothly forward and catch her in my arms as she collapsed.

"Jikai—" Folly looked troubled as she helped me put the princess down. "She has a terrible temper. You are in grave danger."

"Tell me what's been going on, Folly. Where are you from?"

"It has been an awful time." She spoke simply. There was something different about her from Syblians I'd met before, and that long slender dagger had something to do with that. "As for me, I come from Wenhartdrin. You'll never have heard of it."

Now I had a problem. I debated for a moment with myself, and then decided I'd better stick to coming from the Great Plains. As for Wenhartdrin, an island off the south coast of Vallia, that was where excellent wine was made. Folly told me a raid had captured her and others and from then on she'd passed from hand to hand, bought and sold, slave. Polly, the other girl Sybli, had come from some part of Havilfar.

"All our guards were slain, then the Jikai Vuvushis. In the end only the mistress was left."

"And you."

"Oh, yes. But I'm a slave."

What, I wondered, would Folly make of Vallia now?

When Princess Licria roused herself I gave her no time to get back in the saddle of her high zorca.

"We must march, princess, and march well. Now, let us get on!"

Her lips tightened up. She saw my face. She hitched up her shoulder, swung about and started off without a word.

Well, she had spirit, no doubt of that, by Krun!

I said: "If we're lucky we ought to find a room with somewhat of victuals pretty soon."

Folly said, on a breath: "Oh, I do hope so. I am so thirsty."

Without thinking over it, I said: "Me, too. I could do with a nice flagon of best Nardi's Wenyellow. That would go down like a treat!"

She gave me a quick startled look. Of course! Oh, well, if any more came of that lapse, then it would. No doubt her mention of Wenhartdrin had brought that particular wine to mind, Nardi's Wenyellow being a famous vintage of the island. Mind you, it was sent overseas.

Walking on and talking, I noticed how these two tested appearances before venturing too far. They'd been through nasty times, and it showed. Folly told me that the little group with the Princess Majestrix had become separated, she'd no idea how, and they'd been hurrying to catch up with the main expedition. This tied in with the evidence I'd followed. Queen Satra had brought down a huge expedition. Folly didn't know how many people there were; but she said: "Thousands!"

They'd been down here a long long time, and the rumors were that the queen wished now only to return. The trouble was, no way out was found.

In her position as handmaid to the princess, Folly often saw the queen. She said: "She's not like she is at all."

Sort the pips out of that one, Dray Prescot!

Folly wanted to know about the Krozair brand. She'd given it a look when I'd buckled on the scabbard. I said: "It is a blade, Folly. You tell me about the dagger."

"Dagger, master?" Oh, with what innocence that was said!

Her wrap around over her breechclout was long enough to conceal a Vallian dagger. I fancied she'd be slain out of hand in the normal course of events if discovered with a weapon in the presence of the princess or queen. Down here would be slightly different. She said: "You will not tell the mistress?" I shook my head. "I found it down here among corpses. It is a type of dagger I know."

"That Magor—"

She shivered. "I thought this was the end and confided myself to Mother Delia—and then you were there."

Delia of Delphond, the ancient Mother Goddess—she was still known and revered at this time. I felt I liked Folly more and more.

The whole situation was now laid out. When shouts ahead told us we'd at last caught up, I felt even more strongly the sense of destiny. We'd ventured down here by chance. I'd been cut off from my companions. I'd met a princess who might be a lead to the queen. Now the Star Lords had required me to save Mul-lu-Manting, who wanted a return to the old Empire of Loh, calling her schemes the New Empire of Loh. In my arrogant foolishness I'd decided that Mevancy would make an excellent queen ruling as Empress of Walfarg.

Guards approached, tough men in armor who looked as though they'd kill anything first before asking questions. They saw Princess Licria. There

223

was a quantity of Lahalling and general genuflecting. I stood to the side with Folly, thinking grandiose schemes concocted for the Everoinye.

Licria pointed at me. "Seize up this shint! Chain him!"

There was no stopping the efficiency the guards showed. As I was lapped in chains, I was realizing the depths of the Star Lords' schemes.

If they really did want a New Empire of Loh and needed a figurehead, they'd brush aside my choice of Mevancy. Oh, no, Queen Satra was here. Who better to be a new empress than a real Queen of Pain?

Sixteen

Wa-Te's tail hand whisked in from nowhere and caught my bicep. The tail hand hauled and I straightened up. I had been prevented from stumbling by Wa-Te's quick reactions.

"Thanks, Wa-Te," I said in that low slave monotone that has to be learned deuced quickly if one wishes to avoid ol' snake.

Ahead of us and to the rear in the rock corridor stretched the lines of slaves. The smells were offensive for a time; after that they went away unless some fresh scent brought back the sense of smell. The noise of shuffling feet and the clink of chains was broken only by the occasional smack of a whip or the thud of a cudgel. The pervasive pearly light shone down with ironic benevolence on slave and slave driver alike.

Over my shoulders the wooden yoke was trying to rub through the cloth padding and raise blisters. Some of the poor devils down here had shoulders red raw. A needleman had been assigned the slaves; but he could do little apart from ointment and a needle or two to take away the pain.

At each end of the yoke swung a basket. What the baskets contained I had no idea for they were covered with leather and strapped down with brass buckles.

Wa-Te's straw-colored hair hung down lankly. His two left arms could be used one to help support his yoke, the other to scratch or brush his hair. It is highly unusual to see Pachaks as slaves. For my part, I value Pachaks above many other fine races of diffs of Kregen.

"Here comes that greesh again," he whispered.

Greesh is a term of utter contempt used by slaves and the poor folk for slavers and masters. It is formed from that infamous word grak and the word kleesh, one of the worst insults of Paz. Booted feet hitting the stone floor with an arrogant crack, crack, crack, heralded the passage of Yaka, clinking with weaponry, armored in iron, swinging a thick black whip. To his sinuous tail was strapped six inches of bladed steel.

When Yaka the Stripe passed on along the column we slaves breathed out sighs of relief. Yaka had the charming habit of taking ten strides and of then slamming out with his whip at the nearest slave. Ten more strides and another stripe, ten more and another... We here in this little group had been lucky this time. Yaka had been overheard to say that the ten paces a blow technique smartened up the slaves remarkably.

Just how long I'd been marching now was difficult to judge. I'd eaten and slept six times. The column proceeded slowly, and then speeded up so we had to totter along under our burdens, and then we'd come to a halt. "Trouble up front," would go the whisper back down the column.

Well, by Krun! I wasn't at the front, so the traps and the monsters up there, at least, couldn't get at me.

When we debouched into a vast cavern the slaves showed no delight or wonder at the fantastic sight. Glistening stalagmites and stalactites formed growing columns between floor and roof. The air breathed cooler and fresher. Kataki slave drivers bellowed for us to rest and we slumped down thankfully. Guards of all manner of races of diffs prowled. Quite clearly Queen Satra protected her goods. The treasures mattered, not the slaves.

A slender graceful form flitted along the rows. Folly knew where I was stationed, for she had visited me twice before. This time she brought a bundle with an onion and a chunk of moist cheese with a heel of bread. I thanked her and she put a rosy finger to her lips. "All your gear is safe, Drajak, jikai. The mistress insisted it be kept intact and separate. I do not know why."

She glanced around, saw a Kataki glaring at her, flushed up, and ran off.

I split the food with Wa-Te. We were chained up two by two, yokes over-lapping, and Folly had been cautious. No one had seen the food passed.

"I thank you, Drajak. But there is something strange here."

"Aye."

"I have been a paktun for many seasons. I have been abroad in the world. But I have not seen a Sybli like her before."

I told him that Folly was the daughter of a Sybli woman and an apim father, a sea captain. Almost always such a union is fruitless; sometimes a child is born. This explained Folly's actions. As for Wa-Te, he'd been with a party attacked by Magors. They'd fought well. All the Pachaks save Wa-Te had been slain, and the lord they protected had been seriously injured. He'd lived. In reward he'd sent Wa-Te into slavery. "Trylon Ge-fu-Schian. That was his name. I shall not forget."

"Some of the high ones of the world are not all evil," I said.

"Ha! By Hlo-Hli! Not many!"

When we were roused out with kicks and blows and stumbled to our feet and marched on, we passed dead bodies and dead Magors.

This, together with Wa-Te's story, proved that somewhere up at the head of the column marched someone who was capable of negating the stasis spell. So, that was the problem. If, somehow, say by asking Folly, I made contact with whoever it was—well, by Vox! and who might it be?

Once I could get a glimpse of the person or persons bringing sleeping perils to life I could make a decision.

Also, a point I had neglected to check with Deb-Lu or Rollo—once we'd resurrected a person down here, could they in turn bring others back to life?

Maybe Princess Licria was creating all the dangers in front.

Material traps, of course, would function anyway.

There were a number of females of various races in the column and most wore the mustardy-yellow slave breechclout. I still wore the scarlet, although it was a trifle grubby by now and at the first stream I'd give it a good wash. Many women, though, wore the waist to knee wrap-around in various colors. I just hoped no one would find the Vallian dagger hidden under Folly's wrap-around.

Either by searching the girl or finding it sticking in their guts.

"By Papachak the All-Powerful!" Wa-Te nodded his head. "It's getting almighty dark!"

I'd noticed the diminution in the pallid light. I could see quite well; but from the way the slaves stumbled and the exclamations, I gathered they could not. Presently word came down to halt. No one sat down—unless they fell down from fatigue—for to do so would bring ol' snake cracking about their bare backs. After a long wait we were told to sit down. The yokes were not removed, so up front they regarded this as only a temporary halt.

Now, as I have mentioned, these damned Kataki slave-drivers are experienced man-managers—and woman-managers, too, although that disgusting discipline varies—and fooling them is a specialized art. I'd had practice, Zair knows! So there were no keys to our fetters. The iron was banded around and then struck through with rivets.

We were lucky. An ages old slaving trick is to drive the rivet through a bone. That is unpleasant.

Also, because the passageways wound about and narrowed and widened into caverns, we were not yoked fore and aft, which is an exemplary way of keeping poor doomed slaves in marching order.

Treading on our heels stumbled a Gon and a Brokelsh. The black bristle body hair of the Brokelsh contrasted starkly with the thick sprouting chalk white hair of the Gon. This white hair of his plunged the Gon into the deepest shame. His eyes were lackluster and his lips drooped.

I said to them during a short break: "Doms! When I shout 'Greesh!' you must duck your heads very quickly."

They stared at me as though I were bereft of my senses. Well, perhaps I was. Here I was, supposed to be the great and puissant emperor and I was chained up, slave. In addition, it was now clear that the whole train of events from the Star Lords flinging me down to save Mul-lu-Manting to now, all tended in one certain direction. And here I was, chained up like a leem in a lord's baiting pit. I mentioned Makki-Grodno and the Divine Lady of Belschutz to myself—frequently, by Krun!

Our next halt lengthened. Presently a Rapa with his beak missing and his feathers drenched in blood staggered back to find the needleman. He was a guard, not a slave. "A big one up front," said Wa-Te.

"Aye."

A couple more wounded came back. Then Yaka the Stripe appeared flicking his whip suggestively. He directed the tame Ochs to release our own chains from the main chain. "Single file!" he bellowed so the echoes rang. Amid much shuffling and very little cursing, for the slaves were cowed, we sorted ourselves out. The light had improved a little since the darkness in the ways after the cavern of the stalagmites. Wa-Te stood to my front, the Gon to my rear.

We shuffled on to the sound of meaty thuds and cracking whips.

The cavern which we entered was, I judged, fairly gloomy, although I could see what the fuss had been about. The air was humid and stank of decaying flesh and vegetable matter which sliced through our own slave stink. The left hand wall stretched ahead, studded with dark openings just over man height. The right hand side of the cavern was choked with syatras, this time growing up from the floor. They were reaching out to the column of people, fleshy tendrils waving. There were no bodies on the floor, for any folk snatched up would have been popped into those coffin growths. Bits and pieces of syatra scattered about spoke eloquently of the fight to clear a passage through.

We moved on and the flashing white of eyes rolling fearfully at the syatras rippled along the column as I looked back.

Well, this was ponsho and leem time.

Yaka the Stripe was walking up along the column shoving the slaves against the wall. A tendril swiped at his head and missed, and the Whiptail laughed and sliced with his blade. There was nothing wrong with the bastard's courage in this situation. He would be accountable for his slaves and he did not intend to lose any here. "Grak!" he bellowed and snapped his whip. "Grak!"

I projected a whisper to Wa-Te before me. "Ready?"

His tail hand lifted to signal he understood—and was ready.

Yaka stalked on as I turned back to watch him. He strutted past me and his whip licked out to catch the Fristle walking in front of Wa-Te.

Putting all my force into the action I swiveled my body around, legs braced, swinging to the right, and I spat: "Greesh!" The left hand basket at the end of the yoke smashed around like the arm of a trebuchet, parallel to the ground.

At that word of contempt Yaka turned back, facing to the column, and the basket hit him smash full in the chest. He catapulted bodily backwards.

The syatra scooped him up gratefully.

"Wenda!" I yelled at Wa-Te. The Pachak responded instantly and I hurled myself after him into the nearest left-hand slot of darkness.

"I'm dumping the yoke, Drajak!" he called back.

I could see him quite well and was able to hurdle the yoke and its baskets. I shoved my yoke off with a feeling of freedom.

The fetters between my ankles hindered me considerably. Hobbling, I charged after Wa-Te, plunging into utter darkness.

Seventeen

"Crack!" slapped rock against rock, and the bottom rock flew into splinters.

Neither of us felt like cursing. "Here," said Wa-Te and handed across another sharp piece. I fitted the point against the end of the rivet holding his fetters with my left hand and brought the chunk of stone in my right down hard and accurately. The rock did not split. The rivet—I thought, I hoped, I prayed!—moved. Just a fraction, but it moved. It had to.

A soft pearly light hazed all about us in the small cavern. We'd hobbled here expecting pursuit to come baying along the dark corridor after us. No one followed us. We guessed that for the moment there was more concern and turmoil among the guards over the sudden demise of Yaka the Stripe than over checking the slaves. I struck again. Again and again I hit the damned stone, breaking some, finding more, until, at last, at heavenly last, Wa-Te's fetters fell free.

"Thank you, Drajak. Now it is my turn."

The Pachak removed my fetters with neat methodical strokes that had less power than my smashing blows but that did the job economically. Oh, yes, as I say, I do like Pachaks.

"Thank you, Wa-Te. Now, what next?"

"Food and weapons."

"Aye."

"We will find a way out, as Hlo-Hli Herself smiles on us."

He was perfectly confident. He'd been through far more than had I down here. He was a mercenary, a zhanpaktun entitled to wear the golden pakzhan on its silken cords at his throat. He'd always been a mercenary, ever since his father had trained him up and assigned him to the band. When he gave his nikobi, his pledge of honorable service, he would not break it lightly. Pachaks discharge their service loyally until death.

After that we were very lucky.

Moving forward with great care, for we were weaponless as regards steel weapons, we traversed a passage and entered a chamber where tables and chairs and tapestries indicated we were entering once inhabited areas of the complex. There was food, rough fare suitable for guards.

We ate and drank prodigiously. Then Wa-Te, using the leg of a chair, forced open the lid of a chest. There was no trap.

"This must be a guardroom," he said. "Look at these. Rusty!"

Many of the weapons in the box were rusted together. We found five swords that would serve, and with spit and dust cleaned them up.

As I only have two arms, I took two swords. Pachaks have two left arms and a tail hand, so Wa-Te took three swords.

He flexed his right arm, which as usual was marginally stronger than his two lefts. "This feels good, by Papachak the All-Powerful!"

Swinging the two lynxters about, I agreed.

Speaking gravely, the Pachak said: "I would not use my name whilst I was slave. I am Nath Wa-Te. Lahal, Drajak the Sudden."

"Lahal, Nath Wa-Te. I think I shall continue to call you Wa-Te."

He smiled, there in that place of horrors. "Yes, there are very many Naths in the world."

Pachaks form their names from the first syllables of their parent's names; if a daughter the mother's first, if a son the father's. When Nath Wa-Te had a son he would be called a first name, and then Na- and the first syllable of Wa-Te's wife's first name.

Now I faced a dilemma. Was it fair to allow Wa-Te to accompany me? He was cheerful now he had won back his freedom and supremely confident he could march and fight his way out of the labyrinth. If he went off on his own he would face only traps, apart from any monsters already awoken. If he stayed with me, I'd keep bringing perils alive which he otherwise would not encounter. He solved the problem for me by saying: "We must stick together, Drajak. It is the only sensible course of action."

He was right as he saw it, of course. In the end, weakly, I felt we would stand a better chance together.

Just as I'd reached that dubious conclusion, a reverberation echoed through the chamber. It seemed to emanate from the walls. The plates and jars upon the tables rattled. The sound continued, hollow, echoing, rumbling on for a long time.

"By Hlo-Hli! It must be—"

"Aye. The Drums."

The booming vibrations of the Drums echoed away to silence. We stared at each other. What did that ominous sound portend?

Well, whatever that menacing beat of drums did or did not portend, my way ahead was plain enough.

Actually reaching that destination was an entirely different kettle of fish. We went on when we'd rested. We encountered various monsters of the smaller kind and either avoided or finished them. Avoidance was by far the better plan. Here we were venturing into chambers with cut walls, draped in tapestries—mostly torn and in poor condition—with increasing signs of human occupation. The light continued evenly beaming upon us. After the slave column we were slowly recovering a proper sense of smell, and the scents that I brought in mingled with those of people long gone these many seasons. The conviction grew upon me that the People of the Drums must number very few. Every now and again the booming roar of the Drums battered at our ears. After a time it was clear they were growing louder.

Although the whole place was drenched in sorcery, as Rollo had said, we so far had encountered only material monsters and traps. Magic had been non-existent. Again, this was a puzzle.

Wa-Te, a few steps in front of me as we pressed on along a passage, abruptly halted opposite an open door. I stopped. He very very cautiously put his head around the doorjamb, ready on the instant to jump back.

He motioned with his tail hand. Silently I joined him.

The room was of reasonable size. Down the centre stood a long table. The walls were tapestry-covered. At the table men sat, frozen in the act of eating and drinking. They were all Chuliks.

Their arms and armor gleamed bright and slightly oiled. There were a couple of dozen of them, their pigtails dyed red and yellow, their tusks banded in gold and silver, and they looked a mean bunch.

"What is the matter with them?" breathed Wa-Te. "Are they all dead?"

"They're well-preserved, if that is the case."

We went on quietly. Evidently, those Chuliks did not possess enough kharrna for me to awaken them at that range.

After a way, the Pachak said: "Well, for good or ill, they're in our rear now."

"Aye."

Neither of us had volunteered to go in and check, probably to take some of the fine weapons and armor. Caution becomes ingrained when you go delving.

We prowled on and reached an intersection. One arm of the passage stretched ahead, the other to our right, and both were well lighted.

"Toss a blade?" suggested Wa-Te.

The sword came down indicating we should continue ahead.

This passage went on and on in almost a straight line. The cut walls gave way to rough rock and soon we were walking through a tunnel.

"I have an idea, Drajak, the sword lied."

"I think you are right." To be honest, I thought the sword had indicated the truth. It looked to me as though this tunnel might lead to an exit some distance from the City of Eternal Twilight. "There is a corner ahead. Let us—"

"I'll lead on."

At the corner we discovered a large irregular cavern, poorly lit. Nothing moved. "Not a copper ob here. We'd better go back."

"Right," I said. Then I checked. "Hold on a whick."

Wa-Te didn't ask a fatuous question like: "What is it?" He stood silently, waiting, as I peered intently at the far end of the cavern.

The far wall rose sheer. Before it bits and pieces of yellow strewed the ground. Nearer to us the vague forms of men stood, motionlessly. And, nearer still, the crouched shape of a vorlind indicated why those men had halted, and formed a line. Many had bows lifted. Quietness and death brooded over the macabre scene.

What had transpired here was obvious enough.

I took another step forward and the vorlind, lethal, sprang to life. He didn't care there were a dozen men there, with bows. His feral hunger drove him on relentlessly. Now I had started him moving I had to push on quickly so that the line of men would unfreeze and so save the lives already pawned to death.

The archers stirred. Muscles unused for a long time creaked as the bowstrings drew back. A couple of men tottered, taking unsteady steps, and one fell. The others discharged their shafts and the vorlind, riddled, collapsed.

An uproar began, men shouting, women shouting, and a voice above all, bellowing: "By Sasco! Silence!"

Now we were in for it. I advanced boldly, holding up my hand. As I passed the dead vorlind, I saw a fellow scrambling up from the ground where he'd been crouching, in mortal terror of his life. He wore a long black robe and sandals and a jeweled fillet confined dark hair. His face expressed terror to the utmost degree, a face pale and thin, with downdrooping whiskers and a small and too-red mouth. He squeaked when he saw me.

"Where—?"

The big voice battered again. "Silence! By Spikatur Hunting Sword! Must I have you all whipped, guard and slave alike?"

I'd got him spotted now. He stood in the forefront, hand on the pommel of one of his swords, glaring about with his one good eye. His left eye was covered by a diamond and emerald studded patch. Thin he was, thin as a lath with a ferret face and dark hair cropped short. Quick, active, he moved with controlled spasmodic effort. The last time I'd seen him he'd been sitting in an armchair stripping leaves from a plant and scaring Vad Noran half to death merely by his presence. That had been in Huringa, capital city of the island of Hyrklana—before my lad Jaidur became king.

The man in black at my side moved with an odd sliding gait. He ran off, away from the confusion ahead, vanishing past a buttress of rock.

Obviously in answer to a question, the big voice battered again: "I do not know! By Sasco, it is past understanding!"

He must have been wrought up to a frenzied pitch to speak like that. He was a swordfighter, a Bladesman as I surmised, and his quiet icy manner chilled those he encountered. I walked on and called out in a firm voice: "Llahal, doms!"

With Wa-Te at my side I marched up and halted. Beyond him guards and slaves were running back to the bits and pieces of yellow. Now I could see they were skeletons. The uproar continued but in a lower key after the lord's harsh words concerning whipping.

He gave me a look as though he were lunging the rapier at his waist into my guts. "Llahal. You do not address me as dom. I am Vad Gochert, and you call me notor."

I knew his name was Gochert. That he was a vad, next step down in the nobility from a kov, was intriguing.

I said: "This is Kyr Nath Wa-Te, I am Drajak the Sudden—notor."

His one eye sized up the Pachak, and then me. The diamond and emerald eye-patch glittered in that poor light as he turned his head.

"Can you explain what has happened? We entered a shaft and the wall closed at our back. The vorlind was about to attack a man in a black robe. We advanced, ready—and the vorlind is dead, the man in black is gone, and many of my party are now skeletons. By Sasco! It is unbelievable!"

"We have been wandering for some time, notor."

"So you are of no help in unriddling this puzzle. My men are dead!"

I had enough puzzles of my own to keep me busy; the answer to this one was easy enough. After what Gochert had described had taken place his neat line of men had stepped forward into the aura of the stasis spell. Some slaves had been up with them. The rest had seen what happened to them. It seemed to me the edge of the spell was not a sharply defined line, so that a number of people had stepped into the aura. The ones left behind had no idea what it was about. Some had run forward and become frozen. The rest had cowered back, quite unable to force themselves forward to what they must have considered certain death. So they'd waited and waited and so died one by one and were now skeletons.

"You have my condolences, notor. You are sure there is now no way out there?"

"None. I told you. The shaft's wall closed up."

His guards were clustering round now, listening avidly. He had a fair proportion of Khibils in his party, and Hytaks, all solid professional fighting men and women. He had no Rapas and only a few Fristles. One of the Hytaks, bulky in banded kax, stepped up.

"Notor. All the provisions with the skeletons are spoiled. Yet those with the slaves with us are still fresh."

By this time I was looking about among this gaggle of people for a person I assumed he must have brought with him on his expedition.

When a couple of hefty Hytaks walked up carefully carrying the slender form of a girl on their crossed arms, their other arms supporting her back, I saw the answer to that also explained Gochert's fragmented responses to the situation. She wore a long blue gown girdled in silver, with soft slippers on tiny feet. Her pale brown hair was drawn tightly back in a bun to reveal a round innocent face, devoid of makeup. Her eyes were closed. She breathed shallowly. She looked as though the Hytaks could have carried a dozen of her and still not felt the weight.

"Merlee!" said Gochert, anxiously. All his icy manner fled.

She opened her eyes. They were gray-green. She tried to smile, her pallid lips soft and trembling.

"It is all about, notor, all about. So much, so very much!"

A fat high-busted woman bustled up and between them they put the girl safely down on a pile of rugs. She leaned back and licked her lips. Gochert looked down at her. His hand fondled the hilt of his rapier as though seeking the answer there.

Now girls like this Merlee do not like being called witches.

That is their proper name, of course; but it has fallen into disrepute. She was a Witch of the Demaskar Persuasion, and Deb-Lu had told me they had some very real powers. Now the sorcery drenching the Realm of the Drums had overcome her. Once she had come to terms with her surroundings and recovered her powers, she was the one very important person any party needs when they go delving.

"Bring wine!" ordered Gochert. He was making visible efforts to control himself. Once he had recovered, he'd be ice and steel.

Fristles were going around bashing the slaves back in line. Gochert, at least, did not employ Katakis for that disgusting occupation.

I couldn't see Gochert playing any part in the Star Lords' plans; but then, by Krun! you never could tell with them. He'd be useful to Wa-Te and me in providing us the protection of his party. I would have to find out why he had come down here to the Realm of the Drums. If his reasons were merely those of plunder then he could be discounted. Often in the past I'd wondered what had happened to him and why he hadn't crossed my path again, as I had felt so strongly he was fated to do. He'd come down here and stood frozen, waiting through all those seasons to be released.

A minor puzzle was why there were any provisions to spoil left among those poor people who had not dared venture ahead to stand, as they thought, in death. What a horrible predicament that had been! At least Merlee had stepped in to escape death then. The trapped and doomed wretches could all have committed suicide, I supposed. As for Gochert, he must have flown here aboard a Hyrklese voller. He must have a map. Now, where had he obtained that map?

Gochert took a long swig of wine. His one eye fixed Wa-Te and me. "Since you have been down here, you had better lead on. We must find the Drums."

"You'll hear them, notor, from time to time," said Wa-Te.

"Well, by Havil! Get on with it!"

So he was regaining his composure. I gave the Pachak a glance and we started off, followed by Gochert and some guards. Merlee was carried in her litter, the slaves trailed on, and guards brought up the rear.

Up ahead, Wa-Te said: "That was a strange business. I could not see clearly, but I could swear by Papachak the All-Powerful they were all standing like statues."

"Aye."

He gave me a puzzled look. Then he said: "You called me Kyr."

Kyr and Tyr are honorific titles, like 'sir' and carry some weight. He went on: "Kyr can only be given by a king or emperor. Tyr may be given by kovs or high nobles. So, Drajak the Sudden?"

As I say, I have always liked Pachaks. I said: "Believe me, Kyr Nath, that is in my power. But I would prefer to say no more."

"By Hlo-Hli Herself! This is indeed a—"

"Now, Wa-Te. Please."

"Very well. But you must promise to tell me some day."

"When we are safely out of this."

"Done. And this party—they are Hyrklese. One can tell by their weapons and gear. Although some is strange."

The rapier and main gauche were newish imports to Hamal and Hyrklana. They were now known in some parts of Loh; but that must have occurred after Wa-Te's time.

We reached the intersection where we had tossed a blade.

Wa-Te said: "The sword did not really lie. That was the way out."

I made a noise halfway between a grunt and a snort. "Yeh. But it was a way in only, by Chusto!"

Here we turned left and went on cautiously. A clanking at our backs brought Gochert's Khibil captain of his guard. He wore the insignia of a Jiktar, well enough, with armor and swords and a shield. He was a Khibil, understand, and he wasn't going to let us forget that. That, to him, was more important than being the vad's cadade. He shouldered up.

"You two know what you're doing?"

They are so damned cocksure, these foxy-faced Khibils.

I said: "If you wish to take the lead, pray do so."

"You call me Jiktar, yetch!"

I stopped. "Quidang!"

Anyway, we went on and this Khibil cadade, hight Romano the Sharp, assigned a couple of his men to go with us. We were lucky we came across no traps, for the guards marched on with very few precautions.

Debouching onto a ledge along a vast and eroded wall, we saw we'd reached a cavern of considerable size. The ledge stopped halfway and a narrow rope bridge extended before us at right angles, strung across the cavern to a ledge and an opening on the other side. Below us spumed and boiled a river, the water rushing along in streaks and lines of green fire.

The two Khibils started across the bridge at once. Wa-Te said: "That won't take much weight."

"No. Few of 'em at a time."

"Yeh."

We halted at the edge and stopped the traffic, allowing groups of guards across. Almost at once Gochert was up with us, icy with fury.

"What is the hold up?"

The litter containing Merlee swayed and was set down on its legs. Four Brokelsh stood at the carrying poles. The cadade, Romano, bustled up.

"Go across now! There is trouble in the rear."

Gochert snapped out: "Go on!"

If there was trouble at the back then Wa-Te and I were ready to cross right away and get out of it. We started over. The bridge swayed.

Halfway across I felt the bridge swinging even more. I looked back. Gochert and Merlee's litter were following, and a crowd of people were pressing on after with the cadade urging them on.

Wa-Te yelled: "There's too many of 'em!"

"Make it sharpish!" I said.

We started to move as fast as we could over the rotting wooden slats between the rope supports. I suppose I guessed from the wild movements of the bridge that we wouldn't make it.

The ropes parted with brittle twangs. Everybody on the bridge was flung helplessly, end over end, into that rushing boiling water far below.

The thunderous boom of the Drums beat above the roar of the river, their sonorous tones quickening into a rataplan of mocking triumph.

Eighteen

Swirled away with eyes and nostrils and mouths filled with water we shot helter-skelter downstream to plunge into the green gloom of a tunnel. Wa-Te had his tail hand wrapped about my waist and I gripped him so that we clung together in the millrace. Bright light smote down and we sluiced out into water that gradually lost its speed. Around us stretched a lake under an unseen roof, with exotic plants growing and birds flying everywhere.

Those birds flying and chirruping away up there made me think.

Usually it is not healthy to linger in unknown waters on Kregen. There are jaws that bite. So we swam for a little pinkish beach where already some of the survivors were crawling out onto the sand. We joined them.

The cadade was nowhere to be seen. That would probably have been fortunate for him if Gochert was there; the icy swordfighter was not present. Nor was the Witch of the Demaskar Persuasion. I felt a pang for Lady Merlee and hoped she would fare well and survive among the terrors.

The people were running about dazed, not sure what to do. I saw one slave, a hefty Rapa, creep up at the back of a guard Rapa and give him a right tasty smack over the ear. The guard fell down and the slave started to kick his rib cage in. I said to Wa-Te: "Do you wish to remain with this rabble, my friend, or shall we seek sweeter pastures?"

The Pachak swirled his wet hair back. He grimaced. "I'm with you!" This beach curved around and with the backing of green and colored foliage made a pretty picture. Wa-Te and I started to walk along towards the far end where we could just discern a black domed shape which must be a tunnel exit. We could not see where the river left the cavern, if it did. Movement across the lake caught our eye. Over on the opposite shore people were dancing up and down and waving. So that must be some more of Gochert's party.

"I really think, Drajak, that we fare better on our own."

I was about to reply when the four Hytaks who had followed us all burst out shouting. At last one of them said: "We are very sorry to hear that, for we want to go with you."

"What about Vad Gochert?"

"We serve faithfully for good masters. The vad has not paid us since we entered Loh."

Wa-Te might very well get on his high zorca now, for, as you know, Pachaks give their nikobi and then serve—if they don't get paid until the very end of the contract they will still remain loyal right through.

I said: "I am able to give you employment. I will pay you the going rate, plus a bonus, when we reach my party. Agreed?"

The bokkertu thus concluded we six went on towards the exit.

All four Hytaks were crossbowmen. Their spokesman was hight Lurgan the Vandour. As we left the cavern I reflected that it was nice to travel alone, but a little more comfortable, in these circumstances, to have a companion, and much more reassuring to have four hefty fellows at your back.

We went on smartly enough and found tunnels and caves. Now Wa-Te and I had to remember that these fellows had not been down here long. They would gain experience—if they lived—but for now the Pachak and I had to look out for them like Sunday School teachers and their flock.

Also, and this I marked with an exceedingly severe mark—birds and animals were already alive as I approached.

We debouched into a vast cavern and abruptly the booming roar of the Drums enveloped us. The noise continued, filling the cavern with sound. When it ceased, my ears, for one, rang like those famous old Bells of Beng-Kishi. As for my skull, I felt as though it bounced about on my shoulders.

A vague movement ahead past some tree ferns brought my attention back in focus. No time in a labyrinth to bemoan the state of your health, by Krun! The movement was repeated and I made out the figure of a man in armor walking across the cavern at right angles to our direction. He was followed by others. Their armor and dress reminded me of those soldiers Seg had pointed out to me in the Hostile Territories, remnants of the Empire of Loh. This evidence, then, pointed to this party belonging to Queen Satra.

Slaves filed past carrying burdens, followed by more guards. At my side Wa-Te whispered: "There's that shint, Trylon Ge-fu-Schian. I don't want to tangle with him, by Papachak the All-Powerful!"

These people marched near the centre of the column, for presently sumptuously attired people strolled past as though on a picnic outing. The way had been made safe for them. I'd seen the cost of that making safe. Litters were carried past, draped with gold tassels. There was even a band with gleaming instruments; they were not playing, for which I was thankful.

"They live high on the vosk!" growled Lurgan the Vandour.

Just then, walking along with an arrogant swing, the armored form of Princess Licria drew my attention. A few paces to her rear walked Folly. They went on and the procession of nobles continued to pass by. Folly had said there were 'thousands' in Queen Satra's expedition. I was beginning to think she had not exaggerated.

"Look at 'em!" said Lurgan in a choked voice. All of us understood just who and what the figures were who went by now. Some reclined in litters, others walked for a period of exercise. I counted. Dressed in a variety of robes and costumes they might be, they were all of one cloth. There were four Wizards of Loh and six Witches of Loh.

Wa-Te wasn't even looking at them.

After that a body of strapping fellows in marvelous armor stalked by and I began to fancy the queen herself must put in an appearance soon. This experience, in itself, of sitting in the front seats, as it were, and watching the entertainment, was weird.

In the next heartbeat I felt my eyes pop out and my heart give a thumping great kick. I gaped for that heartbeat like any loon; then I saw what had occurred. A great gush of relief swept over me.

A body of men marched past fore and aft of a man and a woman. Their uniforms were quite unlike those of the Lohvians, for these fine fellows in armor wore bright yellow jackets.

I stood up.

Wa-Te said: "Careful!"

Immediately I hunkered down again, the blood thrumming in my veins. But I had to think of the Pachak. I said: "Will that shint of a trylon recognize you?"

"Possibly. He was never over careful of his men."

"H'm. Then you must adopt a name. You can be Nath ti Zanda. That's a nice little village where the apples are juicy. Now, come on!"

I stood up as Wa-Te said: "But what are you about?"

I shouted: "Hai! Hai, my old dom. What kept you?"

Seg and Milsi swung about and stared directly at me, and Seg's bow was off his shoulder, the arrow nocked and the string drawn back before he'd finished swiveling around. Milsi shouted: "It's Dray!"

The parties of EYJ fore and aft of Seg and Milsi moved towards me so that the column might proceed. They sent up a yell, a disciplined cheer, all as one: "Hai, Kendur!"

Well, this was a fine kind of homecoming! I hurried forward. Milsi kissed me and Seg said: "I bet you've been having fun!"

I said: "Where is she?"

Immediately all the fun and frolic left Seg's face. He ground out: "She is not with you? We thought she was."

"No. Perhaps she is with Inch and Sasha."

"No, my old dom. We all fell down a shaft together, with EYJ. Inch is up front now, for we take turns."

So they hadn't found the way we four had entered here. There were lots of entrances, and Seg confirmed that there was a message about the fire. "She must be with Karidge and EDLG." I felt my lips were puffy.

"Yes," said Milsi. "I'm sure she is."

After that the pappattu was made and I told Lurgan the Vandour to report to EYJ, knowing they'd sort him out. Wa-Te, as Nath ti Zanda, coped with the situation admirably. He was unlikely to be recognized, for his Pachak comrades were dead and in the thousands in the column—well, who would remember one fellow? Then Seg shattered me yet again: "We are engaged to dine at the next stop with the queen."

"Queen Satra? You—A Queen of Pain? Wha—?"

Milsi laughed. "She's not like she is at all."

"That's what a little Sybli friend of mine said."

"We have not told her about the lapse of time."

"Well, by Vox, she'll have to know one day. I've an idea there are plans afoot for her. It seems that there are forces who wish to reinstate the old Empire of Loh—"

"Do what!" snapped Seg. "The whole of Erthyrdrin rejoiced when the yoke of Walfarg was thrown off."

"The idea, I think, is to create a strong central force to resist the Shanks."

"That's sensible enough, I suppose." Seg's handsome face expressed the utmost concern. "But I think that force should be Vallia."

"Or, Seg," I said, most mischievously indeed, "Pandahem."

He gave me a withering look. We joined the column and marched on and still the notables had not all passed and still the queen's litter remained in our rear. There must be another damned army following on, too. Seg, Milsi, Inch and Sasha had missed me in the building of the dome and gone looking. With the lads of EYJ they'd tumbled down a shaft they could not climb and so had marched on into the maze. They'd either been fortunate or my companions had been unlucky, for Seg's party reached deeply down without a hint of trouble and they'd bumped into Queen Satra's expedition, and here they were.

"A damned Queen of Pain!" I said. "How d'you—?"

"You wait until the dinner, Dray." Milsi twinkled, her face bright.

"A real Queen of Pain," confirmed Seg.

"So that lets Mevancy out," I said to myself.

The lead pastang of EYJ returned and their relief went up forward. Satra's forces were pleased that they'd found some other reckless fellows to take the lead. Inch and Sasha came back with the pastang and great were the reunions. "We're approaching what I think must be the centre." Inch set his tall form down on a convenient chest, for the column had stopped and preparations for what would have been evening were going ahead. "I think so, too," added Sasha. "And there are those Ngrangi-forsaken Drums again!"

The Drums boomed and roared and volleyed through the camp.

Milsi and Sasha insisted that I dress up in some foolishness of costume from the chests presented to them by the queen. She carried on down here just as though she were in her own court in Walfarg. In the end I found myself wearing a slashed tunic of a nice soft brown color, like mahogany. I'd told them my escapades and why I didn't have my weapons and where they were. So, of course, dressed up and escorted to the queen's tent by a detail of her guards, the first person I encountered as I stepped in was Princess Licria.

Before the polite Lahals could be made, she screamed out: "Drajak the Sudden! I'll have you! Seize him up, guards!"

With a shocking abruptness a rapier point rested against Licria's throat. The guards froze. Seg, in whose capable fist the hilt of the rapier was gripped, said: "I think you make a mistake, princess."

She gargled something. Seg hadn't pricked her throat. If he had to, to make her see reason, he would. "Now, princess. We are honored guests of the queen. So is Drajak. You do ill to cross your aunt."

The guard detail commander, a hikdar, cleared his throat. "Permission to speak?"

I said: "Spit it out, hik!"

He rolled his eyes at Licria, motionless under the rapier threat.

"Come on, man!" I snapped. He was a Hytak, solid and reliable, so I could do business with him. "We shall not harm the princess. There will be no blame attaching to you. Just that I do not want to be—"

"Seized up!" snarled Seg. "What kind of bitch princess is this?"

At that awkward moment the curtains over the tent's inner opening swished open and a little Och lady waddled through. She was not really looking at what she saw, wrapped up in her duties, so she squeaked out: "Please come through, the queen awaits—" Then her brain registered the tableau, and her squeak went up into bat's frequencies.

"Let us all go in to see the queen." Seg spoke pleasantly.

The guards were not allowed past the curtained opening, and when they stopped as we went through, Seg took the rapier away from Licria's throat. I said to the Hytak Hikdar: "Don't worry, dom."

Easy words, I know; but I intended to honor them.

The table was spread in a fashion to arouse the most intense desires. I shall not describe the details. Suffice to say that if they have banquets like that in Paradise, then Paradise is well worth striving for.

The famous silver trumpets of Loh pealed.

The curtains at the far end opened and Queen Satra walked through.

She was astonishing.

She wore robes of simple cut and style, fashioned from the most expensive fabrics. Her jewelry sparkled demurely. Her hair still came forward in that widow's peak over her forehead. That hair was pure white. Her face was a round dump, with creased cheeks, and dimples, and a little pink mouth from the left hand corner of which peeped the tip of a tooth slightly askew in her jaw. Her eyes, dark and brilliant, seemed to me to bear an emotion I couldn't fathom. She was just such a housewife as you might meet going to market with her basket on her arm. Those arms were pink and chubby. Her hands were very small and the fingernails polished. Her whole demeanor was mild, demure, modest.

This—this was a famous Queen of Pain of Loh?

Licria burst out in a blazing fury, the words pouring out in a frenzied torrent: "Aunt! This man—defiled—disgusting—whipped—sent to the Death Jungles of Sichaz—torture—I will not tolerate—"

"Control yourself, child!"

The queen's voice sounded mild, soft and a little breathless. I did not miss the hardness of honed steel in her words.

Milsi said: "Oh, majestrix, there has been some terrible mistake!"

"Yes," confirmed Sasha. "This is our dear comrade Dray and he would never insult a lady's honor."

"He's Drajak the Sudden, Drajak the Defiler!"

"If," said the queen in that soft mild voice that snicked in like a rapier, "you cannot control yourself, Licria, until I get to the bottom of this imbroglio, you had best return to your tent."

Licria gasped. She paled. And she kept quiet.

That was your power. That was your Queen of Pain!

"Now, Milsi my dear, tell me all about it."

"Well, majestrix, it is like this." Milsi went off into the story we five had fabricated. You see, quite clearly an Emperor of Paz was a ridiculous idea at this time. If anybody were to rule Paz then it would be the ruler of the Empire of Loh. Undeniably. Pandahem was owned and controlled by Walfarg as part of the empire. Milsi, who was Queen of Croxdrin, would be totally unknown to Satra. Likewise, any Emperor of Vallia was a potential enemy to the Empire of Loh. Havilfar defied Loh, and was about two hundred seasons after Queen Satra's time to be instrumental in the empire's downfall. Hyrklana, too, resisted. Now our equipment differed from that of these people, and so we fancied we might get away with claiming to come from almost anywhere, Donengil, Balintol. In the end we'd decided to be truthful. We acknowledged, proudly, that Vallia was our home.

Of course, Tall Inch and Sasha from Ng'groga in the south east, and Seg from Erthyrdrin in the north, were nominally subjects of Queen Satra. The institution of mercenaries included in its tenets the notion that a person could settle down in an adopted country. We were Vallians.

As the banquet proceeded Licria ate little, toying with and savaging her food, glaring at me in a way that can only be described as baleful. We all had estates and titles in Vallia, and used them. I fancied this mild-seeming little queen was trying to worm information about Vallia out of us for future use—future offensive use.

In a diplomatic way we were able to assure her that Vallia had no intentions of conquest across the sea. Holding the island was the job. The wine went around and the queen relaxed a trifle. We spoke politely of this and that and soon the queen was explaining things that puzzled me.

"Queens of Pain?" she said, her voice only slightly slurred from the wine. "Oh, yes. I was a wonderful QuoPa! Marvelous! The poor wretches I had tortured—hundreds, thousands. I rode my zorca into battle. I cut down my enemies. Oh, yes, by Lingloh, I was a true, right and puissant QuoPa!" She stared at Licria. "This princess who aspires to be a Queen of Pain is a pale shadow of what I was. She is milk and water, when I was fire and iron!"

Licria's convulsive reaction caught a glass and sent the red wine into a blood red stain across the tablecloth.

There were slaves everywhere, naturally, to minister to our every want at table. Licria snarled at the little Och girl, who shrank away from the stain, holding her cleaning cloth.

"That's right, Licria! Let the blood stay!"

Queen Satra had been downing the wine. I didn't keep count; but she had drunk deep of the grape.

She went on: "I have had ten husbands. Just think of it. Ten of the pompous fools. Oh, no. It is a woman's world, right enough."

Milsi said: "Men have their uses, though."

"Oh, aye, by Lingloh! All my children dead. All of them. Every single one." I happened to be looking at Licria as the queen spoke. A tiny movement curved her lips. I felt sorry for Satra's children. She went on: "Whose child are you, Licria? I can never remember whose grand-daughter you are. At any rate, you're the last of the descendants."

Licria found another goblet and did not answer. The shaft of pure hatred that sprang from her face for a half a heartbeat only portended great evil for the queen. Satra went on maundering about her life, recounting great deeds, famous battles, territories won. Then she said: "All that is past. I am no longer a QuoPa. I have repented of my evil ways. No longer will the silver trumpets of Loh shrill out over foreign dead as our armies sweep on to victory. No, no more, no more."

She was not sick with chivrel, so her white hair must be a sign that her life was well past the two hundred mark. Very soon now she would slip away. If the plot worked as Licria wished, she'd ship out faster than that!

If the Star Lords were serious in their intentions to recreate an empire here in Loh, and wanted Queen Satra to become the empress, maybe they hadn't quite reckoned on her change of heart. She was no longer a Queen of Pain. She was now a mild little old lady anxious to get her life right with Hlo-Hli Herself, or any of the secret pantheon known to her, before she went shuffling off to the Death Jungles of Sichaz. So that left the charming Princess Licria. She would be a Queen of Pain! By Krun, she'd be a QuoPa to outdo any QuoPa who'd ever lived!

What price Dray Prescot as Emperor of Paz with Licria as Empress of Loh?

Satra sighed and nearly went to sleep and was escorted to bed by her slaves. She was smart enough to give orders that we were not to be disturbed.

Licria flounced out without a word. We five, pleasantly filled after the banquet, our senses about us, went along to the tents given over to our use. The jurukkers of EYJ formed a comforting shield. I went off to check that the four Hytaks had settled in and found them happy enough in this new situation. "Where's Nath ti Zanda?"

"He was called out by a little Sybli. Very pretty, by Kyfar!"

"Did she wear black beads around her neck?"

"Aye, lynxor, she did."

Now what did Folly want with the Pachak? I went off along the lines looking for them.

The soldiers of Loh were smart, no doubt of it. I remembered the army we'd seen in the Hostile Territories. 'Great Beasts of the Air' as we'd called them, then had destroyed that army. The downfall of the Empire of Loh was a complicated and not easily explained fact of history.

In contrast my lads of EYJ just got on with the job and were as smart as they needed to be to meet that particular situation. Should some fancy foreign bigwig come visiting and it was necessary to turn out a guard of honor to escort him or her, then my lads of EYJ or ESW would put on an eye-watering show that would make these parade ground soldiers of Loh look like new recruits with straw in their hair straight from the farm.

Turning the corner of a tent and glancing back I saw the usual activity, with soldiers lounging and slaves scuttling. I turned back and there was Wa-Te hurrying towards me. He looked wrought up.

"Drajak! Thank Hlo-Hli I have found you—the Sybli girl, Folly—"

Now I heard the first footfall, I think. I swung about and the dark cloak of Notor Zan fell and enveloped me in blackness.

Nineteen

The men in black hurried us through secret narrow corridors and down steep stairs slashed sheer through virgin rock. They did not speak. They urged us on with knotted ropes. I'd come to my senses under a treefern, with Wa-Te on one side and Folly on the other. The men in black bound our wrists with ropes, and struck us with their knotted ropes, and drove us on willy-nilly. So much for Queen Satra's orders that I was not to be disturbed!

We had been stripped naked. Now I am used to running about on bare feet, and so too was Folly. The Pachak, more used to a pair of stout army boots or studded sandals, made a few faces as stones cut him. But he was not a soft city man who never went barefoot. He could handle this.

Every now and then we were allowed a short rest. The men in black did not talk; they did not object when we spoke together.

"Well, Folly—tell me—"

"The mistress. She was demented! I heard her talking to Trylon Ge-fu—"

"That shint!" exclaimed Wa-Te.

"Oh, yes, he is a great villain. He aspires to Licria's hand and to become Emperor of Loh."

"One of ten, I expect," I said, amused.

"You know about that?" Folly shook her head at the evil of the world. "Most of them went into the river in a weighted sack."

"Folly warned me, but we couldn't find you. When we did—"

"I was as slow as a ponsho attacking a leem."

"Where, master," whispered Folly, "are they taking us?"

The rock quivered and the booming roar of the Drums smashed down. "There's your answer."

Folly shivered. Then she shook herself and lifted her chin.

"I refuse to be frightened by a noise. As for the trylon, you ought to know, Wa-Te, that Licria merely uses him. It's the weighted sack for him when his days are numbered."

"Sichaz extend its Death Jungles for him!"

Then we were knouted up and struggled on. Down and down we went.

Now and then other parties of men in black with captives joined us. I asked Folly if there were a trade in this from the column, and she could only say that often folk were missing and none knew where they'd gone. I saw no one I knew in the new arrivals. We pressed on.

All the men in black resembled the first one I'd seen transfixed with terror by the vorlind in the chamber where we'd met Gochert. Pallid of face, downdrooping of whiskers, with slack features and small, too-red mouths. They wore different kinds of jeweled fillets in their hair.

These, then, I said to myself, are the folk of the Realm of the Drums.

The noise of the Drums when they spoke did not so much grow louder as we neared as become more distinct. The sound traveled throughout this labyrinthine complex. Reasoning from that, I realized that we had not heard the drums until we'd been down for some time. That meant that someone had penetrated to the depths and aroused the sleeping men in black.

A final sharp set of stairs brought us to a tunnel stretching left and right in a circle so that the ends curved out of sight. We went to the left and reached an iron door. Over the door a gilt statue of a xichun spread his wings, and flailed his tail and stretched out his sinuous neck. His eyes seemed to regard us as we passed under, the needle teeth ready to tear the flesh from our bones.

Beyond the iron door the whole aspect of the place changed.

244

The walls were smooth ashlar, crisp where they were not covered by tapestries. The by now familiar pearly light took on a pinkish tinge. Soon we were walking on carpets. More doors followed, each with a xichun set above the architrave. I began to prepare plans if I had to fight one.

The Drums burst out with a rolling thunder; but the sound was no louder than it had been. As though this were a signal, the men in black plied their rope's ends and hurried us on.

The smell of sulfur hung thickly on the air.

We came out onto a ledge high above a cavern. At first it was difficult to take in all the details. A rail guarded the edge and people were filing down past it to the right. I looked over the rail. At the centre of the floor of the chamber the stone was cleared of any obstructions. A round black hole some four paces across gaped like the eye of a Cyclops. Tiers of seating were arranged in a horseshoe, the seats strewn with rugs and shawls. At the moment the stand was empty. Various small buildings stood about, columned, domed, like shrines. I looked up for a moment and saw an odd arrangement of boulders supported by an incurve of the roof. Up between the boulders a shaft appeared to go straight up; but the light failed there and details were lost.

A dais stood to one side of the horseshoe-shaped stand, supporting a throne, with steps leading up to it. A larger platform on the other side held broad tiered steps. There were no rugs there.

The ledge which we descended curved around and when we reached the bottom further details became apparent. Naked men and women of various races were pushed forward into a compound, railed in. To our immediate left lifted the throne. Under the larger platform a door was now visible, presumably leading back into a tunnel through bedrock.

There were many people crowded in so that Wa-Te put his tail around Folly and I put my arm about his shoulders. We did not feel like being separated just now. The stinks of sweat and fear rose in a miasma.

A woman wearing a black robe with a huge yellow xichun emblazoned across back and front stepped out from under the throne. She picked the mallet up from its brackets under a bronze gong. She hit the gong. The metallic sound, so different from the roar of the Drums, convinced me that the gong was not the origin of that gigantic noise.

As the reverberations gonged away to silence, men and women emerged from the door under the platform. They split left and right and climbed the steps to fan out along the terraces. They remained standing. They were dressed in black gowns, emblazoned with the xichun, and they carried Lohvian longbows.

At the same time people began to fill the seats of the horseshoe. These were dressed in a motley of colors, robes of varying cut. All had the yellow xichun somewhere about their clothing. They were talking and laughing, very animated, and many had goblets and parcels of sweets with them.

"Quite a day out for them," observed Wa-Te.

"I must say I don't care for all this."

"I think," began Folly. Then she said: "I will not think what I think!"

After a wait, marshals in black led out two naked men into the area between the arms of the horseshoe. That expanse was sanded.

A deep silence fell. From the rear of the throne dais emerged a procession. Everyone was clothed in black except for the glittering figure all in gold. He walked along with his arms extended and supported by helpers. His face held all the old look of absolute authority I so much detested, as hard as the stone about him. On his head blazed a crown of many jewels, diamonds, emeralds, sapphires. There was just the one red gem. It coruscated from the centre of the crown, lustrous, scintillating, blood red.

So there was the object for which we'd come all this damn long way!

The gong sounded again. The two naked men advanced towards each other and began to wrestle. One had some skill, the other had not. Very soon the skilled forced the unskilled down and so held him trapped in a lock.

Two men in black whipped the two men up. The man who had lost the fight stared with pale hopeless eyes. One of the men in black struck him through with a sword and he fell, his blood staining the sand. He was dragged away. The victor looked about. Men in black surrounded him. He was lifted up horizontally and in a twinkling, as the gong crashed out, he was run towards the hole in the floor and hurled in. His shriek of mortal terror howled up, dwindling in eerie echoes.

The fellow in gold with the ruby of the Skantiklar in his crown held up a hand. Silence fell. We waited. Presently the fellow gestured.

Two more men were thrust out onto the sand. They looked at each other, and shook their heads. They were twins. It was clear to all that they would not fight each other.

A woman with a red patch across her black gown emerged from under the throne. She held a slate in her left hand. She looked up at the fellow wearing the crown. Some of her words were lost; but I caught: "...at least four more, majister..."

The golden-clad arms lifted. Pale hands moved in a mystic gesture. The man's eyes were like live coals, burning upon the two men. The change that overcame them was frightening in its rapidity and intensity. One moment they were staring at each other with brotherly love, the next their faces evinced the most intense hatred. Snarls broke from them. They leaped at each other, and they fought like maniacs—men possessed.

Their fists were knotted about each other's throats. So they gripped and choked. One twin must have been a fraction stronger than the other, a tragic fraction. One man collapsed and the other staggered away, hands to his own throat, retching. As before, the loser was struck through and the winner hoisted and hurled down the black shaft.

Again silence fell.

The woman wearing the red patch consulted her slate. She looked up at the throne and shook her head. Once more the gong crashed out.

This time two naked women were thrust out onto the sand. I did not care to watch, and so took more notice of the details of this hell hole.

The platform to my right contained bowmen, and no doubt they would take delight in shafting any poor crazed wretches who tried to run for it. The steps leading up to the throne on the left had rugs scattered upon them.

The woman with the slate and the woman with the gong stood just to the side. Just what title that fellow up there called himself, I couldn't know. But I bet it was a real fancy string of pomposity. As for the crowd lolling on the horseshoe shaped benches, they struck the most incongruous note in this place of barbarity and terror.

A couple of husky fellows wearing the black gown and the xichun symbol with crossed swords embroidered in yellow below it stood just below the High One in his throne. These two carried swords, not the Lohvian lynxter but an interesting double-curved sword rather like a kris. Their faces looked dull and doughy with good living. The notion was borne in on me that I'd have to do something sharpish if this imbroglio wasn't to be the end.

I heard Folly whisper: "The beasts!" When I looked back the fight between the women was over. One had been struck through and the victor was being hurried to the pit.

"The trouble is," said a distinguished-looking man standing next to Wa-Te. "We have no way of knowing what lies in the pit. Is it a dreadful death? Or is it an escape? Certainly, having a sword stuck through you is final enough, by Amintal the Benevolent!"

We agreed and the argument over which was preferable spread through the prisoners. We stood, as I say, near the left hand side, by the throne; prisoners were picked out from anywhere at random, it seemed, and the next pair of women were selected from the far side by the platform of bowmen.

The fact to remember here was that this was a scene that rightfully belonged some five hundred seasons ago. Then the City of Eternal Twilight was not a Lost City of Chem. It had trading links all over Loh. There was no difficulty in finding people, no mystery how all these folk came here.

The distinguished-looking man added to that by saying that he wished, now, by Amintal the Benevolent, he'd never ventured here after treasure. Like many of the prisoners he appeared unnaturally calm. I, too, felt a numbness between my ears. He finished: "As true as my name is Nath the Thirsty, I am a strom and yet this creature on his throne ignores me."

The women struggled together, breast to breast, and I looked away.

Wa-Te said: "I think the sword will be the easier death, Drajak. Should we be chosen to fight, I shall kill you with sorrow and joy."

"I, too, believe the shaft to be a hideous death. Therefore, Wa-Te, I shall most certainly defeat you."

"Ha!" he said, firing up in that Pachak way. "We'll see!"

When the girl who had triumphed was hurled down the pit the silence fell. I could feel the expectancy in the air, the sizzle as of lightning through rain, the pulse of blood loud in my head.

The woman with the slate gestured and two more men were driven out by the marshals, to fight, and to lose and lose. The man who had won let rip a shriek of animal fear as he went headfirst into the pit. This time the silence pressed down like a leaden helmet.

I felt prickles all over my skin. Folly put her arm about my waist, and I reciprocated, and the touch of her skin vibrated in my fingertips. We all waited on the verge of some great catastrophe.

A red light grew in the pit. At the moment when the red light began to glow, the people sitting in the horseshoe, the bowmen and the people by the throne, gazed upwards. Instinctively, I glanced up. A shaft of light, a sparking, sizzling, flaming bolt of fire smashed up from the pit. It made no sound. Silently it licked its flame upwards. The tip of the flame struck that odd shaping of boulders high in the shaft.

The boulders swung across and clashed together, and then rebounded. Through the cavern, dinning in our ears, the sullen reverberations of the Drums rolled sonorously.

The flame soared up, striking the boulders, smashing out the roar of the Drums. The tip of the flame recurved, spread, descended from the shaft's opening to spread out in a net. That fire had changed. Throughout the gossamer of flaming filaments danced golden motes, sprites of energy that sparked and scintillated dazzlingly. The whole vibrant mass of light descended upon the horseshoe of seating and upon the bowmen's platform and on the throne.

The people there were galvanized into frenetic action. They danced in abandon, flung their arms and legs about, their mouths open and gasping as though they greedily drank wine from a spouting fountain. They were drinking the flames! Their faces shone, sweat poured from them. Crazy scenes were being enacted everywhere among the people in bright clothes. Those in the black robes, drinking in the flames, remained more sober. I caught the immediate idea that they took it in turns, thus to guard, thus to imbibe—imbibe whatever it was they were drinking from the flames!

With a last tremendous clang from the Drums, the flame died.

No one could speak. The silence now was the silence that falls upon a stricken battlefield after all the wounded have died.

The woman in the red patch with the slate was the first to rouse herself. She adjusted her clothing, and then commanded the gong mistress to strike. The gong note rang out peremptorily.

The holiday-attired people, the king's procession, the bowmen, all descended and marched off. The marshals and guards before the prisoners changed over. We waited, without food or drink. Strom Nath the Thirsty licked his lips. "These rasts buy their pleasures dearly!"

I said: "I think, doms, it is time we thought of escape."

"If we don't get somewhat to eat and drink soon," said Wa-Te, "I, for one, won't have the strength to lift my feet." He was, as we all knew, exaggerating. But there was an ugly truth in what he said.

The bowmen returned to their platform, the merry-makers crowded the horseshoe, and the damned procession re-appeared, with the golden form wearing the ruby of the Skantiklar in his crown. I glared on him with some disfavor.

The gong clamored out demandingly.

Marshals were advancing to the far side of the sanded area to pick the next pair of combatants, so we over here could breathe again. The smells were not helped by the perfume everywhere floating into the still air. That damned flame that created the Drums had not been hot—at least I'd felt no heat from it. People sweated from fear, the prisoners, and expectant enjoyment, the holiday crowd.

Down on the edge of the sanded area a man walked along looking at the prisoners. He passed by a marshal and the marshal took no notice of him. This figure wore a plain gown of a crimson hue, and carried a varnished staff. He wore a turban which balanced perfectly on his red Lohvian hair.

I felt—well, I tell you, by Zair, I felt emotion course all through me! Deb-Lu-Quienyin walked on by and he did not look up; he was looking at the front row of prisoners. Presently he walked back and disappeared. Out on the arena two men fought, and died, and one was shafted by a sword and the other was just shafted.

I said to Wa-Te: "When we make our break do not be surprised if we receive unexpected help."

"Oh?"

"You recall those lads with yellow jackets?"

"I should welcome them with open arms!"

Folly said: "Oh, yes, please!"

Wa-Te clicked his tongue and said: "You call them lads. They're the toughest bunch of hard men I've ever met."

"ESW would question that, Wa-Te!"

"What—?"

But I was not listening to my comrade. I was staring at the sanded arena and the marshals shepherding two girls out. The women had their arms about each other's waists. They walked closely together, leg striding for leg, heads touching. The marshals tried to pull them apart and, somehow, two marshals were lying on the ground, rolling over and over.

Rope's ends thwacked down and I jumped at each blow. The women were torn apart and turned to face each other. They stood, defiantly, one foot braced before the other, arms crossed. One of those girls had forearms deeply pitted—but there were many granules still filled with bindles.

The king-like figure on his throne lifted his hands and made his gestures and—lo!—the faces of the women changed. In a heartbeat they were no longer haughty, defiant, radiating love one for the other that would not be broken—now their faces drew into animal snarls, savage downdrawn brows and writhing lips.

I didn't care how they were to die, by sword or pit; that they were to die at all mattered.

Once in hand to hand combat, Delia could easily overcome Mevancy. But Mevancy had only to shoot her bindles and Delia would no longer have a face.

With hatred disfiguring her features, Mevancy began slowly to lift her forearms, pointing at Delia.

Twenty

Red roaring madness engulfed me. I felt choked. Naked as I was I felt as though a metal helmet enclosed my head, crushing my temples, constricting my throat. All I could see in the whole universe was Delia. She stood at the centre of vision and all about her stretched nothingness. Half crouched, her hands extended, she looked lithe and vibrant, quick and lethal as any hunting cat—and across her face spread a demonic look of utter hatred.

I had to tear my whole being away from Delia. I had to control myself, I had to think. I had to—I was out on the sand and somehow the broken body of a marshal lay strewn behind me and I was running for the steps to the throne. If arrows were shot off at me, they all missed.

The two guards with their double-curved swords came down for me and I had one of their swords in my fist and they were reeling back with their guts hanging out. I kicked them aside and sprang up the rest of the steps to the platform where the throne reared. The king in his golden robes still continued to stand with arm extended.

The knowledge flamed in my head that I must not kill him.

Up to his back I leaped, gripping his extended arm in my left fist, and fitting the curve of the sword snugly about his throat. I jerked the sword. I cut him. Oh, yes, I cut the bastard!

"Cancel the hatred spell instantly or I will slit your throat."

I spoke evenly, not panting, and my words shot out like steel darts.

He started in with some expected nonsense like: "You are already dead—let me go!"

I cut him again. I took a vicious and sadistic pleasure from that, Zair forgive me. I dare not look down on the sand. I dare not...

He yelped and I twisted his arm down. If the bones snapped, so much the worse for him.

An arrow clanked onto the arm of the throne. He yelled then, lifting his voice: "Stop! Stop shooting you shints!"

No more arrows flighted in.

I put more pressure on his arm and abruptly it snapped down. He shrieked out something I couldn't understand and tried to twist away in my grasp. He didn't succeed but his movement took his head out of my line of sight. And so I looked down onto the sand.

Marshals were running about and a bunch were starting for the steps up to the throne. So it had been quick, then.

I yelled at them: "Stop still! His head will roll off if you do not!"

Out of concern for him, or fear—who the hell cared?—they stopped.

So I could look at the two women.

Mevancy was flat on her front on the sand. Her right arm was twisted up behind her and in some mystical way her head was being hauled back. Delia was half kneeling on her, and had her in a grip that I recognized as a variation of a Krozair technique with a nasty little extra from the Sisters of the Rose flung in. Blood speckled Delia's arms.

As I gazed with the blood thumping in my temples and the feeling of suffocation nigh on choking me, Delia abruptly let go. She jumped up. Mevancy rolled over, dazed. Delia hauled her to her feet and the women collapsed into each other's arms. They hugged each other, laughing and crying and kissing. What I felt—I do not know what I felt.

Over to the side a black clad marshal suddenly went flying up into the air. He landed with a splat on his back. An enormous figure burst from the crowd of prisoners waving a double-curved sword. He went hell for leather for the next pack of marshals.

As that bulky powerful figure charged, I felt the numbness between my ears falling away. The big fellow was yelling as he charged.

"Hack 'n' Slay! I'll have you, you cramphs! Hack 'n' Slay!"

Following him leaped a rascally gang who went tearing into the black clad men. All were naked. But I recognized most of them. First Emperor's Sword Watch were in action!

The fellow in my grip was blathering on, shrieking over his broken arm, as the greasy blood dripped down from his throat. I twisted him again. "If your Bowmen of Loh shoot, you kleesh, I'll slit your throat."

That instruction proved superfluous in the next turn of events. Everything had happened at a hectic rate. Shafts began to fall among the clustered bowmen on their platform—and each shaft was fletched with the red feathers of the zim korf of Vallia!

The lads of EYJ came running in, perfectly controlled, in tight formation, hurtling on to send the rabble of black-gowned men and the holiday crowd into a shrieking panic. How they scuttled, those drinkers of the flame of the Drums!

Seg and Inch were there, in the lead, roaring the swods on.

Llodi had a spear and was rapidly following old Hack 'n' Slay as they cleared their end of the arena. As for that young rip Rollo, he'd found himself a bow and was merrily shooting anything black that moved.

So engrossed was I in the fantastic scene in the cavern that I took no notice of a hissing squawk overhead. The fleeting thought crossed my mind that if the Star Lords had sent their Gdoinye to spy on what I was doing for them, he'd turned up a bit too late, by Djan!

Now guards of Queen Satra's expedition appeared, joining in.

I whooshed out a breath. Seg and Inch reached Delia and Mevancy. Scarlet and gold cloaks enveloped their nakedness. Milsi and Sasha ran across, half-sobbing, half-laughing, to be embraced. Well, then! Things were turning out well, by Krun!

The four Hytaks led by Lurgan the Vandour who had joined us from Gochert's party, together with Wa-Te, had caught the gong mistress and the woman of the red patch and the slate. They had not slain them. Being professional paktuns, they were touchy on points of honor.

Everything was on the point of being under control. Our forces fanned out to occupy the place and make sure we were secure. The fleeing mobs in black or bright attire would be scuttling away to their bolt holes. We'd have to deal with them in due course.

So, then—and belatedly, by Vox!—I bethought myself of this king fellow's golden crown and the ruby of the Skantiklar glowing at its centre.

Again that hissing squawk spat from above me. I looked up.

A golden flash, a fleeting glimpse of wide spread wings—and I ducked! The golden-feathered xichun darted his sinuous neck past my downbent head and as I rolled sideways so the xichun's fanged head snatched the crown. His wings beat powerfully and he was up and curving for the radiance of the roof.

I yelled. "Seg! Rollo! Shaft him!"

My shout burst above the hubbub. People swung about to stare. The xichun was a mere glinting golden speck, driving past the boulders of the

Drum. A shadow among the cunning balance of stone took my immediate and appalled attention. There was no chance of a shot now, even a Bowman as superlative as Seg could not blast a shaft through solid stone.

Up there the xichun fluttered to a landing on the boulder. It did not move under the weight. A man appeared. There must be a tunnel leading to the Drums through the rock of the roof. He looked down.

I knew him. Oh, I knew him all right!

Deb-Lu appeared up the steps of the throne. He was real. He panted out: "He's got it, Jak! He's got it!"

The king stirred in my grip and I released him, staring up in bitter frustration. This king fellow must have recognized the end for him and his ways. He must also have been brave. With an inarticulate cry he jumped down the steps. The movement made me instinctively follow him with my gaze. He ran with his golden robes flapping about him, he ran straight for the pit of the flame. He jumped in.

His body was not enough to trigger the blast of spitting fire. The pit remained black. His last desperate fling had failed.

Deb-Lu said: "Look, Dray!"

Up there on the boulder of the Drums the bulky figure of Na-Si-Fantong worked on the helmet. He untwisted the ruby of the Skantiklar and held it aloft in triumph.

Then, with a gesture of supreme contempt, he hurled the crown down, and it bounced and trundled across the sand.

"He's gone!"

The Wizard of Loh, Na-Si-Fantong, disappeared.

With him went the ruby, went the reason we had suffered all the perils down here in the Realm of the Drums.

SCORPIO TRIUMPH

DRAY PRESCOT

The picture we have of Dray Prescot, as painted by himself in his narrative and by one who has seen him on Earth, is at once enigmatic and intriguing. He is a compelling figure, dynamic, dominating, demanding, yet there is in him that odd vulnerability. He is a man over middle height, with brown hair and level brown eyes, with enormously broad shoulders and powerful physique. There is an aura about him of abrasive honesty and indomitable courage. He moves like a savage hunting cat, quiet and lethal, sudden. Reared in the harsh conditions of Nelson's navy, he has been transported to the exotic and barbaric, beautiful and cruel world of Kregen, four hundred light years from Earth, under the double star Antares, the twin Suns of Scorpio.

Paz, the hemisphere of Kregen where Prescot has adventured and succeeded, is threatened by the reiving Shanks from Schan, the other half of the planet. He has been pitchforked into the job of organizing the resistance, a so-called Emperor of Paz, and has managed—temporarily—to drive off the Shanks and their mentor, the mysterious Carazaar. In all he undertakes, he is immeasurably assisted by Delia, Delia of the Blue Mountains, Delia of Delphond. Their family are now generally about their own affairs.

To his great surprise, his comrade Wizard of Loh, Deb-Lu-Quienyin, tells him he must concentrate on finding the rubies forming the Skantiklar. These have been scattered in seasons past, and if brought together will confer stupendous sorcerous power on the possessor of the Skantiklar. Down in the continent of Loh expeditions have ventured below the City of Eternal Twilight into the Realm of the Drums in search of one of the rubies. A Wizard of Loh, Na-Si-Fantong, has been collecting the rubies, and it is believed he wants them for no good purposes. He has succeeded in obtaining a ruby and vanishes into the maze of tunnels under the city. Not really convinced in the importance of the Skantiklar, Prescot has to go in pursuit. Alone, he threads his way through the labyrinth, already feeling he will never catch Na-Si-Fantong...

Alan Burt Akers

One

I, Dray Prescot, Lord of Strombor and Krozair of Zy, crawled painfully along a narrow and jagged tunnel with dust clogging my mouth and nostrils and stinging my eyes and every now and then my head would go thwack! against a damned rocky outcrop in the roof. By Makki Grodno's disgusting diseased black-fanged winespout and deliquescing dangling left eyeball! I'd wager that clever Na-Si-Fantong hadn't crawled along here. Oh, no! He'd have used his sorcerous powers to create a smooth marble avenue and strolled along without a care in Kregen.

As for me, I'd hared off after the mage when he'd snatched the ruby and—of course—a whole world of rock and rubble had avalanched down at my back, shutting my friends away and shutting me in.

All I could do now was crawl on as best I could. There was a little light, either from some fungus or perhaps some clever magical scintillant stone—I didn't give a damn which it was. I could just about see where I was going—and where that was I'd no idea at all, at all, as the song has it.

"Sink me!" I burst out to myself. "What the blue blazing hell am I doing, scrabbling about miles underground after a stupid magic red ruby when the damned Shanks are organizing a powerful expeditionary force against us?" I moved my right knee up and then my left and surged forward and—thwack! went my head against the roof. I mentioned the Divine Lady of Belschutz and forged on. Oh, no, I should be out in the fresh air and the light of the Suns of Scorpio, planning horrible retribution upon the fishy heads of the Fish Faces and their whiptailed Kataki allies.

The little kris-like curved sword I'd snatched up kept on getting in the way; but I felt disinclined to abandon the weapon. It would come in useful if I encountered any of the habitual nasties frequenting the labyrinth. I'd had no time to snatch up any clothes. In a somewhat turbulent frame of mind I pressed on along the raggedy tunnel.

As San Blarnoi says: "A day short of Eternity is still Eternity." In the end I reached the point where the tunnel led onto a large cavern. Before I plopped out of the opening I screwed my head around checking to see what reception committee might be awaiting.

The universal mellow pearly light shone down from the overhead. The air hung still and breathless. I could hear no sound apart from my own breathing, inaudible otherwise. The floor of the cavern was artificially smooth. Set around the walls stood nine sarcophagi. I stared at them and my heart sank. Now what mumbo-jumbo nonsense was I in for?

When I was satisfied that no one else was around I stepped down from the opening. Lumps and shards of rock in a fanfall indicated that whoever had made the tunnel had broken through into this cavern.

Immediately I moved away I saw one of them. The poor devil lay alongside a sarcophagus with his head stoved in. Now—because this place, this Realm of the Drums, had been sorcerously held in suspended animation for the best part of five hundred years, this fellow might have died yesterday, or five hundred years ago.

He wore a ragged breechclout and his arms and hands were covered in scratches. He was apim, Homo sapiens sapiens, like me. In the dust at his side lay a hefty crowbar.

A foot in a sandal projected past the end of the coffin and on walking carefully around I saw another fellow, a Rapa, whose beak and feathers of his head were scrunched down between his shoulders.

Strewn across his body were portions of two other men, as best I could judge a Brokelsh and a Moltingur. Whoever had slain them must have had colossal strength.

That was the point at which I made up my mind I wouldn't try to open a sarcophagus.

In the opposite wall stood an opening. It had been bricked up with large blocks and enough had been pulled down from the centre to make a hole large enough for a person to duck through.

That looked to be, apart from the tunnel down which I'd crawled, the only way out.

Very very carefully—as you may well imagine!—I went across and squinted through.

The pearly light revealed what could only be a shrine.

Dark stains disfigured the basaltic altar block. The statue above bent its gilded wedge-shaped head forward, narrow jaws armed with rows of needle teeth, its scaly wings wide spread, its lizard-like body crouched as if to spring, its barbed tail extended. The xichun whose aerial domain lay high above the rain forest had led me on to danger before. The flying animal was clearly some kind of totem down here. I gave it a glare; it did not move.

The feeling possessed me that I'd do well to keep the corner of one eye focused on that golden xichun.

Just for the moment I did not venture into the room of the shrine. There were two doors, one each side of the basaltic block, and each had its own gilded xichun above the architrave. These two flying lizards might be smaller than the fellow over the altar; they'd bear watching with the same attention to self-preservation. A gaggle of chests half-covered with rugs to the side seemed as though they might have been used as seats. I turned back to the main chamber and broodingly surveyed the situation.

The narrow, rocky and damned uncomfortable tunnel through which I'd reached here must have been for most of its length a natural fault. The tomb robbers needed only to break through the last few paces, as the extent of the fantail of rubble indicated. To my mind, then, this meant they must have a map.

If the two doors in the shrine room were the only way out, then whoever had bricked up the opening intended the nine sarcophagi to be sealed in. There might be further bricked up doors in there. The more I looked at the situation the less appealing it became.

Deb-Lu-Quienyin had negated the spell that held everyone down here in stasis only in a local aura around us—that is, my companions and me. So when I came across a living person standing stock still in suspended animation I woke him, her or it up. So that meant these four dead tomb robbers must have died just before the spell was cast five hundred years ago. I walked across—carefully!—and looked at them again.

The apim wore a torn mustardy breechclout. The Rapa wore a green lap-lap, a thigh-length wrap-around. That was fastened by a leather belt with a cheap brass buckle. The Brokelsh and the Moltingur had also worn mustardy breechclouts. After a careful search I found no map.

Again I stared at the torn down brickwork. At first, because the brick blocks spilled into the cavern I'd assumed the wall had been pushed in from the other side. Now it began to look as though it had been torn down and pulled in. Why?

There was, undoubtedly, something highly nasty in that shrine room.

The tunnel at my back was blocked. That left the two doors in the shrine room as the only ways out.

"By the Black Chunkrah!" I said. "Trust that vosk skull of a Dray Prescot to drop himself in it!"

Well, as they say, you must accept the needle, and needs must when you come to the fluttrell's vane. If that was the only way out, then, By Krun! that was the only way out.

Before I came to push of pike I had another look at the sarcophagi. Each was about five feet high, fashioned from marble with rather pleasant patterns. Each lid was adorned with an over-life-size effigy of a warrior. There were an apim, a Fristle, a Rapa, a Chulik, a Hytak, a Pachak, a Brokelsh, a Relt and an Och.

Each one's armor was carved in considerable detail and their weapons were as carefully represented. Of those nine carvings, one of the races of diffs intrigued me by his unexpected presence.

There were no signs I could make out along the junction of lid and coffin to indicate the crowbar had been used. If whatever had destroyed these four men had emerged from the sarcophagi then it had returned and closed the lid or lids without a trace.

Or, perhaps, by Vox, it had torn the brick blocks down and escaped into the labyrinth! That was not a pleasant thought.

Well, then, it must be a damned tidy monster, for it had replaced its lid neatly enough. If one monster had risen and escaped perhaps there were eight more undead waiting for some unsuspecting wight to release them. I felt a prickly itch down between my shoulder blades.

With great care I removed the dead apim's mustardy-colored breech-clout and the Rapa's leather belt. They were dusty but clean enough, so the men had died quickly. The power of the blows that had destroyed them was once again reinforced in my mind.

Picking up the crowbar in my left hand and hitching up the belted breechclout with my right, I took up the little curved sword and started for the jagged opening in the brick block wall.

One, two, three cautious steps brought me into the room of the shrine. Nothing happened. I took a breath. The air hung flat and stale. The feeling of pressure on my temples increased. Menace threatened, I could feel it tangibly, a sensation of imagined horror I had to push away.

Now, then, which door? Left or right?

Both doors were built of balass wood, hard and black, beautifully inlaid with ivory of Chem in geometric patterns. There appeared not a whisker of difference between them.

Neither had a handle, so you were supposed to push them open. If, that is, they weren't locked and bolted from the other side.

Standing midway between those enigmatic doors directly before the altar I made another careful inspection. The dark stains looked most unhealthy. The glint of gold just above the surface of the stained block in the back wall of the shrine took my attention.

An inscription had been carved there and the letters filled with gold. Instead of the beautiful Kregish script, the letters were blocked out in a style used in ancient documents for important headings. Now, of course, I must give the letters in terrestrial form, and have translated the words.

The golden inscription read:

U Q M K B Q
H L R H U O

For some time I stared at the inscription, summoning up the letters of the alphabet in my mind. Then I gave a little nod.

I'd never liked the idea of those two doors. This offered what I considered a better chance. Of course, if I was wrong, then whatever fearful thing had emerged to wreak devastation on those poor devils might well leap out to deal with me.

Anyway, the presence among the warrior effigies of that one particular race of diffs had caught my absorbed attention. I went back into the main chamber. If I was right, there was not a single sign of the person or persons who had attempted to push open the doors. Mind you, there were the stains on the altar...

This was where I had to summon up the blood and harden the sinews all right, by Krun! I positioned myself at the side of the sarcophagus I'd selected. I put my hands on the lid. I took a deep breath. The marble face with its exquisitely carved beak and surrounding feathers looked calm and relaxed, quite unlike the look of ferocious power on the marble face of the Relt's cousin the Rapa. I pushed.

The squeal of marble against marble held an unusual soft sound. The lid slid aside quite easily, and held and did not topple to the ground. I was pleased about that, not being in the business of desecrating tombs.

I looked inside.

The pearly light of the chamber was washed away and eaten up by a pale green glow. The inside of the coffin held no wrapped corpse, no skeleton. The crowbar and the sword in my fists struck me as particularly inappropriate, singularly out of place in that moment of revelation.

There appeared to be no bottom to the sarcophagus. Just that pale green glow radiating up from an immense depth.

Nothing stirred in the chamber.

"Here we go!" I said, cocked both legs over the coffin and dropped plumb into the radiant greenness below.

Two

Enveloped in radiant greenness I fell. Inevitably the comparison occurred to me. The weird parallel in thus dropping through greenness when I was much more accustomed to flying upwards enveloped in blueness, of course, rushed in on me with somewhat more than I liked of a choking feeling.

The drop did not last long. I realized I was no longer falling and that I was lying on a hard surface with no sense of having hit it with any force. The green glow which had cushioned me faded and died. I was lying full length surrounded by stone walls almost touching my shoulders. The tops of the four walls were only some three feet above my head, so I sat up, shoved up, and got my hands on the stone lip.

I pulled myself up to see where I might be.

A good-sized cavern surrounded me, containing eight other sarcophagi. The pearly light showed me the details and, by Zair, I admit it, my heart sank. I was back in the same damned cavern!

For only a heartbeat that miserable realization pressed in on me. Instead of a bricked-up opening, that doorway was now open and surrounded by a golden architrave. There were no dead bodies. The air still hung musty and stale; it smelled quite pleasant after the first shock.

"Djan Kadjiryon smiled on me then, by Djondalar!" I said to myself.

When I'd climbed out of the coffin the decision not to interfere with any of the others was automatic. I was in the business of avoiding trouble, not seeking it.

The shrine room looked exactly the same except for the absence of stains on the altar. Instead a superb golden bowl held flowers arranged by the hand of a great florist. They were perfectly preserved, fresh as the daisies of the field. I felt sorrow that in passing them I would bring them back to life, to wither away and dry into ugly brown stalks.

Hefting the sword and the crowbar I put an eyeball around the left hand door and immediately jumped back and glared up at the three xichuns.

The flying lizards did not stir.

Beyond the door lay a squared-off corridor illuminated by the pallid light. A repetition of my antics showed a similar corridor beyond the right hand door.

Which way I went had no meaning, for I was completely lost, so I went to the left. If going to the right would take me out of the labyrinth then I'd chosen badly, that was all.

The inscription above the altar, this time, read:

BEWARE THE PIT OF THE FIRE FOR THE DRUMS ENSLAVE

"H'm," I said under my breath. "They didn't heed that warning!"

The situation now appeared clearer to me. I fancied this part of the labyrinth under the City of Eternal Twilight had been inhabited by a people before those who'd bathed in the radiance of the Fire as the Drums roared. Perhaps there had been a bloody war. At any rate, those black-garbed priests of the Realm of the Drums had taken over. We had dispersed them; I didn't doubt that some would rally and continue after we had left.

That was, I corrected myself, if we ever did find a way out and did manage to leave this damned maze.

The squared-off passage led on for some distance, turning various corners, and I went along with exquisite caution. By this time I was ravenously hungry. Well, by Krun, I've been ravenously hungry plenty of times before and, Kregen being Kregen, will no doubt be hungry again.

All these various passageways were cut neatly and the floors lay smooth and clean. Almost every door was closed. One or two that were open showed neat living spaces of a simple yet comfortable kind, and all were empty. A larger door revealed a room very similar to the room of the shrine I'd left, and a glimpse of the corner of a sarcophagus through the far opening. On I went to come out to a lobby. Here the head of a staircase with wide steps leading down did not tempt me. I wanted to find the way up and out.

263

Some distance on past more living rooms and two more shrines, a faint green glow ahead seeped into the pearly light.

Approaching stealthily, for I had no idea what I might wake up from a five hundred year sleep, I halted at the edge of a jagged crack across the floor. This fault was the result of an earth tremor, and I was thankful to see that I could leap the gap without difficulty.

Before I did that I stretched out on my stomach and looked down.

The scene displayed below was touching, noble and yet, given what I had run across so far, not entirely unexpected.

The crack in the floor gave me a view of an extremely extensive chamber below. No doubt originally it had been a natural cavern; these people had worked on it, beautifying it, turning it into a temple.

Hundreds of worshippers knelt with bowed heads, frozen in time in the instant of prayer. The high altar blazed with flowers. Priests and priestesses in white vestments had been caught in the act of prayer and blessing. Around the walls and stationed at the many doors stood armed guards. They were of many races of diffs, and were armed and accoutred like the effigies on the sarcophagi. The worshippers carried no weapons. Clearly, these people were concerned lest they be attacked during their devotions. Absolute stillness and silence below created a sense of awe.

These, then, were the folk who continued to live down here under constant threat from the black-garbed degenerates of the Realm of the Drums.

No one stirred, so I was not near enough to arouse them.

Standing up I consigned their fortune to Opaz, and walked on.

After half a dozen paces I abruptly halted and stood stock still.

Onker! Here was I, lord of this and that, Prince of Strombor, King of Djanduin, Strom of Valka, a fellow who had been the Emperor of Vallia and was now supposed to be—or become—the Emperor of Emperors, the Emperor of Paz. I'd had plenty of practice deciding issues, using what skill I had in imitation of the Wisdom of Solomon, acting as a judge. That I did not care overmuch for that side of being an emperor had nothing whatsoever to do with it. I should have seen the situation and its ugly outcome instantly. And here I was calmly walking on! Talk about Pontius Pilate and the washing of hands!

Without any further hesitation I turned around and went back at a run.

Reaching the lobby I went haring down the steps four at a time. The problem of traps and monsters here did not exist. The foot of the stairway led out into a cavern filled with agriculture and flowers. There were no syatras, no Spiny Ribcrushers, no Cabaret Plants, no crowpins and no slaptras in the many pleasant pools. Everywhere as I passed the gorgeous perfumes of the flowers scented the air.

At the far end a series of constructions held gardener's tools. The corridor continued and if the directions I held in my head were right then just up ahead and to the left should lie the temple chamber.

Around the expected corner I trotted and instantly broke into a rapid dash. The two Hytaks on guard at a door stood as they had stood for five hundred years, leaning on their strangdjas, the spiky-headed polearms glittering with edge and point. As each one woke up he had no time to wonder about the stiffness in his muscles, for a thumb pressed just so under his ear sent him back to sleep again.

Now it was necessary to proceed with caution, for the door led onto the balcony around the temple about fifteen feet up from the floor. The balcony was not as crowded as the nave below. A deep breath whooped into my lungs... I set myself... Then I was off, sprinting as fast as I could around the balcony, leaping kneeling devotees, hurtling around clumps of people, rushing on and on until I returned to the door.

The air filled with song. That hymn faltered, almost died, and then regained fullness and power. These people prayed in song. Their quality showed in their reactions. They might feel odd, stiff, with aches here and there; they went on singing their devotions.

There was no need to look back. The temple was now filled with life, with a proud people making their covenants with whatever god they had chosen. And the guards were alert and ready for any sneaky attacks from the black-robed priests of the Realm of the Drums.

Straight down the corridor and up the stairs four at a time and out onto the landing above I hurtled. Along the corridor—a quick look through the green glowing crack to confirm all was well—and then I was rushing on.

Well, now! Perhaps these people might regain the Realm they had lost. So, on I went and gradually the habitations fell away until I was finding my way across rocky caverns and through jagged tunnels, always going up.

A waterfall and a stream impeded me a trifle; but I found a way up drenched in spray to come out onto more tunnels. Still, I was going ever upward, thank Opaz.

Around then I felt as though each leg was encased in lead, weights hung on my arms, and my poor old backbone was bent double under the millions of tons of rock pressing down above. A small cave with only one entrance which could be blocked up promised a decent rest. Ignoring the protests from my inward parts I shut my eyes, thinking as always my last thought before sleep, and opened them again to the same pearly light. I must have slept for I felt refreshed. I was still damned hungry, though, by Krun.

Hungry and thirsty, and only a trifle stiff from sleeping on a rocky floor—something I have had to grow accustomed to as a slave on Kregen— I pushed on. When I saw the corpse on the trail ahead of me, at the time I was crossing a deserted cavern, I bucked up. The poor fellow had been stripped of his worldly possessions, which was a disappointment for me;

but he indicated I was regaining touch with one of the parties wandering about down here. Just which bunch it would be lay in the lap of any of the many magnificent pantheons of Kregen.

Again a stream crossed my path and a long cool drink refreshed but could not satisfy those grumbling inward parts. Grass grew here with pretty white daisy-like flowers. There were going to be syatras and plenty more of the ferocious carnivorous plants of Chem up ahead. Maybe, instead of the plant eating me, I'd eat the confounded thing, by Vox!

So, in not a very happy frame of mind I came out to a clearing with the cavern roof lost in that pearly haze, to see a man sprawled between two trees. He wore a grey breechclout which was of no interest to me. But, in his hand, he clutched a small leaf-wrapped parcel. If I knew my slaves, that would be a trifle of food he had saved for himself.

Now there is no excuse for my conduct. None at all. I am supposed to be a mighty and puissant fellow, a mercenary, a warrior prince and all the rest of it. I just let rip a holler and leaped forward to grab the parcel of food. Food!

The leaf-wrappings were in my hand. I was ripping away to get at the food when a great swishing and swashing brought me up too late, far too late, and the folds of a net descended about me.

Instantly I was rolling over and over and trying to get the little curved sword out of my belt to hack at the strands. They were tough stuff. A sharp point prodded me. A boot kicked me. A hoarse voice said: "Lie still, dom, or I'll stick you through, as Havil is my witness!"

Flopped over on my back I stared up balefully at the fellow prodding me with his spear. His companion kicked me again. They were both apims, wearing armor and weapons after the fashion of Hyrklana, so I knew whose party I'd fetched up with—Vad Gochert, him with the gem-encrusted eyepatch and the icy manner, a dedicated swordsman, a man who worked for Spikatur Hunting Sword in the fight against Hamal. Well, he'd come down here to be frozen some good time ago, and the matter of Spikatur Hunting Sword had been concluded and Hyrklana along with Vallia were allies of Hamal.

He came striding up with his foxy-faced Khibil guards. So, as I say, there is still no excuse for my further conduct. Yes, I was starving hungry, I wanted to get out of this hell hole, and now I'd been trussed up like a chicken in a net and prodded and kicked. I was, I make no bones about it, in an evil mood.

"Hey, Gochert!" I yelled. "Get these clowns of yours off me. Bratch!" Now, for a start, one does not usually address a vad, the second highest rank of nobility, in quite those terms, at least, not unless you are a kov or prince or king with little sense of propriety. Also, that word bratch, meaning get a move on, jump to it, can be offensive.

His gemmed eyepatch glittered on me. As I glared up I saw a flicker of shadow on the jewels—no, rather, a flicker of movement behind the gems. His narrow ferret-like face, although he was an apim, and the spareness of his supple body, held all the suppressed energy of which I knew he was capable. He was all oiled-steel and ice.

"Don't just stand there like a loon!" I bellowed. "Get this confounded net off!"

In that oiled-steel voice, sharp and meticulous, he said: "I remember you now. I puzzled over you when we met here in the maze."

"Well, then, you hulu, get this confounded net off!"

His expression did not change. I was still wrought up so that just what this situation was in reality escaped me. The truth was that a powerful noble was being grossly insulted by a common fighting man.

He made a sharp gesture and the two apims started clumsily to pull the net off. I struggled out, boiling with exasperation. I rapped out: "Kick me, would you, you rast!" And: "Prod me, would you, you cramph!"

One I hit on the nose and the other in the eye. They staggered back, yelping, and I swung about to see a Khibil's rapier point at my throat.

"Stand still—" he started to say. He was that same Romano who was Gochert's captain of the guard, a Khibil cadade with a very high regard for himself. That he had a rapier at all told eloquently that he fancied himself, for rapier and main gauche work were—in his time—comparatively new in Hyrklana. He started to speak, and then the rapier was in my fist and the point at his throat.

"You stand still, you yetch!" I roared. I was, as you can see, most wrought up, in a right old paddy.

He stood rigidly, and his whiskery fox-like face tightened.

Gochert's icy voice reached me.

"Your insults offend me. By Sasco! Just who do you think you are?" I jumped away from the cadade and swung about to face Gochert. He drew his rapier and main gauche with the practised ease of your true Bladesman. "You have a sword, I see. Now it is time I taught you a lesson that you will not forget." He advanced, rapier and dagger poised.

Just then—and only then—I realized what an onker I'd been and what I'd let myself in for. Our blades met and crossed in a chingle of steel.

Three

Those first testing movements gave me time to step backwards, and backwards again as he pressed. I gave ground rapidly, flicking and flailing the rapier in a way that suggested I was more used to a heavier vertical sword rather than the lighter horizontal rapier. His men scattered away and then formed a ring. They started to shout, and even in those moments of tension, I recognized the quality in their encouragements to the lord their master. I'd known plenty of guards and retainers who'd have been overjoyed to see some stranger stick their lord, by Krun!

The ring of shouting men and women meant I had to circle to keep away from Gochert. The blades clashed and I saw he was not trying to thrust home. He was, as he had said, going to teach me a lesson. That would entail, I guessed, a considerable number of weals and cuts and dints on my body. Enough of my evil mood persisted for me to know very well I wasn't going to let that happen.

"You took that sword, and you hurled the insults." He made a neat little passage which should have ended with his point just nicking my left side. I let my own blade flop over to ward off that stroke as though mere chance guided the weapon. His smile could only be described as thin. He went on: "Normally I am over-patient with fools. They take advantage of my good nature. But you, I think, have overstepped the mark."

He whipped in a quick double-beat and then slashed and I had only to step back to allow his blade to whistle past my stomach.

His lips widened a trifle. "Yes, I remember you now. Jak, your name, wasn't it? You helped Vad Noran with the schrepims."

As I have mentioned, there are swordsmen who like to chatter when they fight. That is their privilege. Usually I allow the sword to take over and so let myself sink into that mystic rhythm that enables the true swordsman to fight blindfolded. And, yet, still, the sword does not take over entirely. Always, I hope and believe, there remains enough of Dray Prescot to keep the combat on human terms. So, now, I let him chatter on. I did say: "Drajak, known as the Sudden."

"Drajak. Well, Drajak the Sudden, when I have taught you your lesson your suddenness may be considerably lopped."

A fresh onslaught saw me back-pedaling and keeping his brand out. His smile remained, and I guessed that was a fixed rictus of his fighting habit, a piece of psychological warfare to intimidate his foe. Two little vertical lines appeared between his eyebrows. Again he pressed and again I slipped away, letting my blade drive his down and out to the side. At that point I could have thrust him clean through the bread basket.

He saw that. He saw his error and he leaped back, rapier lifted. So far the left hand dagger had played no part in the combat. I thought I knew why. Gochert fancied himself as a Bladesman; I had the one sword, so he would use just the one.

He said: "I bear you no personal ill will. This is a matter of honor as between a noble and a commoner."

He leaped. I slid away. This time he used both weapons, the rapier and main gauche, known as the jiktar and the hikdar.

Hung on my belt and thumping away at me the crowbar was my only other weapon, the little curved sword having been flung off with the net.

I said: "You are using two swords."

"The lesson must be done."

I hauled out the crowbar with my left hand and hefted it. I wondered what the Bravo Fighters of Zenicce or the Bladesmen of the Sacred Quarter of Ruathytu would say if they could see me now. Laugh? They'd rupture themselves laughing, by Krun!

Still, armed with rapier and crowbar I fought Vad Gochert with rapier and left hand dagger. By this time I'd sussed out his quality. He was very good, that followed of necessity. He would have acquitted himself well in a Bravo brawl in Zenicce, which is high praise. As always when I go into a fight I am ready to meet an opponent who is better than I am, having already had that experience with Mefto the Kazzur. This Gochert was good but not good enough. So now I had to work out what to do about him and his people.

As you can see, I was fighting objectively, and keeping a tight control on my reactions. The longer we went on the more he would see he was outclassed. Then what would he do?

Round about then I came to the conclusion that I'd have to speak up. As we fought I beat down his attacks with techniques he'd never dreamed existed and gave myself time to chatter.

"I did not think you believed poor old Noran. Did you honestly believe he had fought off those schrepims?"

He lost that artificial fighting smile. His ferret-thin face drew even thinner and longer. "You dare to speak of the noble lord Noran in these terms—!" He came in with a swingeing attack that I had to flick away and let my point leap past his side and so draw back without hitting. I said: "Just listen to what I have to tell you, Gochert. No—" as he essayed another onslaught. "No, no. Just listen, confound you, you onker!"

His icy manner and disdainful superiority were evaporating. I said: "I shall not kill you, Gochert, for I believe any man who stands for Spikatur must have some good in him. You would do well to order your people not to shaft me. There is much for you to learn."

His retainers and guards had stopped yelling some time ago. They were talking quietly among themselves, I guessed, their eyes riveted to what was happening to their lord and employer.

Gochert did not cease in his attempts to get his point past my defense. The crowbar was acting as a splendid main gauche. Suddenly he drew back. "I found it hard to credit Noran with victory over the schrepims. I see. You are a great swordsman. So be it. I own I cannot lunge past your guard. But that is something else not touching your insults."

"Look here, Gochert. How would you feel if you'd been traipsing through this damned labyrinth all alone and starving hungry and thoroughly lost and you found a packet of food in the hand of a poor dead slave and then nurdling great idiots drop a net on you and kick you and prod you with a spear, hey? Answer me that."

"I will answer. Yes, I see your position." The icy voice had regained its usual oiled-steel quality. "I would be annoyed—"

"Annoyed!"

"You were so angry you could not think straight. You knew me. You know the correct forms of address. You call me notor, lord. No, you cannot be excused your conduct on those grounds."

"I do not need to be excused my conduct on any grounds. Do not forget, Gochert, if you are taking refuge behind rank, you are only a vad."

His gasp was a perfectly genuine reaction of shock.

Perhaps, in that moment, I felt I might have gone too far. He could lift a hand and his people would shaft me. Oh, sure, I'd knock down some of the arrows and bolts, enough would get through to pincushion me. Now—I felt I'd taken the measure of his mettle. My very first assessment of him had been drastically modified, not least by his conduct during this recent meeting and the fight. We were now standing with our weapons ready facing each other and talking.

Before he'd finished that shocked gasp I went on in my old gravel-shifting voice. "I fought Hamal. The great empire Thyllis ruled is now justly governed by the Emperor Nedfar. Spikatur Hunting Sword fell into—"

He had spirit and fire, ice-cold though he might be. He rallied from the devastating shock of being told he was only a vad. He came back with: "You are talking nonsense. What do you know of—?"

"You ventured into the City of Eternal Twilight and tumbled down into the Realm of the Drums. You think you'd just entered when my Pachak comrade, Wa-Te, and I, met you. Yet many of your party were skeletons."

"Magic." He had caught the underlying seriousness of this situation now and he stood, wanting to know the answers.

"Oh, surely, there is a great deal of magic down here. And I may add that I am highly pleased to see your lady Merlee is safe. The full extent of what has gone on is remarkable and you will find it hard to credit it." I hefted my crowbar as he opened his mouth. "No, Gochert. Just let me tell you what has been going on in the world outside whilst you have been stuck down here."

He shook his head, not in negation but, I guessed, somewhere between astonishment and dazed resignation. I felt I had not misjudged him. Some lords I'd known would have had me shafted and finished by now. So, I told him the history of his part of Paz since the time he'd come down here, of which you have been apprized in my narrative. He listened without speaking and after a time sheathed his unmarked blades and called for wine.

270

He did say: "I have heard of Loriman, the Hunting Kov; I have not, to my misfortune, had the pleasure of meeting him."

He shook his head over the sad fate of Spikatur Hunting Sword, and grunted when I related—only in partial detail—the death of Csitra.

"And she was the wife of the Hyr Notor?"

"Aye, my friend. That Wizard of Loh, Phu-si-Yantong, and his uhu off-spring, were thoroughly bad even though we always attempted to find some good in them. As for Csitra—well, she was pathetic, really."

"But all of 'em evil—I saw what that bastard the Hyr Notor did."

"Yes. Although Csitra—no, she wasn't all evil."

By this time slaves had brought table and chairs and the wine went around. The lady Merlee joined us and listened intently. A freer atmosphere gave me a feeling that I'd cracked a very tough nut. There was always the chance that Gochert, seething with fury and frustration at my treatment of him, was merely playing me along. Once he'd heard my fairy story he'd have me done away with. Still, would a high and mighty noble stay his hand from vengeful slaughter just to hear a fairy story?

Quite clearly there was no way I could prove this yarn that purported to be the history of Paz. When I told Gochert and Merlee of Queen Satra's enormous expedition into the Realm of the Drums, they exchanged a quick glance. Also, by this time, I was convinced Gochert's left eye was not lost. He looked out through the gemmed patch for reasons, possibly, of sheer devilment when facing an opponent, another example of his psychological attack, along with that fixed smile. I said: "I need to meet up with the queen again, for personal reasons. When we do so, then, of course, you'll see my fantastic fairy story is true."

"We heard of Queen Satra when we were planning the expedition." The lady Merlee spoke carefully. "She was reputed to come here five hundred seasons ago."

"Yes. She believes the Empire of Loh still exists."

On a little gasp, Merlee said: "A real Queen of Pain!"

"Oh, aye, my lady. She is as she is, as they say."

She favored me with a quick upward glance, a slanting look that saw a great deal. "You have told us this story. We may either believe the fantastic farrago or not. If it is all true—and I make no judgment at this point— your part in this turbulent history is unclear."

"Um," I said.

"Yes, Drajak the Sudden." Gochert's slicing voice held sudden new suspicion. "You have told us what would be known to the world; you have also told us things that would be known only to kings and emperors."

In a tone I tried to make as smooth as possible, I said: "I am very willing to call you notor and to respect your rank. Suppose I tell you I was placed in a very high position in the retinue of an emperor?"

As soon as I had spoken I wished I'd said king or prince.

"This new Emperor Nedfar, you mean?" Merlee continued to stare.

In for a preysany, in for a zorca. "The Emperor of Vallia."

Gochert put his wine cup down. "That raving Clansman Dray Prescot?"

"Aye—notor."

"His new model army was doing well, as I heard it, against Thyllis's forces up north. And there is Pandahem—"

He was interrupted by Merlee, who touched his hand. "If what Drajak says is true, that is all over."

"Of course." He put his other hand over hers.

I said: "Dray Prescot is no longer emperor. His son, Drak, is emperor with Silda as empress. They prosper."

"How did Prescot die?"

"No, he is still alive. He and the divine Delia abdicated."

"You astonish me. That is perhaps the most fantastic part of your whole fantastic story!"

"A burden well relinquished, notor. Drak is a far better emperor than ever I—that is, than ever Dray Prescot was."

I stared at them. Chattering on like this always drops you slap bang into trouble, by Vox! Seeing a way out, I added: "I was about to say that Drak is a better emperor than ever I gave credit to Dray Prescot; but that implies personal criticism which might be inappropriate. So I merely quoted general opinion." The lady Merlee was giving me a real gimlet stare.

She said: "You are a mercenary, I see. You must be a zhanpaktun to have witnessed so much employed by the emperor."

Deliberately, I put a hand to my throat. That is very often the natural gesture of a paktun, a mercenary touching the golden pakzhan or silver pakmort, when they are mentioned in conversation.

"Yes, my lady."

Gochert, still all ice and cold steel, took his hand from Merlee's and picked up his wine cup. "I find you a remarkable man, Drajak the Sudden. If you are tazll and seek employment I would welcome you to join my guard. I fully and freely forgive you for those insults shouted under dire provocation, for I see you are a man of spirit, accustomed—perhaps overly accustomed—to the company of emperors and kings and therefore forgetful at times."

Now you couldn't say fairer than that. I found great pleasure in the reflection that I'd judged this Vad Gochert aright.

Opening my mouth to make some suitable reply, I was stopped by Merlee in her soft breathy voice. "You said, Drajak, that the lord Gochert was only a vad. I think I see what you meant in the heat of the moment. Why don't you tell us your rank and who you really are?"

The moment hung, palpable with renewed doubts and obvious suspicions held by this little Witch of the Demaskar Persuasion that I did not relish at all, at all, by Zair!

A sharp and high-pitched voice cracked out: "Notor—!"

Another voice, booming with authority, roared: "Stand stock still, all of you, or you are all dead!"

We whipped about to see dark agile figures ringing Gochert's huddle of people, bows lifted, the light glittering off sharpened steel.

Four

No one moved. Under the threat of those bows only the biggest fool in all Kregen would have attempted to do anything at all not sanctioned by those marksmen.

A man came striding through Gochert's people. He looked neither right nor left. He wore completely plain armour. The great Lohvian longbow was held in that apparently lazy, effortless way of your true Bowman of Loh. His brilliant blue eyes beamed on us. Around his waist he wore a flaunting red sash, the only flamboyant mark about him. His face, bronzed, handsome, commanded instant obedience. He marched lithely up to the table.

"Well, my old dom, and you are still in one piece?"

"Oh, aye, majister," I said, and stood up, and clasped his hand which, as he was a Bowman of Erthyrdrin, could grip the shaft and draw and loose before you could detect the movement. "Oh, aye, and among friends."

"Then, by the Veiled Froyvil, that is as it should be."

I turned to Gochert and Merlee: "You have the honor to be in the presence of Seg Segutorio, the King of Croxdrin and Hyr Kov of Balkan. Majister, may I present Vad Gochert and the lady Merlee?"

"Lahal," said Seg. He gave me a funny old look. He and I both, we loved to play act with titles when they served a purpose. Anyway, dear old Seg, the truest blade comrade a fellow could have, was a king and hyrkov.

"Lahal—majister," said Gochert and Merlee. They looked just a trifle apprehensive.

I said: "Majister—is—?"

"Blooming! More lovely than ever—and in a right old paddy over your whereabouts. By Vox, my old dom, you're in for a bit of stick when you get back!"

"Where are—?"

"Each is leading a party. We have arrangements to meet up again without getting lost. It is my good fortune to have found you."

"Any news of the Wizard of Loh?"

Here I referred to Na-Si-Fantong who had vanished with the red ruby of the Skantiklar.

Seg shook his head. "Disappeared in a puff of smoke, I shouldn't wonder."

I said: "I think, majister, the lads can relax now and we can make the pappattu with Vad Gochert's people."

Out there the swods of First Emperor's Sword Watch would keep a very sharp eye on anything that went on around their Kendur, their emperor. So everybody relaxed and the wine was passed, and I had another enormous meal to attempt to fill the hollow between my ribs. There was little anybody could tell anyone else. Na-Si-Fantong had taken the ruby and escaped. That meant he now had at least two, and possibly more. Out of the nine rubies there was still the one in Makilorn and the one in Vallia. As for the others, well, that was up to Deb-Lu-Quienyin to discover.

Our conversation on this subject, although Seg and I tried to be circumspect, could not help but be understood by anyone who possessed the knowledge of the Skantiklar and its supposed magic potency.

So, only half surprised, I heard Gochert say: "I gather you have lost the ruby. It cannot be a secret that we came here for that, also."

"Tell me, vad," said Seg in his grandest kingly manner. He didn't wink at me; I knew he wanted to!

Gochert's story was simple enough, yet vastly intriguing, by Krun! Because Spikatur Hunting Sword was a loose organization—if that—of people devoted to resisting the Empire of Hamal, any assistance was desperately needed. A Wizard of Loh in Hyrklana had offered to help. His name was Phar-Si-Wyrnon. He'd said that if someone would fetch him the ruby from the Realm of the Drums under the City of Eternal Twilight, it would immeasurably increase his powers to assist Spikatur. Gochert had volunteered.

Seg rubbed his chin. "That's bad news. Another party is in the hunt for the Skantiklar."

Gochert, sharply, said: "There is no legal right of ownership here."

"Also," pointed out Merlee, "you have lost the ruby."

"Tell us about this Wizard of Loh," I said.

"Strange, as they all are. I must admit I was not altogether certain he could be trusted. But the advantages he offered were great, very great. He was supposed to send his assistant; but at the last moment he could not come."

"Another wizard would have been useful," I said. Then quickly I added: "To aid the lady Merlee."

"I didn't care for him much," she said, with a toss of her head. "He was big and bulky and he always took a breath and nodded his head before he said anything."

"By the Black Chunkrah!" I said. "Na-Si-Fantong!"

"Yes, that is his name."

"And he's the mage who made off with the ruby."

"Oh!" said Merlee, and put a hand to her mouth.

"Precisely. Spikatur Hunting Sword is gone now, so he wants the ruby for his own purposes. He already has one we know about. If what we fear is correct, then he intends great mischief."

Gochert looked surprised. "There is more than one?"

"Nine," said Seg. "Nine of the dratted things."

"He waited a long time before he came down here," I pointed out. "That could be because his master, Phar-Si-Wyrnon, held him back after Gochert's failure to return. It's my guess Wyrnon is dead now."

"And by the hand of Fantong!" Merlee sounded quite sharp.

"Right." Seg stood up from the table. "It's no good lollygagging about here. It's time we were off. There are people who want to know you're all right."

Gochert and Merlee arose swiftly enough after the king. If they knew the place of underlings beneath them, they equally knew their place in the presence of royalty. I must confess, I joyed in seeing Seg receiving the proper treatment that was his due, and in that feeling of pleasure subsisted a degree of sympathetic understanding that he detested kow-towing as much as did I. Neither of us forget the times we'd been slaves together.

There was a very great need for me to march over to the lines of 1ESW and greet and be greeted as was seemly in these circumstances. "Hai Kendur!" rang out, followed by a roaring hubbub as everyone joined in and we had the beginnings of a right royal shindig. Only the swods of the emperor's Guard Corps addressed their emperor as their Kendur. As I shouted greetings to old friends, I realized anew the convenience of that. After their break out in the Cavern of the Fire they'd quickly rounded up their uniforms, armor and weapons, and gone haring off after me with Seg in the lead. Inch had taken First Emperor's Yellow Jackets. Delia, Milsi and Sasha had led Empress's Devoted Life Guard and her Jikai Vuvushis. Others of my comrades and new found friends had joined in. What Queen Satra, with whose expedition my people had been marching, had thought of all the fraught comings and goings that must have gone on before the search parties took off, I didn't know. But I fancied it had given her muchly to think.

We set off confidently with our scouts up front. Seg told me that the lads had settled into the procedures for delving down here with calm professional expertise, as we knew they would. There was not the chance of a woflo in a Herrelldrin Hell of the Guard Corps allowing me to take the lead. "We've done it," said Seg, "and they know it, and know it's their turn now."

"I just hope none of 'em gets himself killed, that's all."

"Aye."

"I still can't reconcile myself to the idea that a stupid red ruby is so important. By Vox, Seg! I know magic is magic and all that, but it's hard to view this Skantiklar with the fear and veneration it appears to warrant."

"Deb-Lu says it is so, and that means it must be."

"I suppose so. I just have the itch to be about our other business."

"Blattering Shanks. Aye, my old dom. That's our normal priority."

"But not now?"

"Deb-Lu is convinced this Na-Si-Fantong, if he gets his grubby little paws on the Skantiklar, will do us as much, if not more, mischief as the damned Fish Faces."

"Yes, well." I rolled my shoulders around as we marched. "We'll just have to get after him sharpish."

"Aye. Once we know where he's gone."

"More wizard's work."

Seg changed the subject, I suspected by intent to get my mind off fretting over what we were doing instead of bashing Fish Heads. "These people are wondering who you are. Drajak the Sudden won't hold up for ever."

"Well, again, I suppose so. Although who and what I am or supposed to be won't impress Queen Satra."

"When she finds out her Empire of Loh vanished three hundred seasons ago, she's likely to believe anything."

"Ha! You've hit the Chunkrah's eye there!"

At that point the column halted and faintly from ahead we heard shouts and ferocious yells. Presently we started up again and Nath the Burly came back nursing a gash in his arm.

"It's nothing, Kendur," he said as I accosted him. "A pesky vorlind insisted on trying to bite us."

"All the same, Nath, get it seen to. Vad Gochert has a needleman."

"Quidang, jis!"

He trundled off, a hard, human, devoted member of 1ESW.

Nothing else of importance occurred, at least to my knowledge, before we reached Queen Satra's encampment. Her tents and marquees had been set up in a sizeable cavern, and the size of her expedition meant many of her people were camping out in the corridors adjacent. We marched through, and Balass the Hawk, beaming all over his handsome black face, came up to greet me and to direct us to our camping area. The lavishness of Satra's entourage down here in the labyrinth continued to impress me. She was a woman who had wielded terrible power almost all her life. We had to break the news to her that her puissant empire was no more.

That, I felt strongly, was where Delia could exercise her charm and subtlety, and in being gracious mitigate the shock.

The rapier I'd borrowed from the cadade Romano had been handed back and I'd repossessed the little curved sword. The crowbar was hung on my belt. Seg had given that a look, and said nothing, hoping, I knew, to tantalize me by his incuriousness.

I said: "As soon as Milsi gets back, Seg, would you ask her to ask the queen for my gear? That conniving bitch Licria took it all. As a princess, she's bad news. If she knocks the queen off and becomes a Queen of Pain herself, we could be in for a great deal of trouble."

"Milsi has sized her up. The little Licria will find herself in more trouble than she can handle if she doesn't behave."

These few words gave me a deal of comfort. Milsi, as the Queen of Croxdrin, I felt, had experience in dealing with unruly princesses.

We reached the tent and there stood before the opening a young fellow from First Emperor's Life Churgurs. His frame was broad and powerful, his head small by comparison. He was young, the down still on his cheeks. He held himself rigidly upright, shield with the brave devices and spear at exactly the correct angles. His whole demeanor spoke of a young fellow drilled and disciplined, and anxious and willing to live up to the expectations formed of him. My lads kept the Guard Corps regiments well filled up, and this likely lad would fill in splendidly for the future.

About to pass him with my usual greeting, I stopped. I didn't know him. He'd been told about me, that I knew. I looked at him and he flushed painfully clear up to his forehead under the brim of his helmet. He'd have soft brown Vallian hair. His freckles stood out as though someone had splattered his young face with red ink.

I said: "Your name, jurukker?"

"Nath, Nath the Tumbs, if it please you, majister."

So easily then I could have blasted his ears off. What kind of way was that for a jurukker, a tough guardsman, to speak? I clamped my lips shut and I heard Seg move at my back. I spoke in a flat and neutral tone.

"Nath the Tumbs. You are a valued member of my Guard Corps. You have certain privileges not accorded others. You do not need to call me majister. To my swods of the guard I am their Kendur. You call me Kendur, or jis." His face was now almost all red ink. "You never speak as a slave speaks—you know damn well we do not have slaves in Vallia."

"Yes, jis."

I asked him a few more questions—where his home was, how long he'd been in the Life Churgurs, how his mother and father fared, simple questions. I refuse to feel shame at this shameless manipulation. I did not ask simply because I was supposed to be a great ruler, and condescended to his people—oh, no. Every single swod in the army was precious to me. At last I said: "Very good, Nath. I compliment you on your turn out. Carry on like this and very soon you'll be a Deldar, no doubt of it."

"Quidang, jis—thank you."

So when I went into the tent Seg said: "He'll get himself killed now because he's a Life Churgur and—"

"I know, Seg. It is necessary for the good of Paz—and that means the people, including that young Nath's mother and father—that fine young fellows like him fight the enemies of Paz." I bashed a fist into my palm. "Don't you think I'd love to finish with all this fighting and destruction and send all the lads home and go back to Esser Rarioch with Delia?"

"You don't have to convince me, my old dom. Except—well, the old sweats in the corps have one home only, and that is in the Guard Corps."

"Yes, and that young Nath will grow into their ways. Oh, sure, he'll willingly die for me. I'd sooner he lived for me."

Seg started to take off his armor and we let that conversation lapse. My chiefs of the Guard Corps selected likely well set-up young lads and trained them hard, devilishly hard, by Vox. The traditions of the corps held old hares and red necks in a unity of purpose and dedication. What Seg said about the kampeons of the different regiments knowing only one home was absolutely correct. Everything they did was centered on their unit within the Guard Corps. Well, the whole impressive organization had been set up by my comrades in the first instance to keep any daggers out of my back. With the passage of time more regiments had been added to the original Sword Watch and then the Yellow Jackets, ELC, EFB, EZB, ERV, and others in the pipeline together with artillery batteries and medical and supply columns. That original notion had not been mine and for a time I'd been troubled by the creation of an elite force within the army and subsequently had done all I could to meld all the parts together. Another elite force, of course, was Nath na Kochwold's Phalanx. I had taken the decision not to incorporate a Phalanx unit within the Guard Corps. The Vallian Army co-operated well, and we had fostered that spirit of mutual help and comradeship.

The news of my return had gone out and one by one the search parties marched in. As you may imagine there were many scenes of reunion as I greeted my comrades old and new. As for Delia—I held her close, close!—and not for the first time wondered why on Kregen I was such a fool as ever to leave her. Milsi and Sasha showed their relief that I was safe and very quickly thereafter a bunch of Delia's Jikai Vuvushis stalked in led by Milsi. They carried my gear. Milsi smiled a smile that was almost a smirk.

"The queen indicated to me, my dear Dray, that she was not happy with the young madam."

"Oh, yes," amplified Sasha, bending her head under the tent roof. "That little she-leem needs her claws clipped."

"That will not be an easy job." I sounded serious, and both beautiful women lost their smiles at my tone. "She is dangerous. If she has the queen assassinated and takes over—look out for squalls."

"This grizzly graint of a husband is right. But I think," said Delia, "that we have a Princess's Swordsman to bring on that will surprise her most splendidly." In the game of Jikaida the Princess's Swordsman can be brought on at the last extremity when the opponent is about to capture the princess—as the game is played in LionardDen, known as Jikaida City. My friends had been regaled by my tales of what had happened to me there—and by the missing tail hand of Mefto the Kazzur I'd been a very lucky fellow. Here in Loh, the piece called the king or princess would be termed the queen. So Delia's comment was apt, even if it brought up a few hairy memories to me.

"If you mean me—" I began.

"Oh, no, Dray!" Milsi had her secret smile back now. "Oh, no."

"You might as well know what we know." Delia brushed a hand through her brown hair where the pearly light through the tent opening brought out those outrageous tints of auburn. "Your friend Mevancy has a scheme."

I looked at Delia's forearms where the pricks made by Mevancy's darts were fast healing. I shuddered, deep down, and merely nodded.

"Mevancy is a funny girl," said Sasha. "But I think she's as nice as Milsi says."

"Yes," said Seg. "And now you've got your gear back, my old dom, perhaps you'd tell us—"

"Yes," put in Inch. "That crowbar?"

I laughed and told them, whereat they laughed, too.

All the same, as I drew up the brave old scarlet breechclout and fastened the dulled silver buckle of the lesten hide belt, I did feel better for that. The drexer and rapier swung on their own belts at my left side, the main gauche went on the right and a hefty knife snugged over my right hip. The Krozair longsword and the Lohvian longbow and quiver could be snatched up in an instant and strapped on. So, by Zair, I felt equipped again. All the same, that jolly old crowbar had served nobly in the office of hikdar.

As for Mevancy's scheme, if I asked her and she did not wish to confide in me, she wouldn't tell. She considered herself the leader in our dealings for the Star Lords, and as a kregoinya she showed fire and spirit so I willingly went along with that notion.

When, somewhat diffidently, I mentioned to Delia that she might like to break the astonishing news to Queen Satra that her empire had blown with the wind, she laughed and looked affectionately at Milsi.

"Oh, I think Milsi has the queen's ear."

"It does seem so," said Milsi. She sounded surprised it should be so.

"If that's settled, then, thank you, Milsi." I own I felt relieved the matter was going to be handled with tact.

"She wants to know all about what happened, Dray. I expect we'll be invited to dinner tonight. I'll go along and find out."

"A good time," Seg nodded. "We'll all be there and can confirm the preposterous story."

Later on when Milsi returned she said the dinner invitation had been immediately extended. Then she added: "That unpleasant Trylon Ge-fu-Schian will also be there."

"And," said Seg, glancing at his wife.

"Oh, yes. The little madam will be there, never fear."

"Well, now," said Delia in her most charming way. "I really believe we can all look forward to a most pleasant dinner engagement tonight!"

Five

"A most interesting tale, Milsi, dear. Absolutely fascinating."

"But it is all true—"

"Oh, come now! I love a good fairy story. I positively dote on them. But, naturally, one cannot believe them, can one?"

Queen Satra, plump and dumpy, her white hair jutting forward in a widow's peak, leaned forward on one dimpled elbow. Her round face with its little pink mouth from one corner of which peeped the tip of a tooth bore the faintest trace of a flush. Her dark brilliant eyes sized up Milsi as she spoke so quietly and insistently.

"Whatever gods you wish me to swear on—"

"Really, Milsi! You shouldn't go so far!"

Delia said smoothly: "It is a strange story, majestrix, strange and true."

"You all confirm what Milsi says, I hear you. But you are all Vallians. I suspect this is wishful thinking."

Trylon Ge-fu-Schian laughed a scornful bark of contempt.

"Vallians would swear on any god or spirit and forget in the next instant. Treat them as they deserve, my queen."

He was a well-fleshed fellow, and had eaten and drunk his fill. There was plenty of food down here in the Realm of the Drums when you knew where to find it. He wore lounging robes of dazzling cut and color, all oranges and reds, with far too much gold. Rings loaded his fingers. Yet he looked to be a fighting man, well set-up, harsh, with a sallow face and a twist to his mouth that—at least to me—indicated he didn't care how many people he thrust through or how many heads he lopped off.

He carried a curved dagger in an unwholesomely decorated sheath. We Vallians wore our rapiers and left hand daggers, which indicated the power wielded by Satra, an authority vested in her guards standing alertly by door and canvas walls.

"When we reach the surface, the facts will be proved." Delia continued to speak calmly. She did not look at me.

"The facts of your pitiful attempts at lies!" rapped out Schian.

I said: "You and Princess Licria had me and my friends rapped over the head and carted off as sacrifices for the degenerate priests of the Pit of the Fire. I'll overlook that in the presence of the queen. You insult my wife again and I'll—"

"Dray!" said Delia, sharply, very sharply.

I glared at Schian and that old Devil Look of Dray Prescot must have flamed in my face. Grimly, utterly determined, I went on: "Very well. Just remember, Schian."

He colored up to his hair. His hand whipped to the hilt of the dagger. "You can't talk to me like that, you shint!"

Licria, stirring the trouble, said in her hissing way: "This shint insults us, and we do nothing! Aunt! We cannot allow this."

Queen Satra, I saw with, at first, some amazement, was enjoying this. Then I saw the reason for that. She had been one of those fabled Queens of Pain, a real true Queen of Pain of Loh. She'd probably had more people done away with than this rast Schian had had hot breakfasts. She had grown fat and indulgent, and she didn't much care for her niece. Oh, yes, she'd sit and watch, as a cat watches a mouse.

Sasha said: "Really, majestrix, this is a quarrel that is entirely unnecessary. After all, Trylon Ge-fu did have Drajak kidnapped and sold to the people of the Drums. That was not very nice."

Inch glanced across at his wife. He nodded his head atop that tall lanky frame, but he did not say anything.

"What I do, I do!" blared Schian.

Licria licked her lips. She glanced under her eyelids at the queen. She was a cunning shrew and must by now have grown to judge her aunt's moods. She saw which way the wind was blowing.

Princess Licria with her chalk white face and her dark red Lohvian hair coming forward in its widow's peak was, no doubt, a beautiful girl. She was, I believed, a Jikai Vuvushi. The trouble was, the more you looked at her the more you saw that beauty was barely skin deep. It was more properly cosmetic deep. Her eyes, kohled, dark, brilliant, showed her relationship with the queen. Oh, yes, this little madam Princess Licria wanted to be a Queen of Pain and Empress of Loh, and she'd do more than kill to gain her heart's desire.

She said: "Perhaps the men can settle this question when we reach the surface and prove the Vallians to be liars all."

Queen Satra just picked up a ripe plum, and bit it, and said nothing. She gave the faintest of nods.

Delia took an even breath. "When we reach the surface you will find the truth of our story. I well understand you cannot believe it now."

Schian fairly snarled out: "When we have conquered Hamal and the rest of Havilfar falls to us, we shall march on Vallia."

Seg, who'd been idly toying with a piece of bread and saying nothing, lifted the bread to his mouth. He and I, we do not waste food. Before he ate, he said in a voice like a whiplash: "You will march across the sea to face the Hamalese airboats and the Vallian galleons."

Licria in her sharp way, snapped out: "We have fleets of ships."

"Yes, but I told you," Milsi piped up. "The Hamalese flying ships destroyed your fleets of sea going ships. They—"

"We have many Wizards and Witches of many persuasions. None can resist the power of their kharrna."

"Yet, majestrix," said Milsi in her calm and dignified way, "they failed. Do not ask me how. History simply says the Hamalese routed and destroyed the Lohvian armadas."

"Rubbish!" snapped Schian, his face still beetroot red.

The queen looked slowly at Milsi. The queen had taken to Milsi. This was probably because when Seg and I had met her she'd been a trifle older, in physiological terms, than us. We'd bathed in the waters of the Sacred Pool of Baptism in far Aphrasöe and were as old, physiologically, now as we had been then. Chronologically, a great deal of smoke had blown with the wind since then. We'd all matured—even that roaring maniacal reprobate Dray Prescot had grown some sense in the thick vosk skull of his head—but we were all young. Milsi shone out as the dignified mature grand lady among us, and, to our delight, she was picking up our rip-roaring ways.

"It would be interesting," said Queen Satra in a voice artificially small, a teasing, goading voice, "if we knew exactly why our Witches and Wizards of Loh failed. Why the detestable Hamalese won. Then—"

Licria knew when to jump in. "Of course, aunt! How clever! Then we could take measures, and stop it all." She laughed, a metallic laugh of utter malice. "If the nonsense were true, that is."

"If you must interrupt when I am speaking, child, pray do not do so in the presence of others."

Licria, squashed, retired in confusion.

Satra went on: "How say you to that, Milsi dear?"

"A question for the philosophers! Could one change the future?"

Schian fairly snarled out: "The future for Loh is settled. We shall dominate all of Paz. It is our manifest destiny."

I said to myself: "As they say in Clishdrin, by Krun!"

Just then a guard marched smartly in, saluted and shouted: "My queen! San Mar-Win-Naltong has arrived!"

Before the queen had time to nod or say anything an impressive figure stalked into the dining tent. This Wizard of Loh was clearly not going to hang about outside waiting for permission to enter. He was, in a way I found unimpressive, arrogant. Certainly, I'd never dream of keeping Deb-Lu or Khe-Hi waiting. Yet they'd come in, as it were, properly. This fellow with his lavishly embroidered robes and gold and gem-smothered turban simply exuded self-satisfaction and overweening pride. Maybe, if he was representative of the Wizards of Loh current during his time, that explained their failure.

"San Mar-Win." The queen motioned and an attendant ran a chair up to the table. With a great swishing of his robes and angling of his jewel-encrusted staff to catch the lights and glitter, he sat himself down beside Satra. He gazed about on us Vallians down his nose.

"Magic is being used, queen. The magic within this Realm of the Drums is weakening. A new thaumaturgy has been detected."

"Has the college any—?"

He interrupted without any anticipation of a rebuke similar to the one administered to Licria. "We are resolving the situation. There is a weak source approaching us, and a somewhat stronger locus some way off."

I saw no reason to suggest to them that one of these might be the Lady Merlee, a Witch of the Demaskar Persuasion. If that were the case then who or what was the second?

A faint blue began to grow in a corner of the tent. A single glance at the locus of radiance told me this was not the Scorpion of the Star Lords— thank Opaz! As the familiar kindly features of Deb-Lu appeared and his figure thickened into visibility I decided that this was not the weak source. Deb-Lu was anything but weak, by Zair! So there were two other witches or wizards wandering about out there.

"Lahal, all. Pardon my intrusion. There is News of Some Import."

He spoke pleasantly, and those clearly audible Capital Letters told my friends and me that what Deb-Lu had to tell was important.

As a matter of common courtesy we Vallians immediately stood up as Deb-Lu appeared. As for the others—instant confusion followed.

The queen's Wizard of Loh, Mar-Win-Naltong, jumped up, swinging his staff in a glittering arc before him. Licria dived away from her chair and scuttled to crouch behind Naltong. Schian kicked a couple of chairs out of his way as he followed, raving incoherent words. The queen continued to sit, shielded by Naltong.

What happened next lay on an aethereal plane beyond the ken of non-sorcerers. Deb-Lu did begin to say: "There is no need for alarm—" Then he stopped speaking and held up his free left hand. He became still. Naltong's staff continued to whirl in a flashing circle before the Lohvians. Some of the guards stood, mouths hanging, riveted. Others ran out of the tent. The attendants fell to the carpets, clapped their hands over their heads, and sobbed and slobbered, too frightened to scream.

Only moments later two more Wizards of Loh entered the tent and four Witches of Loh. They were all attired in gorgeous and flamboyant robes; their faces expressed absolute power and knowledge of that power. They ranked themselves alongside Naltong, and span their staffs. Quite clearly they were exerting enormous thaumaturgical pressure upon Deb-Lu.

I own I gave a breath of relief when two pillars of light materialized beside Deb-Lu. As the radiance coalesced there stood Khe-Hi-Bjanching and his wife, Ling-Li-Lwingling. Our three comrade Wizards and Witch of Loh stood stock still, staring at the other sorcerers. I felt a prickly itch all over my skin. Heat grew in the tent. Vast quantities of kharrna were being hurled about the tent, energies beyond our comprehension.

Fascinated, we stared upon this thaumaturgical contest.

How could one judge which way the combat flowed? No visible signs of distress appeared upon the faces of the mages at first. The looks of lofty disdain upon Satra's sorcerers slowly vanished. Our three comrade mages exhibited nothing in their faces but absorbed concentration.

Seven against three! How could our friends prevail? And what would be the price of failure?

There was some comfort in the thought that between these sorcerers of Satra's and our friends lay five hundred seasons of progress. Surely, I tried to tell myself, bolstering my hopes, surely they must have learned a few tricks of the trade unknown to Naltong and his gang? Surely?

A fourth glimmer of blue began fitfully to shine beside Khe-Hi. It thickened, wavered, died, returned, coalescing. Like a column of heated air it shimmered there uncertainly. What—or who—was this?

A face appeared momentarily, and vanished in a whorl of light. Rollo! Rollo as ever was! Rollo the Runner whose real name was Ra-Lu-Quonling, an apprentice Wizard of Loh. His form focused and he stood there, and he wavered like a blown candle flame. Grimly he stuck to his task. He said he was no great hand at going into lupu and projecting his image; but he had done so, and manfully he was trying to assist us now. Good old Rollo!

The silence remained profound for all the slaves had retreated into absolute terror. We all stood as though as petrified as the people out there still under the thrall of the suspended animation spell.

A star of light appeared under the turban of one of Satra's wizards. The light shifted and rolled down his temple. The mage was sweating! A witch's lips twisted, revealing brown teeth. She caught her lip between those teeth, and clamped them shut. Another wizard actually gasped.

Now all of Naltong's gang were sweating. What powers, what kharrna, what sheer raw thaumaturgical energies were being expended—only the inhabitants of the Seven Arcades might know.

Naltong reeled. He staggered back. He dropped his staff. A cry, strangled, awful, gargled from his throat. He fell.

The other six mages collapsed.

"Well, now," said Deb-Lu in his cheerful old voice. "I feel they Brought That on Themselves."

"Beastly lot," declared Ling-Li.

"They deserved that for their own impoliteness and stupidity." Khe-Hi sounded severe.

"All I wanted to tell you, comrades," said Deb-Lu, "is that I am happy to report we have broken through the magic here. We can show you the way out."

"Splendid!" I said. "What about this sorry lot?"

Noise had returned and of that noise the greatest row was spurting from Princess Licria. She was howling her head off in terror.

"They'll live." Ling-Li was most laconic.

I said: "I was overjoyed to hear of your twins, Ling-Li. You and Khe-Hi have my deepest felicitations. It's splendid!"

"Thank you, Dray. And you know of our arrangement over their names?"

"Absolutely," said Delia, smiling, perfectly unruffled by all this magic. "And we shall fill their shoes with gold, as is proper when babies enter the world."

Queen Satra stood up. She was breathing heavily and her lips trembled. She started to speak, licked her lips, began again.

"I cannot believe what I have just witnessed. The college is the most powerful in Whonban and that means in all Loh and Kregen. Yet—"

"The college formed by these seven has much to learn," said Deb-Lu in his driest way.

Rollo's form was now flapping like laundry on a line. "I think," his voice said, faintly, "I really think I must depart."

"You have our thanks, Rollo." Deb-Lu half-lifted his staff. "But you really must work on lupu. You make such hard work of it."

"Of course, san—" With an inaudible plop Rollo vanished.

The seven Lohvian mages remained sprawled on the carpets.

Seg said: "My money was on you all the time, Deb-Lu."

Sasha said: "Not a doubt in all Paz!"

Milsi said: "It's lovely to see you all again."

Inch said: "And you know the way out. Capital!"

The forms lax on the carpets failed to elicit any sympathy. I gave them a nod. "I was absolutely confident you'd learned some tricks of your arcane trade in the five hundred seasons separating you."

Deb-Lu rubbed his nose and then immediately shoved his turban straight. "Assuredly, Jak. Assuredly."

Queen Satra emitted a little puff of sound from her moist lips. "I do not believe. Oh, no! By Hlo-Hli, I cannot believe!"

Delia spoke reflectively. "It is most odd. I own to a feeling of sorrow for you. You have been kind to us down here. Yet your empire was oppressive, so we learn at school, and deserved to die." Delia's hand made a graceful gesture before her face. "You have my sympathy, Satra."

Just what this high and mighty queen might have made of that was not to be known, at least, just yet.

Ling-Li said in her precise voice: "There's that other locus out there, growing nearer."

"Could it be the Lady Merlee?" said Delia.

"Too strong for her." Khe-Hi's projected image vanished and then reappeared next to his wife on the other side of Deb-Lu. "Anyway, the mage is masculine."

"We'd better—" began Deb-Lu. The other two nodded and the three said together: "Remberee, all!" and vanished.

Six

The new locus of magic turned out to be a Wizard of Cromal. He walked in with an altogether new expedition unknown to us. They were not in good case, having suffered considerably from the horrors down here. They had few porters left and their warriors looked grimy and battered. All the same, the leader, a one-eared Khibil called Vad Valadian, was prepared to be as haughty as any damn-you-to-hell Khibil considered he had every right to be.

The sorcerer wore robes that had once been impressive. His narrow face bore a shrewd look owing more to knowledge of the world and native cunning than arcane thaumaturgical understanding. He called himself Tse-Tsu-Luenling. He was not a Wizard of Loh. Oh, surely, he'd been born in the continent of Loh down south in Shirnlee, not in Whonban. Now it is essential in order to avoid confusion to grasp the delicate distinctions of territorial claims and magical attainment in Loh. This fellow Luenling was a member of the Cult of Stortingen. He could call himself a Wizard of Stortingen. Now if he traveled abroad and people addressed him as a Wizard of Loh, he'd make the most of that chance. There had been occasions in which I'd been astonished at the actions of a Wizard of Loh, and no doubt this deception explained them.

Absolutely no detective work was required to guess why Vad Valadian had ventured down into the Realm of the Drums.

What my comrades and myself wanted to know was—who had sent him, who was he working for, what new party wanted the ruby of the Skantiklar?

This information was not forthcoming.

There was now a whole great gang of us clustered down here, all thoroughly frustrated by the disappearance of the ruby clutched in the hot little hands of Na-Si-Fantong.

"The best thing we can do is to get out of it," said Delia, and she pursed up those delectable lips.

"Quicker than a shaft from the bow of Erthanfydd Himself," agreed Seg.

In the aftermath of the Conflict of the Sorcerers, a markedly different attitude was observable on the part of Satra and her people. Gochert heard all about it, and apart from a casual comment—and how typical of the icy character that was!—simply ignored the whole thing. He was as anxious to reach the surface as we were.

The Lady Merlee, so Delia told me, had mentioned in her faint voice that she was glad she hadn't been there.

"I'll bet!" I said, and twisted my lips into a smile.

Vad Gochert with his usual cool calculation had decided not to confirm we Vallians' preposterous story. "When we reach the surface," he said, and his jeweled eye patch glittered. "Then the truth cannot be denied."

As I say, a cool customer and a fellow to have on your side.

Satra's seven witches and wizards had recovered and each had a headache that brought tears to their eyes and immediate recourse to the needlemen and the Puncture Ladies. What had happened to them was something like walking slap bang into a brick wall.

The concourse of tents and marquees was struck, the porters and slaves were loaded like pack animals, the guards prowled ahead—and we were off. The lads of the Guard Corps tended to form solid and bristly walls about their Kendur and his comrades. A few words in the right ears saw Mevancy, Llodi, Kuong and Rollo included along with Fan-Si's fristle Jikai Vuvushis and friends. A messenger, young Tyr Nalgre ti Mailinsmot, all pink ears and bright eyes, only just learning not to entangle his sword between his legs, trotted up to say that Vad Gochert and the Lady Merlee would like to walk with us for a time.

This was useful and they joined our party to be fully introduced and to learn more of what had gone on in the world since they'd been frozen down here.

"You are, I think," said Gochert in his precise way, "a hyrpaktun. A zhanpaktun, rather than a mortpaktun—"

"Oh, aye, notor," I interrupted in my growly way. "Time was when a fellow had to earn the right to call himself a paktun, a renowned mercenary. After that he could aspire to become a hyrpaktun and receive the pakzhan from his peers. Nowadays any young lad from the farm can pick up a spear and put a boiled leather helmet on and call himself a paktun without ever seeing a battlefield."

"Times change." Gochert said this with more than its obvious meaning.

"Despite all," said Delia, "one has to believe for the better, surely?"

We were walking through a cavern high and vast, its roof lost in the evanescent pearly light. Somewhere up ahead Satra was being carried along in her palanquin, and to our rear Vad Valadian and his people trailed on. Now Gochert gave me a shrewd look, the light striking from the facets of the jewels covering his left eye.

"Yes, I believe you are a zhanpaktun. But you are more than that. No one can miss the way you are treated."

This, of course, was something about which I could do nothing. My lads weren't going to have anyone—anyone!—treat their Kendur with less than the respect they considered his due. In that case, capital must be made out of it.

"We are all of Paz, Gochert. It is absolutely vital we all join together to fight the damned Shanks."

"I concur."

"Good. Well, it seems the people of Paz require a figurehead to be their leader. Some poor benighted simpleton to be their Emperor of Paz."

He digested this for a time as we marched on. Then he said: "I doubt that some nations of Pandahem would welcome that."

"The Bloody Menahem?"

"Among others."

I told him that recently Menaham had gone on the rampage against their western neighbors and that Vallia was actively assisting in resistance. He nodded and added: "And a considerable more from Havilfar. Particularly the Dawn Lands."

"The Dawn Lands are in a mess," said Delia, with finality.

We'd told Gochert that many countries of the Dawn Lands, down south in Havilfar, had banded together with us to defeat Hamal. Still, his remark held weight. Some of those crusty kingdoms down there would take a deal of convincing to accept some kind of emperor to co-ordinate them. "All that is for when we escape this maze," said Gochert in his sharp voice. "Queen Satra has accepted my invitation to dine with me when we next camp. Would you care to join us?"

The look I gave him must have resembled a Jikaidast observing a cunning and clever gambit in his opponent. I said: "Do you think you know my name, Vad Gochert?"

He waved a negligent hand. "I must needs be blind in both eyes not to."

"Then," I said, "as you are blind in neither, there need be no more pretence between us."

The Lady Merlee gave a little half-stifled laugh at this. I went on: "We shall be happy to accept your kind invitation."

That 'we' meant my friends; it was not a royal we.

Now, as to what followed when we did next camp—I must stress what I have repeatedly emphasized. Killing people is not the proper business of any man or woman. That killing occurs is lamentable, regrettable and explainable. Life is what counts. If a society throws up thugs who go around the streets bullying and fully prepared to murder, that is fair comment on that society. That other people in that society are entitled to protect themselves seems unassailable logic. When Vallia was attacked I had no hesitation in resisting. I may add that I have no fear of the old saw, 'He who lives by the sword dies by the sword.' For a start, I do not live by the sword, and for the second, when I, as they say in Clishdrin, pop my clogs, what more expected fashion could there be?

Gochert's plans for a pleasant rest period entertaining the queen were to be dashed. Up ahead the trail left the cavern by an opening wide enough for two people abreast. Bits and pieces of a crowpin lay about, some still twitching, the vegetable horror hacked to shreds before it had a chance to snatch a passing victim. Mind you, crowpins had to live, too. At the side stood an audo of Satra's personal guards, with a hikdar two paces front and centre. He saluted punctiliously, his clothes, armor and weapons impeccable after all the time he'd spent down here.

"Lord Gochert. A message from the queen."

As the hikdar spoke, Gochert's icy face reflected nothing of his feelings. An expedition had been encountered up ahead seeking the way out. The leader was known to the queen, a certain Chan Holomin, Strom of Wioldrin. She might very well, I fancied, be a trifle cross with Strom Chan, for he had sneaked down here after her without her permission—or so I had been led to believe. Whatever the truth of that, the outcome was that the queen would receive Strom Chan at dinner when we next halted. She must therefore decline Vad Gochert's invitation and would in turn invite him to attend her entertainment.

At the end of the hikdar's recital Gochert simply nodded his head curtly and said: "Tell the queen I am engaged to entertain the King and Queen of Croxdrin and party. I shall attend with them."

"Quidang!"

Handsomely done, I said to myself, handsomely done, by Vox!

Then I experienced a hilarious reaction at all this stuffy protocol and polite society manners—down here among the magics and horrors of the Realm of the Drums!

As to those weighty matters, though, the magics were being taken care of by the assembled mages, and the horrors by the advance guard. This included detachments of Vallians, and therefore inanimate people and monsters of the animal or vegetable creation were being awoken as we progressed.

There were other ways of dealing with the situation, and of Satra's skepticism, naturally; this happened to be the way things fell out.

When we halted to camp and the fires burned up and the smells of cooking wafted and we could take our ease, it was perfectly understandable that to us, despite the pervasive pearly glow, we should think of this time as evening.

As we dressed for the queen's dinner party, Delia said: "Gochert knows who you are, now, and yet he is pussy-footing around the subject."

"Aye. I think the idea of an emperor of emperor's sticks in his craw."

"If I read him aright he will come around. There will be others who will not."

"The Star Lords are hard taskmasters. Willy-nilly, I have to sew the whole of Paz together. I shall," I said with a bombast that amused me and brought a little smile to Delia's lips, "I really shall have to find a kingdom for Inch and Sasha."

"They are perfectly happy—"

"Of course! But Seg feels it, I know."

"Yes."

As she buckled up her rapier, Delia added half musingly: "Mind you, dear heart, I doubt if we can make all our friends kings and queens."

There was not a hint of megalomania in this conversation; there might be a touch of fear. We did what we did because the Star Lords commanded, and we knew only too dreadfully well what happened if I disobeyed. My defiance of the Everoinye had to be conducted in much more subtle ways.

Queen Satra set up a sumptuous banquet. Huntsmen had brought in plenty of game, there were still amphorae of wine untouched; we sat down to a gourmet's repast.

Gochert and his party were welcomed in and we sat at the long table. The throne-like chair at the head of the table remained empty. Across from me sat Strom Chan, his brown seamed face and stiffly jutting black beard as I remembered. We exchanged a few polite words, clearly understood between us the fact we would get together later and compare experiences. Trylon Ge-fu-Schian and Princess Licria, of course, were seated at the table, and a right unholy pair they made, by Krun!

A fanfare of the famed silver trumpets of Loh heralded Satra. Dumpy, plump and homely she might appear; she still commanded presence. We all stood up and when she was seated sat ourselves. Tiresome to recount the meal in all its sumptuousness. We ate and drank well. At one point Satra leaned on a rounded elbow and spoke quietly. We listened.

"My twin sister—oh, yes, I had a twin, as so many of us do in the world. Princess Satra and Princess Csitra." At this name I sat up. "I loved her and she me. We were inseparable. She was the elder. When we were six we learned that one day, when Csitra grew up, she would become the Empress of Loh." The queen took a long draught of wine and a slave girl wiped her lips. "The very next day—oh, it was sad, sad!—poor little Csitra tumbled all the way down the grand staircase. Her skull was split open. I cried at the mess."

Delia's eyes met mine. So that was how a Queen of Pain got started!

A fat major domo, his girth swathed in a violent sash of madder and gold, waddled in and bent to whisper in the queen's ear. She gave me a sliding glance and then nodded. The major domo strutted up to me.

"There is a Lady Mevancy outside who wishes to have a word with you, my lord. It is a matter of the utmost urgency."

A guard detail of my lads had accompanied us to the queen's camp area where the queen's retainers had taken over. I welcomed the idea of getting out of this hot-house atmosphere and having a few words with my jurukkers.

I stood up and made the necessary floridly polite excuses and Satra waved a white plump arm and I was at liberty to leave. Seg was looking fixedly up the table and I turned as I left to give a swift glance there. Schian was leaning back in his chair and wearing a look of extreme pleasure. They'd placed the Lady Merlee beside him at table and he'd been trying to win her attention during the meal, and now she was beginning to melt. Licria leaned forward sharply, so sharply she knocked over a goblet of wine.

Anyway, what in a Herrelldrin Hell did Mevancy want now? Moodily I supposed it had something to do with the Everoinye.

Two of Satra's impeccably clad guards stood each side of the tent opening, the four being armed as churgurs with blazoned shields; the two guards on the other side of the opening were Bowmen of Loh. I gave them a curt nod as I passed into the canvas-enclosed anteroom. Like any thoroughgoing crew of chamberlains and major domos, Satra's lot surrounded the queen with as many barriers to the outside world they could contrive. Without massive stone walls and only canvas to work with they still managed an impressive maze. Hitching up my rapier I went off along the tented corridor.

They really should have waited until I reached the junction of tents at the far end. There were four men and a woman and they were far too eager. Much too forward. Movement in the mouth of the cross tunnel took my gaze away from the five would be assassins. Mevancy stood there, her arms twisted up her back, her face black with fury. She was held by two more men and another woman stood at her side, holding a dagger to Mevancy's throat. So the whole picture was there to read.

All of these people wore tunics of so dark a blue it appeared black. They had the courtesy to wear black half-masks. What the quality of assassins in Satra's time might have been I wasn't sure. Probably very high, given the employment opportunities of the times. These stikitches had turned up in droves to deal with one girl and one man.

My right hand crossed my body to the left and my left hand crossed to the right. I moved slowly and deliberately. I did not draw in a showy flashing Bladesman's draw for action. The rapier and main gauche were not out of their scabbards when the first fellow gave a small and surprised grunt.

He carried a lynxter, the straightish cut and thrust sword of Loh. He dropped it. He put both hands to his chest to clutch at the long Lohvian arrow sprouting there. The fletchings were red and gold, just like the fletchings of Queen Satra's personal bodyguard of Bowmen of Loh.

Before this fellow fell to the canvas floor the man next to him, the woman, and the fellow on the other side, were all struck through with accurate shafts. I did not think these arrows had been loosed by any of Satra's guards. "Would you care to stand a mite to the side, my old dom—?"

I complied and a shaft whipped past to bury its head in the face of the fifth stikitche.

"I hope," I said without turning my head, "I sincerely trust you did not damage Satra's bowmen."

"Not at all! Not at all! The second one was most happy to lend me his bow, most happy indeed."

I didn't care to ask about the first one. I was staring at Mevancy as she was forced out from the tented junction towards us. That dagger at her throat looked damned sharp—the damned sharp dagger was no longer pressing against Mevancy's throat—it was flying through the air and the woman was shrieking with an arrow through her hand.

Before I—a mere swordsman in all this—could do anything, two more arrows finished off the stikitches. They were not all dead, Seg wasn't that stupid, although it was obvious who had contracted with them for this work.

"Now we'll see the quality of stikitches they have around here," said Seg. He stepped up beside me, giving the bow a little shake. "Not a bad little juicer, not bad at all." From Seg that was high praise.

The woman made no attempt to pull the arrow free—that would have ruined her hand for good—instead she gripped that wrist with her other hand, sprang about, and started to run off.

Seg said: "I don't really believe..."

I said: "No more nor I."

Mevancy shrilled out: "Shoot the vicious shint!"

The woman whipped around a canvas corner and the chance was gone.

"No need to ask if you are all right, then, pigeon."

"All right! I—I—" She panted a bit and swung her hair up out of the way. "I tell you, cabbage, when that woman's dagger kissed my throat, it was like—well, look!" She took her hand from her throat. The fingers shone wet. "The shint cut me!"

"Not deep, Lady Mevancy," said Seg. "Not deep."

"Of course not! if it had been deep she'd have slit my throat!"

Although everything had taken place at such speed we could expect inquisitive guards at any moment.

I said: "The guards will be here soon—"

"Of course they will," said Seg in his bold bluff confident way. "I should hope so! Let them see the disgraceful way they take care of the queen's guests." I felt the bubbles of amusement rising—it was not often after a fracas like this I didn't have to run off sharpish, by Krun!

Mevancy said: "They would have killed you, then me, saying they discovered me in the act. And you let her run off!"

"If we wish to find her, that should not be too difficult." Seg wasn't going to argue ethics. "A woman with an arrow through her hand."

"I suppose," said Mevancy with extreme sarcasm, still panting, still wrought up, "if it had been a man you'd have shafted him without thought."

Whether or not Seg was now prepared to argue ethics, and with them the peculiar reversal of values in the female viewpoint on certain issues, I didn't know. Across the canvas floor-covering a little reddish-brown scorpion trotted along, his eight legs going up and down like organ keys, his sting high and curved and arrogant. He cocked his head on one side and those bright beady eyes beamed brilliantly up.

I took hold of Mevancy around the waist and I shouted to Seg: "We're off now—tell Delia—"

My words died in the hollow coldness that descended as the enveloping blue folds of the giant Scorpion closed about Mevancy and me. The Star Lords had sent for us. Hurtling into a long blue void, feeling the rushing of unseen wings all about, up we went, up with the phantom blue Scorpion of the Star Lords.

Seven

Existing through the experiences of sitting down to a formal dinner with all the trimmings when I was down in the earth surrounded by monsters and magics, and having to put up with a clumsy assassination attempt, impinged on me with a high degree of Unreality. How could I take all that nonsense seriously? It was all Unreal.

Going up to see the Star Lords—I felt as though a fluid weight had sunk through my body—that was Real. I was back in Reality once again.

The cold blueness swirled all about me and the warm firm feel of Mevancy's body was gone. We had been torn apart. Head over heels I went up in the blue mist.

"And mind you don't drop me again!" I bellowed up. "You nurdling great apology for a Scorpion!"

In the next instant I expected to go tumbling across the deck of a boat to find myself alone in a broad ocean. Up and still up I went.

All right, then—if there were to be no boat then I'd see fireworks splattering all across the firmament as Star Lord argued with Star Lord, the red of what I thought of as the establishment and the acrid green of Ahrinye the rebellious trouble-maker. Still up and up in the blueness I went.

Was I, then, to be transported in a hissing chair through multicolored veils? Would I walk into the room of the three silver-framed pictures? Perhaps they would dump me down in that cool oval room with a comfortable chair and a table bearing a flagon of fine wine. The Everoinye might, as they had indicated, send me to the bacra area, a weirdly mysterious place of squared off metal boxes being eaten up by horse-sized caterpillars. Or, there must be a chance they'd hurl me to that damned freezing-cold cave of the ice winds and, if they did so, I wouldn't want to hang around in conversation too long as I'd foolishly done before. And, finally—and probably most scary of all—they might just fumble-finger and I'd wind up casually chucked down any old where and languish until I starved to death.

Still up and up in the blueness I soared.

There was no use worrying about Mevancy. The Star Lords had called us and she'd be seen just as I'd be seen—if, that was, the ancient dodderers got it right and we ever did arrive where we were going.

"By Makki Grodno's pustular—" I started to say to myself. Then I stopped. My heart wasn't in it. I just wanted to discover what the Everoinye wanted this time. The truly awesome elements of power and control had been blunted for me over the seasons; now I saw more clearly just what was really happening in this Reality. Where were these places to which the Everoinye summoned me? They were ancient beyond memory, what was their true history? Their power was so vast it must clog the breath in one's throat.

My feet hit cold hard stone.

The blueness all about swirled and swayed and parted gradually to reveal an angry crimson sky. That sky looked like the sky above a burning city. I turned about slowly on the cold stone. I had no clothes, no weapons; that was normal in places like this. I had never been here before. As I finished turning about to face my original direction a series of rounded humps began to become visible ahead. They rose slowly, black and stark against that ominous crimson. Just as the notion occurred to me they looked just like the heads of a gathering of people, in each separate shape two spots of scarlet fire abruptly flashed. Eyes! Eyes of the Everoinye, studying me like a specimen.

On my right side three humps rose, rounded, black against the red. I just stood, limp, waiting. The three shapes flashed their eyes—green! The acid green of Ahrinye, acridly shared now by two companions.

The Everoinye before me, the establishment as I thought of them, clustered the domed shapes in a way reminiscent of amphitheatre seating. Tier on tier they rose, extended from side to side. Could Ahrinye stand against this colossal display of power?

The twin scarlet eyes in each head—did the Star Lords have heads, then, as they once must have done?—lowered balefully on me.

The voice was familiar, hoarse, resonant, clanging.

"Dray Prescot! You have incurred our wrath! We are displeased with you, with your arrogance and presumption."

The sheer volume of sound after the deathly silence preceding struck like a whiplash. I pressed my feet against the stone, and tilted up my head.

"How?"

I expected them to rant on about my own plans for Paz which included designs like making Inch and Sasha a king and queen of some suitable country which would then join our alliance. That was power-crazy, I suppose, to people unable to see past their noses.

The voice deepened, rumbling like a volcano.

"You have the arrogance to pursue other ends than defeating the Shanks. You have the presumption to put your life at risk for no cause."

"Hold on!" I shouted up. "If you mean the Skantiklar—that's important to our resistance to the blasted Shanks, confound you!"

There ensued one of those long silences that punctuated conversations with the Star Lords. Each time I imagined details of grisly punishments they were debating. Finally the hiatus was broken by: "And your presumption?"

"My life was at risk long before I started working for you."

"You misunderstand, as onkerish as ever! Some petty quarrel and assassins could deprive us of a kregoinye. That is your presumption."

I could not stop myself from saying: "You mentioned before my life was valuable to you. That's pretty new! You see I have some value to your schemes. You've just found that out. Well, it's a damned pity you couldn't have found out earlier, when I was almost killed time after time chasing after your mistakes!"

The silence this time held, at least for me, a more mellow tang.

There was no doubt the lowering presence of those tiered rows of heads, brooding down on me with fiery eyes, the eerie feelings cobwebbing this place, produced most profound feelings. The violence of the sky blood-red over all, the gimlet punctures of Ahrinye's green malevolence, the very absence of sound, all were calculated to intimidate, to frighten, to cow.

These superhuman beings could fling me four hundred light years back to Earth, debar me from Kregen for ever. I'd never walk in the streaming mingled lights of Zim and Genodras, never look up to She of the Veils among the stars, never see my Delia again—never! Never! That must not happen! I must remember the scheme I'd promised myself of acting humbly before the Star Lords, of kowtowing—I must hurry to speak.

I said: "The quarrel and the resulting assassination attempt were not of my doing. I did not initiate this problem."

The answer rapped out straight away.

"Yet you were involved. Your life was needlessly risked. The Shanks press closer. You are guilty of presumption."

"So if some rast insults your wife you don't—" Then I hauled up, flaming with passion. The very excuse was muddled with the cause and could finish me off. Anyway, did these superhumans have husbands, wives?

"Enough! You have been called the Prince of Onkers, and we find you to be the Emperor of Onkers." Oh, yes, the rows of them up there all hunched and glaring red-eyed down on me, oh, yes, that was a Court, a Court sitting in judgment.

"Then give him to me!"

The acidity of the words, the sheer nerve-scraping screech shattered into my mind. Ahrinye! I swiveled like a puppet to see the green eyes flaring brighter, malevolent, demanding, ruthless.

If Ahrinye was allowed to control me—run me, as he phrased it—he'd kill me off in no time with impossible demands.

"Give me Dray Prescot and you will see!"

His searing voice scythed into my brain.

I could feel my heart up in my throat. I could feel—I do not know—I could feel nothing.

A softer voice said: "I think not, Ahrinye."

Even before I switched around from facing the green eyes of Ahrinye to stare across to the left of the tiered Everoinye I knew what I would see.

Joy burst up in me. The shape was not hunched and domed, the shape was that of a beautiful woman. All about her hung a shimmering cloud of yellow, so that she seemed to float in a shimmer of gold.

"Zena Iztar!" I fairly shrieked out her name. "Zena Iztar!"

"Perhaps you have been foolish, Dray Prescot, perhaps not. I have been away. I must go away again. But Ahrinye shall not have you."

I tried to speak, and gargles came out, so I started over.

"Zena Iztar—there is much to tell. The Kroveres prosper—"

"Yes. Continue." The voice changed from that soft tone to a sharper demanding note. "Is the decision made? Or must I—"

"No," The hoarse voice interrupted. "No, Zena Iztar, you have no need. The decision is made."

"Against me!" screeched Ahrinye.

"For the good of Kregen."

Flashes of green light struck fanlike up from my right and Zena Iztar's yellow brightened on my left. Sparkles irradiated the air with color. The violent sky washed lambent crimson over all, yet green persisted. Yellow and green, one against the other, with red holding the balance.

Zena Iztar was a more mysterious figure than the rest of this lot put together. Regarded by the Everoinye with reserved condescension and uneasy apprehension she was treated by them with cautious respect. They had spoken ill of her, contemptuously, yet I fancied she'd have the last laugh over them.

"Very well!" With the suddenness of a slammed door on a lighted room, the green radiance vanished. The three forms of Ahrinye slowly sank down.

"The Skantiklar—" I said.

Zena Iztar interrupted: "Find it. Then destroy it."

"Is that wise?" said the hoarse voice.

"It is of little practical value as humans weigh these things."

"Then?"

The golden yellow halo about Zena Iztar's form flickered, began to fade. Her voice sounded as soft and warm as when she first spoke.

"Then what will happen will happen. Yes. Probably that will be for the good, also."

The beautiful shape bathed in golden glow vanished.

"Rembaree, Zena Iztar!" I said to myself.

"Dray Prescot! You have heard the judgment. Do not behave stupidly again." The menace in the clanging voice rang unmistakably.

"I cannot hold myself responsible for fools who force quarrels on me. Surely you can see that?"

"We see you are a kregoinye. That is what to remember."

Just then I could vividly remember Zena Iztar. Her aims for Kregen were less penetrable than the designs of the Star Lords—or, at least, so it appeared to my understanding. Zena Iztar was unique.

About to speak again I paused. A single crystal gong note rang out. The red sky flickered. The hoarse voice said: "What? Again?" The clanging voice replied: "It is necessary. Send him now."

The blueness took me up so swiftly I still had my mouth open as I crashed headlong into bedlam. Naked and surrounded by a confused tangle of naked arms and legs and bodies I felt the ship surge up and lie over on her beam ends. Vomit washed about under foot, and the packed slaves screamed and wailed and shook in their chains. The stink of this slaveship hold took me by the throat, so that I gagged and clamped my mouth shut. The feel of the ship told me she was sinking, sluggish, her recovery slow. Water poured dark and green from the narrow gratings in the overhead.

In mere seconds she'd be gone, dragging down with her her freight of chained slaves.

The Star Lords had catapulted me here. In all this hideous confusion—who was it I had come to save?

Eight

Dark water ran across the deck underfoot as the ship rolled. The smells, the noise, the shaking feelings of insecurity coiled into a daunting sensation of inescapable doom.

"Sink me!" I burst out, fractionally aware of the very aptness of the remark in these circumstances. "I don't know—so—all of 'em!"

Staggering as the ship lumbered back, I hauled myself up.

The slaves were chained individually to the long main chain. Forcing my way to the end I balanced with the movements of the vessel, my old sea legs back in action. The chief staple was bolted. Well, by Vox, somebody must have the key!

More water smashed down through the gratings. There must be one hell of a storm raging out there. The water in the hold was now visibly rising. If we didn't overset we'd be dragged down. The ladder to the deck was in my fists. I went up like a monkey.

A solid sheet of water slashed down at me, shining and green. Doggedly, I held on. Shaking my head free and blinking, I clawed on up.

A pair of legs and feet encased in tall boots washed over the coaming, pushed by the water. Pushing my way up past him, I saw he wore mesh link of a style I recognized. Most of his harness was scarlet. The top of his skull had been cleaved in by an axe. Crouching, I stared across the deck.

Dark shadows flitted across the vessel. She was clearly done for. Her two masts had both gone by the board and a raffle of tangled rigging encumbered the footing. The deck ran with seawater that poured in every time she rolled. The noise of the wind shrieked in my ears. This storm was a rashoon. Movement huddled against the bulwarks brought my attention to what was left of the crew.

They had discarded their armor. Naked except for green breechclouts they had given up the attempt to launch the longboat. That lay in a twisted mass of splintered timber. The wind and the waves battered at reason. The freshness of the spindrift-laden air shocked after the stench below decks. I stepped carefully over the dead fellow half-pitched down the companionway. He had dark curly hair, and moustaches that normally thrust arrogantly upwards but which were now wet and bedraggled. I stared malevolently at the men clustered by the bulwarks.

Oh, yes, I knew where I was, and who these people were.

The key! I had to find the key and find it fast, before the ship foundered.

There was no finesse in my approach. I scuttled across the deck suiting my rush to the violent movements of the ship, grabbed the first wight around the neck, shook him like a drenched rat, kicked his fellow who reeled away, shrieking. I bent to place my lips close to his ear.

"The key!" I bellowed. "The master key to the slave chain!"

"By Goyt!" he spluttered. "You're mad!"

"The key, you cramph, and fast before I snap your spine!"

Three or four of the crew were trying to lever themselves away from the side. Their eyes like white marbles rolled in their heads. I shook the fellow in my fist again and he gargled.

A pile of wet clothing lay tangled beside the shattered longboat. I ignored the clothes, the armor, the weapons. I threw the fellow away and dived at the bundle, kicking tunics and mail shirts and longswords out of the way. The key had to be here!

"Grotal the Reducer take you!" screeched one of the crew. He did not leave his post clinging to a stanchion. Seawater poured in over us. Wet clothes scattered away as I continued my frantic search. The ship's movements were now more sluggish than ever. She wallowed like a pregnant duck. Water ran in shining sheets across the deck. The shadows that flitted across were tinged with penumbras of red and green, twinned shadows, shadows flung by Zim and Genodras, the twin Suns of Scorpio.

A curve of metal took my eye. I snatched it out and keys jangled.

The key ring clutched in my hand, I didn't even bother to look back at the crew as I dived headlong for the companionway. Seawater drove me on.

I practically fell down the ladder. The dead man lay tumbled in a heap at the foot and I jumped over him, and even then I remembered to say a hasty: "May Zair have you in his keeping."

The first key—the largest—did not fit. I tried the second, twisting desperately, it turned and the lock snapped open.

The staple came free as I dragged on it with all my strength. The nearest slave lay writhing and his chains were all entangled. I gripped him by the shoulder and hauled, cleared the mess, started to run the chain through.

A huge fellow with a massive dark beard yelled. "Pur Dray! By Zim-Zair! Pur Dray as I live and breathe!"

I shouted back. "Lahal, Pur Zanad. For the sweet sake of Zair, start these people moving. Help with the chain!"

He didn't waste words. He freed his own chain and then together we went along hauling the chain and releasing slave after slave.

Another fellow with dark curly hair and whiskers shouted: "Pur Dray!" He leaped out, alert and lithe.

"Lahal, Pur Thazdon! Pitch in and help!"

Now the slaves began to sort themselves out as they always do. Those who had been slave and expected to be slave all their lives screamed and ran about and then scrambled madly for the ladder. Those who were prisoners of war, captives made slave, looked about alertly, ready to seize the best opportunities. The ladder was choked by manic scrambling bodies.

"Up for'ard!" bellowed Zanad. He started off. We followed, and I saw more than one face I knew. These men were Krozair brothers, most famed of all the corsairs of the inner sea, the Eye of the World of Turismond. Clearly, they had been taken in a battle lost.

Then I saw the figures I sensed must be the cause of my appearance here. A woman with flowing dark hair and sweet eyes, a matronly figure, stood up. Clutching her hands, two children, twins, a girl and boy, were struggling to hold back the tears. All three were obviously terrified; yet they were not panicking.

"Lady Thynzi," shouted Thazdon.

"Give me the children," I said, and snatched them up into my arms. "Get on! Get on!" We all hurried forward after Zanad.

There was another ladder. We went up one by one, in order, not pushing. The feel of the vessel was now so ominous that I passed up the children, waiting at the foot of the ladder.

The last man to grip the rungs and go up was Zinkardo the Stern. His face bore marks of battle, scars, a broken nose; his eyes were bright and his beard jutted, his whiskers already brushed up. He paused.

"We have not always seen eye to eye in the past, Pur Dray Prezcot. But from this day on I walk in true comradeship with you."

"As I with you, Pur Zinkardo. By Zair! Shorush-Tish has sent us a rashoon to outdo all others."

He went up one rung, waiting for the way to be clear. "We were outmatched, four swifters to ours, and taken. What puzzles me is how you got here, Pur Dray, for, by Zinter the Afflicted, you were not aboard my Princess of Zulfiria. No, that I swear, may Zagri take me else!"

"My ship was wrecked and I was washed aboard here. Up you go, Pur Zinkardo, and may Zair be with us all!"

Out on the reeling deck with the twin suns trying to shaft down shards of emerald and ruby fire through the massy black clouds we saw that the end was almost here. The wind shrieked through our hair. We had to grip onto handholds. Directly before us a black-fanged coast showed intermittently through spray, huge clouds of white water driven upwards and smashed horizontally by the force of the gale. Iron rocks waited to rend us.

The slaveship was now so low in the water she touched bottom before reaching the rocks. She flew to pieces on the instant. We were clinging to planks, baulks of timber, anything that would float. The Lady Thynzi clung on beside me as we went hurtling through the breakers. The children nestled between us, and Thazdon gripped on to help.

Zair had us in his keeping, for we tumbled pell-mell between the rocks. Black shining bulks swept past like stampeding chunkrahs.

Over and over we tumbled amidst the uproar, ripped from our precarious holds, scattered up onto a beach of black sand, driven and pummeled and half-deaf with the wave smash and the wind shriek.

Black shining forms were dragging themselves out of the water. We were drenched loons, gasping for air amidst the never-ending racket of the sea and struggling on wavering legs over that hostile black sand to the crest beyond the beach.

A few sparse bushes, gorse and spinzal, whipped in the breeze. The two children clung to me. Thazdon assisted the Lady Thynzi. By his demeanor he showed he held the lady in great respect. His wife, the Lady Zalfi, was a charming girl, a lively sprite. Now we all slumped down in the scant cover afforded by the bushes. We were bedraggled, panting, stained with black sand, bruised and buffeted—but we were free.

There were not as many of us now as there had been in the slave deck.

Zinkardo the Stern roused himself. He drew a deep lungful of damp air. When he spoke and I heard him easily I realized the worst of the rashoon was past. The breeze was materially easing.

"We have been saved by the courage of Pur Dray. Now we save ourselves by our own efforts. Can any of you see any Zair-forsaken Grodnims?"

No one had. Where the crew had gone we did not know. Lucky for the crew! Had any come ashore within spitting distance he'd have felt the heavy arm of Zairian justice.

"Out of green Magdag, they were," spat Zanad. "May their bellies swell and their livers rot worse than Makki Grodno's."

I looked at the children, sitting cross-legged and demure, much daunted by their horrendous experiences yet bearing up wonderfully. I essayed a smile and they did not flinch back. Their names, I gathered, were Zilvi and Nafren. When young Nafren became a Krozair, as he would one day if he lived, and became a famous kampeon, a corsair of the Eye of the World, he'd be honored with the zed, becoming either Nazren or Nafrez. By the cut of his jib he couldn't wait for that day. He'd carry on the great traditions of the Zairians and their Krozair brothers, fighting for the red against the green. I could not, just then, allow sensible and regretful thoughts of the folly of this continual hatred and warfare to enter my mind. I'd saved him and his sister at the behest of the Star Lords. That was the vital issue here.

We were cast away on one of the group of tiny islands to the south of the western end of the inner sea, known to us as the Seeds of Zantristar. To the Grodnims of the north they were known as the Seeds of Ganfowang. They were off the coast of Shazmoz, a Zairian fortress-city.

"Provided a damned green patrol does not sail past and spot us," said Zinkardo, with great confidence, "we shall be picked up in no time."

There was a certain amount of piratical activity among these islands. Inland there could be found fresh water and food. These folk could survive until rescue found them. Practical, hard-headed professional seamen, they knew their trade and how to take care of themselves. Four to one, they'd fought the Magdaggian swifters, defying the Overlords of Magdag, may Beng Marzubel twist their inward parts into cat's cradles, and now they were free once more and confident of returning home.

Zinkardo the Stern stood tall and commanding. He turned to me. He started to say: "Pur Dray Prezcot! In the name of Zair we thank you, and we give you the Jikai—"

The blueness coiled about me. I felt the coldness and the rushing sensation both of falling into a bottomless pit and of being swept up into the air. The Star Lords would contrive a natural explanation for what the people here could see in the wind and the turmoil. To my own confusion, I own another detail would be added to the legend of Dray Prezcot, Krozair of Zy.

Up I went, headlong, over and over, and so thumped down into a seat.

The chair in which I sat moved. It hissed. It carried me off, sizzling, through a long red-lit tunnel to resume my interrupted conversation with the Everoinye.

Nine

Veils of colored mist swathed the tunnel and the chair carried me hissing through them, brushing them aside like gossamer wings. There was a sweet smell of lavender on the air, most refreshing after the stinks I'd just experienced. I slumped back, still wringing wet, my hair a sodden lump. I pushed it back and my hand dripped water. Used though I was to these extremes of change, all the same, by Zair! a poor ordinary fellow needs to let his pulse settle and get his breath back!

The chair whistled up to a cross passage and slowed.

Another chair cut in from the side, sliding eerily of its own volition. I caught a glimpse of a red foxy face, fiery whiskers, and the bright twinkle of knowing eyes.

"Pompino!" I yelled. "Pompino!"

Scauro Pompino, known as the Iarvin, let his clever mouth drop open. He gave me a most hard and suspicious stare.

"Jak!" Like the Khibil comrade he was, he broke out with a huge laugh and added: "Or Majister Dray, if you wish!"

"All is well?"

"My dear lady wife has moved up three or four bottles, is all. But you—look at you! Like a drowned rat. How you manage to contrive to stay in one piece without me to guide you I cannot imagine."

"I try."

"Well, may the good Pandrite have you in his keeping."

The chairs hissed as though animate and conscious of our words and dashed on again. Pompino was swept away up the cross corridor. I yelled: "Remberee, Pompino!" and the echo floated back: "Rembereee!"

Well, now! By Vox! That self-opinionated and marvelous comrade, Pompino, up here and clearly ready for an excursion for the Everoinye. I'd welcome him along with me, that I knew, when next I was flung down all naked and unarmed to sort out a mess the Star Lords had made for themselves.

The chair sizzled and burbled and dashed around a curve and so tore through hanging veils of silky mist to bring me into a room where the light glowed down warm and pink and the scents had changed to violets.

"Dray Prescot!" The hoarse voice resonated eerily between the walls. Nothing else existed in the room save the chair and myself. "We were unavoidably interrupted."

"I saw the kregoinye you'd sent. His head was clove in by an axe."

"Elten Ranjat. A great and sad loss."

Almost, I burst out with: "By the Black Chunkrah! Will you express sentiments of a similar nature if I get my comeuppance?" But I did not. I kept my old black-fanged winespout shut.

"The decision is reached. You may continue the search for the Skantiklar. However, the Shanks must be dealt with."

I rather cared for that 'however'. It summed up nicely the predicament I fancied the Star Lords found themselves in. Well, I wanted to go and blatter Schtarkins. Deb-Lu just had to be right about this.

Just how long ago I'd been sitting at Satra's dinner party I couldn't say. I licked my lips. "A modicum of throat moistener would go down well at the moment."

Before I'd even finished there was a soft plop! at my elbow. A small round table with a single central leg appeared from nowhere. It bore a goblet of wine, a pale yellow, and although I'd been thinking of a better beverage than wine, I took it up and sipped appreciatively.

"By Mother Zinzu the Blessed! I needed that!"

Quite deliberately I did not wipe the back of my hand across my lips as is the custom when uttering those sacred words. Instead I said: "Thank you."

Silence existed with the fragility of a moth's wings. The Star Lords had expressed regret over the death of their kregoinye Elten Ranjat. This did not prove they still retained human emotions, merely that they appreciated the loss of a valuable servant. Or—perhaps in their dotage the Everoinye were becoming senile, entering their second childhood, regaining feelings submerged for thousands of years. Ahrinye, for one, wasn't senile. The Everoinye protected me from his coarse ambitions, and I felt thankful for that. Mind you, how long could that situation last? As these brooding thoughts swirled around in my old vosk skull of a head the Star Lords spoke and immediately negated any idea they were senile.

"The wizard Na-Si-Fantong is dangerous only to a limited extent. You have at your disposal powers to contain him. The being Carazaar is of greater consequence. His ambitions are reckless and inordinate."

I was still sitting in the chair, still sipping wine, still in the here and now. Yet I felt the dizziness seize me. The Star Lords were actually dealing with issues in a simple practical way instead of their usual vague generalities and threats and orders. I croaked out: "Carazaar was actively assisting the Shanks—"

"He arranged for the Katakis to be employed by them, yes."

"He did, did he?" I heard the savagery in my own voice.

"Our decision regarding the Skantiklar stands. If Carazaar should obtain the nine—gems—our task would be infinitely greater."

I digested that. The hesitation over the word gems indicated the nine rubies were not ordinary jewels. Well, I suppose that must have been obvious from the first. And if that bastard Carazaar stepped in to collect them, as the Everoinye clearly suspected and, perhaps, feared, the Shanks would become far worse, far worse a peril for Paz.

The wine was finished. I placed the goblet on the table and instantly, quicker than the blink of an eye, it refilled.

I let it stand for a moment. "So the rubies do have a real power?"

They could have been sarcastic in response, or not deigned to reply at all. Instead the clanging voice said: "Only to those who know how to create the force. Then they must learn to control it. Carazaar most certainly will know how. It is dubious in the case of the wizard."

The Star Lords never had had much regard for Wizards of Loh.

The voice went on: "There is a task set to your hands. It is a matter of observation. You will see what you need to know."

As the voice rang to silence the chair rotated. I snatched up the goblet, spilling only a little of the yellow, and saw an iron-bound chest sliding along towards me. It stopped about a pace away and the lid flew up.

"Dress!"

This interview had been odd and was now growing odder still. I stood up and looked into the chest. A leather jerkin studded with brass. A tan breechclout. A pair of strapped sandals with iron studs. A leather belt. A round leather helmet with a turned up peak. A plain dagger. A spear and a small round target-like shield. There were also a pouch and a water bottle.

I made a face.

"It is not for you to argue or to question the dictates—"

"I know, I know!"

So, willy-nilly, I put on the gear and took up the equipment. I was dressed as many and many a poor wight had been dressed on many a battlefield when he was whisked off to the Ice Floes of Sicce. A spearman in the ranks—well, this wouldn't be the first time, by Krun!

"Is there no sword?"

"No."

Any Kregan fighting man likes to carry as many weapons as is practicable. A simple spearman is always on the lookout to add to his arsenal. About to try to argue, vainly as I knew, I felt myself whirled up into a blue mist. Head over heels I went blindly tumbling into infinity.

Hard ground slogged into my studded sandals and I staggered forward.

"Whoa up, dom!" The wheezy voice breathed in my ear and a fist caught my upper arm, steadying me. "Beng Dikkane has borrowed your legs, by Quintrell the Licentious!"

My sight cleared. A white-painted wall reared on my left and an animal trough stood across a cobbled street. The fellow holding me up must have just walked around the corner as I appeared. All he'd seen was a drunk toppling into him.

"Thanks, dom—no. Beng Dikkane is beyond my means just now."

"You're ill?"

"No, thanks to—no, not ill."

He gave me a shrewd scrutiny from close-set eyes. He was a Hytak, very correct, grim in armor much like mine. He carried a sword at his side, and his tail was bare of bladed steel.

"They don't care who they recruit, dom."

This was a very direct reference to my avoidance of mentioning any deity or spirit. We stood in the entrance to a side street and soldiers and townsfolk passed along the main road ahead. Shadows limned in red and green lay long over the cobbles. The Hytak fished about in his purse.

"Here, may Hlo-Hli smile on you, dom."

He passed across four copper obs, and I took them, touched by this gesture but aware I must continue as I had started.

"My thanks, dom, may Hlo-Hli have you in her keeping."

He stalked off, compact, a fine fighting man, a typical Hytak. Over his shoulder he called: "Remberee."

"Remberee," I said, and added: "Your name, dom?"

"Nath the Jarvis."

"I am Kadar the Hammer. Remberee, Nath."

"Remberee, Kadar."

He went off around the corner and I looked down at the four coins.

The pouch given me by the Everoinye contained ten silvers and fourteen coppers. I made the obs up to eighteen and closed the pouch. Then I started off to find the recruiting Deldars.

An army was being formed here, and it took little time to discover I was in Tuansmot in the coastal land of Shirrendrin. This was one of the countries in southern Loh which had become independent after the fall of the old Empire of Loh. The town was all abustle as mercenaries from all over marched in to sign up and the townsfolk did their best to fleece them of their worldly possessions before they marched out. Rumor had it that Kov Sing-Lee was assembling this army to march on the neighboring land of Kronenvar. What the reasons might be for this attack no one seemed to know or care. All the talk was of booty.

The climate here was most refreshing after the compost stinks of the jungles. It was a trifle warmer than in my kingdom of Djanduin, over the sea south in Havilfar. I did not expect to see many Djangs here for they do not as a rule venture off as mercenaries. They do get considerable fighting experience, though, not least against the damned Gorgrens infesting the borders. There were all manner of diffs in the town, paktuns with the glitter of silver or gold at throat. I had not been provided with a pakmort or a pakzhan so I was a simple mercenary. There must be a reason for that.

Before I rushed off and signed up, I decided, I'd go for a wet and a meal and find out what the form was.

After the Great Hamalese Wars, as those confused conflicts sprawling across continents and islands were coming to be called in retrospect, there were many mercenaries left tazll and seeking employment. There were a lot of Hamalese in the town, a deuced lot, by Krun!

Knowing Ruathytu, the capital of Hamal, as I did, I fancied I'd be a Hamalese. That was one deception I could carry off without fear—particularly if I claimed to be from Paline Valley.

For a time after the end of the Witch Wars with the death of Csitra, I'd flown around Paz visiting those parts to which I owed allegiance. Nulty, at Paline Valley, had shown me a splendid time. As Hamun ham Farthytu, Amak of Paline Valley, I owned a real and genuine identity. I'd been to Djanduin, Strombor, visited my Clansmen, and all in all a most uproarious time had been had, not least with my two favorite rogues, Nath and Zolta in Sanurkazz. That made me wonder what mischief those two splendid imps, Zilvi and Nafren, whom I'd just taken up out of a Zair-forsaken Magdaggian slave ship at the behest of the Star Lords, were being preserved for in the future.

The twin suns were declining and a little breeze was getting up. As I walked along in search of a suitable tavern I could feel the atmosphere of

Tuansmot, for the town as it were seethed with suppressed energy. Everyone could sense the onset of great deeds. There was to be war. Immense booty would flow into the town. Well, as you know, I detest and hate war with a detestation and hatred great under the suns. Why sensible people can't gather around a table and discuss their problems like civilized folk escapes me. The trouble here was, these people wanted to loot the towns of Kronenvar, their next door neighbor. If I was any judge, the inhabitants of Kronenvar would object. Their objections would be made with edged steel.

The Everoinye had sent me here on a matter of observation. When I saw what the matter was I'd know. I most certainly had no wish to get mixed up in some stupid local war. So, as I walked below the black-beamed entrance to The Squish and Queng, I felt great reluctance even to talk to a recruiting Deldar.

Now these thoughts must have cast a nasty expression over my features, for a passing Och gave me a most apprehensive glance. I straightened my shoulders and thrust dark thoughts aside, anticipating a meal and a flagon, and I put on a most pleasing and simple expression. I had no wish to attract unwelcome attention.

Had, I wonder, the Star Lords sent that scared little Och?

The last of the daylight fell through cluttered windows. The floor was wood and well-polished. The tables and chairs were not broken and not dusty. The serving girls were all pleasing and properly dressed. It occurred to me, somewhat belatedly, that I might not have enough cash to pay for a hostelry of this quality. Hesitating, standing in the doorway, I heard a chair crash over.

Instantly, I sprang about. An enormous numim was charging towards me, his lion-man features ablaze, his golden mane flying. He bellowed.

"Hamun! By Krun! Hamun!"

He seized my hand and began pumping it up and down and he clapped his other lion-man's hand about me and battered me on the back. His face was one enormous beam of gold. He went on roaring.

"Chido! Look who's here—it is beyond Havil, I swear. Chido! Where are you?"

The sound of a chair been kicked away preceded a voice saying: "Where am I, Wees? Falling over your chair, that's what. And I do believe it is Hamun, for I see him with my own two eyes. Hamun!"

"Rees! Chido!" I was engulfed by both of them and we were all talking at once, Chido's once-aimless, watery-eyed face now strong with experience beaming as Rees's lion-man face beamed. Somehow we settled at a table, the chair righted, and the wine passed. There was a great deal to talk about and news to pass.

I said: "I flew across to the Golden Winds, Rees, and—"

"Aye, I know. By Krun, I know! All blown away."

"And I flew down to Eurys, and they told me you'd gone—"

"Gone adventuring with Wees. Aye, by Kwun—for the old fellow wefused to accept my hospitality any longer. He was for a paktun—so—"

I shook my head. "So off you both went. By Krun! What a pair!"

Rees ham Harshur, Trylon of the Golden Winds, and Chido ham Thafey, Vad of Eurys, Hamalese both, were good comrades. They knew me as Hamun ham Farthytu, for I'd lacked the courage to tell them my true identity. So we talked on in a welter of reminiscence and information. Chido, who turned R into W—although I do not always report him as such at length—called for more wine.

Cautiously, I said: "I fear this place may be a little too rich for my purse."

"Nonsense, Hamun!" The golden numim roar shook the flagons. "We have done well in the mercenary trade. Opaz has had us well in his keeping."

"Quite wight!" rattled Chido. "Our treat!"

So they'd now openly avowed Opaz! I felt great joy at that, knowing how dubious they'd been about Havil the Green, the official religion of Hamal.

I said: "My thanks—"

They shouted that down. Then Rees said: "I must say we noticed your dress. A spearman? In the ranks? By the Blade of Kurin, tell us, what happened to bring you so low?"

I couldn't help give a glance at the rapier and main gauche each wore. Bladesmen of Ruathytu, we were—or had been.

"Only temporary. You recall the business of the Battle of the Incendiary Vosks?" They'd both been there, I'd seen them in my capacity as Emperor of Vallia, and they had met me as Hamun. They nodded. I went on: "I've a feeling the damned Shanks are due to hit here soon."

"By Kwun—that is wotten news!"

"This army is for Kronenvar." Rees pulled at his golden beard. "Kov Sing-Lee is raising it at the behest of a powerful mage." He lifted his flagon. "He will not be pleased to be diverted from that task."

"That sounds interesting. A mage is raising this army?"

"Wight. A famous Wizard of Loh. Most mysterious feller."

"Yes, we're going to attack Kronenvar at his command. When he gets here. But if the Shanks descend on the coast—"

"We'll have to fight the confounded wotten Shanks, won't we? Even Na-Si-Fantong must see that."

Ten

The rain beat down steadily on our entrenchments before the castle of Samral jutting out on the western side of the town of Miliksin. Everyone was wet. We kept our weapons dry as best we could. The smells of the encampments, at least, were half-washed away by the rain.

Rees walked up as I stood staring out at the grey walls of the castle. He wore a massive hooded cloak and the water ran glistening to add to the pools underfoot. Every now and then a rock or an arrow would plummet down onto our entrenchments. Rees shook himself.

"Just lost Nalgre the Foot. Arrow clean through his eye."

"They shoot well, these Bowmen of Loh."

"They do."

Rees and Chido had brought a little force of around thirty men with them, now they were down to twenty two, plus me. I'd willingly agreed to join their band. Because I knew the Star Lords had a purpose in outfitting me as a spearman, I'd insisted I serve in that capacity. Chido in his best military way insisted I take a longbow, so to that I'd agreed. The reason the Everoinye had, I felt sure, was to keep me inconspicuous. They did not wish to attract the attention of Na-Si-Fantong to my presence in his army.

"Kov Sing-Lee will have to order the assault soon." Rees didn't sound happy about that. We'd done very little against the walls, and the breach was an apology for an opening. "We'll lose men."

I said: "He'll probably send the Chuliks in first."

"Makes sense."

Our army was a rag-tail affair, with little formal organization. Mostly it was composed of small personal bands, like that following Rees and Chido. A small but, thankfully, competent artillery force was provided by a contingent of Hytaks. They kept battering the walls, concentrating on the breach. The trouble was, their catapults were not powerful enough for the task. As we watched, a rock arched from our lines to crack against the grey stone masonry of the curtain wall. A stone was dislodged, and fell into the ditch. At this, a great roar of triumph welled up from our ranks. Rees made a disgusted sound.

"The first today. We'll have to take the so-called breach as it is. Our food won't last much longer."

"I hear Startigern the Amstrad has fever in his people."

"Aye."

The greyness of the sky, the never-ending rain, the mud, the foul rations—and now disease. Truly, this was soldiering as it really is, and not a pretty sight at all, by Krun.

One reason why I persisted lined the road to Miliksin. Every fifty paces or so, each side of the road, a stake had been set up, and some poor wight had been impaled. This was the handiwork of the lords of the town, putting down a pathetic rebellion of the peasants that had started up as soon as the army from Shirrendrin had marched into Kronenvar.

"If only we had some air!" exclaimed Rees, thumping fist into palm. The small voller in which he and Chido had flown in had suffered the fate of far too many airboats. Her silver boxes had gone black, losing all lift and power, so that she was a mere useless hulk.

"What does the kov have—half a dozen vollers?"

"Five. Tyr Nath Ingling's broke down today. Anyway, these people of Loh don't understand vollers."

"Well, put five in, loaded with troops. That should cause enough confusion to let us scale the breach."

"Scale! Too right, by Krun!"

Chido walked up along the trench behind the palisade, hunched against the rain. His feet were lost in the water and mud. He greeted us glumly. "It is nearly the hour of mid."

"Damned Kronenvars!" said Rees in an ugly voice.

Spot on the hour of mid the expected missile flew up from the walls of the town and arched over into our entrenchments. The missile was the body of a man. His throat had been slit after he had been tortured. He was one of a small band of our scouts captured in the first days of the invasion.

This time the missile screamed as he flew through the air. "So they've refined their devilish practices!" Chido sounded wrought up. "I weally do think, if the attack is not successful, we shall have to leave."

"If the attack fails," said Rees, a little too drily, "we might not be here to leave."

Since leaving Hamal they'd adventured through the Dawn Lands and elsewhere. Both now expressed deep distrust of their decision to fly here and join Na-Si-Fantong's expedition. The honor of a mercenary would not be imperiled if he gave formal notice of departure in the wake of disaster. Until that catastrophe, honor compelled them to continue to serve.

I'd not seen the Wizard of Loh, and this was understandable. A spearman in the ranks might see the Kapt of the army when he rode along the ranks with the standard at the commencement of a campaign. The grey eminence at his back would keep himself—or herself—veiled.

The flap of canvas over my position vibrated under the rain and spilled waterfalls every now and again. We were adequately shielded from a bowshot here. When the rain eased I'd have to take shots at any figures moving on the ramparts. They would, of course, shoot back.

A far cry, this, from the whirling romantic dash of a cavalry charge!

So, this was the pattern as we besieged Miliksin.

Naghan the Bristle arrived to take over the watch. He carried his longbow in a round black leather case and his bristly face looked ugly.

"Lahal, Naghan," I said. "You keep time."

"L'al," he replied in his surly Brokelsh way. "By Bakkar! You can take this land and keep it. Better—dump it all down in the Furnace Fires of Inshurfraz. I hate it."

"The assault will be going in soon, Naghan." Rees spoke with a hard edge to his voice. "You can enjoy yourself then."

"I will, notor. By Havil, I will!"

We left Naghan to his post and went off towards the encampments. As is the nature of these things the rain stopped just then. A straggly column of ponshos wandered along towards the camp from the rear, so at least there would be fresh meat tonight. Finding food for an army is a constant nightmare to the quartermasters. Rees must have caught the same thought for he said: "Kov Sing-Lee does his best; but I could wish the Wizard of Loh would open his purse wider."

I said: "Out here in Loh the folk have little time for their own wizards."

"That's wight! Funny old business. They weckon the Wizards of Loh should have whacked us when we blattered them."

"I think most of these countries were glad to see the back of Walfarg," said Rees as we reached the encampments.

"So you give no chance to a revived Empire of Loh?" I gave Rees and Chido two swift looks as I spoke. "With or without the mages."

"Not a chance in a Herrelldrin Hell!" and: "Sooner climb back from the Ice Floes of Sicce!"

The various subjects of these casual conversations were let lie there; but one unspoken but immensely important function of Na-Si-Fantong remained. There was a sorcerer of some kind in the castle of Samral. He or she could have played merry hell with our besieging force if Na-Si-Fantong hadn't been along to afford protection. So far, as we understood it, he had done nothing actively hostile against the castle or town, so the chances were that he was being baulked in his turn.

With the easing of the rain the shards of ruby and jade could strike through and begin to steam the ground. Just as we finished eating and were chewing our handful of palines, a messenger called Rees and Chido. Although you could not really call the army Kov Sing-Lee had raised for Na-Si-Fantong a heterogeneous mob, for the troops were all paktuns of one description or another, we were certainly a most disorganized force. There were no regiments or brigades, instead the commanders of each little warband reported to Sing-Lee and took orders direct. Rees and Chido came back from the briefing and their demeanor told me instantly that the assault had been decided on.

"At least the clever Wizard of Loh has done his job." Chido plunked himself down and took up the tankard I had ready filled.

"He's seen off the sorcerer in the castle." Rees did not sit but, tankard in fist, strode up and down. "We go in at first light."

With seven moons in the sky of Kregen, very often night affords no real cover. This night, although not a pitch dark Night of Notor Zan, would see all but the three smaller moons below the horizon at dawn.

"Although that breach is an apology for a way in," I said. "I'm glad the thing is settled."

"Aye."

In a somewhat sombre frame of mind, we made our preparations.

I entertained no hope that we'd surprise the garrison. The star light was bright enough for them to see our columns debouching from the entrenchments. Our ace had to be the five vollers. If they could cause confusion enough to get our Chuliks up into the breach, then we'd stand a chance. Chido and Rees's band were stationed about half way back and our mission was to push forward come what may after the Chuliks.

Silently we shuffled forward in column. I put the little round shield up slanting over my head, everybody else did the same, and we went forward like an animated flower bed. Almost at once the arrows rained down.

Men were struck, and screamed, and fell, kicking. We pushed stolidly on. Noise spurted up from the van, the grim and hideous sounds of strife.

Gradually the light brightened, crimson and emerald flooding in long mingled swathes, streaming colored shadows. Well, many a poor devil on both sides of the walls would never see the Suns of Scorpio rise again.

Now we trampled forward over bodies sprawled face down. Arrows stood thickly everywhere. The screams and shouts and the tinker-hammer of weapons clattered in our ears. Now we were stepping past the bodies of Chuliks, and for all their martial skills, they lay there as dead as any Fristle or Rapa. We approached the breach and found ladders in place and climbed up after the fellow in front and so tumbled over the smashed masonry.

Incoming arrows ceased and I was able to take a cautious glance up. The backs of the fellows going on ahead pushed up and down as they climbed the rubble slope. The brilliant deep green of small branches of vepid bushes we wore tucked into helmet or cap shone as though varnished. A recognition sign was vitally necessary in a ragtail army like this, otherwise we'd be hacking one another to pieces instead of the enemy. The sight reminded me, even then, that I'd felt no particular emotion about that hard brilliant green after my recent experiences in the Eye of the World.

With the rising of the suns the raw stink of freshly spilled blood grew on the air. Soon the stench would be nigh unbearable.

Our little band led by Rees and Chido pushed on with the rest. The orders were simple. Break in, slay the enemy, loot. Chance had not brought me to this time and place, for I was here for a reason and I knew that if I allowed myself to be carried with the tide I might miss the mark. Believing in the hand of Fate is all very well, you have to give a few hard strokes yourself to cut across the tide from time to time.

My heart leaped as I saw a tall armored form face down and sprawled in death. That quick involuntary moment of terror for Inch was unnecessary as I knew. There was no need to turn him over. A party of Ng'grogans served with the army, for Ng'groga was just along the coast. I pushed on.

Down from the walls with a maze of streets ahead and the castle to the side, the triumphant besiegers began to fan out, chasing running foes and searching for booty.

The scenes that follow an uncontrolled sack of a town are unpleasant. I stared about, wanting none of that. Rees and Chido were following orders and heading for the inner gates to the castle. The rest of our band were clearly torn between loot and duty; but Rees maintained a high level of discipline. Anyway, you could almost see them thinking, there'd be more and better treasures in the castle of Samral. I judged my objective lay there, too.

Our fliers had done their work, disgorging a surprise party, and we came up to the inner gates in time to see the last of the enemy and the victorious forward rush of our Chuliks.

We all rushed into the castle.

The place was in no wise one of the great and marvelous castles of Kregen. Its grey stone walls enclosed a sizeable area, roofed in timber and tile, and there'd be a maze of corridors and rooms, no doubt. All the same, I was not impressed by the castle of Samral.

As is the nature of these things in a confused assault, parties are split up and nice starting organizations dwindle into one or two fellows prodding ahead with little contact with their comrades. We came out to an inner ward, and the courtyard looked abruptly ominous. Deep shadows lay all along the eastern walls and the glow of red and green burned on the west.

At my side Horvil ham Vaherne gave a little surprised grunt. I did not turn to look at him but dodged back instantly into the shadows of the gateway through which we'd just walked. Another shaft glanced off the masonry, and a third pinged up off the flagstones where I'd been standing.

Vaherne collapsed. The Lohvian shaft through his neck above the corselet rim snapped as he pitched forward and rolled over. Abruptly, the assault on the castle of Samral had turned ugly, in a personal sense.

At my back Chido said: "Poor old Horvil. He was down on his luck when he joined us."

"We won't cross that open courtyard," I said. "Where's a door?"

In the side of the gateway a narrow door led onto a spiral staircase leading up. Chido had with him the twins, Orgren and Nath Fernon, a couple of hefty Rapas, loaded with weapons. Their grey feathers bristled, and Nath's beak was bent lopsided from an old wound. Chido rapped out: "Up with you!"

They went up willingly enough, shields high. Chido flung me a glance.

I started up after them, half-turning to ask a stupid question.

"Where's Rees?"

"Opaz alone knows. He rushed off roaring—"

"He'll be all right."

Up we climbed to come out into a long gallery that led around the court-yard below. Narrow windows on both sides indicated the builders of the castle anticipated making a stand in this place. The defenders had abandoned it already, withdrawing to the far side from which the arrow had spat to kill Horvil ham Vaherne. We hurried along the deserted gallery.

Around the corner of the yard the gallery led into a series of rooms all deserted and very few with anything worth pocketing. Orgren Fernon said: "Where's the loot? By Havil, there must be better stuff than this."

"Clear that Bowman away and we'll see." Chido spoke with a rasp. How changed he was from the dear old goggling-eyed, chinless Chido I'd first met!

Now we went along with very great caution. We were approaching the point directly opposite the gateway. If the set up of rooms was not favorable—and any builder of defensive works would make sure they did not favor an attacker—then we could be in for a nasty surprise. Chido pushed forward to the front. Whilst I was not happy about that, it was a requirement of the job.

In the event we rushed into the target room to find it empty. An over-turned bowl of squashed palines remained the only evidence of anyone having been here and shooting Horvil ham Vaherne.

"By Rhapaporgolam the Reiver of Souls!" spat Nath Fernon. He was strung up with nervous anticipation, and he showed his disgust forcibly. "This place is as useless as a one-handed archer!"

"Try the other door." Chido spoke perfectly calmly.

Orgren and his twin checked the door and we went through into a room overlooking the next courtyard. Besides being deserted the place was dusty and smelled of damp. The evidence now was pretty clear that this part of the castle had been unused for some time. Chido looked through the win-dow and gave a tiny gasp of surprise. We joined him.

The courtyard was a shambles. Dead and dying warriors lay everywhere. The slant of the suns threw up the grisly details pitilessly.

"Theirs and ours," snapped Chido.

"Someone got here first." I was gazing down hoping not to see the dead form of a glorious golden numim sprawled among the blood.

The two Rapas were now in an extremely ugly mood seeing their chances of loot evaporating with every moment that passed. Sounds of fighting carried to us from both left and right. Chido spoke harshly.

"You'll get your crack at some booty. Let's push on."

We rushed back through the rooms we'd already traversed, turned at the

314

corner and headed deeper into the castle. At the end of a long picture gallery—although all the pictures were absent and only rectangles of darker color along the walls showed where they'd been—we found a heap of dead men jamming the doors open. Past them more bodies at intervals told us we were nearing the fighting in this part of the castle as our forces pushed the defenders back. A wounded Chulik sat with his back against the wall stoically binding up his leg from which the blood dropped. One of his tusks had been snapped off at the silver band and his face shone bloodily.

"Who is leading up front?" demanded Chido.

"Likshu the Treacherous may know, notor. I do not."

We left him and pressed on. The noise up ahead grew.

Dead and wounded littered the floor as we advanced through chambers that increased in richness. The two Rapas brightened up, although Nath did growl: "They'll be pocketing everything in sight before we get there."

Now the rooms were sumptuously furnished, with tapestries and couches and statuary. The only treasures left were those too heavy or bulky to be snatched up as the fighting went forward. A golden statue could always be taken up after the victory. A priceless carpet of Walfarg weave could be rolled up and carried off later on.

We were still a floor up from the ground so that when we came out into an imposing vaulted chamber we could look down from a railed gallery. This place was used as a banqueting hall and must also be the room from which the lord of the castle dispensed justice, for a fancy throne occupied a dais at the far end. Across the floor men fought and died. The brilliant green of vepid leaves glinted in the light falling from arched windows. Our men were surging forward over the floor, and the defenders resisted with a desperation that suggested they intended to fight to the death. The two Rapas let out yells of rage and triumph and dashed down the stairs to join the combat. Chido looked at me. I shook my head.

"It's just about all over."

"That's vewy twue, Hamun, but—"

"But nothing. You'll get your share as a lord when the booty is divvied out. No sense in getting killed in a stupid fracas like this."

"It's Wees I'm thinking of."

"I know. But he's not down there. Anyway—"

Then I stopped speaking abruptly. A bunch of Chuliks hammered into a last knot of defenders, cutting them down and scattering the few who ran. As I watched, the bulky form of Na-Si-Fantong broke from his bodyguard of Yellow Tuskers and dashed for the throne. He bent over the seat and what he did I couldn't see. In the next instant he straightened up, turning so I could see clearly. He grasped a small wooden box in his left hand. He flipped the lid open and I swear his eager face glowed with reflected redness.

So, there before my eyes, was the reason for this whole army and war and siege and conquest. Right there, and grasped in the clutching hands of the Wizard of Loh, Na-Si-Fantong!

Eleven

At my instinctive reaction and instant movement, Chido said: "I understood you to say it would be inadvisable to go down there."

My gaze was fixed on the sorcerer below on the throne dais with the box clutched in his hands. His Chuliks surged about him, forming a wall of protective steel. I paused on the top step and turned my head back to shout something to Chido. His appearance astonished me. He was staring up over my head and on his face was such an expression I could not put a name to it. He held his shield up in a reflex action, as though warding off a blow.

I whirled. The cause of Chido's consternation jumped into focus, and then out again, so that I blinked as though a powerful light had abruptly shone into my eyes.

High on the wall between the narrow arched windows a round black spot glowed. The ebon darkness pulsed with a radiance that emanated black light. The spot grew. It swelled like a bubble of shining inky shadows.

Swiftly it bloated and now glinting sparkles of silver shot through the blackness like fireflies on a night of Notor Zan.

The uproar in the chamber died. I did not look down; but I guessed men were standing, gaping, staring in utter fascination at this awesome apparition. Chido said something and burbled away into silence. That silence held the entire banqueting hall in thrall.

In the exact centre of the black hemisphere a brilliant nodule of green burst into existence. The nodule sparked and spat, changing into a star shape that broadened, peeling back the black like the skin of a grape.

For a heartbeat as the green star flowered I tore my gaze away and snatched a fleeting glance down at the dais. Na-Si-Fantong stood, tall and bulky, clutching the wooden box to his chest. His thick face glared up with a mad look of passion and resentment and—I could not be sure—and perhaps a touch of apprehension.

When I swiveled back the green star had displaced the ebon radiance. In a vertical line in the centre of the star the greenness thickened. Then I saw it was not thickening but that some tall thin object was forcing itself through the green—through the solid stone of the wall. As though that was a signal that released the superstitious fears of the mercenaries, shouts of terror spurted up. Some of the paktuns were running, some stayed rooted to the spot. The Chuliks clustered about their employer and, give them their due, they stuck there. Now I was able to switch my observation from the Wizard of Loh back to the green star and then back again. Na-Si-Fan-tong lifted his right hand. He made a gesture. Instantly I stared at the wall where the tall thin object now projected high into the chamber.

Recognition hit me. It was the prow of a ship!

The bows swelled as more of the craft sailed through the solid stone wall. She was not overlarge, and her double keel quickly curved up as she eased through to flaunt up into a high stern. The vessel sailed into the air and turned and settled to the floor.

Now I could look down on her. She had a flat deck and this deck was crowded with Katakis, glittering with armor and steel. Their fierce down-drawn brows and menacing eyes glowered on the Chuliks. Then I saw who sat at the stern of the vessel, resplendent, imperious, dominating and utterly in command of this situation.

From artificially widened shoulders his robes swept away like a sullen cloud of smoky red. His scaled shirt glistened and his bone white hands grasped the haft of a double-handed axe. Bone white his face, with a thick brown beard, no moustache, a lipless mouth clearly revealing fang-like unhuman teeth, nostril slits—yes, I knew that devil face!

On this occasion he did not have with him his followers, naked and half-naked girls in chains, weird other-dimensional creatures, worm-like entities, little scurrying tailed horrors, all claw and fang. He sat in a chair of simple proportions, covered with skins, and he radiated such an aura of absolute contempt and power as to overwhelm.

I forced myself to look at his axe. Double-handed, it was not a great Saxon pattern axe such as that used by Inch. It was double-bitted and each blade curved fantastically, pierced and re-curved and each edge was serrated in sawtooth jaggedness. A very imposing and magniloquent weapon—yes, of a surety. A practical fighting man's implement? I'd bested him when he used a more serviceable axe—was this new one in a differ-ent class, possessed of magic, invincible when pitted against a mere mortal man's cold steel?

The ship settled and the Katakis, bladed daggered tails high, leaped for the dais.

My estimation of this fellow's axe play had dropped drastically when we'd had our little dust up. Now I questioned his tactical skill. His Katakis swarmed up onto the dais where the Yellow Tuskers met them with a feroc-ity to equal and overpower theirs. He'd have done better to have dropped down on them, with the advantage of the high ground.

He wore the helmet that could so easily confuse with its high crown-like curve of tridents, its peaked visor like a barracuda's head in gold, its centre a ferocious fish-head, all exposed needle-teeth. Again I took the fancy that a swift, scared glance would confuse all too easily—was this a man with a fish-face helmet, or was he a fish with a man's face as a neck ornament? Man or Fish, he had brought only Katakis to do his physical work; there were no Shanks with Carazaar.

Chulik and Kataki clashed in a bitter struggle. I stepped back onto the gallery and unlimbered the longbow Chido had given me.

Clean and swift the draw and loose. The shaft sped true. The long arrow struck squarely into Carazaar's unhuman face. The shaft caromed from the skin-covered chair back, splintered into the air. Again, Carazaar was an illusion, projecting his image here by his kharrna. He was in lupu somewhere, sitting in his throne, and yet he was here commanding his minions to his bidding.

And that bidding sent a trembling feeling of frustrated anger through me. The devil had at last shown his hand. Carazaar, too, coveted the Skantiklar.

What he wanted it for, what he might accomplish with it, I did not know. I did know no good would come of it, none at all.

At my back Chido let out a yell followed instantly by the scrape of steel against steel. I whirled. Four warriors hurled themselves along the gallery and Chido was engaged with two of them whilst the other two made for me. None wore bright green vepid in their helmets. With some of Seg's speed I nocked a fresh arrow and shafted the first fellow. The longbow swung back out of the way, the little round target shield snapped forward and the spear slanted up. I charged forward.

These fellows were churgurs, sword and shield men. They were absolutely confident they could knock Chido and me over and escape the disaster. They were not apims, being bulky, two-armed, tail-less zaffims. Their faces were lumpy, as it were unformed, with large brow ridges and squashed noses, and their jaws were narrow to the point of nonexistence. Yet in those sharp jaws stood snaggly teeth that could tear off a fair old chunk of flesh. This zaffim decided he'd just rush me, knock me down with his shield and trust my little targe would never deflect his lynxter as he stabbed home.

In that first flashing glimpse of them I'd decided their shields really were too large for inside work. All right for the line, yes; now I sidestepped and as he blundered past stuck him with the spear. He wore a banded corselet and the spear point snugged in above the neck rim. I withdrew with alacrity, fearing for Chido in his unequal fight.

Dear old Chido handled himself superbly. He'd wounded one of them and was tinker-hammering at the other, trying to get past that damn great shield. I rushed across and gave the wounded zaffim an almighty kick up the rear and yelled in the old foretop hailing roar: "Get off out of it, fambly, before you get dead!"

He yelped more in consternation than anything, gave me a single shocked glance and then scampered off towards the exit. I hit the other one a shrewd and unfair blow, using the butt to thump him in the back whereat he staggered forward so that Chido, quick as a leem, smacked him down.

"No need, Hamun, I judge, to kill the hulus." Chido spoke with the slightest hint of puffing. His face was bright with passion; but he was in command of himself.

"Yes."

The fellow I'd shafted was gone; but the other one with a hand to his neck where the blood dribbled, was staggering away. Chido hauled his man up and pushed him off. The zaffim needed no further urging and ran.

"Perhaps," I said, with meaning, "they were not the yetches who catapulted our fellows."

"Perhaps." Chido was already wiping a rag along his sword. "I wish I knew where Wees was."

I worried over our comrade Rees, but I leaped for the gallery rail and stared down into the chamber.

Many dead Katakis lay on the steps leading up to the dais, and some Chuliks were dead and a few wounded. The remaining Katakis were crowding back. Well, that was the expected outcome of that confrontation.

Chido joined me and, in that instant, he said: "Opaz!"

The Chuliks were moving slowly, more slowly, and then they stopped. They stood like statues. Na-Si-Fantong, hand high, showed a purple and congested face up to Carazaar in his seat aboard his boat, for the devil had lifted off and was floating above the floor. Na-Si-Fantong clutched the little wooden box to his chest. He shook like an aspen. The Katakis stopped retreating and a bunch moved back up the steps. The Wizard of Loh shook himself, and then his trembling fined out and he, too, stood stock still.

Chido said: "Confounded magic—"

A Kataki took the box and in the moment it left Na-Si-Fantong's grasp the lid snapped open in the Kataki's hand. A red streak lanced from the box up to Carazaar—and vanished.

In a bunch the Whiptails ran back, the boat lowered for them and they climbed aboard. There were less now than when they'd begun; but that had never upset a Kataki before and was not likely to now. They held life cheap, including the lives of fellow Whiptails.

The boat lifted and began to revolve.

I said to Chido: "I fancy that concludes the entertainment for today. Step back out of sight."

"Is there nothing we can do? No, of course not."

Now the reason the Star Lords had given me a little shield and a spear became crystal clear. I attracted no attention after a fleeting glance. I was just a simple spearman in the ranks. We stepped back and, just for a moment, the stern of the vessel lifted into sight as she nosed out through the green star in the stone wall. The star vanished, the black globe of radiant darkness formed and dwindled and died. Carazaar was gone—and with him another of the rubies of the Skantiklar.

I was left to contemplate the unpalatable fact that I'd failed to obtain the ruby. Worse than that, instead of Na-Si-Fantong as our chief adversary for the possession of the Skantiklar, we now had to face Carazaar, the éminence grise behind the Shanks.

A voice roared out in triumph at our backs. "I've done it! By Krun, I've done it! Hoko has at last turned his face away and fortune has—"

"Do be quiet, Wees, old fellow. There's nasty magic down there."

"Magic?" The booming numim voice softened. "Hanitch take it."

Very carefully I put an eyeball over the rail. The dais was empty.

The last of the Chuliks trailed off out of the far doorway.

There was no point now chasing after the sorcerer. From what I knew of his character he'd already be planning ways and means to regain the ruby. The ugly thought occurred to me to wonder just how many of the red baubles this devil Carazaar now had in his possession. My job now was to rejoin my friends and consult with our comrade Wizards and Witch of Loh.

"Phew!" said Chido on a breath. "Can't say I've ever liked messing about with confounded magics."

"Nor me!" agreed Rees. Then, in a light eager voice: "Look at this!"

We turned to him. He'd been in a fight all right, but his sword had been cleaned and was back in its scabbard. His shield was thrust up on the point of his left shoulder. He held out a brass-bound balass box.

"A Jikaida box," said Chido. "Aye. And, see, look what's in it!"

The moment I saw I felt an enormous gladness for Rees well up in me. The box was jammed with gems of every description. It was a fortune.

"Splendid!" cried Chido. "Now the estates of the Golden Wind will—"

"They've all blown away long since." Rees swelled his chest. "I'll start afresh, somewhere else. Opaz will aid me, I know."

Now after the Battle of the Incendiary Vosks when I'd parted company with Rees and Chido I'd been exceptionally busy over the business of Csitra and the Witch War. When that dust up had finished at the hunting lodge in Yumapan known as the Eye of Imladiel there had been time to go back to see Nedfar in Ruathytu. Nedfar was a man of the utmost integrity. Where in many men to be seated on the throne of empire by another person and his armies would bring resentment rather than gratitude, Nedfar had simply thanked me and we had gone forward together as allies. So I'd put in a word for Rees. Nedfar was aware of the good work Chido and

Rees had done in the battle, and before, and made immediate arrangements to find a vacant estate or two.

Since the golden lion man had taken himself off abroad, and Chido with him, nothing had so far happened. I had to be careful when I spoke.

I said: "The last time I was in Ruathytu I picked up all manner of gossip. You know how it is. I did hear that the Emperor Nedfar was mightily pleased with your actions at the Incendiary Vosks. He knew of your difficulties with the wind blowing your estates away. I think he has in mind to find you others, a vadvarate of a certainty."

Before the numim could speak Chido burst out: "Marvelous! I've always said, Wees old fellow, you are worth more than a trylon, a vad at least and a kov for pweference. We must return at once."

"We-ell—"

"That seems a good idea," I put in, my work done.

"You'll come with us, Hamun? Of course you will!"

"Ah, well, now—" My future tasks lay in Loh, of that I felt convinced. I'd like to go roistering with these two in the Sacred Quarter of Ruathytu once more. The dichotomy in apparent character of the Hamalese had always fascinated me. When they'd been the enemies of Vallia we'd always seen them as a miserable folk, singing mournful songs, obsessed with their Laws. Yet the Bladesmen ruffled in the Sacred Quarter and there were many bright sparks like Rees and Chido. Oh, yes, I'd had some splendid times.

"We'll set Wees up in his new lands and then we'll—"

"I can't be certain of that until the new emperor confirms it." Rees shook his golden-maned head. "We were siding with old Hot and Cold."

"Oh Wees! Only because the damned Vallians poked their long noses in."

"I suppose so. Old Hot and Cold was no good for Hamal, anyway. I saw the Vallian Emperor, on the battlefield. His people fought magnificently. He was—impressive. Funny thing, he reminded me of someone. I could have sworn I'd met him before, yet, of course, that's impossible."

I kept my old beakhead placid and my black-fanged winespout shut.

"First thing is to collect our men and then see what Na-Si-Fantong is up to. We'll have to tell him the campaign is over for us."

I couldn't help saying: "The fellow who became Emperor of Vallia was dragged at the tail of one of Queen Thyllis's calsanys through Ruathytu."

"And I've told you before I considered that disgusting at the time."

"So you did, Rees, so you did."

"A wotten thing to do, even to a Vallian."

I stared at dear old Chido and I knew, somewhat heavily, that even now I couldn't unburden myself, tell him and Rees I was not only a Vallian but was that self-same Dray Prescot who had become the Emperor of Vallia.

What they'd say to the notion of an Emperor of Emperors, an Emperor of Paz, I just couldn't contemplate. I remained Hamun ham Farthytu, the Amak of Paline Valley.

We went out, and went cautiously, for who knew how many of the defenders lurked in the shadows thirsting for revenge.

This red ruby of the Skantiklar was gone, and that depressed me with the terrors and horrors that must follow. I tried to take some comfort from my comrade Rees's good fortune—but I made heavy weather of it, I can tell you, by Krun.

Twelve

For one awful moment of terror I imagined, as the blue glow of the Scorpion faded, that I was back on Earth.

The whitish yellow radiance falling about me did not come from a little yellow sun but from concentric rings of lamps, shining upon a pleasant glade among rhododenrons and hydrangeas. The air tasted full of the fragrance of many flowers banked in solid beds of colour. The grass shone a lustrous green. Butterflies flitted by. Above the lamps the sky remained aloof and indistinguishable. I was not on Kregen, of that I felt confident, so I stared about, alert for what might chance next.

The phantom blue Scorpion had taken me up as we rested after the siege of the castle of Samral. Rees and Chido would wonder where I'd gone. Would the Star Lords fashion another excuse for my absence?

Now I have mentioned that although it appears I spend my time with the Everoinye slanging them rotten and attempting to keep myself from being contemptuously hurled back four hundred light years to the planet of my birth, the truth, of course, is that the whole situation is so fraught with terror and the anticipation of terror that my mind is held in a kind of stasis. The Star Lords wield power of so immense a scale it surpasses normal imagination. My reflexes become automatic. Yes, there were many questions I could think of in more rational moments on Kregen, but to bring them to mind facing the Everoinye is an altogether different order of rationality.

So, now, when the clanging voice resonated through the clearing I felt once again that familiar tightening of all my senses.

"Dray Prescot! Where is that which you observed and were sent for?"

I swallowed down hard. "I expect you know. That benighted Carazaar took it—"

"Oh, yes, we know, Dray Prescot."

A hissing at my back brought me about sharply. A wooden brass-bound chest skimmed across the grass and halted at my side.

"Replace your dress."

It was borne in on me that I still wore the leather gear and carried the little targe and spear. Philosophically, I shrugged them off and dumped them all back into the chest. This was more normal, facing the Star Lords stark naked.

The sequence of automatic actions must in some way have unclogged my brain, or jolted it into action. I remembered a question the answer to which I would like to hear from these superhuman beings. I kept that question like a little nugget of gold in my head, hugging it, concentrating on it, ready to spring it when I judged the time right.

"We warned you Carazaar was a formidable opponent."

"He's that, all right."

If they thought I was going to plead guilty and beg forgiveness then they had another thought coming. Sure, I'd changed my attitude to them—or attempted to—but I felt instinctively they'd not believe a new cringing Dray Prescot after the uncouth rough with whom they were familiar.

I did feel it prudent to speak up, saying: "There was nothing I could do. The fellow has an impressive amount of kharrna."

If I found myself back on Earth in the next heartbeat I wouldn't then be surprised. As ever, that calamity must be prevented.

I said: "Touching these ideas of a new Empire of Loh—"

Whether or not the ploy to distract their attention actually worked or not, I, of course, couldn't say. Probably they were prepared to talk on this subject in any case. I felt a genuine gush of relief when the clanging voice spoke. "You preserved the life of Mul-lu-Manting and she fanatically desires this new Empire of Loh. You have met Queen Satra who regards herself still as the Empress of Loh, a true Queen of Pain. Between them they may accomplish..." The voice paused and when the Star Lord spoke again I marveled. Did I detect a note of humor in the words, like that last bubble in a glass of champagne? "Well, Dray Prescot, the human who has the yrium. What is your opinion?"

If my mouth hung open foolishly I wouldn't have been surprised.

Well, sink me! I'd let 'em have it, both barrels!

"There are advantages and disadvantages. Many of the people of Loh, and particularly of Walfarg and Tsungfaril, are listless, lackadaisical. One has to judge that they would not give a good account of themselves in any confrontation with the Shanks. Should Walfarg be re-united into the empire and be provided with strong leadership, resistance should follow."

"Yes?"

"It is my view that most of the other independent nations of Loh would resent any attempt by Walfarg to impose their old empire."

"Go on."

"Against that one must set the unsettling effects. Should Walfarg persist, then we'd end up fighting among ourselves instead of fighting Shanks."

"That is an eventuality you must prevent."

I clamped my harsh old lips shut. The kind of jobs these Everoinye handed out were mind boggling in their immensity.

"How in a Herrelldrin Hell would I do that?"

"You have the yrium."

"And that's supposed to be enough?"

Silence fell.

I broke that uncanny quietness. I spoke up brashly.

"Tell me, Star Lords, do you or do you not want the Empire of Walfarg or the greater Empire of Loh to be reformed?"

If they came back with their infernal chorus: "That is not for you to know," I honestly felt I'd crash to the ground and start tearing up fistfuls of grass and chewing on them like a demented man.

Instead: "One balances the other. The Shanks remain the priority. Anything forwarding that end must be used."

"All right. So Mul-lu-Manting doesn't antagonize the people and Satra gets to run her new Empire of Walfarg. Yes, we'd stand a better chance against the Fish Faces. But the unpleasant consequences—"

"That is a question for the Emperor of Paz."

For a black instant sheer disgust overwhelmed me. Not so much despair as angry denial. How the hell was I supposed to cope with all these problems? For a start, I couldn't see Satra taking orders from anyone, let alone that she-leem Licria if she got to take over.

I got out, half-choking: "Very few folk want to know about any footling Emperor of Paz."

"Then you must make them."

"I've seldom been in the business of making people do anything—"

"In that, Dray Prescot, patently, you lie."

Because they were who they were I couldn't smack a glove into their faces and challenge them to a duel or sequence of duels. Anyway, I suppose what they said was true enough. I could remember times when folk had done what I wanted—as you who are listening to my narrative can testify—without any real understanding on my part why they chose to do so. This was all bound up with that mysterious and frightening power, the charisma Kregans call the yrium. The opposite, the evil power, is called the yrrum.

The scents wafted fragrantly, a little breeze blew and the varnished leaves of the rhododendrons rustled harmoniously. The resonant voice echoed about the clearing. "As to Carazaar and his interest in the Skantiklar, all things must eventuate in each epoch. Ways will be found."

I wondered, if the next eventuation was to take place in the next epoch, how they expected me to be still around to find any ways.

A familiar hissing spurted and I turned to see a battered wooden chest bound in black iron trundling over the grass. When it stopped at my side I didn't lift the lid. I waited.

"Dress."

Up went the lid on the instant and I saw the brave old scarlet breech-clout. Well now! Yes, my kit was there, all of it was there. The lesten hide belt with the dulled silver buckle, the heavy Bowie-type knife I persist in calling my old sailor knife, the rapier and main-gauche—I pulled them out one after the other. And then I stopped stock-still. I felt utter shock.

The Lohvian longbow and quiver were there, and the Krozair longsword. But they were placed over and half concealed another scabbard, another sword.

I pushed aside the longbow and longsword. I reached out for the scabbard.

I did not recognize the hilt. By that I mean, this sword was not one I owned, and I had only one, that of Alex Hunter, back in Esser Rarioch.

Slowly, reverently—and this is not blasphemous in connection with an instrument of destruction—I drew the blade from the scabbard. A one handed sword, this, fitting the fist and becoming a part of the body. The cunningness—the genius—is this, that when you strike with a Savanti sword which is lightness personified, in the instant of contact the lightness becomes weight, becomes heavy with devastating force. Oh, yes, there is no sword I knew of on Kregen—including the great Krozair longsword—to equal the Savanti Blade.

Did I hear a murmur of laughter, mingling with the rustle of the leaves?

"There is much for you to do, Dray Prescot. Even the Savanti, misguided though they are, secluded in far away Aphrasöe, have their uses."

I said: "The Savanti sword is used only for good."

"In that we would like to concur."

Slowly, thoughtfully, I strapped on my gear. I had been thrown out of Aphrasöe by the Savanti, tossed, as I'd believed, out of Paradise. I'd found new paradises in Kregen. I suspected that the Savanti wished for all of Kregen to become the domain of apims like themselves, like me. They saw no future for diffs, the splendid array of folk who were not Homo sapiens sapiens. If the Everoinye meant that the Savanti were misguided in that, then I agreed.

"You will pursue the search for the Skantiklar and you will resist the Shanks. The two tasks are now intertwined."

I opened my mouth and the world drenched itself in blue. The gigantic shape of the phantom Scorpion hovered and drew me up into its embrace. Head over heels, up I went, enveloped in blue coldness. Hurtling I went thumping down onto a damned hard chunk of rock that knocked all the wind out of me. I lay there, and if I mentioned Makki Grodno and the Divine Lady of Belschutz, I fancy I had just about every right in the book.

"Stop lollygagging around skulking down there, cabbage. Get up here and pitch in!"

Fighting the dizziness that wanted to turn my head around on my shoulders and twist my inward parts outward, I clawed up and stared about.

Another damned cavern! A blasted cave with hard rocks and syatras and an omnipresent pearly glow. I was tumbled down a little cleft. On the ledge above me Mevancy was swishing and swirling her sword very prettily against half a dozen fellows in black robes, with red brilliant eyes, all lethally intent on chopping my comrade into bite-sized chunks. One of them screeched and tumbled backward with his face a red pudding, so she had some of her bindles left. I levered myself up, unlimbered the Krozair brand and charged into action.

Do not ask why I did not draw the superb Savanti Sword. I just whirled up over the ledge and cut the first two down with diagonal slashes that were controlled to a nicety and I whirled to slip a blade that whirred past and then I ducked and came up with my sword snouting and so swirled after the blade thrust and withdrew into a long slicing cut that doubled-up the next. Mevancy had seen off the last and so we two stood there, staring at each other among the tumbled corpses.

Her color was high and her breast rose and fell under the mail shirt. Her forearms looked nearly empty of bindles. Oh, yes, not a great and stunning beauty, my comrade Mevancy, but splendid and great-hearted with her beauty shining from within. Oh, and, yes, she had a cutting way with her and a sharp tongue that I relished.

"Well, cabbage, and where have you been?"

"Round and about. I'll tell you—but you are all right, pigeon? We were whisked off and then you—"

"You mean you!"

"Um," I said. There was so much to say and catch up with. She would see our separation as me leaving her. Selah! "What did—?"

"Oh, I had to go to assist a kregoinye, Strom Irvil—"

At this I burst out with a raucous bray of laughter.

Her eyes widened and she looked thoroughly shocked.

"Cabbage!"

"Strom Irvil of Pine Mountain! So he was in it again, was he? And I'll bet he called you Zaydo—"

"He did, the presumptuous onker!"

"You're here, so everything went well."

"Yes. I arrived to be attacked on the instant and then you fell down that cleft and lay there taking your ease like a—like a—"

"Back to the old cabbage days, right?"

"Oh, you!"

So we were comrades once again and ready to face what might come.

What did come revealed itself as Mevancy gasped: "The shints!" Advancing towards us among the rocks and clearly illuminated by the pearly light, a whole bunch of men in black robes surged on, weapons glittering.

Thirteen

Firmly, she said: "We'll have to run for it, cabbage."

Without hesitation or any stupid suicidal heroics, I agreed.

Mind you, by Zair, that brash young Dray Prescot who'd first landed on Kregen might well have gone whooping down on the black-robed fanatics brandishing his sword. Had I been alone I believe I might well have seriously considered that as an option. Running away from enemies was not a habit of mine. Discretion, as they say in Clishdrin, may be the better part of valor; but Valor, as they say in Valka, is the better part of the Person.

We hopped and skipped over the rocks and darted aside from the clutching tendrils of that damned unhealthy syatra and so went running helter-skelter into the mouth of a tunnel.

A foul stench gusted up, as of congested sewers. A partially decomposed corpse deliquesced just inside the tunnel, riddled with darts. In the wall a wooden flap dangled from a dark slot.

"Poor devil!" rapped out Mevancy and she leaped over. "Thank Gahamond he tripped that trap."

"And thank Opaz the people were petrified and so didn't come along and reset the devilish contraption."

What, also, this meant was clear. Some of our party had been this way already, resuscitating those held in the stasis spell. We sped on.

The slapping of leather sandals on the rock at our backs echoed eerily. The walls shone with nitre. The air gradually sweetened. We ran on and debouched into a cavern where a fountain played at the center and a pool lapped almost to the sides. The ledge was wide enough for one.

"Have a care, cabbage."

"Oh, rest assured, pigeon, I shall. But you—I recollect you seem to like—" and then I shut up. What the hell was I thinking about to remind a lady of the time she'd fallen in the water and deadly jaws stuffed with razor-sharp teeth had bitten for her? Onker! I finished: "Two openings up ahead. Left or right?"

"When I've looked at each I will make the decision."

"Quidang!"

The first opening led onto a featureless tunnel, as did the second.

I looked back across the pool. The opening through which we had emerged was just visible past the fountain. The fanatics following us would probably split their party here to check each tunnel. I unlimbered the Lohvian longbow, gave the string a few testing pulls and then selected an arrow.

"What the blue blazes are you up to, cabbage?"

"A spot of target practice will actively discourage them, and might knock enough off to make them change their minds about pursuit."

"We-ell—"

Over the splashing tinkling of the fountain the sound of hurrying footfalls brought the bow up. The first fellow through the opening halted and then started to edge carefully around. I let him go and the next and the next. Four of them were walking delicately around and others appeared.

"What are you waiting for, onker? Shoot!"

"All in good time. Erthanfydd, as Seg would say, demands perfection in target selection as well as speed and accuracy."

"Oh, you!"

The bow drew smoothly and I let fly. The shaft hit the black robe at the mouth of the tunnel. Both he and the man immediately pushing on to his rear fell, the shaft skewering both. The little knot just ahead and to the side along the ledge did not panic until two of their number pitched into the water. They attempted to crowd back, knocking another one in and yelling blue murder to one another. I shafted the rest of that bunch and turned my attention to the four originals on the ledge.

After our experiences at the hands of these people it was hard to feel sympathy for them. The rearmost one simply turned around and made a wild dash for the safety of the tunnel. He tripped on the bodies of his companions and went screeching into the water. The next one was spitted through. The penultimate black robe glared about, his head turning, and I could see the mad red glitter of his eyes. He took a shaft through his middle so that left the one who'd first emerged into the cavern of the fountain.

Give him his due. He had courage. He was nearer to us than to his compatriots. He lifted his sword and charged. Well, sympathy has its place; I fancied that here and now any loose sympathy lying about ought by rights to belong to Mevancy and me. He went over screaming.

"H'm," sniffed Mevancy. "Very pretty." She nodded across the pool. "They do not seem keen to follow us."

"I wonder," I said, putting the bow back. "Would they have gone round that ledge so readily if they'd seen me? The fountain hid me pretty well until I shot."

"Heroes or cowards, it doesn't matter much now. Come on, cabbage."

They could have been heroes or cowards, I said to myself; they were certainly a most unlovely lot.

We went along the second tunnel and as we walked, looking everywhere about most carefully, we told each other what had befallen us in our latest dealings with the Star Lords. Strom Irvil of Pine Mountain's problems had been straightened out and Mevancy returned. I gave her a greatly bowdlerized version of my escapades. Both of us felt the Everoinye could clearly foresee some vast and confused confrontation. "It's this devil of a Carazaar. By Spurl!" exclaimed Mevancy. "He's in need of a few bindles."

She had indeed shot off a lot of the little darts from her forearms and she'd need to eat up well to replace them as quickly as possible. That made me think about food and a wet—and, of course, that was a disastrous thought to occur.

Around us in the sourceless light the rock walls glittered with nitre and a stream tinkled along under trees and bushes. A couple of syatras, bloated, tendril-waving, waited at the exit to the cave. Among the ordinary vegetation I could see none I recognized as edible.

I said: "I wonder what those dratted syatras taste like?"

"Probably like the soles of a calsany herder's sandals."

"Aye," I agreed moodily. "Probably."

"You're not hungry, are you? I had a splendid meal just before I returned."

That's it! I said to myself. That's bloody it! Those puffed-up Star Lords couldn't even fix me some grub! And they expect me to run about at their beck and call. Well, by the puss infected nostrils and swollen liver of Makki Grodno! Next time I saw 'em I'd—I'd—Well, then, what would I do? Sure, I was getting back to my raucous old self; the Everoinye remained the aloof powers they had always been.

A little gasp puffed from Mevancy's lips and she stopped stock-still. I'd been walking a little to the side and rear and now, wrapped up in my complaints anent the Everoinye, I collided with her shoulder. About to blurt out something about standing in people's way, I stopped as Mevancy said: "By Spurl! I don't believe it!"

A swift glance at the exit from the cave convinced me that if Mevancy didn't believe, I did.

The vague form of a person stood by the exit and the syatras were going mad. They kept sweeping their tendrils to wrap the person up and transfer the body into the internal organs for leisurely digestion. They kept on doing that. And, each time, the tentacle simply went flailing on through the figure.

The figure wavered about so much and flickered blue and grey by turn it was impossible to recognize the face. I fancied this was Rollo. By this time I felt that Mevancy knew Rollo was a Wizard of Loh—well, all right, an apprentice sorcerer—all the same I did not call out.

For a brief instant the phantom shape coalesced into the body of a well set-up young man wearing a yellow veil across his face and nondescript clothes of some hue between fire-ash grey and bruise blue. There followed the briefest of sounds, something like a chicken's headless squawk, and the figure wisped away.

The syatras were inconsolable.

"What—?"

"Those damn plants look edible to me, pigeon." I was being horrible to her, I suppose, in our comradeship, yet I feel strongly you will understand. Whipping out the old sailor knife I started across.

"Oh, you!" she yelled. Then: "Come back, you fambly!"

Stopping and half-turning I called: "All right. Won't be long now before someone comes for us."

She nodded, abruptly firm and purposeful. "Yes, exactly what I thought. There are very few people who are entirely at their ease around sorcery. And next time you want to play games, cabbage, I'll play harder."

Only moments later, there stood dear old Deb-Lu-Quienyin, leaning on his polished staff, beaming at us. His turban rested on his head exactly level; a spirit level couldn't have lined it up straighter.

"Lahal and Lahal!" he called, walking up. The syatras at his back flailed a couple of tendrils in his general direction. Then they gave up and flopped back in frustrated disgust.

"Lahal, san." Mevancy held herself very upright. "We are most pleased to see you."

"Yes, yes, my dear, as I you. Now, this is the way out."

He gave us directions that would last for a couple of burs or so and promised to return then. We followed his instructions and just at the moment we were faced with three possible routes, Deb-Lu appeared and told us the correct one. The strongest feeling was born in on me that nothing else was being said and no news exchanged because they must wait until we reached the surface.

At his next appearance Deb-Lu gave us directions which he explained would last us a considerable time. So long as we went in the same general direction and continually upwards, we'd be well on the way. In addition, he steered us into a cave where fruits grew and tubers and many of the little animals darted about. So we were able to lunch along the way.

Feeling replete, we went bravely on, ever upwards. Nothing untoward occurred. Time went by. The Realm of the Drums where we'd been lay a damned long way underground, by Vox. Eventually, we entered a cave where idols of a malignant and ferocious appearance clustered around the walls. An altar block bearing familiar and horrible stains stood at the center. Over on the far side Deb-Lu appeared before an idol whose mouth leered with uneven teeth. The thing held a statue of a naked girl in his clawed hands.

Mevancy said nothing; but she drew in her stomach tautly.

Deb-Lu pointed to the girl's dangling foot. He had no need to tell us what to do. I went across, aware of Mevancy's feelings, and pulled that pitiful foot.

The statue revolved. A dim wash of amber and verdigris light spilled into the cave mingling with the omnipresent pearly radiance.

We went through and the statue revolved and closed at our backs.

A grotto surrounded us with walls packed with the most amazing clustering of small statues of an incredibly varied number of life forms. Many dead leaves lay blown across the floor. At the far end a low overhang draped with dependent foliage admitted a weak light—but that light was ruby and jade, the streaming mingled radiance of Zim and Genodras, the twin Suns of Scorpio.

Mevancy started to run across and on the instant I followed.

I need not have fretted. She was by now an old campaigner. At the mouth of the overhang she paused and stood stock-still, looking out.

Joining her I peered between the hanging vines. Jungle. Well, by Krun, and what else apart from the City of Eternal Twilight did I expect to see?

Fourteen

Delia said: "I am glad to see you are still in one piece, husband."

And I said, and I opened my mouth—and I could say nothing. I took her into my arms and felt the powerful grip of her arms about me, a quick passionate convulsion of energy, crushing me to her and then releasing. Oh, yes, Delia is a most fiery lady!

After a space there in the aft cabin of *Vendayha Lady* she let me go and, lightly, said: "And I suppose you will tell me some of it?"

We flew on through thin air and I told her some of it. Mevancy was being looked after and a flushed young subby—a sort of leutnant zurluft— was turned out of his cabin to make room for her. She'd given Delia such a look as the voller picked us up as would have curled me up inside if I hadn't known the exact score. I may say 'Poor Mevancy!' from time to time; for all her problems and her despairing hopes, her friendship with Delia dispelled any lingering jealousies—after all, it seems to me perfectly obvious that every woman on Kregen—and on Earth if they knew—would be jealous of Delia. It is to Delia's personality and charm and her supreme tact that she sails serenely above petty jealousies. When the big ones come, as in her dealings with Nyleen Gillois, why, then, my Delia is a lady leem!

So, as I say, we sailed on and brought ourselves up to date. I wanted to know the reactions of Queen Satra to reality.

"Her lips tightened up. She made a little sign with her fingers." Delia made the sign in the air as we sat at ease. "Of course when we emerged into the city all the people came awake—what a sight!"

"I'd like to have seen it."

"Licria fainted clean away. That unpleasant trylon Schian fellow went quite green about the gills. Seg laughed."

Delia had waited for me in the admiral's aft cabin. Captain Erlik had welcomed me aboard after Deb-Lu had guided the suspended basket to where Mevancy and I stood by the grotto. Now she held onto my arm as we talked.

"Seg would. So, by Vox, would I!"

"He also expressed his opinion that he regretted he'd not put a comfortable wager on it. That made Inch laugh."

"Those two! They're with the Tambu Force so we'll soon have news of Fish Faces running."

As I'd stepped aboard observing the fantamyrrh, Captain Erlik had addressed me as strom, for I was the Strom of Valka. Oh, yes, I might be the kov of this and the king of somewhere else and have been the Emperor of Vallia, but to the people of Valka I was their strom and that was the beginning and end of it. To further the campaigns ahead the Valkans had made a huge collection to pay for this splendid new vessel, *Vendayha Lady*. She'd been built in the spanking new yards at Vondium. The silver boxes had come from Balintol. She'd been destined for Drak's forces operating in Pandahem. When news of the plight of their strom in the jungles of Chem reached Valka, they'd simply dispatched *Vendayha Lady* south to assist.

I said: "We can't have that, my love! Drak needs all he can lay his hands on. Much though I love the folk of Valka, they are part of Vallia, and their duty is to the emperor. If *Vendayha Lady* was assigned to Pandahem—"

"Hush, hush! Drak sent word to retain her. He was as worried as anyone over your—um—whereabouts."

I gave her a damned sharp glance. She was paler than usual. I said: "Tell me."

"It's so silly—well, it's not, really—"

I took her hand off my arm and put my arm about her, arranging ourselves comfortably on the settee, her head on my shoulder. "Spit it out."

"We're both young still, aren't we? But—but I find it more and more difficult to—to accept—our rackety way of living."

"The Star Lords command me and the Sisters of the Rose you."

She remained silent for a moment and no doubt was using some choice phraseology regarding the Everoinye. Then: "Yes. I am a Red Sister. I might have been the chief of the SoR had I so wished."

I couldn't help myself from blurting out: "So you didn't succumb!"

She did not know that I knew what I did about the SoR through the Star Lords. One day I would tell her, for we'd had enough secrets between us. "Well, husband, I shall renounce active duty with the SoR."

"I joy over that. I can't chuck off the damned Everoinye."

"And I cannot much longer endure our separations." She moved restlessly. "By Mother Jinju the Possessed! I want a proper life with a husband at my side."

You may well imagine that I felt like a samphron crushed between rollers so that the rich oil might run out. Personally, I could do nothing to halt what the Star Lords commanded; personally, I would do anything—anything at all!—for my Delia. The impasse was complete.

The need to clear my throat before I could speak did not surprise me. "Once we have stopped Carazaar, solved the Skantiklar mystery, and defeated the Shanks, I think the Star Lords might well give me a rest."

"Until the next time?"

"I was thinking of a more permanent rest."

She twisted around at this, her hair a tumbled glory, and glared at me, her brown eyes bright with moisture, those gorgeous red lips trembling. "That sounds dreadful, Dray!"

"Oh, I didn't mean that! Come on, let's go on deck."

"Very well, after—" And she kissed me very thoroughly.

So it was some time later that we went up on deck.

We were flying north and still over jungle. "I thought we'd be flying westerly, chasing over to Tambu—"

"All in good time, all in good time. We've been staying with Queen Satra. The whole situation is fascinating. Deb-Lu advised, so I did."

I grunted. "H'm, well you can't really argue with Deb-Lu."

Then I said: "Hold on a mur. What about the people of the City of Eternal Twilight when they woke up from the enchantment? What about the wedding and that bungling oaf casting the spell—?"

Delia smiled. "They acted like the other people we woke up. The sorcerer saw his spell had failed and then he was recognized and jumped on." She was holding onto my arm with the grip of a zhantilla's jaws. "They were most surprised and dismayed to see one of their towers with its top blown off."

"Deb-Lu certainly did a fine job there."

"Na-Si-Fantong had left an apprentice there, somebody like Rollo. Fantong charged him up with extra kharrna; but, of course, he failed."

"Made you do a spot of aerobatics, though."

"Quite exhilarating, if you must know!"

So she was getting back to her usual splendid form, thank Zair. She went on to tell me how Queen Satra and some of her retinue, flown home to

Hiclantung courtesy of the Vallian Air Service, had been received. The bulk of her forces were marching. One fine day they'd arrive in Hiclantung.

"They do seem a miserable decayed lot, these Walfargians. I don't think more than half a dozen folk raised a cheer when Satra made herself known."

Very often the habit of Queens of Pain of Walfarg when ascending the throne of the Empire of Loh was to lavish vast sums and immense labor on building a new capital. The old capital might decline a trifle but would remain a powerful city. This habit was known on Earth, obvious examples in the Middle East coming to mind. As a result, when the empire washed away, great cities remained standing in various parts of Walfarg. That helped to explain the fragmentation of Walfarg after the catastrophe. Satra had simply resumed her occupation and command of her capital.

"And the incumbent king—what's his name—King Hwangin, wasn't it?"

"I notice you say 'wasn't' rather than 'isn't.'"

"Oh, aye, my love. We're getting the feel of our Satra."

"Quite. Mind you, every overlord of a great city or goodly lands calls himself a king these days, as the overladies call themselves queens." She made a little moue with those gorgeous lips. "He vanished. It was given out he welcomed Satra and had abdicated."

"Inside a sack in the river, I expect." I shook myself. "Well, I don't want to know much about that."

"His guard and soldiers—such as they are, the broken-down creatures—cheered for Satra. Gold was spent."

"So now she'll start up a great war of re-conquest to regain her lands in Walfarg. I don't know. I admit to being uneasy about that."

"Judging by the apathy of these Lohvians she'll have to hire paktuns."

"So she will. I don't care to dwell on what would happen if the Shanks put in a really serious attack."

As we talked so we walked arm in arm up and down the area of the poop immediately forward of the aft fighting tower. This was Admiral's Country and we were not disturbed. Without consciously realizing the fact, I took stock of *Vendayha Lady*. A fine flier, with three decks, three fighting towers, and two fighting galleries below on each beam, she represented aerial might of a kind relatively new in Vallia, for she had been built at home. Hamal continued to experience difficulties in obtaining supplies of the ingredients for the silver boxes. Hyrklana, too, could not build ships fast enough. The supplies of silver boxes from our friends in Balintol, meager though they were, were absolutely vital. King Filbarrka na Filbarrka and Queen Zenobya had worked wonders on behalf of Vallia out there in Balintol.

A smart young Air Cadet ran up the ladder and saluted with a snap.

"The captain's compliments, majestrix and majister. Would you care to join him for dinner?"

I cocked an eyebrow at Delia and she smiled and said: "That would be nice." Her smile appeared to transfix the cadet with rapture.

I said: "Your name, cadet?"

He jumped and swallowed and stuttered out: "Jankwa, majister, Larghos Jankwa ti Fakwald."

"From Hawkwa Country, I see."

"Aye, majister. I have heard all the tales of Jak the Drang."

A small rictus at the side of my mouth might have passed as a smile.

"Those were the days. Well, Larghos, there are days like those ahead."

"Aye, aye, majister!"

He ran off, sliding down the ladder rails. One day, and Opaz alone knew, he might become the Lord High Admiral of the Vallian Air Service, perhaps taking over from Vangar ti Valkanium as he was about to take over from the Lord Farris.

We dressed elegantly and soberly and as the Suns of Scorpio declined in washes of ruby and jade went down to dinner. The rest of the quick flight to Hiclantung passed uneventfully, pleasantly, in good company and much talk. "Hiclantung," I said to myself. "Well, Queen Lilah's city was well-named."

The reception committee sent by Queen Satra not only met us just outside Wayfarer's Drinnik, they accompanied us into the city, showed us around, insisted on taking care of our every want and, in short, they treated us like royalty. We were housed in a palace. You'd take all week to count the slaves and servants. Anything you wanted was at your elbow almost as soon as you'd asked. The servants moved about sharply. The guards looked alert.

"She's quite a lady, this Queen of Pain," I said.

"She's put a fire under their tails, all right. When I flew off to get you and Mevancy out of the jungle in a basket—" At this I made a face at her and she went imperturbably on. "The people were losing their listlessness but in this short time I can see a new difference."

We were standing on a high balcony overlooking the city with the suns slanting their emerald and ruby fires across that strange Walfargian architecture. The heavy shadowy arcades supporting their piled masses of buildings, the domes coated in green copper, the twisted spires, the sense of suffocation and yet of ease of movement throughout the city always struck me as strange. Covering the surrounding land the walled villas extended a long way, bowered in trees. This city of Hiclantung had been the greatest; it was still rich and Satra quite evidently intended to recover all she had lost.

"Yes," Delia nodded. "She'll grab it all back. But there's more to what she's doing than that."

"Reaction to the truth? Action to counter the shock?"

Delia tilted her head and gave me a slanting smile. She wore a loose-fitting lavender dress and the light caught radiantly in her hair—ah, well, I cannot repeat often enough, there is no one in two worlds to compare to Delia of Delphond, Delia of the Blue Mountains. "Trylon Ge-fu-Schian—"

"Djan rot his socks!" I put in.

"Quite, my love. He went off to his trylonate and came back with a bloody nose."

"Haw!"

"Now he's fawning around Satra wanting money to raise an army."

"She might. If he remains loyal to her."

"We've not seen much of Licria."

"Mevancy said you'd concocted a plan—"

"That's all down to your little pigeon. It'll be her show."

"H'm," I said, half frowning. "She's capable enough and she's as courageous as a zhantilla. You can't tell me—?"

"Nope." Her smile sent a breeze from my heels to my scalp. "She specifically made us promise not to tell you until she was ready."

"Yeh," I said. "She's another right little madam!"

"Talking of your various lady friends—" As she spoke I arched my eyebrows. She just went on with that mischievous smile curving her lips. "Fan-Si. I asked her if she and her group would like to join my Jikai Vuvushis but she said she wanted to go off to Tambu with her friends."

"Moglin the Flatch and Larghos the Throstle."

"Yes. Seg and Inch were pleased to take them."

"Oh, sure!" I grumped. "That's where I should be—"

"They will cope splendidly, as you very well know, my love. The pot is boiling nicely here. Anyway, Trylon Kuong and Llodi the Voice went with their people." She gave me a quizzical look. "They're still a trifle—ah—uneasy—about..."

"Yeh, I know." I heard the annoyance in my voice. "When I met up with you and our comrades I ignored those new friends in a most stupid and obnoxious way. Mind you, Llodi's all right."

"He and Larghos the Throstle gave us a beautiful concert."

"I'll bet."

A familiar step at our backs brought us around to see Deb-Lu-Quienyin walk into the suns shine of the balcony. A moment later Rollo joined him. Both their faces were grave.

"Deb-Lu." Delia put her hand on my arm. "Is the news so bad?"

The Wizard of Loh nodded and his turban fell clean off revealing his brilliant red Lohvian hair. He spoke harshly.

"We suspected Carazaar could summon a vast amount of kharrna to expend on a project. We are now confident he is able to do this and increase his powers enormously. Then he must rest and recuperate."

"Makes himself better than he is for a single shot," I said. "Go on."

"He smashed our defenses in Vondium. The ruby of the Skantiklar in the imperial regalia of Vallia is gone."

Fifteen

Queen Satra was raising an army. She was far too busy to entertain us; but she sent a polite note in explanation with a promise of a banquet in a sennight's time. We sent back a proper reply thanking her for her hospitality. With both Milsi and Sasha away in Tambu, it was my opinion, and one I was convinced was correct, that Satra didn't care to be overshadowed by Delia. That, of course, was perfectly understandable in a powerful Queen of Pain, especially one who intended once more to be the Empress of Loh. But, then, the trouble is, as you know, no one can compare with Delia. If that brings jealousy and hatred to the bosoms of many a fine lady, then selah! Delia can handle that!

And, by Zair, in the nicest and kindest way possible on two worlds.

So, because Deb-Lu continued to insist we remained in Hiclantung, we had some time to ourselves, and time to explore the city.

Along with Deb-Lu and Rollo, Mevancy had her own quarters in the palace given over to our use. I said to Delia one fine morning: "What the deuce is Mevancy up to? We hardly ever see her."

"Plans."

"Oh."

"Plans," she repeated, with that firmness of tone that could stop a vove cavalry charge at fifty paces.

"Does Deb-Lu know?"

"No."

Well, now, I said to myself. The little minx may be involving the Star Lords in this pretty plot of hers.

As the barracks and outlying camps filled up with mercenaries, the vast majority not from Walfarg, we had to face the unpleasant consequences of Carazaar's seizure of the ruby from Vondium. Deb-Lu explained that the attack had been almost entirely magical, only a small force of Paktuns being used once the defenses had been breached. That was a similar system to the one he'd used in the Castle of Samral down in Kronenvar.

"Once he has regained his full power, he will become a dangerous enemy again." Deb-Lu was clearly greatly concerned. He hadn't liked the cauls of protection he and his comrades had erected being penetrated.

"And you say he can, as it were, pump himself up with extra kharrna to go out and do something similar?"

"Yes, Delia, that he can and will."

"Makilorn," I said.

"Naturally." She lifted her glass, for we were at a small supper. Rollo was off doing his exercises like a painstaking apprentice should. "Is there nothing we can do, Deb-Lu?"

"Khe-Hi, Ling-Li and I are collaborating even more closely. We are sure we can defend the ruby in Makilorn—or wherever we may hide it—but that will take time."

"So it's a race." I spoke glumly.

Delia flashed me a brilliant glance. "Deb-Lu will win!"

On that note of whistling in the dark we retired for the night.

The next morning Nath Karidge, commander of the Empress's Devoted Life Guard, reported in that they'd caught an assassin trying to climb in through a window of the palace. Although my Guard Corps had gone off to Tambu to fight Shanks, as under the circumstances was perfectly proper, EDLG had refused to desert their prime duty.

"Unfortunately he insisted on striking Jurukker Erlon the Biceps' rapier with his stomach."

"That Erlon!" said Delia, shaking her head. "Still, I'm sure it couldn't be helped."

"Erlon specially asked me to say he regretted the incident."

"I'm sick and tired of that Schian!" I burst out. I felt hot and cold. If a damned assassin got in and Delia— "He's got to be sorted out."

Delia flashed Nath Karidge a swift glance. I felt my blood turn to ice. I stared at them both. When I spoke, my old gravel-shifting voice had never sounded uglier.

"So this isn't the first time? The cramph has tried before—when I wasn't here?"

"Now, Dray—"

I glared at Nath who drew himself up, your splendid beau sabreur to the life. I said: "Your duty was to tell me, Nath."

"No, my heart. I asked Nath not to."

"I see." Nath Karidge's life, as of his regiment, revolved about the empress. He just stood there, handsome, trim, and I could not fault him.

"Very well." About to go on with some dangerous bombast about my going to settle this with Schian once and for all, I closed my black-fanged winespout.

"You should know, jis," Nath said in a firm voice. "There have been three attempts on the queen's life. All failed, and the assassins were killed before they could be questioned."

"They might all be sent by Licria, or only some," said Delia.

"Whatever," I said, "that little madam must be getting very frustrated. The queen's got her measure well enough."

"I'm not sure." Delia made a graceful gesture for Nath to help himself to the parclear on the breakfast table. That reduced the temperature of our conversation. "Licria is cunning. The queen simply does not believe she has the gall to make an attempt on her life. You can see her point of view."

"Is that what Milsi thinks?"

"Yes."

A paline twisting in my fingers burst and the sweet juices ran down my palm. I licked them off. "Licria and Schian! What an unholy pair!"

"The regiment is on full alert." Nath drank his parclear.

He needn't have said that, for he'd know I assumed that after attempts on the life of the empress EDLG would be very much on the qui vive. Oh, no, Nath Karidge had been shaken by the ugliness of my reactions.

I turned to Delia. "You have your rapier and main gauche and daggers, of course. Your Claw?"

"Yes, my love." Her voice was particularly mild.

"Good. Then keep it by."

Her Claw, a most vicious and unpleasant instrument of destruction, would be kept in its jikvarpam instead of the balass box. That I knew.

Nath Karidge said: "With your permission, maj, I'll cut along now. Things to do."

"Of course, Nath."

He slapped up a salute of such smartness it nearly took his head off, and stalked out. I guessed he'd be chasing tails all morning. The use of the diminutive of majestrix as maj instead of jes was rather pleasing. I found I preferred it to jes, although I'd remain jis to our comrades.

Shortly after that a message arrived to say the queen wished to see us urgently at the palace.

We had planned on watching the quarter finals of the regimental hikc-hunkazzarn competition. Delia and I looked across at each other as Nath Karidge gave orders for the escort and messenger to leave. I believe we all shared the same thought.

Nath said: "I came back with the messenger, maj, studying her. As far as she is concerned, the message is genuine."

"Well," I said, flatly, not moving. "I think it's madam at work."

The others nodded, and Delia said: "We'll go, though."

"Maj!" Nath was not so much flustered as apprehensive. He'd go marching off into the jaws of a Herrelldrin Hell to save the empress; he didn't relish one single little bit the idea of her following him.

He now had two sets of twins, bonny lads and lasses, and a beautiful wife and a comfortable marriage. Delia and I, for our parts, would not readily forgive ourselves if Nath Karidge was killed.

Nath tightened up his lips and then burst out: "Very well! I'll roust out a guard detail right away."

Delia called: "Nissa!"

Instantly a slip of a girl stood at her side. I hadn't seen from whence she'd sprung. "Maj?"

"The bag with the red roses, my dear."

Nissa was off at once. She had pale blonde hair, closely cut, and a sweet round face that would in a few seasons blossom into a maturity of beauty to do more than one poor fellow's business for him. She wore a trim outfit of russet, and a necklace of flowers looked cool and fragrant at her throat. Also, she wore a long Vallian dagger on her thigh. Almost at once she was back bringing the sack with the red roses embroidered upon it.

"Here, Nissa, let me help," said Nath.

I saw they'd done this before. The Claw was brought forth and strapped up over Delia's left hand and forearm. It glittered with menace. Those razor sharp talons could take a villain's face clean off.

Delia made a little helpless moue at me. She was not altogether enamored of the Claw of the Sisters of the Rose, preferring the rapier and dagger; but she well knew its effectiveness to those trained in its use from childhood.

With Delia's left hand hidden in the folds of her cape, with Nath leading and the guard detail around us, we set off through the strange avenues of Hiclantung. People gave us the occasional glance; mostly they remained indifferent. Much though they had changed from the listless lot they'd been, Queen Satra still had much work to do to turn them into a nation that would fight for her—as she thought—or fight the Shanks—as we desired.

The mid morning rays of the suns lay streaming their mingled lights of jade and ruby across the city. Green copper domes shone refulgently. Dark shadows under the arcades looked as though all the Perils of Prandar the Pernicious lurked there. Up ahead a bridge of houses crossed the avenue.

Nath halted and our little party closed up.

The lights of the suns were completely extinguished under the bridge.

Quietly, without pointing, Nath said: "Under the bridge. I caught an odd flash of movement, quickly stilled."

"Nets," said Delia, firmly.

"Aye, maj, my thought exactly—" Then Nath Karidge had no time to finish the sentence. Black figures burst against us from each side. They'd been waiting in ambush for us to be trapped in the nets, and we'd spotted the trap and halted, so now they were going to finish us where we stood.

They did not holler or whoop but came in with feral silence.

Instantly a swirling fight developed. Nath was not to be baulked from his position protecting the empress, not even by her husband the emperor. Screams began to racket up and the harshness of spilled blood smoked into the air. Using the rapier and main gauche I put a big feathered Rapa down and flicked a quick look at Delia. Her Claw scintillated silver in a slanting slash and swung back gleaming redly. Nath thrust a fellow away from the side and then I had to skip a blow and thrust and whirl and when I could look again Delia was just withdrawing her rapier from a bulky Brokelsh. I charged over towards her. The noise of the fight had not attracted the attentions of any passersby. Quite the opposite. Ordinary citizens simply made themselves scarce when stikitches were earning their living.

Abruptly, just as I reached Delia by way of another Rapa, a Chentoi and a Fristle, there seemed to be hundreds of EDLG swarming everywhere. The assassins were so overwhelmingly outnumbered that very few were able to escape.

To my horror I saw young Nissa in there swinging an ironwood quarter staff, and cracking the last few assassins over their heads. Her round face was no longer sweet, it was suffused with fighting rage.

"Delia!" I yelled. "What kind of mortillas are you raising now?"

She saw Nissa, and frowned, and then immediately gave me a little smile.

"We are as Opaz fashions us." She shook red drops from her Claw. "Nissa is seconded to me as handmaiden from the SoR. She is a good girl; but I cannot say I relish this much frowardness."

Nath Karidge, splendid in the light of the suns, wheeled up.

"They've gone. We'd better clear off, too."

"Right," I said. Then: "And what about all these lads of yours?"

"Ah, well, jis. I considered it a reasonable idea to—ah—as it were—ask them to follow along. Just in case."

"H'm. I remember when you disobeyed orders at the Sign of the Headless Zorcaman."

He brightened up. "Fine, rollicking days!"

"Aye, Nath," I said, somewhat heavily. "Aye."

The jurukkers of EDLG took care of their own; the sprawled corpses in the black clothes of their calling were left to rot. I looked down on one with the blood greasy from his beak. A clean sword lay at his side, his hand lax. I needed that sword, for it was a lynxter, the usual weapon of Loh. Unbuckling the dead Rapa's belt I hauled it free and scabbarded the blade. Then, on an impulse, I ripped open the black cloth at his throat. Yes, the silver pakmort, a trifle tarnished, was indeed at his throat on its silver cords. This was one paktun who, wandering the Death Jungles of Sichaz, must rue his decision to give up the mercenary life for the assassin's.

The troops were jostling into formation and Delia and Nath were waiting as I took the pakmort and stuffed it and its silver silken cords into my pouch. Now I'd made the decision I felt as though a scouring wind had blown through my old vosk skull of a head, freshening up my brains.

We marched back in good order, and Nissa twirled her quarterstaff.

Later on that day I said to Delia: "I have to go out tonight."

She shook her head with a little helpless gesture that caught the breath in my throat. "Is there anything I can say that will—?"

"Probably, yes, there is. But we both know this nonsense has to be stopped."

"The queen—"

"Yes. This is just the first step in a logical progression that I am the first to admit may lead to disaster. But I will not stand for that cramph Schian any longer. Once I've warned him off, and I hope in the process given him the fright of his life, then maybe the queen can help."

Because she was Delia, she lifted her chin and said: "Then I shall go with you. Naturally."

It took a hell of a time to convince her I'd better go alone, a hell of a time. Her lower lip trembled with passion, her blood was up and her eyes transfixed me with a brilliancy that blinded. But I held doggedly on.

She found a grey slave breechclout, which I felt would attract less attention, even, than the mustardy brown ones. A simple leather tunic and boiled leather helmet, the Rapa's silver pakmort at my throat and his lynxter at my side, sundry other possessions a mercenary would carry, and I stood up, ready for the off.

"You look the part, my love."

I kissed her and so sealed any possible last minute pleas. Then I just ran off, feeling my heart thudding, ran off so that, just in case she called me back, I would not hear.

Sixteen

Motionless and barely breathing I waited in the shadows cast by a giant ceramic pot, growing flick-flick plants, for the double rank of guards to march past. Apart from them the corridor lay empty, for Deb-Lu, whose phantom image had guided me here, had vanished.

This corridor in Trylon Schian's luxurious villa was well enough lit, confound it. The guards were all from those who had been trapped down in the Realm of the Drums. They were smart enough to challenge a lone paktun. Once I'd got in and Deb-Lu had begun to guide me there'd been no place where I could shuck off the leather and appear as a slave. I waited for the guards to march past—and the double rank halted with a clash and just stood there.

There was absolutely no use my fuming with annoyance over this situation—but I did, anyway.

"By the hairy upper lip and pendulous belly of the Divine Lady of Belschutz!" I snarled to myself. "What in a Herrelldrin Hell are they hanging about here for?"

Although the double rank of guards faced me, they couldn't spot me in the pot's shadows if I remained still. They couldn't hear me, either. So, I just stood there quietly.

A fly buzzed along and alighted on my nose.

With the stoicism and courage of your true hero, I did not move.

The blasted thing plonked his nasty little legs up and down my hooter and I had to hold my muscles in bands of steel to prevent perfectly natural reactions. In a heartbeat or two I'd sneeze. I could feel the itch developing. A single sound, a movement, mysteriously coming from the shadows of the plant pot would bring the instant attention of the guards. Oh, I'd try to sweet talk them out of sticking me there and then, and if I failed I'd fight 'em all, of course—a light feather touch brushed my nose and was gone.

A flashing glimpse of the flick-flick plant flicking out a tendril, flicking up the fly, and flicking it into an orange cone-shaped flower—oh, yes, all praise to Opaz the Cultivator who sent down flick-flick plants to Kregen when the world was young!

A brisk voice yelled: "Brassud!" and the guards snapped to attention. The next moment, as though the flick-flick plant had commanded them, they right turned and marched off. Now they guarded a young woman and her attendants, so I knew I was close to where I wanted to be, although not yet there.

Deb-Lu appeared, without a trace of blue shimmer. He rubbed his nose and I—I confess—I laughed.

"Esser Rarioch is maintained in so clean a condition," he said, "you have to breed flies specially for the flick-flick plants. Is there not a contradiction in that situation, Dray?" We walked along the corridor towards a junction where the lighting, if anything, shone more brightly.

"Assuredly, Deb-Lu. But if man interferes with nature by keeping his house so clean flies can find no sustenance, then surely, as Opaz would wish, he must then care for those plants dependent on flies?"

"Only partially. They can live without—"

"But in what case!" We'd reached the junction and found no one there. For myself, I found nothing incongruous in carrying on a kind of philosophical discussion in these circumstances, and neither, I am sure, did Deb-Lu.

"Oh, I agree absolutely we must care for the creations of Opaz." He gestured with his staff. "It's down here."

"A flick-flick plant denied flies is like a skychunner denied purchales."

His amused chuckle coincided with our arrival outside a door of balass with ivory of Chem inlays. "Very important little fellow, this, Jak."

"Then I shall go in and pay him a visit." I pushed the door open.

"Oh, he's not in. Arranging an orgy for tonight."

The stink of stale perfume lingered on the air in this fussy apartment. The chamberlain fellow must be of some importance judging by the vulgar ostentation of furnishings and fittings. I padded across a carpet of Walfarg weave—which I judged to be of the third grade only—until Deb-Lu called: "There."

Straight ahead of me the wall was clothed by a tapestry depicting the ritual slaughter of San Sin-Sin-Yarelving. The thing was not an object I'd even think of tolerating in any of my homes. I pushed it aside and touched the button and the secret door slid aside.

"Thank you, Deb-Lu."

"I do not wish to use very much more kharrna at the present time. Satra's college of mages is not without some skills."

"Quite."

Deb-Lu winked out and I walked into the corridor beyond the secret door. As in most Kregan buildings of importance the secret ways had been provided by the architect with vision slits so that the passage, only a trifle dusty, lay barred in stripes of light. I debated whether or not to become as a slave, decided against it, and went on as a paktun. On one notable occasion I'd been betrayed by the chingle of a pakai, and although the dead Rapa assassin, who'd provided me with his lynxter, pakai and pakmort, did not have too long a string of victory rings, there were enough for me to take it off and stuff it into the pouch. Each of those silver rings had once fixed a pakmort to its silken cords. There were only two gold rings, triumphs of the Rapa over zhanpaktuns.

Each shaft of light falling across the narrow corridor allowed vision of a room or chamber, sometimes different views of the same space. We'd ascertained that Schian had an important interview towards the hour of dim and I intended to attend. Moving along quietly and cautiously and negotiating the many twists and turns and ladders and stairways, I came at last to an observation slit showing me Schian's study cum library. The place did have a few books and scrolls in it, at that. The main feature was a large couch with a table handy loaded with drinks.

Now I remembered the patience learned stalking my supper in the wild. My irritations and annoyances vanished. Composing myself, I settled down to wait.

If the Star Lords were watching me now I might expect a scorpion to waddle out of a crack in the wall. I refused to allow myself to worry over that eventuality. No doubt they'd thunder in their hoarse clanging voice that I was being impertinently impudent, or impudently impertinent in thus risking my life on a mission that did not affect their plans. Ah! I'd say in reply; if I'm assassinated, then your plans for me and my confounded yrium go up in smoke.

No little reddish brown scorpion waddled arrogantly out to confront me.

The hour of dim approached, voices sounded and the door of the study was thrown open. Four guards—fine tough Chentois—stalked in, their sallow faces and sharp eyes peering for assassins lying in wait for their lord.

When they were satisfied, Trylon Ge-fu-Schian walked in. He wore his clashing colored lounging robe, a dagger, and he was munching on a handful of palines. With him tripped Princess Licria, looking radiant in a revealing gown of silver mesh. Both of them had eaten and drunk well, that was evident.

They flopped on the couch facing me and the guards took station around the walls. Now you know my feelings about and views on hired guards. They take their pay and they do their job. I do not willingly harm them, for I have stood my turn of watches in the dark hours. There was a good chance I could burst in and deal with the guards before turning on Schian and Licria. But that would inevitably take a little too long, and the alarm would be raised. Patience, again, was my tactic here.

"If he's as good as is claimed," Licria was saying, "something might be accomplished at last."

"Aye, Hlo-Hli take it, at last." Schian sounded sullen.

"He will be busy."

"I still want that devil Dray Prescot and his precious Delia first on the list—"

"I think not, Ge-fu." She spoke sharply. "The queen first, then some of her most trusted advisers—we know who they are well enough—and then all who oppose us will be bereft of the queen's protection."

He shifted on the couch and reached a flagon from the table. "Well, I suppose so." Suddenly he brightened up. "When the queen is gone, you are right, princess. Why, we can arrest Prescot and I shall have the pleasure of cutting him down. His Delia can be thrown to the Rapa guards."

"Yes. I shall watch that." Her tongue licked her lips.

"Of course, there are her guards."

"A handful only. The army will crush that regiment instantly."

H'm, I said to myself, by Vox! Nath Karidge and the lads of EDLG will have something to say about that first!

They sipped wine and presently a Khibil stalked in, magnificently dressed, haughty, flushed, clearly elated.

This Khibil sported but one ear. Licria nudged Schian, and reluctantly the trylon stood up to acknowledge the presence of a vad.

Licria, as a princess, remained seated.

Immediately, before any lahals, she said: "You have him, Vad Valadian?"

"Aye, princess. He is willing to earn his hire. I have him outside—"

"Then bring him in at once!"

On this signal the doors opened again and a smart young fellow marched in. As was to be expected he wore a plain olive-colored cloak over his black clothes. His black mask covered his entire head and the eye-holes held shadows darker than the clothes themselves. He carried himself alertly. He wore no visible weapon.

"Master Fu-Ming-Fung," was all Vad Valadian said by way of introduction.

That name sounded idiotically ridiculous. This stikitche, then, required an alias. He bowed gracefully and stood, silent and waiting. So they discussed terms for the disposal of the queen and her chief ministers. The whole conversation was repugnant to any normal person.

The one-eared Khibil, I had ventured to believe, was not a villain. Now, it appeared, he was, and a thoroughgoing one, at that. No doubt this unholy pair had promised vast rewards for loyal service once they became empress and emperor of Loh. So he'd found a top-class assassin for them.

When the bokkertu had been concluded the vad and the stikitche left bowing and scraping. Licria sprayed perfume into the air and the place stank like a rest home for Sylvies. The glance she flashed Schian and her abrupt order to the guards to leave were unequivocal. Now was my time to burst in and tell them their fortunes.

Just at that critical moment a soft shushing footfall sounded along the secret passage. Instantly, quicker than thought, I was flat against the wall in deep shadow away from the light through the spyhole.

There were three of them, creeping cautiously along. As they passed bands of light I saw they wore dark clothes and weapons glittered. So the devils had followed me in here! They were an inconvenience. We were bound to make a noise. Still—the lynxter loosened soundlessly in the scabbard.

The three black-robed men halted before the spyhole. One peered through. At once I saw the truth of the situation, and my unwanted part in it. By the pustular armpits and infected nose of Makki-Grodno! What a mess!

Even as they burst into the room beyond the spyhole so I charged.

It was all a confusion of action and swirling capes and glittering steel, of Licria screaming and Schian swearing and trying to draw his sword and of the stikitches abruptly aware of the peril at their backs trying to switch targets. Schian did for one and I stretched the other two out. The guards smashed into the room, breaking the little bolts.

"It's all over!" I shouted, and I used all the authority I could muster. The guards halted, uncertain, and I stared at Licria who was climbing to her feet from the cover of the sofa. "Tell them, princess. Your life is safe, and so is the life of the trylon." If she read a double-meaning into the words that was my intention.

Her face, always pale, resembled the ashes of a fire dead before dawn.

She trembled. "The shints," she mumbled, and she bit her lips, and stared at the corpses. She gestured. "Drag them away!"

Schian lifted the bloody tip of his sword towards me.

"Where—how did you get here?"

"As to that, I will tell you—and the princess. Now, do as you are bid!"

He jumped and fairly snarled at the guards. Now was another moment of crisis, this time a personal peril. If he said: "Kill him!" what would then eventuate?

He did not. Licria took a huge draught of wine, and choked, and more collapsed on the sofa than sat down. Schian looked uncertain.

I said: "You have had a lucky escape. Had I not come to talk to—"

Schian snorted his contempt. "Talk, you shint! You came to kill us."

"Had I wanted you dead would I have stopped the stikitches—onker!"

He flushed up. He was still more shaken than he realized. I went on in my old gravel-shifting voice: "I wanted to tell you to stop sending assassins against us. I have overlooked your impertinence, your treachery and your pathetic assassination attempts. But my patience is not unlimited." I nodded my head towards the door. "Those fellows were sent by someone who had no doubt suffered from your attentions in the past."

Licria looked up. She whispered. "The queen?"

Staring at her, I saw the way her cosmetics were flaking and running.

"Hardly. She has no need of that to discipline you."

That made her angry, her blood thumping in reaction to the scare. She flung her head up and opened her mouth and I cut in: "Your life has been saved by me before this. Or have you forgotten?"

She was looking up at me. She stood up, swaying only a little. In a small voice, a wondering voice, she said: "No, I have not forgotten. And if what you say is true, you have saved my life again." She was staring at me. "I had not realized just what—what kind of man you are."

Schian started to say something and she snapped out: "Do be quiet, Ge-fu!" With the dark stains of kohl ruining her face—a fact of which she must have been unaware—she looked at me. Now I have seen that kind of look on women's faces before. And, always, by Krun, it means trouble.

I said: "I have told you why I came to see you. Leave us alone. Now—remberee." I started for the secret passage.

"Wait—" she called.

Schian snarled out: "I'll have that bricked up, by Hlo-Hli!"

"It's no use, princess." I spoke hard. "No use." I ducked my head and stepped into the passage and started off along briskly, very briskly, by Vox! If Schian sent guards after me, well that would be in his nature. Also, he had completely missed the byplay. There was no doubt at all that if ever their plans came to fruition he'd wind up in a sack weighted with chains in the river.

If this new assassin was as good as Vad Valadian claimed then Queen Satra was in trouble. Whatever she might believe about her ability to protect herself and however much she might shrug off Licria as a real threat, she'd have to be warned. The assassin looked competent. That smart, well set-up young fellow exuded menace. It hung like an aura of bright darkness about him.

In the event I cleared off out of the villa without trouble.

What Delia said when I walked in I will not repeat. After she let me go I told her what had happened. When I'd finished, she said: "They might take heed. Oh, and Mevancy is here with a friend."

"Oh?"

"Yes. From Vallia. Caspar Del Vanian. A famous artist. He's come to paint Queen Satra's portrait."

Seventeen

Mevancy reclined in a graceful posture on a chaise longue with the radiance of the Suns of Scorpio reflecting in from the high north window. She had a filmy scarf cunningly draped about her back with the ends beautifully folded about both her forearms. Her bindles were thus concealed. Apart from the scarf she wore no other clothes.

Her usual high color burned into a brilliant rosy flush as I barged into the room. "Cabbage! Get out!"

The lively young fellow in the painter's smock had his back to me, working at his easel. He turned his head, saw me, and dropped his charcoal.

"Majister!" he said, his pleasing face with the brown hair and eyes frank and not over-awed. "You completely fooled me."

"Are you going to go, cabbage, or are you going to gawp?"

"Now then, pigeon. This isn't the first time I've seen—"

"No! Well, you needn't assume—"

"I'll see you both at the second breakfast."

I took myself off, and if I say I was chortling away inside, I am sure you will understand and forgive.

At the second breakfast Delia said: "Will you tell us all the news of Vallia, Caspar? We've been a little out of touch lately."

"I'm afraid, majestrix, I too, have been out of touch. I've been—"

About to burst out: "Knocking off more targets, I suppose?" I did not. I clamped my black-fanged winespout around a handful of palines.

Caspar gave me a quick glance and went on: "Painting in the aracloins."

Well, that was what he wanted to do, instead of painting portraits of the empty-headed lords and ladies of Kregen. I gave him a mean stare.

I said: "How'd you come to meet Vad Valadian?"

He jumped. Calmly, he said: "Mevancy arranged it."

Swiveling to look at her I lifted an eyebrow.

Mevancy looked hard at me and then glanced at Delia.

"Pigeon!" I snapped, and I own I heard the sharpness in my voice. "The Empress Delia knows about the Everoinye. There are no secrets now."

"Yes," she nodded her head. "Yes, this was arranged with the knowledge of the Everoinye."

"Well, what the blue blazes do they think they're playing at? Surely they know that she-leem Licria will be far worse than Satra?"

There ensued a little pause, and then Caspar said: "Mevancy—when did you tell Drajak—I mean the emperor—?"

"I didn't."

"You can knock off the majister bit, Caspar. Drajak will do."

"But how—?" they both demanded. Delia laughed.

When she'd finished telling them, Mevancy blew out her rosy cheeks. "I've read the stories about Dray Prescot and—well, now, by Spurl, I really believe every last one!"

"The queen didn't send the assassins last night."

"One of her ministers," Delia observed.

"Too scared to tell the queen the truth," said Mevancy.

"All the same," I said, shaking my head. "I don't think putting Satra out of the way is altogether a bad idea if someone worthy could be found to be empress." I looked at Mevancy. "But Licria—"

"Drajak." Caspar leaned forward. "The plan is to prove to the queen that Licria is plotting against her. Simple revenge ought to follow."

"Oh," I said, feeling faintly foolish.

Then, with a little laugh that probably sounded like the growl of a goaded zhantil, I added: "So that explains this mysterious Princess's Swordsman you women were so secretive about."

"Caspar the Peaker—in person!"

With a fresh bunch of palines balanced on my palm I said: "So how do you prove to the queen that what you say is true?"

"No problem—"

"No, no problem when you admit you're a stikitche in private with her! She'll have the guards in and your head off so fast your feet won't, as they say in Clishdrin, touch the ground."

"I'm sure Caspar will be convincing—"

"Maybe, pigeon. But he'll have to be convincing pretty damn quick!"

"This is not the first time this deception has been played." Caspar moved his empty fruit juice glass on the table, making patterns. "I must claim, with due modesty—and I am not a modest person—that I know how to conduct myself in these circumstances."

With that assurance I had to be content. Delia said that she was sure Caspar would handle the whole business admirably, and that gave me confidence.

Having to be as content as I could be with the situation over the succeeding days I turned to other affairs that pressed in. Many letters were written—a whole library of correspondence, by Vox!—and so I was able to keep my finger on the pulse of what went forward in Paz. The speed with which Queen Satra re-imposed her will on Walfarg impressed me as it awed everyone. Her activities meant she was too busy to sit for a portrait. No doubt she felt she had to accomplish much in little time—a feeling with which I was only too familiar. This meant that Caspar was not called to the palace and so the plan could not go ahead. Mevancy's portrait bloomed.

"Trylon Schian is becoming so impatient I think he'll burst a blood vessel." Caspar wiped his brushes as he spoke, head on one side regarding his easel. "As for the little Licria—she bides her time like a syatra."

"The queen will want the portrait soon." Delia spoke positively. "She knows her time is drawing to a close and she will use it as propaganda. Her army grows larger every day."

"Once she has all Walfarg," I said somberly, "if she marches across the frontiers, that will—"

"What will happen then is in the hands of Opaz."

"And the Everoinye."

The very next day Satra sent for Caspar.

Just after he'd gone off with servants to carry his artist's gear and a bunch of Delia's lads of EDLG as guards, Deb-Lu-Quienyin walked in on us as we were thinking about the mid-afternoon meal. He looked grave.

After greetings he said: "As you know we have set cauls of protection about the ruby of the Skantiklar in Makilorn."

"Not—?" exclaimed Delia, somewhat crossly.

"Not yet, thanks to the Ones of the Seven Arcades. Carazaar has been attempting to break the seals, and failing."

"Thank Opaz—and you—for that!"

"It is evident that he has not yet rebuilt sufficient kharrna. But we believe he soon will. What he is doing is to use force."

"Shanks?"

"Yes, Dray, unfortunately. Seg and Inch will be flying in soon from Tambu. They have fought the damned Fish Faces there and succeeded admirably in driving them off—so Carazaar is busy transferring them to attack Makilorn."

"This is a crisis, then." Delia slapped the hilt of her rapier. "Another one, confound all the Opaz-forsaken Fish Faces on Kregen!"

I said: "It looks as though we'll all have to go down to Tsungfaril and see about defending Makilorn." I snorted. "What a prospect, by Vox!"

"If we can prevent Carazaar's forces from taking the city and breaking into the palace where the ruby is hidden, his kharrna may be overcome." Deb-Lu pulled his ear. "I say may be. He will be most powerful, most powerful indeed."

"You mean the nearer he is to the damned red stone the greater he can work on your protection?"

"Exactly."

"Then we'll just have to stop him, blatter him good!"

Around then I would not have been in the least surprised if a scorpion the size of my hand had stalked in with his eight legs going up and down and his flaunting tail curving up, its black sting and purple sac of poison very nasty. As I've said, Kregish scorpions have these eyes on stalks, not usual, and when the scorpion of the Star Lords makes eye to eye contact, it is, I can testify, a most spine-erecting feeling. As for hunting by sound, there is on Kregen a swift little arachnoid of which it is said he can hear your muscles moving your bones about inside your body. This eenlan, all glistening brown, yellow and black, gives rise to the old-fashioned saying: "As noisy as an eenlan."

No scorpion appeared so the Star Lords were not going to interfere— at least, not just yet—although they hovered near, damn near, by Bunje Kazar the Effable!

Caspar arrived back well pleased with the first sitting, saying that, as usual, he was painting the queen's head and her clothes would be worn by a slave or a lay figure. He saw the graveness on our faces.

"It looks as though I won't be here for you to complete my picture, Caspar." Mevancy held down her annoyance very well.

"Oh?"

When we'd told him the news he screwed up that young fresh face, making his few remaining spots dance about. "You'll need armies, then."

Rollo, who'd joined us for the evening meal, interjected: "And mages."

"Quite," said Deb-Lu.

"One interesting thing I heard," said Caspar. "The queen told one of her ministers—that bloodthirsty vorsim, Pallan Quincing—that if any Hlo-Hli forsaken Shanks marched into her territories she'd string them up, make all of 'em dance on air."

"Only," I grunted sourly, "they won't march. They'll fly."

Delia said: "Satra has no real experience of Shanks."

All the same, what Caspar said cheered me a trifle, for obvious reasons.

Knowing that Deb-Lu was maintaining contact with our forces in Tambu, I asked him: "When do you expect Seg and Inch and the others back, Deb-Lu?"

"Oh, now they know where the Schtarkins are going they intend to follow as soon as they've regrouped their forces."

I cannot say I felt too pleased about that, by Vox. Regrouping of forces is usually a euphemism for a process following highly unpleasant occurrences.

Delia put her hand over mine. "Nothing frightful. We'd have heard."

"I suppose so."

So, as you can see, the situation was much like the curate's egg. We all cleared off for the night and sleep, for once, did not come easily. If only— if only! Well, if 'if onlys' were not ifs but facts, two worlds of which I know a little would not be the same places.

Here was a situation where I could do with having the Everoinye use their powers to put me in two places at once. Deb-Lu's insistence that we remain in Hiclantung was about to be proved correct in the fascinating plot cooked up by the women to defeat the charming Licria. I wouldn't want to miss that. At the same time I had to go down to Makilorn and blatter Fish Heads. If Carazaar laid his claws on the ruby there—well, by the dripping nostrils and blackened teeth of Makki-Grodno!—how many would he have then?

Although without the aid of the Star Lords I could not be in two places at once, other remarkable innovations were taking place in Loh that would have astonished almost as much. Queen Satra was actively creating a flying service. Her air service was to be modeled on that of Vallia. Delia told me how much Satra had been awed, impressed, and eventually angered by her flight aboard *Vendayha Lady*. Out of sheer politeness—and because Delia is the kindest person on two worlds—Delia had put *Vendayha Lady* onto a regular shuttle ferrying the balance of Satra's army and entourage to Hiclantung. Satra grasped the war potential in that, by Krun!

"So that means another customer for vollers in the market," I said.

"It's all progress, my heart!" I saw she was teasing me, although the matter was serious, and I understood she was right. We had to maintain a perspective on all our diverse problems. "We have a decision to make. Caspar and the little Licria's comeuppance, or Makilorn and Carazaar."

"No matter what Deb-Lu may say now, there is no choice, is there?"

"Of course not."

"I just hope Seg and Inch are all right. I don't like the sound of that regrouping."

"How many more times, you onker of a fambly! We'd have heard."

The only answer to that was to kiss her, which I did with great zeal and thoroughness. She kissed me back with a hungry passion that spoke eloquently of her fears for the future.

When Caspar returned that evening from his painting session with the queen he stood in the doorway of the room we used as a lounge and stared at us all in the lamplights. A stray shaft of radiance caught the corners of his eyes and for a moment his eyes glittered. We all sensed the significance of the moment. Only for that instant he stood, rigid and somehow taller than his height, then he stepped forward into the room and the spell was broken.

Rollo couldn't be contained. "Well, Caspar?"

"It is done."

Deb-Lu let out a breath; but he did not speak.

"You'd better tell us about it, then, Caspar." Delia was brisk.

He nodded, crossed to the table to pour the evening wine for himself and began speaking at once. "As planned. There was absolutely no peril in it for me." As to that, I wondered; there were no overtones in his voice to indicate he minimized his danger. "The proofs proved themselves, Schian's ring, Licria's order to the sentries. My part, of course, was as a humble painter enrolled as a part-time stikitche."

"What of Vad Valadian?" I spoke in my growly voice.

"A dupe, acting out of misguided friendship."

"And—?" said Delia, somewhat sharply for her. Of course, what Caspar the Peaker was saying was important and interesting, what Delia's 'and' meant was the vital issue.

"They have both been taken up. Schian will probably go in the river. Licria to an establishment of little sisters of a stern persuasion."

"So the queen is squeamish after all!"

"Licria is," pointed out Delia, "the last of her line."

Who could say how much Satra had already known? High office and almost unlimited power, as I have before said, addle people's minds. Her very pride in her bloodline would keep her fanatically determined to ensure that one of her descendants ascended the throne after her. If that was Licria's daughter, Satra would be well pleased. As I opened my mouth to voice these thoughts, Delia said: "Licria will be married off and her daughter trained up. As for the little she-leem herself—I suppose one must feel for her."

Mevancy, who up to now had been sitting twiddling her wineglass, broke out: "Feel for her!"

Her color was high and she looked charged with emotion.

"She's had her day and her race is run," said Delia mildly.

"Yes." Mevancy spoke slowly. "In that sense, yes, I see that."

"Right," I said. "Well done, Caspar. Now we're free for Makilorn."

"I have—other plans."

Caspar the Peaker was a kaogoinye working for the Star Lords. If he had other plans then the Everoinye were dispatching him on a new mission.

"Of course, Caspar." Delia smiled. "Thank you."

The evening meal ought to have been a cheerful occasion for we had cleared up one of our more pressing problems; the good friends gathered at the table were not, it seemed to me, in a celebrating mood. Nath Karidge had been invited and he responded to that atmosphere. He told me that he'd asked Deb-Lu to communicate with Vallia to request airboats for EDLG.

"The Emperor Drak is kindly sending down sufficient fliers to transport the whole regiment. I am a trifle concerned—"

"Oh?"

"Aye, jis. Suppose Queen Satra lays her hands on them?"

"A cogent point, Nath. A secret rendezvous?"

"That'll be the best plan."

He smiled his Beau Sabreur smile and I knew he'd see to that item.

All the same, Satra's greed for vollers presented an unwanted further complication in our already complicated lives. Two problems had baffled and continued to baffle the famous Wizards of Walfarg of Loh. One— the manufacture of gold from base metals. Two—the means of levitation. Stories of flying carpets were well-known on Kregen, although naturally differing somewhat from our terrestrial versions. Flying carpets were unnecessary in lands where airboats were used, except and unless they were readily and cheaply available to the masses. There was no doubt that some mages could levitate themselves and perhaps a few followers; events had occurred strongly suggesting this theory to be correct. In general, flying remained a mystery. Of course, I felt pretty well convinced that Carazaar was using some form of sorcerous aerial navigation rather than any mechanism based on the silver boxes of vollers.

"By the silk-clad legs of the Lady Diwina!" burst out Delia. "Give us a song, Rollo, and cheer us all up."

So he sang a little ditty, 'The Sweet Flowing Water,' composed by Pitir Ng'gland from Ng'groga some five hundred seasons ago. After that we had 'Bear up your Arms' and the 'Lay of the Ponsho Farmer's Daughter' and a few more of the old favorites. When we were all yodeling out: "No idea at all, at all, no idea at all!" we'd sung ourselves back into a better humor.

On parting for the night, Deb-Lu said: "Satra's banquet may well prove an interesting occasion."

"She'll be on top form," prophesied Delia, with a smile.

"Oh, Nath," I said, bringing up something that had been puzzling me. "I'm surprised Drak can spare any vollers from the Pandahem campaign."

"That's just about over now, jis. Yumapan and Lome joined in and the Bloody Menahem were well and truly trounced, aye, by Lasal the Vakka!"

"Queen Lush?"

"Kept on getting in everyone's way, so the news said—you know, jis."

I found, to my astonishment, that I laughed. "I know."

"She made a sensible decision in the end. Appointed a noble from Yumapan to command the combined armies. Fellow called Kov Loriman."

My amusement increased. "The Hunting Kov! I'll bet Nath the Impenitent laughed at that one."

"Chuktar Nath Javed. Oh, aye, jis. Trust him."

Yes, by Vox, I said to myself. Old Hack 'n' Slay would never forget the time he'd had to drag and carry the Hunting Kov through the horrors of the Coup Blag. The news that the Bloody Menaham had been tamed, if only for a while, would come as a relief to all, and especially to Pando the Kov of Bormark in Tomboram. An unkind thought occurred to me—who was winning in the bottle race between Tilda the Beautiful and Scaura Pompina?

There is no need for me to relate the tedious details of Satra's banquet. It all went off in style. She was, as Delia had prophesied, in top form. She was full of her plans for the new empire. At a suitable break in the proceedings, I said to her: "And if the Shanks attack?"

"They will be dealt with, all of the Fish Faces."

"We are leaving for Makilorn in the morning. The Shanks are massing an army there—"

She stared at me with those deep eyes, her white widow's peak, as it were, thrusting forward with determination. She summed me up, she summed up the situation. "That is in the south, past Chem."

"Once they have conquered, their fliers will strike north."

She knew what I was getting at. She sat quietly, pondering. When she lifted her head she said: "Let me know their strengths as soon as possible."

She would not be drawn any further, so with that I had to be content.

It appeared clear to me that my role, unwanted and thrust on me by the Star Lords and those folk who believed in me, as Emperor of Emperors, Emperor of all Paz, was one of conciliation, of argument and of persuasion. I could not order Satra to send her army south to fight Shanks. I would have to persuade her to see that that decision would be her best course.

In the morning we prepared for the off.

To my surprise the one-eared Khibil, Vad Valadian, and Strom Chan with his beard just as stiffly jutting, came to see us off. They said they'd asked Satra if they could go with us but that she had refused permission. She'd said she needed both them and their paktuns for her new armies.

In his arrogant Khibil way, Valadian said: "I think she will come around. It is very clear to us, in any case."

"Very clear, majister," added Strom Chan grimly.

"I thank you both. Now it is remberee."

"Aye, Remberee, Dray Prescot, Emperor of Emperors!"

With that, *Vendayha Lady* soared up into the brilliance of the Suns of Scorpio.

Some way out we picked up Nath Karidge and EDLG from the secret rendezvous and our little squadron headed south.

I feel it completely unnecessary to relate the uproarious welcome we received from our comrades when we reached the camp outside Makilorn.

They were there, the men and women whom you have met in this narrative of mine. Seg and Inch, Milsi and Sasha fell on us, laughing. Nath na Kochwold, stern and living proof of the invincibility of his Phalanx, old Hack 'n' Slay for whom, as Delia remarked, estates and a title must soon be found, greeted us with news that an enormous shbilliding was organized for tonight. My new friends greeted us in a much more restrained fashion, Kuong, Llodi, Larghos the Throstle all looking down at the mouth. Moglin the Flatch was not there, neither was Fan-Si.

"Tell me," I said in the old gravel-shifting voice.

"She was wearing her armor an' all, just like you always said. Proper mail an' everything."

In a heavy voice, Kuong said: "Yes. The bolt went clean through her throat above the mail rim."

"And Moglin?"

"Went berserk. Charged and was cut down."

I could say nothing. The little Fristle fifi, Fan-Si—gone. Moglin the Flatch—gone.

How many more good friends were to die before all these horrors were over?

Eighteen

One has, in these latter days, to be tolerant of other peoples' religions, unless, I suppose, you belong to one of the great proselytizing faiths of two worlds. The religion of Tsungfaril was enough to drive any preacher, fanatical or not, into hysterical action. The best I could hope to do, and I trusted Opaz Beneficent would smile, was to imply to some of the more zealous in the ranks that our first priority was dealing with Shanks. People are touchy about their faiths. I wanted no in-fighting, no bloodshed between the forces we were trying to muster to resist the Fish Faces.

Burrowed over many seasons within the escarpment fringing the wasteland and paralleling the River of Drifting Leaves the tombs of generations of the dead of Makilorn reminded me, as I have said, of Petra. I paid a visit to the tomb set aside. There were no flowers, for land is so precious in Makilorn and flowers and timber scarcer than gold pieces in a barracoon. The gods of Tarankar were not those of Tsungfaril, nor those of Walfarg, and I commended the ibs of Fan-Si and Moglin to them. Then I went back to the city.

This was on the second day after our arrival. The enormous feast and celebration had duly taken place. Any crusty old kampeon, any fighting man or woman is accustomed to the death of comrades. Death is a mere part of life.

The city of Makilorn remained as I remembered, white roofed, built after the style of the tomb of Genghis Khan, narrow along both banks of the river. You may well imagine how Lunky's heavy face brightened when he greeted me.

"I always knew, majister, there was more to you than perhaps even a Diviner could scry." His thick lips twisted into a smile almost of self-mockery. "And you the emperor all the time!"

"And, san, still your friend, I trust?"

The narrow tired face of San Chandro broke into its attractive smile as he said: "Friends? By Tsung-Tan the Mighty! It is you who do us the honor."

These two dikasters, the Diviner and the Repositer, guardians of the religion of Tsungfaril and of the paol-ur-bliem, the accursed, were most anxious to do all they could to help. Kuong and Mevancy chipped in to explain as we walked in the coolness of arcades. Deserts surrounded the city, yet it was now obvious to us all that the Shanks would use their airboats to fly over the barrier deserts. Already we suspected they had adapted to fresh river water. In any case, driven by the sorcerous energy of Carazaar, they could mount a sudden vicious attack, seize the ruby, and be gone back to their seas.

We turned about at the end of the arcade and the stumps of our twin shadows marched with us until we passed under the overhang. Deb-Lu appeared at the far end. He walked swiftly towards us, his brown polished staff high.

He looked animated. "Lahal, all. Dray! Astonishing!" He bent forward and peered hard at Lunky. Dressed soberly, as always, the Diviner wore the habitual fawn gown of Tsungfaril. Deb-Lu put out his hand and with a quick upward movement of his head that almost dislodged his turban, said: "May I?"

"San," said Lunky in his heavy way. "May you what?"

"Oh, of course! You have an—ah—object on your chest. I suspect it is strung about your neck—"

"Yes. I cannot tell you—"

"Of course. That I understand. May I please see it?"

Slowly, Lunky pulled a gold chain up from the front of his gown to reveal a golden trinket. In shape it vaguely resembled a formalized representation of Tsung-Tan although fuller in the body. Instantly, I remembered a burning building, flames everywhere, and a dead and charred man, and a girl to be rescued.

Before Deb-Lu could speak I burst out: "But the drikingers took it!"

Mevancy snapped out: "Cabbage! I was right. Leotes' men did retrieve it."

Deb-Lu swung on me. "You've seen this before?" He almost squawked his amazement.

"If it is the same one. San Tuong Mishuro lost it in a burning building and after that bandits seized it."

"There is only one." Lunky held it reverently.

Deb-Lu straightened up. His kind wise old face looked triumphant. "The ruby of the Skantiklar in Makilorn is hidden among nine of the queen's necklaces. That we know—"

"So does that devil Carazaar!" flashed Mevancy.

"Agreed. What he does not know, what we did not know until we were close enough to ascertain is—there is a second ruby in Makilorn. And it is concealed within the icon of Tsung-Tan around San Lunky's neck!"

Oh, yes, there was consternation at this, pleased confusion. Then I growled out: "All the more reason to resist Carazaar."

Mevancy gave me a demanding look and after a time we were able to have a few words in private. She said: "The Everoinye, then, must have known all along!" To which I replied: "Oh, I don't know. They weren't at all interested in the confounded Skantiklar then, were they?" And: "Cabbage! You always—" And: "Pigeon! I sometimes think they're senile!" And—a gasp of horror.

"Miscils, palines, sazz and parclear!" called Kuong. Mevancy and I gave each other two good long fighting stares, then, shoulders back, heads high—and Mevancy's face a rose of color—we marched in for refreshments.

As you will by now be aware, it was vitally necessary for me to hold an impressive parade of the army. This meant all of the Vallians present in the army, not just the Guard Corps. Perhaps you may imagine the pomp and circumstance of the occasion, held outside the walls on the flat and dusty desert. They were there—oh, yes, they were there! The swods in their disciplined ranks and files. Many of them you have met in my narrative. Many names have appeared and then vanished, good men and women gone down to the Ice Floes of Sicce, to be met by the Grey Ones and so try to make their way to the sunny uplands beyond. Before this business of the Skantiklar and the Shanks was done, many more would follow.

We were greatly cheered by the arrival of Queen Kirsty. She and Rodders had cleared Tarankar out pretty smartly. Her mercenary army had grown. Now she breathed fire and slaughter against the devil Shanks who dared to attack her capital city. Also, she was actively goading the apathetic citizens to take up arms and fight for their city.

Inevitably, as we were in Loh, questions of archery arose. There were competitions held every day. The Bowmen of Loh were skeptical of men and women of other lands who used the famed Lohvian longbow. I own I was smugly satisfied to note that many of the prizes went to my lads of Valka and Vallia.

As a matter of interest, First Emperor's Foot Bows were mainly longbows; there were a pastang of crossbows and a pastang of Valkan compound reflex bows included. All the ranks were full up. My chiefs organized a constant shuttle of fliers bringing in provisions, supplies, provender. Feeding an army is always a nightmare; feeding an army in a desert is purgatory.

Now we had two rubies of the Skantiklar, the question in the minds of all those in on the secret was—how many did Carazaar have?

Once he got his claws on all nine, all hell would break loose.

Mind you, by that time we'd all probably be dead.

Korero kept polishing up his shields, and he carried extra weaponry. Balass the Hawk had been saddened by the loss of Fan-Si and Larghos; but like us he was inured to pain of that kind without becoming callous. My chiefs of the Guard Corps, Nath na Kochwold and his Phalanx, and the Chuktars of the line moved about the camp with grim determination. Everyone knew that the imminent battle would be the big one, the culmination of all their efforts.

The Hamalian forces flew in under the temporary command of Kapt Hargon ham Hurlving, for Fleet Admiral Harulf ham Hilzim had returned to Ruathytu to attend the Emperor Nedfar. A new force commander would be sent out as soon as appointed by Nedfar.

Our scouts reported in regularly. On the day when we'd finished reviewing the Hamalese I made up my mind. We were very thin on the ground and in the air. Taking our refreshments when we could I was chewing the last of a section of vosk pie and battling my way past the chunks of gristle therein. Delia saw me chewing and smiled. In a fashion I hoped was not too surly, I said: "I'm going off to Djanduin and then to see the Clansmen."

"I agree. All Paz is in this. I'll welcome the trip."

In his big breezy way Seg chipped in. "Too true! All Paz has to stand as one."

Inch nodded his head atop that lanky frame. He didn't speak for he'd broken one of his astounding taboos and couldn't utter a word until nightfall.

So, the very next day, aboard *Vendayha Lady*, we sailed for Djanduin.

Again, needless for me to relate the joyous proceedings as my Djangs welcomed their king and queen. Kytun Kholin Dorn and Ortyg Fellin Coper, the best of comrades both, agreed instantly that the Djangs must be represented in this struggle. I particularly wanted the flyers, young men and women astride the superb flutduins, the best flyers in my view in Paz. As for the four-armed Djang warriors, they had already beaten Shanks in fair fight and were thirsting to show the Fish Faces the errors of their ways. A sizeable force was quickly mustered and dispatched aboard Djanduin vollers.

Then it was all the long way east across continents and islands and

oceans to Segesthes. We stopped off briefly in Strombor which was compe-
tently run in the absence of Gloag fighting Shanks in Mehzta, and then we
soared out over the Great Plains. Well! My Clansmen led by the wild Hap
Loder went mad with joy and great were the rejoicings. This time I was
after armored chivalry mounted on the earth-shaking voves. My clanners
responded and, once again, a force mustered and flew out, this time with
Vendayha Lady in company. We all met up at Makilorn.

So, now there were five separate forces here. The Armies Gathered.

Seg and Milsi, Inch and Sasha, were not in the camp. I was not in the
least surprised when they turned up with another army. These were fighting men and women from Milsi's and Seg's realm of Croxdrin, reinforced
with a goodly gang of bean-pole tall, axe-armed Ng'grogans recruited by
Inch and Sasha.

Now there were six armies mustered on the sands outside Makilorn.

"If poor old Queen Satra gets it right," observed Delia, "that will make
seven armies."

"And we need every single swod in every army." Inevitably, there were
rumbles, and sporadic arguments leading to quick fights between soldiers
of one race or army and the others; in general the troops behaved themselves. All were only too well aware of the stern tasks that lay ahead.

In the event the seventh army turned up aboard Hyrklese vollers. Delia's
face brightened up wonderfully at the thought of seeing our lad, Jaidur,
King of Hyrklana. I felt for her—and, by Krun! for myself—when Jaidur
turned up missing. The forces from Hyrklana were led by Vad Gochert.
His eye patch glittered on me as the greetings were exchanged.

"The king entrusted me with the army. I am honored, majister."

"Indeed," I said in my gruff old way. If I confess to pleasure at the thought
I'd read this man aright from the beginning, then I make no apology for
that. "And we are honored to have you and the Hyrklese army with us."

Later on Delia, with rather a long face, told me that she'd had confiden-
tial information from some of her people she'd earlier sent to Huringa to
keep an eye on Jaidur that the marriage did not prosper. "Nothing too serious yet, that cannot be mended; but, my heart—"

"Jaidur is a right tearaway. Vax Neemusjid. Aye. Well, like his brothers he
has married. As for the girls—"

"Lela—or Jaezila as you will call her—and Tyfar will be splendid! That I
know. As for Dayra—Ros the Claw—she has things to do yet."

"And little Velia, who is not little any more, and Didi—"

"They are promised to the Sisters of the Rose."

"Aye."

The next army to arrive gave me great pleasure. He came stamping up to
our tent in his bash on, bully-boy way, full, fleshy, choleric. I said: "Lahal,
kov. It is good to see you and the army of Yumapan and Lome."

"Lahal—majister."

Oh, yes, Kov Loriman the Hunter had come a long, long way since the days of Spikatur Hunting Sword, when we'd groped our way around among the magics and monsters of the Moder. A figure appeared at his side, wreathed in a trembling blue radiance.

Instantly, futile though the gesture was, my fist gripped the hilt of my sword.

Another blue-shimmering figure ghosted into existence, and dear old Deb-Lu, very quickly, said: "It is perfectly all right! He felt he would prefer to stand before you in lupu at first. Afterwards—"

"You vouch for him, san?"

"I do. He recognizes the situation. He appealed to Kov Loriman because they have worked together before."

"I see!"

The astonishment I felt was tempered by caution. If Deb-Lu said a thing was so, then it was a safe bet that that thing was so.

"The requirements of the Skantiklar have changed. San Na-Si-Fantong has uncovered further information which he has shared with me. It seems that the Skantiklar's powers are uncontrollable by a single mage. The power for self-destruction is so great as to make the thing deadly. It is our view, shared by Khe-Hi and Ling-Li, that the Skantiklar had best be destroyed."

There was no need to say that this information tallied with what I had learned from Zena Iztar and the Star Lords.

"You have the ruby safe, the one you snatched in the Realm of the Drums?" I spoke with a hard edge to my voice.

"Aye, majister." Na-Si-Fantong, as ever, ducked his head and took a breath before he spoke. "And the other two."

"Then Carazaar can only have four."

After that the real Na-Si-Fantong walked in with Deb-Lu, and I found to my astonishment that my astonishment died. We were all of Paz, in this great struggle together.

"If you don't count Turismond, which is, anyway, remote and cut-off," pointed out Delia, "we now have representatives of all the islands and continents."

Thinking about creeping along the dusty passages of the Realm of the Drums after this clever sorcerer, Na-Si-Fantong, had disappeared, I answered a little absently, if sharply: "Loh, where the battle is to be fought, is not represented by the central power—the Empire of Walfarg."

Milsi in her gentle way said: "Give Satra time, Dray."

"Give her enough time and she'll be too late."

"She has a task, though, be fair."

"Look, Milsi, dear, why don't you and Seg nip up to Hiclantung and spell it out for the old biddy? If she fiddles about regaining all her realms and the Shanks win, then she'll lose 'em anyway. If she comes down here and chips in, then, if things work out, we can help her."

Seg roared out: "Why don't you finish the sentence properly, my old dom?" He was laughing at me, his handsome face beaming.

"Finish the sentence?"

"Aye, my old dom! Properly. Finish with: 'Dernun!'"

"Oh," I said, chastened.

"A very good idea, Dray." Milsi was quite unperturbed. "We'll go."

"And do be quick," said Delia. "The Shanks' power grows."

"They'll wait," grunted Seg, "for me to shaft a few of 'em."

We shouted up the remberees when Milsi and Seg and a bodyguard lifted off for Hiclantung. Now if from all this coming and going, with armies being wafted into Tsungfaril from all over Paz, you gain the impression that we had vast fleets of aerial ships at our bidding, I must immediately disabuse you of any such notion. An accretion to our strength came with the vollers from Djanduin, certainly. But we were short of air still. For example, most of the clanners from Segesthes were lifted in Hamalese vessels. Among these were a few brand new craft; most were battle-worn. Kapt Hargon ham Hurlving told me that the Emperor Nedfar had appointed a kov to command the land forces and that Fleet Admiral Harulf ham Hilzim would be returning to command the air. This pleased me. Harulf was a fine sailor and a good man.

During this brief period Na-Si-Fantong was much in Deb-Lu's company. Whilst I cannot go so far as to say I felt uneasy at this close association, I had a few words with Khe-Hi and Ling-Li when they arrived in the camp. They'd had to attend to their twins' education back in Whonban so that they would in the fullness of time become a full-fledged Wizard and Witch of Loh.

Khe-Hi laughed. "Oh, Deb-Lu will get the best of anything that goes on there!"

Ling-Li agreed. "There is always something more to learn under the Seven Arcades."

I heaved up a grunting kind of sigh. "Yeh. As in life. The more you know the more you understand how little you know."

In the camp there were, of course, plenty of other sorcerers of various persuasions. Like the troops, they had their quarrels and, like the swods, they got over them and learned toleration under stress. My view was quite simple. In our struggle against Carazaar we'd need every damned mage we could lay our hands on.

Kuong had taken Llodi and comrades off to his estates at Taranik to maintain contact and pick up supplies of dried fruit. I made it a point of comradeship to ride out to greet his returning caravan. They trudged up to Wayfarer's Drinnik smothered in dust, dry, and many limped as they marched.

Kuong was boiling with fury.

"Damned Glitchers! By Lohrhiang of the strangdja and kazz! I'd string 'em all up, make 'em dangle, Tsung-Tan rot their eyeballs!" He was in a right old paddy.

"I'm sorry to hear that," I said as we rode together.

"Oh, we shafted 'em and drove 'em off. But we lost good men and animals. Poor Naghan the Miserable—a most cheerful merry fellow—will never ride with us again. Tsung-Tan rot 'em!"

"And the supplies?"

"We lost some dried berries—it's the lads that sadden me."

The Glitch Riders, raiding down from the north, flamboyant in their sand scarves and their robes, flashing steel expertly from the backs of their mounts, sticking their slender lances with deadly precision, remained a constant threat to the caravans. We just did not have enough air to cover everywhere. So, once again, I made up my mind.

As I was issuing instructions for a small expedition, Mevancy came in to see me. My hardened jurukkers by now knew who had immediate access to their Kendur. I looked up from the list.

"Mevancy? You look—ah—"

"It doesn't matter what I look like, cabbage. May I borrow a small airboat? Please?"

"Of course."

"You don't ask me what for?"

"If you intend to tell me, you will. If not—"

"Oh, you!"

Her color rose blooming in the tent and she wouldn't look me in the eye.

"I'm going home to Sinnalix." As I said nothing she went on: "Oh, I'm not deserting! Just that—well—I've some business." Her eyes looked everywhere but at me. She was acting in a most shifty fashion.

"Very well, pigeon. Take who you like; but take a bodyguard."

She took a pace forward and now she looked at me. I felt her gaze burning on me. "Thank you, cabbage. You are—kind." That was not, I judged, the word she'd intended to use.

The order for the voller was quickly written and signed and Mevancy took herself off. I had a damned shrewd idea what that was all about. Poor Mevancy! Still, my plans for her remained. If she married Kuong after she returned from Sinnalix, and if we beat the Shanks, and when Satra died— well, who would venture to foretell the future? I relished the sound of Queen Mevancy, Empress of Walfarg. Yes, by Zair, I liked that!

Even so, I, Dray Prescot, a simple sailorman, could laugh at myself for all these extravagant notions of queens and empresses.

The expedition was quite small, half a dozen swift vollers crammed with my lads. Delia, of course, insisted on going along, and with her Nath Karidge and some of her Jikai Vuvushis. We flew north. There is little need to go into great detail. The Glitch Riders in general stuck to their own clans and only occasionally united under a nominal leader. The first encampment we visited was thrown into panic at our arrival. We dropped a few firepots on the desert as a hint of our power. Then I landed.

The local chieftain, after a thorough talking to, was happy to co-operate.

He pointed me in the direction of the encampment where lived the fellow they'd choose as their nominal leader. Following the same procedure we quickly had him eating out of our hands.

I said: "Chief Wan-fuong. There are greater enemies to fight than are to be found guarding the caravans. If your young men are the renowned warriors they claim—and I have thrashed them in my time—you will send them to join the warriors fighting the damned Fish Faces."

He heard me out as I elaborated. He was a dignified old soul, no doubt with the blood of many and many a caravan guard staining his past. He took a deep breath and the mass of silver chains draped over his chest chingled and caught the lamplight in the tent.

He fingered a scar running down his cheek. Slowly, he said: "We are not so remote here that I have not heard of you. You may destroy our tents with your fire from the sky. We would fight you to the death—"

"Uselessly and to no purpose. The Shanks are all our foes."

I saw that he was already in agreement but that he must be persuaded in order to maintain his pre-eminent position here. I persuaded him. At the end he nodded that desert-hawk face. "I will send our young men and we will fight alongside the paktuns of Queen Kirsty. It is agreed."

Standing up, for I'd been sitting cross-legged on the carpet, I gave him a nice formal answer, and praised him and his warriors. Then I cleared off into the fresh air and observing the fantamyrrh climbed aboard the voller.

Chief Wan-fuong hadn't asked about pay for his young men. He was clearly perfectly satisfied they could look after themselves in the camp of their erstwhile enemies and victims. As for pay—the Glitchers were well-accustomed to taking what they wanted from the prostrate forms—dead or alive—of those they had beaten in combat.

I knew what Kirsty or Kuong or anyone of Tsungfaril would say at this turn of events. "Let the Glitch Riders and the Fish Faces kill one another, the more the merrier, Tsung-Tan rot 'em all!"

All the same, I felt personally very pleased at the outcome of this spot of business. If this was a sample of what an Emperor of Paz could accomplish, the game might be well worth the candle. After the battle—always assuming we won—there would be a very great need for a whole fresh look at the situation. It might well be intractable; but, by Krun, we had to try to organize life in this part of Loh so that people could live freely.

Our little expedition turned for Makilorn. Towards the hour of mid a hail rang out from for'ard, the Kregish equivalent of: "Sail ho!"

Up in the bows that young scamp, Ensign Nalgre V'ron'v pointed. The dark shape of a voller sped south west on a closing course.

Now as to names in Kregish—well, Nalgre's family often wrote their surname as Vronv. No names on Kregen, contrary to some pig-ignorant critics, are unpronounceable. Here on Earth some of the ancients wrote only consonants and omitted all vowels. When reading you simply supplied the vowels as you went along. Two or three consonants in a string can easily be separated by the briefest little vowel sounds. Although Vronv is perfectly pronounceable as it stands, you can always say Veronev. Enough of that, by Krun!

We closed the other voller which was of Hamalese build.

The little craft did not waver or change course but bore on steadily.

Side by side we sailed on. From the staffs above our heads floated our flags. The Great Union of Vallia, Delia's personal tresh, my Old Superb, other standards denoting who was aboard. From the strange voller floated two banners I recognized.

A surge of exultation welled up in me. By Krun! This was splendid!

The Llahals rang across the gulf, the challenges, and from our side roared out: "Delia and Dray Prescot, Empress and Emperor of All Paz!"

The stentor might as easily have shouted Valhan instead of Prescot, either was correct. The answering shouts lifted my emotions, I can tell you, by Krun, yes!

"Kov Rees ham Harshur, Commander in Chief of the Hamalese Army!" and: "Kov Chido ham Thafey, Chief of Staff of the Hamalese Army here in Loh!"

Rees and Chido as ever were! I turned to Delia and she saw my face and she smiled. "Very well, Hamun ham Farthytu," she said in a whispering voice, for I had long since told her of that real identity from Paline Valley. "Will they recognize you?" She put her head on one side. "And it is time, high time, we were properly introduced."

"If ever there was a time, my love, it is now."

"Yet—?"

The vollers sailed on side by side.

"And it is high time I told them the truth. Mind you, I intend to keep Hamun as a real identity, that is far too useful to throw away."

"They will keep the secret—from all you have told me of them."

"Also, it is in my mind to play them a trick. They caught me hopping in The Squish and Queng down there in Tuansmot. Now it is my turn!"

I yelled at the helmsman. "Lofty! Lay us alongside!"

"Quidang!"

Our voller edged closer, and Nudger the Bottom, the Ship-Deldar handling the ropes on the beam opened his mouth to yell. He'd roar out: "Coming aboard! Emperor of Paz!"

"Belay that, Nudger!" I snapped, very sharply. He gave me a look, then went on flicking his ropes in and out. "Just say: 'Coming aboard.'"

I was wearing a simple fawn tunic and sandals in the heat of the desert, with rapier and main gauche and the Savanti sword. Heavy clobber is to be avoided in these climes when the slipstream hits you like a blast from the Furnace Fires of Inshurfraz. I handed the Krozair longsword to Delia, and she said: "Mind you invite them to dinner tonight."

"Positively."

Nudger yelled as ordered and with my hand up to my face I moved to the bulwark. Under cover of my hand as I faced outboard I changed my features into those of Hamun ham Farthytu. That face now was a trifle hardened from the one I'd assumed seasons ago in Ruathytu, changed as Chido's had changed, despite the fact that Kregans change so little and slowly over their span of years. Experience must leave its mark.

I leaped across onto the deck of the Hamalese voller.

They saw me and they gaped.

I bellowed out: "Well, you two famblys! Have you no greetings for an old comrade in arms?"

"Hamun!" and: "By Krun! Hamun!"

In the next instant we were clapping one another on the back and fairly dancing about the deck. This was all wonderful stuff and I joyed in it—and yet—and yet! Wait for the next act in the drama!

The voller lurched.

She staggered in mid air.

Instantly Chido sprang to the controls and then ripped the cover over the shaft to the silver boxes below. He straightened. His face betrayed it all.

"Black."

All forward motion ceased. The airboat shuddered as though trying one last time to remain airborne. She dropped. Straight down she plummeted.

We fell through thin air towards the hard desert sands waiting hungrily below.

Nineteen

"So it is Lahal and Remberee in a breath." Rees's lion voice rang hard.

"I'm wondering," observed Chido, "if the weather's improved along the Ice Floes of Sicce at this time of year."

"We must," said Rees, staggering slightly as the voller plummeted, "have a last toast." He crossed to a side locker and gripped onto the gunwale. As he pulled out a flagon and goblets I looked up at the circling Vallian fliers. She was up there, all I ever really wanted. I'd not deserved her, of course not. One of the vollers detached itself from the squadron and plunged vertically shooting down under power faster than us in free fall. Oh, I'd tried to do my best; all those times the Star Lords had sent me off on their hare-brained schemes I'd fought, clawed, bit and scratched, to get back to her. And, then, she'd be off with the Sisters of the Rose. No, our life had not been smooth.

"Here, Hamun. By Krun, if this is the end of it all, then let's go with flagons in our fists!

"Aye, Wees! A toast!"

I gripped the goblet and stared at these two. We stood facing in towards one another, forming a triangle. We lifted our right arms up, goblets high, and—I found nothing uncanny in it—as one we roared out: "To us!"

For a few moments as the flier plunged we stood like that, goblets high, challenging the dark fates of the universe.

We drank and at the precise instant the wine touched our lips the sound of a hollow gong blasted into the hot air. The airboat kicked like a calsany. We tumbled together, clasping our free arms about one another, and, by Krun, we did not spill a drop!

Again that bumping lurch sent us reeling.

Holding on we felt the voller's mad descent checking. We were slowing! Gripping on, we drank up the toast and Rees bellowed: "I was going to throw the goblets overside in the last toast. But not now. I prize them."

"They're vewwy handsome, Wees."

Now we were going down still at a rate of knots but nowhere near our original speed. All the same, if we hit flat on like this we'd still be splattered. At last we condescended to take notice of what was going on. We tumbled over to the gunwale, gripping on, and looked down.

"Damned close, Hanitcha the Harrower take it," snarled Rees.

The yellow and brown of the desert sprang up towards us. Around the outline of our little voller another flier's outline showed. The brave flags would all be broken away from their masts. No doubt the deck was in a hell of a mess. We slowed. Closer and closer—slower and slower—someone down there was doing some consummate flying. When we hit the thump was enough—at last—to topple us off our feet. We sprawled along the gunwale, laughing.

I stopped laughing damned quickly. My clever scheme had gone seriously awry. I stood up and gave them two hard stares.

"There are things I must tell you. That's why I came aboard, so as to have some time alone with you."

Rees puffed out his cheeks and pulled himself up. "And I'm going to have a few words with the pilot of that voller. Stupendous! Whoever he is I'm going to shake his hand and stand him a bumper."

"I believe," I said in a flat voice, "that particular voller pilot to be my wife."

Their mouths hung and then snapped shut. Both of them: "Your what!"

"Please do not call me Hamun. No one knows I am Hamun ham Farthytu here, except my wife, of course. Please call me Dray."

Chido was still sitting on the deck. His face could no longer properly be described as chinless; he certainly looked a trifle vacant now.

"Dray?" He started to stand up. "That's a Vallian voller. By Kwun, Hamun, what's going on?"

Chido did not, naturally, say 'Dray.' He said: 'Dway.' The near approach of death had driven all traces of Hamun's features from my face. As I looked at them, two blade comrades, Bladesmen with whom I had ruffled it in the Sacred Quarter of Ruathytu, I felt something of that old Dray Prescot Devil Look spread across my old beakhead. I spoke brusquely. "Vallian, yes. They do not know I am Hamun ham Farthytu. I am known as Dray. By Vox! Remember to call me Dray—please." The last I added as graciously as I could.

"Damned Vallians," said Chido. "Dway, is it?"

"Aye."

"Your wife flew that voller?" demanded Rees.

"Aye—so I judge by the skill."

"You look damned different Hamun—Dway."

"Then, by Krun, you've married a girl of parts!"

There being no suitable reply to that I started to say: "Dray it is then—" A thunderbolt burst up over the gunwale and fairly hurled herself at me. She clasped me about the waist and gripped me hard. She trembled.

"You great fambly!" she cried. "Why do you do things like this to me?"

Over her shoulder I could see other figures climbing aboard. The uproar flowered up into the desert sky. They were all clamoring about me now. Among the yells were: "Kendur!" and: "Majister!" and: "Jis!" with one or two "Drays" thrown in. I sighed. Fat chance now of breaking the news gently to Rees and Chido. I said to Delia: "It'll go hard with them."

"Then, my heart, let us do it right now."

At once she freed me and swung about. Among the people all clamoring about us we looked for them—and could not see them.

"Nath!" She spoke rapidly to Nath Karidge. "The two who were aboard, the numim and the apim—where are they?"

"They were rather pushed aside in the rush, maj. I trust they were not trampled down."

He spoke in jest, I saw; but there was more than a grain of truth in what he said, by Zair!

Eventually the pair were spotted walking along side by side out across the sands. Their heads were bowed and they were clearly in deep conversation. Delia gave me a swift glance and I nodded.

I held up my hand and instantly silence fell.

"Thank you, friends. We have had a wonderful escape from death. Now prepare to proceed. Check any damage." They'd know exactly what to do.

There was no need to assist Delia over the side. Agile as a jumping jimnu she was up and over and waiting for me. I clambered after and, arm in arm, we walked off towards Rees and Chido.

"I don't much care for this," I said in what was really a mumble.

"I believe what you have said of them. They will handle the situation. It's their attitude to Vallia that troubles me."

"Aye."

They saw us coming, turned to face us, and stood, waiting.

I made the pappattu in the correct form and sequence; but I did not mention anything about empresses. Rees bowed deeply.

"We are indebted to you for our lives. I give you our profound thanks."

"Our most profound thanks," amplified Chido, head up. His bow had not been as deep as Rees's. He studied me. "Dway? Delia?"

"All right! All right!" I fairly snarled it out. "By the diseased and decomposing liver and lights of Makki Grodno! Yes, yes, and yes! I am that Dray Prescot and this is that Delia Valhan Prescot, Delia of Delphond, Delia of the Blue Mountains, of whom you have heard tell. So? Does that affect our comradeship? Well, Rees, well, Chido?"

They remained silent and I could feel sympathy for them. Into the little hiatus Delia spoke in her soft voice. "The other fliers watched. They told me you three stood together, and drank a last toast. That must have been a sight to see."

Nath had obviously been told and had told Delia in all the uproar. The two, numim and apim, stood a little helplessly, I thought, not looking at us.

Chido spoke. "A damned Vallian all the time. And the damned Emperor of Vallia as well." He held out his hand. "But still a Bladesman and a comrade."

We shook hands, at which I felt remarkably embarrassed, and Rees boomed: "A Bladesman and a comrade," and wrung my hand in his turn.

I said: "I am Hamun ham Farthytu in Hamal. I would beg the favor—"

"Yes, yes, Dway! We understand and we'll wemember."

"Aye, Dray. That we shall."

The double meanings there rang loudly between the words.

"So you two are kovs now. My sincere and warmest congratulations."

Rees favored me with a leery look. "The Emperor Nedfar told us that we had been commended to him by a very close friend."

369

"He did not say who the vewwy close fwiend was—now I think we know."

"That's it. If you're going to go maudlin on me—"

"Dray!" said Delia, half laughing.

In his most courtly way, Rees bowed to her. "You have my condolences, majestrix, for having to suffer such a fellow."

"Insufferwwable!"

The high ringing notes of a trumpet blasting into the hot air took our instant attention. The call was 'Air Alert!' Chido and Rees would most likely not recognize the Vallian trumpet call; but they looked up with us. They were up there, three of them in a tight vee formation, flying fast into the north west. Their black hulls cut blots of darkness in the bright sky.

"Looks as though we've arrived just in time," remarked Rees.

"Oh, the big one's coming up, no doubt of that, by Krun."

We started off back for the group of vollers and my lads were already fanning out across the sands in a protective ring. Others were hard at work on the airboat. Delia made a face. "What a mess I made of her."

Then Chido made a remark that convinced me we were truly back to our old comradeship. "Splendid flying, majestrix—for a Vallian!"

Delia laughed easily, and then said: "For that, Chido, you may call me maj in company and Delia when we are with friends." Oh, yes, by Zair, Delia knows how to sort out scamps!

Feeling much relieved I walked back with my comrades and surveyed the damage. Our voller would still fly, of course, although her upperworks were ground down. The bright flags were salvaged and rigged on jury masts.

Briskly, Chido walked over to the flier that had caused all this trouble, saying: "We'll get our gear. A salvage team can fly up from our fleet."

Rees joined him and Delia called: "And you two are invited to dinner."

"We accept with pleasure—maj."

If there was going to be a running battle of wits between them, I wanted to stay out of the middle, I can tell you, by Vox!

With commendable rapidity we were all ship shape and Vondium fashion and took off for Makilorn. Rees and Chido took a last long look at their abandoned flier, alone on the deserted sands. The introductions were not long drawn out affairs. Folk came up and shook hands and said who they were. The Pappattu was made informally and gracefully.

Chido kept on shaking his head. "A damned bunch of scallywag Vallians."

"I saw you, Dray, on the field of the incendiary Vosks."

"Aye, Rees, aye. I was glad that Vad Garnath did not die by your hand."

"At the time—then, afterwards—yes, I was glad, too."

"I'd have given his corpse a kick or three," said Chido sturdily. If he meant it or not, I didn't know. Chido had changed. I wouldn't put it past him now.

In the camps outside Makilorn the newly arrived Kapt and his chief of staff of the Hamalese forces made themselves known. They'd itched to be here and had taken the small flier without waiting for Hilzim. He turned up the next day in an enormous skyship that was a capital addition to our fleets.

"Eight armies," I said at the second breakfast. I spoke fretfully. "Where in a Herrelldrin Hell is Satra?"

Deb-Lu said: "We could well do with her college of mages."

"I just hope Milsi and Seg—" began Sasha, then stopped talking.

"Trust old Seg to look out, my love," said Inch in a mild manner. As I have said, when Seg and Inch talk gently and mildly it scares the pants off anyone who even remotely knows anything about them. The strongest possibility existed that if Satra had harmed Seg or Milsi, Inch would sort her and her army and her sorcerers out first—and then start on the Shanks.

Inevitably a certain distant friendliness subsisted between my two sets of comrades. They were not exactly cool, one to another, as wary, ready to test the others' mettle. I tried not to make the mistake I'd made with Kuong, Mevancy, Llodi and company. We all shared meals in the ornate tent my lads considered fitting for their Kendur. And—there was no word of Mevancy.

A couple of days later a squadron of vorlcas sailed in, flying argosies of sail coasting through thin air and settling gracefully to the desert. Vallians disembarked, and Valkans, tough fighting men and women. To our joy Kov Turko led them to join the Vallian expeditionary force. I shall not go into the shenanigans that followed; believe me, we held a shbilliding to rock the stars in the night sky of Kregen and make all the seven moons dance.

Nothing would satisfy Turko but he must try a few falls to the glory of Beng Drudoj, and Korero joined in, and many and loud were the falls thereof. Rees, watching, offered a wager—but of that outcome I will not speak. As you may see, despite our manifold problems, we kept fit, we entertained ourselves, and we trained for the big day.

Some of the contests that took place were stupendous in the extreme. After all, Khamster, Kildoi, Djang, Clansman—all in camp together!

And still Mevancy did not return.

One day Kuong said to me in a troubled frame of mind: "I really think I shall have to go and find out."

"Trust her. Let's ask Deb-Lu."

After Deb-Lu had gone into lupu in his easy way and scryed, he told us Mevancy was well and unharmed. "She has not yet completed her business."

With that calm assurance to ease our minds, we could turn to our business. An orbat had to be worked out. Every single swod had to know exactly where he must be and what he must do. Our scouts reported regularly and we were in no apprehension of a surprise raid catching us unawares.

Each army considered it had the right to the right flank. Failing that, then the center was the favored position. These decisions were down to me.

The leaders of the various armies and their chiefs were assembled and I spelled it out to them in words that meant I brooked no arguments.

Each army and each unit of each army was told exactly where they were to form up. I went on: "We must react swiftly. It is doubtful if the Shanks under a leader like Carazaar will miss any tricks. Their object is to take the city. That is practically indefensible from the air. We resist within the city, we strike them outside, and our air will clear their air."

As soon as the assembled chiefs left, Delia and I took Inch and Sasha and Deb-Lu to a second, smaller meeting. Present were Queen Kirsty and Rodders, Lunky, and Na-Si-Fantong. Wine was served and then I spoke.

"You have between you five of the gems of the Skantiklar. It has been agreed that the thing is too evilly powerful and must be destroyed. I would ask you, now, to destroy the gems you have."

Lunky gasped, and automatically his hand grasped the icon on his breast. Kirsty frowned. Na-Si-Fantong shook his head. I glared at him, and he said: "It is not possible, majister. Let San Deb-Lu-Quienyin enlighten us all."

Deb-Lu pushed his turban straight and scratched his nose. "Quite right, Jak. The whole thing must be destroyed as a whole. Single rubies will not perish by fire or any other means of which we know."

"Confound it!" I said. "Confound and blast it!"

"We just have to win the battle to protect the gems." Delia put a slim finger to her lips. "Even if we do not succeed in gaining the other rubies from Carazaar, he will not make the Skantiklar."

"Then the threat will always remain."

"As Zim and Genodras rise each morning."

"Sink me!" I burst out. "Who'd be the Emperor of all Paz!"

Deldar Ornol the Mischievous put his head around the flap of the tent to roar: "Master Rollo requests a word with San Quienyin. Urgent." Ornol, as the guard Deldar, bellowed like all Deldars bellow, bright of face and powerful of lungs.

Deb-Lu perked up. "Ah! That'll be about Seg. I put Rollo onto him."

"Send him in, Ornol."

"Quidang!"

Instantly Rollo more ran than walked in, disheveled and eager.

"Lahal—San—Seg has done it! Satra requests vollers to transport her army here as soon as possible."

"Excellent!"

Inch stood up. "I'll organize that."

Fleet Admiral Hilzim and Kov Loriman detached ample fliers to bring in Satra's army and we awaited their arrival with keen interest.

I said: "So that makes it nine armies."

Nine is the magical and mystical number on Kregen. At the Gathering of the Armies, then, we had nine armies. Nine armies to fight against the Shanks and Carazaar and all his dark power.

And still Mevancy had not returned.

"Although," I said quietly to Delia, "I fancy it is Milsi who's accomplished this great stroke of fortune for us."

"Yes. She has a way with her."

To our three sorcerous comrades, Ling-Li, Deb-Lu and Khe-Hi, I said: "When Satra arrives I'm going to have to try to be strict with the old biddy. Sort her and her army out. I'd rather like you to take a tough line with her mages. It would be nice if we could form a kind of super college. I am only making suggestions, you understand—"

"Oh, Dray!" broke in Ling-Li, half-laughing. "When you try to be humble you look as though you've constipation."

The two Wizards of Loh smiled in complete agreement.

H'm, I said to myself. I suppose the confounded Star Lords can see that, too.

"We have a considerable gathering of thaumaturgical expertise." Deb-Lu was looking chippy, and I guessed that was in anticipation of dealing with Satra's sorcerers. "A super college will be formed. Carazaar is in for one big surprise."

"All the same," pointed out Khe-Hi, with a glance at his wife. "He is normally very powerful. With his enhanced abilities—"

"We will check him, my dear," said Ling-Li. "We have to."

She said 'We will make him bare the throat' which is the same thing.

Again, there is little need to detail our joyous reunion with Milsi and Seg. Satra's troops landed and marched to their appointed camping grounds. She and they were received with much pomp and circumstance. A large and of necessity formal dinner was held that night, and I more or less itched all the way through the tedious proceedings. We had a great battle to fight. All the same, functions of this kind formed an integral part of the political process.

At a suitable point I stood up and lifted my glass. "A toast!" I bellowed in the old foretop hailing voice. "To the Nine Armies of Paz!"

They drank it down without, as they say in Clishdrin, any heeltaps, and Seg and Inch stood up. Seg called out: "To our glorious victory!" and Inch shouted: "Coupled with the utter discomfiture of all our foes!"

There was no hint of bad luck in this, on Kregen, and many more toasts were drunk in brimmers and bumpers.

The singing was curtailed by the earlier length of the banquet. I insisted that we yodel out 'The Bowmen of Loh' which we did with full throats.

After that we went to bed and the next morning the Shanks arrived.

"They darken the sky!" exclaimed young Ensign Nalgre V'ron'v. He looked up, his face flushed. I did not detect any greater fear in him than was to be expected in these frightening circumstances.

To be truthful, there were a lot of them. One hell of a lot of them.

Our preparations were all long since made. Our fleets swarmed out to meet the Schtarkin airboats and all too soon flames and black smoke gouted hideous death across the sky.

I'd told the chiefs: "We do not simply sit back and resist in a defensive role. We must go over to the attack. The Shanks will not like fighting on foot in the desert. Our biggest single problem will be a sharp and sudden raid into the city. Carazaar will probably send his phantom image to lead Shanks and Katakis. Whatever dweomer he may use, he can be foiled if his tools are eliminated."

To that end strong guards remained steadfast about the five gems, and we placed other guard formations at strategic points so as not to draw attention to the rubies' locations. I remained in the city with 1ESW and 1EYJ under my hand to rush instantly to any threatened spot. The balance of my Guard Corps stood under arms to give support. Queen Kirsty and Rodders had their army within the city, manning the walls in company with a good proportion of Queen Satra's troops. Nath na Kochwold and his Phalanx with associated formations were ready to march out and bash any ground troops for they would be of limited use in the narrow alleys of the city.

K. Kholin Dorn came stamping up the stairs to the high tower where I'd perched a temporary headquarters. Like any fighting Dwadjang he carried an arsenal of weapons. He pulled a bright orange kerchief from under a strap and wiped his lips where the wine shone from the goblet in his fist, he grasped a djangir, the short broad sword that is the racial weapon of Djanduin, and with his free fist he punched me lightly on the bicep. "Well, now, king—where are these Fish Faces marching in hordes across the desert whom we will show these Clansmen on their voves how to despatch to the glory of Djan Kadjiryon of the Bright Flame? Eh, where?"

Hap Loder, just as ferocious although, like me, he had only two arms, following on, said: "By the lights of Zim and Genodras, Kytun, we shall turn the lesson the other way around. All the same, Dray, where are they?"

Out over the dusty plains the aerial combats continued. The sandy floor remained barren of marching troops.

"When you are dealing with a fellow as slippery and sly as Carazaar," I said, "It behooves you to watch every direction at once."

"You mean they'll burrow under the ground and come at us out of tunnels?" demanded Kytun, and he took another swig at his goblet.

"That is not at all impossible for Carazaar. By Zodjuin of the Silver Spear, not impossible at all!"

That made them stiffen up their spines!

Among the vollers swirling and rising and falling and—horrendously—bursting into flames, darted swift-winged shapes like clouds of annoying insects. Delia said: "Your young flutduinim are doing splendidly, Kytun."

He nodded, pleased. Such was his pride in his flyers, however, that he had to pass it off somehow. "That, my queen, is to be expected of Djangs. I give praise to the young people of Valka who fly quite well."

Delia laughed. That laugh can always run spider-fingers up and down my spine. I remembered my early days on Kregen when a laugh was a rare commodity, hard to come by and harder to produce.

There was no doubt that Fleet Admiral Hilzim was holding the Shanks. A few vollers broke away, diving for the city, to be caught and snuffed out by the reserve squadrons of Hyrklese fliers. In the air, the battle was going our way. Our scouts had not reported a vast army on foot, nor had we expected them to, for had they done so our fleets would have sailed out to drop fire pots on them. The foot troops would have to land from the air.

A small airboat came whistling over the desert, close to the ground, fleeting in from the opposite direction from the battle. Instantly a pair of fast patrolling fliers swooped on her. Without turning my head, I said: "Deb-Lu! Would you kindly send a message to those patrol craft—"

"I have already done so, Jak. Look, they are escorting her in."

Shortly thereafter Mevancy climbed the stairs to headquarters.

"Lahal all," she said in a most prim and proper way. She was dressed in her mail shirt and her forearms were bare. Some of the little bindle sockets were empty. She looked somehow different. She'd changed in some subtle way. There was about her an aura of joy much subdued by sadness.

Delia was the first to speak. She said: "We are glad to see you safe, my dear. And, too, I see you were successful."

Mevancy's face took on the color of the setting Zim. "Yes."

One or two other of the folk welcomed her; I didn't say anything until she spoke to me directly. Then I said: "Kuong is somewhere along the walls, trying to run the whole defense by himself. He'll be glad to see you."

"Of course. Thank you. When the battle is won I shall see you again."

After she had gone I realized that neither cabbage nor pigeon had passed our lips.

Because on the beautiful and terrible world of Kregen women as well as men fight as soldiers, women rise to high rank in the military hierarchy. Many and many a Jikai Vuvushi's name is written in the histories of war. There were Lady Chuktars in our ranks. Mevancy's position was vague in our establishment order. I'd given instructions that she held the rank of Ord Chuktar, that is, she was eight grades up in the rank of chuktar which took her higher than the equivalent brigade commander and into the area of divisional command. Yet she had no command within our army. The most sensible course for her to follow would be to stand with Kuong. I hoped she'd picked that up from my few words.

The observation I'd made concerning Kuong trying to run the show by himself was not strictly true, for Rodders with vastly more experience stood in command there. All the same, I'd wanted to stir Mevancy up a trifle.

A sharp and quickly muffled cry splattered from the group of brilliantly clad officers and aides at our back. I half-turned, then killed my instinctive smile. An enormous four-armed Djang carrying Delia's shields carried on talking to Korero. He was completely oblivious of the fact his massive boot rested on Nissa's dainty foot.

She gave him a sharp nudge into his armor with the end of her quarter-staff. Korero said: "Lift your foot, Tandu, if you wouldn't mind."

Dalki, Tandu's son, who carried Delia's personal banner, let rip a snort of amusement born of long experience of his father's little ways.

The aerial combat out there claimed my attention. The locus of the fighting drifted away from Makilorn. I refused to think of the fine young men and women burning and falling and dying in the skies above the desert. Somebody called out: "We're winning! They're flying off!"

Delia said: "I wonder."

As a matter of common sense before a battle I'd strapped on a harness of armor although I'd not yet donned the Mask of Recognition provided by my people. I began to feel claustrophobic with all these folk clustered around. Also, it was hot.

Delia said: "Look at Deb-Lu."

In a space apart to himself the Wizard of Loh sat on the stool we'd insisted he use. His eyes were closed and his face held the rapt look that indicated thaumaturgical processes were at work. We waited, uncertain what this might mean, and the buzz of conversation died away. At last Deb-Lu opened his eyes and looked at us. He used his staff to stand up.

"The college we have formed is extremely powerful. Under the Seven Arcades I doubt a stronger has existed in Loh." His face looked strained. "We now have definite intelligence that the Shanks have ceased their attempts to invade Mehzta. It is certain they have flown to join Carazaar."

No one spoke at this disastrous information.

Deb-Lu went on: "Khe-Hi and Ling-Li have located Carazaar's main force. Just below the horizon diametrically opposite from the air fight. They will hit any moment—land troops inside the city."

"So the cunning devil has faked a withdrawal and dragged our air off. Now he has a clear run in—except for the Hyrklese and Djang vollers."

376

Almost immediately screeches of alarm burst up all along the walls and towers. Like a cloud of insects the Shank fliers swarmed across the desert to hurl themselves on Makilorn.

They were cunning in their attacks. Our few Hyrklese and Djang pickets were swept aside. Fliers settled over the city like flies. Others disgorged troops onto the sands outside clearly with the intention of keeping our exterior forces engaged and so prevent them assisting in the city.

There were all manner of Fish Heads represented—Shants, Schtarkins, Schturgins and many others, including those called Vakstirns who rode any saddle animals they could steal in the lands they invaded. Instantly, the whole city was enveloped in combat.

Among the hordes dropping onto the city were many Whiptails. These Katakis would after their victory round up the population as slaves, that was their business. Until then they furnished the Fish Faces with invaluable assistance in dealing with the inhabitants of Paz, of knowing customs and of winkling out pockets of resistance and hiding places. The Chuliks in our ranks ran their thumbs up and down their tusks and promised dark deeds versus Katakis. The Yellow Tuskers were in the mood for a fight.

All over the city along the banks of the river the fighting boomed. Seg and Inch and Turko were down there, and Loriman and Kuong and Mevancy and others of my friends and comrades. I began to fret.

Delia said: "If you do, I shall."

How I hate all this business of fighting and killing! Battles, despite their undeniable academic and intellectual attraction, are anathema to any rational person. Yet we had to resist the Fish Faces. This was a doom and a destiny forced on me and not only by the Star Lords. If only the Makki-Grodno pus-loving Shanks would leave us alone!

Thus kept summarily out of the fight I watched from the tower top. Mind you, I could see what went on and give orders and conduct myself as an emperor should. I'd always tried to be an emperor who looked after the folk in his care. Perhaps I should have employed paktuns to fight for Vallia.

I was fidgeting about and gripping onto the hilt of the Savanti sword and then feeling to make sure the great Krozair longsword was securely at my back.

"By Lingloh!" rasped out one of the aides. "We're winning!"

"I believe we are at the moment," said Delia in her equable voice.

Certainly as the reports flowed in they were all of hurling the damned Fish Faces and their contemptible Whiptail allies back in bloody confusion.

The Shank forces outside who drove on to reinforce their fishy fellows within the walls were met by Clansmen in earth-shaking vove charges, by Nath na Kochwold's Phalanx which drove in crimson and bronze through the trident-wielding ranks like an avalanche devouring a village. Oh, yes, we were winning.

"I don't like this," I said. At the startled looks flung at me, I went on: "That Opaz-forsaken Carazaar has something nasty up his sleeve."

"Yes, Jak, and it has started." Deb-Lu spoke firmly, standing up from his stool. "He is casting. Very powerful. Very powerful indeed. Our forces will be driven back unless our new college can resist effectively. We can grip and hold him for a space—"

"And then?"

"They will roll over us."

"Then you must send me to—wherever in a Herrelldrin Hell it was."

"Last time he ran off—escaped to another plane."

"And that won the battle for us."

"Yes, Jak. If you go—"

"Oh, I'm going!"

Delia put her hand on my arm. Looking at her and devouring all her gorgeousness, as it were, in one huge draught, I said: "It's the only way."

"Yes."

The transition was swift. In the next heartbeat I was standing swaying about on insubstantial clouds. A silver sky encompassed me.

Directly ahead across the cloudscape underfoot loomed the throne of Carazaar.

Twenty

The throne bulked as I had seen it before, stupendous, barbaric, evil. Scale-covered draperies swept away, golden ornaments glinted in the silver light. The shadows lay at angles that corresponded to my own shadow—my own single shadow. Carazaar was here, then, on the same plane as myself. He was surrounded by his retinue, naked and half-naked girls of surpassing beauty. Monstrous shapes hovered vaguely at his back. The little scaled creature chained with the silver collar crouched against his right leg. N'gil, an obscenity of fish belly whiteness and gaping crimson mouth, huddled at the side, and the corpse-rotten thing hissed at my appearance.

Carazaar himself brooded on me, apparently entirely unshaken that I had sprung from nowhere onto this private plane of sorcery.

His face, scraped chalk-white, with paper-thin skin stretched gauntly over bones, with lipless mouth revealing a twin row of fang-like teeth, jagged as those of a shark, and with narrow nostrils pulsing, remained still a countenance from nightmare. And his eyes! Blue-black, they blazed with the mad red light of rhodopsin. His dark beard rested on his skeleton-like hands folded across the haft of his impressive and gilded axe. His gaze lowered on me. He did not speak.

He had his bevy of round-faced and barracuda-sharp Bowmaids of Loh in attendance, bows half-bent, ready to loose those deadly shafts into my guts.

They were not my immediate concern, for forward waddled the macabre shape of Arzuriel—Arzuriel with his four tentacles, each tipped by a fang-filled head. This multi-dimensional creature might be real or it might be a mere apparition. I had the strongest feeling the thing was real.

Fish-man or man-fish, Carazaar leaned forward to watch the contest.

The obscene thing waddled forward on bandy legs ready to rip chunks of bloody flesh away. I intended to stand no nonsense. With the smooth practiced movements of a Krozair of Zy I drew the great longsword. Arzuriel lurched forward, grasping for me, and I struck four shrewd blows.

Four fang-filled heads rolled upon the clouds. Before Arzuriel let rip a single screech I brought the brand down vertically and cleft him. In the next instant and without thought I leaped violently sideways. Four long Lohvian arrows passed through the space I had just vacated.

Without stopping, bounding from one foot to the other, I plunged on. Another bevy of shafts whistled past. These girls were good! There was really only one answer. I might bat arrows away as I had done in the Jikhorkdun of Huringa before I hurled a bloody leem's tail in fat Queen Fahia's face; that I'd surge forward to handstrokes was most doubtful.

Arzuriel had collapsed and I swirled back to him and gave my sword two cleansing swipes on his body. Sheathing the sword and hauling the Lohvian longbow forward took a mere moment. It was vitally necessary then to deflect incoming arrows with the bowstave before I could spring aside and whip out an arrow and nock it. My first shot struck the end Bowmaid. She just simply burst. Bits of skin and bone splattered through the air, a greenly-black cloud of nauseous gas sent a disgusting stench into my nostrils. The second shot did the same for the next of Carazaar's archers; the thing exploded in a gusting stink.

By the time I'd dealt with two more the form of Carazaar and his throne and retainers began to shimmer. He did not offer to waddle down and confront me with his axe. He'd tried that before and been bested. Now he thinned above the clouds, thinned and dissipated and vanished.

Yes, I admit it. As I stood there breathing lightly, there upon the clouds, slowly releasing the pull on the shaft I'd not loosed, I felt elation. Like any simpleton I experienced a great gush of joy. We'd done it!

The return transit proved as rapid as my arrival and in a twinkling I staggered just a few unsteady steps along Makilorn's western wall. The air rang with shouts of triumph. All about me the swods of our armies were

379

yelling their heads off in victory. Deb-Lu had not brought me back to the HQ tower; but in those heady moments with the battle won I gave that no thought. Away past the cultivations and over the desert the hosts of Carazaar fled. His fliers spiraled up and away—those who could escape the destructive fangs of our vollers. The Suns of Scorpio shone refulgently down in their glorious blazes of jade and ruby and altogether the scene made a wonderful picture.

Turning to look back into the city I saw a number of fires had been started but that our damage control parties were hard at work to contain the blazes. In the general excitement I had gone unnoticed. A ferocious bellow brought me around and a giant vove of a fellow waved one arm in my face and pointed with the other three out over the desert. I didn't know him.

"King!" he fairly erupted. "Look at the nulshes!"

A single look told me the story. The Shank vollers swarmed back into the attack and our fliers recoiled. Hordes of Fish Faces and Katakis flooded towards the city. I looked more closely—and I saw the full horror of what Carazaar was accomplishing.

A whole regiment of our churgurs swayed and toppled over. They fell lazily, like slow-motion dominoes falling. But they crashed to the desert sands, and immediately after their sister regiment brigaded with them fell.

Deb-Lu's voice at my side said: "Yes, Jak. His power is enormous. He can send key formations into catalepsy—"

"I sent him packing!" I fairly snarled out.

"Aye, Jak, aye, so you did. He has fled to another plane—"

I gave Deb-Lu a leery look. He sounded positively chirpy. "And?"

"Our new college also has power. We can send you after him—"

"Then, Deb-Lu—do it!"

As the transition swept me up I realized why Deb-Lu had not brought me back to the HQ tower. My feet hit hard stone, wreathing mists cleared, and there loomed Carazaar's damned throne. At once I skipped sideways and the Lohvian shafts whistled past. I'd no idea where we were. I shot two more of the Bowmaids so that they burst into clouds of nauseous gas. I moved diagonally and shafted the rest. That left it between Carazaar and me.

Ha!

The thing coalesced from the coils of mist. It thickened and swelled and grew into a shape I recognized. Oh, yes, I knew what this monster from a diseased nightmare had been, and was, and now was again.

This time there were no throngs of blood-lusting Ullars and Harfnars, banked on their seats, no gore-soaked sand beneath my feet, no ring of perching Impiters. This time—thank Zair!—Delia was not spread all white and naked upon a triangle of wood. And, this time, I did not swing a bunch of chains; this time I could shoot the damned Ullgishoa with a Lohvian longbow and smash in with a Krozair longsword.

Carazaar had summoned up this horror from my past and no doubt hoped to unnerve me thereby. The Ullgishoa, squamous and writhing, its upper half a hemispherical carapace of scales, its lower a contorted snakelike mass of tentacles, each tipped with an oozing protuberance, moved towards me. Its single huge eye, mucous dripping, yellow and ruby, had once been burst by the swing of chains. This time two Lohvian shafts obliterated the orb and it burst into a fountain of scarlet and yellow. I remembered, oh, yes, I remembered the barbaric savagery with which I'd dealt with the Ullgishoa. Latterly I'd tried to calm that primordial fury, gentle my own savagery. Well, if Carazaar played this game then once more I'd revert to that half-crazed Dray Prescot who'd first been transported to Kregen.

The Ullgishoa's tentacles writhed and oozed and it screeched its own death-throes—and then it faded and vanished. I stared at the throne.

For three heartbeats Carazaar's face lowered on me, the parchment skin stretched so tightly it seemed the bones must break through at any moment. Haziness engulfed the throne and the dais and its occupants. The mist concealed all before me. A swirling commotion in the fog focused above my head. I knew what thing it was that thrust through, for I'd met it among the rocks of Delia's Blue Mountains. Then I'd wielded a huge sword of war, blunt as a lead razor, and had a hard fight taking out the four eyes.

The shorgortz lumbered forward from the mist on its twelve legs. Its scales glistened with a crimson iridescence, their centers green-black, its four eyes blinked in rapid succession, and its tendrils groped forward to snatch me up so that the claws of the forelegs could stuff pieces of me down the parallel jaws. Carazaar had summoned a much more dangerous creature this time. Four Lohvian shafts were required to take out the eyes. The thing exuded a vomit-like stench, and thrashed about, seeking its prey. To get at Carazaar I must pass the shorgortz. Away went the longbow and with a subtle sibilance out came the Krozair brand.

I leaped.

Tendrils slashed and the claws raked and I struck powerful shrewd blows, almost overwhelmed by the stinks alone. The work was accomplished swiftly. I had no feelings either of compassion or hatred for the shorgortz. Driven by its own destiny like everyone else, it merely did what its nature compelled. I surged on past the limp tail out of the mist.

Carazaar's throne had vanished. In the same instant I felt the ground lurch beneath me and in the next I stood in a grassy glade surrounded by trees. Framed between mossy trunks ahead stood the damned throne.

What would be the next monster from my lurid past Carazaar would throw at me? Zair knew, there were enough of them. Two leems stalked out from the trees and stood, sizing me up. One had a black tuft to the end of his tail, similar to the second, who wore a silver collar. I wondered at Carazaar's reasoning here. Yes, leems are lethal, feral, vicious killers; they stood little chance against a fully-armed and experienced leem-hunter.

With the thought that Seg might fancy the two shots I sent two shafts from the bow. Care had to be exercised to hit the leem's main heart. Both creatures rolled over. Carazaar's face brooded on me.

I lifted the bow again ready to take a shot at him and he was gone!

So, too, was I. Deb-Lu's college hurled me in close pursuit and this time my feet hit sand—silver sand. I thought, then, I knew my next antagonist.

Mountainous, sixteen legs, eight tusks, whiplash tails, and a mouth like a river dredger lined with rows of jagged shark's teeth. Its four blackly-red nostrils quivered as it picked up my scent and its two saucer eyes swiveled to regard me. A boloth. The silver sand beneath my feet was a nice touch. Over that silver sand, once, had raced four friends of mine, bringing me help. So even as I reached up for a shaft I realized why Carazaar had put in those two leems. I knew, before my fingers touched the feathers, that I had but one arrow left.

With that last shaft from the Lohvian longbow I blotted out one eye.

Being a frugal old paktun I did not throw down the bow but slung it over my shoulder out of the way. You never knew when shafts would come your way. The way ahead now lay with the Krozair longsword.

No need to detail that combat, for I used my usual system in dealing with poor hostile creatures who, in seeking to fulfill their destiny, try in the process to eat me. Piece by piece the enormous monster was finished. By the time he was on the point of collapse I tried so to work it that I'd be as close as possible to the throne when at last the boloth fell.

The bellowings and screamings—for the boloth has no trunk—filled that pleasant glade with the sounds of horror, and the blood and stench with disgust. Carazaar sat still half-leaning forward resting on his axe. I was as close to him as I was going to get before he saw through my stratagem.

With the Krozair brand all smeared and slimed, thrusting forward, I leaped for Carazaar.

"You're an onker, Dray Prescot, an onker of onkers, a get-onker!"

The onward rush carried me forward with all the impetuosity of a numim lad chasing a Fristle fifi. His derisive shout echoed in my ears—"A get-onker!"—and I swear my blade touched a down-draped silk, for the damned throne took off and shot into the air before vanishing. I stood there like a veritable loon, like the onker I'd so often been dubbed.

"By the disgusting diseased tripes and innards of Makki Grodno! And also by the unmentionables of the Divine Lady of Belschutz! Deb-Lu—get me after him!"

I stood in a vast hall dimly lit by braziers which cast thick shadows from fat and rotund pillars. Incense stank on the air. Furtive movements filled the shadows with menace. And—there stood that confounded throne with Carazaar and his retinue waiting for me.

He hurled a couple of risslaca at me, which I bested, and strode on.

Various creatures stalked from the shadowed aisles, and I cut them down, and moved on. Syatras sought to ensnare me from the pillars, and I hewed my way past them. Animal and vegetable horrors were defeated. I marched on. The kreektizz nearly got me. When I'd fought him in what I always recalled as the adventure of the flame-haired siren he'd nearly got me then. I had to draw the old sailor knife to hack off the tail with which he'd lapped me. Most annoyingly he'd chewed up some of the leather bits and pieces of my armor. Still, I kept on moving forward towards Carazaar.

The floor tilted. It definitely tilted. A pillar crumbled across in a puff of mortar and brick dust and lunged for my head. The ceiling fell in as I dived desperately out of the way. A single flashing glance showed me a chunk of brick hitting that gaudy canopy over Carazaar's throne. Before I had time to marvel at that event the throne vanished. The floor still rocked like a swifter in a rashoon. I dragged in a breath and rolled away from falling debris and splashed into waves rolling up a sandy beach.

By this time, among all the purposeful rage I felt to get to grips with Carazaar, a tinge of tiredness crept. I know tiredness is a sin; but I had been rather leaping and prancing, hacking and hewing about, recently.

The forms of Khe-Hi-Bjanching and Ling-Li-Lwingling appeared hovering just above the edge of the surf.

"Where is the old devil, then?" I demanded. The beach lay deserted for as far as I could see in both directions. There was not a sail in sight—but the twin Suns of Scorpio flooded mingled streaming lights.

"The battle fluctuates, Dray. We are weakening him; but—"

"But what? Where in a Herrelldrin Hell is he?"

"Temporarily we've lost him—"

"Lost him!"

"We will find him. He is planning a different attack. And, as Seg would say, my old dom, you need the breather."

"H'mf," I grumped. "I suppose so. But for the sweet sake of Opaz find the rast fast!"

Before the last word was out of my mouth away went sea and sand and sky and with them the friendly familiar Suns of Scorpio, and in their place a great and vasty darkness lay over the land.

Into that blackness pricked dots of red fire. Oh, yes, they have been likened to the Watchfires of Hell, the red rhodopsin eyes of schrepims. There were eight eyes, four pairs of them, the same number of schrepims that had escaped in that adventure with Unmok the Nets, and if some light was not shed shortly upon the proceedings then I'd be—I stopped my maundering.

I could make out the forms of the green-scaled lizard-men. I could see them in the darkness with remarkable clarity. I recalled as I stalked on that previously I'd been surprised at how well I saw down various dungeons. Then I recalled something—this was the handiwork of the Star Lords!

Schrepims are incredibly quick and agile, they are also reputed to have the Powers of the Dark, although this I doubt. If this was a sample of Carazaar's new approach then he'd upped the scale of his attack a thousandfold. What, clearly, he didn't know was that the Everoinye, in response to my request, had bestowed that gift upon me. The Slacamen started to stalk me and I went bald-headed for the nearest and upset him a trifle and so chopped him. In that old fight I'd had a thraxter. Now—the difference resulted in the rapid disintegration of the schrepims and an equally rapid transference to another plane. So fast are these lizard men one had sliced his thraxter cunningly enough to sever the breastplate straps on one side and the thing dangled down so that I had to discard it. I threw the kax down and stared upon my new surroundings.

Familiarity, as they say in Clishdrin, breeds contempt. The awesome power wielded by these mages of hurling people through immaterial planes of existence could never be taken for granted. Each shift of scene represented vast amounts of kharrna expended. The very thought of what was taking place was enough to send shivers down one's spine. I own I felt that most strongly—the sheer overbearing awesomeness of this whole experience.

Now I must relate what have to be some of the most painful passages of my life upon the cruel world of Kregen.

I stood in the dear familiar garden of Esser Rarioch my home above the city of Valkanium in Valka. Far below me the bay glittered in the streaming mingled radiance of the Suns of Scorpio. As I gaped about Carazaar and his infernal throne reared up among the rose bushes that were Delia's particular pride. Starting off towards him I was filled with such fury that—well, it is all highly painful. There were six of them and they came at me each in his own particular fashion. Balass the Hawk. Turko. K. Kholin Dorn. Hap Loder. Rees and Chido. Comrades all, they charged forward to slay me.

Difficult—oh, aye, difficult!—to recall let alone relate. I fought them. And, yes, I slew them all, every last one. They did not explode into disgusting bits and pieces stinking to high heaven. They remained sprawled on the grass in that quiet garden, lax and limp in death, the blood bright upon them. My comrades, slain by my hand, all bloody and dead. I gazed stupidly.

"By the glass eye and brass sword of Beng Thrax!" I stared at Balass. "By

Djan-kadjiryon!" I stared at Kytun. "By the Black Chunkrah!" I stared at Hap Loder. "By Morro the Muscle!" I stared at Turko. "By Krun!" I stared at Rees and Chido.

The combat had been intense and ferocious and they'd nicked me a few times and done for the rest of my armor. Blood-spattered, I stood forth clad only in the old scarlet breechclout.

Shame filled me. There had been six of them, six of the finest fighting men Kregen could boast, and I'd beaten them. Prowess—don't talk to me about prowess, think of the misery the pursuit of prowess brings. I was tired, oh, yes, tired to the bone—but there was more to be done!

Twin shadows moved upon the grass and a great glittering golden Kildoi fronted me. For a heartbeat I imagined I had to fight Korero the Shield.

Then I saw the truth.

I felt that recognition like a vove hoof in the guts.

And—the bastard had his tail hand all present and correct.

The splendid golden Kildoi with his four arms and handed tail carried shield, spear and three swords. With only one sword he had proved he could best me. Always, as you know, I am prepared to meet a better swordsman than I am. I have never claimed to be the best swordsman of two worlds. In this arrogant Kildoi I had met a better swordsman, if not, as I had been assured, a greater.

A throaty cackle of laughter gusted from Carazaar's throne.

If this was the end of my adventures on Kregen, then this was the end. He had to be played as I played a many-tentacled or many-legged wild beast. He had to be deceived by cunning other than the feints known to swordmasters. I started on him and allowed everything that is and has ever been Dray Prescot to flow into the great Krozair longsword.

Of course he was very good, he was the very best I'd ever met.

His tail hand went first, chopped as he tried to stab past the scarlet breechclout.

He was hitting me. I did not feel the cuts. All the Krozair disciplines flowed into a single continuous effort. In the end he was done for. He went down to one knee and the shattered remnants of his shield held aloft vainly tried to keep out the Krozair brand. No hatred for him and no compunction; just the last cleansing blow to allow me surcease.

His name? That, surely, is unnecessary? I spared him a grave salute with the bloodied blade. "Go to whatever gods will have you, Prince Mefto A'Shanofero, Prince of Shanodrin—Mefto the Kazzur!"

With the sword lifted so ridiculously I looked across the garden and saw, and felt—I do not know what I felt. They walked slowly towards me, splendid, lithe, clad in war harness, handsome, lethal. The shorter did not say: "Well, my old dom!" Instead he lifted his bow. The taller swung his axe.

My strength was draining away and yet I could not rest. I knew exactly what they'd do, for we'd done it a thousand times together. I might flick away the first two, even three arrows. By then the Saxon pattern axe would be carving me into pieces. There was but the one chance.

My right hand left the hilt of the sword and the haft of my old sailor knife snugged sweetly. I drew and threw. Two streaks criss-crossed. The Lohvian longbow shaft caromed off the upheld Krozair brand. The knife slugged into that strong virile face. No thought! No thought! Axe and longsword twirled and licked and then I stepped back, panting, and stared with self-loathing horror upon the two corpses on the grass.

What to say! What to think! Nothing—nothing in all the ghastly world of Kregen. If I thought I had plumbed the depths of horror the movement by the red roses showed me that horror has no depth, there is no end, there is no worse, no worst of hell and horror and damnation.

She stepped forward with that heartbreakingly beautiful swing. The rapier, the Jiktar, glittered in her right hand. Her left was covered by the wickedly sharp talons of her Claw, her jikvar. She half-smiled in the old familiar way. The light of the suns caught in bright radiance in her hair. I stood. I just stood.

The Claw swept towards my head in a cunning blow that would remove my face. Instinct alone caused me to slide away, pivoting, avoiding the rapier thrust. The Krozair brand hung limply in my left hand, dangling. I was gasping for air I could barely draw into my lungs. I must stand still, must accept the needle. She moved with that graceful undulating movement towards me again.

A voice from the air snapped: "Dray Prescot!"

Refulgent yellow light blossomed. I knew that yellow radiance. The voice went on: "Stand away. Look at your comrades."

I looked. The pathetic twisted heaps splattered with the blood of my making lay scattered on the grass. They sloughed. Flesh dripped and bones glinted yellow and pink; then they exploded into gouts of green and black ichor stinking nauseatingly in that fragrant garden.

"They are in Makilorn, fighting Fish Faces. This is not Delia. You must make the final effort, Dray Prescot. You must!"

"Zena Iztar!"

"The battle is nearly won. Carazaar's power will be gone with this last throw. Nerve yourself to strike down Delia of Delphond, Delia of the Blue Mountains—so that you may save and return to her!"

The Claw hissed past my face and the rapier scorched my ribs.

This was not Delia! This was a black phantasm from the kharrna of Carazaar. I brought the great Krozair longsword up, cunningly, swervingly, brought the superb brand down in a killing blow.

The Claw flashed to intercept. Like a chunkscreetz it caught and trapped the bloodied blade. The great and superb Krozair longsword snapped.

The Krozair brand snapped clean across.

The fact registered with such a colossal shock I felt the rapier's kiss as I desperately slid aside.

Carazaar's throaty laughter echoed in the garden of my home.

The Claw ripped bloody flesh from my side.

All I had ever really wanted in life was Delia. All the rest had been thrust upon me by fate, or the Scorpion, or the Savanti and the Star Lords. I recall little of what followed. I drew the Savanti sword. I used the Savanti blade. I fought. When it was over the yellow radiance washed upon the phantasmal corpse of Delia and I closed my eyes.

Zena Iztar said: "Carazaar's power is broken. The Fish Faces are defeated. Now, Dray Prescot, you must rest."

Yellow warmth engulfed me and when I opened my eyes and orientated myself I discovered I was back on Earth. Zena Iztar must have patched me up enough to survive. I was in Africa. I did what I could until the Scorpion snatched me up again to return to Kregen.

The Star Lords summoned me to their presence and I detected—or imagined I detected—the faintest note of approval. The Shanks had been decisively driven away. Oh, yes, we all expected their return some day. As for Delia—how can you imagine my feelings when I saw her again? I told her the whole story. "And I clawed you, my heart?"

"Aye, most damnably!"

She gave that impish laugh that betides a mischievous intent. "And my little Claw broke your great Krozair longsword?"

"Aye."

"Still, the Savanti sword—"

"Well, that is another matter."

Shortly after that on the way to Valka the Everoinye dispatched me off to Earth where I am now. They dropped me in Munich where I used a whole heap of cassettes to relate this section of my story on Kregen. I have also, incidentally, seen the books. And very nice they are, to be sure. I know I shall be summoned by the Scorpion soon and am glad to have had the opportunity to tidy up the events that occurred in Loh.

Mevancy, by the way, married Kuong and gave birth to beautiful twin girls, both of whom will grow bindles on their forearms.

As for me, I await the summons of the Scorpion.

There is, after all, only Delia who matters in two worlds.

We-ell, yes. That is undeniably true. But you who have faithfully followed my narrative will be well aware of other people who mean much to me.

I am sending these cassettes off to Alan Burt Akers for I feel the Star Lords looming near and I wish to complete this section of my history. To follow are some uproarious goings on in Balintol and Tarkinlass and the reckless proceedings of Joldo Ironhand, the Kov of Low Vreng, so there is still much to relate. As for the Skantiklar, Carazaar and the Shanks, well, of course they are controlled and tamed at the moment; but I know they are up there on Kregen waiting for my return.

Who can foretell the future?

As I never tire of saying, all I ever really wanted was Delia, Delia of Delphond, Delia of the Blue Mountains.

Twenty-one

My name is Drak Valhan Prescot, and I am the Emperor of Vallia. My wife, Silda Segutoria Valhan Prescot, is the Empress of Vallia.

I must confess I found it extremely difficult to believe my father's fantastic stories of a world with only one yellow sun, with only a tiny silver moon, and with no diffs at all but only apims like ourselves. Now, I have to believe. For me this all began one pleasant evening as we strolled along the balcony after dinner in the palace of Vondium the Proud City.

A squawk in the air drew my attention. Up there flew a scarlet and golden raptor, a giant hunting bird of remarkable aspect. I'd thought I'd seen such a bird as a youngster; but my father pooh-poohed the idea. Now I know the raptor to be the Gdoinye, the spy and messenger of the Everoinye. In the next instant I was upended in a blue radiance, the enormous form of a blue Scorpion seized me away and I recovered my senses to find myself in this city.

The Star Lords had provided me with decent clothes and local currency and to my amazement I could converse with the inhabitants in their own language. The reason for these extraordinary occurrences must, it is clear, be that what happened to my father and mother should be made known to Mr. Alan Burt Akers, and thence to you who listen to the cassette tapes I am recording in my hotel room. I shall post them at once, and return—I trust, by Vox!—to Kregen.

There is no doubt about it, I do not think I could ever become used to living on a world with only one sun.

To begin on a personal note, I'd just returned from a long and arduous campaign in Pandahem during which we'd dealt with some severity with the Bloody Menaham. There were stupendous celebrations when the victors of the Lohvian campaign around Makilorn joined us. The religious observances continued for days, and the winding processions chanting 'Oolie Opaz' filled the boulevards and avenues bordering the canals of Vondium.

Subsequently and in grave conclave agreement was reached. Seg

Segutorio and Milsi were to become Emperor and Empress of Pandahem. This would unite the island and ensure peace.

I well remember my father exclaiming with a sigh of resignation: "Well, by Krun, Inch and Sasha are King and Queen of Hyr-Thoth-Ghat-Loh, now Milsi and Seg have been saddled with an empire—" And my mother softly interrupting: "Oh, you grizzly old graint, we'll find an empire for them, as Dee-Sheon is my witness!" She really is the most remarkable mother anybody can have. And I now recognize that should be 'in two worlds.' She went on: "Very soon Mevancy, your little pigeon, will be Empress of Walfarg."

"And," growled my father in his gravel-shifting voice, "she won't be your detestable Queen of Pain, either, by Zair."

When he says: 'By Zair,' I own it as a Krozair of Zy. 'By Vox' is good Vallian. I often wonder, though, about his frequent use of the Hamalese 'By Krun.' I really do.

He added: "All these kings and queens and emperors and empresses cavorting about me, a simple sailorman—by Zim-Zair, it's uncanny!"

In this I think his reference to a simple sailorman is a trifle—well, on Kregen we'd say "Hesink," which is similar to 'de trop', too much. I've seen the kings and queens reduced to a quivering jelly merely because he looked at them in his Dray Prescot way.

Trouble erupted over in Tarkinlass and there was nothing for it but that he must fly off there immediately to sort things out. Mother spoke to him most strictly. Other people pointed out various facts. In the end, grumbling like Muruaa, he agreed to let the army go and sort things out as was their duty.

"I'm becoming just like Mevancy called me," he burst out. He mentioned Makki Grodno and the Divine Lady of Belschutz. "Just a damned cabbage!"

A nesting of new flutduins had just come to their prime. These superb birds, originally from Djanduin, were capable of easily carrying two people. I value our Vallian aerial cavalry as highly as our Phalanx, as my guard corps.

"That's it!" declared my father on a morning when the suns shone quite nicely. "A flight! Delia, my heart, let's fly aloft and get some fresh air into our lungs!"

"We'll take a picnic."

"Capital!"

"You remember the impiter, and flying from Umgar Stro?"

"Aye. Aye, I remember. And all the rest, all the rest. Those days will never be forgotten—"

"Particularly when there are innumerable puppet shows, and plays and books, recounting the astonishing adventures of Dray Prescot."

My father let rip that astounding noise he claims is a laugh. "Most of 'em are downright lies!"

"Not all. Not all."

The flutduin was brought to the high terrace. He was a truly magnificent bird, brilliant of plumage and with a spirit—perhaps—to match his passengers. They climbed aboard, laughing, and fixed the clerketers. The bird gave two enormous beats of those curved wings and soared aloft.

As, shading our eyes against the suns, we stared up, a scarlet and golden bird, small beside the flutduin, spiraled overhead.

In these latter days my father had told me of the Star Lords and the Gdoinye. Silda held my arm. Up and up soared the flutduin.

I saw it all, clearly, without hindrance, and marveled at the wonder.

Blueness grew about the bird. The shape of a giant Scorpion formed. Hovering, gigantic, the Scorpion lowered over the soaring bird. Redness shone down lambently.

So often my father had said it. Delia, Delia of Delphond, Delia of of the Blue Mountains, and Dray Prescot, Lord of Strombor and Krozair of Zy, Empress and Emperor of Paz, were carried up in the blue radiance of the Scorpion into the scarlet infinity of the Star Lords.

I know exactly what he was saying.

"By Zair! What now!"

A Glossary to the Lohvian Cycle

Compiled by Els Withers.

References to the six books of the cycle are given as:

SRB: *Scorpio Reborn*
SAS: *Scorpio Assassin*
SIV: *Scorpio Invasion*
SAB: *Scorpio Ablaze*
SDR: *Scorpio Drums*
STR: *Scorpio Triumph*

NB: Previous glossaries covering items not included here can be found in Volume 5: *Prince of Scorpio*, Volume 7: *Arena of Antares*, Volume 11: *Armada of Antares*, Volume 14: *Krozair of Kregen*, Volume 18: *Golden Scorpio*, Volume 22: *A Victory for Kregen*, Volume 26: *Allies of Antares*, Volume 32: *Seg the Bowman*, and Volume 37: *Warlord of Antares*.

A

Accursed of Tsung-Tan: those sentenced to live one hundred lives before admittance to Gilium.

Afflatus, Path of: one of the paths of Alternative Magic.

Alternative Magic: theory of magic which attempts to perform the same work as that done by sorcerers (magic) and by gods (miracles) solely through one's own human powers.

Ankharum: city at the western edge of the Great Salt Desert.

Annorpha Aigrette: prize in an archery tournament at the Springs of Benga Annorpha.

Annorpha, Springs of: hot springs located in the oasis town of Orphasmot.

ham Armit, Taranto: the Rango of Firthlad, Khibil Jiktar aboard *Dovad Daisy*. SAB

Arngalf Galfarn: a legendary warrior who was tested by the god Schnurrdun the All-seeing.

Aron the Ferry: a ferryman on the River of Drifting Leaves in Makilorn. SRB

Artifices of the Sword: Krozair treatise written some 2,500 years ago by San Zefan, Krzy.

Arzuriel: demon employed by Carazaar, with four tentacular appendages instead of arms, each having a pseudo-head at its tip, a bulb-like growth containing two eyes set beside the fanged mouth.

Asatha, Deldar Paline: Jiktar Vuvushi wounded by Shanks. SAB

"Asleep by the Desert Lily": a plaintive little tune from Tsungfaril.

autmoil: stranger.

Avenue of Splendid Arches: a street in Makilorn.

B

Bakkar, by: oath used by Naghan the Bristle.

Bargrad the Pellin: Brokelsh whom Prescot recruited in Taranjin to resist the Shank occupation. SIV

Bargray the Tumbs: a deckhand on the vessel *Quaynt's Fortune.* SIV

Bella Chuan-Hsei: an actress traveling with Mevancy in the Farang Parang. SAB

Beng Frust, Law of: law stating that when you urgently need an item you cannot find it.

Benormy: Brukaj retainer in the retinue of Chan Holomin. SDR

bindles: spines biologically generated in the forearms of Sinnalixi women, dischargeable at will.

Blanky: preysany ridden by Prescot.

bliem: life.

blotto: Kregish for "ditto."

Bog: the name given to a fellow handy at bashing evildoers.

Boromir of the Ashes: place where Caspar the Peaker was sent by the Everoinye.

Borrakesh: kovnate in Tarankar.

Braga: Brokelsh retainer in the retinue of Chan Holomin. SDR

brellam: a variety of tree. They grow straight up and very tall. They spread wide branches and turn up their leaves in serried masses of cups. They prevent most of the rain and suns-light from falling to the surface, holding the liquid within their cellular structure. Consequently the ground beneath is relatively bare of lesser vegetation.

bronze boxes: the vollers built by the Shanks use bronze boxes rather than silver boxes for lift and motive power.

C

Cabbage: Mevancy's nickname for Prescot.

Caran, San: Repositer and would-be murderer of Kuong Vang Talin.

Carazaar: a sorcerer who seems to be connected with the Shank invasion. Described as having parchment-white skin, smoldering red eyes, a full brown beard, a lipless mouth with double rows of fangs, and mere nostril slits for a nose. SRB, SAB

"Carnation Pink and Iris Blue": a song of Houdondrin in Loh.

Caspar the Peaker: nickname of Caspar Del Vanian.

Chaadur na Dorfu: known as Chaadur the Striker, Kurinfaril, alias used by Prescot in Tarankar.

Chandro, San: one of the Queen of Tsungfaril's Repositers. SAS

Chang-So: helmsman of the vessel *Garrus*. SIV

Chang-So, San: court wizard of the Queen of Tsungfaril, who nurses a grudge against Prescot. SAS

Changwutung: town where Prescot was dropped by the Star Lords into the middle of a walled garden.

Chanshong: a city of Walfarg.

Chardaz: homeplace of Mevancy.

Chasserfic: snakelike water animal, with eight limbs, a fish's tail like an eel's, hinged jaws, and fangs all the way up to its throat.

Chem: territory of jungles and hostile inhabitants in the equatorial latitudes of Loh.

Cheng, San: Repositer of Trylon Kuong after the death of San Caran, with a sharp nose and rounded chin. SAB

Chentoi: a race of diffs.

Cheryl: daughter of the jewelsmith Hwang Tei; eloped with Naghan the Cheerful against her father's wishes and was miraculously saved by rain.

Chiako the Gut: cadade of Tuong Mishuro's guard. SRB

Chikitto the Unerring, by: an oath used by thieves in Makilorn.

Ching-Lee: female companion of Wink. SAS

Chuan-Hsei, Bella: an actress traveling with Mevancy in the Farang Parang. SAB

Claransmot: oasis to the west of Orphasmot.

Clishdrin: home of aphoristic people.

Clovang: region of Tarankar consisting of mountains and valleys.

Clovangjin: chief city of Clovang.

Coram the Flatch: a dwa-Hikdar from 2ESW. SIV

Cromal: yet another school of wizardry.

crowpin: type of carnivorous plant.

Csitra: twin sister of Queen Satra; died in childhood.

D

Dahemin: exceedingly ancient name given in southern Loh to the twin moons of Kregen.

Dalendin, Song of: song of the triumph of lovers Ornol and Vilia through adversity.

"A day short of Eternity is still Eternity": saying attributed to San Blarnoi.

Deliverance: name given to the jury-rigged flying craft stolen by Prescot and his friends from the Shanks. SAB

Del Vanian, Caspar: a kaogoinye charged with killing Queen Leone of Tsungfaril; also a painter. SAS

Demaskar Persuasion: a magical order having some very real powers.

Dien-sing the Droopeyed: character in the song of Dalendin.

dikaster: in the religion of Tsung-Tan, those trained to recognize a reincarnated paol-ur-bliem.

diviner: dikaster

Din'nagul: country in southern Loh.

Djondalar, by: oath used by Prescot.

Domesti: Och retainer in the retinue of Chan Holomin. SDR

Dondo!: a way of saying, "Good!"

Dovad Daisy: Hamalese airship sent to fight the Shanks in Tarankar. SAB

Drajak the Sudden: alias used by Prescot in southern Loh. SRB

Dravka: Brokelsh retainer in the retinue of Chan Holomin. SDR

Drifting Leaves, River of: a dry river which once flowed southwards through Makilorn.

dwaprijjers: swift piratical vessels that ply the trade along the Ivilian Keys.

Drums, People of the: Inhabitants of the Realm of the Drums. Pallid of face, down-drooping of whiskers, with slack features and small, too-red mouths. They wear different kinds of jeweled fillets in their hair.

E

eenlan: swift little arachnoid, all glistening brown, yellow, and black, which is said to be able to hear your muscles moving your bones about inside your body.

Erlik: captain of *Vendayha Lady*. STR

Erlon the Biceps: Jurukker in the Empress's Devoted Life Guard. STR

Eternal Twilight, City of: an ancient city in the jungles of Loh, under a time-freezing spell.

F

Fang, Ron Dang: also called Rodders; a mercenary, a Bowman of Loh, companion to Kirsty. SAS

Fansi: a Fristle serving-maid in the palace of Makilorn. SAS

Fan-Si: a Fristle member of the band of Nath the Ron and Layla. SIV, SAB

Fantong, Na-Si-: Wizard of Loh, seeking the Skantiklar. SAS

Farang Parang: wastelands between Ankharum and Makilorn.

Farantino, Orlon: known as the Rekarder, a Khibil retainer of Layla na Borrakesh. SIV

Fardo the Splitter: brother of Fan-Si, taken by Shanks.

Fariang, Laygon: a lord with a stutter who traveled with Mevancy in the Farang Parang. SAB

Fashti: a shapely Fristle maiden, a member of Rikky Tardish's troupe. SRB

Fenella: Puncture Lady who attended Prescot when he was paralyzed. SRB

Ferlie: a follower of the New Empire of Loh in Shamfrin. SDR

Fing-Na: a thief of Makilorn. SAS

ham Finral, Hangol: a Hamalese Strom, cadade of Vad Leotes' guard, adherent of Lem, who took an intense dislike to Prescot. SRB

Finsi the Silver: a member of Prescot's guerilla force in Tarankar. SIV

Flamdi: name of slouncher on which Prescot crossed the Gleek Frankai. SRB

flamin: south-Lohvian term for a sand scarf.

flang: a type of vermin.

Flarvil: a Fristle member of 1ESW. SAB

Flesh, Path of the: one of the paths of Alternative Magic.

flitchlak: a variety of tree similar to a syatra, which uses sticky tendrils to whip its prey up to the flower to be eaten.

fluttclepper flick: hell for leather—very fast and risky speed.

Foke the Clis: Fristle whom Prescot recruited in Taranjin to resist the Shank occupation. SIV

Folly: slave of Princess Licria, frozen together with her in the underground Realm of the Drums, daughter of a Sybli mother and an apim father.

Fu-Ming-Fung: alias used by Caspar Del Vanian.

Fwang, Wei: needleman who cared for Llodi when he was wounded by Lady Pulvia. SAS

G

Gal-ag-Foroming: teacher of Ra-Lu-Quonling. SIV

Galfarn, Arngalf: a legendary warrior who was tested by the god Schnurrdun the All-seeing.

Gandil the Mak: a crony of Strom Hangol, a beetle-browed fellow with black hair and a bad skin, who habitually carried sword and axe. Killed by Prescot. SRB

Garrus: vessel on which Prescot took passage downriver from Ternantung. SIV

garsun: flour made from the roots of the gola-gola plant.

Gdoinya: sister bird to the Gdoinye.

Gdoinyi: the Gdoinye and Gdoinya.

Ge-Fu-Schian: a Trylon, original employer of Wa-Te. SDR

Ghat Gate: a gate in Taranjin.

Gilium: paradise in the religion of Tsung-Tan.

glahber: a "poor devil."

Glarkie Dunes: one of the names given to the desert to the east of She of the Sundering.

Gleek Frankai: the Great Salt Desert in southern Loh.

Glima: a Gon girl who escaped from the Shanks with Prescot and his friends. SAB

Glinting Charm, River of: river running through the town of Changwutung.

Glitch Riders: a nation of nomads living to the north of the Farang Parang.

gola-gola: a plant whose massive roots are ground to yield flour.

gorse: a type of bush.

Goyt, by: oath used by Grodnims.

Great Salt Desert: desert found in the southern part of Loh, also called the Gleek Frankai. SRB

Grotal the Reducer: a Grodnim deity.

Guishsmot: home town of Walfger Olipen.

Gurong: a Deldar in the caravan of Vad Leotes. SRB

H

Hamish ham Thanstrer: Kapt of the Hamalian air fleet sent to fight the Shank occupiers of Tarankar.

Hamparz, Sternum: Ship Hikdar of *Dovad Daisy*. SAB

Hangol ham Finral, Strom: cadade of Vad Leotes' guard, a Hamalian, adherent of Lem, who took an intense dislike to Prescot. SRB

Hanjhin: oasis to the west of Orphasmot.

Hanshar, Ortyg: the chief priest of Makilorn. SAS

"Happy the Day of the Shearing": a Lohvian song.

Hargon, San: one of Strom Hangols' cronies. Had Tuong Mishuro killed, and was killed in turn by Prescot. SRB

Havil Resplendent: Hamalese airship sent to fight the Shanks in Tarankar. SAB

Havil Resurgent: Hamalese airship sent to fight the Shanks in Tarankar. SAB

Heart: oft-used Lohvian term for the Chunkrah's Eye.

"Her Hair as Red as the Robin's Breast": an old Lohvian song.

"Hesink": expression meaning "*de trop*", "too much."

Hiclantung: Lohvian city, home of Queen Satra.

Hien-Mi, San Nalgre: one of the Queen of Makilorn's Repositers. SAS

Hilzim, Harulf ham: Vad of Quinvarn, Fleet Admiral of the Hamalese fleet sent to fight the Shanks in Tarankar. SAB, STR

Hinjanchung: a town on the River of Glinting Charm.

Hirrume Warrior: Hamalese airship sent to fight the Shanks in Tarankar. SAB

Hlo-Hli: god of the old Lohvian Empire.

Hoban the Brows: varterist aboard *Dovad Daisy*. SAB

Holi and Hola: most common Lohvian name for the twin moons of Kregen.

Holomin, Chan: Strom of Wioldrin, encountered by Prescot in the underground maze beneath the City of Eternal Twilight.

ham Homath, Nath: Hikdar in the Hamalese fleet sent to fight the Shanks in Tarankar. SAB

Hondar the Frogan: ship Deldar of *Dovad Daisy*. SAB

Horvil ham Verherne: Hamalian mercenary in the army of Na-Si-Fantong. STR

Hosifi: see Shiang, Hosifi.

Houdondrin: a country in Loh.

Hsienu, Nath: also called Nath the Bollard, master of the vessel *Garrus*; addicted to Jikalla. SIV

H'siung Garden: a restaurant at the Springs of Benga Annorpha.

Huang: a contestant for the Annorpha Aigrette. SAS

Hurlving, Hargon ham: a Kapt, temporary commander of the Hamalian fleet in Loh. STR

Hwang: one of two guards who watched Prescot fall from the sky into a carp pond. SIV

Hwang, Pling-Fe-: noble of Tsungfaril whose newborn baby was supposed to receive the spirit of the assassinated Queen. SAS

Hwang Tei: jewelsmith whose daughter Cheryl eloped with Naghan the Cheerful.

Hwangin: king of Hiclantung. STR

hyrzim: one of two styles of scabbard for a Krozair longsword, highly decorated.

Hytak: race of diffs each having two arms, two legs, and a sinuous tail to which an edged blade is often strapped. The backbone of many armies and many mercenary bands, hytakim are valued as fighting men and women. Their armor and weapons are maintained in impeccable condition.

I

Ib, Path of the: one of the paths of Alternative Magic, in which the tenth corner is of special significance.

Ibdrin: spirit-land, where the souls or spirits of murdered or violently-killed people are believed to cluster, waiting for vengeance

Inglewong, Lady Floria: companion to Trylon Nanji Tawang. SRB, SAS

Inky: Valkan boy with whom Prescot flew a kite. SRB

Ishti!: a Shank war cry.

"It's no good crying after you've upset the calsany.": No use crying over spilled milk.

Ivory Lorn: an abandoned city in the Farang Parang.

Iwanhan, San: philosopher who suffered at the hands of well-intentioned torturers.

J

The Jeweled Crook: a lodging house in Larishsmot, where Prescot stayed when he was paralyzed. SRB

Jimjim the Randell: a slave in Shank-occupied Taranjin. SIV

K

Kadar the Hammer: alias used by Prescot in Loh. STR

Kang the Hook: a fisherman of Makilorn. SRB

kaogoinye: an assassin working at the behest of the Everoinye.

Kaopan: in the religion of Tsung-Tan, a ceremony to ensure that a dead paol-ur-bliem will not be reincarnated.

Kaour: death-dealer.

Kei-Wo the Dipensis: a thief of Makilorn. SAS

Kendur: name used for the Emperor by the Emperor's Sword Watch.

khan: a silver coin of Tsungfaril.

Kirsty: cousin to Leone, later Queen of Makfaril. SAS

Koo, Kling: a woman of Makilorn.

Koskei of the Daggered Tail, by: a Kataki oath.

krad: patriotic bronze coin minted by the Presidio of Vallia in the Times of Troubles and which forms the main part of the Vallian Freedom Army's wages.

kreektizz: a type of ferocious beast.

kregoinya: a female agent of the Star Lords.

Kronenvar: land neighboring Shirrendrin.

krosturr: one of two styles of scabbard for a Krozair longsword, plain and unadorned.

Kuong Vang Talin: Trylon of Taranik, recently come of age. SRB, SAS, SAB

Kwang: a bandit who attacked Prescot's caravan in southern Loh. SRB

L

laiker: Lohvian variety of shortsword.

Languin: see Nuong-Hi.

Lanlo the Plump: a follower of the New Empire of Loh in Shamfrin, husband of Milly. SDR

Lao-Chan the Staver: bowright in Taranjin who was killed for making defective bows. SIV

lap-lap: a thigh-length wrap-around garment.

Larghos: bosun of *Garrus*. SIV

Larghos Jankwa ti Fakwald: cadet aboard *Vendayha Lady*. STR

Larghos the Lame, Kapt: a soldier poet killed in an ambush 1500 years ago.

Larghos the Throstle: a member of the band of Nath the Ron and Layla, with a fine singing voice. SIV

Larghos the Trevoilyan: a Hikdar aboard *Shankjid*. SAB

Larishsmot: town at the eastern end of the Old Lorn trail.

Larrigen: see Parfang.

Lavonth: predatory beast, about the size of a greyhound, a pelt patterned in zigzag of tawny and umbre.

Laygon Fariang: a lord with a stutter who traveled with Mevancy in the Farang Parang. SAB

Layla na Borrakesh, Kovneva: fought against the Shanks in Tarankar. SIV

Leone: Queen of Tsungfaril, paol-ur-bliem, assassinated in her bath. SAS

Leone: female companion of Wink, paol-ur-bliem, one of three heirs to the throne of Makfaril. SAS

Leotes: see li Ningwan, Leotes.

by Lhun: an oath used by Mul-lu-Manting.

Licria: Princess Majestrix of Walfarg, frozen for hundreds of years in the underground Realm of the Drums by a magic spell until released by Prescot.

lictrix: a saddle animal native to Loh, related to the sectrix.

Lin: one of two guards who watched Prescot fall from the sky into a carp pond. SIV

Lindy-ma-Sendiyin: a follower of the New Empire of Loh in Shamfrin. SDR

Lingli, Mistress: puncture lady who attended to Wink when he was stabbed by a thief. SAS

Lingloh, by: an oath used by Whonbim.

Lingshi: mistress of the Jeweled Crook. SRB

Lisa the Forthright: leader of the Pilgrims.

lisehn: variety of tree from which the fine Vallian bowstaves are built.

Llodi the Voice: a guard in the retinue of Vad Leotes, known for his singing voice and splendid fissured nose. SRB

Loctrux: a deity worshipped in Tsungfaril before the advent of Tsung-Tan.

Lohrhiang: a priest of Tsung-Tan who conquered the followers of Loctrux.

Lola the Assandra: a follower of the New Empire of Loh in Shamfrin. SDR

Loptyg the Muncible: serving in the Emperor's Sword Watch. SIV

Luan-Chi the Flexible: Thanko thief recruited by Prescot in Taranjin to assist in sabotage. SIV

Lulli Quincy: proprietress of a lodging house in Makilorn. SRB

Lunky: apprentice to Tuong Mishuro, later succeeding him as a dikaster. SRB, SAS

Lurgan the Vandour: Hytak crossbowman in the retinue of Vad Gochert. SDR

Lush Bonhomie: a tavern in Makilorn where Prescot foiled a theft. SAS

Luxurious Rest, Chambers of: suite in the palace of Makilorn, the old Chemzite Chambers.

Luz: Lohvian name for the red sun of Kregen.

lynxor: Lohvian term for lord.

lynxora: Lohvian term for lady.

lynxter: variety of sword used in Loh.

M

Magor: swamp-dwelling crocodilian predatory beast, red-eyed. It is not known whether they are intelligent.

Makilorn: city of roughly a hundred thousand inhabitants in Tsungfaril.

Mangarl the Sofirst: a swod aboard *Shankjid*. SAB

Margon the Ron: a zhanpaktun traveling in the caravan of Trylon Kuong. SRB

Mar-Win-Naltong: Wizard of Loh in the retinue of Queen Satra. STR

Meimgarum: oasis city on the eastern side of the Gleek Frankai. SRB

Mellow Moonlights: one of the many Kregen expressions for "Good evening."

Merkaller: a manufacturer of first-class carriages.

Merle: a member of the Sisters of Voxyra. SAB

Merlee: a Witch of the Demaskar Persuasion, beloved of Vad Gochert. SDR

Mevancy nal Chardaz, Lady: a kregoinya who befriended and looked after Prescot when he was paralyzed. SRB, SAS, SAB

"The Milkmaid's Song": a Lohvian song.

Milly: a follower of the New Empire of Loh in Shamfrin, older sister of Tilly. SDR

ming: a gold piece in southern Loh.

"The Miscil Returned": a little ditty about the farmer who paid ten gold pieces for a slave and married her and demanded the gold back from her owner as her dowry.

Mishuro, San Tuong: a dikaster, assassinated by Pulvia. SRB

Moggers: nickname of Moglin the Flatch.

Moglin the Flatch: a Fristle member of the band of Nath the Ron and Layla. SIV

Mother Molly's: lodging house where Prescot and Quonling stayed in Hinjanchung.

Mul-lu-Manting: a Witch of Loh who publicly advocated the re-establishment of the Empire. SIV

mytzer: a draft beast.

N

Nafren: son of Lady Thynzi. STR

Na-Ku, Sandar: a Pachak warrior aboard *Shankjid*. SAB

Na-Si-Fantong: wizard of Loh seeking the jewels of the Skantiklar. SAS

Nafty: giggle-prone assistant hired by Mevancy. SRB

Naghan: a bandit who attacked Prescot's caravan in southern Loh. SRB

Naghan the Bristle: Brokelsh mercenary in the army of Na-Si-Fantong. STR

Naghan the Cheerful: eloped with the jewelsmith Hwang Tei's daughter Cheryl against his wishes and was miraculously saved by rain.

Naghan the Chik: a thief of Makilorn. SAS

Naghan the Hammer: former assistant to Shan-lao Ortyghan. SIV

Naghan the Marbut: a slave overseer for the Shanks in Taranjin. SIV

Naghan the Omurdour: cousin of Nath Hsienu, suspected to have been killed or captured by Shanks.

Nalgre the Erkensator: crewman of *Shankjid*. SAB

Nalgre the Foot: soldier in the army of Na-Si-Fantong. STR

Nalgre the Frunicator: one of Strom Hangol's cronies, killed by Prescot. SRB

Nalgre Hien-Mi, San: one of the Queen of Makilorn's Repositers. SAS

Nalgre ti Mailinsmot: a messenger in the retinue of Vad Gochert. STR

Nalgre ti Mornlad: a cadet aboard *Dovad Daisy*. SAB

Nalgre V'ron'v: Ensign with the Vallian fleet in Loh. STR

Nan-ni-Oboling: a follower of the New Empire of Loh in Shamfrin. SDR

Nardi's Wenyellow: a famous vintage of Wenhartdrin.

Nath the Burly: a member of 1ESW. STR

Nath the Dorvenfull: the archer of 1EZB.

Nath Fernon: Rapa mercenary in the army of Na-Si-Fantong. STR

Nath the Graintjid: legendary warrior slain by Arngalf Galfarn.

Nath ham Homath: Hikdar in the Hamalese fleet sent to fight the Shanks in Tarankar. SAB

Nath the Horizons: traveled with Mevancy in the Farang Parang. SAB

Nath Hsienu: also called Nath the Bollard, master of the vessel *Garrus*; addicted to Jikalla. SIV

Nath Ingling: Hamalian mercenary in the army of Na-Si-Fantong.

Nath the Jarvis: an inhabitant of Tuansmot. STR

Nath the Lump: a guard in the employ of Tuong Mishuro. SRB

Nath the Ready: alias used by Ra-Lu-Quonling. SIV

Nath the Ron: Kov of Borrakesh, leader of a band rivaling that of Layla na Borrakesh. SIV

Nath the Rumpador: apim whom Prescot recruited in Taranjin to resist the Shank occupation. SIV

Nath the Thirsty, Strom: Prescot's fellow captive of the People of the Drums. SDR

Nath the Tumbs: a member of 1ESW. STR

Nath the Twist: alias used by Prescot at the Springs of Benga Annorpha.

Nath the Uttarler, San: chief Repositer of the Queen of Makilorn. SAS

Nath the Veins: a Deldar aboard *Shankjid*. SAB

Nath ti Zanda: alias used by Nath Wa-Te. SDR

Newsat, Naghan ham: Strom of Livhavil, affianced to Rangicha Taranta, an adherent of Lem. SAB

N'gil: a leechlike creature attending Carazaar, appearing to be the repulsive product of miscegenation between apim and Shank. SAB

nik-armorer: assistant armorer.

Nik-Whonban: a country in Loh.

Nikki the Lame: lookout at Clovangjin. SIV

Niliin: a wine from down the River of Drifting Leaves.

Ningwan, Leotes li: Vad of Sabiling, in whose retinue Prescot and Mevancy traveled for a while in Southern Loh. SRB

Nissa: handmaiden of Delia.

Nol the Arm: a Deldar in 1ESW, eaten by a flitchlak. SAB

Nola: a follower of the New Empire of Loh in Shamfrin. SDR

Noring the Ovoinach: Kanzai Warrior Brother encountered by Prescot and Mul-lu-Manting. SDR

Notesov: a country of Loh.

noumjiksirn: the Kregen form of a wake, a serious yet carousing way of remembering fallen comrades.

Nuong-Hi: family in Ankharum who sell animals, carts, and carriages to travelers arriving from across the Gleek Frankai. SRB

Nuong-Hi, Languin: see Nuong-Hi.

O

Oglin Vandar: a swod aboard *Shankjid*. SAB

"Oh for the Sword of my Lover": a sad little ditty filled with long cadences and the drawn out vowels of sadness.

Old Lorn Trail: trail running from Larishsmot to Makilorn.

Olipen: a merchant from Guishsmot.

Oneness, River of: river running south through Ankharum.

Onso the Gnat: a companion slave to Prescot in the Shank armory.

Orgren Fernon: Rapa mercenary in the army of Na-Si-Fantong. STR

Orlon Farantino: known as the Rekarder, a Khibil retainer of Layla na Borrakesh. SIV

Ornol Skobog: an old kampeon in the Emperor's Yellow Jackets. SIV

Ornol Wanlicheng: a wandering scholar, an adherent of Alternative Magic. SIV

Orphasmot: town located a few days' ride to the west of Makilorn, site of the Springs of Benga Annorpha.

Ortyg Hanshar: chief priest of Makilorn. SAS

Ortyghan the Dagger: a Fristle member of 1ESW, prone to strapping a dagger to his tail. SAB

P

Palandi the Iarvin: Khibil who designed an incendiary device for burning a Shank warehouse in Taranjin. SIV

Paline Asatha: Jiktar Vuvushi wounded by Shanks. SAB

Pancheen Gate: a gate in the walls of Makilorn.

Pandarun: Caravan master of Vad Leotes. SRB

Paol-ur-bliem: the Accursed of Tsung-Tan.

Paramdan: homeplace of Ornol Wanlicheng.

Parfang, Listi and Larrigen: a newlywed couple of Makilorn.

Pathfinders: also called Pilgrims or Wayfarers, adherents of Alternative Magic.

peaker: a dagger with grooves for poison.

Phar-Si-Wyrnon: Wizard of Loh in Hyrklana who offered aid to Spikatur Hunting Sword; erstwhile master of Na-Si-Fantong. STR

Pigeon: Prescot's nickname for Mevancy.

Pilgrims: also called Wayfarers or Pathfinders, adherents of Alternative Magic.

Pimpim: a thick green wine from Chem, cloying as syrup.

Ping: a thief of Makilorn, a runt of a fellow with a yellow-scarred jaw and bad teeth. SAS

Pling-Fe-Hwang: a noble lord whose baby was supposed to receive the soul of the assassinated Queen of Makilorn. SAS

punklingling: a melodious musical instrument.

Pondo: surly assistant hired by Mevancy. SRB

Pondro the Pin: bosun of the vessel *Quaynt's Fortune*. SIV

Pontior: a man saved by Mevancy for the Star Lords.

Porstheimer: manufacturer of first-class carriages.

Prang: companion of Wink. SAS

Pride of Hanitcha: Hamalese airship sent to fight the Shanks in Tarankar. SAB

Pride of Ruathytu: Flagship of the Hamalese fleet sent to fight the Shanks in Tarankar. SAB

Princess of Zulfiria: Zairian ship commanded by Pur Zinkardo.

Pulvia the Ringlets: assassin hired by Strom Hargon. SRB

Pynsi: fickle girl of whom Ra-Lu-Quonling was enamored. SIV

Q

Quando the Iarvin: Khibil who escaped from the Shanks with Prescot and his friends, of considerable physical strength. SAB

quanim: a race of diffs having long ears and a pointed chin.

Quaynt's Fortune: boat on which Prescot took passage from Changwutung. SIV

Queen's Matrons: court ladies who provide the queen with information about her past lives unknown to male Repositers.

Quincing: one of Queen Satra's ministers.

Quincy, Lulli: proprietress of a lodging house in Makilorn. SRB

Quintrell the Licentious, by: oath used by Nath the Jarvis.

Quinvarn: see ham Hilzim, Harulf.

Quonling, Ra-Lu-: a Wizard-of-Loh-in-training who was thrown out for failing an exam. SIV

R

Rafael: a kregoinye who worked with Mevancy, killed in a fire. SRB

Rafe the Ponshim: one of Prescot's force of guerillas in Tarankar. SIV

Raffi of the Lightning and Thunder: a Lohvian goddess.

ragamo/ragama: a kind of general insult usually employed when you're not sure if the person you are addressing is a real shint, or just a hulu or a fambly.

Ranal Shang-Li-Po, San: one of the Queen of Makilorn's Repositers. SAS

Ranjat, Elten: kregoinye killed in service to the Everoinye. STR

Realm of the Drums: inhabited tunnels and caverns beneath the City of Eternal Twilight.

reedkhansix: headdress of silver coins worn by girls of Taranik, serving also as dowry, handed down from mother to daughter.

Rendi the Keel: master of the boat on which Prescot took passage down the River of Oneness. SRB

Repositer: in the religion of Tsung-Tan, one trained to draw forth the memories of a reincarnated paol-ur-bliem.

Rhagran: Rapa captain of the guard in the retinue of Chan Holomin. SDR

riffim: a race of diffs, who had invaded and taken over Tarankar.

Rikky Tardish: master of a traveling entertainment troupe who employed Prescot as a clown. SRB

rispa: a sweet variety of fruit.

Rodders: nickname of Ron Dang Fang.

Rogrifor: a Rapa guard in the retinue of Chan Holomin. SDR

Rollo the Runner: alias used by Ra-Lu-Quonling

Romano: cadade in the retinue of Vad Gochert, captain of the guard. SDR, STR

Ron Dang Fang: also called Rodders; a mercenary, a Bowman of Loh, companion to Kirsty. SAS

Ronal the Waspish: a Hikdar with the Vallian force in Loh. SDR

ronil: a purple-red jewel of great price.

S

Samral: castle on the western side of the town of Miliksin.

Sandar Na-Ku: a Pachak warrior aboard *Shankjid*. SAB

Sandeater: zorca ridden by Prescot from the Springs of Benga Annorpha to Makilorn. SAS

Sardanar: town located at the mouth of the River of Glinting Charm, with massive sea walls and fortifications dating back to the early days of the Walfargian empire.

Satra: former Queen of Pain, frozen for hundreds of years by a magic spell in the Realm of the Drums beneath the City of Eternal Twilight. SDR

Scanda: a Hikdar, a member of the Sisters of Voxyra. SAB

Seeds of Ganfowang: Grodnim name for the Seeds of Zantristar.

Seeds of Zantristar: group of tiny islands to the south of the western end of the Eye of the World.

Schnooprins: a synonym for Shanks.

Schnurrdun the All-seeing: legendary god who tested Arngalf Galfarn.

Scrimshi the Sturr: A guard in the retinue of Vad Leotes. Killed by bandits. SRB

shal-armorer: assistant armorer.

Shamfrin: a city in Walfarg.

Sharn: name of an ibdrin.

Shan-lao Ortyghan: head of an armor shop in occupied Taranjin. SIV

Shang-Li-Po, San Ranal: one of the Queen of Makilorn's Repositers. SAS

Shangsha: a town of southern Loh.

Shankjid: voller sent by Vallia to fight the Shanks, rescued by Prescot from a shuckerchun and flitchlak. SAB

She of the Blushes: a name used in Loh for the fourth moon of Kregen.

She of the Sundering: river in southern Loh forming the western boundary of the desert.

Shenlitz: a variety of liquor.

Shernly: Kovneva of Shamfrin.

Shiang, Tsun and Hosifi: potters, parents of a baby supposed to be the reincarnation of the assassinated Queen of Makilorn. SAS

Shirrendrin: a coastal land of Loh.

Shorush-Tish: Zairian storm deity.

shuckerchun: predatory animal which sucks its victims below the earth.

Sichaz, Death Jungles of: Lohvian term for the Ice Floes of Sicce.

Siloni: a woman of Makilorn, mother of the reincarnated Vad Leotes. SRB

Sindi-Wang: a thief of Makilorn, a woman of enormous development casually displayed between the folds of her dress. SAS

Sing-Lee: a Kov of Shirrendrin.

Sinnalix: home country of Mevancy, south of Murn-Chem in Loh. Once advanced in culture, but now little better than barbarians; also the inhabitants of this country; the women have the ability to discharge darts from their forearms, while the men are brutish, misshapen, and ugly.

Sinnalixi: plural of Sinnalix.

Sin-Sin-Yarelving: renowned martyr of Lohvian history.

Skantiklar: a set of nine jewels yielding unimaginable sorcerous power.

Skobog, Ornol: an old kampeon in the Emperor's Yellow Jackets. SIV

Skull Charger: Hamalese airship sent to fight the Shanks in Tarankar. SAB

Slezen: needleman who attended Prescot when he was paralyzed. SRB

slikker: a boat similar to a dhow.

slouncher: animal native to the deserts of Loh, similar to a camel, but with eight legs and three humps. Will kill anyone attempting to molest their young.

Snarlendrin: a country of Loh.

snizz: to backfire, go awry.

Snuffles: lictrix lent by Mevancy to Prescot. SRB

Sooey: a thief of Makilorn, killed in the raid on Shang-Li-Po's secret villa. SAS

spinzal: a type of bush.

spotty-lind: nickname for a vorlind.

Spurl, by: oath used by Mevancy.

Squish and Queng, the: a tavern in Tuansmot.

squonch: a variety of fruit.

stangsi: predatory cave-dweller, wide and flat, like a cartwheel of tentacles and stingers and unpleasantnesses. It drops upon its prey from above.

Sternum Hamparz: Ship Hikdar of *Dovad Daisy.* SAB

Stinja: name given by Larghos the Throstle to his polearm.

Stinkback: beast with four red eyes, with a scaled hide, humped in shape with prongs on its back.

Stortingen, Cult of: another Lohvian school of wizardry.

strank: twin-finned shark frequenting the rivers of southern Loh.

Sundering, She of the: a river marking the western boundary of the trylonate of Taranik and the eastern boundary of Tarankar.

Suringlas: a kregoinye who worked with Mevancy.

Susy-Lee-Sarin: betrothed of Chan Holomin.

"Sweet Flowing Water, The": song composed by Pitir Ng'gland from Ng'groga some five hundred seasons ago.

Swiggletoe: lictrix purchased by Mevancy for Prescot in Ankharum. SRB

T

Takroti, by: a Kataki oath.

Talin, Kuong Vang: Trylon of Taranik, recently come of age.

Tan: the prophet of Tsung in the religion of Tsung-Tan.

Tanch, Tiny: an Ng'grogan member of the troupe of Rikky Tardish. SRB

Tanki the Stitch: saddler in the caravan of Vad Leotes. SRB

Taranik: Trylonate to the west of Makilorn.

Taranjin: capital city of Tarankar.

Tarankar: country to the west of Tsungfaril, where the Shanks launched their invasion of Loh.

Tarankar Army of Liberation: guerilla force organized to fight the Shank occupation by Prescot acting as Prince Chaadur.

Taranta: Rangicha of Firthlad, sister of Taranto ham Armit. SAB

Tardish, Rikky: master of a traveling entertainment troupe who employed Prescot as a clown. SRB

Tawang, Nanji: Trylon of Fuokane, a disagreeable fellow. SRB, SAS

Tei, Hwang: jewelsmith whose daughter Cheryl eloped with Naghan the Cheerful.

Telsi: a lady of uncertain occupation, Lunky's fiancée.

Ternantung: a town located on the River of Glinting Charm.

Thalna, Lady: one of three heirs to the throne of Makfaril. SAS

Thana ti Vincentsmot: a Jiktar with the Vallian force in Loh. SDR

Thanko: a race of diffs with a mop of dusty hair and a drooping nose.

ham Thanstrer, Hamish: Kapt of the Hamalian air fleet sent to fight the Shank occupiers of Tarankar.

Thazdon: Krozair rescued by Prescot from a sinking slave ship. STR

Thynzi: Zairian lady rescued by Prescot from a sinking slave ship.

Tighten your scabbard: slang for "Don't lose your temper."

tikshvu: "missy"—a word often used to threaten and cow a young girl who has been rebellious.

Tilly: a follower of the New Empire of Loh in Shamfrin. SDR

Tim Timutorio: Bowman of Loh who lost three fingers and now lifts a shield at Seg Segutorio's back in battle. SAB

Tomecdrin: a country in Balintol.

Tongo the Lash: a Deldar in Prescot's force of guerilla fighters in Tarankar. SIV

Tongwan the Slow: a guard in the employ of Tuong Mishuro. SRB

True Trog: a deity of Tarankar.

Tse-Tsu-Luenling: a wizard of Stortingen in the retinue of Vad Valadian. STR

T'sien-Fu: Crebent left in charge of Taranik by Kuong. SIV

Tsien-Ting: master of the vessel *Quaynt's Fortune*. SIV

Tsungfaril: country in southern Loh.

Tsung-tan: universal deity of Tsungfaril.

Tuansmot: a village of Shirrendrin.

Tuco: a Brokelsh enslaved by the Shanks. SAB

Tuftytail: preysany ridden by Prescot in Tsungfaril. SRB

Tun-du-Haffyien: art master at a school for Wizards and Witches of Loh. SIV

Tuong Mishuro, San: a dikaster, assassinated by Pulvia. SRB

Twang: a bowyer and fletcher of Makilorn. SRB

U

Ul-ga-Sorming: wizard to whom Pynsi gave her favors. SIV

Umblers: a funny race of diffs, erratic, incompetent, leaving behind them a trail of accidental damage. Skilled only at raising goats.

V

Vakstirn: type of Shank who ride any saddle animals they can steal in the lands they invade.

Valadian: a Vad, a Khibil, with one ear, leader of an expedition in the underground Realm of the Drums. STR

"Valor is the better part of the Person": a saying of Valka.

Vandar, Oglin: a swod aboard *Shankjid*. SAB

Vangar ti Valkanium: admiral of the Vallian fleet sent to fight the Shanks in Tarankar. SAB, SDR

Vangli ti Trishnar: a Hikdar in the guard of the Queen of Tsungfaril. SAS

Vankari: a race of diffs of powerful physique, of practically no forehead, of spatulate nose, of wide gap-jawed mouth, of a stooped posture that emphasizes their brooding hunched menacing aspect. Like many a member of the poorer folk they chew Cham all the time. Reputed to be fond of Fristles, and the Fristles do not reciprocate, which amuses everyone except the Fristles.

Varankey, Slender: a juggler in the troupe of Rikky Tardish. SRB

Varnion: country known for mussels.

Vasama: fat fussy woman who controlled Yoshi. SAS

Vendayha Lady: Valkan flying ship dispatched to Loh. STR

Vengali: type of Sorcerer from Vinkleden.

Vilia: character in the song of Dalendin.

Vinkleden: home of the Vengali sorcerers.

volail: a variety of blue and white flower.

voltigeurs: unarmored or lightly armored light infantry.

Vondal ti Dernsmot, Ortyg: a Jiktar with the Vallian force in Tarankar.

vorlind: a beast with six legs, a spotted hide of orange and black, and pads and claws that can remove your head as neatly as a headsman's axe.

Voxyra: a minor and semi-secret religious sect of Vallia.

Vutch-Ikar: a pagan god of Walfarg, with a pot-belly and staring eyes.

W

Walfarg: ancient empire consisting of all Loh, Pandahem, and vast lands in the east of Turismond.

Walfarg, Wizard or Witch of: Lohvian terms for Wizards and Witches of Loh.

walfger: Lohvian term for mister.

walfgera: Lohvian term for madam.

Walig: Lohvian name for the green sun of Kregen.

Wan-fuong: a chieftain among the Glitch Riders. STR

Wanlicheng, Ornol: a wandering scholar, an adherent of Alternative Magic. SIV

Wa-Te, Nath: fellow-slave to Prescot in the retinue of Princess Licria. SDR

Wayfarers: also called Pilgrims or Pathfinders, adherents of Alternative Magic.

wegener: saddle animal with six legs, narrow flanks, and a spiky head.

Wei Fwang: needleman who cared for Llodi when he was wounded by Lady Pulvia. SAS

"The Well that Never Ran Dry": a Lohvian song.

"When a Wizard meets a Wizard, Sailing through the Air": a song of Loh.

Whonban: homeplace of the Wizards and Witches of Loh.

Whonbim: an inhabitant of Whonban.

Wielder of the Brass Rod: one Kregan expression for a slave overseer.

Wink: a young man stabbed by a thief in the Tavern of Lush Bonhomie. SAS

Wioldrin: a Lohvian province.

Winkal the Horknik: a Shank prisoner rescued by Prescot's guerillas. SIV

World, Path of the: one of the paths of Alternative Magic, in which the seventh corner is of special significance.

Wr.: abbreviation for walfger.

Wurzam, by: a Lohvian oath.

X

xichun: flying animal something like the xi of the Stratemsk, with green and gold red-edged scales, deeply curved iridescent wings, sinuous necks, whiplike tails, and small wedge-shaped heads with jaws stuffed with needle teeth.

Xinthe, Lady: student, nurse and cook to Ornol Wanlicheng. SIV

Y

Yaka the Stripe: Kataki slave overseer in the retinue of Princess Licria. SDR

Yakwang, by: an oath of Makilorn.

Yango, San: one of the Queen of Makilorn's Repositers. SAS

Yoshi: a diviner of Makilorn. SRB, SAS

Yriang: a purple-faced, jewel-bedecked Stromni who traveled with Mevancy in the Farang Parang. SAB

Ysbel: woman of Makilorn who assisted in rescuing Mevancy from the river.

Z

zaffim: race of bulky, two-armed, tail-less diffs, characterized by lumpy, as it were unformed, faces, with large brow ridges and squashed noses, and jaws that are narrow to the point of nonexistence holding snaggly teeth.

"Zair lays many a trap for the unwary feet of the boastful": a proverb of Sanurkazz.

Zalfi: Zairian lady, wife of Pur Thazdon, rescued by Prescot from a sinking slave ship.

Zamran: a pretty market town in the kovnate of Zamra.

Zamrarn: country in southern Loh, source of black pearls.

Zanad: Krozair rescued by Prescot from a sinking slave ship. STR

Zanath na Zenrik, Pur: inventor of a neat and subtle twin attack with the Krozair longsword three hundred seasons ago.

Zefan, San: Krozair author of the treatise the *Seventh Circle of the Artifices of the Sword*, approximately 2,500 years ago.

Zilfi: daughter of Lady Thynzi. STR

Zinkardo: Krozair rescued by Prescot from a sinking slave ship. STR

Zinter the Afflicted, by: a Zairian oath.

The Zinul and Queng: a tavern of dubious delights in Hinjanchung.

Zunida the Laudable, Lady: prayer-idol stolen from the Sisters of Voxyra.

About the author

Alan Burt Akers was a pen name of the prolific British author Kenneth Bulmer, who died in December 2005 aged eighty-four.

Bulmer wrote over 160 novels and countless short stories, predominantly science fiction, both under his real name and numerous pseudonyms, including Alan Burt Akers, Frank Brandon, Rupert Clinton, Ernest Corley, Peter Green, Adam Hardy, Philip Kent, Bruno Krauss, Karl Maras, Manning Norvil, Chesman Scot, Nelson Sherwood, Richard Silver, H. Philip Stratford, and Tully Zetford. Kenneth Johns was a collective pseudonym used for a collaboration with author John Newman. Some of Bulmer's works were published along with the works of other authors under "house names" (collective pseudonyms) such as Ken Blake (for a series of tie-ins with the 1970s television programme The Professionals), Arthur Frazier, Neil Langholm, Charles R. Pike, and Andrew Quiller.

Bulmer was also active in science fiction fandom, and in the 1970s he edited nine issues of the New Writings in Science Fiction anthology series in succession to John Carnell, who originated the series.

For more details about the author, see www.mushroom-ebooks.com.